Red Sky in the Morning

&

Without Sin

Born in Gainsborough, Lincolnshire, Margaret Dickinson moved to the coast at the age of seven and so began her love for the sea and the Lincolnshire landscape.

Her ambition to be a writer began early and she had her first novel published at the age of twenty-five. This was followed by eighteen further titles, including *Plough the Furrow*, *Sow the Seed* and *Reap the Harvest*, which make up her Lincolnshire Fleethaven trilogy. Many of her novels are set in the heart of her home county but in *Tangled Threads* and *Twisted Strands* the stories include not only Lincolnshire but also the framework knitting and lace industries of Nottingham.

ALSO BY MARGARET DICKINSON

Plough the Furrow

Sow the Seed

Reap the Harvest

The Miller's Daughter

Chaff Upon the Wind

The Fisher Lass

The Tulip Girl

The River Folk

Tangled Threads

Twisted Strands

Margaret Dickinson

Red Sky in the Morning & Without Sin

PAN BOOKS

Red Sky in the Morning first published 2004 by Pan Books.
Without Sin first published 2005 by Pan Books.

This omnibus first published 2005 by Pan Books
an imprint of Pan Macmillan, a division of Macmillan Publishers Limited
Pan Macmillan, 20 New Wharf Road, London N1 9RR
Basingstoke and Oxford
Associated companies throughout the world
www.panmacmillan.com

ISBN 978-0-330-44367-8

3 5 7 9 8 6 4 2

A CIP catalogue record for this book is available from
the British Library.

Printed and bound in the UK by
CPI Mackays, Chatham ME5 8TD

Red Sky in the Morning

For Zoë and Scott,
my daughter and son-in-law

Acknowledgements

My grateful thanks to Graham and Liz Jarnell for answering all my questions about sheep. Any errors, of course, are mine and not theirs! As always, my love and thanks go to my family and friends, especially my husband, Dennis, and those who read the script in the early stages: Robena and Fred Hill, David and Una Dickinson, Linda and Terry Allaway and Pauline Griggs. Your constant support and encouragement mean more to me than you can ever know.

Special thanks to the best agent any writer could have – Darley Anderson. Thank you, too, to all the 'team' at Macmillan, headed by my lovely editor, Imogen Taylor. You're all absolutely wonderful.

1946

One

The girl was standing in the middle of the cobbled marketplace. She had been there for hours whilst the busy market bustled around her. All day the raucous shouts of the stallholders had rung out, each vying with the others to attract the attention of the shoppers, but they had not gained hers. It was two weeks before Christmas and the stalls were laden with holly wreaths and mistletoe, bringing colour to a drab, wet day.

Now it was growing dark and the traders were packing up and going home. Home to a warm fire and a hot drink, no doubt liberally laced with whisky to drive out the chill and to thaw frozen hands and feet. The rain had been falling steadily since early morning and the girl, just standing there so quiet and still, staring ahead of her and looking neither to right nor left, was soaked to her skin. Her long black hair was plastered against her head. The bottom button of the shapeless coat she wore was missing and the garment flapped open, revealing the swelling mound of her belly. Yet she didn't seem to care about her condition, or even about the discomfort she must be feeling. She seemed unaware of everything and everyone around her. Her thin face was white and pinched with cold, and devoid of expression. Her blue eyes, so dark they were almost violet, were lifeless.

'A' ya goin' to stand there all night, lass?' The last

market trader to load his wares into the back of an old van shouted across the wet cobblestones, shining now in the pale glow from the street lamp. She did not even glance in his direction. It was as if she hadn't heard him. The man wiped the back of his hand across his face and shrugged. 'Please ya'sen,' he muttered and turned away. He looked longingly towards the public house, the Shepherd's Crook. Even out here in the cold and the wet, the buzz of conversation could be heard through the open door. A haze of pipe and cigarette smoke drifted out into the night air. The market trader hesitated for a moment, seemingly torn between the inviting hospitality the place offered and the thought of home, where his wife would be waiting with a hot meal and warm slippers. The pull of home won and he bent to swing the starting handle of his battered van. The engine spluttered into life and he moved to the driver's side of the vehicle, slinging the starting handle into the well in front of the passenger seat. He glanced across at the girl, then shrugged again and climbed into the van.

When the noise of the motor had died away the marketplace was deserted, except for the girl. The only other living creature was a pony, harnessed to an old-fashioned trap and tethered outside the Shepherd's Crook. It looked as wet and miserable as the girl felt. Just once she licked her lips, tasting the rain.

The laughter and the noise from the pub spilled into the street as three men came out, lurching along the pavement, bumping into one another, laughing and joking and filled with the merriment of the festive season. They didn't even notice her. More men left the pub in twos and threes, yet the pony still stood there, occasionally pawing the ground, his metal-clad hoof scraping the cobbles. He shook his head and water droplets showered from his rain-soaked mane.

'Time to go home, Eddie. You can't stay here all night.' There was a disturbance in the doorway of the pub and, for the first time, the girl's glance focused on the two men there. One was very unsteady, reeling from side to side and being steered towards the waiting pony and trap by the other. 'Come on. Your pony'll tek you home. Good job he knows the way better'n you when you're in this state, in't it?'

For a moment the drunken man leant against the trap, then he grasped the side and, with the aid of the other man, heaved himself into the back. The pony lifted his head, perking up at once now his warm stable was almost in sight.

'On you go, then.' The publican raised his hand, about to untether the pony and slap its rump to send it on its way, when the man in the back mumbled, 'Wait. Wait a mo'.'

Through the blur of drink and the steadily falling rain, he had caught a glimpse of the girl standing in the middle of the square. He raised a shaking finger and pointed. 'Who's that?'

'Eh?' The landlord glanced over his shoulder. 'Oh, her. Bin there hours. Some tramp beggin', I 'spect. Well, she needn't think she's goin' to get a bed at my place.'

Eddie was scrambling out of the trap again.

'Now, now,' the other man remonstrated. 'On you go home, Eddie. You're goin' to be in enough trouble with your missis as it is. Don't be bothering yourself with the likes of that little trollop.'

Eddie shook off the man's restraining hand. 'You can't leave a poor lass standing there in this weather,' he mumbled and began to shamble towards the girl.

The landlord shrugged. 'Have it your way, then. I've better things to do with me time. Goodnight to you, Eddie Appleyard.'

The landlord went inside and slammed the heavy door of the public house. The sound of the bolts being shot home echoed in the silence.

Still the girl had not moved as Eddie reached her and stood before her, swaying slightly. He peered at her through the gloom. 'Nowhere to go, lass?' His voice was gentle and caring and the girl, who had thought she was empty of all emotion, felt tears prickle behind her eyelids. It was the first kind word she had heard in weeks, months even. Slowly, she shook her head.

He touched her arm lightly. 'Then you'd best come home with me.' Without waiting for any sign of agreement or otherwise from her, Eddie turned and reeled back towards the trap. But before he reached it, he stumbled and fell to the cobbles. The girl watched for a moment and then, when he made no attempt to rise, she moved at last. Her limbs were stiff with cold and for the first few steps she hobbled like an old woman. She bent and grasped his arm. He grunted and, leaning heavily on her, struggled to his feet. They staggered towards the trap. The man scrambled into the back and then turned, holding out his hand towards her. 'Come on, lass. You can't stay out here all night.'

She hesitated and then put her hand into his. When she was sitting beside him on the floor he said, 'Giddup, Duke.' The pony moved and, as the trap swayed, the girl clung on to the side, but the man merely shifted himself into a more comfortable position. Curling his body to fit into the confined space, he lay down. With a satisfied grunt, he rested his head on her lap and, almost at once, began to snore.

The pony bent its head against the driving rain as it plodded up the steep hill, leaving the lights of the town behind them. Beneath the slight shelter the sides of the trap afforded and with the warmth of the man close to her seeping into her chilled being, the girl's eyelids closed. Her head drooped forward and soon, draped across the man, she too slept.

Two

'Who the hell's this?'

A woman's strident voice startled the girl awake. The pony and trap had come to a halt in the middle of a farmyard. Farm buildings and a house loomed through the darkness. The woman, a raincoat over her head, was standing at the back of the trap, poking the sleeping man with her forefinger.

'Eddie – wake up. Who's this, I'd like to know? Some trollop you've picked up at the market?' She prodded him viciously. 'You've a nerve and no mistake. Come on.' She began to pull at him. 'Stir ya'sen. I want an explanation. And it'd better be good.'

The man grunted and lifted his head. His face now on a level with the woman's, he murmured, 'Bertha, my dearly beloved wife.' He grinned foolishly, but even in his drunken state the girl could detect the sarcasm in his tone.

'I'll "beloved wife" you,' the woman shrilled as she dragged him from the trap. He fell to the ground on his hands and knees, but she made no effort to help him up. Instead she pushed him with her toe. 'Get up, ya daft beggar. And as for you,' she added, glaring up at the girl still sitting on the floor of the trap, 'you can be on ya way—'

'No – no.' Hanging on to the back of the trap, the man dragged himself upright. He swayed slightly, but his voice was less slurred now. 'No, she's stayin'. She's nowhere to go.'

'What's that to do with you? Who is she?'

The man shrugged. 'Dunno. She was standing in the marketplace getting soaking wet, so I brought her home.'

'Oh, a real knight in shining armour, aren't ya? Get on inside.' The woman pushed him again. Then she jabbed her finger towards the girl. 'And you. You'd better come inside an' all. Only for a minute, mind. I want to get to the bottom of this.'

The woman, small and very overweight, nevertheless marched towards the back door of the farmhouse with surprising agility.

'Come on, lass,' Eddie said. 'We'd better do as she says.' He held out his hand to her and, stiffly, she climbed out of the trap. As they began to walk towards the house, the girl spoke for the first time. Her voice was low and husky.

'What about the pony?'

'Eh?' Eddie blinked. 'Oh aye.' He lurched back towards the animal, still waiting patiently, and patted its neck. 'Poor old Duke. You always get the rough end of the stick, don't you?' His voice was low as he muttered, 'Reckon we both do.'

The man began to grapple with the harness and the girl moved to help him. As soon as the pony felt himself released from the shafts, he trotted towards the building on the right-hand side of the yard. The man gave a wry laugh. 'He knows his way home all right.'

They left the trap in the middle of the yard and went towards the house.

'If she – if she won't let you stay in the house, lass, the hayloft above Duke's stable is dry and in the morning—' He wiped his hand across his face and then shook his head as if trying to clear it. 'I'm not thinking too straight, but I'll sort summat out for you in the morning.' They stepped into a scullery and through that into a warm kitchen, where the smell of freshly baked mince pies still lingered. 'I'll see if I can get her to—'

'So? What's all this about?' Bertha was standing with her fat arms folded across her bosom. Her mousy coloured hair was straight and roughly cut into an untidy bob. Parted on one side, the long section of hair was held back from her face by a grip. Her florid cheeks were lined with tiny red veins and her mouth was small, the thin lips lost in the fatness of her face. Only in her mid-thirties, yet already she had a double chin. As she stood awaiting her husband's explanation, her pale hazel eyes sparked with anger.

Behind the woman, in the doorway leading further into the house, stood a young boy in striped flannelette pyjamas. He was no more than ten years old and his large brown eyes were darting from one to the other between his parents, but they seemed oblivious to his presence.

The girl shivered and glanced towards the glowing fire, longing to kneel before it and hold out her hands to its heat.

'Well? I'm waiting.' The woman's glance raked the girl, taking in her bedraggled state. Then her mouth turned down in disgust. 'I might 'ave known. She's in the family way. Is it yours, Eddie Appleyard?'

'Don't talk daft, woman.' Her accusation brought a brief spark of retaliation. 'I ain't even seen her afore tonight.'

'Huh! Expect me to believe that.' She stepped towards

the girl. 'Well, you can be on your way, whoever you are.'

The man said nothing, but he made a motion with his head as if to remind the girl of his earlier offer for her to sleep in the hayloft.

'I saw that. Ee, there's more going on here than you're letting on. I can tell.'

Eddie ran his hand agitatedly through his thick brown hair. He was a tall, thin man in his mid-thirties, yet slightly stooping, as if the years of farm work were already bending his back. His face was weather-beaten and there were lines around his brown eyes.

'There's nothing going on, as you put it,' he said wearily. 'She's just a poor lass who's got nowhere to go. Surely, you can show a bit of—'

'And why's she got nowhere to go?' Bertha flung her arm out, pointing at the girl's stomach. 'Because 'er family – if she's got any – has slung the little slut out, that's why.'

Eddie sighed. 'You don't know that.' They were talking about the girl as if she was not there. 'You don't know anything about her. No more than I do.'

'Aye, but I can guess.'

'It's the truth I'm telling you,' he said quietly, yet there was a note in his tone that implied he knew she wouldn't believe him.

Bertha turned towards the girl. 'What's your name then?'

The violet eyes regarded the woman steadily. 'Anna,' the girl said softly.

'Anna what?'

The girl hesitated and looked away, avoiding Bertha's probing, hostile eyes. She ran her tongue nervously round her lips. 'Anna Woods.'

But Bertha had noticed the hesitation. She sniffed in disbelief. 'Oh aye. Well then, Anna Woods – or whatever your name is – you'd better take yourself off, 'cos we don't want the likes of you hanging around here. Go on.' She flapped her hand. 'Be off with you. And don't come round here again.'

'She can sleep in the stable,' Eddie put in. 'You can't turn the lass out, specially when it's nearly Christmas.' Sadly, he added, 'No room at the inn, eh, Bertha? Now look, love, why don't you find her a blanket and—?'

'I aren't finding the little trollop owt.' Bertha whipped round on him. 'And as for you, Eddie Appleyard, you ain't heard the last of this.' At that moment she noticed the boy still standing in the doorway. Instantly Bertha's whole demeanour changed. She stepped towards him and put her arm around his shoulders. 'What are you doing down here, Tony? Go back to bed, there's a good boy.'

Anna saw the boy glance briefly at his father as he murmured, 'Yes, Mam,' and then he scuttled out of sight. She heard his light footsteps on the stairs and then the sound of his bare feet pattering across the floor above.

'There.' The woman rounded on her husband again. 'See how you upset him? He can't sleep till he knows you're safely home. He's the same every week. Though why he should bother himself after the way you carry on beats me.'

Sickened by the woman's ranting, Anna turned and stepped out of the warm kitchen and through the scullery. As she opened the back door, she shivered again as the coldness of the wet night hit her once more. She bent her head against the rain and hurried towards the barn door through which the pony had disappeared.

Halfway across the yard, she jumped as a dog, chained outside its kennel, barked and tried to run towards her. She couldn't see it clearly in the darkness, but she made soothing sounds in her throat. The dog ceased its barking, whined and then returned to its shelter. *Even he doesn't like the wet*, she thought wryly.

Inside the barn, it was cold but dry. As her eyes became accustomed to the dark, Anna felt her way around, her icy fingers touching the brick walls. She heard the sound of the pony and her fingers touched a coarse blanket thrown over the boarding at the side of his stall.

'Sorry, Duke,' she murmured and stroked his rump, 'but my need is greater than yours tonight.'

Hugging the blanket, which smelled strongly of horse, she felt her way up a ladder and into the hayloft. She removed her wet coat and wrapped herself in the blanket, then lay down on the hay, burrowing beneath it to find what warmth she could.

Exhausted, she was asleep in seconds.

Anna was awakened by the sound of someone climbing the ladder to the loft. She stretched and raised herself on one elbow. It was not the man whose head appeared, but the young boy's. They stared at each other for several moments in the pale light of a cold dawn, before Anna lay down again and closed her eyes. She hoped he would go away once his curiosity had been satisfied. She had not yet made up her mind what to do next. She wished she could stay here for ever. She was warm and snug for the first time in weeks.

In fact, she thought, *this would be a nice place to die.*

She was about to drift off into sleep again when she heard the boy climb the rest of the ladder and creep, on hands and knees, across the hay towards her. There was a long silence before he whispered, 'I've brought you something to eat.' Another pause and then he added, 'And some milk.'

She opened her eyes again and looked up at him. He was holding a roughly wrapped parcel and had a small milk can hooked over his wrist. 'It's only bread and cheese.' He was apologetic. 'It's all I could take without me mam finding out.'

Now Anna sat up, reaching out thankfully to take the food. She had been ready to give up, to succumb at last to an overwhelming desire to close her eyes and never wake up, but the physical ache of hunger revived her instinct to survive.

The boy watched her as she ate ravenously, his brown eyes large in his thin face. 'Are you going to have a baby?' The question was innocent enough, but the girl scowled at him and did not answer. Yet it was the first time her face had registered any kind of emotion. 'Where have you come from?' Again, no answer. 'Where are you going?' To this she replied only with a vague lift of her shoulders. 'Haven't you got a home? A mam and dad?'

Anna lay down again. 'Thanks for the food,' she said flatly, deliberately ignoring his questions. Her words were a dismissal, yet the boy did not move. He sat quietly beside her and she could feel him watching her.

They heard a noise below and, startled, the boy scrambled away towards the ladder. Anna raised her head. He was peering down the open hatch, his eyes wide and fearful. Then she saw him relax, the sudden tension in his limbs drain away.

'Hello, lad.' Eddie Appleyard's voice drifted up. 'Come to see if our visitor's still here, have you?'

The boy nodded as the man began to climb up towards him. 'I brought her some bread an' cheese, Dad. And some milk. But don't tell Mam, will you?'

Eddie appeared at the top of the ladder. Even through the poor light, Anna could see that he was smiling. He reached out and ruffled his son's hair. 'No, son, course I won't.' His grin broadened and Anna had the feeling it was not the first secret that father and son had shared. 'As long as you don't tell her I've raided the larder an' all.' He handed up a blue-and-white-check cloth bundle as he glanced across to where the girl lay. The boy took it and moved back to her side. 'Me dad's brought you something too.'

The man levered himself up the last rungs of the ladder and stepped into the loft, bending his head to avoid the low rafters. He dropped to his haunches beside her as, now, Anna sat upright.

'It's very kind of you,' she said huskily as she unwrapped the cloth. There was a slice of pork pie, two cold sausages and two slices of bread, spread thickly with butter.

'And here's a couple of apples,' the man said, fishing in his pocket. 'From our own orchard. We lay 'em out on newspaper in the loft to last us through the winter.'

Now they both sat and watched her eat. When she had finished, the man said kindly, 'Now, lass, what can we do to help you? Are you heading for somewhere? I could mebbe take you there, if it's not too far away?'

There was a long silence whilst the girl seemed to be struggling inwardly. She saw the man and his young son exchange a glance, but they waited patiently for her answer. At last she said haltingly, 'No, I'm not going anywhere.'

'Are you looking for work?' Eddie asked. 'Is that it?'

'I suppose so, though—' She hesitated, before adding bitterly, 'I won't be able to work for very long.'

'Do you know owt about farm work?' Eddie asked, carefully ignoring her brief reference to her condition.

The girl regarded him steadily, seeming to weigh up the consequences of her answer before uttering it. Guardedly, she said, 'A bit.'

'Can you milk cows?'

She shook her head, her eyes downcast. Her reluctance was obvious, but at last she admitted, 'Sheep. I know about sheep.'

The boy clapped his hands excitedly. 'We've got sheep. Lincolnshire Longwools,' he added with a note of pride. 'And it'll be lambing time soon. She could help with the sheep, Dad, couldn't she?'

'Well—' Now the man was doubtful. 'I wasn't thinking so much of her staying with us.' His expression was both apprehensive and apologetic at the same time. 'I was just wondering if we could find her a place on a farm hereabouts.'

The boy's face fell.

'It's all right, Mister.' Anna moved to get up from her warm nest in the hay. 'I don't want to cause you any bother.' She glanced at him shrewdly as, remembering the previous night, she added softly, 'No more than I have already.' In a shaft of early morning light slanting through the rafters, she could see that Eddie had a scratch on his left cheekbone. A scratch that had not been there the previous evening.

Eddie made a dismissive gesture with his hand, but she could see the wariness deep in his eyes. The boy was still glancing from one to the other, biting his lip. Suddenly, his expression brightened again. 'What about the cottage, Dad? Couldn't she stay there?'

The man looked at him, at the girl and then back to his son. 'But it's nearly falling down, lad. It's hardly weatherproof.'

'You could mend it, Dad.' The boy's face was alight with eagerness. 'You could do the walls.' He glanced at Anna. 'They're only mud.' Now he looked back again to his father. 'And Mr Wainwright could do the roof.' Once more he explained to Anna, 'It's a thatched roof and Mr Wainwright does thatching. He mended the corner shop in the village. It's got a thatched roof an' all. Oh Dad, do let her stay. Please. She's got nowhere else to go.'

'Is that right, lass?' the man asked her quietly and when she nodded, he sighed.

His brow furrowed, he sat deep in thought for several minutes until a shout made them all jump. It was Bertha's shrill voice in the barn below them.

'Eddie? Where are you?'

The boy made a sudden movement like a startled fawn, but his father put his finger to his lips.

Bertha was at the bottom of the ladder. 'Are you up there, Eddie Appleyard? 'Cos if you are—'

It sounded as if the woman suspected that Anna had spent the night in the hayloft. Like statues the three of them were motionless, the boy holding his breath, his father looking guilty. Anna watched the man with detached curiosity. *He's afraid of her*, she thought with a flicker of surprise. Never before had she seen a man fearful of a woman. The other way about, yes, oh yes . . .

She closed her mind against thoughts that threatened to overwhelm her.

Bertha's voice, still calling her husband's name, was further away now. 'She'll be gone in a minute,' the man said in a low voice, 'then you can go down, Tony.'

'What if she asks where I've been?'

Eddie's smile flickered briefly. 'Well, I wouldn't tell her you've been up here with this lass. Don't worry, I don't think she'll ask you. It's me she's after.' He looked at Anna. 'She'll be wanting the trap harnessed. She always goes into the town on a Thursday to see her sister and do a bit of shopping.' He chuckled, a deep rumbling sound, and his face looked suddenly much younger, laughter lines wrinkling around his eyes. 'For all the things I've forgotten to bring from the market the day before when I've had one too many.'

He stood up and brushed the hay from his clothes. 'Come on, Tony. Time you were getting ready for school.' He turned back to Anna and smiled down at her. 'You stay here. When the wife's gone, I'll come back and take you down to the cottage.' He pulled a wry expression. 'But it's not much to look at.'

The man descended the ladder first and the boy followed, pausing briefly to smile back at her. Anna raised her hand and curled her fingers in a kind of wave, but could not summon an answering smile.

Three

'It's not much of a place,' Eddie said again as they walked up the slope away from the farm, 'but it's in a good spot near the woods. Sheltered, but very isolated.' Anna felt his glance. 'It'll be lonely for you.'

That'll suit me, she thought, though she said nothing.

She had waited in the hayloft until she heard the trap rattle out of the yard, the sound of its wheels on the roadway receding into the distance. Only a moment later she had heard the man calling softly from below. 'Coast's clear, lass.'

They walked on, but near the top of the hill Anna paused and looked back towards the farm where the man and his family lived. Cackle Hill Farm, for she had seen the name on the gate as they left, was set against a background of trees, beyond which was the rolling countryside of the Lincolnshire Wolds. She turned and followed the man, who was still plodding to the top of the rise. When they reached it, they both paused to take in the view below them. The land sloped away again and at the bottom of the track on this side of the hill Anna could see the outline of a cottage nestling against a wooded area on the right from where she was standing. The land was cold and stark, the trees naked against the grey sky, but in spring and summer she guessed the view would be idyllic. Just beyond the cottage she could see a stream bubbling down the hillside and disappearing round the far side of the wood. Sheep dotted the sloping fields and, for the first time in weeks, Anna smiled.

'You like it?' Eddie asked gently. Anna jumped. For a moment she had forgotten he was there.

'Oh! Oh yes.' She nodded. 'It was the sheep. I – I like sheep,' she added diffidently.

Eddie nodded. 'Mek you feel at home, d'they?'

Her smile faded and at once her face took on a closed look. 'Something like that,' she murmured and the man knew he had said the wrong thing. Silently, he vowed not to mention her home, nor question her about her background. But he liked this lass. He wanted to help her. She was like a lost sheep herself and his tender heart reached out to her. He sighed. If only his wife would be as kindly disposed towards her.

They were nearing the cottage now and Anna could see that it was as tumbledown as he had said. It was a small, lime-washed, mud-and-stud, thatched building with a central front door and a window on either side. To the left of the door, there was a gaping hole where the mud had crumbled away, leaving the wooden slats of the framework exposed. On the same side of the cottage the thatched roof was badly in need of repair. Several of the windowpanes were broken and the front door leant drunkenly on its hinges. When Eddie pushed it open, it scraped the mud floor.

'This place is only used at lambing time. I stay here, specially if the weather's bad. My lad comes too – if his mam'll let him.' The last few words were murmured, almost as if he did not intend the girl to hear them.

The door opened into a tiny hallway with steep stairs, more like a ladder than a proper staircase, leading to the upper floor.

'It's two up and two down, but I only ever use this room,' Eddie said, leading her into the room to the right. He laughed as he jerked his thumb over his shoulder towards the other room. 'I put the sheep in yon one.' He stood looking about him. 'But it's not too bad in here. At least it's weatherproof. We'll get a fire going in there.' He nodded towards the grate, beside which, built into the brickwork, was a bread oven.

Anna glanced around. It was like stepping back into the last century – or maybe even the one before that. There were no rugs to clothe the coldness of the beaten-earth floor. In one corner there was a rusty iron bedstead, but there was no mattress on it. A wooden rocking chair stood near the fireplace, and in the centre of the room there was a table and one kitchen chair. But to the girl, who had lived rough for months in barns and outhouses, the promise of somewhere dry and warm was heaven-sent.

'It's a bit sparse.' Eddie smiled apologetically. 'But we don't need much when we stay here. Anyway, I'll fetch you the feather mattress I use. It's in our loft at the moment.' He pointed. 'That door there's the pantry. I'll soon get that stocked up for you. And this one' – he opened another door that led directly out of the kitchen at the side of the cottage – 'goes outside to the privy. It's down the path there. And you'll have to fetch your water from the stream, I'm afraid. But it's fresh and clean. Comes from a spring up the hill.'

Anna nodded.

'Like Tony said,' Eddie went on, 'I can repair the walls and the windows. I'll rehang the front door and I'll ask Joe Wainwright if he—'

'I can't pay for work to be done,' Anna said at once. Then, realizing she might have sounded ungrateful, she gestured with her hand and added, 'It's – it's very kind of you, but I – I have nothing.'

Gently, Eddie said, 'I wouldn't expect you to pay, lass. The cottage belongs to me and it's high time I got it repaired up.'

'But I can't afford to pay you rent, at least not at the moment.'

The man dismissed the idea. 'Don't you worry about that, love. Besides, you're going to help me with the lambing.' He paused significantly, as if he realized he was forcing her to make up her mind, before adding quietly, 'Aren't you?'

They regarded each other steadily for several moments before she nodded slowly.

When Tony arrived home from school it was already dusk. He rushed into the kitchen and skidded to a halt, surprised to see his mother standing behind the table unpacking her shopping. Before he could bite back the words, he said, 'You're home early. I didn't think you'd be back from Auntie Lucy's yet.'

Bertha smiled. 'I couldn't wait to get back to show you what I've bought you. Here – ' she held out a brown paper bag towards him – 'open it.'

Tony sat at the table. 'But it's not Christmas yet.'

His mother smiled at him. 'Oh, that's just a little extra one from your mam.'

Inside the bag was the usual bar of chocolate she always brought him after her trip to town, but today there was another present. A Dinky toy.

'Aw, Mam – thanks! It's that tractor I wanted.' He opened the box and ran the toy along the table, imitating the sound of a real vehicle. 'Chugger-chugger-chugger.'

Bertha watched him fondly. 'That's all right, love.' She sat down opposite him and rested her arms on the table. 'Now, tell me,' she said, 'what you've been doing at school today.'

'We had writing this morning and sums and then we played footie this after.' The boy reeled off the events of his day.

With deceptive mildness, Bertha asked, 'And did you enjoy the piece of pork pie and the cold sausages as well as the sandwiches I packed for you?'

The boy sat very still. His eyes were still on his new toy, but now he was not moving the tractor or imitating its sounds.

'You can tell your mam, Tony love. I won't be cross. I just want you to tell me if you took them. That's all.'

The boy's lower lip trembled. He opened his mouth once, then twice, but no sound came out. The back door opened and closed and there was the sound of Eddie removing his boots in the scullery.

He appeared in the doorway into the kitchen and stood there for a few moments, glancing between the two seated on either side of the table. 'What's up?'

'Nothing.' Bertha snapped. 'Me an' Tony are just having a little chat. That's all.'

'Oh aye. What've you been up to now, lad? Not in trouble at school, are you?' Eddie moved into the room and went to stand beside his son's chair. He smiled down at the boy and ruffled his hair. Tony shook his head but still did not speak. Instead he stared miserably at his new toy as if all the joy had been taken out of the gift. Eddie looked across the table at his wife, a question in his eyes.

'I was just asking him if he'd enjoyed the pork pie and sausages that's gone missing out of my meat safe in the larder. That's all. Simple enough question, I'd've thought, but it seems as if he doesn't want to answer me.'

'Ah.' Eddie let out a long sigh. 'Now I get it.' Heavily, he said, 'Go out and feed the hens, there's a good boy. Me and ya mam need to talk.'

Tony scrambled from his chair, leaving his new toy on the table. Quietly he closed the door from the kitchen into the scullery, but he did not leave the house. Instead, he stood with his ear pressed to the closed door. He could hear every word clearly.

'You know very well the lad didn't take the food, but it's your way of trying to find out. You shouldn't *use* him, Bertha. It isn't his fault you an' me don't get on nowadays.'

'And whose fault is it, I'd like to know? *I* don't disappear off to market every week and come home rolling drunk, after being with goodness knows how many trollops in the town. And then you have the gall to bring one of 'em home with you. Into my house.' She beat her chest with her fist.

Wearily, Eddie said, 'Bertha, I don't go with trollops, as you put it. In fact, I don't go with other women at all—'

Bertha snorted. 'Spect me to believe that. I know what men are like.'

Eddie regarded her with pity and shook his head slowly. 'Bertha love, I wish you'd believe me. We're not all the same. Just because your dad was a ladies' man—'

'Don't you say things about my dad, Eddie Appleyard. You're no saint.'

'The whole town knew about your dad and his carryings on, love.'

'I aren't sitting here listening to you calling my dad

names just to mek ya'sen feel better.' She wagged her finger in his face. 'He didn't get drunk and come home and knock his wife about.'

Appalled, Eddie stared at her. 'Bertha, I've never—'

'Oh 'aven't you? How do you know what you do when you're sow drunk?'

Eddie dropped his head into his hands. He couldn't believe it. He was not a violent man. Never had been. And though things were not right between him and his wife, he couldn't imagine that he would ever attack her physically. But then, he had to admit, he did get 'sow drunk' as the locals called it, a state that resembled a snoring, snorting pig. And, to his eternal shame, Eddie had to admit that he could not remember what he had done when he was in that state.

He couldn't even remember having brought the girl home from the town until Bertha pulled him from the trap and there the girl was, just sitting there. But that was something he was never going to admit. Not to his wife and certainly not to that poor lass. He didn't want her to think that he hadn't meant to help her, that he couldn't even remember making the offer.

'So?' Bertha was leaning towards him. 'What did happen to my pork pie and sausages?'

'It – it wasn't Tony,' Eddie stammered. 'It was me. I – I was hungry. In the night.' He wasn't used to telling lies. That was yet another thing he hadn't known he was capable of doing.

'If you expect me to believe that, Eddie Appleyard, you're even dafter than I thought you were.' She paused and her small, piercing eyes were boring into his soul. 'Is she still here? Is she still in the hayloft?'

Now he could answer honestly and even Bertha could detect the note of truth. 'No, she isn't.'

'Well, good riddance is all I can say. And if that's the truth, Eddie, then we'll say no more about it. And now I've got work to do even if you haven't.' She levered herself up and turned away, leaving her husband sitting at the table, his head still in his hands, vowing that as long as he lived he would never touch another drop of drink.

Four

From the scullery the boy heard his mother's chair scrape along the floor as she got up from the table. He scuttled out of the back door. He was halfway across the yard when the collie, chained up near its kennel, barked a greeting. The boy hesitated, glanced back towards the farmhouse and then hurriedly released the dog's collar from the chain.

'Come on then, boy.' Together they ran across the yard and out of the gate. In the gathering dusk the boy began to run up the track, the dog loping at his side. At the top of the hill Tony stopped to look down to where the cottage nestled against the trees. He could see a dim glow from the windows and knew that the girl was there.

He shivered, but whether from the cold or the misgiving he felt he could not be sure. Yesterday's rain had gone and stars shone in a clear sky, the moon a gleaming orb. There'd be a frost tonight. Though he was only ten, Tony knew about the weather and the changing seasons. He bent and pulled up his knee-length grey socks. He hadn't had time to change from his short school trousers. Nor had he stopped to put on his wellingtons. His mam'd scold if he messed up the leather lace-up boots he wore for school. He didn't want to make his mother cross with him. She seemed to spend a lot of the time cross these days, but mostly with his dad. The boy frowned and chewed on his lower lip. He couldn't understand why his mam and dad argued so much. But maybe all parents did. He didn't really know. He had some school pals whose homes he sometimes visited. He went to a birthday party now and then and one or two of the boys in his class had been to Cackle Hill Farm. But he still didn't know if other mams and dads carried on at each other like his did.

A gust of wind nibbled icily at his knees and his mind came back to the girl. *She'll be cold*, he thought. Without making any conscious decision, he began to walk slowly down the hill towards the cottage.

Anna had lit a fire from the kindling Eddie had brought her. Thoughtfully, he had also left a box of matches. She had drunk the milk and eaten most of the loaf of bread he had brought too. The hurricane lamp he had given her hung from a hook in the ceiling, casting eerie shadows around the walls.

'I'll bring you some more bits and pieces as soon as I can and I'll start work on the repairs tomorrow. I reckon the chimney'll need sweeping an' all.'

She'd looked him straight in the eye then. 'What about your wife? I don't want to bring trouble on you, Mister. You – you've been kind and I'd like to stay here for a few days. But maybe I'd better move on when I've rested a bit.'

'No.' His retort was swift and surprisingly firm. There was no way he was going to allow this girl to be turned away, especially not just before Christmas. 'No,' he said more gently. 'I – I want you to stay. Bertha needn't know. Not if we're careful. She never comes up this way. She never – ' there was a bitter tone to his words now – 'goes anywhere about the farm. The only time she goes out the house is to town. She dun't even use the village shop. Says she dun't want to give the gossips any more to chatter about. She – she dun't mix wi' folk easy.' He had smiled then, his eyes crinkling with a spark of mischief. 'But that's all to the good. She'll never know if I get things for you from the local shop, will she? And when I go into town next market day, I can get you some more bits of furniture.'

'Furniture? However are you going to get that past her?'

His smile broadened to a grin, his face looking suddenly years younger. 'I don't have to. The road to town runs yon side this wood and there's a track that comes round the other side of the trees to here and then on to our farm.' He gestured with his left hand in a vaguely northerly direction. 'We don't use this way, because the gate from our farm' – now with the other hand he pointed southwards – 'leads out onto the road between the town and the village.'

Anna could not hide the fear in her eyes. 'So – so does anyone use this track past the cottage?'

'Not many, love. Just farm workers now and again and mebbe – ' he chuckled suddenly – 'a poacher or two.'

She had dropped her gaze and breathed more easily.

And now, as the early darkness of a cold December evening came, she sat huddled against the fire. He had been right. The chimney did need sweeping, for every so often smoke puthered into the room, making her cough and her eyes smart. Once that was cleaned, she would be able to build up the fire to use the bread oven, and when the holes in the walls and the roof were mended she could make this a very cosy little home.

If only . . . Her thoughts started to drift but she shook herself physically and pulled herself back to the present.

It was then that she heard a scuffle outside the door from the kitchen and her whole being stiffened. It was too late to turn out the lamp and hide. She jumped at the soft tap on the door. She could not move, could not call out. She just sat there rigid with fear as, slowly, the door opened.

The boy stood framed against the darkness, blinking in the light from the lamp. They stared at one another for a moment and then the girl shivered in the frosty air coming into the room from the open door. The boy stepped inside and closed the door.

'I guessed you might be here. I came to see if you was all right. I – I thought you might be cold.'

She could see the man's features in the boy's face now; similar dark brown eyes and brown hair and a thin but well-shaped face. The boyish features would strengthen into a firm jawline and the father's kindness was already showing in the son's concern for her.

Anna summoned a smile. 'Does your dad know you've come up here?'

He shook his head. 'No.' He bit his lip and then blurted out, 'They're – they're rowing.'

Her smile faded. 'Over me?'

Tony shook his head. 'Not – not really. She thinks you've gone.' He moved closer and squatted down in front of the fire, holding out his hands to the meagre warmth the few sticks were giving. 'I'll get you some logs from the woods tomorrow before I go to school.'

'She doesn't know I'm here, then?' Anna asked softly.

He shook his head. He glanced up at her briefly and then looked back into the flames. Haltingly he said, 'I – don't reckon me dad wants her to know either.' Tony was reluctant to tell her that his father had lied to his mother over the food he had given the girl. He knew why his father had done so, but he wasn't happy about it. He felt torn between his parents. He didn't want his mam to be upset, yet he could understand why his father wanted to help this girl. What he couldn't understand was why his mother didn't want to help her too.

But Anna seemed to know, for she said quietly, 'No, I don't suppose he does.'

After a few moments Tony stood up. 'I'd better go. I've the hens to feed before I go to bed. It's one of me jobs,' he said importantly. 'And – and Mam might be looking for me.'

Anna nodded.

He hesitated a moment and then pulled a crumpled bar of chocolate from his pocket. Holding it out to her, he said, 'You can have this. It's mine. Me mam brought it for me from town. She won't know.'

Anna took it, unable to speak for the sudden lump in her throat. She had thought she had been past all feeling, past caring. Yet the actions of the farmer, and now his young son, made tears prickle behind her eyes.

'And I've brought someone to keep you company.'

For a brief moment her eyes were panic-stricken. 'I don't want . . .' she began, but already he had opened the door. In answer to his soft whistle a black and white collie trotted into the room and stood close to the boy, looking up at him with adoring, obedient eyes.

Tony fondled the dog's head. 'Stay, Rip. Stay here

with the lady.' He glanced up and smiled at her. 'He'll look after you.'

'Won't your mam miss him?' Anna asked, torn between wanting the animal's company and yet not wanting the boy's kindly action to bring him trouble.

Tony shrugged. 'She might, but I'm just hoping she won't.'

Anna tried to raise a smile, anxious to let him know that she appreciated his gesture.

'Thank you,' she said, her voice hoarse with gratitude. She held out her hand to the dog. The animal did not move until the boy nodded and said, 'Go on.' Then Rip padded across the floor and allowed himself to be patted by the stranger. He lay down on the floor and rested his nose on his paws, but his eyes once again sought his young master.

'Stay,' Tony said firmly and though, as the boy went out of the door, the dog gave a little whine, he did not move from his place beside Anna.

'Well, now,' she said softly, stroking the dog's head, 'it looks like we're both going to sleep here on the floor for the night.'

Wrapping herself in the horse blanket she had brought with her from the barn, she lay down between the dying fire and the dog. The animal's warm presence against her back soothed her chilled limbs and brought unexpected comfort to her lonely soul.

Five

The dog was scratching at the door, whining to be let out. Anna roused herself from heavy sleep and dragged herself up from the floor. She was stiff and cold. The fire had died out in the night and the room, never really warmed, was now freezing.

'All right, boy, I'm coming.' She opened the door and the dog ran out. She watched him streak up the hillside towards home. She closed the door and looked around the room in the pale light of early morning. There was little she could do except wait and see if the boy came as he had promised. What was his name? Tony, that was it. Maybe, later in the day, the man would come to see her too. Maybe he would bring her food. Maybe . . . Maybe . . .

She sighed, irritated to find herself dependent on these strangers for her survival. And she was afraid too. The man seemed kind, but why was he prepared to do so much for her? He was even risking trouble within his own family. Was he expecting something from her in return for his generosity? More than just helping him with the lambing? She shuddered and shied away from such thoughts. And how safe was this place anyway? The cottage was certainly isolated, nestling in a vale and obscured from the road by the wood. And it was on the farmer's land; that would offer some protection.

But was it enough?

It would have to be, she told herself. For now at least. If she rested here for a while, then, when she was feeling stronger, she could move on. Further away. She must get further away . . .

She heard a voice outside and looked out of the grimy window. She saw Tony with the dog bounding around him, leaping up to lick the boy's face. She could see that they were overjoyed to see each other again. The boy was laughing. 'Down, Rip, down. Good boy. Good dog.'

She opened the door and stood waiting until they reached her.

'I've come to get you some wood,' Tony said, smiling at her. 'Like I promised.' His face fell a little as he said, 'I'm sorry, but I couldn't get you anything to eat this morning. Me mam . . .' He fell silent, not wanting to sound disloyal to his mother, yet wanting to help the girl. 'Anyway, Dad's milking just now, but he gave me this to bring up. He'll be up later, he said, when he comes to the sheep.' The boy held out a can of milk.

'Thanks,' she said, taking the can eagerly and drinking thirstily.

'You're hungry, aren't you?' the boy said. 'I wish I could . . .'

'Don't worry,' she said at once. 'This is lovely. Really.'

There was a brief pause before he said awkwardly, 'I'd best get you the wood. I don't want me mam to miss me and it'll soon be school time.'

'I'll come with you and then I can find it for myself.'

He led the way in amongst the trees. The girl, still clutching the blanket around her, followed. The dog ran ahead, investigating the exciting smell of rabbit.

'I should have brought a sack,' Tony said, his arms soon full of twigs and broken branches.

'It's all right,' Anna said, taking off the blanket from around her shoulders. She shivered as she felt the loss of its warmth. 'We'll use this.' Together they collected enough kindling and larger pieces of wood to last her the day and carried their haul back to the cottage.

They tipped it onto the hearth and Tony squatted in front of the fireplace. He began to put the twigs into the grate. 'They're a bit damp. I don't think they'll catch light.'

'I'll see to it. You'd best be off.'

He stood up, for a moment feeling suddenly shy. 'Ta-ta, then.'

She nodded and managed a smile. 'Ta-ta,' she echoed.

'Come on, Rip.'

She watched them running up the track until they disappeared over the brow of the hill.

The boy had been right; the sticks were too damp to catch light and after the torrential rain she doubted there'd be anything in the woods that would be dry enough. And the dry kindling that Eddie had provided that first day was all gone. So, hugging the blanket around her again, Anna decided to look around the cottage. There just might be an old piece of wood she could use. There was nothing in the other room, where damp patches marked the floor and the wind whistled in through the broken windows. But when she climbed the ladder-like stairs and stepped into the two rooms under the roof, she found the floor littered with leaves that had blown in through a hole in the thatch and drifted into a corner. The leaves were brittle dry.

She filled the pockets of her coat and climbed down the ladder. Within minutes, the leaves caught light and she picked out the least wet of the twigs to pile on the top of the leaves. The fire smoked as before, but at least it was alight.

She drank the last of the milk and tended the fire. When she looked out of the window again, she was surprised to see that it was fully light, the winter sun pale in a watery sky. For a while she watched the sheep grazing on the slopes and then she saw the man coming down the track carrying a basket over one arm and two blankets under the other.

'Here we are then, lass,' he greeted her. 'I bet you're ready for this.' He held out the basket. There was bread, butter, cheese and more milk. 'Sorry it's not more. I'll go to the village shop later . . . Oh, you've got a fire going. That's good.'

'Your son came up earlier,' Anna said in her soft, husky voice. 'I hope you don't mind.'

Eddie pulled a wry expression. 'I don't. But if the wife finds out—'

'You – you'd better tell him not to come then. I don't want him getting into trouble on my account.'

The man shrugged. 'I don't reckon Bertha'll guess. He roams all over the farm with that dog of his. Gone for hours sometimes. Look,' he said, returning to the matter of her welfare, 'I'll mebbe manage to bring the tractor and trailer up this way later. I can't get into town until next market day without it looking odd, but I'll see what I can find in the outhouses. There's always bits and pieces we've thrown out.'

Later that day Eddie's tractor came chugging down the track with a loaded trailer behind him and pulled to a halt outside the cottage. To Anna, who had nothing, Eddie's barn seemed to have yielded a treasure trove.

'There's a kettle, a few old pots and pans and an armchair. It was me dad's.' His eyes clouded. 'Bertha threw it out the day after he died. And I've managed to get the old feather bed down from the loft when she was in the dairy,' he added, dragging it off the trailer. 'It'll be a bit damp. You'd better let it dry out before you use it.'

Remembering her soaking of two days earlier, Anna smiled to herself, but said nothing. She was hardly likely to take harm from a damp bed, she thought. But the man meant well.

Lastly he unloaded three sacks. 'There's potatoes from our own store and a few apples. And I've been to the shop for you. You'll have to let me know if I've forgotten anything you need.'

Anna stood, shaking her head in wonder. 'It's – it's wonderful. I don't know how to thank you.'

'No need, lass. You're working for me now, aren't ya?' He glanced at her and winked. 'And I always look after me employees.'

'I'll work for you, Mister. Oh, I'll work as hard as I can, but . . .' She touched the mound of her belly briefly.

He nodded sympathetically. 'Don't worry about that, lass. We'll cross that bridge when we come to it.'

But what would happen when they did come to that particular bridge, as he put it, even the man dared not contemplate. 'And now,' he said, trying to divert their thoughts. 'I must see to me sheep.'

'Can I help?'

'No, no, lass. You get ya'sen sorted out. And then – well – we'll see tomorrow, eh?'

Anna nodded. 'All right,' she agreed in her low, soft voice, 'but from tomorrow I want you to tell me what needs doing. And if you don't . . .' She smiled suddenly and the man stared at her, unable to take his eyes off her. She was a pretty lass, though a bit thin at the moment to his mind, but when she smiled her whole face seemed to light up. Even so, it was not enough to drive away the sadness in the depths of her dark eyes. 'And if you don't, Mister, then I'll *find* something.'

He laughed. 'Right you are then, lass. It's a deal.'

As he drove his tractor and trailer back towards the farm to fetch bales of hay for his sheep, Eddie was still smiling.

The following morning Anna walked across the meadow in front of the cottage towards the next field, where she could see the sheep contentedly munching long stalks of kale. She moved stealthily. Sheep were nervous creatures, easily panicked and bunching together in the face of danger and most of Eddie's ewes would be in lamb; the last thing she must do was to startle them.

Shading her eyes, Anna glanced round the edge of the field. There were several gaps in the hedges where the sheep could easily push their way into the neighbouring field. Anna began to smile. Here was something she could do to repay the farmer for his kindness. When the tractor and trailer chugged down the track later that morning, Anna was waiting for him.

'I don't suppose you've left those holes in the hedges for a reason, have you?'

'No, lass,' Eddie said wryly. 'I just haven't had time to repair them.'

'Right, then. You can bring me a billhook and a hedge knife too. Oh, and a few stakes.'

Eddie laughed. 'You're not going to try plashing, are you?'

Anna nodded.

Now he eyed her sceptically. 'Are you sure you can do it?'

Anna gave him one of her rare smiles. 'That's for you to say when I've had a go. I'll do one small gap first and then, if you're not satisfied, you can say so and I'll let well alone. All right?'

Eddie looked mesmerized. To him hedge-laying was a skilled art and one, he had to admit, that he had never been able to master properly.

Whilst he fetched the tools, Anna chose one of the smaller holes and began to clear the hedgerow of weeds and long, dead grass. By the time Eddie brought back the items she had asked for, Anna was ready to position two stakes in the gap. Then, taking up the billhook, she chose the thickest stem she could find in the existing hedge to the right of the hole and began to chip off all its side shoots.

'I'll – er – leave you to it, lass. I'll – um – come back later and see how you're getting on. Only don't tire ya'sen, will you?'

'I'll be fine, Mr Appleyard. It's nice to have something to do.'

Concern was still plainly written on the man's face, though whether it was for the pale waif who had come into his life or for his hedge, even Eddie could not have said. He glanced at her again and now his anxiety was wholly for her, but he was gratified to see a healthy pink tinge to her cheeks this morning. And the way she was wielding the billhook showed no sign of any ill effects from the cold night she must have spent in the cottage.

'I'll be off then,' he said again, still reluctant to leave his hedge. He sighed as he turned away. *Oh well*, he was thinking, *I don't suppose she can make a much worse mess of it than I would.*

A surprise awaited Eddie on his return to the field with Rip trotting beside him, pink tongue lolling, eyes ever watchful and alert. They stopped before the hole in the hedge – or at least where the hole had been. The thickest stems from the existing growth had been cut diagonally a few inches from the ground to a depth of about three-quarters of the thickness and bent carefully over so that the stem did not break. The branches then lay one above the other at angles of about thirty degrees across the gap in the hedge and were neatly woven in and out between the stakes. In time, new shoots from the old wood would form a thick hedge once more. Even the top had been neatly finished off.

Eddie stood gaping. He took off his cap, scratched his head and then pulled it on again, whilst Anna stood by, smiling quietly. 'By heck, lass, it's as good as I could do. No, if I'm honest, it's better. Where on earth did you learn to lay a hedge like that?'

Anna's smile faded and she turned away, but not before Eddie had seen tears fill her eyes.

'I had a good teacher, Mister,' she said huskily. 'A

very good teacher.' Then she took a deep breath and called to the dog. 'Come on, boy.'

As she bent to pick up her tools and move on to the next gap, Rip bounded alongside, leaving Eddie staring after her and then, glancing back to his newly repaired hedge, marvelling again at the young girl's workmanship.

Tony came each night after school to see her, always managing to bring something useful for her. And every night he ordered his dog to 'stay' with her.

'We've broke up from school today,' he told her near the end of the week following her arrival. 'It's Christmas next week.'

'Is it?' Anna said, surprise in her tone.

The boy stared at her. 'You hadn't forgotten?' he asked. To the boy, who had been counting the days, it was incredible that anyone could not know it was almost Christmas. Even his mam, who usually scorned merrymaking at other times, always loved Christmas. She had been mixing the puddings and baking mince pies all this last week. And last night she had helped him put up paper chains, looping them along the picture rail around the best parlour, which they would use on Christmas Day.

In answer to Tony's question, Anna shrugged. 'I've been travelling. I'd forgotten what date it is.'

'How long have you been travelling?' he asked with a boy's natural curiosity. 'Where d'you come from?'

Even the ten-year-old boy could not fail to notice the fear that sprang into her eyes at his question. She bit her lip and turned away. 'Oh, a long way away. You wouldn't know it.'

'I might,' he insisted. 'We've been doing geography at school on the British Isles and learning where lots of places are. I *might* know it.' He was trying to wheedle an answer from her, but now the girl said nothing and deliberately turned her back on him and his questions.

A few days before Christmas Tony brought her a hot mince pie. 'Me mam's just finished baking. She didn't notice I took an extra one.'

Anna bit into the light pastry with the warm juicy mincemeat inside. 'It's lovely,' she said. 'I wish I could send a message to your mam.' She smiled and suddenly some of the pain that was always in the depths of her violet eyes, lightened. 'But I'd better not.'

Tony was staring at her. 'You're ever so pretty when you smile,' he said with the innocent candour of a young boy. 'Haven't you got funny coloured eyes? I mean,' he added hastily, 'they're nice, but I've never seen anyone with eyes that colour before.'

At once the smile fled from her face and the anguish returned. Her words came haltingly, almost as if she were trying not to speak them, but an innate politeness was forcing her to do so. 'They're the same – colour as my – mother's.' The last word was spoken in a strangled whisper and, to the boy's horror, tears welled in her eyes.

'I'll be off,' he said gruffly, pushing his hands deep into the pockets of his coat. There was an embarrassed pause before he said, haltingly, 'I'll have to take Rip back with me tonight.'

He bit his lip. He didn't want to explain to the girl that there had been an awkward moment at home the previous evening. He had been sitting in his pyjamas in front of the kitchen range drinking cocoa when his mother, coming in from the outside privy, had said, 'Where's Rip? He's not chained up.'

Tony had felt his heart miss a beat and then begin to pound. He licked the line of chocolate from his upper lip and said, 'He – he wouldn't come home with me. He – he went off chasing rabbits, I think.'

'At this time of night? That's not like him. He's a very obedient dog usually. Specially with you, Tony. Oh well, mebbe it's not only rabbits he's chasing,' she added dryly. 'He's male, after all.'

Tony buried his nose in his mug to finish his drink. Then he stood up. Going to his mother, he put his arms around her and gave her an extra tight hug, trying to assuage his guilt at lying to her. 'Night, Mam.'

She had kissed his hair and patted his back. 'Night-night, love.'

Now, in the cottage, he commanded, 'Come on, Rip. Home, boy.'

The dog wagged his tail, but made no move to follow. Instead, Rip glanced at Anna and then sat down.

Tony slapped his own thigh. 'Come *on*, Rip.'

The dog flattened his ears and lay down, crawling on his belly, not towards his young master, but towards the girl.

Now it was the boy who had tears in his eyes. 'He's *my* dog,' he said. 'Not yours. I only lent him to you.'

'I know you did,' Anna said quietly, her own misery forgotten for the moment. 'Rip is confused, that's all.' She bent and stroked the dog's head and he licked her hand. 'Good dog. Go with your master now, boy. Go with Tony.'

As if understanding he had been released from any

obligation, Rip sprang up, barked and ran to the boy, leaping up to lick his face. Tony knelt and put his arms around the dog, hugging the wriggling body to him. Without another word, he turned and began to run up the hill, the dog racing ahead and then coming back to him.

Anna heard the boy's joyful laughter and the dog barking. As she closed the door against the dusk of approaching evening, she was already missing Rip's comforting presence in the cottage.

Six

Anna did not see the boy for the next three days, but each morning, when she opened the side door of the cottage to visit the privy, a small pile of wood was neatly stacked against the wall just outside. Later in the day Eddie would come to check on his sheep and would bring her food.

'All right, lass?' was his usual greeting and, as he left, he would say, 'Now, don't you go overdoing it, love.' It was the closest he ever came to referring to her advancing pregnancy.

Anna was surprised how much she missed seeing Tony, but there was plenty of work for her to do. She was kept busy collecting more wood to keep her fire burning through the cold nights and cleaning the inside of the one room in the cottage. She swept the floor and cleaned the windows and scrubbed out the bread oven. But, apart from the brief visits from Eddie and Rip, she saw no one. She had thought that solitude was what she wanted. She had believed she wanted to hide herself away from the world and all its cruelties, yet the farmer's kindness, and especially the boy's, had melted her resolve. Besides, she reminded herself, she had been desperate. Standing in the marketplace that night with nowhere to go, no money and hunger gnawing, she had known she could not hold out much longer.

If the man had not brought her to this place that

night, she doubted she would still have been alive by now. When she felt the child within her move, and in the moments of despair that still racked her, she wondered if it wouldn't have been for the best if she and the child had not survived. But the tranquillity of this place was already seeping into her wounded heart and bringing her a measure of peace. She was not happy – she doubted she would ever feel real happiness again – but she was no longer in the depths of misery. The instinct to survive was strong again within her. And now she had a place to stay. It was only when darkness closed in and she was alone in the cottage that the fear threatened to overwhelm her once more. Maybe she should ask Eddie for strong bolts for the two doors into the cottage. Perhaps then she would feel safe.

'I bet you thought I'd forgotten all about mending the walls,' Eddie called to her one afternoon, as he climbed down from his tractor and went to the trailer behind it to unload tools, wood and what looked suspiciously like a pile of wet mud.

Seeing her looking at it with a puzzled expression on her face, Eddie said, 'It's subsoil. I dug a hole ovver yonder near the stream. It's just right for this.'

Anna leant closer. 'What are all the bits in it?'

'Chopped-up pieces of barley straw. Now, all we need to do is mix it with a bit of sand and water and we'll be ready.' He smiled at her. 'Good, ain't it, when you can provide your own building materials? And it dun't cost me a penny,' he added, to reassure her that her presence in his cottage was not costing him a fortune.

Fascinated, Anna stood watching him nailing the

thin laths of wood into place and then plastering the mud mixture onto the wooden framework.

'I could do that,' she murmured, after watching him for a while.

He glanced up at her. 'Now, leave me summat to do, lass, else I shall start to feel I'm not needed.'

'Oh, you're needed, Mr Appleyard,' she murmured softly, thinking what might have happened to her by now if it hadn't been for this kind and generous man.

'Tell you what,' Eddie said. 'You'll be able to do the whitewashing when the mud's dried enough. How about that?'

By the time dusk came creeping across the field, the other downstairs room was already weatherproof.

'Joe Wainwright's promised to come early in the New Year to see to the roof,' Eddie said, straightening up to ease his aching back. 'That should make the upstairs rooms inhabitable if you should want to use them.'

Silently, Anna thought: *I won't be here by then*, but she did not want to seem ungrateful. Instead she asked, 'Do you think you could spare some whitewash for the inside walls? I hate asking for anything – you've been so good, but—'

'Course, lass. I should have thought of it mesen.'

'And – and could I have a snare? I could catch rabbits in the woods then.'

Now Eddie looked doubtful. 'I'm not too keen on setting traps or snares for wild creatures, love. I don't like to think of poor animals suffering, you know?' He pulled off his cap, scratched his head and then replaced his cap. Anna was beginning to notice that this was a habit with him when he was perplexed or anxious, or maybe even embarrassed in some way. 'Oh, I know I'm a farmer and I raise animals to be killed for meat, but that's done in a humane way.'

'I'm sorry,' Anna said swiftly. 'I shouldn't have asked.'

On Christmas Eve, in the late afternoon, there was a knock at the door. Anna's heart beat faster and her throat was dry as, standing in the shadows, she edged close to the window to see who was standing outside. When she saw the slight figure of the boy, she let out the breath she had been holding and opened the door with a genuine smile of welcome that widened when she saw the expression of apology on his face.

'I'm sorry,' he blurted out.

'Whatever for?' Anna said, pretending not to understand and, so that he would not have to explain his earlier childish petulance, she added swiftly, 'I know you can't come every day to see me.' She pulled the door wider, inviting him inside. 'But it's nice to see you when you can.'

She became aware that his coat was bulging, as if he was carrying something clutched to his chest.

'I've brought you a Christmas present,' he said.

'You shouldn't have . . .' Her voice faded away as she realized that the 'something' he carried was wriggling and pushing its way out from beneath his coat. A tiny wet nose appeared and then the silky black and white head of a collie puppy.

'Oh!' Reaching out with trembling hands, she whispered, 'For me? Is it really for me?'

The boy nodded, grinning broadly now, his earlier awkwardness forgotten. 'Me dad knows this farmer whose bitch had puppies a while back. It's all right. It's ready to leave its mother.' He handed the squirming creature to her.

Anna held the puppy against her breast and stroked its head, whilst it licked at her hand. 'Oh thank you, Tony, thank you,' she murmured. 'He's lovely.'

'You'll have to think of a name for him and when he's bigger you can train him to be a good sheep dog. Rip is,' he added proudly. 'Me dad trained him. He'd tell you what to do.'

For a brief moment, the girl's eyes clouded and seemed to take on a faraway look.

'What are you going to call him?'

Without even stopping to give thought to her choice, she said at once, 'Buster.'

'Buster,' the boy repeated, trying out the name aloud. Then he grinned and nodded. 'Yeah, it's a nice name. Buster. I'll bring you an old basket out of the barn tomorrow and—'

'It'll be Christmas Day. You mustn't come tomorrow. Your mam—' Her voice trailed away.

'Well, as soon as I can then.'

Rip was barking outside the cottage and the boy said, 'I'll have to be off.'

The puppy made all the difference to Anna. He demanded her constant attention and his antics brought the long-forgotten smile more readily to her mouth.

Tony landed with a thump on the end of his parents' double bed. 'Wake up. Wake up. It's Christmas Day.'

There were grunts and groans from both his mother and father.

'Whatever time is it?'

'It's not light yet. Go back to bed for a bit. There's a

good lad.' Eddie was burrowing further beneath the covers, trying to recapture sleep.

'But I want to open my presents.' A plaintive note crept into the boy's tone. 'Don't you want to see me open my presents?'

Bertha roused herself and threw back the covers. 'Course we do, love. Come on, Eddie, stir ya'sen. T'ain't Christmas every day.'

She pulled on her old dressing gown and pushed her feet into well-worn slippers. 'I just 'ope Father Christmas has remembered to bring me summat an' all.'

'Oh Mam,' Tony laughed. 'There isn't a Father Christmas.'

His mother pretended to look scandalized. 'What do you mean? Course there is. Who else do you think brings you all them presents? Enough to fill a pillow-case?'

Tony grinned and bounced up and down on the end of the bed. 'You do, Mam.'

'Well, I believe in Father Christmas,' she declared, her slippers flapping across the linoleum-covered floor. 'Not much else to believe in,' she muttered in a low voice so that the boy would not hear. 'Come on, then. Let's go an' see what he's left you.'

As the woman descended the stairs, grunting with each heavy tread, the boy scrambled to the top of the bed. 'Dad, Dad!' he whispered urgently. 'What about the girl? She'll be all alone. And it's Christmas. Are you going to see her today?'

Eddie yawned and stretched. 'I'll try, lad. But don't you go. Not today. Your mam'll want you to stay here today.'

'I took her the puppy. She – she was ever so pleased.

I could tell. She'd got tears in her eyes. But pleased tears. Not sad tears.'

'Had she, son?' The man put his hand on the boy's shoulder. 'I'm glad. The little chap'll be company for her, won't he?'

'Well, yes.' The boy was not convinced. 'But it's not the same as being with other people and having presents to open and a nice dinner and . . .' His voice trailed away as he thought about their own day ahead here in the cosy farmhouse. It was a stark contrast to the draughty cottage and the meagre fare that Anna would be facing.

Eddie patted his son's shoulder again and said, 'Run along. I'll be down in a minute. I'll see what I can do later.'

The next few hours were spent happily. Even Bertha was delighted with the gift that Eddie had bought her, a warm dressing gown and cosy slippers. Luckily, she couldn't know that, as she slipped them on and paraded around the parlour, his thoughts were not on her, but with the lonely girl in the cottage over the hill. Hidden in the barn were some clothes for her. Useful, serviceable clothes and not new, but his desire to see her face when he presented them to her, the delight he hoped to see in her expression was in the forefront of his mind. But he played the part of dutiful husband and doting father. The latter was not difficult, for Tony's pleasure in the day was obvious and even Bertha had gone to a lot of trouble over the Christmas dinner. Goose and all the trimmings followed by Christmas pudding and brandy sauce.

But all the time he was eating it, Eddie was wondering how he could take some to the girl. He didn't guess that, as they sat side by side at the table, his son was worrying about exactly the same thing.

In the afternoon Tony played with his new toys whilst Eddie helped Bertha wash up. It was the only day in the year when he lent a hand in the kitchen.

'You've spent your morning cooking for us, love,' he always said. 'It's only fair I give you a hand to clear up. Not much of a Christmas Day for you otherwise, is it?'

Later, as Bertha played a noisy game of Snap with Tony, Eddie said, 'I'd better nip out and check the animals. Feed Duke and Rip. I reckon they deserve a Christmas dinner an' all.'

'There's some scraps on the side for the dog,' Bertha said absently and then shouted loudly, 'SNAP! You missed that one, Tony. You weren't watching.'

'Sorry, Mam,' the boy mumbled and looked down again at the cards, but not before he and his father had exchanged a meaningful glance.

This time it was Tony who shouted loudly, 'SNAP!' Now he was happy to pay full attention to the game for he knew from the look that his father was going to take a plateful of Christmas dinner to the girl.

Seven

In January the weekly ration of fresh meat for each person was cut yet further. And there were gloomy predictions that there would soon be a cut in the bread ration, with no hope of any increase either in eggs, bacon or fish.

'You'd've thought they'd be increasing rations now, not cutting 'em further,' Bertha grumbled. 'The war's been over two years come May.'

But Eddie was more philosophical. 'That's one advantage of living on a farm,' he told Anna later and winked conspiratorially as he smuggled more food to her without Bertha knowing. 'Always a bit extra for us that no one need know about.'

The girl was staring at him, a stricken look in her violet eyes.

'I'm sorry, lass,' Eddie said hastily. 'I didn't mean to worry you.'

As she turned from him, she lifted her hand in a gesture of reassurance. 'It's all right. It's just . . .' But she did not finish her sentence and moved away, leaving Eddie staring after her with a puzzled expression. He waited for her to turn back again, to say more, but no explanation was forthcoming.

What on earth could he possibly have said to make that look of fear leap into her eyes once more?

Eddie sighed. The lass was a mystery and no mistake.

Towards the end of January, freezing weather gripped the whole country in its icy fingers. Power failures plunged towns and villages into darkness, whilst the temperature dropped lower and lower.

Cackle Hill Farm had its own generator, but Eddie was concerned for the girl in the cottage. Every few days he took a bag of coal with him on his trailer, hidden beneath the feed for his sheep.

Anna looked out of the cottage one morning to see a slate grey sky. She lifted her face and sniffed the air. *Snow*, she thought. *There's snow coming and a lot of it.*

'How many sheep have you got?' she asked Eddie later when he came on the tractor with bales of hay for his flock.

'About fifty. Why?'

'I reckon we're in for some snow, Mr Appleyard.'

Eddie glanced at the laden sky and then at the girl. 'Aye,' he agreed, marvelling at her knowledge. 'I was thinking the same mesen.' Just who was this girl, he was wondering, and where had she come from? She was certainly knowledgeable about the countryside and about farming. The image of her hedge-laying was in his mind. She was looking about her now, glancing over the sheep, which were grazing with placid contentment unaware of the threatening weather. Eddie was sure that the girl was thinking the same thing he was – his flock ought to be under cover before the snow came. It was the most animated he had seen her, the most conversation they had had. Even over the hedging, she had not been quite so interested, so concerned, so – alive!

He smiled, thankful to see the change in her. 'Call me "Eddie". Everyone does. Meks me feel old to be called "Mester Appleyard".' For a brief moment she looked uncertain, as if, suddenly, her growing trust in him had been threatened. He saw her glance at him and he couldn't mistake the suspicion in her eyes. And something else too. Could it possibly be fear? Hastily, he added, 'Only if you want to, of course. Mebbe I ought to call you "Miss Woods". But to hear mesen called "Mester Appleyard",' he went on, trying to make a joke of it, 'meks me think me dad's come back.'

Her expression lightened a little and there was even the ghost of a smile as she said softly, 'No, no. "Anna" is just fine . . .' There was a long pause before she added almost inaudibly, 'Eddie.'

'Now, about these sheep,' Eddie said, deliberately changing the subject, his gaze roaming over the nearby slopes, 'we could be in real trouble if the snow comes. We're due to start lambing any time.'

Horrified, Anna stared at him. 'As early as this?'

Eddie nodded. 'I usually plan it to start in February, with a batch of about twenty.' He tapped the side of his nose. 'Then I can get them to market by late June or early July when the prices are good. The rest lamb in March and April. Those lambs get the clean grazing, the new grass that year. Then I can sell them any time I want or keep a few to add to my own flock.'

Anna smiled and began to say, 'That's what—'. She stopped and bit her lip. Sensing her thoughts were again turning to a troubled past, Eddie tactfully hurried on. 'They lamb outdoors unless the weather's bad, then, I take them down to the barn. But as soon as the lambs are strong enough, I bring 'em back to the field.' He paused and then laughed wryly. 'Course, some of 'em are awk'ard beggars and drop too early. That's when we end up in your cottage.'

'It must be a busy time for you,' she murmured, her eyes still with a faraway look.

'Tony helps when he can.' He laughed. 'I forget sometimes just how young he is. He's a good lad.'

'Mm, I can see that,' Anna murmured. She did not ask if Bertha ever helped for she'd guessed the answer.

'Mebbe' – Eddie was glancing worriedly at the sky and thinking out loud – 'I ought to get as many as I can of the flock down to the yard. I can't get all fifty under cover, but at least they'd all be in one place.'

'It'd certainly be better than them getting buried in the snow out here. We'd never find them. And when those that are due start lambing—'

'I'll bring Rip and Tony up tomorrow and we'll start rounding them up. One day off school won't matter.'

'There's no need to keep him off. I can help you.'

Eddie nodded. 'All right then, lass. I'll see you bright and early in the morning.'

'Eddie,' she said suddenly, as he began to climb back onto his tractor, 'leave me your crook, will you?'

He eyed her speculatively. 'Course I will. But what do you want with it? I mean, you didn't ought to be tugging about with sheep. Not in your . . .' His voice trailed away, but when he glanced briefly towards her stomach she understood. 'Now, promise me you won't.'

Touched by his concern, she smiled, though as always the smile scarcely reached her eyes. The deep sadness in them was something that haunted Eddie Appleyard even when he was not with her.

'I'd just feel better if I had one,' she answered, neatly

evading giving her promise and knowing he would not deny her request.

Eddie reached into the trailer behind his tractor and handed her his shepherd's crook.

'This isn't your only one, is it?' she asked softly, running her hands lovingly up and down the polished wood.

He laughed. 'Lord, no. I've two more and Tony's even got his own little one. I had it specially made for him.'

Anna closed her eyes and sighed, and when she opened them again Eddie was startled to see tears brimming. Her voice was husky as she said, 'That's nice.' Then swiftly, she turned away.

As he drove up the track, Eddie was filled with acute sadness, yet he didn't quite know why. Every so often something was said or something happened that seemed to remind the lass of her past – something that brought tears. He wished she would open up, that she would tell him more about herself. He sighed. There was nothing more he could do except look after her – no matter what it cost him.

As he drove into the yard and climbed down from his tractor, he saw Bertha standing in the doorway, her arms folded across her bosom. Scowling, she shouted, 'And what's so interesting up yon track, might I ask?'

As he walked towards her, he forced a smile. 'Me sheep,' he said and added mildly, 'Any tea in the pot, Bertha love?'

The snow came that night. It began stealthily, falling innocently enough at first and clothing the world in a thin, white sheet.

The following morning Eddie, Anna and Rip rounded up thirty-three sheep and drove them down to the farmyard, though Anna was careful to stay out of sight of the house. Another ten wandered down to the cottage of their own accord and sheltered near the walls or beneath the trees. By dinnertime the snow was coming thick and fast.

'There's still seven missing,' Anna panted, leaning on her crook and screwing her eyes up against the huge flakes that settled on her face. They clung to her hair and covered her shoulders.

'You go in now, love. You're beginning to look like a walking snowman. You'll be soaked through.' He didn't refer to the day he had found her and brought her home, yet it was in both their minds. She had changed even in that short time. Now she had a home, she was warm and well fed. Now she was able to laugh and retort, 'So do you.'

Beside them, Rip shook himself vigorously, the snow from his coat showering them both with even more.

'We must find them,' Anna insisted as her thoughts returned to the missing animals.

'Me an' Rip'll keep looking, but it's pretty hopeless in this lot. We can't see more than a few yards in front of our noses, never mind trying to see sheep across the field. If it'd only stop snowing, we might have a better chance.'

'But seven,' Anna said, 'that's a lot to lose.'

'I know,' Eddie said soberly, 'but think of all those we've saved. Besides, they might be all right if it stops soon.'

They both glanced at the sky and then at each other, but neither spoke. They didn't need to. The sky was so heavy with snow that it was almost like the dusk of evening even though it was only midday. They both knew that the snow would keep coming until it was ankle deep, then up to the knee and, finally, almost too deep for anyone to wade through. They were facing day after day of blizzards that would shroud the countryside and bring transport, movement of any kind, to a halt. The lanes and then the roads would soon be impassable and only tractors or vehicles with heavy chains on their wheels would be able to move anywhere. Children from outlying areas would not get into the village school. Isolated farms and houses would be snowed in and would have to rely on their own food stores.

That first evening, when Eddie returned, wet through, aching in every limb and disconsolate because he had not found even one of his missing sheep, Bertha was already fretting. 'I'm going to be trapped 'ere, not knowing if me sister's alive or dead.'

'I'll take you into the town on the tractor, love, if it gets that bad and you're worried about her,' Eddie offered.

His wife's retort was scathing. 'Spect me to ride on that thing? I'd be a laughing stock.'

'Nobody's laughing, Bertha. We'll have to get about as best we can.'

'Aye well, you're all right, aren't you? You can still get into town of a Wednesday.' She leant towards him, wagging her finger. 'Only thing is, Eddie Appleyard, you can't drink like a fish no more, 'cos the tractor won't know it's own way home like that poor old pony.'

Eddie turned away without replying. There was no talking to the woman sometimes. He couldn't believe that she had not noticed by now – and he certainly wasn't going to remind her – that he had not come home drunk, not once, since the night he'd brought the girl home. He had kept his silent vow of abstinence, but Bertha hadn't even commented on it.

In the cottage, Anna didn't mind the weather. In fact, it made her feel more secure. No one could reach her now. No one would find her hidden away in a snow-covered cottage near the wood. And she had all the supplies she needed. In the weeks since Christmas she had built up a woodpile in the next room and, thanks to Eddie, she had a good store of tinned food in the larder. She and the puppy would be fine – the only thing that concerned her was Eddie's sheep.

Gently, young though he was, Anna had begun to train the puppy. She would whistle softly in different tones and different pitches and repeat the words of instruction that the shepherds used. When he grew bigger and spring came, then she would take him into the fields and teach him properly.

But sometimes the tears overcame her and she buried her face in his soft coat, remembering that other dog called Buster who had been hers in that other life.

The following morning Anna looked out to see a white world outside her window. But, for the moment, the snow had stopped falling. After a hasty breakfast, she pulled on her warmest clothes and the wellingtons Eddie had brought her.

'Now you stay here, warm and cosy by the fire,' she said to little Buster, who, sensing that he was going to be left alone, whimpered. 'It's a pity you're not bigger like . . .' she began and then faltered, blinking back sudden tears. Then she added bravely, 'You could be a great help today.'

With a final pat, she opened the front door. Normally, she used the door from the kitchen, but today she had another idea. At once a deluge of snow that had drifted against it during the night fell in and it took the girl several precious minutes before she could get the door closed again and then begin to dig a path away from the cottage.

'This is worse than I thought,' she muttered, resting on her spade for a moment. Digging away the snow was hard work and the ever-increasing bulge of her stomach hampered her. But the thought of the sheep buried out there in the fields spurred her on. 'Worst of it is,' she muttered to herself, 'they're such silly creatures. They might not be together. They could be anywhere.' But her words were spoken fondly. She had a great affection for sheep and it was this that was making her disregard her own safety – even the well-being of her unborn child – in an effort to save the rest of Eddie Appleyard's flock.

First, she dug her way round to the back of the cottage, to find the sheep huddled against the back wall of the cottage, their long coats matted with snow.

'You poor things, you do look miserable. Come on, let's get you in the warm.' Grabbing hold of the nearest one, she began to lead it round the side of the building and in through the front door and pushed it into the empty 'parlour' of the cottage. Two had followed her of their own accord and, with three similar trips, she soon had all the sheep under cover. She counted them. Ten. Yes, she had been right. Somewhere on the snow-covered hills were seven more. Already the little room looked crowded, but Anna was determined to find the others and bring them to safety.

'Now for the difficult bit,' she murmured, taking up the crook and plodding round to the front of the cottage.

Snow was falling again, but only light, small flakes. Even though the sky looked laden, at the moment she could still see across the fields. Anna scanned the slopes. Taking a deep breath, she pushed her way through the deep snow towards the side of the field. Sheep tended to look for shelter and when the snow began the hedgerows would be the most likely place to find them.

She had unearthed two by the time she heard a shout and looked up to see Eddie, Tony and Rip struggling to reach her.

'I thought – you promised me . . .' Eddie panted as he neared her, 'that you wouldn't do this.'

For the first time Anna laughed aloud throwing back her head, the joyous sound echoing around them. For a moment, Eddie and Tony stood looking at her and then, unable to stop themselves, they laughed too.

Anna was shaking her head. 'I didn't actually answer you.' Then she looked at him with an expression that was almost coy. 'But I expect you're used to being obeyed.' And she nodded towards Tony.

Eddie smiled, but there was a wry twist to his mouth now. 'By Tony, yes. Well, most of the time.'

He looked at the two bedraggled sheep standing miserably in the snow. 'I'm surprised they're still alive.'

'Luckily, they weren't buried very deep, but we'd better get on looking for the rest . . .'

'Oh no! You're doing no more. You take this pair back to the cottage and . . .'

Her face was suddenly mutinous. She shook her head. 'Not until we've found the others.'

The man and the young girl stared at each other, whilst the boy looked from one to the other, watching the battle of wills between them.

'You need my help,' Anna said, her expression softening. 'Let me repay you for your kindness when I can. Please?'

He sighed. She was right. He did need her help, but he was worried about her. Even in the short time he had known her, her belly had swelled. She couldn't have much longer to go, he thought.

'Well,' he said still doubtful, but weakening. 'All right, but promise if you feel tired you'll stop.'

'Yes, I'll promise you that.'

'Right. Tony, you take these two down to the cottage . . .' Eddie said and Anna added, 'In through the front door and into the other room. The one to the left.'

Eddie stared at her. 'You've got some inside?'

She nodded. 'The ones that were sheltering at the back of the cottage.' She laughed. 'They're guests in my front parlour now.'

They worked – the three of them – until late afternoon, until all but one sheep had been accounted for.

'We'll have to leave it at that. I'll take these down to the yard if they can make it through the snow. Mebbe she'll turn up.' Eddie's thoughts were still with his one lost sheep. 'Mebbe she's wandered off and found her own shelter somewhere.' But his tone was not convincing.

'I wanted to find them all,' Anna murmured, her gaze still roaming the hillsides, but in the gathering dusk she could no longer see very far.

'We've found more than I dared to hope thanks to you, lass,' Eddie said. 'Can you manage with those twelve? I really can't get any more into the barn.'

'It's a bit crowded, but yes. They'll be fine.'

'I'll bring some feed for them, but now into the cottage with you and get yourself dry and warm.'

'I will, but first . . .' Letting her crook fall, Anna bent and scooped up a handful of snow. Then she moulded it into a ball. 'Let's have snowball fight.' And she lobbed the ball of snow at Tony, catching him full in the chest.

For a brief moment, the man and the boy stared at her in amazement. Then, with a whoop they began to fling snow at her and at each other until a blizzard of snowballs was flying through the air and their laughter was echoing through the dusk and the gently falling snowflakes.

At last, breathless, they stopped, bending over to catch their breath. As she straightened up, Anna's laughter turned into a cry as pain stabbed at her stomach and she fell to her knees in the snow.

'What is it?'

She was bending double, crouching in the snow and groaning. 'It – hurts,' she gasped.

'Let's get you inside. Then I'll have to fetch the midwife from the village. I reckon it's your bairn coming, lass.'

She clutched his arm and looked up at him with terrified eyes. 'No – no. I don't want anyone else here. And I don't want the baby.' Her voice rose to a hysterical pitch as she gripped Eddie's arm with an intensity that frightened him. 'I won't have it. I won't.'

Eight

They helped her back to the cottage. The man was worried and the young boy's eyes were wide and fearful. All Tony wanted to do was to run as far away as possible.

'Let's get you into the warm and lying down,' Eddie said, aware of how inadequate warmth and comfort were in the snowbound, isolated cottage.

'Shall I go and get Mam?' Tony asked.

'No,' the girl cried. 'No. I don't want anyone.'

As another spasm of pain gripped her, she grasped Eddie. 'I don't want anyone else. Promise me. I don't want anyone to know I'm even here.'

He didn't answer her, but pushed open the door and half carried her inside the cottage. 'Lie down,' he commanded. His voice was gentle, but there was a note of firmness in his tone. 'Now, look here, lass. I respect your feelings. Whatever reason you've got, I know you don't want other folks around. But this is different. I can't manage on me own . . .'

'Why not? You know about sheep – about lambing . . . aah . . .' Her words ended in a cry of pain and she held her stomach.

Eddie could not help a wry smile. 'This is a bit different, love, than helping a few lambs into the world.'

'I don't see why,' she panted, as the contraction faded.

Eddie shook his head. 'I'm going to the village to fetch the midwife. I'll ask her not to say owt. Pat Jessop's a good sort.' His face sobered. 'I'd never forgive mesen, if owt happened to you – or to the bairn.'

Anna closed her eyes as she whispered dully, 'It wouldn't matter. It wouldn't matter to anyone. Maybe it'd be for the best.'

Eddie took her hand and squeezed it. 'Don't say things like that, lass. It'd matter to me. To both of us.' He turned and looked at his son. 'Wouldn't it, Tony?'

The boy nodded. He was still frightened. He'd seen lambs and calves born all his young life. But, like his dad said, this was very different. At his father's next words his fears increased.

'Now, son, you stay here with Anna while I go back to the farm and fetch the tractor. I'm going to tell your mam that I've got to stay up here with the sheep. Then I'll go to the village and fetch Mrs Jessop and when I get back with her, you can go home.'

Seeing the boy's terror, Eddie put his hand on Tony's shoulder. 'Don't leave her, lad. I'm counting on you. I won't be long.'

The boy's voice trembled as he asked, 'What if Mam comes looking for me?' He put out his hand to fondle his dog's head. Rip had come to sit beside his young master, his attention divided between Tony and the boisterous puppy. Buster was leaping around him, giving excited little yelps, inviting the older dog to play. But Rip sat obediently to heel.

'She won't,' Eddie replied, trying to sound more confident than he felt. Bertha would never venture out to look for her husband, but Tony was a different matter. She just might be worried enough about him to brave the weather.

'Please, oh please, don't go,' Anna moaned, but Eddie was adamant. 'I have to, lass.'

'But it's coming. It's coming.' Her voice rose in anguish.

'No, it isn't. If I know owt about these things, you're going to be a while yet. Specially . . .' He had been going to add 'with your first', but he thought better of it. Instead, he patted her hand encouragingly and turned away. 'I'll be as quick as I can.'

He trudged back through the snow to the farmhouse.

'Where's Tony?' was Bertha's first question.

'He's all right.' Eddie managed to sound convincing and, as much as he could, he determined to keep to the truth. His lies would sound more convincing. 'We've got all the remaining sheep into the cottage, bar one. And one or two of them look as if they're going to start.' If only she knew just who it was that was 'lambing', he thought wryly. 'I'll have to stay up there for a bit, love. I've come for the tractor. I – I need some bits and pieces from the village. Anything you want while I'm going?' he added swiftly, hoping to divert her from asking too many questions about what was happening in the fields.

'No, no, I don't think so,' Bertha said abstractedly, then, returning to her main cause for concern, she added, 'You're not to keep Tony up there all night.'

'No, no, love, of course not. I'll make sure he comes home well before dark. But,' he added, with more truth than she could ever know, 'I know he's only young, but he's a great help to me.'

'You don't have to tell me that,' Bertha said and there was pride in her tone. For a moment she softened. 'You get off to the village and I'll pack you some food up now and you can call for it on your way back.'

Eddie swallowed, feeling trapped. He hadn't planned on coming back this way, but on taking Mrs Jessop further along the lane and in by the track round the far side of the woods to reach the cottage. He couldn't risk Bertha seeing Pat Jessop riding on his tractor complete with her midwife's bag. But all he could say was, 'Righto, love. That'd be grand.'

As he rode into town on his tractor, Eddie worked out a plan. *I'll take Pat straight to the cottage, then double back round by the lane and into the farmyard. That way I can collect what she's packed up for me and then go back up the track from the farm to the cottage.* It was lucky, he thought, that the lane was not visible from the farmhouse. Bertha wouldn't be able to see him going past the gate and then coming back again. Not unless she was out in the yard near the gate. And he very much doubted she would be. Not in this weather! He smiled to himself, beginning to enjoy the intrigue.

'Who'd have thought it?' he muttered aloud. 'Quiet old Eddie Appleyard having a bit of excitement in his life.'

Left in the cottage with Anna and the two dogs and with twelve sheep now huddled in the next room, Tony was mentally counting the seconds from the moment his father left.

'Can I – get you anything?' he asked tentatively.

Anna, lying quietly for the moment, with her eyes closed, shook her head. 'I'm sorry,' she said, 'that you're having to see this. You shouldn't be here.'

Tony shrugged, suddenly feeling important. 'S'all

right. I've seen lambs and calves an' that born. I know all about it.'

Anna smiled weakly. Did he? Did he really know the whole process? How a lamb, a calf, a child was conceived? Perhaps he did, she thought. He lived on a farm. Had done all his young life. He must have seen the ram in the fields with the sheep, the bull with the cows and maybe Eddie even allowed him to watch when the boar visited. For an intelligent boy it wouldn't be too great a step to imagine what happened between a man and a woman . . .

Anna groaned and covered her face with her hands, trying to keep the memories at bay.

'Is it hurting again?' Tony asked.

She let out a deep sigh and tried to relax her body. 'Not just now.'

But only a minute later she was doubled up again and thrashing about the bed in agony. Tony backed away from her, standing pressed against the far wall, wanting to run, but knowing that he could not, must not, leave her.

He had promised his dad.

Rip whined and pressed against the boy's legs. Even the puppy's lively scampering was quietened. Giving little whimpering cries, he nestled between Rip's paws.

If only, Tony agonized, she would stop crying out in pain.

Eddie banged loudly on the door of the village midwife's little cottage. Wintersby village was lucky to have a trained district nurse cum midwife living there. Not all villages had one and a trip to the market town of

Ludthorpe would have been impossibly slow in this weather, even on the tractor.

The door was flung open and the tall, buxom figure of Pat Jessop stood there.

'Eddie.' She smiled in welcome. 'What brings you here? Something wrong, ducky?'

'I need your help, Pat.' At her gesture of invitation, he knocked the snow from his boots and stepped inside the door. As she closed it, he pulled off his cap.

'Slip your boots off and come into the kitchen. Tell me all about it,' she said leading the way.

Eddie and Pat Jessop, Pat Anderson as she had been then, had attended the village school at the same time. They had played together as children and Pat had loved nothing better than visiting Cackle Hill Farm and helping with the harvest or, as she had grown older, lambing time. She always said it had been that experience that had led her into nursing. Yet, because she had gone to train in the hospital on the hill in Ludthorpe and had lived in the nurses' home there, the tender romance that might have blossomed between her and Eddie had withered. Pat had fallen in love with a handsome night porter on the hospital staff and, eventually, Eddie had married Bertha. Pat's husband had been killed in the recent war and sadly there had been no child from the union for Pat to love and cherish in his memory. Her loving nature could now only find fulfilment in the care of her patients and nothing gave her greater joy than bringing a child safely into the world.

'I've a bit of trouble on, Pat.' Eddie stood awkwardly in the tiny kitchen, turning his cap through restless fingers.

'Sit down, Eddie, and have a cup of tea.'

'I'd love to, Pat, but I can't stay. I need your help.'

Swiftly, he explained how he had met Anna and taken her home with him. 'Bertha doesn't know she's staying in me cottage. And,' he added pointedly, 'she mustn't.'

'Oh, Eddie,' she murmured, shaking her head at him in gentle admonishment, 'you and that big heart of yours. It'll get you into real trouble one of these days.'

With wry humour, Eddie ran his hand through his hair. 'I think it already has, Pat.'

Pat pulled a face. 'I have heard the tittle-tattle in the village. Not that I take any notice of it,' she added swiftly, 'or repeat it.'

'I know you wouldn't, Pat,' Eddie said softly.

'Anyway, right now we must think about this girl. You think she's gone into labour, Eddie?'

'I'm sure of it.'

'Just give me five minutes to put me warmest clothes on and get a few things together and I'll be with you.'

It had begun to snow again as they started on the journey back to the farm, which lay about a mile outside the village. Pat, muffled in a mackintosh, scarves and wellingtons, sat on the mudguard over the huge back wheel of the tractor. She had dispensed with her official district nurse's uniform in favour of slacks and jumpers. She knew just how long this night might be.

Dusk was closing in as they reached the cottage, to see Tony standing in the doorway. There were tears running down the boy's face and as soon as the tractor stopped and Eddie and Pat climbed down, he ran towards them and flung himself against his father.

'Come quick. She's screaming and screaming all the time now and – and there's water and blood too—'

'Oh my God!' Eddie muttered, but already Pat was hurrying into the cottage.

'Now, ducky, here I am. You'll be all right. Let's have a look at you.'

The man and the boy stood in the shadows, feeling helpless but unable to tear themselves away.

Anna was bathed in sweat and clutching the sides of the mattress. She was crying out and writhing in agony.

'Now, now, calm down. I'm here now and everything will be all right,' Pat was saying, soothing the terrified, pain-racked young girl. Pat examined her swiftly and looked up, smiling. 'It's only your waters broken, ducky. Everything's just fine. Baby will be fine. Now, when's your due date?'

The girl's head moved from side to side.

'When did the doctor tell you your baby would come, ducky?' Pat persisted gently.

'Never – seen – a doctor,' Anna gasped. 'I don't want it.' Her voice rose. 'I don't want it.'

Briefly, Pat left Anna's side and crossed the small room to Eddie.

'This isn't going to be easy,' she whispered. 'She's fighting it. Send the boy home, but you'll have to stay, Eddie. I'll need you. Get that fire built up. Plenty of hot water and—' Her eyes fell on the two dogs in the corner. She pointed in horror. 'And get them out of here this minute.' At that moment bleating came from the next room and Pat's eyes widened. 'Oh, Eddie, don't tell me! You've got sheep in there, haven't you?'

Eddie nodded.

Pat sighed and shook her head. 'Eddie Appleyard, what am I to do with you? This is hardly the ideal place anyway for the lass to give birth, but with animals a few feet away . . . I don't want her getting an infection.

So,' she went on, rolling up her sleeves, 'get me a bowl of hot water and the first thing we'll do is wash in disinfectant. Both of us. Where's my bag? Ah, there it is.' As she turned she added, 'You still here, Tony? Off you go and take those dogs with you.'

Tony cast a wide-eyed glance at his father. 'I can't take Buster home. What'll Mam say?'

'Put him in with Duke. She never goes in there.'

Tony picked up the puppy. Like his father, he knew that Bertha never went anywhere near the pony unless it was safely harnessed between the shafts of the trap. Buster made little yelping noises and licked the boy's face, ecstatic to be fussed.

'Have I time to take the tractor back and pick up some food? Bertha was packing summat up for me. I – I don't want her to wonder why I haven't gone back.'

Pat could only guess at the full story from the brief outline Eddie had given her, but, knowing his wife, she realized the importance of Eddie's request. 'Yes, go on, but be as quick as you can.'

Eddie put his hand on his son's shoulder. 'You run on home, son, but not a word to your mam.'

The boy nodded and turned towards the door, but before he left he gave one last glance at the girl on the bed. Then he was out of the door and wading through the snow as fast as he could. As he went, he heard Anna's last, despairing cry. 'I don't want it. Let me die. Just let me die.'

Nine

The birth itself was straightforward enough. The baby was small, a little early, Pat thought, but it was the girl's attitude that concerned her. Anna screamed and writhed, fighting the pain.

'When you get a contraction, you've got to push,' Pat told her, but irrationally Anna would only shout, 'I don't want it. I don't want it.'

Kindly, but firmly, Pat said, 'Well, you can't leave it in there, ducky.'

Eddie kept the fire built up and soon the room was hot and stifling. He fetched and carried to Pat's commands and, as she brought the child, kicking and screaming, into the world, he was standing beside her, holding Anna's hand and mopping the girl's brow gently.

'You've a lovely baby girl, Anna. She looks a bit premature, but she's beautiful and what a pair of lungs!' Pat laughed and held up the wriggling infant. Swiftly, she wrapped the baby in a piece of flannelette sheeting. 'I'll see to you in a minute, my pet,' she murmured. 'Here, Eddie, you'll have to hold her for a moment. I must get the placenta.'

'Me?' Eddie looked startled.

'Yes, you, Eddie Appleyard. I don't see anyone else handy.'

Eddie sat down in the battered old armchair he had

brought from his barn for Anna and held out his arms. Gently, Pat laid the tiny infant in the crook of his elbow and watched Eddie's face soften as he looked down at the baby girl. If Pat Jessop had not known Eddie so well that she believed every word he had told her implicitly, at that moment she could have believed that the child was indeed his. Watching his tender expression and the gentle way he held the child, as if she were the most precious being on God's earth, brought a lump to Pat's throat. There were going to be plenty of the village gossips who would believe that he was the father once this news got out. But no one would hear it from Nurse Jessop.

'Now then,' she said briskly, turning back to the new mother, who was lying quietly with her eyes closed. Anna's cheeks were red with the effort of giving birth, but it was not the colour of robust health. The young girl was very thin and Pat wondered if she would have enough milk to feed the child naturally.

'Now, Anna, you're lucky you don't need any stitches, but we've got to get the afterbirth away. I'll have to massage your tummy.' Drowsily, the girl opened her eyes and frowned. 'That hurts.'

'Sorry, love, but I have to do it.' When that did not produce the desired effect, Pat said, 'Can you cough, ducky?'

Anna made a little noise in her throat.

'Come on, Anna. A real good, deep cough. Right from your boots. That's it. Good girl,' Pat exclaimed as the placenta came slithering out. 'That's what I wanted. Now we'll get you cleaned up and you can rest while I wash the baby. Then you can hold her.'

Pat glanced at the girl, but she had closed her eyes again. She lay passively all the time while Pat washed her and changed the sheets, which the nurse had had the forethought to bring with her.

'It's amazing how many times I have to use me own sheets.' Pat laughed. 'And I've brought you some baby clothes too. I keep a few spares. Now, you have a little sleep whilst I wash the baby and then you can hold her.'

To Pat's dismay the only response Anna made was to turn her face to the wall.

When she had washed and dressed the baby, Pat sighed as she sat in the chair beside the warm fire, holding the child close. She brushed her lips against the tiny infant's downy hair and asked softly, 'What's going to happen to you, little one?'

The firelight was a soft glow on Pat's round face and glinted on her blonde curls, which were usually tucked neatly away beneath her district nurse's severe hat. Her blue eyes were troubled as she looked up and asked quietly, 'What's going on here, Eddie?'

Eddie moved closer to the fire to sit beside Pat. He passed his hand wearily across his forehead. 'I don't know, love, any more than you do. All I can tell you is – ' he glanced across to the bed in the corner, but Anna was now sleeping – 'it looks like she's run away from home. She's desperate that no one should know she's here. She didn't want me to fetch you, even though she was obviously in pain. She's terrified someone is going to find her. Her family, I suppose.'

Pat nodded and sighed. 'Same old story, I expect. She's got pregnant and her family's given her a hard time about it. She's either run away or – ' her tone hardened – 'they've thrown her out.' There was silence between them before Pat added angrily, 'You'd think, wouldn't you, after what we've all been through in the war, that folks would have learnt to be a bit more understanding. It breaks my heart to think of all the poor little bairns born in the war that'll never know their fathers, even some of 'em born *in* wedlock ne'er mind those that weren't. And there's a few of both sorts round here, let me tell you. Ee, what's the world coming to, Eddie? What's the world coming to?'

Eddie was silent, unwilling to admit, even to Pat, that his own wife had shown the same lack of compassion towards Anna.

'But you'd better be careful, Eddie, letting her stay here. She can only be seventeen or eighteen at the most. Legally, still a minor.'

'Well, I'm not going to report her, if that's what you're suggesting.'

'I'm not,' Pat said swiftly, 'but you ought to talk to her when she's stronger. Make her see that she should at least get in touch with her family.'

'She's never mentioned anything about her family, and when I've tried to ask her about herself she clams up.'

Pat glanced across at the bed in the corner. 'Mm. Something's not right, Eddie. Have you seen that scar on her fingers?'

Eddie stared at her and then shook his head.

Pat held up her right hand and with her left forefinger, made a slashing movement across the first two fingers on her right hand. 'She's got a nasty wound across here. A deep cut, I'd say. It's healed now, but it's not an old scar. I reckon it's been done about six or seven months ago. About the time,' she added pointedly, 'that she would find out she was pregnant.'

There was silence between them, each busy with their own thoughts, until Eddie said, 'I'd better check on the sheep.'

Minutes later, he put his head round the door. 'There's one going into labour and there's not much room in there—'

'Well, you can't bring it in here.'

Eddie shrugged and was about to disappear again when he paused and asked, 'What about you? Do you want me to take you home?'

'No, no. I'll stay here the night.' She cast a coy look at him. 'Though what it'll do to my reputation, I daren't think.'

'Well—' Eddie scratched his head.

Pat laughed. 'Go on with you, you old softy. I'm only teasing. I must stay here till morning anyway and make sure Anna knows how to feed her baby.'

'Oh, right,' Eddie said and looked relieved. He grinned at her before disappearing back into the neighbouring room.

How nice it was, Eddie was thinking as he knelt beside his ewe, to have a woman with a sense of fun and a bit of sparkle about her. Yes, that was the word he would use to describe Pat Jessop. Despite the sadness she had experienced in her own life, there was always a sparkle about her.

It was two o'clock in the morning before Eddie came back into the kitchen, washed himself thoroughly in the sink and sat down wearily in the chair beside the fire. 'The rest seem OK for the moment. What a day!' He leant his head back against the chair and closed his eyes.

'Sorry I couldn't offer to come and help you. It'd've been just like the old days,' Pat said softly. 'How's the lamb?'

'Fine and healthy and suckling straight away.'

'Mm,' Pat said dryly as she glanced towards the sleeping girl in the corner of the room. 'I've always said the animals can teach us a thing or two.' She paused and then said, 'Tell you what, Eddie, you nurse this little mite for a moment and I'll make us some tea and then you get a bit of rest.'

'What about you?' Eddie asked as Pat gently placed the sleeping infant in his arms.

'Me? Oh, I'm all right. Quite used to the odd sleepless night, but you'll have to take me back to the village in the morning. I've me rounds to do. In fact' – she smiled impishly – 'you'd better get me back home before it's light, else there'll be gossip.'

Eddie chuckled softly, but his eyes were now on the baby in his arms. 'She's a bonny little thing, ain't she?'

'She is,' Pat agreed, once again watching the gentle expression on Eddie's face and feeling the prickle of tears behind her eyelids.

In her job, Pat Jessop rarely let her emotions get the better of her. It didn't mean she didn't care. Far from it. Her compassion was what made her so good at her job and loved by all her patients. But the whole village knew that Eddie's marriage was not all that it might have been. And Pat's tender heart went out to the man who had been her friend since childhood.

'Funny woman, that Bertha,' was what the gossips said. 'Her dad was a right 'un. Affairs? He 'ad more women than I've had 'ot dinners. And what he didn't get up to in the war was nobody's business.' Here, the storyteller would tap the side of his nose and nod knowingly. 'Black market. Mind you, if you wanted owt, you knew where to go. There wasn't much that Wilf Tinker couldn't lay his hands on.'

'Where is he now then? Dead?'

'Oh no.' The teller would warm to his tale, saying triumphantly, 'He's inside.'

'Never!'

'S'right, but the family don't want folks to know. As if we don't all know already.'

'What happened?'

'It was near the end of the war. Several of the farmers were having ducks pinched in the night. Course, good source of food, weren't it, on the black market? Well, Wilf's driving his old van one night along a country lane in the middle of nowhere when the local bobby stops him. "I ain't no ducks," Wilf ses straight away and then, of course, the bobby looks in the back of the van and finds half a dozen of the little beggars. Still alive, mind you, in a sort of coop and covered over with sacks to muffle the quacking. Daft part about it was – ' at this point the storyteller would be almost overcome with mirth – 'the bobby'd only stopped Wilf 'cos one of his headlamps was showing a bit too much light. He weren't even looking for ducks.'

All this ran through Pat Jessop's mind as she watched the infant lying in the strong arms of Eddie Appleyard. She felt guilty that she had played a part in his present unhappy marriage. Much as she had adored her husband and never once regretted falling head over heels in love with him and marrying him, she did regret that this had perhaps precipitated Eddie into taking up with Bertha Tinker. If only he hadn't, she reflected, then maybe now . . .

'Here's your tea, Eddie,' she said, placing it on the

floor beside him. 'Let me have her.' She held out her arms once more for the child. 'Drink that and then get your head down for an hour or two. You're going to have a few busy days and nights ahead of you.'

In the early hours, before it was quite light, Pat woke Anna.

'I'll have to go soon, ducky, and I want to make sure you know how to feed the little mite.' Whilst Anna made no effort to resist Pat unfastening her clothes and putting the baby to her breast, she made no attempt to hold the child against her. She refused even to put her arms beneath the baby to support it. The baby girl nuzzled against the reluctantly offered breast but made no attempt to suckle.

'They sometimes take a bit of time to learn how to do it. Come on, love. You must hold her. She can't do it all on her own.'

But the girl lay with her head turned to one side, her eyes closed, and refused even to look down at her child.

Pat sighed but continued to support the child, holding her so that the tiny mouth felt the red nipple. After what seemed a long time to the man watching, the baby began to suck.

'There's a clever girl,' Pat talked soothingly to the child. 'That's wonderful. Sometimes they take a lot of coaxing,' she told the new mother, 'but this little one knows what's good for her. Don't you, my precious?'

Eddie looked on, glancing anxiously from child to mother. It was all right whilst Pat was here, but what was going to happen once she had to leave? Would the girl go on rejecting the child? He knew what to do in the animal world when the mother acted this way, but if it came to dealing with a human being he was lost. He thought about the night Tony had been born. Pat had brought him into the world too and he remembered Bertha's arms reaching eagerly for her son. Whatever else she might be, Eddie could not fault Bertha as a mother. The only sad thing about it was that whatever love Bertha had to give was centred upon the boy and there was none left for her husband.

Pat lifted the baby away from Anna and immediately the infant opened her mouth and began to yell.

'My, my, you're letting us know you like it now you've got the hang of it, aren't you?' Pat laughed and put the baby to her mother's other breast.

Still Anna made no move to look down at her child and Pat and Eddie exchanged a worried glance.

At last the baby's hunger was satisfied and she fell asleep.

'There now, Anna, you can go back to sleep again. You must mind you get plenty of rest. I think she's going to be a very demanding baby. But you're young and strong and you'll cope as long as you're sensible and take care of yourself as well as the child.'

Anna lay with her eyes closed. She made no sign that she had even heard Pat, let alone understood what she was saying.

As the light of dawn filtered into the cottage Pat wrapped the child and laid her in the deep armchair. 'She'll be safe there till you get back, Eddie.' She cast an anxious glance back towards the bed. 'I'm worried about that lass, though,' she said quietly. 'I think I'll ask the doctor to take a look at her. If he can get out here in all this lot.'

Eddie nodded. 'Whatever you think best, Pat. But once I've taken you back, I shan't leave her for long.

I might have to go down to the house . . .' They exchanged a look. 'But I'll come straight back.'

'Fetch me again tonight, Eddie.'

'If you're sure?'

Pat nodded firmly. 'I am. Besides by the look of some of those ewes in there, you could use another pair of hands.'

Eddie returned to the cottage later, bringing the puppy back with him from the stable, just in case Bertha heard its yapping and decided to investigate. As he opened the door, he found the baby crying again, but Anna had made no effort to get up from her bed. She was just lying there with her eyes closed, a tiny frown furrowing her brow as if the noise was irritating her.

At once the puppy trotted across the floor and, taking little runs, tried to jump up onto the bed, barking excitedly. Anna opened her eyes, leant down and lifted it onto the bed. She fondled its silky ears and even smiled gently at it. Eddie watched in disbelief to see that the girl could fuss a dog and yet turn away from her own child. Determinedly, he crossed the room and lifted the puppy from the bed and carried it to its basket in the opposite corner.

'Stay,' he instructed sternly. The little thing whimpered, but lay down obediently, its nose resting on its paws, its eyes large and appealing.

Then Eddie picked up the child and carried her to the bed. 'This is the one you should be taking notice of. You must feed her, love. You're all she's got. Come along now.'

But Anna turned her face towards the wall again and refused to answer.

'Look, lass. I don't want to have to do what the midwife did—' He bit his lip at the thought of having to put the child to the mother's breast himself. He took a deep breath. 'But I will, if you force me to it, 'cos I'm not going to stand by and see her go hungry.'

Suddenly, she turned her head to face him angrily. 'I don't want it,' she cried out passionately above the noise of her child's crying. 'I *hate* it. I don't care if it dies. And me along with it. Just leave us. Let us both die. It'd be for the best.'

Appalled, Eddie stared at her. Then he said firmly, 'This little mite doesn't deserve to be spoken about like that. *She's* done no wrong.' He couldn't prevent the obvious emphasis, but immediately he regretted his words.

Anna raised herself on one elbow. For the first time there was real spirit in her tone. 'What right have you to judge me? You don't know the first thing about me. You don't know what happened.'

'Then tell me.'

'It's none of your business.' She lay back down again. 'I don't know why you're bothering with us, anyway. Just let us be.'

'If I just "let you be" as you put it, you'll let this little one die, won't you? And then you'll be in trouble yourself.'

'No, I won't,' she muttered. ''Cos I won't be here either.'

'Don't talk silly, Anna,' Eddie said. 'Sit up and feed this little one. Come on.' His tone was authoritative now, but still it had no effect. The girl turned her whole body away from him and her child and lay on her side facing the wall.

Eddie sighed and laid the baby back in the big

armchair. There was nothing else for it. He'd have to feed the child himself the way he sometimes fed motherless lambs.

For the rest of the day Eddie tended the baby and his sheep. He warmed milk on the fire and dipped a teaspoon in boiling water to cleanse it. Then, when it was cool enough, he sat with the child on his knee and painstakingly spooned the milk into the baby's mouth.

He kept his eye on Anna, but spoke to her only briefly to give her some food.

'Anything else you want?' he asked abruptly. Anna shook her head, unwilling to meet his gaze.

It wasn't that he was deliberately punishing her, it was just that he didn't know how to deal with her callous treatment of the child. To see her fondle the puppy but turn her back on her baby had made him angry.

Late in the afternoon another ewe gave birth to a healthy lamb. Eddie placed the newborn creature to the mother's teat and at once the lamb began to suck, the mother patiently giving herself to her young.

From her bed, Anna heard the bleating and could picture the scene – the new mother and her offspring. When Eddie came back into the room, Anna had raised herself on one elbow and was looking across the room towards her own child, lying quietly now in the chair.

She glanced briefly at Eddie, but then lay down again and closed her eyes. She was sore and ached all over. And she was tired, so very, very tired. All she wanted to do was lie here and not have to move ever again. For months she had tried to ignore the inevitable. And since Eddie had brought her to this cottage, she had begun to feel that, perhaps, she could begin to live again, that the nightmare would begin to fade. But now, after the birth, she would have a daily reminder. Every time she looked at the child, the memories would come flooding back. Anna was fighting an internal emotional battle that the man could know nothing about, nor even begin to guess at.

Ten

That evening Eddie again fetched Pat Jessop from the village on his tractor.

'I hope, for your sake, nobody sees us,' Pat said.

Eddie shrugged. 'They'll just think I'm taking you to some outlying place 'cos of the weather.'

'Which you are,' she smiled. 'Just as long as they don't guess exactly *where* it is you're taking me. Anyway, how is she?'

Pat's face became anxious as Eddie explained what he had been obliged to do to feed the child. 'She doesn't want owt to do with the bairn, Pat. I'm worried sick.'

Pat put her hand briefly on his arm. 'Don't worry, Eddie. If the worst comes to the worst, I'll bring the child back here and look after it myself. I've a good neighbour who'd look after her whilst I'm out on my rounds. She's seven of her own.' Pat laughed. 'She'd hardly notice another one to feed. Jessie'd take it all in her stride.'

Eddie smiled briefly, but said, 'Well, I hope it won't have to come to that.'

'I hope so too. Come on, we'd better get back there and see what this night brings.'

To their disappointment, it brought no change in Anna's attitude. True, Pat was able to make her feed the child, but she could not coax Anna to hold the baby nor even to look at it properly.

In the early morning Pat found herself in the neighbouring room, delivering a lamb whilst Eddie attended to another ewe.

In the cosiness of the cottage, cut off from the rest of the world by the swirling snow outside, Eddie and Pat smiled at each other. 'It's just like when I used to come and help you and your dad when we were little, Eddie.'

Eddie's dark eyes held her gaze in the flickering light from the hurricane lamp. Her lovely face glowed in the soft light and her gentle eyes held such compassion, such understanding and, yes, love. He was sure he could see love in her eyes. 'Aye,' he said softly. 'I remember.' He sighed and murmured, 'Oh Pat, if only—'

She touched his arm. 'Don't, Eddie,' she whispered, a catch in her voice. 'Please don't say it.'

They gazed at each other for a long moment, each knowing instinctively what the other was thinking, before Pat stood up and deliberately broke the spell.

But it was a moment between them that she would cherish.

When Eddie and Pat left just before dawn, the cottage was quiet. Slowly, Anna sat up and looked across to where her daughter lay. The child was quiet now, full of her milk, which, the midwife had told her, was going to be plentiful.

'You must drink plenty of milk yourself and eat well,' Pat had urged her and had left a bowl of cereal and a glass of milk beside the bed. 'And please, ducky, try to feed the bairn yourself.'

'It – hurts,' the girl had said. She had touched her own breasts. 'They're hard.'

'It's the milk coming.' Deviously, and keeping her tone deliberately casual, Pat had added, 'It would help that feeling if you fed her.'

But, yet again, Anna had turned away. Now, in the stillness of early morning, she lay back and drifted into sleep again but was awakened by the door opening very quietly. For once, she could not even summon up the terror that usually assailed her. She just lay there keeping her eyes closed. Whoever it was, she had not the strength to do anything about it. Just as before, she had not had the strength . . .

She winced, screwing up her eyes tightly to block out the terrifying memories.

Tony tiptoed across the floor, pausing to look down at the baby lying fast asleep in the chair. Then he came to stand by the bed.

'Are you all right?' he whispered, afraid to wake her if she was sleeping.

Anna nodded, but did not speak. She did not even open her eyes.

'Where's me dad?'

Again, there was no answer.

He tried again. 'Is it a boy or a girl?'

Silence. A little more loudly he repeated his question.

Anna licked her dry, cracked lips. 'A girl.'

'What are you going to call her?'

Anna let out a long, deep sigh that seemed to come from the very depths of her being. 'I don't know,' she said dully.

'You'll have to call her something,' the boy said practically and wrinkled his brow thoughtfully, as if the whole burden of naming the child rested with him. Perhaps it did, for the mother was uninterested. 'What about Alice?' he ventured. At school, the teacher had just been reading *Alice's Adventures in Wonderland* to the class. It was the first name that came to his mind.

There was no response from Anna. 'There's Rose or Janet or Mary . . .' He ticked the suggestions off on his fingers, naming the girls in his class. At last, as if wearying of his persistence, Anna opened her eyes and said, 'Maisie. Her name's Maisie.'

'Maisie,' the boy repeated, sounding the name out aloud. 'Maisie Woods. Yes, it sounds nice. I like it.'

The child began to whimper and Tony grinned. 'See, she knows her name already.'

Very gently, he picked up the child and carried her to the bed. 'She wants her mummy, don't you, Maisie?'

He tried to lay the child in Anna's arms, but she made no move to take her. 'Come on,' he said a little impatiently. 'She's hungry. She wants feeding.'

Anna stared down at the child. The baby's crying ceased for a moment. Dark blue eyes stared at her mother. Whether or not the tiny infant could really see her, Anna did not know, but it seemed as if she could. The baby's face worked, stretching and grimacing.

'Look, she's smiling at you,' Tony said, his knowledge of human babies too sketchy to think otherwise.

Slowly, tentatively, Anna slipped her left arm beneath the baby's head. With her right hand she gently pulled down the shawl and looked upon her daughter for the first time.

When Eddie returned to the cottage, Anna was feeding her daughter and Tony, without a shred of embarrassment, was sitting on the end of the bed watching her.

To the young boy, it was perfectly natural to see a mother feeding her young.

Eddie felt relief flood through him. Only later would he learn that it had been his son's prompting that had finally broken down Anna's defences.

He came towards the bed, smiling. 'All right, lass?' Anna looked up, managed a weak smile and nodded.

'I've brought a few things to stock up your pantry.' He glanced at Tony. 'You'd better get back home, lad. Your mam knows I'm going to be up here for the next few days. With the sheep,' he added pointedly.

The boy stared at him for a moment, then looked away. He understood his father's unspoken insinuation. 'Can I – can I come up each day? I shan't be going to school 'cos of the roads, but I can get up here, specially now your tractor's made some tracks.'

'Only if your mam ses you can.'

The boy nodded eagerly. 'She'll want to send you some food anyway.'

Eddie put his hand on Tony's shoulder. 'Now, you look after your mam. Let me know straight away if she needs owt. All right?'

The boy nodded, grinned at Anna and then reached out and gently touched the baby's head. ''Bye, Maisie,' he whispered softly.

As he left, Eddie asked, 'Is that her name? Maisie?'

Anna's voice was husky. 'Yes. Tony – wanted me to decide on a name.'

Quietly, Eddie said, 'It doesn't matter yet, but you do know you'll have to register her birth, don't you? It's the law.'

Anna looked at him with startled eyes. 'How – how would I have to do that?'

'Go into town and—'

'Oh, I couldn't.'

'But you must register her.'

Her eyes were wide with fear. 'I couldn't go into town.'

Eddie sighed and let the matter drop for the moment. Perhaps he could get Pat to deal with the problem.

Pat beamed with delight when she entered the cottage that evening to find Anna sitting up in the bed, cuddling the child to her breast. She stamped the snow from her boots and shook her coat.

'It's snowing again,' Pat remarked as she crossed the room towards Anna. Making no direct comment about the change in the girl, she merely enquired, 'All right, ducky?'

Anna nodded. 'Thank you,' she said huskily, 'for all you've done.'

Pat shrugged. 'It's me job, love.' But the look in Anna's dark eyes told the midwife that she understood Pat Jessop had done far more for her than was usual.

'Now then,' Pat said briskly, 'we'll banish Eddie to the other room while I help you have a good wash. I've brought you some clean sheets and a nightie. And there's some clothes for the bairn. Now, off you go, Eddie, and see to your sheep.' Pat smiled at him and flapped her hand to dismiss him.

Eddie grinned as he closed the door behind him, marvelling at how Pat Jessop got her own way without even raising her voice. With her merry face and good-humoured banter, people just did as she asked them without arguing. He shook his head thoughtfully, unable to prevent himself once more comparing Pat's methods to his wife's sharp, demanding ways.

With a minimum of fuss, Anna was soon washed and lying in a clean flannelette nightdress between crisp, sweet-smelling sheets. Then Pat turned her attention to the baby. For a while, Anna lay watching her bathing the child in a tin bath that Eddie had brought from his barn, murmuring endearments to the wriggling infant all the while.

'You're a lovely little thing, aren't you, my precious. With those big eyes and such a lot of pretty hair.' Pat glanced up at Anna and smiled. 'I think she's going to be a real carrot top, love. Just look at her pretty hair.'

Anna's eyes widened and her lips parted in a gasp. With a noise that sounding suspiciously like a cry of despair, Anna turned her back on them both and buried her head in her pillow.

Pat watched her, biting her lip and frowning worriedly. *Now what have I said?* she thought.

She laid the child down in the deep armchair and went towards the bed. Touching the girl's shaking shoulder, she said softly, 'I'm sorry, love. I didn't mean to upset you. Would you like to tell me about it?'

The girl's only reply was to shake her head.

Pat sighed. In all her years of experience, she had never come across a case like this before. She'd dealt with mothers who had rejected their children initially, but once they came around, as she had believed Anna had done, then they didn't often lapse back into withdrawing themselves from their child. Yet now, it seemed, she had unwittingly touched some raw nerve that had made this girl turn her back on her child once more.

She patted the girl's shoulder again, feeling powerless. It was a feeling she did not often experience and certainly did not relish. She liked to be able to help people and, most of the time, she did. 'I'm a good listener, love. And I never judge folk. Whatever it is that's upsetting you, it'll not be anything I've not heard before. So, if you ever want a kindly ear, you know where I am. Your secret – whatever it is – would be safe with me.'

The girl's shoulder was rigid beneath Pat's touch and she made no movement, gave no sign that she had even heard the nurse's words.

Later, when Anna had fallen into a restless sleep and the baby was quiet, Eddie and Pat sat before the fire.

'I said summat to upset her, Eddie,' Pat whispered. 'Just as she seemed to be coming round an' all. I could kick mesen.'

'What did you say?'

Pat sighed and shook her head. 'I was just talking to her about how pretty the child is. With big, dark eyes and that she's going to be a redhead.'

They sat in silence for a moment before Eddie said thoughtfully, 'Perhaps it reminds her of someone. Someone she'd rather forget?'

Pat stared at him. 'Oh. The – the father, you mean?'

Soberly, Eddie nodded. He opened his mouth to say more, but at that moment there was scuffling outside the back door.

With a worried expression, Eddie got up, 'This can't be Tony. Not at this time of night. Surely—'

As he moved across the room, the door was flung open and a rotund figure, wrapped in thick clothes and covered in snow, stepped into the kitchen. Behind her came a much smaller figure, a figure that scurried into the room and flung itself against Eddie.

'I tried to stop her coming, Dad. Really I did,' Tony cried, tears running down his cold face and mingling with the snow.

Eddie put his arm about the boy, 'It's all right, son. It's all right,' he said gently, as he looked up to face his wife.

Eleven

Bertha's glance took in the girl in the bed, now awakened and sitting up, her eyes fearful. The commotion woke the baby, who began to wail, and Bertha's face contorted into a look of loathing. She swung round and, with surprising agility, flew at her husband, her arms flailing, her hands reaching to slap and punch and scratch. He tried to defend himself as her blows rained upon him, whilst Tony pulled at her coat, crying, 'Mam, Mam, don't. Please, don't.'

Pat hurried forward to intervene, but Bertha shrieked, 'You keep out of this, Pat Jessop. I might 'ave known you'd be in on this.' Then she raised her hand and dealt her husband a stinging blow on his cheek that sent him reeling. Before he had time to recover his senses, Bertha had whirled about and was moving to where the child lay, her hands outstretched, her eyes murderous.

Pat moved, but there was someone even quicker than she was. Anna flung back the bedclothes and seemed to fly across the room. She snatched up her child and hugged her close. 'Don't you touch her. Don't you dare lay a finger on her.'

Her eyes blazing, she faced the irate woman and even Bertha faltered in the face of the lioness protecting her young.

'Bertha, please—' Pat began, but Bertha now turned and vented her anger on the midwife.

'I told you, keep out of this. You've done enough. I suppose you know all about his goings on, do you? And if you know, then the whole village'll know. Aye, an' half Ludthorpe too, I shouldn't wonder.'

'You've no cause to talk to me like that, Bertha.' Pat bristled. 'And you're not being fair to Eddie—'

'Oho, "Eddie", is it? Summat going on between the two of you, is there?' Her face twisted into an ugly sneer. 'Now the war's over you'll have to look a bit nearer home for fellers, won't you?'

Pat was furious. 'How dare you—?'

'Oh, I dare all right. It was common gossip about you cycling up to that RAF camp *and* afore your husband was killed, an' all.' Her mouth twisted and she flung her arm out towards Anna. 'You're no better than that trollop there, Pat Jessop, so don't try to play the innocent with me.'

Pat was shaking her head sadly now. 'You're not right in the head, Bertha. Do you know that? You're twisted, saying such things. I'm a district nurse, for heaven's sake and the camp was in my district.'

Bertha's mouth curled with disbelief. 'Expect me to believe that? They'd got their own doctors and nurses. So why would they need your – ' she paused deliberately – 'services?'

'Oh, there's no reasoning with you, Bertha. I was often called to the families of RAF personnel who lived near the camp. And I'll tell you something, whether you want to hear it or not. I don't care what you say about me, but you've no call to make such horrible insinuations about Eddie.' Pat shook her forefinger in Bertha's face. 'You've got a good man there, and you're a fool not to see it.'

'How would you know?'

'Come off it, Bertha. I've known Eddie all me life. Do you really expect me to call him "Mr Appleyard" now? 'Cos if you do, then you've another think coming.'

All the time the heated exchange was taking place between the two women, Tony had clung to his father. Anna clutched her baby to her, patting the child's back and trying to soothe her crying.

'If you're so clever, then, Nurse Jessop, p'raps you'd like to tell me what's really going on then with this girl here?'

'Like he told you, Bertha. She was in the marketplace in town with nowhere to go and he took pity on her. That's all.'

Bertha snorted. 'If you believe that, then it's you that's the fool. Not me.'

She turned and held out her hand to her son. 'Come on, Tony. You an' me's going home. You're not to come up here again. You hear me?'

Tony cast a helpless glance at his father. 'But – but we haven't told him why we came.' He glanced nervously at his mother, yet he was determined to speak out. 'It's the sheep in the barn. There's one or two of them dropping their lambs. And one – well – you ought to come, Dad.' His voice petered away as his mother added, 'Oh, he's far more important things to do up here, Tony love. I see that now. And I also see why you tried to stop me coming.'

The boy hung his head and shrank against his father, but Bertha was holding out her fat arms towards her son. 'But I don't blame you, lovey. It's not your fault. You're not old enough to understand. Come on, love. Come to your mammy.'

Eddie gripped the boy's shoulder understandingly

and then gave him a gentle push. 'Go on, son,' he said quietly.

'But what about the sheep, Dad?'

Eddie nodded. 'I'll come down.'

With obvious reluctance, the boy moved towards his mother. She put her arm about his shoulders and drew him to her. Her eyes narrowed as she said, 'You and your carryings on, Eddie, are one thing, but involving your own son in your lies and deceit is quite another. I'll never forgive you for that. Never.'

And then she was gone, out into the wild night, dragging the boy with her and leaving the three adults staring after her, mesmerized and beginning to wonder if it had all really happened.

'I'm so sorry,' Anna began. 'It's all my fault. I should never have let you bring me with you that night. I'll go.'

Eddie spread his hands in a helpless gesture. 'You can't go anywhere in this lot, love.' He sighed heavily as he sank into the armchair, weary and dispirited. He dropped his head into his hands as he muttered. 'Wait till the weather improves and you're feeling stronger, then we'll see.'

The truth was that, deep inside him, he didn't want her to go anywhere. Eddie wanted Anna to stay right here in his little cottage.

Pat seemed to recover her senses. 'Get back into bed, love. Here, give me the bairn. There, there,' she crooned as she took the crying child into her arms. 'All that shouting's upset you, hasn't it, my little love? There, there. It's all over and your mammy's going to feed you now.'

Anna climbed back into the bed and soon a comparative peace was restored as the infant's cries were silenced while she sucked hungrily. But the cosy, intimate atmosphere of the little cottage was gone, spoiled by Bertha's bitter wrath.

When mother and child were sleeping, Eddie and Pat sat before the fire, their heads close together.

'What are you going to do, Eddie?'

Eddie closed his eyes and sighed wearily. Then, as the baby stirred and gave a little snuffling sound in her sleep, he smiled. He seemed to straighten up as he glanced towards Anna lying in the bed. 'D'you know,' he said, as if he was as surprised as Pat to hear himself saying the words, 'I reckon I'm going to stand up to Bertha for once in me life.'

Pat touched his hand. 'Good for you.'

'The lass and her bairn can stay as long as they want. If – if she wants to go – ' Pat saw a fleeting expression of disappointment in his eyes – 'then – so be it. But if she wants to stay, then she can.' He stood up and pulled on his coat. 'I'd best be off and see to me sheep.' He paused at the door and turned to say solemnly, 'There's one thing Bertha was right about, though.'

Pat raised her eyebrows. She couldn't think of a single thing that the vitriolic woman had been right about.

Eddie went on, 'Tony. I shouldn't have involved him. I'll have to tell him not to come here any more.'

Pat smiled as she said softly, 'You can try, but I don't think either you – or Bertha – will be able to stop him.'

The snow ceased at last, but then came the thaw and, with it, the danger of flooding to the surrounding district.

'You can't stay here. You'll have to go into the village,' Eddie told Anna. 'Pat's said she'll have you and the bairn. I'll take you—'

'No!' Anna's voice was sharp and determined. She was up and about now and able to care for herself and her child and even the puppy, but she was not yet fully recovered from the birth and had not ventured outside the cottage except to visit the privy. 'We're going nowhere. Not yet, anyway. Not until I'm well enough to move on. To get right away.'

Eddie spread his hands. 'But this cottage lies almost at the lowest point in the vale. The stream will overflow. There's no doubt about that happening, and when it does the water could back up as far as here. It'll get into the cottage—'

'Then we'll go upstairs.'

'You can't do that. The whole place would be damp. You wouldn't be able to keep the bairn warm. You can't light a fire up there.'

'Can't you bring me a paraffin heater, or something?'

'I could,' Eddie agreed reluctantly, 'but it would hardly keep you warm enough up there.'

'We'll be fine.'

'You might be, but what about the baby?' He eyed her thoughtfully. She seemed to have come round now and to be caring for her child properly. Pat had no worries, but Eddie couldn't stop the dreadful suspicion that the girl was just biding her time and that perhaps she still hoped something would happen to the child. To both of them, if it came to that. He lay awake at night, alone now in the spare bedroom to which Bertha had banished him, thinking of the young girl in the cottage and wondering . . .

'Maisie'll be fine,' Anna was insisting now. 'I'll keep

her warm.' She must have seen the anxiety in his face, for she added, in her soft, husky voice, 'I promise.'

As the snow melted and the earth began to show through in brown patches, it was still too wet for the sheep to find grazing, even though they were out on the hillside again. Each day Eddie brought hay for his sheep, but each night Anna still found them huddled against the cottage wall, as if asking to be let in. And each night she would open the door wide and usher them into the room, comforted by the sound of their soft bleating in the middle of the night.

'The stream's overflowing like I said it would. I've brought you some sandbags, but I don't reckon it'll hold the water from getting into the cottage.'

Anna nodded. 'I saw. I went out for the first time today. I took Buster for a walk.' She laughed. 'But he doesn't like getting his paws wet.'

Eddie smiled, though the worry never quite left his eyes. 'He's only little.'

'I've got everything ready in the room upstairs.'

'I'm sorry now that I didn't get Joe Wainwright up here to the roof afore Christmas.'

Anna shrugged and smiled. 'One room's all right. That's all we need.' She glanced at him, teasing. 'I wasn't thinking of taking the sheep up there an' all.'

Eddie laughed. 'No, I don't think they'd manage to climb the ladder. Not even with Rip barking at their heels.' He watched her for a moment. It was the first time that Anna had said something light-hearted and now he saw that she looked better – calmer, he thought, and not so afraid.

'Are you happy here?' he asked before he stopped to

think. To his chagrin, the smile faded from her face and the haunted look was at once back in her eyes. She returned his gaze, but avoided answering his question directly.

'I'm very grateful for what you've done for me, Eddie.' Suddenly, she was on her guard again as she added, 'I'll – I'll always be grateful to you, but I can't stay here for ever.'

'Why? Why not, love? You said you'd nowhere to go.' He paused, then when she did not answer he pressed on. 'Or is it different now you've had the bairn? Is that it? Are you going home—?'

Almost before the words were out of his mouth, she had spat back. 'No, no. Never.' Then she faltered. 'I – I have no home.'

'All right, lass, all right.' He spread his hands, trying to placate her. 'I didn't mean to upset you and I'm not trying to pry. It's just that – ' he took a deep breath – 'it's just that I'd miss you if you did go and – and – well—' He was floundering now and the words came out in a rush. 'If you really haven't anywhere special to go, you're welcome to stay here.'

'What about your wife?' Her unusual dark eyes were regarding him steadily.

He shrugged. 'She's said no more about it. The only thing she has done is to stop Tony from coming to see you.' He forbore to tell Anna that his wife had also banished him from her bed. Not that it was any great loss. She had not allowed any 'marital relations', as they called it, for years, he thought bitterly. The only thing he did miss was the warmth of her bulk next to him on a cold night. But a brick heated in the oven, wrapped in a piece of blanket and shoved into the bed was a good substitute! Now he smiled mischievously.

'But I don't expect for one minute that she'll be able to stop him sneaking over the hill to see you now and again. That lad will find a way, if I'm not much mistaken.'

Anna's small smile chased away some of the guarded look on her face. 'Well,' she said slowly, 'I'd like to stay for a while longer, but I don't want to cause you any more trouble.'

'You won't,' he said briefly and silently added to himself: *No more than I'd already got afore you came.*

Twelve

The snow continued to melt and the rushing stream became a torrent, which overflowed its banks and flooded the land. Nearer and nearer it crept to the cottage and Anna was obliged to move upstairs, though she could wade through the water if she needed to in her wellingtons. Eddie helped her take her bedding up the narrow ladder and lift the armchair onto the table, so that it would not get soaked.

'I still wish you'd go and stay with Pat Jessop. She asked about you again yesterday.'

'That was kind of her,' Anna said carefully. 'But we'll be fine up there, specially now you've brought us that little stove. As long as I can keep Maisie safe and warm and fed, we'll be all right.'

'But can you?' Eddie asked worriedly.

Anna regarded him steadily. 'If I can't, Eddie, I promise you I'll give in and let you take us to Nurse Jessop's.'

'That's all right then, lass.' He smiled with relief. 'And now I'd better get these sheep onto higher ground.'

'How's the lambing going?' Anna asked. 'I wish I could be more help to you.'

'Considering what we've had to cope with, very well, really. I've still several ewes to drop, but I've already got a good few healthy lambs.' He raised his hand. 'Must get on, lass. See you later.'

''Bye,' Anna murmured as she watched him whistle to Rip and begin to round up the sheep that had been her companions for several days. She was sorry to see them go.

The water was now lapping at the walls of the cottage and against the sandbags across the thresholds. As Anna sat on the floor at the top of the ladder with the puppy beside her, the water began to seep into her home. Buster yapped excitedly, as if he could drive back the thing invading the cottage. They watched tiny rivulets creep beneath the door and spread out, until the whole of the earth floor was covered. And still the water kept coming.

She felt a moment's panic, imagining it rising so high that it engulfed the whole cottage and drowned them.

And suddenly she wanted to live. She no longer felt the craving to lie down and let a welcome oblivion overtake her. Now she had something, or rather someone, to live for. She had another human being dependent upon her. She hadn't wanted the child. It had grown within her against her will and she had hated it. Hated the thing inside because of how it had come to be there.

But now the child was no longer an 'it'. Maisie was a tiny human being in her own right, already with a character that was evident when she bellowed for attention. Anna smiled fondly as she glanced over her shoulder to where her child lay sleeping in a Moses basket that Pat Jessop had brought. Where had she heard the phrase 'They bring their love with them'? Well, it was certainly true of her Maisie. Now Anna loved her daughter with a fierce, protective passion. And, ironically, it had been Bertha Appleyard who had made her see that.

If only – Anna's face clouded – the child had not been born with red hair.

She glanced down again at the water, still rising below her. Rationally, she worked out that, because of the lie of the land, the water could not possibly rise above a certain depth. Up here, they would be quite safe.

That night Anna lay down on the soft featherbed mattress on the floor and cuddled her child to her.

Though the water lapped beneath them, she felt safer than she had done for weeks. Cut off from the outside world by the flooding, no one could find her.

'Still visiting ya little bastard, are ya?'

Eddie sighed deeply and cast a sideways glance at Tony sitting at the table, head bowed and toying with the food on his plate.

'Bertha, the child's not mine. How many more times—?'

Bertha snorted. 'She's got brown hair. Just like you. I saw that much that night.'

Holding onto his patience with a supreme effort, Eddie said, 'No, she hasn't. It's red. Ginger. And her eyes are blue.'

'That's nowt to go by. All newborn babies have blue eyes.' She nodded knowingly. 'Its eyes'll be brown and its hair'll go darker. Like yours.'

Bertha pursed her small mouth until it almost disappeared into her fat face. She banged Eddie's dinner onto the table in front of him and then took her place opposite, beside Tony.

'Don't you worry, love.' She patted her son's arm. 'You've still got me, even if your dad is so taken up with his new daughter that he hasn't any time for you now.'

'That's not true, Bertha—'

Bertha's tone was vitriolic. 'Isn't it? You're off up that track two or three times a day and you don't come back for an hour or more. And don't try telling me you're with your sheep all that time, 'cos most of 'em are down here in the barn or the yard. I bet you're off up there to watch her feeding her kid. Getting an eyeful, are ya? Disgusting, that's what you are.' Her mouth twisted. 'Disgusting.'

Tony's head hung lower as he felt the colour creep up his own face. He'd watched Anna feeding little Maisie. He'd not thought it wrong. So was he 'disgusting' as well, then, in his mother's eyes?

He'd not go to the cottage again, he vowed silently. He didn't want to upset his mam – didn't want her to think that about him. And he didn't want to see the baby any more. Not if his dad was going to love her more than him. Yet he liked going to see Anna and the puppy, and the baby, too, if he was truthful. He'd helped name the little girl. He'd begun to feel she belonged to him a little bit as well. But his mam was so angry. Angry at his dad, angry because the girl was even there. It seemed to him that she hated Anna and the little baby. But he still couldn't understand what his mam meant when she said the baby was his dad's.

The young boy, with a tumult of emotions going on

inside his head that he couldn't really understand or rationalize, pushed the food around his plate and chewed each mouthful round and round, unable to swallow for the lump in his throat.

'You all right, lass?' It was Eddie's voice shouting through the front door.

Anna climbed down the ladder and stepped into the water. She pulled open the door and smiled a welcome. As Eddie stepped inside, she said, 'We're fine. Managing to keep warm and dry.'

'Pat wants to come and see you. Check on you and the bairn, but—'

'Tell her not to worry till this lot's gone. We're all right. Honestly.'

Eddie nodded, but the worried look never left his eyes.

'There's something else, isn't there?' Anna said.

Eddie smiled ruefully. 'I don't think Tony'll be coming to see you any more. His – his mam's put a stop to it.'

'Well, I expected that. I'm sorry, though. I'll miss him.'

'Aye, an' I reckon he'll miss you. He keeps asking about you and Maisie, but—' His voice trailed away.

'But what?' Anna prompted.

Eddie sighed. 'Oh, nothing really.' He didn't want to tell Anna about the full extent of Bertha's spite, though he knew she would guess most of it.

Her presence in the cottage was causing Eddie Appleyard all sorts of problems that he had not foreseen when he had brought the girl home that night. He hadn't known what he was doing, he thought wryly, in more ways than one!

But, despite it all, not for one moment did he regret that Anna had come into his life.

Thirteen

It was late the following afternoon when Anna heard movement outside the cottage and then someone hammering on the front door at the bottom of the ladder. She climbed down and stood near the door, but did not open it.

'Who is it?' she called.

'Me,' came Tony's voice. She pulled open the door, rippling the water further into the cottage.

The boy was breathless from wading through the flood to reach her.

'What are you doing here? You shouldn't–'

'Me dad sent me,' he interrupted. 'He ses can you come down to the farm? He needs help and he ses I'm not big enough to do it.' For a moment, the boy's mouth was a disgruntled pout and there was resentment in his eyes as he looked at her, as if she was personally to blame for taking the place he believed was rightfully his. 'He's got two ewes dropping at once and they're both difficult. He needs help and I can't get to the village–'

'Of course I'll come, but I'll just have to get Maisie wrapped up warm–'

'Dad said not to take her.' His head drooped sulkily. 'I – I'm to stay with her, he said.'

Anna bit her lip, uncertain whether to trust the boy in his present mood, though she really had no choice.

Eddie Appleyard had been good to her. In fact, he had probably saved her life and that of her child. She couldn't refuse his plea for help.

'All right then. She's just been fed, so she'll be all right for some time and she's asleep. But don't touch the stove, will you?'

'Course I won't,' he said, vexed that she could doubt his common sense.

She followed him up the ladder and dressed herself quickly in the warmest clothing she had, then, with a last glance at her child, she descended the ladder again and left the cottage. Once out of the water, she hurried up the track towards the farm. She was gratified to find that she had almost recovered from the birth of her child. She was not quite as strong as normal, but youth had helped her to heal quickly.

She paused at the top of the hill to look down at the farm below her. In the low-lying parts of the land, water stood in small lakes, and as she set off down the track she could see that part of Eddie's yard too was under water. As she waded through it to reach the barn, she glanced apprehensively towards the farmhouse, hoping that Bertha would not catch sight of her.

She reached the huge barn door, pulled it open and stepped inside. There were two makeshift pens at one end with straw bales where Eddie could attend to the ewes in labour. Anna pushed her way through the flock, patting a head here, stroking a woolly back there until she reached him.

'I've got a bad one here,' Eddie said. 'Breech and I reckon it's twins.' Then he nodded towards the ewe in the next pen. 'I want you to have a go at that one. The forelegs are presented but there's no sign of the head. Do you know what to do?'

Anna nodded. 'I think so. Push it back very gently and try to manipulate the head into line with the forelegs?'

Eddie gave a quick smile. 'That's it. Your hands are smaller than mine. Tony tried, but his wrist wasn't quite strong enough.'

As she squatted down beside the ewe, Anna smiled ruefully. 'He's not very happy at me taking his place.'

'I'll talk to him later. At the moment I've more to think about than Tony having a mardy.'

There was silence between Eddie and Anna as they struggled to help the ewes. The only noise the bleating from thirty or so sheep.

'There!' Anna said triumphantly, as the lamb slithered safely from its mother. Swiftly she cleaned its mouth. 'It's not breathing, Eddie.' But without waiting for instruction, Anna bent her head close to the tiny creature and blew into its mouth. After a few attempts she looked up, smiling. 'It's fine now.'

'Well done, lass. Mind you dry it well and don't forget to see to the navel.'

'How are you doing?'

'Not good. I think I could lose this ewe. She's quite old and, like I thought, it was twins. I've got them both and they're OK, but she's not cleansing properly.' He shook his head sadly and ruffled the sheep's coat. 'Poor old lass. You've given me a lot of healthy lambs, though, in your time, haven't you?'

'Mine's all right. She's cleansed and I've checked her udders. Do you think she'd take one of those lambs?'

Eddie looked doubtful. 'I'd sooner rear these by the bottle and let her feed her own. One strong lamb's much better than two weaker ones. Mind you,' he said, scratching his head thoughtfully, 'I don't know how I'm going to cope. I've two lambs in the house already and Bertha won't have owt to do with them. Tony's been looking after them, but now the snow's gone he'll have to go back to school. The lane to Wintersby village isn't too bad with flood water.'

'I could take them home with me,' Anna offered.

In the warm cosiness of the barn, they looked at each other. In the soft glow of the lamplight, Eddie marvelled at the girl's beauty. Her eyes were dark pools and in the light from the lamp her skin was a golden colour. And, it was not lost on either of them that she had referred to the tumbledown cottage as 'home'. Tremulously, Anna smiled. 'I've nothing else to do – apart from looking after Maisie – and I could manage to carry them up the ladder.'

'Well, if you're sure, it would help if you could take at least one. I'll bring you bottles and everything you'll need for feeding.'

He glanced at the ewe near Anna. 'Tell you what,' he said, suddenly coming to a decision, 'Let's risk it. She's young and healthy. Let's try her with one of 'em and then you can feed the other. If we can get hers and one of these twins to suckle, we might trick her into thinking she's had the pair of them.'

Eddie picked up one of the lambs and passed it over to Anna, who rubbed some of the adoptive mother's afterbirth fluids over the orphan. She gave it to the ewe to lick first and kept the animal's own offspring back from her until she had accepted the other lamb.

'That's it,' Eddie murmured, not needing to give advice and amazed, yet again, at the young girl's knowledge. *She's been brought up on a farm*, he thought briefly. *She must have been. And she's been taught well.*

It wasn't until late at night that both lambs were

suckling contentedly. Anna stood up and eased her aching limbs. She glanced towards the other pen, an unspoken question on her face. Eddie shook his head. 'Gone, I'm afraid,' he said of the ewe and sighed.

'I'm sorry,' she said. Then she glanced around the barn. 'If there's nothing else I can do, Eddie, I'll be getting back. Maisie must be hungry by now and—'

'Another minute won't hurt, love. Here, sit down and have a drink first. There's a flask of tea I brought out somewhere. Ah, here it is. I reckon we've earned this.'

They sat side by side, leaning against a bale of straw, and sipped the warm, sweet tea gratefully.

'What a night,' Eddie murmured. 'I couldn't have managed without you, lass.'

'We've still lost a ewe, though,' she said sadly.

'Aye, but I'd likely have lost more if you hadn't been here.' He bit his lip, wanting to ask her about her past, wanting to ask how she knew so much about sheep, but he held back the words, knowing that if he so much as mentioned the subject, she would withdraw into silence.

Anna was sitting watching the newborn lambs, a gentle smile on her face. 'Isn't it wonderful—?' she was beginning when the big door of the barn opened and they looked up to see Bertha standing there.

'Eddie? Where are you? Oh, there you are. What do you mean by keeping Tony up all night?' At that moment, she became aware that it was not Tony sitting beside Eddie, but the girl. 'You! What the hell are you doing here?' She glanced around the barn. 'And where's Tony?'

Eddie sighed and struggled to his feet. Wearied by the night's events, the last thing he needed was a confrontation with Bertha. But there was no way out this time. Flatly, he said, 'We've had two difficult births and Tony couldn't help so I sent him to fetch Anna.'

'Oh aye,' Bertha said sarcastically. 'Any excuse.'

'It's not an excuse, Bertha. It's the truth. She's saved me a lamb and possibly a ewe as well, to say nothing of getting this ewe to adopt—'

'Never mind all that. Where's Tony?'

'Looking after Maisie.'

'Maisie?' Bertha glanced around the sheep. 'Which one's Maisie?'

Eddie almost laughed aloud, but the thought of what was going to come in the next few seconds killed his laughter. 'Maisie is Anna's baby.'

For a brief moment Bertha stared at him in disbelief. 'You – you've sent him up there to look after this trollop's bastard?'

'Bertha—' Eddie began, but his wife was in full flow. 'Well, that takes the biscuit, that does. I've heard it all now. I must be the laughing stock of the village. You and your carryings on. For two pins I'd pack me bags and go.' She wagged her forefinger at Eddie. 'And take Tony with me. But I'm not going to, 'cos that's just what you'd like me to do, isn't it? And then you could set up home with your fancy piece here. Well, you aren't going to get what you want, 'cos I'm staying put. I'm not going to see my son done out of his rightful inheritance. Oh no!'

'Bertha, you've got it all wrong.'

'Oh, I don't think so. I'm not blind. But you've a nerve, Eddie Appleyard. Parading your love child for all the world to see as if you're proud—'

'The child isn't his,' Anna said huskily. 'What he's

told you is true. He'd never met me before that night he brought me here. Why won't you believe him?'

Bertha stepped closer and thrust her face close to Anna's. ''Cos I know men. Dirty buggers. Only after one thing.' She prodded a vicious finger into Anna's stomach. '*You* ought to know that.'

Even in the half-light, Eddie could see that Anna's face had turned white.

'That's enough, Bertha. There's no call to say such things to Anna.'

'I've every right. She's no better than a whore and a marriage-wrecker and, mark my words, if the old customs still survived, I'd have her ran-tan-tanned out of here. Yes, that's what I'd do, I'd get the whole village up against her.'

'I'll go,' Anna murmured and picked up the lamb.

'Yes, you go. Get out of my sight and off my boy's land. The quicker you and your bastard leave the better.'

'You'd best go on home,' Eddie said in a low voice. 'I'll bring all the paraphernalia you'll need for feeding.'

As Anna moved away towards the barn door, she could feel the woman's malevolent gaze following her like a knife in her back. And as she hurried across the yard and up the track, her heart was pounding. *We'll go*, she promised herself. *As soon as the flood waters have gone and the weather improves, we'll go.*

It wasn't until she reached the cottage that she began to breathe easily again.

Tony was peering down from the upstairs. 'What happened?' he asked eagerly. 'Is everything all right?'

Huskily, Anna told him, 'I'm afraid we lost a ewe, but she gave us two healthy lambs. Here.' She began to climb the ladder, holding up the lamb. 'Take this one. We managed to get the other ewe, which only had one lamb, to take one of the orphans and I'm going to look after this one.'

Tony took the lamb and held it close. 'Why?' he asked and his eyes were belligerent once more. 'I can look after it. I've already got two at home.'

'That's just it,' Anna said reasonably. 'You've got enough to cope with and you'll be going back to school soon.'

The boy pulled a face but could not argue.

As she stepped off the ladder, the puppy sprang up from his place by the Moses basket, where he had been sleeping, his nose resting on his paws. He galloped across the floor, sliding and tumbling in his anxiety to reach her. He jumped and made little yapping sounds of pleasure.

Anna smiled down at him and fondled him, but her attention was on Tony as she watched him cuddling the newborn lamb. 'They're still your lambs,' she said softly, 'not mine.'

He shrugged and tried to say with grown-up common sense, 'They'll be going for slaughter as soon as they're old enough anyway.' But there was a tremble in his voice that the young boy could not hide. 'Dad always tells me I shouldn't treat them like pets. We're farmers.'

'That's right. Rip's your pet, but—'

'Not really. He's a working dog.' He nodded towards Buster, still jumping and barking excitedly. 'He's growing, isn't he?'

Anna nodded. 'Yes, and he'll be a working dog too, but it doesn't mean I can't fuss him now and then.'

'You'll have to start training him soon, then,' the boy said, knowledgeably.

'I already have.'

Tony's eyes widened. '*You* have? You know about training sheepdogs?'

Suddenly, the wariness was back in Anna's face and she turned away from him. 'A bit,' she said shortly and then deliberately changed the subject. 'Now, we'd better get somewhere sorted out for this little chap to sleep. Let's go and look in the other room.'

They inspected the other upper room together, but both declared it far too cold and draughty for the young lamb.

'We'll all stay in here,' Anna declared. 'And keep each other warm.'

The weather improved at last, the flood waters drained away and Pat Jessop was able to cycle from the village to see Anna. She came up the lane and rode boldly through the farmyard. Leaving her bicycle propped against the barn wall, she took her bag and climbed the track to the top of the rise and down the other side to the cottage.

'I'd like you to see the doctor. Maisie ought to be checked over and you certainly should be.'

'We're all right—' Anna began at once, but Pat interrupted firmly. 'I wouldn't be doing my job properly, love, if I didn't insist. Now, do you want to go into town or have him come here?'

Her eyes wide with fear, the young girl looked around her, as if casting about for some way to escape. 'I—'

'Look,' Pat said gently. 'Why not let Eddie take you

into town next market day? You've got to register the child anyway. You must do that. It's the law.'

'I – I know, but—'

'I'll come with you, if you like.' Pat chuckled. 'I'd quite like a ride in Eddie's old pony and trap again. It wouldn't be the first time.' Her tone grew wistful. 'Mind you, it was a different pony in those days.' Then she became businesslike once more. 'I'll speak to Eddie, and if it's a nice day next Wednesday we'll all go. I'll make an appointment at the doctor's for you and we'll go and see the registrar too.'

There was no getting out of it. When Pat Jessop was in her most persuasive mood, there was no arguing with her.

Anna sighed. 'All right then.'

Pat beamed. 'Good. I shall look forward to our little jaunt. And now I must go. See you next week.'

Pat was already late for her rounds that morning. The cycle ride out to Cackle Hill Farm would put another hour on her routine, but she was not ready to leave yet. There was someone else she wanted to see first.

Pat knocked on the back door of the farmhouse, summoning her most forbidding expression. It was not an easy thing for the district nurse to do, for she was a buxom, pleasant-faced young woman with a ready smile and a teasing, jovial manner. Her long blonde curls were tucked up neatly beneath her cap and the navy blue uniform gave an impression of a severity that was not really part of her nature, though she could, when necessary – as she had been that morning – be firm and persuasive with her patients.

'Oh, it's you,' Bertha said unnecessarily when she opened the door.

'Yes, it's me, Bertha. Can I have a word?'

'What about?'

'Oh things,' Pat said airily evasive. 'How about a cup of tea? I'm parched. It's a long ride out here.'

'It's not a cafe. I haven't time to be making tea.'

'Oh come on, Bertha, there's a dear. Surely, we've known one another long enough—'

'Oh aye, we know enough about each other not to need cosy chats over my kitchen table.'

But seeing that the nurse was not to be budged, Bertha turned away, muttering, 'Oh, come in then, if you must.'

Pat stepped into the warm kitchen, drew off her gloves and held her hands out to the roaring fire in the range. How different was this kitchen to the meagre surroundings in the little white cottage over the hill. Yet Pat could feel that there was already far more love in the tumbledown haven near the woods than there ever would be in this house.

For a brief moment she wondered if Bertha was right. Was there an affair going on between Eddie and the girl? Perhaps the child *was* his. But then she dismissed her fanciful notions as being just that. She had seen them together and whilst there was no doubting Eddie's concern for Anna's welfare, it seemed to be no more than that.

But who knew what the future might bring? For a moment she felt a pang of sympathy for Bertha, who was at this moment banging cups and saucers onto the table with bad grace.

'This is very kind of you, Bertha. It's cold riding

about the countryside on that bike in this weather.' But Pat's words were only greeted with a belligerent glare.

When the tea was ready, they sat down together on opposite sides of the table.

'What is it you want, then? Come to talk me round about that little slut up yonder?' Bertha jerked her head in the direction the cottage lay. ''Cos if you have, you're wasting your time.'

'Not really, Bertha,' Pat said, taking a sip of tea and then placing her cup carefully onto its saucer. She looked up and held Bertha's gaze. 'I just wondered what you know about her.'

Bertha shrugged her fat shoulders. 'Nowt. Nor do I want to.'

'Why not?' Pat's question was direct and pointed.

'Why d'ya think?'

Pat leant ever so slightly towards her. 'I don't know, Bertha. That's why I'm asking you.'

Bertha clattered her own cup into its saucer. 'It's obvious, ain't it? She's Eddie's bit on the side. He's got her into trouble and she's coming knocking at his door. And him being the soft fool he is—'

Pat was shaking her head, unable to believe the tirade of abuse coming out of Bertha's mouth. 'Bertha, your Eddie's not like that.'

'How do you know?' Bertha's retort was like a whiplash. 'Men are all the same. Only after one thing. And even when they've got it on tap at home, it's never enough.' Her small mouth twisted into a bitter sneer.

Pat was appalled at what she was hearing. Eddie's home life must be far worse than she had imagined. Whether or not Eddie had looked for comfort elsewhere, Pat couldn't be sure, but she knew one thing now.

If he had, she wouldn't blame him.

She stood up, unwilling to listen a moment longer to Bertha's twisted logic. The whole village had known for years that Bertha's father had been a 'ladies' man'. Pat had grown up hearing the gossip, witnessing the men's nudges and winks and the women 'tut-tutting' in sympathy with his poor wife. But what she hadn't realized was the terrible effect her father's philandering had had on the young Bertha.

'Do you know something, Bertha? I feel sorry for you. Really I do. But you're a fool. You've got a good man in Eddie Appleyard. There's never been a hint of gossip about him and other women that I've heard. And, believe me, in my job I'd hear it. I carry a lot of secrets for folks round here. And that's what they'll always remain. Secrets. But I'm telling you now, Bertha, Eddie's a good man and I believe him. He felt sorry for that lass and tried to help her.' She leant towards Bertha to emphasize her point. 'And that's all.'

Bertha heaved herself to her feet. 'Get out of my kitchen, Pat Jessop. You're another of his fancy women. Oh, don't think I don't know that you an' him went together afore you found yourself a better catch. And now your husband's dead, you're trying to worm your way back in with Eddie. Well, you won't get the farm. I'll tell you that. I'm his wife and all this' – she waved her arms to encompass the house and all the land that lay around it – 'will one day belong to my son.' She jabbed her finger into her own chest. '*My* son.'

Pat shook her head. 'Oh Bertha,' she said sadly, 'is that all poor Eddie is to you? A good catch?'

Bertha's eyes narrowed. 'I told you, get out of my kitchen, Pat Jessop.'

Pat pedalled away from the farm with a heavy heart.

Poor Eddie, she was thinking. *Poor, poor Eddie. And that poor lass, too*, for she was sure that Bertha Appleyard was just biding her time and that one day, when the opportunity came, she would cause that poor lass a whole barrowload of trouble.

Fourteen

'I don't want to go. I don't see why I have to go.' Anna's face was mutinous. 'The baby's fine. You've said so yourself. And so am I. We don't need a doctor.'

Pat was patiently adamant. 'But *I* need you to see a doctor. If there was anything wrong, then I'd be for the high jump. You wouldn't want me to lose my job, would you?'

If Pat had hoped to appeal to Anna's sympathy, she was sadly mistaken. 'It wouldn't have anything to do with you. Nobody knows about me. Nobody knows I'm here.' She paused and, almost accusingly, added, 'Do they?'

'No.' Pat was holding onto her patience. 'But like I said, if there was anything wrong and you had to see a doctor – or even go to the hospital – well, questions would be asked.'

Anna frowned. 'What do you mean "wrong"?'

'I like to have a newborn baby checked thoroughly. And only a doctor can do that properly. And you should be checked too, particularly when a doctor didn't attend the birth.' Pat forbore to add: *Especially when the birth happened in such a squalid place.* Instead she added, 'Besides, you've got to register her.'

Anna's frown deepened, but at last she muttered, 'All right, then.'

So on market day the following week Eddie took

Pat, Anna and the child into the market town of Ludthorpe. The baby was snugly wrapped in shawls and her mother held her close for extra warmth.

'We'll have to go in the trap,' Eddie had said. 'I've got to save me petrol for the tractor.'

Above the rattle of the wheels, Pat chattered merrily. 'This is a treat and no mistake. I can get some shopping that I can't manage on my bicycle.' She smiled saucily at Eddie. 'We'll have to do this more often, Eddie.'

He smiled, but did not answer her.

From the moment they had climbed into the trap outside the white cottage, Anna had seemed ill at ease. As they came down the hill towards the church with its tall spire and turned right along a street that widened out into the marketplace, Pat noticed that the girl's nervousness was increasing. Her eyes were wide and dark with fear and her hands trembled. They passed through the busy marketplace and in front of the low, whitewashed Shepherd's Crook. Eddie glanced at it with nostalgia. He'd had some good times in there. He'd had some good pals and he missed their friendly company on market days, but he had kept his vow. He would never again get sow drunk.

Pat put her arm around Anna's shoulders. 'It's all right, love. I'll come in with you, if you want me to.' With kindly bluntness, she added, 'You're not the first to have a bairn with no dad around and you'll not be the last neither. There's just one thing, though. You do know that you can't put the father's name on the birth certificate when you're not married.' She leant a little closer. 'I presume you're not married to the father, are you?'

Anna shook her head with a vehemence that surprised both Pat and Eddie, who was listening. 'No,' the girl almost spat. 'No, I'm not.'

'Well then,' Pat went on placidly, giving no sign that she had noticed the girl's agitation, 'in that case, you have to register the child in your surname. That's all.'

'I – know,' the girl whispered, but Pat could see that she was still disturbed.

'Mr Bowen's not going to judge you. He's just there to do his job.'

Anna hung her head, her dark hair falling down like curtains on either side of her face, hiding her expression. Above her bent head, Pat and Eddie exchanged an anxious glance. Then Pat pulled a face and lifted her shoulders in a gesture of bewilderment.

When Eddie pulled the trap to a halt outside a tall, stone-clad building with pillars on either side of the huge oak door, Anna was still white-faced and trembling. When she walked into the registrar's dingy office, she almost turned and ran.

'Go on, love. It'll be all right.' Pat gave her a gentle push. 'I'll be just out here if you need me.'

Mr Reginald Bowen was a bent, wizened little man with a wrinkled, unsmiling face. He frowned at her over small, steel-rimmed spectacles and his beady eyes seemed to bore into her soul. She felt that he could read her innermost secrets.

But Anna's first impression was wrong. When the registrar spoke, his voice was gentle. When he moved forward and ushered her to a seat in front of his desk, his manner was kind. As she sat down, Anna looked into his face, close to her now as he bent forward and, with a hooked finger, gently pulled aside the shawl so that he might see the child.

'So this is your little one.' Mr Bowen smiled and all

the deep lines on his face seemed to curve upwards so that his whole face seemed to be smiling. His beady eyes were no longer fearsome, but twinkled with pleasure. 'What a little treasure. A girl, is it?'

Anna nodded.

'Well now.' Mr Bowen straightened up and went round to his own side of the desk. He pulled a notepad towards him and, pen poised, glanced up at her. His 'official' face returned and he looked severe once more. Anna was still a little nervous, but no longer frightened of what she must do. It had to be done, for the sake of her child.

'I must ask you a lot of questions,' the registrar explained, 'but I want to reassure you that whatever you tell me is in the strictest confidence.'

Anna bit her lip and nodded.

'There now, shall we begin?'

The child's Christian name, date and place of birth were quite easy to answer, but when it came to Anna's details she hesitated and bit her lip. Mr Bowen glanced up.

'Don't be shy, my dear. I can assure you that nothing can shock me. I've seen and heard it all.'

Have you? Anna wanted to cry. *Is there no story you could hear that wouldn't shock and disgust you? Perhaps if you heard what happened to me . . .?*

Softly, Mr Bowen interrupted her thoughts. 'I take it you're not married?'

Anna shook her head.

'Then we must register your little girl under your surname. We cannot put the father's name on the certificate unless he is here. Are you in touch with the father? Could he – er – be persuaded to come with you?'

Harshly, Anna said, 'I don't want his name on it.'

'I see,' the man said. He cleared his throat and added, 'Have you any identification with you? Your own birth certificate?'

Again, Anna answered with a mute shake of her head.

'Your identity card then or your ration book?'

He bent his head, preparing to write again, but when she did not speak, he looked up once more. Anna was staring at him, her face devoid of colour. Nervously, she ran her tongue around her mouth to moisten her dry lips.

'Y-yes,' she stammered as, with a trembling hand, she pulled the documents from her pocket and held them out to him.

'Ah,' Mr Bowen said as he perused the papers. 'Woods. I see your name is Annabel Woods.'

Anna nodded. Hoarsely, almost as if she were dragging out the words, she said, 'But – but I'm called Anna.'

'Well, that seems to be in order, my dear,' Mr Bowen said, handing the documents back. Anna almost snatched the card and book from his fingers and pushed them deep into her coat pocket.

'So now we can register your little one. Maisie Woods? Is that it? No second name?'

Anna stared at him for a moment and then said slowly, 'Yes. Maisie Patricia. After Mrs Jessop. She's been – very kind.'

Mr Bowen smiled and, for the first time, Anna understood the expression 'wreathed in smiles'. All the lines in his face seemed to join together in one huge smile. 'She's a lovely lady. She'll be tickled pink.'

*

Registering both herself and her child at the doctor's surgery was easy, especially as now she had Pat's comforting presence beside her. The receptionist accepted their names as Annabel and Maisie Patricia Woods. Only one moment gave Anna a brief scare.

'We might need to see your birth certificates at some point,' the woman said, 'but it doesn't matter today.'

Anna breathed again. She turned to Pat, who was now standing by her side. 'I hope you don't mind. I called her after you.'

'Oh ducky . . .' Pat said and squeezed her arm. As Mr Bowen had predicted, Pat really did turn pink with pleasure.

The doctor was young, a junior partner in the well-established practice in Ludthorpe.

'I think you'll get on better with Dr Mortimer,' Pat had told her. 'Dr Jacobs is an old dear, but a bit crusty, if you know what I mean. He's an ex-army doctor and not ever so good with babies and children. He's a big man and his handlebar moustache frightens the little ones.' Pat laughed merrily. 'And the not-so-little ones sometimes, too. But Dr Mortimer's a dear.'

The young man's fresh face beamed as Pat ushered a nervous Anna into the surgery. He bounced up from his chair and sprang around the desk to shake Pat's hand. 'Nurse Jessop. Lovely to see you. Come in, come in. How kind of you to bring me a new patient.' And he smiled at Anna and held out his arms to take her baby. 'Now, let's have a look at little Maisie, shall we?'

Swiftly and expertly, he examined the baby, taking time to murmur endearments to her and even to tickle and play with her so that he gained her confidence. 'Well, she's fine,' he said straightening up at last. He turned towards Anna. 'And how's the new mother coping? Any problems.'

Anna bit her lip, glanced nervously at Pat and then shook her head.

'I need to examine you, Mrs Woods. If you like to undress behind the curtains and then—'

'No!'

There was a startled silence and Pat looked up from where she was redressing the baby. 'It's all right, Anna. I'll be here.'

Avoiding their glances, Anna shook her head. 'I'm fine. I don't mind you looking at the baby, but I don't need—'

'It really is advisable, Mrs Woods—'

'Stop calling me Mrs Woods,' Anna snapped. 'It's Miss—'

There was an awkward silence and then, to their horror, Anna burst into tears. 'I'm so sorry. I – I didn't mean to be rude. It's just – I'm so frightened.'

'Frightened?' The young doctor was genuinely distressed. 'Of me?'

Anna's voice was muffled by her tears, but they both heard her whisper, 'Of you touching me.'

Again, the doctor and Pat Jessop exchanged a glance. A look that said: *There's something going on here that we don't know about.*

'I'll be right with you, love,' Pat tried to reassure her. 'I'll even hold your hand, but the doctor must examine you internally to make sure—'

'Internally?' Anna almost shrieked. 'Whatever for?'

'To make sure everything's as it should be. It is important both for now and for the next time you have a child—'

'There won't be a next time,' Anna interrupted bitterly. 'I'll make sure of that.'

Again a look passed between the doctor and the district nurse, but neither of them said anything.

After a great deal of gentle persuasion, for both doctor and nurse could see that the girl was genuinely terrified, Anna gave her reluctant consent. The examination was difficult. Despite the doctor telling her to relax, Anna tensed every muscle against him. But at last he said, 'Everything seems to be fine.' He could not stop himself adding, 'Physically.'

Anna took no notice and pulled on her clothes quickly, but Pat gave a little nod of agreement.

There was something upsetting this poor girl and she meant to find out what it was. She had grown fond of Anna and she could understand now why the kindly Eddie Appleyard was still taking such risks to help her. There was just something about the girl. Even Pat couldn't put her finger on quite what it was. Anna was a strange mixture of vulnerability and feistiness. *But for some reason*, Pat thought, *she makes you want to put your arm round her and take care of her*.

Pat acted out the thought, putting her arm about the girl's shoulders. 'Let's get you home now. Eddie'll be waiting and, if I know babies, it won't be long before Maisie here starts to let us know she's hungry.'

As she led the girl from the room, Pat glanced back over her shoulder. 'Thank you very much, Dr Mortimer.' She gave a brief nod to the young doctor that said silently: *I'll look after her*.

The doctor smiled but his glance, following the young girl, was full of concern. He wished the girl would stay, would allow him more time to talk to her. He was sure she needed help. He knew he could give it.

But it was obvious she couldn't wait to get away from his surgery. The young man sighed as he promised himself that the next time he saw Nurse Jessop on her own, he would ask her about the mysterious Anna Woods.

'You're home from market early. Couldn't ya find a doxy today?' Bertha paused significantly. 'Or don't ya need one now you've got a live-in trollop just over the hill?'

Eddie had dropped Anna and the child off at the end of the track on the far side of the wood.

'Are you sure it's not too far for you, lass? Carrying the little 'un an' all?' he'd asked, but Anna had shaken her head. 'It'll do me good.'

'I know of someone who's not likely to need their pram any more. I'll see if I can get it for you,' Pat offered.

'I can't pay for it—' Anna began, but Pat laughed. 'It's had seven bairns in it. It's that battered I don't reckon Mrs Dawson'll want anything for it.' Hastily, before Anna might think she was being treated like a charity case, the district nurse added, 'But I'll ask her. We'll do it proper.' Pat waved. 'See you soon, love. Now, Eddie, you'd best get me home. I've still got patients I must see today.'

How different was Pat's attitude towards the young lass, Eddie was thinking now as he faced his wife. He couldn't help comparing the fat, blowsy woman before him, with her small, mean mouth and beady, suspicious eyes, with Pat's warm friendliness and ready laugh.

For once his anger bubbled to the surface. 'Give it a rest, Bertha,' he snapped. He spun round and left the house, slamming the back door behind him.

So, Bertha thought, her eyes narrowing, *I was right. That little trollop is still in the cottage. Well, Mr Eddie Appleyard, we'll have to see about that, won't we? But I'm patient. I can wait. I can bide me time. I can wait years, if that's what it takes. But one day, oh yes, one day. There's summat funny going on there with that little madam and one day I'll find out what it is.*

Fifteen

By the time the snow and the flood waters were gone, Anna had begun to feel a little safer in her hideaway home. Until Joe Wainwright arrived to repair the roof.

Anna saw a lorry chugging towards her down the track from the farm. At first she thought it was Eddie, but as the vehicle drew nearer she realized that the driver was a stranger.

The lorry halted in front of the cottage and now Anna could see the name painted along the side. *Joe Wainwright, Builder.*

The man climbed stiffly out of the cab. He was small and stocky and dressed in corduroy trousers and jacket with a red neckerchief tucked into his striped shirt. He was very bow-legged and walked with a rolling gait as he came towards her, holding out his callused hand in greeting. His face, with three or four days' growth of stubble, was swarthy and lined. Anna couldn't help staring at him as she put out her hand, a little nervously, to shake his.

Joe laughed. 'Aye, I know I'm a funny little feller. I couldn't stop a pig in a passage, could I, lass? But I'm good at me job, else Eddie wouldn't have asked me to come and look at that there roof.'

He squinted up at the holes in the thatch. 'Aye, that's no problem. We'll soon have you all shipshape, lass.' His glance rested on her once more. He gave a little nod. 'So you're the one all the village is talking about, a' ya? The one Eddie Appleyard's moved into his cottage? A bonny 'un an' all.' Joe looked around him, his sharp eyes searching. 'And ya've a babby, ain't ya?'

Anna felt a prickle of fear. It was the first time her privacy had been invaded so boldly. Pat's questioning had been probing, certainly, but it had been done with a feeling of genuine concern. This man was just plain nosy.

'I have,' Anna said shortly. 'But it's not Mr Appleyard's bairn, if that's what folks are saying.'

Unabashed, Joe wheezed with laughter. With blunt honesty, he said, 'Aye well, lass, that's what they *are* saying.' He winked. 'You should hear the owd beezums in the village. Clackety-clack, their tongues are going. Like me to set 'em straight, would ya?'

Anna shrugged. 'I don't care one way or the other. *I* know the truth and so does Mr Appleyard.'

She wondered how the village had heard of her existence in the secluded, tumbledown cottage. Her mouth tightened involuntarily. There was only one person, other than the Appleyard family, who knew she was here. Pat Jessop. And to think Anna had allowed herself to trust the nurse.

Joe interrupted her thoughts. 'Aye, but his *wife* dun't, does she?'

Incredulous, Anna stared at him. 'Are you telling me that it's her spreading the gossip?'

He rubbed his fingers on the bristly growth on his chin. 'Well, who else could it be? No one else knew you was here. 'Cept their lad, Tony.' He gave another wheezing laugh. 'And I don't reckon it's the sort of thing he'd tell his schoolmates, do you?'

Anna chastised herself inwardly. She had been wrong

to accuse Pat. Thank goodness it had only been in her mind and not spoken aloud.

'Where've you come from then?' Joe's prying was not finished.

'That's my business,' Anna snapped, hoping that she could offend him just enough to stop his questions but not enough to prevent him mending the roof. But it was impossible to offend Joe Wainwright. His skin was as thick and impervious as the leather on his boots. He just laughed and countered with another question. 'And are you staying here then?'

'Not for long. Now,' she added, trying desperately to steer the focus of his attention away from her, 'would you like a cup of tea and a slice of currant cake? I've just managed to master the bread oven.'

'I wouldn't say no, lass. I wouldn't say no.'

Joe Wainwright was, as he had said, good at his work. In a few hours the thatched roof was repaired.

As he climbed down his ladder, he remarked, 'I see you've had a bit o' trouble with that there wall. Eddie mend that himself, did he?'

'Yes.'

'Ah well, 'spect he has to watch the pennies like the rest of us. Specially with Bertha Tinker for a wife.' He sniffed contemptuously. 'By, she's a shrew and no mistake. Just like 'er mother. No wonder poor old Wilf Tinker used to look elsewhere for 'is comforts.' He gave a huge wink and tapped the side of his nose as he added, 'If ya know what I mean.'

For once, Anna could not stop a twinge of curiosity. She did not venture any questions, but Joe needed no prompting and she made no attempt to stop him. 'Mind you,' he went on, warming to his subject as he found a new ear to listen to his gossip, 'he's a bit of a lad in more ways than one, is Wilf. Ended up in the nick, he has.'

Anna's eyes widened, but still she ventured no comment.

'Aye, black market in the war, y'know.'

Anna bit her lip.

'Course, lots o' folk dabbled a bit in a harmless sort of way. Most of us got away wi' it.' He winked again, indicating that he, Joe Wainwright, had not been above making a bit on the side. 'But poor old Wilf Tinker was 'is own worst enemy. Couldn't tell a lie, see. Not a convincing one at any rate and o' course when he was faced with the law . . .' He shrugged and spread his hands. 'They saw right through 'im. Pity, really. He's not a bad sort in lots of ways. He certainly wasn't a real crook, if you knows what I mean.' He nodded knowingly. 'There was some hard nuts in the war, lass. Real spiv types that'd sell their granny if they thought they could get a bob or two for her.'

A shudder ran through Anna and she felt suddenly sick. She turned her head away before Joe should read her expression.

'And this Wilf Tinker was Mrs Appleyard's father?' she asked, recovering herself.

'Tha's right. Him and his missis had two lasses. Bertha and Lucy. Lucy did well for herself. Married an office worker and lives in Ludthorpe. Quite the lady, Lucy is. I reckon poor old Bertha envies her. Though give me Eddie Appleyard any time. He's all right, is Eddie. But I dun't reckon I need to tell you that, lass, do I?'

Anna turned back slowly to meet his steady gaze. 'No, Mr Wainwright,' she said. 'You don't.'

By shearing time Maisie was out in the bright, early summer days, sitting up in the deep, black pram that Pat had brought for her.

'Jessie Dawson doesn't want owt for it.'

Anna had eyed the district nurse sceptically. 'Are you sure?'

'Course I am.' Pat laughed. 'Mind you, I had a job to get her to part with it. She shed tears as I wheeled it away. "All my bairns have been in that pram," she said.'

Anna frowned. 'Are you sure she won't want it again? I mean, she sounds very fond of children. She might—'

'I'm sure Jessie'd love another half-dozen given the chance. But she won't have the chance, love. She had to have a hysterectomy after the last baby.'

Anna put her hand onto the well-worn handle. The pram sagged down at one corner where a spring had weakened.

'It's a bit battered, ducky, like I told you.'

'It's fine.' Anna smiled as she rocked the pram gently. 'Maisie will love being outside.'

The local farmers all helped one another at certain times of the year: haymaking, harvest and, for those who kept sheep on the Wolds' hills, shearing. But with Eddie's small flock, only Sam Granger, an acknowledged 'dab hand' at shearing, would come. And, of course, Joe Wainwright, who seemed to turn up at every event, would no doubt be there.

On the day before shearing was to begin in the yard at Cackle Hill Farm, Anna wheeled Maisie into the warm sunshine and parked the pram just outside the gate in the fence surrounding their home. She glanced back towards the cottage garden with a small stab of pride. Despite her intention to leave as soon as she could, she had not been able to stand the sight of the neglected garden. In front of the cottage, she had scythed the small patches of grass and was able to keep it short now with a battered old lawnmower that Pat had brought her.

'I've treated myself to a brand-new one,' the nurse had said, beaming. 'I've got quite a big lawn and this one was too much like hard work. But you're young and strong. You'll cope with it.'

Anna had weeded the flowerbeds and now Canterbury bells, cornflowers and convolvulus sprouted happily, whilst lupins and irises were just coming into flower. At the side of the building, there had once been a square of kitchen garden. Whilst Anna was adamant that she would not be here long enough to enjoy the fruits of her labour, she had nevertheless cleared the ground and planted onions and lettuce.

'Why don't you plant cabbage and caulis?' Eddie had suggested in March. 'And what about runner beans and . . .'

'It's not worth it,' Anna said quietly. 'I won't be here to enjoy them.'

Eddie's face fell.

'Unless you'd like me to plant them for you?' she added.

Eddie shook his head. 'No, lass,' he said heavily as he turned away. 'Don't bother.'

But she had dug the kitchen garden over anyway and

now, unearthed from the choking weeds and nettles, a rhubarb plant flourished in one corner flanked by two gooseberry bushes.

Buster, usually so boisterous, sat by the pram whenever Maisie was outside, as if guarding the child. Today, however, Anna had other work for him.

The sheep had all been washed in the stream a few days earlier in time for their fleeces to dry in the summer sunshine. It had been hard work, for the sheep hated being plunged into the water and had fought and struggled. Panting and soaked through, Anna and Eddie had laughed at each other.

'You look like a drowned rat,' she had giggled.

'So do you,' he had countered, grinning. 'Go on home. Go and get dry.'

'Why don't you come too? There's a sharp breeze. You'll be chilled by the time you walk back to the farm.'

'Aye, mebbe you're right.'

They walked together towards the cottage, Eddie pushing the pram containing a sleeping Maisie.

'D'you know,' he mused. 'I don't reckon I ever pushed our Tony in his pram. Not once.'

Anna laughed softly. 'Not reckoned to be man's work, eh?'

'Wouldn't have bothered me,' Eddie said and there was a note of regret in his tone as if he thought he might have missed a special moment.

As he manoeuvred the pram through the back door, Anna said, 'I'll get a blanket for you. Could you set up the clothes airer? And get those wet things off.'

Eddie grinned. 'Yes, ma'am.'

Anna changed into dry clothes in her bedroom and Eddie sat wrapped in a blanket whilst his wet garments steamed in front of the fire. Anna handed him a cup of hot cocoa and sat down beside him.

'A good job done.' She smiled.

Eddie glanced up to meet her eyes. As he took the cup, their fingers touched briefly. 'Aye lass,' he said. 'A good job done.'

They sat together in companionable silence and even when his clothes were dry enough to put on Eddie seemed reluctant to leave.

He paused in the doorway on his way out and said softly, 'Thanks, lass, for everything.' Very gently, he touched her cheek and then turned and walked away up the slope.

'Oh, Eddie, what a lovely man you are,' Anna whispered to herself as she watched him go. For the first time in many months she suddenly realized that she had not been afraid to be alone with a man.

And now the day for shearing was almost here. Anna surveyed the sheep contentedly grazing in the field near her cottage. Then she shaded her eyes and looked up to the top of the rise, where she could see Tony standing looking down the track towards her. Rip was sitting obediently beside him. She had often seen the two of them at the top of the hill, but not once, since the day he had been sent by his father to fetch her to help with the difficult birth of twin lambs, had the boy visited the cottage.

Now she saw him glance, just once, over his shoulder as if checking to see if anyone was watching him. Then suddenly he launched himself down the hill, running pell-mell towards her, Rip bounding along at his side barking joyfully.

The dog reached her first and jumped up to lick her face. Then Rip capered with the half-grown puppy.

Anna held out her arms and, as Tony flung himself into them, she lifted him bodily off the ground and swung him round.

'Oh, I've missed you,' she said impulsively as she set him on the ground and breathlessly they leant against each other, laughing together. She pulled back and held him at arm's length. 'You've grown. I'm sure you've grown.'

Tony grinned. 'Nah.'

'You have, you have,' she insisted and then laughed again. 'But if you haven't then come and look at Maisie. She certainly has.'

As he reached the pram, Tony gasped. 'Oh. She's sitting up and she's smiling. Really smiling now.' He held out a finger to her. The baby gripped it and tried to pull it towards her mouth, but the boy laughed and gently eased it from her grasp. 'No, no, dirty.'

Maisie blinked at him. Her smile faded. Her chin quivered and she began to whimper, huge tears welling in her dark brown eyes.

'Oh don't. Don't cry, little Maisie. I didn't mean to make you cry, but my finger's mucky.' He leant towards her and tickled Maisie until she chuckled once more.

Watching the young boy's tenderness with her child, Anna felt a lump come to her throat.

'Come on,' she tried to say briskly, though she didn't quite manage it for her voice was unsteady. 'We've work to do.'

Sixteen

'Sam's coming tomorrow to start the shearing,' Tony said. 'And Dad says he wants you to come down to the yard and wrap the fleeces for him.' The boy put his head on one side and regarded her thoughtfully. 'Do you know how to do it?'

Anna closed her eyes for a moment as the memories came flooding back, threatening, not for the first time, to overwhelm her. She knew just how it would be. The yard alive with activity: sheep bleating, men laughing and ribbing one another, yet all the while the fleeces would be falling from the sheep as if by magic under the expert hands wielding the shears. She opened her eyes again, but, not trusting herself to speak, she merely nodded.

'We've to round up about half the flock tomorrow morning. Joe Wainwright comes an' all. He cuts all the clags off and opens up the necks for Sam. We do about half the flock one day and the rest the next.'

'Oh.' Anna raised her eyebrows. 'I'd have thought an expert shearer could do your dad's flock in a day.'

Tony grinned. 'He could easy, but he doesn't start till midday. Ses he likes the sheep to have the sun on their backs for a while. Makes the shearing easier, he ses.'

Anna smiled, for a moment her thoughts were far away once more. 'So it does,' she murmured. 'I'd forgotten that.' Then she brought her wandering mind back to the job in hand. 'So, are you coming to help me round them up in the morning?'

Tony nodded. 'I'll be here early.'

The following morning Anna and Tony worked together, leaving Buster sitting beside the pram. For once, the little dog was restless, wanting to join in the rounding up. At last, unable to sit still any longer, he bounded across to Rip, startling the five sheep the older dog was guiding up the track. Anna and Tony burst out laughing, imagining they could see an aggrieved look on Rip's face.

'Just look at him,' Tony spluttered. 'He looks like me dad when I've done something daft.'

'I know just what you mean. He looks as if he's saying, "Look what you've done. Now I've got to start all over again." '

'And poor Buster hasn't a clue what he *has* done.'

'Here, boy. Here, Buster,' Anna called and the young dog came slowly towards her, head down in apology. But Anna fondled him. 'It's all right, but you've got to learn. Now, stay.'

The dog lay down whilst Anna, holding the crook that Eddie had lent her, moved to the right and began to whistle to Rip. With a series of shouted instructions and whistles, they rounded up the five sheep again.

'Yan, tan, tethera, fethera, pethera . . .' she murmured to herself as her eyes misted over once more. But Tony had heard her.

'Oh, you can count like the shepherds, an' all.'

'What?' Anna turned startled eyes upon him, hardly realizing that she had spoken aloud. 'Oh – er – yes.'

'Then you can teach me. Dad only knows "yan, tan, tethera", then he forgets. How far can you count?'

'Only to about twenty . . .'

'That'll do.' Tony grinned.

Anna smiled. 'You follow Rip up the hill and see he gets them into the barn whilst I get the next lot. And I'll try to get this little rascal to do as he's told.' She turned towards the young dog. 'Come on, Buster. High time you learned to earn your keep.'

Anna felt very nervous about going down to the yard. If it hadn't been for the fact that she owed Eddie Appleyard so much, she would have stayed in her little haven, safe from inquisitive eyes. But, she sighed, she had no choice. So she put Maisie in the pram with a bottle for her feed and set off up the track. Joe Wainwright and a man Anna had not met before were already at work in the yard.

Eddie made the brief introduction. 'This is Sam, Anna.' Eddie made no reference to the baby in the pram, which she had parked at the edge of the yard.

'Morning, lass,' Joe greeted her cheerfully, but Sam glowered briefly at her and then turned his back.

As she was making ready the table where she would lay the fleeces to wrap them, Joe came and stood beside her. 'Tek no notice of old Sam, lass. He's got a daughter of his own about your age. And he's a better guard dog than Eddie's sheepdog ovver yonder.' The man gave a wheezing laugh. He leant a little closer. 'Won't let the poor lass even speak to the young fellers, ne'er mind walk out with any of 'em.'

Anna's mouth tightened as she glanced towards Maisie sitting contentedly in her pram. 'He doesn't approve of me, you mean.'

Quite unabashed, Joe nodded. 'Summat like that,

aye, lass. But you mark my words, he's stacking up a barrowload of trouble for 'issen. The more you try to keep 'em tied down, the more they'll try to slip the leash. 'Tis only nature, lass, 'tis only nature.' Joe laughed again and leant closer to whisper, 'But what he forgets is that some of us round here have long memories. When he was a young feller his wife's father went after him with a shotgun one night.'

Anna turned to stare at Joe.

'You've heard of a shotgun wedding, lass, ain't ya?'

Anna nodded.

'Well, that was a real one, an' no mistake, 'cos their first bairn was born only six months after they was wed.' Joe winked and tapped the side of his nose. 'So Sam's the last one to be disapproving, ain't he?'

Anna said nothing, but let her head drop forwards to hide her face. Then she felt Joe's friendly hand rest briefly on her shoulder. 'Chin up, lass. You'm got a lovely babby there. Be proud of her.'

Then he turned and walked away, but the man's bluff kindness had brought tears to her eyes.

The men worked hard, with Anna alongside them pausing only to feed and change Maisie and to grab a quick bite to eat herself. She watched in admiration as Sam tipped each sheep onto its rump. So sharp were his blades and so experienced his hands that he didn't even seem to work the shears, but swept the blades down with long easy strokes, deftly turning the animal so that the fleece came off in one whole piece. Then it was Anna's turn to pick up the fleece and take it to the slatted table. Taking it by the hind legs, she flung it upwards and outwards, as if shaking a rug, so that dust and loose fibres floated around her. Then she picked off all the bits of briar and grass that still clung to it. She folded the flanks towards the centre to form a rectangle and rolled the fleece from the back end up towards the neck, where she drew out the neck wool to form a tie long enough to encircle the rolled fleece and tuck back in under itself.

All afternoon she worked steadily, until Eddie called a halt and Bertha appeared in the yard carrying drinks for the workers. Anna turned away, but not before she had seen the look of fury on the older woman's face.

It was late in the evening when Anna climbed the track wearily, with scarcely the strength left to push the pram up the slope. Even when the shearing was done for the day and the men had gone, the work was not finished. The sheared sheep had to be driven back to the field and the next lot brought down to the farm for the night, ready for shearing the following day.

'Dad, Dad,' Anna heard Tony shouting. 'There's three lambs can't find their mothers. They're crying.'

The high-pitched bleating of the lambs as they darted from one ewe to another, unable to recognize their newly shorn dams, was pitiful. But Eddie only chuckled. 'It's all right, lad, I'll make sure they've found the right ones afore I leave them. But you run on home now. Ya mam'll be wanting you away to your bed. And you too, Anna, you take that little one home. You look all in, ya'sen.'

'Goodnight, then, Eddie. I'll see you in the morning.'

'Goodnight, lass. And thanks for all your help today.'

Anna smiled and turned away. As she entered the cottage, she leant a moment against the closed door, glad to be back in her little sanctuary. And yet it hadn't been a bad day. Despite Sam's obvious disapproval and Bertha's malevolent glare, Joe had treated her kindly. It had been a good day.

There had only been one moment that had caused her anguish, but no one could have guessed. At least, she hoped no one had noticed that for a moment her heart had seemed to rise into her throat and her hands had trembled.

Joe had unwittingly brought about the stab of fear. He had been admiring Sam's skill at shearing and had commented lightly. 'You remind me of a young feller that lives over Lincoln way. By, I've never seen a better shearer in me life. Like a knife through butter, it is, to watch him and he never leaves so much as a nick on the sheep. But blessed if I can remember his name.'

'I bet you mean Jed Rower,' she heard Sam say. 'I saw him at the show one year. You'm right, he's a clever feller . . .' The two men had continued their chatter, whilst Anna froze for a moment and then her heart began to pound. Her hands were trembling as she carried the next fleece to the table, her face flushing bright red. Biting her lip, she tried to concentrate on the wrapping, but she did it so badly that she was obliged to unfold it once more and begin again. No one seemed to notice and gradually her heartbeat returned to normal and she tried to squash the thoughts that mention of the name had evoked.

But now, in the stillness of the cottage, those thoughts refused to be ignored.

I must go, was all she could think of. *I'm still not far enough away. Once the shearing's finished, I must move on.*

Seventeen

'You coming with me into town?' Eddie asked Anna as they stacked the rolled fleeces into the back of his trailer to take into Ludthorpe. She shook her head. 'No – I – er – I've things to do.'

'All right, then, lass. I'll see you later. Anything you want bringing?'

Anna's heart beat a little faster and her hands were clammy. She didn't like deceiving Eddie, who had been so kind to her, but, as soon as he had left the farm heading towards the town, she intended to leave too, but in the opposite direction. She dared not tell him, dared not say goodbye, for she knew he would try to persuade her to stay. And he would probably succeed. She would leave via the village, Anna decided. She would call in to say her farewells to Pat and to leave a message for Eddie with her. She could even write him a note . . .

'We'll have to dip in about a fortnight's time . . .' Eddie was saying as he climbed up onto his tractor.

Startled from her own thoughts, Anna said, 'What? What did you say?'

'I said, we'll have to dip all the sheep in about a fortnight.' He smiled down at her. 'I'll need your help then all right, lass. Tony's not strong enough to manage them when they struggle . . .'

Anna stared up at him. Oh no, it wasn't possible. Quite unaware of her plans, Eddie had innocently presented her with yet another reason for her to stay longer.

'Oh, er, right,' she murmured and silently promised: *Two more weeks, then. Just two more weeks and then we'll go.*

Anna stood at the top of the rise, watching the lorry taking a batch of the lambs to market manoeuvre its way out of the gate of Cackle Hill Farm. Beside her Maisie lay asleep in the depths of the black pram, blissfully unaware of her mother's inner turmoil. The young woman smiled gently, though tears prickled her eyes. She couldn't help it. It was not the way of a true farmer. Though never cruel to any animal, nevertheless proper farmers were unsentimental about the need to slaughter the livestock they had so carefully reared. But Anna had not been able to stop herself becoming fond of the woolly little creatures that gambolled and leapt about in their joy at just being alive.

Once she had known that kind of joy.

Her gaze roamed over the slopes of the surrounding fields, vibrant in their summer colours. Below her in the cottage garden splashes of colour vibrated against the darkness of the trees beyond, stately white foxgloves, purple lupins, and pink petunias and even a few early red roses. She wished she could plant more flowers in front of the cottage and there was room in the vegetable patch at the side to plant potatoes, carrots, beans – enough to provide for herself and Maisie for months. She could make it into a real home. She already had, really. She could be content here, almost happy. Anna bit her lip. But it was futile to make such plans.

She couldn't stay here. They had to move on. It wasn't safe. She must get as far away as possible. There were too many people now who knew she was living here. Pat Bishop, Joe Wainwright, the doctor and the registrar in the town and, more recently, the vet and then the men who had come to help with the shearing. And it had been then that she had realized she was still not far enough away. The list of those who now knew where she was was getting far too long, to say nothing of the gossips in the village who knew all about her presence in Eddie Appleyard's shepherd's cottage, even if they had never seen her. The more who knew, the more likely it was that word might get back . . .

And most dangerous of all was Bertha, whose malevolent gaze seemed to follow her everywhere.

It was time to go. The dipping was done, the lambs all gone. Now would be a good time to leave.

Her mind made up, Anna turned her back on the idyllic scene and determinedly pushed the pram down the rough track towards the cottage that had been her haven for the past few months. She would go, she resolved, and go now before she could change her mind.

Back at the cottage, she began to gather her belongings together, her own and Maisie's clothes and food for the journey, piling them all beside the pram. Then she stood looking down at the heap. There was far too much to fit on the pram. Its already sagging springs would never take the extra weight. And there was too much for her to carry. Maybe if she put some in the pram and made up a kind of bundle she could carry on her back . . .

From outside, the sound of Eddie's tractor came closer.

'Oh no!' Anna breathed and hurried outside to forestall him coming into the cottage. He was back earlier than she had thought. She had taken too long to get ready.

He drew to a halt and switched off the engine. Climbing down, he came towards her, smiling. 'Well, lass, that's another lot gone and I got a good price.' His grin widened. 'I'll be able to give you a bonus on your wages.'

Anna smiled tremulously and walked away from the door, trying to keep a distance between him and her home. But her ruse was not working.

'Where's Maisie?' He moved towards the back door.

'She – she's asleep,' Anna said desperately. 'Don't wake her. She's teething and – and she's not sleeping very well.'

This was not strictly true. The child was indeed teething, but she seemed to be having little trouble.

'She's very lucky,' Pat had told Anna on her last visit, adding with a laugh, 'and so are you. Most kiddies have an awful time and so do their mothers. Being kept awake half the night isn't any fun for baby or mother.'

'Oh.' Eddie stopped at once. 'Poor little mite,' he said sympathetically. 'I remember Tony crying a lot when he was teething. I used to rub a little whisky onto his gums.' He grinned. 'But don't tell Pat I told you that, will ya?'

Anna tried to smile, but it was a nervous, half-hearted effort. Eddie didn't seem to notice. His gaze was roving over the outside walls of the cottage. 'You know, this could do with a lick of lime wash—'

At that moment, much to Anna's chagrin, they heard Maisie wail.

Eddie's face brightened. 'She's awake. Now I can see her.' He was in through the back door before Anna could stop him.

She sighed and followed him. He was standing quite still, staring down at the pile of their belongings beside the pram. Slowly he turned to look at Anna, disappointment and concern on his face.

'What's this? You – you're not thinking of leaving, love, are you?'

Silently, Anna nodded.

'Aw, lass, why? What's wrong? Is there something you need? What is it? Tell me and I'll get it.'

Anna shook her head. 'It – it's not that, Eddie. You've been wonderful, so good. Too good—'

He stared at her for a moment and then closed his eyes and groaned. 'Aw, lass, you're not thinking I'm going to want summat in return. Aw, lass, don't ever think that. Not of me.'

'No, no, Eddie,' she reassured him swiftly. 'It's not that. Truly. That – that never entered my head.'

He eyed her sceptically. 'Didn't it?' he asked gently. ''Cos it has into other folks' nasty minds.' His voice dropped to a whisper. 'Even me own wife's.'

'Well, maybe at first,' Anna admitted. 'But not now. Not since I've got to know you. You're just a very kind man, Eddie Appleyard.'

For a moment there was silence between them as they gazed at each other. At last Eddie cleared his throat, but his voice was still husky with emotion as he asked, 'Then why, lass?'

Maisie's wailing grew louder and before she answered him, Anna moved to the pram and picked up the child. Resting her baby against her shoulder, Anna patted her back soothingly. Maisie's cries subsided to gentle hiccuping.

'I have to move on. I have to get further away.'

'Why? What is it you're afraid of? *Who* are you afraid of? You've been here months now and no one's come looking for you. Or has summat happened I don't know about?'

Anna lowered her eyes, not daring to meet his steady gaze. Hating herself for lying, she shook her head.

'Then why, lass? You're safe here.' When she did not answer, he added, 'Aren't you?'

Anna closed her eyes and let out a deep sigh. Flatly, she said, 'I don't know. I – I just feel that the further away the better.'

'Further away from where exactly?' Again there was no reply from her, so he prompted gently. 'Won't you trust me enough to tell me that at least?'

In a husky, reluctant whisper she said, 'Lincoln.'

'Lincoln?' Eddie almost laughed. 'Why, that's miles away. No one's going to find you here. To folks from the city, this is the back of beyond.'

Anna smiled thinly but said nothing.

'So will you stay, lass? At least a little longer? It'll be haymaking afore we know it and then harvest . . .'

'And then it'll be winter and I won't be able to go,' she said.

Eddie grinned ruefully. 'Aye, so it will, lass. So it will. You see right through me, don't ya?' They smiled, understanding one another. 'So, will you stay, love? Please say you will.'

With a jolt Anna saw that there were tears in his

eyes. A lump grew in her own throat so that she could not answer. Instead, slowly, she nodded.

Anna and her daughter were still there through haymaking and into the harvest in the heat of August. It seemed as if half the village turned out to help the local farmers get in the harvest.

'It's always happened round here. It's a sort of custom, but more so in the war,' Pat told her. 'With a lot of the fellers away, we had Land Army girls here and the local women helped an' all.' She laughed. 'I reckon we all got to enjoy it.'

'Did – did Eddie have Land Army girls here?' Anna asked.

'Oh yes,' Pat said. 'Most of the farmers did. Some of the girls even stayed on. One girl married a local lad and stayed.' She nodded towards a pretty, fair-haired girl. 'That's her. That's Phyllis. Nice lass, she is. You'd like her. Why don't you let me introduce—'

'No,' Anna said swiftly. 'No, thanks.'

Puzzled, Pat glanced at Anna but said no more. Anna was staring across at Phyllis, almost as if she recognized her and yet she had refused to meet her. In fact, she refused to meet anyone, refused even to try to make friends. Pat sighed. Anna was a funny lass and no mistake.

As Eddie towed the last of the wagons behind the tractor to his stack yard, Pat said, 'There, that's Eddie's all safely gathered in. We've just Ted Bucknall's to do now and that's the harvest home. There'll be a harvest supper in the village hall then. You'll come, won't you?'

Anna shook her head.

'But everyone will be there—'

'No!' Anna was adamant. 'I – I can't.'

Pat sighed as they walked together back towards the farm. 'You will have to mix with folk sometime, love. You can't keep yourself a recluse.' She laughed and nudged Anna's arm. 'They'll be calling you a witch soon.'

Anna smiled wanly.

'And what about Maisie? She needs to play—'

'I play with her.'

'But she needs to be with kiddies of her own age. She needs—'

Anna stopped and turned to face Pat. 'I know you mean it kindly, and I'm grateful, really I am, but I can't mix with folk. And – and I can't let Maisie either.'

'She'll have to when she gets to five years old and has to go to school,' Pat said bluntly. 'You've got to face that, Anna, because it's a fact and you can't get away from it.'

Now Anna smiled. 'I know that, but we'll be miles away from here by then.'

On the evening of the harvest supper, Anna sat alone on the grass outside the little white cottage, watching the sunset. She drew her knees up, wrapped her arms around her legs and rested her chin on her knees. It was so quiet, so still, so peaceful . . .

As the sun dropped lower, emblazoning the western sky with red and gold, Anna dared to feel happy for the first time. The feeling of contentment came stealthily, unbidden, and yet she hardly dared to acknowledge it, to believe that she could ever feel secure and . . .

She heard a movement and jumped, glancing round to see Eddie standing only a few feet from her.

'Sorry, lass,' he said softly. 'I didn't mean to startle you.'

He came across the grass and sat down beside her. 'Lovely sight, ain't it? A Lincolnshire sunset. Nowt to beat it. "Red sky at night, shepherds' delight".'

They sat in companionable silence. For a while, it seemed as if there was no one in the world but them. Then, quietly, Eddie began to talk. 'You must wonder why me an' Bertha ever came to get married.'

'It's not my business, Eddie,' Anna said, not sure she wanted to be the keeper of his confidence. It bound them even closer.

'You might have guessed' – he smiled ruefully – 'that once upon a time I carried a torch for Pat Anderson. Sorry, Jessop she is now.'

'I could see there was a closeness between you,' Anna murmured.

Eddie sighed. 'But she left the village. Went to be a nurse in Ludthorpe and met this handsome young feller at the hospital.' There was no bitterness or jealousy in Eddie's tone, just sadness. 'Couldn't blame her, I suppose. He was a really nice feller.'

'And you started seeing Bertha?'

Eddie gave a short laugh. 'Sort of. She came to work here at the farm. My mam and dad were still alive then, but getting on a bit. Mam needed help in the house and with the dairy work. She was a kindly old dear, my mam.'

'That doesn't surprise me,' Anna said, before she could stop herself.

His eyebrows raised in question, Eddie glanced at her. Anna laughed softly. 'You must take after her, Eddie.'

He smiled and gave a little nod. 'I'd like to think so.' He paused as if lost in thought for a moment. 'Anyway, me mam felt sorry for the Tinker family, specially the youngsters, and when Bertha left school she offered her a job here. And, of course,' he added pointedly as if it explained everything, 'she lived in.'

Anna could imagine how it must have been. A young man, disappointed in love, and a young girl thrown together. Maybe, then, Bertha had been prettier than she was now. Maybe she had fallen in love with Eddie . . .

But Eddie had no such illusions. His next words dispelled Anna's romantic hopes. 'The Tinkers always had an eye for the main chance and my dear wife was no exception. She set her cap at me and I, like a fool, fell for it.' He sighed heavily. 'It wasn't so bad in the early days, I have to admit. She was good to me mam and dad, nursing them in their final illnesses. I'll give her that. But then, after Tony was born, it was as if she gave all the love she had to give to him. So' – he turned to look at her gravely – 'don't ever think, lass, that it's you who's caused trouble between us, 'cos it ain't.'

'I'm very sorry, Eddie,' Anna said huskily. 'There's no happy endings in real life are there? That only happens in books.'

'Don't say that, lass. Mebbe there's not one for me, but for you—'

Anna pursed her mouth and shook her head emphatically. 'No. Not for me either.'

There was a long silence until Eddie said, 'Then I'm sorry too, love. Very sorry.' He paused again before asking tentatively, 'Won't you tell me what happened to you?'

Anna's head dropped forward and she pulled at the grass with agitated fingers. 'I can't. It's – it's too painful.'

'All right, love. But if you ever feel the need to talk, I'm here. I'll always be here for you.'

As if pulled by an invisible string, they turned to look at each other. Hesitantly, Eddie reached out. For a moment, Anna drew in a breath and almost jerked away, but then, seeing the tenderness in his eyes, she allowed him to touch her. He traced the line of her cheek with his roughened forefinger, yet his touch was surprisingly gentle.

'Ya won't leave, lass, will ya?' he pleaded softly. 'Ya'll stay here. With me.'

His face was soft in the golden glow of the sunset, his eyes dark unreadable depths, but she could hear the longing in his voice. Anna trembled. By going, she would hurt this lovely man. This man who had given her everything, yet asked nothing in return. But by staying she risked the safety of herself and her child too.

'Till spring, Eddie,' she whispered. 'That's all I can promise. Till spring.'

Eighteen

Anna did not leave the following spring. Maisie learned to walk on the soft grass of Eddie's meadows on the hillside outside the cottage, whilst Anna helped again with the birthing and rearing of the lambs. Anna planted vegetables in the garden at the back of their home and Eddie renovated the upstairs rooms.

'Maisie needs a room of her own, now she's getting such a big girl,' he said, smiling down at the little girl, who followed him whenever she could, clinging to his legs and gazing up at him. He ruffled her coppery curls and tickled her cheek.

'Tony?' Maisie would ask day after day and Eddie would laugh. 'He's at school, lovey. You'll have to make do with old Eddie today. I know, you can come and watch me do the milking.'

'No, Eddie. She's not to go to the farm,' Anna said, overhearing.

In the past year, she had seen Bertha rarely and, in all that time, had never spoken to her once. The other woman made no trouble now, but on the odd occasions that Eddie had needed Anna's help in the buildings or the yard near the house Anna had felt Bertha's malevolent glare following her.

'It'll be all right—'

'No!' Anna was adamant. 'She's not to go to the farm. Not ever.'

'Bertha wouldn't hurt her, Anna. She's got a lot of faults, but she'd never hurt a child. She loves children.'

'Even *my* child?'

'Oh Anna.' His eyes reproached her. 'She's not a bad woman. She'd not harm your little girl.' He shrugged. 'She didn't like the idea of you being here. Still doesn't, I expect.' He wrinkled his forehead. 'But she's not even mentioned you recently. 'Spect she's got used to you being here now.'

'She doesn't allow Tony to come to see us though, does she?'

Eddie smiled. 'No, but he comes anyway.'

'Not so often now and when he does he comes round by the road and the woods so that she can't see him come up the track.'

'Aye, well, I expect he's only trying to save her feelings. He's very fond of his mam, y'know.'

'Of course he is,' Anna murmured and there was a catch to her voice that Eddie couldn't fail to hear. For a brief moment, her eyes had that haunted, faraway look. 'That's as it should be.' She paused and then added emphatically, 'I'm sorry, but I don't want her to go to the farm.'

Eddie sighed and shrugged. 'All right, love, if that's the way you want it.'

He patted the little girl's head and gently disentangled himself from her clinging arms. 'Ta-ta, lovey,' he murmured and then walked away from them.

Anna bit her lip. He was disappointed, she could see that, but she dared not risk Maisie going to the farm.

She could not blot out the memory of the murderous look in Bertha's eyes at the time of Maisie's birth.

*

They were still living in the cottage when Maisie reached her fourth birthday. And on that day the little girl decided it was high time she investigated what lay beyond the hill up the track from her home. By now Maisie, with her shining coppery curls and dark brown eyes, was bright, intelligent and surprisingly knowledgeable for her age, considering that she had had little contact with the world outside her isolated home.

She knew very few people other than her mother, Eddie, Tony and Pat Jessop. But now the inquisitive child was set on adventure.

'I need to fetch some water,' Anna said. 'Are you coming?'

Maisie shook her head. 'No. I'll stay with Buster.' The dog was now fully trained as a sheepdog and was every bit as trustworthy at looking after the child as he was at guarding Eddie's flock.

Anna shrugged and set off carrying two water buckets. With narrowed eyes Maisie watched her go. When her mother was some distance away, the child went round the side of the cottage and began to climb the hill, hidden from her mother's view if she happened to glance back.

Sensing that his charge was about to do something wrong, Buster began to bark.

'Ssh,' Maisie frowned at him. 'If you make a noise, I'll shut you in the house.'

The dog whined and then leapt around her, trying to shepherd her back home as he would have done a wayward sheep. But the little girl was not as docile as the animals. She wagged her finger at him. 'Quiet, Buster.' Then she added, 'Down!' in such a firm, grown-up voice that the dog obeyed her. Panting, his pink tongue lolling, he watched her climb the hill with anxiety in his eyes. He sensed this was wrong, but he didn't know how to stop her.

At the top of the track, the child, a tiny figure now, looked back. The dog barked and stood up, but Maisie's shrill voice bounced over the breeze to him. 'Stay!' Buster obeyed, though as she disappeared over the brow of the rise he whined unhappily.

The day was bright but cold and blustery and now, in the late afternoon of the February day, Anna sat down for a few moments on an old tree stump near the stream. She looked down into the brook as it bubbled and chattered its way down the slope, past the wood and under the bridge in the lane and on out of sight. Where it went she didn't know, but she felt as if this little stretch of the stream belonged to her. She pulled her coat around her as she watched the bright water. She sighed. She loved this place and now she would hate to leave, but soon they must. This time next year Maisie would be five and, if they stayed, she would have to go to the village school.

Anna couldn't risk it. She would have to get further away. She couldn't risk even more people knowing them. People who might ask questions: teachers, other children and their parents.

She must get away, yet the thought made her feel sad. She stood up, but then, hearing the sound of a bus coming along the lane, she crouched down behind the tree stump until it had passed by. The vehicle stopped and she heard voices. As the bus drew away, she peeped round the side of the stump to see Tony walking along the side of the stream, head down and his hands thrust into the pockets of his trousers. He was whistling and his bulging satchel swung from his shoulder.

Tony, at fourteen, now attended the grammar school

in Ludthorpe. Anna still remembered the look of pride on Eddie's face when he had given her the news. 'He's passed the scholarship for the grammar. Bertha dun't know where to put 'ersen, she's that pleased.'

Anna had smiled. 'And so are you, Eddie. I can see it on your face.'

'Well, course I am. Can't deny it.'

'Is Tony pleased?' Anna had asked softly.

Eddie had shrugged. 'I reckon he is, but he ses all he wants to do is follow me onto the farm. But I tell him he'll have the chance to go to agricultural college now when he leaves there. That'd be something, wouldn't it?'

Anna had nodded, happy to see Eddie so pleased and proud.

Now, as she watched Tony come towards her, Anna realized how much he'd grown and matured in the last four years. He was a young man, already taller than her and almost as tall as his father. He had Eddie's brown hair and dark eyes.

As she saw that he was alone, she rose from her hiding place and waited for him to reach her.

'Hello,' she called and he looked up and grinned at her, his eyes wrinkling in just the same way that Eddie's did.

'Thought I'd come and see Maisie on her birthday.' He dug in his pocket and pulled out a small white paper bag. 'I've brought her some sherbet lemons. It isn't much . . .' he began, 'but she likes them and I've got her a card,' he added as if in apology that his gifts weren't more.

'That's lovely,' Anna reassured him.

Tony grinned. 'Went without me dinner today so I could get her a card.'

'You shouldn't have done that. What would your mother say?'

Tony tapped the side of his nose. 'She'll not know if you don't tell her.' He laughed. 'And you're not likely to do that, are you?'

Anna laughed too. 'Certainly not. Come on,' she said, picking up the buckets. 'Let's go and find Maisie.'

'Here, let me take those,' Tony offered, but Anna shook her head. 'No, I'm fine. That satchel looks heavy enough and, besides, carrying two I'm balanced.'

As they walked back towards the cottage, Anna said, 'She's been a very lucky little girl. Pat brought her a lovely doll and Eddie has made her a wooden cradle for it. They must have had their heads together planning it.'

Tony nodded. 'I know. He's been making it in the shed for weeks. It's from both of us really, but I wanted to get her a bit of something on me own.'

Anna laughed. 'They're her favourite sweets. The only trouble is I'll have to hide them from her and dole them out one by one.'

'Why?'

'If she eats too many at once – and given half a chance she will – the lemon makes her mouth sore.'

Tony laughed too and nodded ruefully. 'Yeah, I've done that too.' As they reached the cottage, Tony added, 'Is she inside?'

'I left her out here, playing with Buster. Oh, there he is. Look, halfway up the hill.' Suddenly, there was fear in Anna's eyes. 'But where's Maisie?'

Nineteen

Maisie skipped down the track towards the farm below her. There was no one about, so she climbed onto the five-barred gate leading into the yard and swung on it as she looked around her. It was lambing time; it always was near her birthday. Only yesterday a ewe had given birth in the field near the cottage. Her mother had allowed her to watch and the child had been fascinated to see a lamb sliding from its mother's tummy and within minutes stand on its own wobbly legs.

'Can we take it into the house to feed, Mam?' she had asked.

Anna had smiled. 'No, darling. This mother can feed her lamb herself. It's only when the mother can't feed her young for one reason or another that we have to do that.'

The child was disappointed, yet glad that the lamb would have its own mother. She wouldn't like to be without hers.

Now, swinging on the gate, she looked across to the large barn in front of her. She could hear the sound of sheep coming from inside. She knew that Mr Eddie, as she called him, took as many of the sheep as he could down to the farm when they were lambing. But he had too many to house them all. He never tired of telling her that she had been born in the cottage alongside several lambs.

Her glance swivelled to the back door of the farmhouse. She ran her tongue round her lips, jumped from the gate and pushed it open. She skipped through it and across the yard. She hesitated only a moment before she raised her small fist and banged on the back door. A few moments elapsed before she heard a shuffling on the other side and then the door swung open and she was looking up into the unsmiling face of the large woman standing there.

Unfazed, Maisie looked her up and down then she smiled her most winning smile. Her dark brown eyes lit up and a dimple appeared in each cheek.

'Hello. I'm Maisie. I live over the hill in the cottage. Who are you?'

The woman gasped and blinked her small eyes rapidly. 'Well, I never did!' was all she could say.

'What did you never did?' the child asked innocently and completely unabashed.

'It's you.'

The child nodded. 'Yes, it's me. But who are you?'

'Who am I?' the woman repeated, rather stupidly it seemed even to the four-year-old girl. 'I'm Mrs Appleyard.'

'That's Mr Eddie's name. Are you his wife?'

Her mouth dropping open, Bertha merely nodded, dumbfounded.

'What's your first name?'

'Bertha,' the woman murmured, as if in a trance.

Maisie beamed. 'I'll call you Mrs Bertha then. I like that. It's a nice name. Mrs Bertha.' She nodded as if satisfied by the sound of it. 'Can I come in?'

Wordlessly, Bertha stood back and opened the door wider, her gaze following the child as if she were utterly mesmerized by her small visitor.

'Ooh, it does smell nice in here. Have you been baking?' The child sniffed the air appreciatively as she stepped into Bertha's farmhouse kitchen.

'Er – well – yes,' Bertha said, waddling after Maisie. Already the child had hitched herself onto a tall stool near the table and was looking longingly at the scones laid out on a wire cooling tray.

To her astonishment, Bertha found herself saying, 'Would you like one?'

'Ooh, yes please. And please may I have some raspberry jam on it? I like raspberry jam best.'

Bertha cut open a scone, spread it thickly with butter and jam on each half. 'Wait a moment,' she said, bustling to the pantry. 'I've some cream here . . .'

A minute later she stood watching as Maisie bit into the warm scone, leaving a smear of jam and cream on her upper lip. 'Mmm, it's lovely, Mrs Bertha. Thank you.'

'You're welcome,' Bertha murmured. She sat down, her gaze fixed on the child. So this was that girl's child. The girl that Eddie had brought home four years ago and taken up the hill to live in his cottage near the wood. She stared hard at Maisie, trying to see any likeness to her husband in the child's face. She had brown eyes like his, but there any resemblance ended. Her hair was copper-coloured, almost ginger, and her features were nothing like Eddie's.

Of course, she probably took after her mother. Bertha screwed up her eyes, visualizing the girl. She'd had black hair and unusual eyes – a deep blue, violet almost, Bertha remembered.

That meant nothing. This child could still be Eddie's.

Maisie had finished her scone and was licking her finger and picking up all the crumbs on the plate. She smiled widely at Bertha, the line of jam and cream still on her lip. 'Are you Tony's mam?'

Bertha nodded.

'He's nice, isn't he? But he doesn't come to play with me very often. I 'spect he's too busy. My mam says he is. Doing his homework and helping his dad and you on the farm.' She paused and leant across the table. 'I'm going to school next year. I'll be five then.'

'So you will,' Bertha murmured absently, her gaze never leaving the child's face, her thoughts in a turmoil.

Maisie jumped down from the high stool and came around the table to stand near Bertha. 'I'd better go home. I'm not supposed to come over the hill. I 'spect Mam'll be ever so cross.'

She smiled as if the thought didn't worry her too much.

Then she put her arms around Bertha as far as she could reach and puckered up her mouth. Bewildered, Bertha found herself lowering her face towards the child to receive a jammy kiss. She was still sitting at the kitchen table, gazing after her as Maisie skipped out of the back door and across the yard.

'Well,' Bertha murmured, 'I never did.'

'Where can she be?'

Anna was almost wild with panic and Tony couldn't calm her down. 'Don't worry. She'll have wandered into the woods. We built a den in there last summer. I bet she's—'

'She's not allowed to go into the woods on her own,' Anna snapped. 'There's poachers' snares in there. Anything might happen. She knows that.'

Tony glanced up the slope again, frowning. 'What's the matter with Buster? He's never moved. I'd've thought he'd have come to us.'

'Buster,' Anna called. 'Here, boy.'

The dog rose reluctantly and came towards them, head down, tail between his legs.

'There's something wrong,' Anna said, her anxiety spiralling. 'Something's happened. I know it.'

Tony fondled the dog's head. 'What is it, boy? Eh?' he murmured. 'You'd tell us if you could, wouldn't you?' He knelt in front of the animal and held the dog's head between his hands. 'Where is she, Buster? Where's Maisie?'

The dog barked, pulled himself free of Tony's hold and began to run up the hill. A little way off, he stopped and looked back, then ran on again. Tony and Anna glanced at each other.

'I bet she's gone up there,' Tony said. 'He's trying to make us follow him.'

Anna's hand fluttered to her mouth. 'Oh no! She would never go up there. I've forbidden her. Someone – someone must have got her.'

Tony frowned. 'Got her? What do you mean?'

Anna did not answer. She was already running up the hill. Tony followed, his long legs loping easily after her. They arrived at the top together. At once they saw Maisie skipping merrily up the track towards them as if she hadn't a care in the world.

Anna ran towards her daughter, almost tumbling in her haste to reach her. 'Where on earth have you been?' She grasped Maisie's arm roughly.

'Mam – you're hurting.'

'I'll hurt you, you naughty girl.' Anna bent and

slapped Maisie's bare legs so hard that red imprints of her hand marked the child's calves. Maisie opened her mouth wide and yelled.

Watching, Tony winced as if he, too, felt the little girl's pain. Anna was still incensed, shaking the girl and shouting, 'Where have you been? Tell me where you've been.' But Maisie only wailed louder.

Tony moved forward and tried to prise her from her mother's grasp but Anna held on tightly. 'No, leave this to me. Come on . . .' She began to drag the screaming child up the track and over the hill. Maisie, tears running down her cheeks, looked back at Tony, whose tender heart twisted at the sight of her pitiful face. When they disappeared he turned and walked slowly down the hill towards the farm.

He must find his dad.

In the cottage, Anna stood Maisie on a chair in the kitchen, their faces on a level. 'Now, you will tell me where you've been or I'll smack you again.'

The child's wails had subsided to a hiccuping sob. 'To see Mrs Bertha.'

'Bertha?' For a moment Anna thought Maisie must be lying, but then she noticed the smear of jam on the child's mouth. 'You've been to the farm?' she asked incredulously. 'You've been inside the house?'

Maisie nodded. 'To see Mrs Bertha. She's Tony's mam. She gave me a lovely scone with jam and cream.'

The surprise was deflating Anna's anger. Whilst the child had deliberately disobeyed her, Anna knew Maisie could not be expected to understand *why* she should not go to the farm.

'Was she – was she nice to you?'

In a strangely adult manner, Maisie wrinkled her brow thoughtfully and then nodded. 'She didn't say a lot. I think she was surprised to see me.'

'I bet she was,' Anna murmured, lost for words herself. Then she pulled herself out of her stunned reverie to say, 'I'm not going to smack you again, but you've got to promise me that you will never go there again. If you do,' she warned, 'I will punish you very severely. Do you understand me, Maisie?'

The child had stopped crying, but her tears streaked her grubby face. 'Why can't I go and see Mrs Bertha again? *She* didn't say I couldn't.'

Anna sighed, unable to find a plausible explanation to make the young child understand. So she resorted to the age-old decree of all parents at one time or another. 'Because I say so.'

It was later that evening when Maisie was in bed in one of the upstairs rooms that Eddie knocked on the side door of the cottage. He stepped into the kitchen and without even greeting her, he demanded, 'What's been going on?' He was frowning and his tone held a note of censure. 'Tony told me you'd smacked Maisie.'

'Huh! I'd've thought you'd've heard all about it from Bertha.'

Eddie shook his head. 'Bertha's said nothing.'

'Maisie went to the farm. If she'll do that, she might take it into her head to go anywhere. She'll be going to the village before I know it.'

'She'll have to soon enough when she goes to school.'

'Oh no!' Anna shook her head. 'We're leaving before she has to go to school. In fact, I've made up my mind. I'll help you with the lambing and then we're going.'

'And where do you intend to go, might I ask?'

'Anywhere as long as it's far enough away from – from here, so that no one knows us.' Her voice dropped as she muttered, 'There's a few too many folks around here know us already.'

'Meaning?'

Anna ticked them off on her fingers. 'You, Tony, Bertha, Pat Jessop, Joe Wainwright and the other fellers who come at shearing and harvest. The doctor in town and the registrar, to say nothing of folks in shops when I've been forced to go into them. Specially the one in Wintersby. The gossip was rife in the village when I first came here. Mr Wainwright told me so.'

Eddie's tone softened. He could hear the panic in her voice. 'You can't live on a desert island, love. Wherever you go, you'll meet other people. And Maisie will have to go to school next year. I know you're bothered about her birth certificate, but they'll ask to see it wherever you go.'

'I'll say I've lost it.'

'They'll only get you to send to the authorities for another.'

Anna stared at him. She hadn't realized that copies could be obtained so easily. She sat down heavily on a chair and, resting her elbows on the table, covered her face with her hands.

'Why can't you stay here? I don't know who or what it is you're so afraid of. You've never told me.' There was a hint of reproach in Eddie's tone. 'But no one's ever bothered you, have they? Not in four years. Surely, you can stay?'

Slowly, Anna dropped her hands and stared into his face. Even though the thought of having to leave this haven and set off into the unknown frightened her, she shook her head sadly and whispered, 'I'm sorry, Eddie, but I daren't stay here. Not now. Not any longer. Not if Maisie's going to do what she did today.'

Twenty

Lambing was almost over. Only two more ewes left to give birth.

'You'll manage now, Eddie. You've been lucky this year. No motherless lambs for me to rear by hand in the cottage.' She smiled. 'Maisie's quite disappointed. She likes feeding them with a bottle.'

Eddie's eyes were anxious. 'You really mean you're going?'

'I'm sorry, Eddie,' Anna said huskily, 'but we must. I – I don't know how to thank you for all you've done for me. For us—'

'You could thank me by staying and making this your home,' he said gruffly. 'I'll even give you the cottage – and the bit of land round it – if it'll make any difference.'

'Oh, Eddie—'

'I mean it.'

She could see he did and tears filled her eyes. 'I couldn't possibly let you do such a thing. What would your wife say? And then there's Tony. It'll be his one day.'

Avoiding a direct answer about Bertha, Eddie said, 'Tony'd agree. I know he would. He doesn't want you to go any more'n I do.'

Anna touched his arm. 'You're such a kind man. I – I didn't know such kindness from strangers still existed until I came here—' She broke off and turned away as if she was afraid of saying too much. 'We're going tomorrow,' she said with a finality that brooked no argument.

They were all packed, ready for the morning, their belongings in neat bundles and loaded onto Maisie's old pram.

'You'll be able to sit on the top if you get tired,' Anna told her, trying to make it sound like an adventure. But tears spilled down Maisie's cheeks. She cried silently, making no word of complaint, no screams of protest, but her anguish at leaving the only home she had ever known was evident on her small face.

'Come on, up to bed with you. We've got a long way to go tomorrow.'

'Where are we going?'

'You'll see,' Anna said brightly, making it sound as if their destination would be a lovely surprise, but in truth she had no idea herself where they were going.

They would just set off and see where they ended up, but after four years of comparative safety, even Anna was a little afraid.

It was completely different from the last time she had run away. Then she had not cared what became of her or of her unborn child.

Now, she did care. Eddie had taught her to care again.

In the middle of the night, Anna awoke to a dreadful noise. Buster was barking frantically and scratching at the front door to be let out. And from outside the cottage came the noise of barking dogs and the terrified bleating of sheep.

'Oh no—!' She flung back the bedclothes and dressed hurriedly. She climbed down the ladder and was pulling on her warmest coat when Maisie, bleary-eyed with sleep, appeared at the top.

'Mammy—'

'Go back to bed,' Anna began and then, with only a second's hesitation, she said, 'no, get dressed. As quickly as you can and come down.'

'Why? We're not going now, are we?' Maisie's lower lip trembled.

'No, but can you hear that awful noise? There are some dogs attacking the sheep. You must run to the farm for me and knock on the door as loudly as you can and fetch Mr Eddie. Can you do that?'

Maisie nodded eagerly, turned and ran back into her room to dress, whilst Anna lit a hurricane lamp and found her crook. She opened the side door and, as the child climbed down the ladder again, they stepped out into the darkness together, Buster streaking out ahead of them.

Outside the noise was even more frightening.

'Thank goodness,' Anna said. 'They're down there towards the stream. They won't see you. Now run, Maisie. Run as fast as you can.'

The little girl disappeared into the darkness and Anna braced herself to walk towards the terrifying noise.

In the moonlight, she could see two dogs attacking one of the ewes still in lamb. Already it was overthrown and unable to rise, helpless against the snapping jaws. Buster was barking and running at them, doing his best to drive the attackers away from the sheep. His sheep.

Anna moved closer and hit one of the dogs on the back, yelling at the same time.

The dog yelped in surprise. Intent upon their kill, neither dog had sensed her approach. The first ran a few yards and stopped, turning to stand and stare at her, panting hard. Now she lashed out at the other dog, but it jumped out of the way and turned to face her, head down and snarling.

They were big dogs, much bigger than poor Buster and in the darkness as terrifying as a couple of wolves. Crouching low, the second dog crept towards her. Buster stood beside her, growling a warning, but the aggressor took no notice of him. Anna held her crook horizontally in front of her to fend it off as it leapt up at her. She felt a sharp pain in her left hand and knew its white teeth, flashing in the moonlight, had bitten her. Now the other dog, emboldened by its companion, came closer. They lined up side by side in front of her, ready to spring. Beside her Buster whined and barked again.

'Down!' Anna cried in the firmest tone she could muster.

They took no notice and leapt in unison, but not at her. With one accord they fell on Buster, knocking him over. They attacked him cruelly, biting and tearing at his flesh. Now Buster was yelping in pain and fear. Anna hit out at the dogs with her stick and managed to frighten one away. But the bolder of the two turned and snarled at her. It grabbed her crook in its mouth, growling all the time. Gradually she drew it away from Buster, but then the other dog crept closer once more towards the injured sheepdog lying on the ground.

'No!' Anna shouted, feeling helpless to deal with both dogs at once. At that moment she heard a shout from behind her. 'Stand clear, Anna.'

She glanced back to see Eddie just behind her, pointing his shotgun at the dog nearest to her.

'Don't hit Buster. He's on the ground.'

'I won't. Drop your crook and move away.'

Anna did as she bade him. A shot rang out. Her attacker shuddered and fell to the ground. At the sound, the other dog ran, but Eddie levelled his gun and fired again. The dog stumbled, rolled over and lay still.

Now there was an ominous silence.

Eddie threw down his gun and held his arms wide to her. With a sob, Anna ran into them and was enfolded in his safe embrace. Behind them, watching, Tony stood holding Maisie's hand. As she became aware of them, Anna drew back.

'Are you hurt?' Eddie asked anxiously.

'Just my hand. It's nothing—'

'Let's take a look—'

'No, no—' Anna pulled away from him and stumbled towards Buster, lying motionless on the ground. Maisie ran forward.

'Oh, Mammy. What's happened to Buster?'

'The bad dogs hurt him, darling.'

Maisie squatted down beside the animal she considered her pet and touched his coat. 'It's all wet, Mammy.'

'Leave him, darling. We'll carry him home in a minute.' Anna rose and moved to where Eddie was bending over his sheep. 'I don't think we can save her,' he said, 'but she's gone into labour. Tony,' Eddie looked up and called across to his son, still standing motionless a few feet away, 'help Anna take Buster back to the cottage.' His glance rested on the little girl crying beside the inert animal. 'And take Maisie away from here.'

Silently, Tony did as he was asked. He spread out his coat on the ground and together he and Anna gently lifted Buster onto it.

'I ought to stay here and help your dad,' Anna said. She couldn't see Tony's expression in the darkness, but his voice was harsh. 'I'll come back and help him. He doesn't need you.'

Anna gasped and knew at once that Tony had read far more into the comforting hug his father had given her than had been meant.

'Tony, you don't understand—' she began.

'Don't I?' he muttered in a low voice so that his father should not hear. 'Oh don't I? Seems me mam was right all along.'

Anna shuddered and groaned. 'No,' she cried. 'It's not like that—'

'What's the matter?' Eddie's voice came out of the blackness.

'Nothing,' Tony called quickly before Anna could speak. 'I'll just help Anna and I'll come back.'

Without speaking to each other now, Anna and Tony carried Buster back to the cottage where they laid him on the hearth in front of the dying embers of the fire. Maisie knelt beside him. Now they could see that his black and white coat was matted with blood. The animal lay still, whimpering occasionally, his dark eyes wide and full of suffering.

'He's not going to die, is he, Mammy?' Maisie sobbed.

'Darling, I don't know.' Anna always tried to be honest with her child, even if the truth was painful.

Maisie sobbed louder. 'Can't we take him to the doctor?'

As if against his will, Tony's arm crept around the child's shoulders. 'We'll take him to the vet in the morning.' His glance at Anna was resentful, but he still kept his tone gentle towards the little girl. 'Dad'll take him.'

Suddenly Tony got up. 'I'll go back to him.' He left the cottage, slamming the door behind him. Anna winced but Maisie, unaware of the undercurrent of emotion between her mother and Tony, continued to stroke the dog's head. 'Don't die, Buster. Oh please don't die.'

A while later Anna heard the distant sound of a single shot. Shortly afterwards, the outer door to the kitchen opened and Eddie and Tony came in.

'The ewe's dead. I had to put her out of her misery. They'd nearly torn her throat out. There was no way even the vet could have saved her,' Eddie said as he came to where Buster was lying. 'How is he?'

Anna shook her head. 'He's still alive but covered in blood.'

'Right,' Eddie said, taking charge. 'Let's see to your hand first, love.'

He rummaged in the cupboard and produced bandages and a bottle of Dettol. As he bent over her hand bathing it and applying the bandage, Anna was acutely aware of Tony's morose expression as he watched his father's tender ministrations.

'You go home, Tony, lad. Thanks for your help, but—'

'No, Dad,' the young man said quickly. His glance rested upon Anna and his eyes narrowed. 'I'll wait for you.'

The following morning, Eddie arranged for the vet to visit Anna's cottage. He stood by whilst the man examined the dog. 'He'll live,' the vet pronounced. 'He's been badly mauled, but with tender care he'll be fine.'

He stood up and looked about him, noticing the bundles of belongings piled high on the pram at the side of the room. 'Going somewhere, were you?'

'We – we were leaving today.'

'Well, if you were planning on taking the dog there's no way he's walking any distance for quite a while.'

When the vet had left, Maisie looked up at her mother. 'Are we staying, Mammy?'

Anna sighed. 'It looks like it, Maisie,' she said flatly.

Despite the terrible events of the previous night, Eddie could not stop his smile stretching from ear to ear.

Twenty-One

'You've found another excuse to stay a bit longer then?'

Later that afternoon Tony stood in the centre of her kitchen, eyeing Anna belligerently.

She sighed, glancing down to where Maisie was sitting on the hearth beside Buster, lying in his basket. The little girl had not left the dog's side all day. Anna opened the front door and motioned to Tony to follow her. Once outside she said, 'Look, what you saw last night meant nothing. It's what anyone might have done in the circumstances. I'm sorry you saw it—'

'I bet you are.' The boy was disbelieving.

'It meant nothing,' she insisted. 'I'd have run to you if you'd held out your arms to me at that moment.'

'You're a bit old for me,' Tony said nastily and Anna closed her eyes, saddened to think that their friendship was at an end. Wiped out in an instant by an innocent hug of comfort between two friends.

'We're friends,' she tried again to explain. 'Your father's been very good to me.'

'Why?' Tony snapped. 'Just why did he bring you here in the first place? I can still remember how upset me mam was when he brought you home. I didn't understand it all at the time.' He paused and added pointedly. 'Now I do. She always thought there was summat more to it than he said. She even thought Maisie was mebbe his. Now – I think she was right.'

'I swear to you, on Maisie's life if you like,' Anna retorted angrily, 'that she is *not* Eddie's daughter.'

'Then whose is she? Tell me that.'

Anna's face blanched. She shook her head. 'No,' she whispered. 'I – can't tell you that.'

Tony's mouth twisted. 'You mean,' he said unkindly, 'you don't know.'

Before she had realized what she was doing, Anna's hand flew up and she smacked Tony's left cheek. 'How dare you say such a thing to me? If you only knew the truth—'

The boy had not even flinched or moved. 'Then tell me,' he persisted.

'No.' Anna stepped back as if even the thought of having to drag up the memories was abhorrent. 'It has nothing to do with you. Or –' she added with a last vestige of spirit – 'or with your father.'

Tony shrugged. 'Well, if you won't tell me, you can hardly expect me to believe you, can you?'

As he began to walk away, she cried after him, 'Why can't you just trust me?'

He paused and glanced back. 'Why can't *you* trust *me* enough to tell me the truth?' he countered. 'I know I'm only fourteen, but I'm not a child any longer. I'd understand, whatever it is. Unless,' he added pointedly, 'it's because you've something to hide. Something that you're really ashamed of.'

When she did not answer, he turned and walked away, leaving Anna staring after him. *If only you knew*, she thought, *how close to the truth you are*.

Of course, there was no way that Anna could leave now, even though after Tony's change towards them she would dearly have loved to go. But she could not leave Buster behind and it was impossible for him to travel in his weakened state.

Mid-morning she heard someone calling outside the cottage and opened the door to find Pat Jessop with her hand raised ready to knock.

The nurse beamed at her. 'Oh, you're still here. I was so afraid you might have set off early. I didn't want to miss saying goodbye, even though I do wish you weren't going.'

Anna sighed and gestured for Pat to step inside. 'We're not,' she said and quickly explained all the night's events that now kept them here.

'I really don't see why you have to go at all,' Pat said, lifting Maisie onto her lap and cuddling her. 'You're tired, my little love, aren't you?' Maisie leant against the comforting bosom of the district nurse, sucking her thumb. 'Why don't you go upstairs and have a little nap, eh?'

Maisie took out her thumb and looked up at Pat. In a serious, adult voice she said, 'I can't leave Buster. He needs me.'

'Of course he does, but your mammy's here and so am I just now. Nurses have to rest and look after themselves too, you know, else they can't care for their patients, can they?'

Maisie regarded Pat solemnly and then slid from her knee. 'All right, but you promise to look after him?'

'I promise and if I have to leave before you wake up, your mammy will stay with him until you do.'

They listened whilst the child climbed the ladder and then Pat leant across the table towards Anna. 'There's something you're not telling me that's upsetting you.'

Anna smiled wanly. 'You're too sharp by half, Nurse Jessop.'

'It's me job, ducky,' the nurse grinned. 'Besides, I'm a nosy owd beezum. Everyone in the village ses so.'

Yes, Anna wanted to say, *but they all know too that their secrets are safe with you.* She sighed. 'It's Tony,' she began and found herself confiding in the friendly woman. 'He's begun to believe his mother's vicious lies. He can't understand why I can't talk about the – the past. I just can't. Not to anyone.'

Pat touched her hand. 'Not even to me?' she asked softly.

Anna pressed her lips together and tears welled as she shook her head. 'No, not even to you,' she said huskily. 'But if I – ever did – you'd be the first. Even before Eddie.'

Pat nodded. 'Well, you know I'm always ready to listen if you ever decide you do want to unburden yourself. And I use that word purposely, 'cos it is a burden you're carrying. I can see that. A very heavy burden. And you know I'd never tell a soul—'

Now Anna smiled. 'I know.'

Pat stood up. 'I'll have to be on my way, but I'll take a look at Buster first.' She wagged her forefinger at Anna playfully. 'Just so long as you remember to tell Maisie I did so.'

A few moments later the nurse said, 'He's doing fine.' She stood up again. 'I wouldn't have wished for any of this to happen, but I have to say I'm glad you're not going.'

Anna's eyes clouded. 'We – we'll have to go this summer. Maisie will have to start school and – and they'll start asking to see her birth certificate and—'

'Listen, ducky. The headmistress of the village school is a friend of mine. And there's only her and her assistant teacher. Why don't you let me have a word with her?'

Anna opened her mouth to protest but Pat hurried on. 'No one else will ever hear about Maisie's birth certificate not having her father's name on it. Only she and her assistant need to know and I suppose the Education Offices at Lincoln—'

'Lincoln?' Anna's head shot up and her eyes widened.

Pat stared at her, her mind working quickly. Anna, realizing she might have given away far more than she intended, floundered. 'What I mean is, why does anyone have to know anywhere else but at the school?'

'That's where the County Offices are. They're a sort of headquarters, if you like, for all the schools. But,' she hurried on, trying to reassure Anna, 'to them you're just a name on a piece of paper. But there'll be plenty of other bits of paper with only the mother's name on, believe you me.'

Anna still looked doubtful.

'It'll be the same in every county. It'd be the same wherever you went,' Pat said and was immediately sorry to see the defeated, haunted look in Anna's eyes that had been there when she had first met her return; a look that had been banished during her years of safety in the little white cottage.

Now the fear was back.

'So you're going to stay?'

Anna couldn't fail to hear the eagerness in Eddie's tone. She sighed and said dully, 'It seems there's nowhere any better.'

He put his head on one side. 'Is that a compliment? 'Cos it doesn't quite sound like one.'

Anna smiled apologetically and repeated what Pat had told her. 'So it seems it'll be the same wherever I go. But I just felt I wanted to be further away.'

'From where?' Eddie asked very gently, but Anna would not allow herself to be caught off guard. 'You mentioned Lincoln once. Is that where you lived?'

'Just further away from this area, that's all,' Anna answered evasively.

They were silent for a moment before Eddie said, 'But you think now that it might be all right to stay here?'

'Well, for a while anyway. Pat's going to talk to her friend at the school, so maybe—' She sighed. 'Oh I don't know. Now there's Tony—'

'What do you mean?'

'He – he read the wrong meaning into you comforting me the night the dogs attacked the sheep and – and poor Buster. When I – I ran to you and you – you hugged me.'

'Ah,' Eddie breathed. 'So that's what's up with him. I'll have a word. You leave it with me. I'll put him straight.'

Anna never learned what Eddie said to Tony – if indeed he said anything. Over the following weeks and months, the boy did not visit the cottage, and if he came to the sheep, he skirted their home and was brusque with Maisie when she ran to him, lifting up her arms to be swung round.

'Tony won't play with me any more,' she told her mother tearfully. 'Is he cross with me?'

Anna shook her head. 'No, darling. It's me he's cross with. Not you.'

'Then why won't he play with me? That's not fair.'

'No, it isn't, but then I'm afraid a lot of things aren't fair.'

It isn't fair, Anna thought resentfully, *that I have to hide myself and my daughter in the back of beyond just because . . .*

Her mind shied away from the bitter memories. She forced a smile onto her face. 'Don't cry, Maisie. I know, let's go and play hide-and-seek in the woods.'

The child pouted and shook her head. 'You don't do it properly. Tony plays hide-and-seek better than you do.'

Anna sighed. 'Oh well, in that case you'd better come and help me round up the sheep. And bring Buster. He's well enough now to be getting back to work. I think he's malingering.'

Maisie, always intrigued by big words, said, 'What's that mean?'

'Pretending he's still poorly when he's not.'

Diverted from her distress over Tony, Maisie fetched the dog from the kitchen. 'Come on, boy,' Anna heard her daughter say sternly to the dog. 'No more mal'gring.'

Anna smiled.

Twenty-Two

The summer passed uneventfully and it was time for Maisie to start school.

'I know she's not five until next February,' Pat said, 'but Miss Drury says she can take her at the start of the autumn term this September, if you like. I told her she's a bright little thing and—' Pat stopped, unwilling to say that she had also indicated to the head teacher that the child needed to begin to mix with other children of her own age. 'She's been well brought up,' the nurse had confided in the teacher. 'She's a credit to her mother, but she's been forced to live the life of a recluse.'

'Why?' the thin, grey-haired woman, who had devoted her life to the education of other people's children, had asked.

Pat had sighed. 'That's all part of the great secret – whatever that is. I can only guess because Anna won't trust anyone enough to divulge anything about herself or her past.' She shrugged her plump shoulders. 'That's her privilege, of course, and I respect it, but it can't be good for the child, can it?'

Edna Drury shook her head. 'No, it can't.' She pondered a moment and then said, 'Well, I can take the child in September if the mother agrees.'

Pat beamed. 'I'll make sure she does.' Now, to Anna, she finished the sentence she had begun, 'I told her she's a bright little thing and Miss Drury respects your desire for privacy. Betty Cussons will be Maisie's teacher, by the way.'

'Is she nice?'

'Lovely. She's only young and the little ones all adore her.'

So Maisie started at the village school at the beginning of September. For the first few weeks Anna met Maisie in the lane just outside the village and listened to her chatter about her day. They always walked the long way round the wood, alongside the brook and up the track to the cottage to avoid going near the farm.

'Why don't you come through the yard and up the hill?' Eddie asked Anna. 'It's much shorter and the little lass must be tired after all day at school.'

'No,' Anna replied shortly. 'I don't want her to think she can come that way. She might be tempted to try to see your wife again.' She forbore to say that Tony's offhandedness was still causing heartache to the child – to them both, if she was truthful.

But it wasn't many weeks later that Maisie said, 'I can walk home on me own, Mammy. I can walk with Geoffrey Johnson. He lives just down the lane from Mr Eddie's farm.' She leant forward as if imparting a confidence. 'He hasn't got a dad either. His dad was killed in the war. That's what Geoffrey said.' There was a loaded pause whilst Anna held her breath. She knew, even before the child opened her mouth again, what was coming. 'Was my daddy killed in the war?'

Her heart was beating rapidly, but Anna replied carefully, 'No. You haven't got a daddy.'

'Not at all? You mean, I've never had a daddy?'

Anna avoided her small daughter's trusting gaze and shook her head. 'No. There's only ever been just you and me.'

The child looked crestfallen and said in a wistful voice, 'Meg's got a daddy. He made her a swing in their garden. She said she'll let me have a go on it if I'll be her friend. She ses I can go to her house for tea. Can I go, Mam?'

'We'll see,' Anna said, but silently determined that she would have to think up an excuse. She didn't want Maisie visiting people's houses in the village. Questions might be asked. 'Now come along, we must fetch the water from the stream. It's bath night.'

Maisie jumped up and down and clapped her hands. She loved bath night on a Friday when her mother put the tin bath in front of the fire and filled it with hot water and then knelt beside it to soap Maisie's sturdy little body and wash her bright copper curls. Afterwards, dressed in a clean nightgown, she would cuddle up with her mother in the big, old armchair and Anna would tell her stories.

Her mother needed no book to read from. Anna had enough imagination to weave a magical world for the child.

'Tell me "Mr Mumble's Gold Walking Stick",' Maisie would plead and Anna would begin, making the story different each time. 'That's not right,' the child would say laughing.

'Isn't it?' Anna would pretend innocence.

'No, last time he lost it on the beach and the sea came and washed it away, but a mermaid brought it back.'

'Oh yes, well, this is a different time. This time he lost it in a snowstorm and . . .' And off Anna's imagination would lead them into another adventure.

*

It was just before Maisie's fifth birthday, when they were already busy with the lambing that Anna rose early to see the red sky of an ominous dawn. The sight unsettled her. She believed in the country sayings and feared the onset of stormy weather. But for Anna there was more to it than that. She tried to quell the memories, tried to forget her own superstition that it was not only troubled weather that such a sky foretold but something more.

She shook herself and told herself she was being silly and fanciful.

'I can't spare the time to take you to school, so you're to walk on your own, but you come straight home,' Anna told Maisie. 'No dawdling and no going to anyone's house. You hear me?'

To Anna's relief the burgeoning friendship between Maisie and Meg had withered and died. As little girls do, they had fallen out the very next day after Maisie's conversation with her mother, but Anna was still not convinced that Maisie would be able to resist another invitation.

'And you're to come round by the wood. You're not to go through Mr Eddie's yard.'

For a brief moment, Maisie eyed her mother and then said meekly, 'Yes, Mam.'

She skipped away towards the brook, the little satchel carrying her lunch swinging from her shoulder. But if Anna had known what was already going through the child's scheming mind she would have felt even more agitated.

Later that morning, Eddie climbed down from his tractor, his face solemn. 'I don't suppose you've heard . . . ?' he began and Anna's heart seemed to leap in her chest and then began to thud painfully.

She'd known by the sky that morning that something awful was going to happen.

'What?' Her face was white, her voice a strangled whisper.

'The King's died – poor chap – in his sleep.'

Anna felt a rush of relief flood through her. She almost said aloud, 'Is that all?' but bit the words back.

'He was a good man,' Eddie was saying solemnly. 'And the poor lass that's to follow him is so young.' He shook his head. 'So very young for such an awesome task.'

Now Anna could not prevent the words spilling out. 'But she's got a husband at her side to help her. She's not alone. Not like—' She bit her lip and dropped her gaze. Guilt flooded through her that she could have been so caught up in her own fears that she had not spared a sympathetic thought for the poor man and his family. She turned away, uncomfortably aware that Eddie was staring at her, shocked and disappointed.

Her words were not only lacking in compassion for the bereaved family, but were insulting to Eddie, who had done everything he could to help her.

And that, Anna thought with shame, was how she repaid him.

Maisie obeyed her mother's instruction for a week. Each morning she walked down the track, turned to the right and walked towards the lane with the stream on her left and the woodland on her right. Turning to the right again, she passed the wood and came to the gate leading into the yard of Cackle Hill Farm. And each evening she returned the same way. It was a long way for the little girl. She had already walked more than twice the distance it would have been if she had taken the short cut through the farmyard.

As Maisie reached the farm gate late in the afternoon of her birthday on her return from school, it was raining hard. Her footsteps slowed and she lingered in the lane near the gate. She could hear clanking sounds from inside the cowshed and wondered if Mr Eddie was in there. She glanced up the hill. Her mother couldn't see her. The cold, wet winter's afternoon was already growing dark as she glanced at the back door of the farmhouse, imagining the warm kitchen and the smell of freshly baked bread and pies and those delicious scones with jam and cream.

It was really Mrs Bertha she wanted to see, but maybe if she pretended to see Mr Eddie in the cowshed first . . .

The little girl pushed open the gate and marched boldly into the yard.

'Mr Eddie, are you in here?' she shouted, knocking on the lower part of the door into the shed. The upper part was open and fastened back to the wall, but the lower part was shut. The noise from inside stopped and she heard footsteps. Then Eddie's head peered over the half door.

'Well, well, and what are you doing here, Maisie?' His welcoming smile faded as he remembered the reason Maisie had been sent to fetch him last time. 'Has your mam sent you to fetch me? Is something wrong?'

Her curls danced as she shook her head. 'No, she doesn't know I'm here.' She pulled a face and then smiled impishly. 'I'll be in trouble if she finds out.'

Eddie chuckled. 'Ah well, I'll not tell her, eh?'

'Is Mrs Bertha at home?'

Now Eddie could not prevent the surprise from showing on his face. 'Why, yes. She is.'

'Can I see her?'

Eddie took off his cap and ran his hand through his thinning hair. 'I don't rightly know, love. I mean . . .' He faltered, not liking to intimate that the older woman might not want to see the little girl against whom she still held such resentment.

'I'm all wet,' Maisie said plaintively.

'I know, but . . .' He sighed and muttered. 'I suppose it can't do any harm. Come on then, let's go and see if she's got the kettle on.'

As they walked across the yard, Maisie put her tiny hand into Eddie's large one and skipped along at his side. And that was how Bertha saw them from her scullery window.

'So you've come to see me again, 'ave ya?' Bertha said as the child perched herself on the stool near the table. 'After my scones, I bet.' And she ruffled the child's curls affectionately.

Eddie stared in amazement. He couldn't believe what was happening before his eyes. Bertha was actually being civil to the child. More than civil, she was being nice to her. Very nice.

Bertha's tone sharpened. 'Well, Eddie Appleyard, ain't you got work to do?'

'Yes, but—' Eddie glanced helplessly from one to the other, not knowing what to make of it. He turned and left the house, shaking his head in bewilderment. He knew his wife was a funny mixture, but this beat all.

As he crossed the yard, he passed Tony returning from the school bus. Seeing the puzzled look on his father's face, the boy said, 'Summat up, Dad?'

Still mesmerized by what he had just witnessed, Eddie shook his head. 'No, lad. At least – I don't think so.' He did not stop to enlighten his son any further and carried on walking towards the cowshed. Tony watched him go, then shrugged and went into the house.

The moment he stepped into the kitchen, he saw the reason for his father's bafflement. Tony stood in the doorway and stared. There was Maisie sitting at the table, munching a scone and chattering to his mother as if they were bosom pals.

'It's my birthday today, y'know,' she was telling Bertha. 'I'm five.'

Bertha looked up and smiled at Tony. 'We've got a visitor,' she said. 'But I don't think I need to introduce you, do I?' There was a hint of sarcasm in her tone that was lost on the little girl, but not on Bertha's son.

Tony's face coloured as he muttered, 'What's she doing here?'

'Just visiting a neighbour, aren't you, lovey?'

Maisie nodded happily, completely unaware of the undercurrent of tension in the room. 'Why don't you come and play with me any more?' she asked Tony, her brown eyes staring candidly at him.

Tony scowled and, embarrassed, glanced at his mother. But she answered Maisie. 'Tony's getting a big boy now. He's at the grammar school in the town. He has ever such a lot of homework and then, of course, he has to help his dad.'

'Oh.' The child looked crestfallen.

'But you can come and visit me whenever you like.'

'You'd best go home now, Maisie,' Tony butted in. 'Your mam'll be wondering where you've got to. She'll be worried.'

Maisie nodded and jumped down from the stool. ''Bye, 'bye, Mrs Bertha and thank you for the scone.'

As the child let herself out of the back door, Tony turned on his mother. 'Mam, what are you up to?'

Bertha adopted her most innocent expression. 'Whatever do you mean, Tony? What should I be up to?'

'I don't know,' he said slowly, 'but it's summat.'

'Don't talk nonsense,' Bertha said, but as she turned her back on her son she was smiling to herself.

'I think it's time you left,' Tony said bluntly. He found Anna busy trying to cope with a ewe and a difficult birth. It was obvious she had not noticed that Maisie had been later home than usual or that she had appeared from the direction of the farm instead of round by the wood.

Her mind still occupied with the sheep, Anna said, 'Fetch your father, Tony. I think he might need the vet to this ewe. The lamb's all right, but the mother—'

'Yes, yes, I'll get him, but did you hear what I said?'

Anna looked at him and blinked, dragging his words to the forefront of her mind. 'Leave? Now? Why?'

'Maisie was down at the farm, sitting in me mam's kitchen as large as life and twice as cheeky.'

'The wilful little—'

'Please, don't punish her. I'm only telling tales – I don't reckon to – because it's for your own good. I – I—' He hesitated, not wanting to sound disloyal to his mother, yet he had this awful feeling that something was not right. 'Me mam's being nice to her and I don't know why. It's – it's not natural. Not when you know what she thinks of *you*.' His brow puckered and he muttered, 'I can't understand it. I'd've thought she'd be horrible to Maisie an' all.'

'Mm.' Anna was thoughtful too. 'So would I. Or at the very least, make it so obvious she wasn't welcome that she didn't visit again.' She eyed Tony speculatively. He was fifteen now and, in a lot of ways, mature for his age.

'Is there anything else you're not telling me?' she asked bluntly.

Tony shook his head. 'Not really. But—' Again he hesitated and Anna probed gently. 'But what, Tony? Tell me. Please.'

The words tumbled over each other in a rush. 'If she – wants to get at you, the easiest way is through Maisie, isn't it?' He ran his hand through his hair, with an action so like his father's that Anna almost smiled – would have done if their conversation had not been so serious. 'Oh, I shouldn't be saying this,' he anguished. 'Not about me own mam. She wouldn't hurt Maisie. I know she wouldn't do that but – but . . . oh I don't know what to think.'

'It's all right,' Anna said huskily. 'Don't worry. I won't be angry with Maisie, but I must impress upon her that she is not to visit the farm. And come the better weather, this year we really *will* go.'

But at the end of the month, Eddie slipped on an icy patch in the yard and broke his leg and even Tony was now forced to ask Anna to stay a while longer.

'He can't work for six weeks and I'd have to stay off school.' He pulled a face. 'And me mam doesn't want that. She'll see to the dairy work if you'd go down and milk the cows—'

'You mean she's agreed for me to do that?'

Unsmiling, Tony nodded and there was bitter sarcasm to his tone. 'Oh yes. Even me mam'll swallow her pride if it gets her out of doing the milking.'

The weeks passed. Eddie's leg mended and then it was almost haymaking, followed by harvest and then another winter was upon them. Although the passage of time did not diminish her fear, Anna began to feel secure in her little cottage haven near the woods and gradually her need to move on lessened. She knew Eddie wanted her to stay. Of Tony's feelings, she was less certain. Sometimes he would be as friendly and caring as ever. But at others he ignored their presence in the cottage for days. He was brusque with Maisie and offhand with Anna. No doubt, Anna thought grimly, his mother had been pouring vicious lies into his young ears and turning him against them. Anna couldn't blame the lad: it was natural that he would believe his mother. She no longer cared what Bertha thought about her. She rarely saw her and, for the most part, she managed to ignore the woman's malevolent presence over the hill.

But, unbeknown to her mother and even to Eddie and Tony, Maisie's visits to see Bertha continued. Not often, but now and again when there was no one about to see, the growing child would skip into the yard and knock on the back door of the farmhouse.

And Bertha would smile to herself and welcome the child into her home, content to bide her time. Bitter though Bertha was, she was a patient woman.

Twenty-Three

On the last day of January 1953, Eddie said, 'I didn't like the look of the sky this morning, lass. Did you see it? A real shepherd's warning. I reckon we're in for some stormy weather.'

Anna glanced skywards and pulled a wry face. 'The wind was rattling round the cottage last night and through the trees in the wood. You should have heard it.' She smiled. 'I could almost imagine it was the sea.'

Though she could not have known it, Anna's words were prophetic.

The wind howled all day. By nightfall it had risen to gale force. Anna sat by the fire in the white cottage, a half-finished peg rug on her knee. She worked calmly at it, pulling the pieces of rag through the hessian, trying to blot out the sound of the raging storm outside. Maisie sat close to her, her brown eyes wide with fear.

'Time you went up to bed,' Anna said, but her daughter only drew closer.

'Can't we sleep down here tonight, Mam? I don't like the wind. It sounds as if it's trying to blow the thatch off the roof.'

'We're safe enough here, darling,' Anna murmured and a small, wistful smile played around her mouth. How could she explain to her young daughter that the elements had never held any fears for her; it was only at times like these, when other people shuddered and shut their doors against the weather, that she felt safer than at any other time.

No one would venture to seek her out in this kind of weather. Anna sighed. Perhaps it was time she stopped being quite so fearful. Six years had passed and, though she had had one or two frightening moments, they had all been in her imagination. She had not been found. No one had come looking for her. Since the early days after her arrival no one had challenged her or asked an awkward question. Eddie no longer tried to probe gently. And Tony, now a tall, thin, sixteen-year-old, due to sit his O level examinations this coming summer, rarely made reference to her past life. Even Pat Jessop, still a good friend, had stopped asking. The village gossip had died down, although, on the rare occasions that Anna ventured into the village, she was still aware of the curious glances.

Maisie broke into her thoughts. 'Buster doesn't like this weather either.'

The dog, now fully grown and already a good sheep-dog, huddled against their feet, whining every so often to remind them that he was there and that he needed a friendly stroke of reassurance. As Anna was bending forward to pat his head, a loud banging sounded at the back door, making Anna and Maisie jump and Buster leap to his feet and begin barking.

In an instant all Anna's resolution fled and her fear was back as strongly as ever. Maisie ran to the window and peered out into the wild, black night. Even she, young as she was, knew that her mother did not like the door opened until they knew who was standing on the other side.

'It's Mr Eddie.'

'You're – you're sure?' Anna persisted.

Maisie nodded vigorously. 'Let him in, Mam.'

Still a little reluctant, Anna shot back the bolt and opened the door, letting the storm into the warm kitchen. Eddie almost tumbled into the room and Anna had to fight the wind to shut the door. He leant against the table, bending over it to regain his breath.

'It's the sea, lass.'

'What do you mean?'

'It's breached the sea wall at Mablethorpe and other places down the coast. People's homes are flooded. There'll be a lot of folk needing help.'

'How do you know?'

'Pat told me.'

'Pat? When have you seen Pat?'

For a moment, Eddie looked shamefaced. 'I was in the village and I just called to see if she needed any help. Don't like to think of her struggling about on her bike in this weather. You know, if there was a babby bein' born somewhere—'

'I know,' Anna said softly.

'She'd got a call to go into Ludthorpe and help set up a rescue centre in the town hall.'

'You're taking her there?'

Eddie shook his head. 'No, someone's picking her up.'

Maisie was tugging at Eddie's sleeve. 'How far will the sea come? Will – will it get here?'

Despite the gravity of the news, Eddie smiled. 'I hope not, love,' he said. 'If it did, then—'

Though the young child did not understand, Anna realized what Eddie meant. If the sea reached Cackle Hill Farm, then half the county would be under water. She put her arm round her daughter's shoulders and pulled her close. 'There's a hill or two between us and the sea. It won't reach us.'

Maisie's lip trembled. 'Are you sure?'

'Sorry, love.' Eddie put his hand on the little girl's shoulder. 'I should have realized you wouldn't understand. No, the sea won't get here. But there is something you can do – ' his gaze found Anna's face – 'that we can all do to help them poor folks whose homes have been invaded by the water.'

'What?' the child asked whilst Anna's heart stood still. Before Eddie put his suggestion into words, she knew what he was going to say and her fear was back one hundredfold.

Oblivious to her feelings, Eddie said, 'There'll be hundreds being evacuated. They'll need somewhere to stay. I was wondering—?'

'What about the farmhouse?' Anna's tone was sharper than she intended. 'You've plenty of room there.'

Eddie's mouth tightened. 'Bertha won't have strangers in the house—'

Anna opened her mouth to retort that, for once, she understood how his wife felt and that she too didn't want strangers in her home. Then she saw the look of disgust on Eddie's face as he spoke of Bertha. Anna closed her mouth, the words unspoken as shame swept through her.

She remembered the night he had found her, soaked to the skin, exhausted and homeless. He had brought her to his own home, given her shelter, fed and clothed her – all against the wishes of his wife. He had done all this for her and now he was asking for that same compassion from her.

Anna touched his arm. 'What do you want us to do?'

Eddie smiled. 'I knew you'd do it, lass,' he said, hoarsely. 'I knew – that whatever it cost you – you wouldn't turn your back on those poor folks.'

Anna glanced away, unable to meet his trusting gaze, feeling very guilty that she had almost allowed herself to be every bit as selfish as Bertha.

Eddie, mercifully unaware of her inner turmoil, said, 'Tony's coming with me. We're taking the tractor and trailer. We should be able to get through the water to rescue folks.'

'Can I come?' Maisie piped up. 'I want to go with Tony.'

Eddie rested his hand briefly on the child's curls. 'No, you stay and help your mammy get ready for some visitors.' He turned back to Anna. 'They'll be cold and hungry. Can you make some soup or a stew?' Anna nodded as he went on, 'And you'll need blankets. I'll see if I can get some more. I must go—'

'Eddie – ' Anna grasped his arm briefly – 'be – be careful.'

With a brief smile and a swift nod of the head, he was gone out into the wild night.

In the early hours of the morning, Anna, who had not been to bed at all, though she had at last persuaded Maisie to go, heard the sound of Eddie's tractor chugging along the track around the wood and towards her cottage. As she opened the door, the blustery wind caught her skirt and tore at her hair. On the back of the trailer, she could see Tony with a woman and two children. One was only a baby, the other a little boy about Maisie's age. As the vehicle drew to a halt, Anna reached up with welcoming hands to help down the refugees.

'Oh, you're soaked through. Come in, come in. There's a good fire and hot food.'

The little boy held out his arms to be helped down, but the woman sat still on the trailer, clutching her crying infant to her but staring straight ahead as if she was unaware of Anna's presence.

Eddie jumped down from the tractor and came to stand beside Anna.

'Poor thing,' he murmured. 'She's in shock, I reckon. Her husband's missing.'

'How terrible,' Anna said and then raised her voice, 'Come along, love. Let's get you and the little one inside.'

At last, with Tony's urging, the woman allowed him to take the baby from her and hand it gently down to Anna. Then, woodenly, the woman climbed down from the trailer and moved into the cottage. But it was as if she was unaware of anything around her. She didn't seem to be aware of her own discomfort or even to notice the crying of her baby.

Anna sat the forlorn little family before her fire, wrapped them in blankets and ladled out hot soup, thick with pieces of meat and sliced vegetables.

'I call this "full-up soup",' Anna said, trying to raise a smile from the little boy. But he was white-faced and silent, the shock and terror showing in his eyes.

Maisie appeared in the doorway, a shawl over her nightdress, her bare feet sticking out below the uneven hem. She rubbed sleep from her eyes and stared at the strangers sitting in their kitchen. Then she sidled across the room to stand beside Tony, but stared wordlessly at the young boy, who was now eating the soup hungrily.

'We're going back—' Eddie said, making for the door.

'Not before you've had a warm and something hot to eat,' Anna said firmly. 'Come on, sit down at the table. You too, Tony.'

'But—'

'No "buts". You can't help folks if you're exhausted yourselves.'

'By heck.' Tony grinned, sitting down. 'She's getting to be a right bossy boots.'

Despite the tragedy that was unfolding all the way down the east coast of Britain, Eddie managed a brief smile. 'Aye, but she's right, lad.'

They tucked into a large bowl of soup and crusty fresh bread, but within minutes they were both rising and leaving the cottage. 'We'll have to go back, lass.'

Anna nodded. 'Take care then. Both of you.'

When they had gone, it was strangely quiet in the cottage. Only the wind, still howling outside, disturbed the silence.

'What's your name, love?' Anna asked the woman, who had scarcely touched the soup. She sat clutching the blanket around her and rocking to and fro. Then she began a strange keening, a kind of dry-eyed crying.

'Don't, Mam.' The young boy stood up and put his arm about his mother. 'Dad'll be all right. The mester said he'd go back and look for him.'

But his mother just shook her head in a hopeless gesture. 'He's gone. I know he's gone.'

The boy glanced helplessly at Anna, who was nursing the baby and trying to spoon some warm milk into the little mouth, all the while wishing that Pat Jessop would walk through the door and take charge.

'What's your name?' Now Anna addressed the boy, who seemed to be recovering from their ordeal more quickly than his mother.

'Peter Warren.'

'And your mam's?'

'Clare. And the babby's called Susie.'

Without warning, the woman suddenly stood up, threw off the blanket from around her shoulders and stumbled towards the door. 'If Bill's gone, I don't want to live—'

Before Anna could reach her, Clare pulled open the door and rushed out into the wild early morning. 'I don't want to live any more,' she wailed, her words caught and tossed callously away by the gale.

'Here, hold the baby, Peter,' Anna said. 'Don't worry. I'll get her back. Stay here.'

Snatching her coat from the peg behind the door and pulling it on, Anna hurried out into the storm leaving the two children and the baby. The woman was stumbling down the slope towards the stream, her arms stretched wide, her lament carried on the wind. A loud, hopeless wailing that chilled Anna's heart.

If she reaches the water, Anna thought, *I'll lose her.*

The stream was a rushing torrent from recent rain and a smattering of snow. The woman could be swept away. She was teetering on the bank when Anna grabbed her around the waist and unceremoniously pulled her to the ground. They rolled over and over, locked together in a desperate struggle, the one determined to end her misery, the other stubbornly refusing to let her throw her life away. They rolled over the edge of the bank and slithered into the icy torrent. The breath was knocked from Anna's body, the water gurgled in her ears, but she held on fast, her arms around the woman's waist. Suddenly Clare stopped struggling and went limp in Anna's grasp. Together, they were carried a few yards, bumping along stones and rocks on the bed of the stream.

Then Anna surfaced, gulping in air. Somehow she gained a foothold and dragged herself to the edge, lugging the dead weight of the woman with her. Panting, she lay on the sloping bank, half in, half out of the water. And still Anna held on to her burden. Gasping, she struggled to heave herself up, but all the time she refused to let go, not even for a second, in case Clare was feigning weakness in an effort to break free when she felt Anna's hold relax. But Anna was determined not to let go.

Just as she had once been saved, now she vowed to haul this distraught and desperate woman back from the brink.

At last they lay side by side on the grass beside the stream. For a moment Anna knelt beside the prone form, bending double to regain her breath. The woman was still and silent.

'Oh no,' Anna breathed and then she screamed and grasped Clare, shaking her. 'No! You can't die. You can't leave your bairns. Think of your children.'

And now, in that instant as she shrieked at the woman, dragging her back to life by the sheer force of her own spirit, Anna realized just what Eddie had done for her. He had saved her life – and Maisie's. And now she had the chance to save someone in return.

'I won't let you die. I won't *let* you!' But there was no spark of life. Anna felt utterly helpless. Again she shook Clare hard. Miraculously, the woman stirred and began to cough, spewing out stream water, and Anna felt tears of thankfulness.

It was several minutes before Clare was sufficiently recovered to allow Anna to half drag, half carry her across the field and back to the cottage. Maisie was watching out of the window and opened the door for them. By the look on her daughter's face, Anna knew that Maisie had witnessed the struggle near the stream.

Much later, when the boy was asleep in Maisie's bed and Clare, washed and resting in Anna's, the little girl confided, 'I didn't tell the boy, Mam. He was by the fire, holding the baby, so he didn't see. And I didn't tell him.'

Anna drew her close and buried her face in the child's copper-coloured curls. 'Oh Maisie, my precious darling,' she murmured huskily. Whilst Maisie returned her mother's hug fiercely, she had no understanding of the tumult of emotions in Anna's heart. Guilt, thankfulness and an overwhelming gratitude to Eddie Appleyard that words could never express.

A shivering Eddie and Tony sat wrapped in blankets before the fire and sipped Anna's hot soup gratefully. A restless daybreak had shown them the full extent of the disaster.

'A lot of the folks that had to be evacuated have been brought to Ludthorpe or other official rescue centres,' Eddie told her, 'but they're trying to find homes willing to take some of them in. Give them a bit more comfort, like. Poor devils.'

'There's lots of families got split up,' Tony put in. 'One poor chap couldn't find his little lad. He was – he was six.' Tony's voice broke as he glanced at Maisie and then, wordlessly, he reached out and touched her cheek. He said no more but his gesture spoke volumes.

'Is there any news of Clare's husband?' Anna asked softly.

Sadly, Eddie shook his head. Then, more briskly, he stood up and shook off the blanket. 'Well, this won't do. There's still more to be fetched to safety. To say nothing of taking feed to stranded animals.'

'You're not going back?' Anna said, before she could stop herself. 'You're out on your feet, Eddie.'

'I've got to, lass. Whilst there's folks still needing help—'

Tony began to stand up too, but Eddie put his hand on his shoulder. 'No, lad, you go home. You've done enough.'

Tony straightened up and met his father's gaze steadily. Quietly, he said, 'If you're going back, Dad, then so am I.'

Anna watched father and son standing together and marvelled at the likeness between them. Tony was so like his father in appearance; brown hair and eyes, tall and thin, but without the slight stoop that years of hard work had brought Eddie. And now the son was showing that same kindness and concern for others.

'Come on then, lad, though what your mam's going to say, I don't know.'

Later that night Bertha had plenty to say.

'You've done what?' she shrieked.

'Lost me tractor and trailer.'

'How on earth can you lose a tractor and trailer?'

Eddie sighed. 'It got stuck in the sand and the mud and now it's been bulldozed into the sea wall.'

'Whatever for?'

'Because they're desperate to shore up the defences and—'

'And they thought they'd use your tractor and trailer, eh?'

'No, Bertha, just listen, will you? We got stuck and they haven't time to be pulling stuff out. It's a race against time. There's an army of lorries bringing stone and slag – anything they can find to shore up the defences. And any vehicle that got stuck has ended up as part of the sea wall.'

'Just think, Dad.' Tony was laughing. 'You'll be able to walk along the sea wall and say: my tractor's somewhere under this lot.'

'You think it funny, d'ya?' For once Bertha rounded on Tony, venting her anger. 'You've not had a thought for me, 'ave ya, whilst you've been busy playing the heroes. Well, I've been worried sick about you.' Her gaze rested on her son and Eddie knew that her anxiety had not included him. Now she turned to her husband. 'You'd no right to take him with you. Owt could have happened to him—'

Tony put his arm around her quivering shoulders. 'Well, it didn't. And Dad couldn't have stopped me going to help. And you'd much rather I'd've been with him, wouldn't you?'

'Yes, but—'

'Oh, Mam, don't be like this. You should have seen all those poor folks. Their homes flooded, washed away in some cases. Some of 'em had only got the clothes they stood up in.'

Bertha sniffed. 'Huh. Next thing they'll be coming round for a collection for 'em, I shouldn't wonder. Well, they'll get short shrift here now we've got a new tractor and trailer to buy.' She shrugged Tony's arm away. 'I'll get your supper. That's unless you're both off out again with the pony and trap.'

Father and son exchanged a glance. 'No,' Eddie said wearily, 'there's nothing more we can do.'

'There is one thing I'd like to do, Dad,' Tony said softly as his mother disappeared into the scullery.

Bone weary, Eddie leant back in his chair and closed his eyes. 'What's that, lad?'

'Go round all the rescue centres. See if we can find that poor woman's husband.'

Eddie opened his eyes and lifted his head. 'Clare's, you mean?'

Tony nodded. 'It's the least we can do, specially after what – ' he glanced quickly towards the scullery and lowered his voice even more – 'Anna did.'

'Taking her in, you mean?'

'Oh no. She did more than that. Maisie told me.' Swiftly, before his mother returned, Tony explained. 'Anna saved that woman's life.'

For a moment, Eddie stared at his son and then slowly began to smile. 'Then the least we can do, son, is what you suggest.' As Bertha came back into the room, Eddie winked slyly at Tony and then raised his voice, 'D'you know, Bertha love, that was a very good idea of yours. Tomorrow we will take the pony and trap.'

His wife stared at him for a moment as if she thought he had gone completely mad. Then with a scornful snort, she banged the plates down onto the table. She turned and stormed out of the room, leaving father and son trying hard to stifle their laughter.

Twenty-Four

The following morning, after milking and feeding all the animals, Eddie harnessed Duke into the shafts of the trap.

'We'll go and see Anna and the woman – what's her name, Tony?'

'Clare. Clare Warren and her husband's name is Bill.'

'Aye, that's right. We'll go and see them first and make sure there's nothing they want.'

'The only thing that poor woman wants is her husband back.'

Eddie's face was sober. 'Aye, aye.' He sighed. 'We'll do our best, but I don't hold out much hope. I reckon, if they'd found him, they'd have let us know.'

Tony was more optimistic. 'Oh, I don't know, Dad. They're all that busy. It's a nightmare for the authorities.'

'I suppose you're right. He might have slipped through the net and be somewhere just as desperate about his family. I wonder if that other feller found his little lad.' Eddie was suddenly still. 'He said his lad was about six, didn't he? And that little lad up yonder is about that age. You don't suppose it was him – the father, do you?'

Reluctantly, Tony shook his head. 'Too much of a coincidence, I reckon. Besides, he'd have mentioned his wife and baby, wouldn't he?'

Eddie sighed. 'Aye, I suppose so. I'm just clutching at straws, I reckon.'

Tony grinned. 'Well, just you keep clutching at 'em, Dad. Keep hoping.'

They visited the town hall in Ludthorpe and were appalled at the number of people made homeless by the disaster. Several families were frantic with worry over a missing loved one. Eddie tried to speak to the organizers about Bill Warren, but they too were now exhausted and overwhelmed.

'He's not here. That's all I can tell you, but you could try all the villages just inland from the coast. They've opened up schools and village halls to help out,' one harassed WVS lady suggested. 'But he could be anywhere. Do you know him?'

'Not exactly, but his wife's given us a good description. Tall, broad, fair hair and a little scar under his left eye from an accident when he was a kid.'

'Well, good luck. Sorry I can't be of more help.'

'You have been. You've given us more places to look for the feller. Thanks. Come on, Tony. We've a long day ahead.'

By milking time that evening Eddie and Tony had still not returned and, of their own accord, the cows were gathering down near the yard, their udders full and uncomfortable.

Anna, standing at the top of the rise and looking down towards the farmyard, chewed her lip worriedly. Ought she to go down to the yard and begin the milking? Two things stopped her. Bertha, of course, and the fact that Anna was uneasy around cows. In the six years she had been here, she had only helped with the milking once or twice. And even then she had scuttled into the byre and out again as quickly as she could, afraid of being kicked by a restless cow, but even more afraid of Bertha finding her. Only when Eddie had broken his leg had she felt comfortable being there.

Above the wind, she heard a distant sound and glanced to the left to see the pony turning in at the gate. She strained her eyes through the dusk of the winter's evening.

There were three figures sitting in the trap. Anna's heart leapt with hope as the three figures alighted and two – Tony and a tall, broad stranger – hurried up the path towards her. Tony spotted her and waved excitedly.

Anna felt a lump rise in her throat and tears prickle behind her eyes. 'Oh thank you, thank you,' she breathed. Then she turned and ran down the track towards the little cottage, stumbling and almost falling in her urgency. 'Clare, oh Clare, come quickly.'

The door opened before she reached it, but it was Maisie who ran out. 'Mam, Mam. She's not here. I couldn't stop her. She's gone out. Into the woods, I think—'

'No, oh no!' Anna was panic-stricken and blaming herself. She shouldn't have left Clare alone.

She caught hold of Maisie. 'Tony's coming up the track with a man and I think it's Clare's husband. Peter's daddy. Now, you stay here, darling, and tell Tony and the man to come into the woods.'

Without waiting for a response from her daughter, for Anna knew Maisie would do as she had asked, Anna ran into the wood. It was dark and cold and the wind tore through the branches overhead, making a sound like rushing water.

'This is the worst place she could have come,' Anna muttered to herself. Maybe, she thought, in her confused state poor Clare had thought the noise was the sound of the sea and she had gone towards it to search for her man.

'Clare,' she cried out. 'Clare. Come back. He's here. Bill's here.'

She was taking a chance on this being the truth, but moments later Tony and the stranger came crashing into the woods behind her. Breathlessly, Tony said. 'We found him. This is Bill. Where is she?'

'I don't know. She can't have been gone long. I only went to the top of the hill. I wasn't away more than a few minutes. Oh, I'm so sorry—'

The big man gripped her arm briefly. 'Not your fault, lass. From what this young feller tells me, you've already saved her life once. Don't blame yourself.'

Tony moved ahead shouting her name and then Bill cupped his big hands around his mouth and let out such a roar that Anna felt her ears ring.

'Clare. It's me, Bill. *Claaaare.*'

They waited a moment, listening. Bill shouted again and then they listened again.

'I heard something,' Tony said, pushing his way through the trees and undergrowth. 'I'm sure I did. This way.'

Bill and Anna followed eagerly. Bill shouted again and this time they all heard a faint cry.

'She's here,' Tony, still leading the way, shouted jubilantly, but then he stood aside as Bill rushed forward to gather his wife into his arms.

'Oh, my darling girl. I thought you were lost. I thought I'd lost all of you.'

Clare was clinging to him as if she would never let

him out of her sight again. 'I thought you'd drowned. I thought you were dead. I didn't want to live. Oh, Bill, I'm sorry.'

He smoothed back her hair and between showering kisses on her face, murmured reassuring endearments. 'It's all right. I'm here now. We're all safe . . .'

Anna was standing transfixed, staring at the tender scene and feeling a mixture of thankfulness and joy for them, yet, for herself, an acute longing.

If only . . .

She felt Tony touch her arm. 'Come on,' he said softly. 'Let's leave 'em to it. They're all right now.'

'Yes,' Anna murmured. 'They're all right now.'

It wasn't until Bertha saw the reports in the local papers that she realized exactly what her husband and son had done. Eddie Appleyard was hailed as a hero for his rescue work.

> Throughout the night he and his sixteen-year-old son, Tony [one of the newspapers reported], ferried people stranded by the rising water to safety. Time and again Mr Appleyard waded through icy sea water, which was sometimes up to his chest, to reach young and old and carry them out of their flooded homes. Then he drove his tractor and trailer all the way to Ludthorpe to the centre there before returning to continue the rescue. Together father and son worked tirelessly to bring people and animals to safety. It wasn't until their tractor and trailer became stranded in the sand and had to be abandoned that this courageous and unselfish pair were forced to give up and accept help themselves.

All Bertha could say was, 'And how do you think you're going to do the ploughing now?'

'I'll think of something, Bertha,' was all Eddie would say. 'I'll think of something.'

But Bertha, keeping herself to herself, had no idea what the locals thought of her husband.

'You wouldn't believe it,' a beaming Pat told Anna. 'They're falling over themselves to help. Mrs Arnold at the village shop has got a collection box on her counter for the flood victims and she ses she has to empty it twice a day. And as for Eddie, he's had the offer of three tractors and five trailers to borrow whenever he wants that I know about. And,' she added triumphantly, 'they're all talking about your brave rescue of that poor woman.'

Anna stared at her. 'How does anyone know about that?'

For a moment, Pat could have bitten her tongue off. It wasn't like her to let herself chatter so much that she was in danger of letting out secrets. But, for once, she had been so excited that Eddie's kind-heartedness had at last been recognized and then at hearing the villagers speak kindly of Anna, that she had let her tongue run away with itself. She knew very well how the news had got out. Maisie had told Tony and he had deliberately spoken of it, hoping it would cast Anna in a good light amongst the locals.

Pat wrinkled her forehead and pretended vagueness. 'Don't really know, ducky. I expect Mrs Warren is singing your praises from the rooftops. And so she should.'

'Mmm,' Anna said, eyeing the nurse suspiciously. 'Maybe.'

'Anyway,' Pat said, turning the topic of conversation, 'all's well that ends well, as they say.'

Now Anna smiled, thinking of the little family who had stayed with her and who were now happily reunited.

If only her own story could have had such a happy ending.

Twenty-Five

'I've passed. I've passed the scholarship. I'm going to the grammar school in town. The same one Tony went to.'

Maisie danced around the table in Bertha's kitchen clapping her hands. She caught hold of Bertha and tried to make her dance too, but the woman, who had grown even larger in the last few years, flapped her hands. 'Oh go on with ya. My dancing days are over.' She sniffed and added wryly, 'If I ever had any.' Then she smiled, 'But I'm real pleased at your news, lovey. And Tony will be too.' There was a slight pause. This was the moment she had waited eleven years for. Bertha's eyes gleamed as she added, with deceptive casualness, 'To think that his sister is following in his footsteps—'

Maisie stopped, her dancing suddenly stilled. She stared at Bertha. 'What – what did you say?'

Bertha shrugged her fat shoulders. 'Surely you know you're his sister, don't you? Well, half-sister.'

As if she had been pole-axed, Maisie shook her head. 'I – I don't know what you mean? How can I be?'

'Mr Eddie's your dad, that's how.'

'But – but I haven't got a dad. Mam ses so.'

Bertha couldn't prevent her mouth twisting scathingly. 'Everyone's got a dad. Hasn't your mother even told you the facts of life yet?'

Dumbly, Maisie shook her head.

'Well, you're a big girl now and it's high time you knew. You'll be going to the big school soon and you'll be laughed at if you don't know. Besides, if you learn it in the playground, you'll learn it wrong. You ought to know the truth. The whole truth. Sit down . . .' She took the girl firmly by the shoulder and pressed her onto the stool near the table. 'Let's get us a cup of tea.' Bertha's thin mouth, almost lost now between the folds of fat, smiled, and her eyes were glittering with a strange excitement. 'And one of your favourite scones. Then we'll have a little chat, eh?'

Maisie walked slowly up the track and over the hill, her head spinning. She forgot completely to go out of the farmyard gate and into the lane to walk the long way home, as she usually did after a visit to Mrs Bertha. This time she didn't care if her mother saw her and guessed where she had been. She didn't even care if her mother shouted at her. She would shout back. And if Anna hit her, she'd probably hit her back the way she was feeling at this minute.

Bertha had spared the young girl nothing in the end. She had begun gently enough, as if she was doing Maisie a favour. 'You know how animals are born, don't you?'

Maisie had nodded. She'd witnessed sheep and cows giving birth and had accepted it as the most natural thing in the world. 'Well, it's the same with human beings.' And then Bertha launched into an explanation of all the facts of life in the most intimate detail. By the end Maisie felt sick, but Bertha was not done yet.

'You want to be careful of men, young Maisie.' She wagged her finger at the girl. 'They're only after one thing and they'll tell you all sorts to get it. Tell you they love you and that they'll marry you. But they'll never be faithful just to you. They're like animals. Like a ram amongst the ewes.'

The vivid pictures Bertha aroused in the young girl's mind made her scramble up from the table and rush outside. She had leant against the wall, breathing deeply, her eyes closed.

Inside the house Bertha cleared away the cups and saucers, smiling as she did so.

Maisie reached the cottage and entered by the back door. To her relief the kitchen was empty, so she climbed the ladder to her bedroom and lay on her bed, staring at the ceiling.

Was it really true what Mrs Bertha had told her? Was Mr Eddie really her father and Tony her half-brother? Had her mother, her pretty mother, done *that* with Mr Eddie? He was an old man in the young girl's eyes. It was disgusting. And the way that Bertha had explained it to her, it was all disgusting. Maisie groaned and turned over, burying her head in the pillow, trying to blot out the images in her mind's eye.

She couldn't ask her mother about it because Anna would then know she had been visiting Bertha and had been doing for years. And she certainly wasn't going to ask Mr Eddie. She couldn't even ask Tony. He was away at agricultural college in his final year there. He would be coming home to stay then, to work on the farm. But he wouldn't be here until the end of June or so.

Maisie sat up suddenly. There was one person she could talk to, who would understand. Nurse Pat.

*

'Hello, ducky. This is a nice surprise. Come in.'

Pat Jessop had hardly altered in the eleven years since Maisie's birth and to the young girl she had always been Auntie Pat.

As Pat ushered her visitor into her cosy sitting room and fetched her a glass of lemonade and a chocolate biscuit, she eyed the girl worriedly. She could see at once that something was troubling Maisie.

The girl sat on the old sofa, twisting her handkerchief in her fingers, leaving her drink and biscuit untouched.

Pat sat down beside her and took the girl's agitated hands into her own. 'What is it, love? Come on, you can tell me.'

Maisie raised tearful brown eyes. 'You won't tell anyone? Not my mam? Not anyone? Promise?'

Pat's mind worked quickly. If the girl had been older she'd've guessed she was in trouble. Pregnant and scared to death. But Maisie was only eleven. It was almost impossible. Not entirely, but most unlikely. But Pat was an honest woman. Carefully she said, 'I won't tell a soul, but I might have to encourage you to tell someone else. I don't know till you do tell me. It depends what it is, but I'm trying to be truthful with you, Maisie.'

The girl nodded. Then the words came out in a rush, all jumbled up and making little sense at first. When at last Maisie fell silent, Pat swiftly pieced the sorry tale together. Her mouth was a hard line, her kind eyes unusually angry. Her wrath was not directed at Maisie but at the unthinking woman who had imparted nature's most beautiful facts to a naive child in such a cruel manner. It could warp the young girl's mind for life, Pat thought, incensed by Bertha's callousness.

She sighed, knowing that she must do what she could to minimize the damage. And she must do it now.

'Now listen to me, Maisie,' Pat began in a kind but firm tone. 'Bertha Appleyard is a bitter, twisted woman.' Over the next half-hour, Pat's gentle voice eased away the girl's horror. She explained that Bertha had had an unhappy childhood because of the kind of man that her father was.

'A father is a big influence, specially on a girl and—'

Maisie raised her eyes to look steadily into Pat's. 'Auntie Pat, is Mr Eddie my father?'

'Only your mother or Mr Eddie could answer you that, but I don't believe he is. Both he and your mother always say that he found her in the marketplace in Ludthorpe just before Christmas with nowhere to go. He brought her home and gave her shelter in his little cottage. And you've lived there ever since.'

'Then – then who is my father?'

Pat took a deep breath. 'I don't know. I'm guessing that your mother wasn't married to him and that she ran away. But why she did I don't know either. Maybe one day she'll tell you. All I do know is that over the years she has tried to remain hidden away. She's terrified of being found, presumably by her family or – or your father. Several times she's talked about leaving. About getting further away.' Pat smiled gently. 'But always something's happened to stop her going.'

Maisie nodded, remembering one or two of those occasions for herself.

'You mustn't believe everything that Bertha told you. There are kind men in the world. I was married to a wonderful man, but he was killed in the war. But we were happy together and – and what happens between a man and a woman who truly love each other is beautiful. Remember that, Maisie, because what I'm telling you is true. What Bertha told you is true from a – a factual point of view, but she made it sound dirty and horrible. And it isn't. Believe me, ducky, it isn't.'

'You evil, wicked, owd beezum.' Pat shouted and actually shook her fist in Bertha's face when the woman opened the door to Pat's banging on it. Before Bertha had time to close it again, Pat had stepped inside. 'You've bided your time all these years. Waited for an opportunity to stick the knife in, haven't you? And now you've done it.'

With troubled eyes, Pat had watched Maisie leave. She hoped she had done enough to minimize the damage to the young girl, but she doubted that Maisie would ever quite forget Bertha's tales. Pat's anger had boiled over and, before she knew what she was doing, the district nurse was pedalling furiously towards Cackle Hill Farm.

'I don't know what you're talking about and you can get out of my kitchen, Pat Jessop.' Bertha glowered at her. 'I don't want your sort in my house. You're no better than you should be. No better than that little trollop over the hill.'

'You're sick, Bertha. Do you know that? Sick and twisted. Oh, I know your dad gave you and your poor mam a rough time, but you've let him wreck your life. And you needn't have done because somehow, Bertha, and God alone knows how, you managed to hook yourself a decent man. A lovely man. And yet you still can't put the past behind you, can you? You've let it blight your life with Eddie and now you're trying to twist an innocent girl's mind and wreck her life an' all.'

'It's not the girl so much,' Bertha muttered and jerked her thumb over her shoulder, 'as her trollop of a mother.' She glared at Pat, her eyes full of bitterness and hatred. 'I'll swing for her one day. You mark my words. I'll swing for her.'

Pat shook her head slowly, more sad now than angry. 'Oh Bertha, why? You don't really believe that Maisie is Eddie's child, do you? He's just a kind and gentle man who helped a young lass in trouble. Look how he was in the floods. He was a hero. Can't you understand? That's just how Eddie is. He puts others afore himself.'

'He's a fool. Look after Number One, that's what I say.'

Pat nodded and glanced around her. 'Well, you've done all right for Number One, haven't you, Bertha? Got your feet well under the Appleyard table years ago.'

'Get out! Get out of my kitchen right now,' Bertha shouted, waving her arms.

'Oh I'm going. I've said what I came to say. Except,' she added pointedly, 'that I need to see Eddie and tell him what's been going on.'

Bertha's reaction was not what she had expected or hoped for. The woman merely shrugged her shoulders and muttered, 'Meks no odds to me. Tell him what you like.'

Pat's anger seethed once more. She thrust her face close to Bertha's. 'And what about Tony? Do you want him to know just what a horrible woman you really are.'

Again Bertha shrugged. 'Tony thinks same as me. He hates 'em. Both of 'em.'

'Well, there, Bertha, I think you're wrong. I think

your Tony is very fond of them. Specially,' she added and she could not prevent a little thrill of malicious triumph, 'Maisie. I think he's very fond of Maisie. And I don't think for a minute that he'll like what you've done. He's got a lot of his dad in him, has Tony.'

Now the look on Bertha's face was exactly what Pat had hoped to see.

Twenty-Six

'Has the busybody nurse told you then?' was Bertha's greeting when Eddie came into the house for his dinner.

Wearily he said, 'Why, Bertha? Just tell me why you want to hurt that kiddie? You must know it's not true. She's not mine and you know it. And then to take the job upon yourself of telling her what her mother should tell her, well – ' he shook his head in disbelief – 'that beats all. It really does.'

Bertha turned away. For once she had no answer. She didn't care what Eddie thought of her, but her son was a different matter.

'It isn't true, love,' Eddie said gently.

He had waited in the lane, watching for Maisie to come home from school.

Maisie didn't pretend that she didn't know what he was talking about. Instead, she returned his steady gaze with her soft brown eyes that, to his sorrow, now held a more worldly look. 'Do you swear it? On – on Tony's life?' Tony was the only person that Maisie could think of on whose life Eddie would not risk tempting a cruel Fate.

Without hesitation Eddie nodded. 'I swear on Tony's life that I am not your father.' Then he smiled gently. 'Though I'd be lying if I didn't say I wished I was.'

For a moment Maisie stared at him. Then she let out a deep sigh and seemed to relax.

'There's never been anything – like that – between your mother and me.' His voice deepened. 'I am very fond of your mam, as I am of you. But I'm nearly old enough to be your *mam's* father, let alone yours. No, lass, I promise you that what my wife said is not true.'

'Some of it is, though, isn't it?' Maisie said in a small voice.

'What?'

'About – about what men – well, some men,' Maisie, remembering Pat's words, amended the sweeping statement, 'are like.'

'Ah,' Eddie said, understanding. 'That.' He paused a moment then went on. 'Well, love, I can't deny that there are some men in the world just like Mrs Bertha told you, but she made it sound as if all men are like that. You see, she was unlucky. Her father was a wrong 'un, so she thinks all men are bad. And they're not. Your difficulty, lass, is going to be recognizing a wrong 'un when you see one. But a good sort will respect you as well as love you.' He glanced down at her worriedly. She was very young to be taking all this in. Silently he cursed his wife for her vicious tongue. 'Do you understand what I'm trying to tell you, Maisie?'

'I – think so.'

'Well, when you're older and the boys start flocking round, you just come and ask me if you've any doubts about 'em.' He patted her shoulder. 'I'll sort 'em out for you.'

Maisie smiled thinly, but said nothing. How could she, an eleven-year-old child in his eyes – in everyone's eyes – tell him that she didn't want a flock of young men, as he put it, round her. There was only one boy she wanted. Only one boy she had ever wanted or would ever want.

Tony.

That was why Mrs Bertha's words had hurt her so much. The last thing that Maisie wanted in the whole wide world was for Tony to be her half-brother.

If Anna had known about Bertha's nastiness, more than likely she would have started to pack their belongings and threatened to leave. And this time she might have really meant it.

But for some reason that was never discussed, no one told Anna what had happened. And, unfortunately, no one thought to tell Tony either when he next came home from college.

If they had, it might have settled the turmoil in his mind about the truth of Maisie's parentage. It was something that had plagued the boy from the night that Anna had first appeared in the kitchen. A story perpetuated in his mind by his mother yet denied by his father.

Tony had never been able to decide whom he believed, and in the meantime Anna and Maisie continued to live in the little white thatched cottage near the woods.

But now Maisie never called at the farm to see Mrs Bertha.

In the September of 1958 Maisie started at the grammar school in Ludthorpe, travelling on the bus that trundled through the narrow lanes gathering up the children from the outlying district. As it had for Tony before her, the bus stopped for her at the bridge over the stream and she walked alongside the wood to her home.

Tony had completed his course at agricultural college and was now working on the farm that would one day belong to him. He bought himself a motorbike and even from their isolated cottage Anna and Maisie could hear the machine roaring through the country lanes, sometimes late at night. When she heard it, Anna could not resist the urge to smile. *That'll not best please Bertha*, she thought.

Maisie grew tall, slim and leggy. Coltish was the word that Pat used. The district nurse still visited the cottage as a friend. In fact, she was Anna's only female friend.

'She's going to be a real beauty,' Pat would say, laughing. 'A few more curves in the right places, Anna, and you'll have 'em queuing down the track as far as the lane.'

'Not if I have anything to do with it,' Anna said darkly.

'Aw, ducky, you've got to let her grow and flourish.' Pat sighed. 'You've kept her hidden away all these years. Never let her have any friends to speak of.'

'She hasn't wanted them,' Anna retorted swiftly. 'She's quite happy with the animals. That's all she needs. We don't need people.'

'Ta very much, I'm sure.' Pat pretended to be offended.

Anna smiled and said, 'You know I don't mean you. You're not people.'

Pat laughed. 'I'm not sure if that's a compliment, but I'll take it as one.' Then she sighed again. 'But you ought to let her mix a bit more. Go to her friends' birthday parties. And as she gets older, you ought to let her go out and enjoy herself a bit. This rock and roll that's all the rage amongst the youngsters now. I wouldn't mind a bit of jiving myself.'

'And what would happen then? She'd get in with the wrong crowd and get herself into trouble.'

Pat put her head on one side and regarded Anna thoughtfully. 'Is that what happened to you?'

Over all the years, Anna had never confided in anyone about her past. And again she turned away, muttering, 'Never mind about that. It's Maisie we've to worry about.'

'Aye.' Pat nodded sagely. 'We have.' But her meaning was not quite the same as Anna's. The kindly Pat Jessop was concerned that the girl was going to be kept as a virtual recluse all her young life. It was bad enough that a lovely young woman like Anna should have chosen such an existence for herself, but to inflict it upon her daughter was little short of criminal. The youngsters of today were a different breed. They had no memory of the austerity of the war. As the Prime Minister said, they'd never had it so good. They demanded, and got, a better standard of living. As well as working, they wanted to play too. *And why shouldn't they?* Pat thought. *Why shouldn't they have a bit of fun in their youth? They'll be a long time grown up.*

She got up to leave. There was time yet for her to work on the problem, but if Anna wasn't very careful, when she was older Maisie would rebel.

And then Anna would know what trouble was.

On Maisie's fifteenth birthday Eddie presented her with a battery-operated radio. Maisie was ecstatic.

'Will it tune into Radio Luxembourg? I heard it at Sally's once. They play all the latest songs.'

'Oh, I reckon it will.' Eddie laughed and winked at Anna. 'She'll probably drive you mad playing all this rock and roll, but I thought you wouldn't mind.'

Anna did not join in. She frowned at the machine and murmured, 'Just so long as that's all she does.'

'What do you mean?'

'I don't mind her listening to the music, but she needn't think she's going to the village dances.'

The previous year the local Young Farmers' Club had started a Friday-night dance for their members. Maisie had begged to go. 'Everyone's going from school, Mam.'

'I very much doubt it,' Anna had replied shortly. 'The village hall wouldn't hold everyone from your school.'

'You know what I mean,' Maisie snapped back impatiently. 'I didn't mean it literally.' For once her soft brown eyes were sparkling with resentment. 'Why can't I go?'

'We keep ourselves to ourselves.'

'But why?' the girl cried passionately. 'Why do we have to live like this?' When her mother didn't answer, Maisie said, 'Do you know what they call you in the village? A witch.'

Anna smiled. 'I can think of worse names they could call me.'

Maisie gasped. 'But it's awful. Years ago they'd have burned you alive.'

Anna chuckled. 'But they won't, will they? And if it keeps them away from here – all the better.'

The girl stared at her. Over the last two or three years she had begun to realize that she lived a very different life from most of her schoolfriends. All her friends, if she was honest. It hadn't seemed as noticeable when she had been at the village school. Several of her classmates lived on isolated farms and the difference had not seemed so great. But now she was older and mixing with youngsters from the town, she had begun to see how odd her own life was compared with theirs.

'Ask your mam if you can stay the night at mine,' her best friend Sally had asked Maisie more than once. 'We could go to the pictures and all meet up in the coffee bar. You'd love it. It's what we do most Saturday nights.'

Maisie had shaken her head. 'She won't let me. I don't even have to ask her. I know what the answer'll be.'

'Well, try.' Sally, a good-natured plump girl with mischievous eyes and curly brown hair, had linked her arm through Maisie's. 'We'd have such fun.'

But Maisie had been right. Anna's answer was 'No'.

Late in the afternoon of her birthday, when she arrived home from school, Tony was waiting for her at the cottage.

'I've brought you these,' he said, handing over two magazines. 'There's some pictures of all those fellers you're always going on about. Elvis Presley, Cliff Richard and Adam Faith, is it?'

Maisie opened the pages. 'Oh, look,' she exclaimed over one of a handsome, dark-haired, moody-looking young man.

'Who on earth is that?' Anna asked.

'Elvis,' Maisie breathed. 'Oh, it's Elvis.'

Tony grinned. 'Reckon I look a bit like him, don't you?'

Maisie laughed. 'Well, a bit, but can you sing like him?'

Tony dropped the magazine onto the table. He adopted the pose of the guitar-playing idol and began to sing 'Are You Lonesome Tonight?'

Maisie laughed and clapped her hands. 'Oh you can, you can. You sound just like him.'

Tony laughed. 'I don't know about that, but I wish I had his money.'

'You wouldn't be any happier,' Anna said quietly. 'Now, Maisie, take these upstairs to your room. I must get the tea.'

Maisie pulled a face, but did as her mother asked. Tony made to leave, but at the door he turned and said, 'Tell you what, I'll take you for a spin on me motorbike on Saturday afternoon.'

Before Maisie could answer, Anna said swiftly, 'Oh no. She's not going on that. Not at the speeds you go. And don't deny it, Tony, 'cos we can hear you from here roaring through the lanes. One of these day's you'll come a real cropper off that bike.'

'Oh mam, please . . .'

'No.'

'I'll be very careful,' Tony said. 'I promise.'

'Please, mam. Just once. Just for my birthday.'

Anna still looked doubtful, but relented. 'All right then. But you're not to take her far. You promise not to go too fast?'

'I promise.'

Maisie clapped her hands and rushed to hug her mother. 'Oh, thank you, Mam. Thank you, Tony.' She turned from her mother and flung her arms about his neck and kissed his cheek. Tony's face flamed and he pushed her away, but in her excitement Maisie did not notice. 'What time shall I be ready and what shall I wear?'

'Er – oh – whatever you like.' His face like thunder, Tony dragged open the door and was gone, slamming it behind him.

For a moment both Maisie and Anna stared at the closed door. Then the girl turned and looked at her mother, with wide, troubled eyes. 'What did I do, Mam? What did I do?'

Slowly, Anna shook her head. 'I don't know, love. I really don't know.'

On the Saturday afternoon, dressed in trousers, a thick jumper and warm coat and scarf, Maisie waited for Tony. And she waited and waited. As dusk fell, she said tearfully, 'He's not coming, is he?'

'Doesn't look like it, love.'

'Have you said anything to him? Have you put him off?'

Anna shook her head. 'No, I haven't. I admit I did think about it, 'cos I'm a bit worried about him taking you . . .'

'That's it, then,' Maisie snapped, pulling off her gloves. 'That'll be why he hasn't come. He knows you're not for it.' Then she added bitterly, 'And *she* won't be either.'

'No, she won't,' Anna said, her tone surprisingly mild. 'But I wouldn't have thought he'd've told her.'

Maisie climbed the ladder to her room and tore off her clothes. She switched on her wireless to play as loudly as possible. Then she threw herself on her bed and lay staring up, dry-eyed, at the wooden rafters of her ceiling.

I won't cry, she vowed. *I won't let him hurt me*. But with Elvis's deep tones singing 'Wooden Heart', she felt the tears welling and trickling down her temples as she lay on her back.

Twenty-Seven

Maisie was out in the fields early the next morning. Two ewes had gone into labour at the same time and Anna could not cope alone.

'You'll have to fetch Mr Eddie, Maisie. Go down to the farm and fetch him.' She paused and added, 'Or Tony.'

'I'm not fetching *him*,' the girl replied moodily, 'but I'll go for Mr Eddie.'

'Just go, Maisie. Get someone, else we'll likely lose one of them.'

Maisie ran.

Tony was in the yard, swilling out the pigsty.

'Where's your dad?' Maisie asked, panting hard from running all the way up the track and down to the farmyard.

'He's taken Mam into town. You've heard of her sister, Lucy, haven't you?'

Anna nodded.

'Well, her sister's husband's very ill. He's had a seizure, Mam calls it, so she's gone to stay for a few days.'

When Duke had got too old to pull the trap any more he'd been 'retired' to the meadow and Eddie had invested in a small truck. But Bertha could not drive, so Eddie now had to take her wherever she wanted to go.

‘’Cos you needn’t think I’m going on them buses. Not with all them nosy parkers. You can take me, Eddie. Every Thursday.’

‘Course I will, love,’ Eddie had agreed readily. He quite enjoyed a day’s peace at home when Bertha visited her sister, even if he did have to make two trips into town, to take her in the morning and fetch her home at night.

Today, however, there was an emergency and Lucy had sent a telegram asking Bertha to go at once.

‘You’ll have to come then,’ Maisie said now. ‘Two ewes have gone into labour and Mam needs some help.’

Tony dropped the yard brush. ‘Right. Come on then.’

They hurried back up the track, Tony loping alongside her with easy strides. ‘I don’t know why me dad doesn’t bring as many as he can down into the big barn. He did in forty-seven.’ He glanced at her. ‘The year you were born in all that snow. But he likes sticking to the old-fashioned way. Now, if it was me, I’d build a big barn to house ’em all every lambing time. But no. “What was good enough for me dad is good enough for me,” he ses.’

Maisie glanced at Tony. He was back to his usual self this morning. ‘What happened yesterday? Why didn’t you come and take me out on the bike like you promised?’

Immediately, there was a wary look on his face. ‘Sorry,’ he said curtly. ‘It – it was getting the telegram from me auntie.’

She recognized it for what it was. An excuse.

‘How very convenient.’ Maisie could not stop the remark and when Tony did not answer, she knew that she had hit the mark. They hurried on side by side, but now neither of them spoke.

With Tony's help, there were no problems and two healthy lambs came into the world. Anna, Maisie and Tony were standing together in the field watching the new mothers when they heard the sound of Eddie's truck drawing into the yard.

'Come on,' Tony said. 'Come down to the farm. Mam's left enough food to feed an army for a week. Come and have dinner with us.'

Anna shook her head. 'Oh no. It wouldn't be right. Knowing how your mother feels about me. About us.'

'Well, I'm going,' Maisie said, beginning to walk away. 'I want to tell Mr Eddie he's got two lambs.'

'Come on,' Tony coaxed. 'It'll be all right. And then I'll take Maisie out on me bike this afternoon.'

Anna eyed him speculatively, said nothing, but began to follow him down to the farm.

'Now, isn't this grand?'

Eddie was beaming from ear to ear as he spread the table with a snowy cloth and got out the cutlery from the drawer. 'She left a joint of beef in the oven that we can cut at for the week. It'll be done now. And there's veg to heat up. Isn't this grand?'

Anna had stepped nervously into the kitchen. This was the first time she had been inside the farmhouse since the night of her arrival. It had taken her a few moments to feel that she could even stay. She still wasn't quite comfortable being in Bertha's home, but she was smiling now as she helped to lay the table, guessing that this was probably the first time Eddie Appleyard had played host in his own home. Bertha never invited guests. As far as Anna was aware, even Lucy and her husband had never visited the farm. As they all sat down together, Anna said, 'Well, this is a feast and no mistake.'

'Tuck in, Maisie lass, tuck in. If you're off out on that moteybike this afternoon, you'll need summat to warm you up.'

Maisie glanced at Tony, who smiled and nodded. 'Yeah. Sorry about yesterday, but we'll go after dinner.'

Maisie, ready to forgive him anything, grinned back.

The wind whipped through her hair and stung her cheeks as Maisie wrapped her arms around Tony's waist and clung to him.

Looking over his shoulder, she watched the lane rushing towards them and disappearing beneath the bike's wheels. Laughing, she shouted in his ear, 'Faster, Tony, faster.'

On a perfectly straight piece of lane, Tony opened up the throttle and the bike leapt forward. Maisie screamed with delight.

At the end of the lane, he slowed, turned round and roared off again back the way they had come. When they returned to the farm, they were both red-faced and laughing. But Anna was waiting for them in the yard, her arms akimbo.

'So much for your promises, Tony Appleyard. We could hear you from here. I might not know much about motorbikes, but I know when one's going too fast.'

'It was only on Long Lane. On the straight.'

'Mebbe. But there's hills and dips in the lane. What if something had been coming the other way?'

'There wasn't.' Tony was getting angry now as Maisie climbed off the pillion and he flung his leg over the bike and propped it up on its stand. He faced Anna squarely. His voice was quiet, but deadly serious. 'Do you really think I'd risk hurting her? Maisie? Of all people?' Then, slapping his gloves together he marched away from them and into the house, leaving both Anna and Maisie staring after him. The one with growing dread in her heart, the other feeling as if she was about to burst with happiness.

In the summer of the following year, Maisie sat her O levels and, as a special treat, Anna allowed her to attend one of the village dances with her friends to celebrate the end of the exams.

'But don't think this is a regular thing because it isn't.'

Maisie hugged her. 'No, Mam. I won't.'

Pat, who had been canvassing relentlessly on the girl's behalf for the past year, listened to the exchange. 'I'll take you into town on Saturday on the bus and buy you a pretty skirt, Maisie. You know, one of those wide ones with lots of petticoats underneath. And some nice shoes for you to dance in.'

'Oh now, I don't know about that,' Anna began. 'It'd be a waste. Like I say, this is a one off . . .'

'Oh please, Mam,' Maisie begged.

Anna sighed. 'We'll see. Now, take Buster out and round up the lambs. The lorry's coming for them tomorrow.'

Maisie's face fell. She hated it when the lambs were taken to market.

As the girl closed the door behind her, Anna said, 'It's very generous of you, Pat but, honestly, she won't get the chance to wear such clothes.'

'She'll get plenty of chance when she goes away to college.'

'What?' Anna screeched. 'She's not going anywhere. She'll stay here with me and work on the farm. Eddie has already said . . .'

Pat sat down at the table without waiting for an invitation. 'Eddie will say anything to keep you here. To keep you *both* here.'

Anna stared at her and sank slowly into the chair opposite. 'Oh Pat,' she said sadly, 'not you too. You don't think there's something between me and Eddie.'

'No, I don't. I believe you. But have you ever stopped to think that Eddie maybe feels very differently? That maybe he would like there to be something between you? He doesn't have a very happy home life, y'know.'

Anna was silent, remembering the scratches on Eddie's face when she had first come here and, over the years, the odd bruise on his cheek. Even a black eye once or twice. And when these happened, Tony would stay away from the cottage for days, even weeks sometimes. Anna would guess that there had been a row between Eddie and his wife, and doubtless the cause had been her continued presence in the cottage. If so, it would throw Tony once more into a conflict of emotions – torn between his parents.

'I know,' she said flatly, 'and it's my fault. I should have gone years ago. I – we – shouldn't have stayed.'

'It's nobody's fault but Bertha's. It's certainly not

yours, ducky, so don't even think it. He'd've had a rough time with her whether you were here or not.'

'Do you think so?'

'I know so. Anyway, we were talking about Maisie and her career.'

'*You* were.'

'She's a bright lass and ought to be given a chance. She wants to be a teacher and—'

Anna stared at Pat incredulously. 'She's told you that?'

Pat nodded. 'Well, yes. I thought you knew.'

Anna shook her head and said slowly and thoughtfully. 'No. She's said nothing to me.'

'I don't suppose you've given her the chance. You've just decided that she's got to bury herself away here and—'

Anna sprang up and began to pace about the room. 'You don't understand. I've got to keep her safe.'

'She's a sensible girl. She – she knows the facts of life,' Pat said, carefully avoiding referring to the unfortunate way in which the girl had learnt them. 'If I had to put money on any of the youngsters around here *not* going off the rails, it would be your Maisie.'

The compliment did not ease Anna's agitation. 'You don't understand,' she repeated. 'It's not *Maisie* herself that's the problem. It's – it's other people.'

'What other people? Her peers, you mean?'

Anna shook her head. 'I can't risk us – being – found.' Then, as always when the conversation came close to matters from the past, Anna clamped her mouth shut and refused to say more.

Pat heaved herself up. 'Well, if you won't confide in me, I can't help you. But after all these years, surely you've nothing to fear now. It's sixteen years, for heaven's sake. You can't still be frightened about your family – or whoever it was – coming after you? You're not still hiding from the past, are you? Not after all this time. Surely, they'll forgive and forget by now?'

Anna swung round, her magnificent eyes sparkling with bitterness and hatred. She almost spat the words out. 'Oh, you don't know the half of it. It's me that can't forgive and forget. Me! Don't you understand?'

'How can I, ducky,' Pat said sadly, 'when you won't even tell me what happened?'

Anna turned away from her and, through gritted teeth, all she said was, 'No, and I don't intend to either. So leave it, Pat, will you? Else you and me are going to fall out.'

Twenty-Eight

'Well, you've been and now you know what it's like. Not all it's cracked up to be, I bet. I expect you were a wallflower for most of the evening. So don't be asking to go any more.'

Maisie gaped at her mother. She had never heard Anna speak so scathingly. Not all it'd been cracked up to be! The village dance had been everything and more that Maisie could have possibly imagined.

Tony had taken her into the village, not on his motorbike but in his father's truck. When they arrived outside the hall, he got out and opened the door for her, just as if she was royalty. 'In you go then. Have a good time. I'll pick you up at eleven.'

'Aren't you coming in?' Her disappointment was obvious.

Through the darkness she heard his chuckle. 'I reckon I'm a bit old for the village hop now. I'll leave it to you youngsters.'

'Don't be silly. Of course you're not old. Auntie Pat still goes sometimes. She told me.' Maisie put her hand through his arm and tried to pull him towards the door. 'Please come in, Tony. You can go if you don't like it. But – but please just come in with me.'

Tony glanced down at the girl. In the light from the doorway, he could see that she was biting her lip nervously.

'All right then. Just for a bit, eh? But I can't do all this fancy jiving stuff.'

Maisie giggled. 'Neither can I.'

'Wait while I park the truck.'

She stood near the doorway whilst Tony moved the vehicle a little way down the road and parked it on the grass verge.

'You goin' to stand out here all night?' Chris Wainwright, Joe's son, swaggered past her on his way in. He was dressed in tight trousers – drainpipes – and a long jacket, which almost reached his knees, and thick-soled suede shoes. His black hair was greased into a hairstyle like Elvis's. But there, sadly, the resemblance ended. Chris had a large, almost hooked nose and a spotty face. But he had other redeeming features. He was nice. He wasn't a bully or unkind and Maisie liked him. She grinned at him. 'I'm waiting for Tony.'

Chris's smile wavered as he said, 'Oh. He's coming, is he?'

'He wasn't. It's – only 'cos I asked him to come in with me.'

'You could have come in with me if I'd known you were coming. Anyway, I'll save you a dance.' Clowning, he said, 'Course me card's full, you know, but I'll squeeze you in somewhere.'

Maisie laughed and gave a mock curtsy. 'Thank you, kind sir.'

Chris went into the hall as Maisie turned to see Tony coming towards her.

'Who was that?' Tony asked, frowning after the disappearing youth.

'Chris Wainwright.'

'What did he want?'

'A dance later on.' Maisie laughed. 'Least I've got one.'

Maisie had more than one dance. A lot more. In fact, she hardly missed one and then only because she was completely out of breath.

Tony stood leaning on the temporary bar at the end of the big room. They were serving soft drinks only and Tony would dearly have loved to go across the road to the King's Head, but he had no intention of leaving Maisie to the tender mercies of this lot. He glanced around morosely, half envious of their youth, half disgusted at their style of dress. Fashions reached the countryside much later than in the city and the village lads were now heavily into the Teddy boy look, complete, in some cases, with bicycle chains and knuckle-dusters. One or two even carried flick knives, but it was all for show – just bravado, Tony believed. He knew most of the kids here and that they would run a mile if anyone raised an 'offensive weapon' in anger. He almost laughed as he watched the boys congregating on one side of the room, the girls on the other. Every so often a brave male would leave the pack and venture across to the female herd to pick a partner. And most of them seemed to make a beeline for Maisie, he thought morosely.

Tony had attended one or two of the dances in his teens, but it had never really been his scene. He was much happier with his own company or about the farm with the animals or going over the hill to see Anna and Maisie . . .

He sighed now as his eyes still followed the whirling, laughing figure of the girl who filled his thoughts and disturbed his dreams.

If only, he thought for the umpteenth time, *I knew the truth about her.*

Maisie did not answer her mother, but turned away before Anna could see the defiance in her eyes. The girl had had a wonderful time, and best of all had been driving home through the July night with Tony. He'd parked the truck in the farmyard and insisted on walking with her up the track, right to the door of the cottage.

'Mam's still up,' Maisie had said as they reached the top of the rise and saw the light glowing in the cottage window.'

Tony laughed. 'Well, of course she will be. It's the first time you've been out as late as this and to a dance. What can you expect?'

'Does your mam still wait up for you?' It had been a long time since Maisie had spoken of Mrs Bertha, so deep went the hurt that his mother had inflicted.

'No, not now. But she used to until I got to twenty-one.'

Maisie sighed. 'It must be nice to be older and be able to do what you want.' She was silent for a moment as they descended the slope. Then, after a pause, she said, 'I wish Mam would let me go out a bit more.'

Carefully, Tony said, 'She's worried you might get into the – the wrong company.' Silently, he sympathized with Anna. He had never experienced such a mixture of emotions as he had watching Maisie dance with one lad after another. Concern, envy and, yes, he had to admit it, jealousy. And yet he didn't agree with Anna keeping her daughter shut away from the world like a hermit.

'They're only lads from the village and one or two

from town,' Maisie interrupted his thoughts, answering his comment. 'I go to school with most of them. Oh, I know they dress a bit daft. All this Teddy boy stuff. But they're harmless.'

'I know,' he had to admit, 'but your mam doesn't know that, does she?'

'Suppose not,' Maisie admitted grudgingly. She sighed heavily. 'I don't suppose she'd let me go to a show in Lincoln. Sal says Billy Fury and some other stars are coming to do a live show at one of the cinemas there in October. I'd love to go.'

In the darkness Tony grinned and, feigning ignorance, asked, 'Who's Billy Fury?'

'Oh he's smashing. Ever so good-looking. He's a singer. Sal gave me a picture of him. I've got it beside my bed.'

'Huh!' Tony feigned indignation. 'I thought you'd've had my picture on your bedside table.'

Maisie grinned. 'I would – if you gave me one.'

After a moment's pause, Tony asked, 'Would you really like to go to see this chap then?'

'Oh yes,' Maisie breathed and even through the darkness he could hear the longing in her voice.

'Then I'll take you.'

'Will you? Oh Tony, will you? Really?'

And before he realized what she was doing, she had flung her arms round his neck and kissed him firmly on the lips. 'Oh thank you, thank you.'

'S'all right,' he said gruffly. 'You'd better get inside now. And don't tell your mam. She'll not let you go if you tell her. We'll just go. Right?'

With breathless excitement, Maisie said, 'Yes, yes. All right.' As she broke into a run down the last few yards to the cottage, she shouted through the night.

'Thank you, Tony. You're the best. Oh thank you. I love you.'

'I've told Mam I'm going home with Sal after school on Wednesday,' Maisie told Tony as they planned their outing.

'And I've told Dad that I can't help with the evening milking 'cos I've got to take me bike into a garage in Ludthorpe.'

Maisie's eyes clouded for a moment. 'Have you?' If there was something wrong with Tony's motorbike, the whole trip might be off.

'Course not,' Tony was saying cheerfully, 'but if you can get out of school at dinnertime, we can get to Lincoln in the afternoon. You'd like a look round the shops, wouldn't you?'

Maisie's eyes shone. 'Ooh, yes, please.'

Her childlike excitement at the thought of such a simple pleasure touched Tony. Anna had no right to keep a young girl like Maisie shut away. Their life was little better than a hermit's. No wonder Maisie had rebelled at last.

'Mind you wear something warm,' he reminded her.

'I'll take my clothes to school with my games kit and hide them in my locker in the changing room.'

They grinned at each other, enjoying their secret. Now Tony had no qualms about helping the girl deceive her mother. Maisie deserved a bit of fun.

The following Wednesday afternoon Maisie was waiting round the corner from the school. As she climbed onto the back of his motorbike, she said resentfully, 'I thought I wasn't going to make it. Mam didn't even want to let me go to Sal's tonight.'

'How does she think you're going to get home from there?'

Maisie giggled. 'I told her I'd asked you to fetch me home.'

Tony chuckled. 'You crafty monkey. Well, I will be, won't I? We should make it back home by eleven and she need be none the wiser. Hold tight, off we go.'

For the first time in her life, Maisie was on her way to see the city of Lincoln.

The shops and the hustle and bustle of the High Street entranced Maisie.

'Just look at all these people,' she marvelled, standing almost open-mouthed on the pavement. 'Wherever have they all come from?'

Tony chuckled as he held on tightly to her arm. He was afraid that she would be swept off the pavement and under the wheels of a bus, unused to crowds as she was.

'Oh, and look at the swans.' The excited girl leant over the parapet of High Bridge.

'Come on, it's time we were making for the cinema.'

As they walked along the street, Maisie saw the queue of young people, mostly girls, outside the building. Her face fell in disappointment. 'We'll never get in. Oh, Tony . . .'

'Don't worry.' Tony patted his pocket. 'I got the tickets two weeks ago. Our seats are reserved.'

Feeling important, they marched to the head of the queue. Standing on the steps outside the doors was a man who appeared to be marshalling the queue.

'Now, now, ladies,' he was saying jovially. 'No need to push. You'll all get in.' He pretended to glance down the length of the line snaking along the pavement. 'Oh I don't know, though.' He laughed loudly. 'It might be standing room only by the time we get to the end.'

'Don't matter, Mister,' someone shouted. 'Long as we see Billy.'

'Oh you'll see him. You'll see him,' the man promised. He was tall, in his fifties, and he was dressed flamboyantly like an old-fashioned music-hall star. His eyes were dark brown and the hair that showed from beneath his trilby was grey with a tinge of the ginger colour it had once been. He sported a pencil-thin moustache, which he kept stroking with the fourth finger of his right hand.

Maisie heard Tony's soft chuckle. 'He looks like Max Miller, 'cept for the 'tache.'

'Who's Max Miller?' Maisie asked innocently. The man must have heard her remark, for he smiled down at her from the top step. 'Max Miller, young lady, was one of the greatest comedians this country's ever seen. Now I could tell you a thing or two about the great Max Miller . . .'

'Ne'er mind about 'im,' a girl at the front of the queue shouted. 'When are we going to get inside? It's draughty standing out here.'

'All in good time, miss. All in good time. The doors will open in five minutes.'

''Ere—' The girl was still not satisfied. 'What about them? They're queue jumping.'

Tony fished in his pocket and produced the tickets and waved them. 'No, we're not.'

'What a sensible fellow,' the big man boomed and,

putting his hand on Maisie's shoulder, he ushered them towards the door. As she passed him, the man touched Maisie's curls and murmured, 'What pretty hair you've got, my dear. What a lovely colour.'

Maisie smiled up at him and then followed Tony through the door and into the cinema, excitement bubbling just below her ribs.

As they climbed the steps to the circle, Maisie giggled. 'Did you hear what that man said to me? He said, "What pretty hair you've got, my dear." He sounded like the wolf out of "Little Red Riding Hood".'

Tony laughed with her, but he glanced back over his shoulder to see the man watching them climb the stairs and his gaze seemed to be fastened on Maisie.

'Well,' Tony murmured, 'I wouldn't be too sure he isn't.'

The show wasn't quite what Tony would have chosen to see. One of the few males sitting amidst a crowd of screaming girls, he felt very out of place. But Maisie's delight was obvious. She screamed with the rest until she was hoarse and even Tony was forced to admit that Billy Fury was charismatic. Suddenly, at twenty-six, Tony felt an old fuddy-duddy.

At the end of the performance, Maisie pleaded, 'Do let's go round to the stage door and get his autograph. I've brought a book specially.'

'Oh I don't know. It's late now—'

'Please, please, please, Tony.'

'All right then, but we mustn't stay too long.'

Outside, special police patrols and even a police dog were waiting in case of trouble from hysterical fans. But the queue in the yard outside the stage door was orderly. This time, though, Maisie and Tony were obliged to tag on at the end of it and wait with everyone else. The minutes dragged by and no one came out of the stage door. Then there was a sudden flurry and the man who had been at the front of the building before the show emerged. A photographer was with him and at the man's direction he began to move down the queue taking pictures. 'For the *Echo*. Like to see your name in the paper, wouldn't you?' He paused every so often and jotted down a few names.

'I don't want me face in the paper,' Tony muttered. 'Come on, Maisie. It's time we were going. He's not going to come out. You can't blame him, love. He worked hard on that stage, I'll give him that.'

'Just another minute, Tony,' she begged. 'Please.'

The photographer was moving closer. 'What'll your mam say if she sees your name in the paper. She'll go spare.'

Maisie grinned. 'She'll not see it. She never takes a paper. You know that.'

'Aye, but someone might see it who knows you. What then?'

But at that moment the camera flashed and Maisie and Tony blinked. 'Now, love, what's your name,' the photographer asked, pencil poised above his notepad. 'And where are you from?'

'Maisie Woods,' she blurted out, answering his question automatically. 'From near Ludthorpe.'

'And yours, sir?'

'Nowt to do with you,' Tony growled. 'And don't you print that picture in the paper else I'll bust your camera for you. Come on, Maisie, we're going.'

Maisie smiled quickly at the young photographer. 'Sorry,' she said. 'We've got to go.'

As they began to move away, the photographer beckoned to the big man still standing in the stage door. They heard a shout and saw 'Max Miller' striding towards them. 'Wait a minute, I want a word with you—'

'Come on, Maisie,' Tony grabbed her arm. 'Run for it.'

By the time they rode into the farmyard at a quarter to twelve all hell had broken loose.

Anxiety had driven Anna to come down to the farm. The three of them – Anna, Eddie and Bertha – were standing outside the back door. It was the first time that Anna had come face to face with Bertha in sixteen years.

'Where are they? Where's Tony taken her?'

'My Tony wouldn't take that little trollop anywhere. Like mother, like daughter, I say. I heard about her at that dance in the village.' Bertha nodded sagely, her jowls wobbling. 'Making an exhibition of 'ersen. Dancing with every Tom, Dick and Harry.'

'He was taking her to Sally's house in Ludthorpe. But she should have been back hours ago. Where is he? Is he here?' Anna was close to hysteria. 'I've been on edge all day. There was a funny sky this morning. I don't like it. Something bad's going to happen. I know it is.'

'Now, now, love. Calm down.' Eddie tried to pour oil on what were becoming very troubled waters. 'Tony wouldn't let any harm come to Maisie—'

Bertha's mouth twisted. 'Oh "love", is it? Oh well, now we know, don't we?' She turned to face Anna, adding sarcastically, 'Of course he wouldn't let any harm come to his *sister*, now would he?'

Anna gasped. 'His – his sister?'

'Well, half-sister?'

Anna stared at the woman for a moment and then began to laugh, but it was hysterical laughter. 'After all this time you still think that?'

Bertha thrust her face close to Anna's. 'Why else would you stay here all these years? Why else would you bury yourself away in the back o' beyond. Unless you were where you wanted to be. With 'im.' At this she jabbed her husband in the chest.

Anna, her anxiety over Maisie forgotten for the minute, shook her head sadly. 'You're mad. Eddie's just a kind man who deserves better than you—'

'Now, now.' Eddie tried to placate the two women again. 'Don't let's get into all that. It's Maisie we should be thinking about—'

At that moment they heard the distant roar of the bike and turned towards the yard expectantly as the sound grew closer and at last turned in through the gate.

Anna flew across the yard. She dragged Maisie off the pillion and fired questions at her so fast that the girl had no time to answer. Then Anna rounded on Tony.

'And as for you, don't you come near her again. Do you hear me? Not ever.'

As Anna dragged her daughter away, Maisie glanced back over her shoulder. Tony was watching her. Their eyes met and held in a gaze until, through the darkness, they could no longer see each other's face.

Eddie ran his hand through his hair and muttered, 'Eh, lad, what trouble have you caused now?'

In the doorway of the farmhouse, Bertha smiled.

Twenty-Nine

'I have my reasons.'

'What? What reasons?'

'You don't need to know.'

'Yes, Mam, I do.' Maisie tried to calm the hysteria in her tone. She was trying very hard to act like an adult. 'I know I'm not a grown-up yet, but I'm not a child any longer either. Why can't you trust me?'

'Trust you? Trust you? When you do what you've done today? Deliberately disobeyed me and deceived me. How do you expect me to trust you after that?'

'Because I can't see why I have to stay shut away from leading a normal life unless you tell me why.'

Anna sat down heavily at the table and laid her head on her arms. She groaned. She was tired, very tired. All the long years of loneliness, the constant fear, which despite the passage of time seemed as sharp as ever. Bringing up Maisie alone with only Eddie and Pat Jessop to turn to for help. And living in the isolated cottage with none of the amenities that most people now enjoyed. It hadn't seemed so bad at first, when Maisie was tiny, but now she was forced to acknowledge the unfairness of their life for her daughter. It was one thing for Anna to choose to hide herself away. It was quite another for her to inflict that same seclusion on the young girl.

Her voice trembling, Maisie said, 'I'm sorry, Mam.

I – I promise I won't do anything again. At least – not without telling you. But will *you* promise *me* something?'

Anna lifted her head slowly. 'Depends what it is,' she said guardedly.

Maisie licked her lips. 'Well, if I promise to tell you exactly where I'm going, who with and what time I'll be home, will you let me go out a bit more? I'm not asking to be out every night, not even every week. I've got my school work to do, specially now I'm in the Lower Sixth.' Then the words came tumbling out in a rush of confidence. 'Mam – I – I want to go to teacher-training college.'

'I can't afford—' Anna began, but Maisie interrupted eagerly.

'You don't have to. There's grants and things we can apply for. The careers teacher said so. And I do so want to be a teacher. The little ones, you know. At a village school like the one I went to here.' She reached across and gripped her mother's hands. 'Please try to understand, Mam.'

'We ought to go away. Get as far away as possible,' Anna murmured. 'We should have gone years ago, but . . .'

'Why, Mam? What is it you're so afraid of?'

Anna pressed her lips together and shook her head. 'I can't tell you,' she said huskily. 'Please don't ask me.' Then hesitantly she said, 'All right. If you do your best to keep your promise, you can go out now and again. But if you want to go to teacher-training college, you'll have to work hard at school.'

'That's why I wanted to stay on and do A levels.'

Maisie could have left school long before now, but Anna had agreed to her staying on into the sixth form.

It had been her way of ensuring that Maisie was at home for another two years.

As if reading her thoughts, Maisie said, 'And even then I needn't go very far away. There's a very good teacher-training college at Lincoln—'

Anna sprang to her feet. '*No, no*,' she shouted. 'You'll not go there. Anywhere but there. Anywhere.'

Maisie gaped at her. 'All right, Mam. All right. There's another year before I have to decide anyway—'

'Get to bed. It's very late. I'll never be up in the morning.'

Submissively, Maisie got up, kissed her mother's cheek and then climbed the ladder to her room, still shocked by her mother's reaction to the mention of the college in Lincoln.

Maisie fell asleep almost at once, but in the other bedroom Anna lay awake until the first fingers of dawn crept in through the window.

'Everything all right?' Eddie asked.

'Sort of,' Anna replied guardedly and then allowed herself a wry smile. 'You?'

'Bertha's giving Tony a hard time. She hit him. First time I've ever seen her go for him.' There was wonder in his tone.

'Oh, Eddie, I'm sorry.'

Eddie shrugged. 'Not your fault, lass.'

'No, but it is Maisie's.'

'Not really. It seems it was Tony who suggested the trip.'

'Yes, but it was for Maisie, wasn't it?' Anna insisted.

'Well, yes.' Eddie was obliged to agree.

'Has she hurt him?'

'Who?'

'Tony? Has Bertha hurt him?'

Eddie laughed. 'Oh that. No.' He chuckled. 'You should have seen it, lass. He's a strong lad, you know, and whilst I've never stood up to her – ' he wrinkled his brow and rubbed his nose – 'never thought about it, really. But he just caught hold of her wrists and held her. She was screaming like a banshee, but she couldn't move. And he held her like that till she calmed down. He told her, quite calmly, that he was a grown man and that he'd do what he liked and that it was nothing to do with her. I don't reckon she'll tangle with him again in a hurry.'

Eddie said no more. He did not want to tell Anna about the rest of the row that had gone on in the farmhouse the previous night.

'You'll keep away from that little slut,' Bertha had screamed at her son. 'You'll have the law on you, if you don't. You could be put in prison.'

'She's sixteen. Old enough,' Tony had goaded her.

'Don't you understand?' Bertha had screeched. 'She's your sister.'

'That's what you say.' He nodded across to where Eddie was standing in the corner of the room. 'But me dad ses different. And he should know.'

'He'd deny it. Course he would. I'm surprised that trollop over the hill hasn't had a brood of his bastards by now. All men are the same.'

'No, we're not, Mam.' Tony's voice was gentle. Now he was older he understood more about his parents' unhappy marriage, though there was nothing he could do about it. A few years earlier Eddie had explained to him about Bertha's father, about his philandering and his lawless ways that had finally landed him in prison. 'We've just got news that he's died in there,' Eddie had said, 'but it won't alter how ya mam feels about him and how it's twisted her view of all men. It's something you'll have to cope with, lad, as you get older. You're all she's ever had to pour her love into and it's going to be hard for you.'

And now Tony was facing his mother's warped reasoning. 'We're not all the same, mam. There's nowt between me and Maisie, I promise you.'

He had not added that he wished with all his heart that there could be. But always there was the spectre of their relationship hanging over him. Just which of his parents was telling him the truth?

He wanted to believe Eddie, but dare he?

'Well, I'm truly sorry,' Anna said now, dragging Eddie's thoughts back from the previous night.

'No harm done, lass,' Eddie said, managing to lie cheerfully and convincingly. 'No harm done.'

That evening, thirty miles away in a terraced house in Lincoln, the big man dressed like Max Miller sat staring at a picture in the local paper. 'Damn,' he muttered. 'They haven't printed the picture I hoped they would. They've put one in of the audience arriving.'

'What are you on about, Dad?' The younger man stood in front of the mirror over the fireplace, combing his hair into an Elvis Presley look-alike style.

The older man smiled. 'Good job I thought to call at the *Echo* offices and get the originals of all the photos taken that night, wasn't it?'

'Whatever do you want them for?'

'I'll show you,' the man answered as he pulled several black and white photographs from an envelope and sorted though them. 'Come and look at this.'

'I'm off out. Can't it wait? I'm meeting someone.' He was dressed in a bright pink Teddy boy suit with a bootlace tie and crepe-soled shoes.

His father glanced at him. 'Bit old for dressing like that now, aren't you?'

'Huh,' the other laughed. 'You're a fine one to talk. Always dressed like something from an old music hall bill.'

'Well, that's me job, son. Got to look the part of the theatre promoter, now ain't I?'

'All right. What is it?'

'Here, look at that. Remind you of anyone?' He jabbed at one of the pictures with his forefinger. 'Her. That girl there.'

His son stared at the photograph. He glanced at his father and then his gaze went to a faded photograph on the mantelpiece of himself as a child of about twelve. He looked again at the newspaper picture as the older man said softly, 'She's got bright red hair, an' all. *Just like you.*'

They stared at each other. 'Could it be?' the son asked.

'It's possible.' He pointed again at the paper. 'And do you see what her name is? Maisie. Now that's a bit like May, isn't it?'

The younger man nodded. 'What are you going to do?'

The big man heaved himself out of his chair. 'A bit of detective work first. Then we'll see. Oh yes, we'll see all right then.'

The two men grinned at each other.

If Anna had known what was happening in that terraced house in the city, she would have packed their things immediately and fled for her life.

Thirty

Two men in a red sports car drove into the yard at Cackle Hill Farm, scattering hens and sending up a spray of slurry. The big man unwound himself from the seat and the younger man jumped out agilely. They looked around them.

'Hello there,' the big man's voice boomed. 'Anyone at home?'

The yard was deserted, except for the hens and three geese that waddled away quickly. 'Knock on the door,' the older man suggested and his son strode towards the back door of the house and rapped sharply.

A moment passed and then the door opened framing the ample figure of the farmer's wife. Visitors to the farm were rare and Bertha eyed them with suspicion. 'What d'you want?'

The older man moved closer and doffed his trilby with an exaggerated show of courtesy. He fingered his moustache. 'Good day to you, ma'am.'

The younger man too made a little bow towards her, though shrewdly Bertha felt it was all an act. An act to charm her. Well, there was no man living who could charm Bertha Appleyard.

She began to close the door. 'Not today, thank you.'

'Oh now, wait a minute, love,' the older of the two began and even had the temerity to put his foot in the door. Bertha glared at him and opened the door wider, intending to slam it against his foot. Guessing her intention, he withdrew his foot hastily. Instead, he put up his hand, palm outwards as if to defend himself. 'Wait minute, Missis. Not so hasty. We only want to ask you a few questions. We reckon you can help us.'

Intrigued in spite of herself, Bertha wavered. 'Go on.'

'We're looking for someone. A girl. Well' – he glanced sideways at his companion – 'she'd be a young woman now. And she'd probably have a youngster. Anna. That's her name. Anna Milton. Do you know anyone living hereabouts with that name?'

Bertha opened the door wider and smiled. Like a spider inviting a fly into its web, she said, 'Come in, why don't you?'

Out on the hillside, Anna wandered amongst the sheep checking them. From time to time she paused and looked back to watch Buster trailing after her, valiantly trying to keep up.

'Poor old feller,' she murmured, bending down to stroke him. 'You're so weary now, aren't you?'

The dog, who had been their faithful companion since just before Maisie's birth, was old and worn out. Both Anna and Maisie knew he could not last many more years. Maybe he had only months.

'If he starts to suffer,' Anna had explained carefully to Maisie, 'we'll have to let him be put down. It's the kindest.'

With tears in her eyes, Maisie had nodded and buried her face in the dog's coat.

Today Buster seemed slower than ever, but his heart

was 'as big as a bucket', as Eddie said, and the dog was still trying to do his job.

'Come on,' Anna said, 'let's get you back inside near the fire and you can rest.'

As they made their way steadily back towards the cottage, Anna saw two men crest the top of the hill and begin to walk down the slope towards them. She shaded her eyes watching them.

Suddenly, her heart began to pound. No, it wasn't possible. No, no, *no*!

She began to run towards the cottage. If she could just get inside before they reached her . . .

'Come on, Buster. Come *on*!' But the dog was too weak. His running days were over. She stopped and picked him up. Despite his frailty, he was still heavy. Clutching him tightly, she struggled and stumbled towards the cottage, desperate to reach its safety. She was almost there, a few yards more and . . .

But the younger of the two men had broken into a run. He was gaining on her. She wasn't going to reach the door. If she had dropped the dog to the ground and run, she could have made it. But, remembering that other time, she held onto him. She couldn't – wouldn't – let the same thing happen to this Buster.

'Now, now, Anna. What's all this? Aren't you pleased to see us?'

He had reached her and was standing between her and her haven. And now the older man was near and he was barring her escape to the side door.

Anna lay Buster on the ground and stood up to face the two men. 'Leave me alone,' she spat at them.

'That's no way to greet us, Anna,' the older man said, 'after all this time. We've been worried about you. Running off like that.'

Anna's eyes narrowed with hatred. The younger man moved towards the dog, lying panting on the ground. He touched it with his foot and Buster growled.

'Still got your brave little protector, eh, Anna?' he sneered. He drew his foot back and aimed a vicious kick at the defenceless animal. Buster's yelp galvanized Anna. She flung herself at the man and began to pummel him.

'Get away. Leave me alone. I hate you. I hate you.'

He was strong and stocky and, whilst Anna was no weakling, she was no match for his strength. He held her by the wrists quite easily. She kicked his shins, but he only laughed. That awful, cruel laugh she remembered so vividly in all her dreams.

Anna began to scream, but he only laughed louder. 'There's no one to hear you, Anna.'

And all the time his father just stood watching.

At the moment when Anna almost gave up the struggle, she heard a shout from the top of the hill and saw Eddie and Maisie running towards her. The man, still holding Anna, turned.

'You get the girl,' he muttered to his father. 'I'll take care of him.'

He turned back and, raising his hand, dealt Anna a vicious blow on the side of her face, knocking her down. The blow had not quite knocked her out, but when she tried to rise she found she was so dizzy that she sank back to the ground.

'Mam!' Through the mists she heard Maisie's cry, but the girl never reached her. She was caught and held fast. 'Now, now, lass. We only want to talk to your mam and you.'

Dimly, Anna was aware that the younger of the two men and Eddie were facing each other like two fighting cocks, circling warily around each other.

The man reached into his pocket and flicked open a knife. 'No!' Maisie cried and struggled, but the big man held her fast. 'Mr Eddie, he's got a knife.'

Dully, her words registered with Anna and she tried to drag herself up. 'No,' she gasped. 'No. Please, no more.' She stumbled towards the one holding Maisie and clung to his arm. 'I'll do whatever you want. I swear it, but make them stop. Don't – don't let him hurt Eddie.'

He looked down at her upturned face, the bruise on her cheek swelling already. His lip curled sarcastically. 'Oh, so the woman was right, was she? You are his fancy piece.'

Anna shook her head, then winced as the pain stabbed. 'No – no, you've got it wrong. I—'

Her words were cut short by a terrifying yell from behind her as the younger man leapt forward, stabbing with the knife.

'No!' The cry came from both Anna's and Maisie's lips at once.

But his blood was up. There was murder in his eyes. Even Eddie, quiet, gentle Eddie Appleyard's face was thunderous. 'I don't know who you are, but you're not going to come here and treat her like that—'

Sudden realization was filtering through Eddie's mind, even in this moment of danger. This, then, was what Anna had been afraid of. One glance at the face and red hair of the man facing him told Eddie all he needed to know. This was the man Anna had run from and, by the look of it, she had had good reason.

There was no denying the likeness. The man threatening him with a knife was undoubtedly Maisie's father.

'Put the knife away, lad, and let's talk this through,' Eddie said, trying desperately to instil calm into his tone, though he would dearly have liked to knock this feller into the middle of next week.

'Talk?' was the scathing answer. 'Talk? What she needs is a damn good hiding. Show her who's boss. By, I've waited years to catch up with that little madam. And now I've found her. Well, she won't escape me again.'

Suddenly he lunged forward, his knife thrusting towards Eddie. It found its mark, entering deep into Eddie's body just below the ribs. Eddie gave a low grunt and his eyes stared in shocked surprise before he crumpled to the ground.

Anna and Maisie cried out together and even the big man shouted, 'No,' as the knife went home. They heard him mutter, 'You damned fool. What do you want to go and do that for?'

His attacker was standing over the still figure, holding the knife covered in blood. Anna and Maisie tore themselves free and flung themselves down beside Eddie. Maisie cradled Eddie's head in her arms, whilst Anna tore open his clothing to see how bad the wound was. Blood spilled out drenching his clothes and hers.

'Oh Eddie, Eddie,' Anna moaned and closed her eyes.

Dimly, she heard one of them say, 'Come on, we'd better get out of here. You're a fool. You've wrecked everything.'

'He was coming for me. It was self-defence.'

'Don't talk daft. He was unarmed.' He nodded towards Anna. 'She'll tell 'em that. And the girl. Come on. Let's get out of here.'

They ran up the hill and down into the farmyard

and scrambled into the car. Bertha came out of the back door. 'Find her, did you? I hope you've come to take the little trollop away—'

'Sorry, Missis. Can't stay.'

The engine burst into life. The older man reversed the car erratically and, turning it, drove at speed towards the gate. Driving out into the lane without stopping to see if the way was clear, the car clipped Tony returning on his motorbike, knocking him off balance. As the sports car roared off up the lane, Tony was thrown off his bike and onto the grass verge. His landing was soft and he was unhurt but very angry. Swearing, he gained his feet in time to memorize the number plate.

'Road hog,' Tony shouted as he stood in the lane, shaking his fist after the disappearing vehicle.

Whilst over the hill, now cradled in Anna's arms, Eddie Appleyard fought for his life.

1939

Thirty-One

'Higher, Daddy, push me higher.'

The child on the swing, petticoats flying, swooped through the air.

Her father laughed. 'You're quite big enough to work it yourself now, Anna.' But the ten-year-old smiled winningly and the man capitulated. 'Hold tight, then.'

'Oh, Ken, do be careful,' May called anxiously, nibbling agitatedly at her thumbnail. 'What if the branch breaks?'

Ken laughed. His tall frame was a little stooped, giving the deceptive appearance of frailty. His long face was thin, with hollowed cheeks, but his grey eyes were kind and gentle. He worked in an office in the city of Lincoln and perhaps that was why his skin had a sallow look. Ken stepped back from the swing, letting it slow down of its own accord.

'Daddy?' Anna cried plaintively, but her father only laughed. 'Enough now, love. Your gran will have tea ready and then we must catch the bus back home.'

Anna pouted, but then her sunny nature drove away the brief moment of petulance. She put her feet to the ground and slowed the swing even more. Jumping up, she ran to her parents, pushing her way between them, and linked her arms in theirs.

Mother and daughter were remarkably alike, with

black, curling hair and smooth skin. But their most outstanding feature was the colour of their eyes: a dark blue, almost violet. Most people, meeting them for the first time, could not help remarking on the unusual, yet beautiful, colour.

As they arrived at the back door of the farmhouse, May's mother, Rosa, met them.

'Perfect timing.' The plump, placid-faced woman beamed. 'Tea's ready.'

They sat down at the huge kitchen table, with Luke Clayton at the head whilst his wife sat at the opposite end.

'The news isn't good,' he began as he carved a huge piece of boiled ham and passed plates around the table.

'Help yourselves to potatoes,' Rosa said. 'Now, Luke, I don't want any talk of war round my table, thank you. And certainly not in front of the child.'

'I thought everything was all right now, Dad,' May put in, 'since Mr Chamberlain came back from Munich last year.'

The two men exchanged a sober look.

'That agreement, or whatever it was, wasn't worth the paper it was written on,' Luke grunted. He turned to smile at his granddaughter. 'That enough ham for you, lass?'

'Yes thank you, Grandpa.' Anna smiled at the weather-beaten face with its deep lines, at the snowy white, bristly moustache that tickled her when she kissed his cheek.

Ken turned towards his wife and touched her hand lightly. 'It was in all the papers yesterday. Hitler has marched into Czechoslovakia.'

May gasped and the colour fled from her face. 'You mean there's going to be a war?'

Again the two men glanced at each other.

May's voice rose. 'Tell me. I want to know.'

'Now, now, love,' Rosa said, passing the vegetables. 'Don't get all het up about things that don't concern us.'

May rounded on her mother, anxiety making her speak sharply. 'Of course it concerns us, Mam. If there's a war, Ken might have to go.' Then, as if contradicting herself, May grasped her husband's arm. 'You won't, will you?' Clinging to any hope she could think of, she said, 'Besides, you're too old, aren't you?'

Ken cleared his throat and glanced round the table in embarrassment, wishing that his father-in-law had not raised the subject. 'There's talk of more recruits being sought to join the Territorials. I – I thought I might volunteer.'

May gave a little squeak and covered her mouth with her hand, staring with wide-eyed disbelief at her husband. 'Whatever for?' she whispered. 'Why do you want to go and do something like that?'

Luke sniffed. 'Well, if you'd take a bit of advice from an old soldier who was daft enough to volunteer for the last lot—'

'Aye, off you went to war and left me with May to bring up. She was only six when you went,' Rosa began, wagging her finger across the table at her husband. Then she smiled. 'Mind you, I was that proud of you the day we came to wave you off. Marching away to serve your country.' She shook her head, remembering. Tears filled her eyes as she murmured, 'And then, all them medals you got—'

'Well, I don't care about uniforms and medals,' May declared. 'I don't want Ken to go. He might not be as lucky as Dad.'

The unspoken words lay heavily in the air.

'Aye,' Luke said softly. 'I was lucky to come back and without serious injury, an' all. I know that.' He turned towards his son-in-law. When Ken had first started courting his daughter, Luke had not been at all keen on the young man. Ken Milton was a city lad, with no interest in the country or the farm. With an only daughter, it had been Luke's dearest wish that May would marry a local farmer who would take on Clayton's Farm in the future. But May had been drawn to city life, though how she could enjoy living in those crowded streets, which were never quiet day or night, beat Luke. Yet now, as he looked at his son-in-law, Luke felt a fondness for the lad he had not known before. Ken was a good husband to May, Luke acknowledged that. And together they were bringing up a lovely daughter, Anna, who was Luke's pride and joy.

'Don't volunteer, lad. That's my advice.' Grandpa Luke's face was unusually grim. 'Patriotism is all very well and I'd be the first to defend me country from attack – even at my age.' He shook his head. 'But volunteering gets a lot of good fellers killed. Wait till you 'ave to go and not afore. Wait till they send for you.' His tone was grim as he added, ''Cos believe me, they will. If it really comes to war, they'll have to bring in conscription – just like they had to last time.'

Anna's wide-eyed glance went at once to her father's solemn face as he rose from the table. 'I'm sorry, but I'm afraid if it does come to war, I shall go.'

At the sound of May's startled gasp, Anna turned to see that her mother's face had turned deathly white.

On the bus home, her parents scarcely spoke to each other. Her mother looked out of the window and her father stared straight ahead. Sitting on the seat in front of them, Anna shivered. The pleasure of the day had turned suddenly cold.

Throughout the summer, preparations for war continued in earnest. Plans to evacuate children from the cities into the countryside threw May into turmoil again. 'Not from Lincoln. Surely they won't bomb us?'

Ken shrugged. 'It's a possibility we'll have to face. There's a lot of industry in Lincoln that'll be involved in war production, I don't doubt. We could easily be a target. But promise me, Maisie darling, that you'll go out to the farm. You and Anna.' Maisie was Ken's affectionate pet name for his wife, used only in their private moments together or when, as now, he was trying to win her round to his way of thinking.

May pulled a face. 'I suppose so,' she agreed reluctantly. 'But I thought I'd got away from all that when I married you. Wearing wellies all day and mucking out the hen house. To say nothing of milking those horrible cows.'

Despite his anxiety, Ken smiled. 'Is that all you married me for? To get away from the farm?'

May laughed and teased him. 'Of course it was. Didn't you know?'

They were sitting on the battered sofa in front of the plopping gas fire, their arms around each other. Anna was safely asleep upstairs and the two adults could talk freely without fear of frightening her.

Ken's arm tightened about May's waist. 'If I do go, I just want to be sure you and Anna are safe, that's all,' he said.

'Well, there'll be plenty of work for us all to do,' May said wryly. 'Dad was saying only last weekend that the government are offering to pay farmers two pounds an acre to plough up grazing pastures to grow more crops.'

Ken nodded. 'They're worried that food imports will be at risk if there is a war.'

'But two pounds an acre, Ken. That's a lot of money.'

Ken laughed softly. 'Like your dad always says, "It's an ill wind—"'

May was not to be diverted so easily. 'Why don't we all go? If you work on the farm, you'll not have to go to fight.'

Ken shook his head. 'May, please try to understand. I want to do my bit.'

People in Britain tried to carry on life as normally as possible, yet everywhere they were reminded of the threat hanging over them all. Houses continued to be built, the King and Queen embarked on a tour of North America and people still went on their summer holidays. Yet news filtered through of Hitler's treatment of the Jews in Germany and rumours began that he had set his sights on Poland. By the end of August war seemed inevitable. Clutching their gas masks and perhaps a favourite toy, thousands of tearful children began to be evacuated from the cities and towns into the safety of the country.

When the day came for Ken to leave, the railway platform teemed with men in khaki. Dotted amongst them were women in flowery dresses, wiping tears from their eyes and clinging to their menfolk's arms.

Anna stood with her parents, holding tightly on to

her mother's hand. She was afraid of getting separated from them and being lost amongst the crowds.

'You do understand, May, why I have to go?'

'I still can't understand why you won't at least wait for your call-up papers – like Dad said.'

Anna heard her father sigh. 'We've been through all that,' he said, sounding weary. And they had. Even Anna knew that because she'd heard them arguing in their bedroom at night, trying to keep their voices low so that she would not hear. But always the arguments would end with the sound of her mother crying.

May was trying to be brave now. Her mouth was trembling and tears brimmed in her eyes and threatened to spill down her cheeks, yet she was still trying her best to smile. 'It's just – just – I don't know how I'm going to cope without you.'

'I know, love. But you must be strong for Anna's sake too.'

'But I'm not strong, am I?' Her voice was muffled against him. He did not answer but drew her close and then held out his arm to Anna to enfold her in a bear hug too. 'You must look after each other. And promise me, May, if we get any bombing in Lincoln, you'll go out to the farm? Go and stay with your parents. Anna can go to the village school. They take them right up to leaving age there.'

May nodded.

'Oh, Daddy.' Anna turned her dark, violet eyes up to look at her father. 'Are there going to be bombs?'

'I'll not lie to you, love. There might be. But we might be lucky in Lincoln. They'll be making for the bigger cities rather than here.'

It seemed a forlorn hope and the two adults both

knew it. Ken was trying to make light of it for Anna's sake. He didn't want to frighten their ten-year-old daughter. The fact that he was leaving them and that they might have to leave their home in the city had been enough to give the imaginative child nightmares already.

As the train whistle blew, May clung to Ken. He bent and kissed her hard, murmuring, 'Oh, Maisie, my darling Maisie.' Then he was sweeping Anna into a bear hug again and she was crying against the rough serge of his coat. 'Don't go, Daddy. Please don't go.' But with one last, desperate kiss he turned from them both and was gone, lost amongst the throng climbing aboard the train.

When May and Anna returned home, the terraced house was strangely quiet without him. It took May days to stop automatically laying a place for her husband at the table and every night Anna went to stand by Ken's chair to say goodnight, only to stand staring down at the empty place.

Halfway through his training, he had a precious forty-eight-hour pass and then, later, a longer leave. The day before he had to return to his unit, Ken told May quietly, 'This has been what they call embarkation leave. I'm to be posted abroad when I get back.'

May buried her face against his shoulder and asked in a muffled voice, 'Do you know where?'

'No, love. I don't.' Ken said no more. Rumours had been rife around the camp before he had left, but no one knew for sure. And even if he had known, he would not have told May. Now he murmured, 'Don't tell Anna till I've gone. Please, Maisie.'

It was bad enough having to tell the wife he adored,

but to see his beloved daughter's stricken face was more than he could bear.

It was not how he wanted to remember Anna.

Ken Milton was amongst the first British troops to arrive in France in the middle of October. At the same time, a general call-up of men over twenty years of age started and May said mournfully, 'Your daddy would have had to go now anyway.' She scrunched up the newspaper and turned to Anna, plastering a bright smile on her face. 'Perhaps he was right to go. First to go, first to come home, eh?'

Ken had been wrong about one thing. Children were not evacuated from Lincoln but brought to the city from other places deemed to be at far greater risk.

'Your teacher's asked us to take an evacuee,' May told Anna. Biting her thumbnail, she said, 'There's thousands arriving on the train from Leeds. It's not that I don't want to help – of course I do – but I think we ought to go out to the farm. It's what Daddy would want us to do. We'll go to Grandpa. He'll look after us.' May shuddered. 'I hate us being here on our own.'

The protest from her daughter that May had expected – probably hoped to hear – was not forthcoming. Secretly Anna was delighted. She loved her grandpa Luke and she loved the farm.

The following day May locked up the house, glancing back as they turned the corner at the top of the road. Would they ever see their home again? she was thinking, but she kept these thoughts to herself, trying to make their evacuation to the country seem like a holiday. Dragging three heavy suitcases, they caught the bus from the city centre which passed through the village close to the farm. Then they walked the last few hundred yards down the lane.

Rosa came out into the yard, her arms held wide. '"It's an ill wind that blows nobody any good",' she quoted and laughed loudly. 'See, if it wasn't for the war, we wouldn't be having you come to live with us for a while, would we?'

May glanced at Anna. Missing her husband and now having to leave her city home were causing May grief, but Anna pulled her hand from her mother's grasp and ran towards her grannie, arms outstretched.

'Can I feed the hens for you and c'lect the eggs?' she gabbled excitedly.

'Course you can, lovey.' Then, catching sight of May's doleful face, Rosa said kindly, 'Now, come along, May. This horrible war will soon be over and Ken will be safely back home. But in the meantime,' she said with a chuckle, 'I can't deny that it's lovely for Grandpa and me to have you here.'

Anna flung her arms around her grandmother's ample waist and pressed her cheek to the woman's comforting warmth. 'Oh, Grannie, I do love the farm and being here with you and Grandpa. And if only Daddy were here too, it would be perfect.'

Above the girl's head, mother and grandmother exchanged a solemn glance.

Thirty-Two

'Anna, this is Jed Rower.' Luke pointed with a gnarled finger towards the youth standing awkwardly near the cowhouse. 'He's Bill Tomalin's nephew.'

Bill Tomalin owned the farm adjacent to Luke's farm and Anna had heard the grown-ups talking about the family.

'Poor old Bill and his missis. Lost their only son in the twenties. Measles. You wouldn't think measles was a killer, now would you? But there you are . . .' Anna remembered her grandfather talking as he carved the Sunday roast.

'Poor little mite,' Rosa had put in, bustling between the scullery and the kitchen table. 'He was so poorly. And you caught it off him, our May. Do you remember?'

May had wrinkled her forehead. 'Was that the time I had to lie in a darkened room?'

'Yes, that's it. They reckoned the illness affected the eyesight and told everybody to keep their bairns in bed and in the dark. Eh dear, what a time it was. And poor little Jack didn't get better. I remember going to the funeral. What a terrible sight it is to see a child's coffin.' The tender-hearted Rosa wiped her eyes with the corner of her apron.

'So now,' Luke had gone on, 'there's only his sister's boy, Jed, for Bill to leave his farm to. Mind you, he's a real good lad. Comes at holiday times and at weekends if he can get here. And he'll help me out if I need it.'

Now, as the two youngsters stood in the yard staring at each other, Luke said, 'Jed's left school now, Anna, and he's come to live at his uncle's. Wants to be a farmer, don't you, lad?'

'That's right, Mester Clayton. Never wanted nowt else.'

Luke beamed at him. 'That's what I like to hear.' He wagged his finger at the young man. 'And no running off to the war when you gets old enough. You hear me?'

Jed grinned. 'Oh I reckon it'll be over long before then, mester.'

'Aye well, that's as mebbe. I 'ope so, lad. I do. But these wars have a terrible habit of going on a lot longer than them there politicians reckon. Any road – ' Luke turned and put his hand on Anna's shoulder – 'at least this war's brought Anna and her mam to live with us for a while.'

Jed, with merry hazel eyes, fair curling hair and a wide grin, glanced at her and nodded. Anna smiled shyly and then dropped her gaze.

'Well now, I can't stand here yakkerin' all day,' Luke said. 'There's work to do.'

'Can I help, sir?' Jed asked. 'Uncle Bill said you was a bit short-handed with a couple of your regular hands going off to the war.'

Luke beamed at him. 'Ya can, lad. We've two Land Army wenches due soon, but in the meantime I'm a bit stretched. So a bit of help'd be worth a lot of pity, as they say. Now, can you milk cows?'

Jed nodded.

'Right then, you set to in there – ' he jerked his

thumb over his shoulder towards the cowhouse – 'whilst I get the next lot from the field. Now where's that dratted dog of mine?' He gave a shrill whistle and a black and white collie came tearing round the corner of the building, sliding to a halt in front of his master.

'Come on, dog, let's get them cows in.'

Anna laughed. 'But he's a sheepdog, Grandpa.'

Luke winked at her. 'Aye, but Buster dun't know that, does he? He just thinks he's got to round up any kind of creature. Have you seen him with the geese?'

Anna shook her head.

'That's what I trained him with. They're every bit as cantankerous and awk'ard as sheep.'

'I don't like geese. They're nasty, hissy things.'

Luke laughed. 'An' you don't like the cows 'cos they kick. What do you like, lass?'

Anna beamed. 'I like sheep.'

Luke put his arm about her shoulders. 'Right, then lass. Whilst you'm here I'll teach you all I know about sheep. How's that?'

Anna glanced up at the wrinkled, weather-beaten face. Solemnly, she said, 'I'd like that very much, Grandpa.'

Soon the country became resigned to being at war. Like the conflict which had begun twenty-five years earlier, it was not over by Christmas. The beginning of 1940 was a bleak time and scarcely a minute of the day went by when May and Anna were not thinking about Ken. But despite the ever-present worry, Anna blossomed in the fresh air and country life. She didn't even mind the heavy snowfall that arrived in February. She revelled in tramping through the deep drifts to rescue 'her' sheep.

'Now, lass, I've got summat for you.' Grandpa Luke's blue eyes were twinkling mischievously beneath his shaggy eyebrows.

'A present?' Anna's voice was high with excitement. 'For me?'

From behind his back Luke produced a strangely shaped parcel – long and thin but wider at one end. Anna ripped away the wrapping paper to reveal a shepherd's crook fashioned in every detail to be a small replica of Luke's own.

The girl gasped with delight. 'Oh, Grandpa, it's lovely. Thank you.' She kissed the old man's cheek and was tickled by his moustache.

'There now, when you go out with Buster to fetch the sheep you'll be a real shepherdess.' Luke wagged his forefinger at her and drew his eyebrows together in mock severity. 'But there is a catch. You've got to earn the title. You'll have to learn to help with the lambing and the shearing and the dipping. Even how to count them the shepherd's way.'

Anna was nodding so hard she felt as if her head might fall off. Her violet eyes were bright. 'I will, oh, I will. I want to learn everything, Grandpa,' the young girl told him solemnly. 'I want to stay on the farm for ever. I don't ever want to go back to the city.'

Tears filled the old man's rheumy eyes as he touched her cheek. 'Aye, lass, I reckon you don't.'

Since his disappointment that his own daughter had turned her back on country life, this was more than he had dared to hope for from his granddaughter.

Her instruction began that day, though at first she wasn't sure whether it was she giving Buster instructions or the dog showing her what needed to be done.

But soon the two became firm friends. It was almost as if the dog now belonged more to Anna than to Luke.

'He's still a working dog, lass,' the old man would remind her. 'And you mustn't make pets of the animals.'

Anna nodded, understanding. 'We're farmers, aren't we, Grandpa?'

'That's right,' the old man said, his voice hoarse with emotion. 'That's right, me little lass.'

The only reminder of the war was the distant drone of aircraft.

'What's that noise, Grandpa?' Anna asked the first time she heard them.

'Planes, lass. Hampdens, so they tell me. There's an aerodrome a few miles north from here.'

'Oh.' Anna was silent for a moment and then, in a small voice, she asked, 'Are they – are they going to drop bombs on the enemy?'

'Aye, mebbe.'

'But – how can they be sure they don't drop them on our soldiers?'

Luke smiled at her, his leathery face creasing into a thousand wrinkles – or so it seemed. 'Oh, they'll mind not to do that, love. They'll be aiming for things like enemy shipping, and if they do go over enemy territory it'll be things like bridges and railways and maybe factories that make equipment for the war.'

'That's what Daddy said the Jerries'd do to us,' Anna said. 'They might bomb Lincoln because he was sure the factories there would be making things for the war.'

'Aye well, lass, I reckon he could be right. Anyway,'

he added, putting his arm about her shoulders, 'that's why you've come here. To be safe with us, eh?'

Every day Luke would give his own weather forecast and try to guess whether they would hear the planes that night. 'Just look at that lovely sunset, lass. Ain't no better sight anywhere than a Lincolnshire sunset, to my mind. Sign of good weather, that is. They'll be flying tonight.' And then, in contrast, he would say, 'Don't reckon we shall hear them planes going out tonight. Bad sky this morning. Reckon we're in for a bit of a blow.'

But sometimes he would be wrong and, distantly, they'd hear the planes going out.

Each night Grandpa insisted that everyone was silent whilst he listened to the nine o'clock news on the wireless. Anna, sitting quietly, was obliged to listen too and so picked up the war news. Some of it she understood, but in her young, logical mind she still questioned the truth of her grandfather's assurances. If both sides were dropping bombs on each other, she couldn't understand how the British, whose army was over there, could be sure not to drop them on their own men.

Every night Anna knelt on the cold floor of her bedroom and prayed fervently for her father's safe return. But when she climbed into bed at last and lay down, she felt no reassurance that her prayers would be answered.

And then, at the end of May, they all listened with horror to the news of the evacuation from Dunkirk. They glanced fearfully at one another, knowing that Ken was out there somewhere.

A week later May received the telegram, forwarded

from their home in Lincoln, reporting that Kenneth Milton was missing, presumed killed.

'It's not fair, Grandpa. It's not fair. Why did Daddy have to get killed?'

Weeks after the news had come, Anna still could not accept it. Helping her grandfather with the haymaking, she walked beside him into the meadow to rake and toss the swathes of grass that had been cut the previous day.

In his gravelly voice, Luke said, 'Life isn't fair, lass. But we all have to make the best of it, whatever comes our way. I was in the last war. I volunteered right at the start. Just like your dad did.' Luke cast a wry glance at his granddaughter. 'He wouldn't listen to me, would he? Had to go an' do the same.' Luke's bushy white eyebrows drew together in a frown. 'Can't blame him, though,' he murmured, his thoughts far away. 'But I was lucky. I came back.'

He stood leaning on his rake, gazing into the distance as if he were seeing a ghostly regiment of long-dead comrades marching past. 'A lot of good men didn't come back. The war to end wars, they called it then, yet just over twenty years after it ended here we are plunged into another. I don't reckon them politicians will ever learn,' he ended bitterly. Then Luke seemed to shake himself and said briskly, 'This won't get the work done, lass. Come on now, put ya back into it.'

Anna spent a lot of time with her grandfather. When she was not attending the local school, she was by his side.

'She's as good as any farmhand,' Luke told Rosa.

'You should see her with the sheep.' He chuckled. 'I reckon she's given 'em all names. All thirty of 'em.'

'How did she take it when the lambs went? And does she know they've gone for slaughter?'

'She understands. I explained it all to her. Aye.' Luke gave a deep sigh of contentment. 'The farm'll be in safe hands when I'm gone.'

Rosa said seriously. 'Let's not talk about anyone else going yet. That little lass has had enough sadness in her life to last her a good few years. And as for our May . . .' Rosa shook her head and sighed. 'I don't know if she'll ever get over losing Ken.'

Luke lit his pipe and puffed at it, getting it well alight before he answered. 'She's young. She'll not forget him. Course she won't. But time is a healer, love. Given time, she'll mebbe meet someone else. Our May needs a man to lean on and I won't be here for ever.' He chuckled. 'Even if I'd like to be.'

Rosa said wryly, 'But what sort of man is she likely to find, eh? We're going to lose a whole generation of fellers again, just like we did last time. And what'll we be left with? You tell me that. The dregs, that's what.'

Luke twinkled at her mischievously. 'Well, I came back last time. Is that what I am then? The dregs?'

Rosa laughed. 'You tek it how ya like, Luke Clayton. If you remember – ' she nodded at him teasingly – 'I was engaged to that butcher feller just afore the last war. And he didn't come back, now did he?'

'Yeah, but if I remember you'd thrown him over before he ever went to the Front.'

They laughed together, easy in the knowledge that it was all just banter between them.

Their laughter faded and Rosa said pensively, 'It'd be nice to think that – in time – May could meet someone nice, 'cos you're right, she does need someone and it'd be nice for that little lass to have a daddy again.'

'But in the meantime – ' Luke opened his newspaper and spread it wide, scanning the pages for yet more news – 'she's got us.'

Thirty-Three

It was a cruel Fate that was listening at that moment to Luke's confident statement. Only three weeks later Rosa began to feel ill.

'I can't understand why I feel so tired all the time,' she said, sitting down in the wooden rocking chair beside the range after a morning's work. 'I can usually go all day without stopping, but now—'

'You're not as young as you used to be, Mam.'

'I'm only fifty-seven,' Rosa responded indignantly.

May eyed her mother. 'You've lost weight, too.'

'I always do in summer. We eat more salads an' that in the hot weather, don't we?' Rosa heaved herself out of the chair in an effort to prove there was nothing wrong with her. ''Spect I've got a bit of anaemia. I've had it before at this time of year.'

'Anaemia doesn't give you a pain in your tummy. I've seen you holding yourself. Look, you're doing it now.'

'It's just a bit of indigestion. Something I've eaten.'

May cast her a wry look. 'I think you ought to see the doctor, Mam.'

'Aye, sometime. I'll go when I've time.'

A week later even Luke was persuading her to go. 'I'll take you into the village mesen and make sure you do see him,' he declared. 'You're not right, woman. Even I can see that. The weight's dropping off you.'

'All right, then. I'll go.'

Luke and his daughter exchanged a startled glance. The fact that Rosa was agreeing to see a doctor was enough for alarm bells to start ringing in both their minds.

They had good reason to be fearful. The doctor sent Rosa into Lincoln for further tests and two weeks later he called at the farm.

'Run along into the yard, missy,' he said in a kindly manner to Anna. 'I need to talk to your grandpa and grannie. May – ' he had known the Clayton family for years and had attended May's birth in this very farmhouse – 'you stay, please.'

He sat down at the table, his face solemn as he explained gently that the consultant had found a growth in Rosa's stomach.

'We can operate, but—' His silence and the unspoken words hung in the air.

'Oh no,' May cried, her hand flying to her mouth. 'Oh Mam, no.'

Luke took his wife's hand and held on to it tightly. 'This operation? If she has it, there's a chance?'

The doctor glanced from Luke to Rosa and back again. He knew them so well, knew that they were strong enough to be told the truth. He wasn't so sure about May. She was crumbling before his eyes. But then, he reminded himself, this was the second lot of terrible news she'd had in a few short months. 'Fifty–fifty.'

Rosa seemed to be taking the news calmly. 'Well, I've had a good life. And May's home now to look after her dad . . .'

'Mam,' May cried, tears flooding down her cheeks, 'don't say such things. You'll get better. You'll have the operation and you'll get better. I know you will. Oh Mam, you have to. I – I can't bear to lose you too.'

Luke walked out of the house with the doctor.

'I'm so sorry, old friend. I wish there was more I could say, more I could do.'

'You've told us the truth and now we know what we have to face.' Luke glanced across to where Anna was playing with Buster. The girl was laughing at the dog's antics, their game driving away some of the sadness from her face. 'Though how I'm going to tell that little lass, I don't know.'

'Like me to do it for you?'

Luke shook his head. 'No. Thanks, but it'll come better from me. If she sees we're facing up to it, then—'

He said no more and the doctor nodded agreement, but he was thinking that May was not going to be of much use.

As if reading his thoughts, Luke said softly, 'She's stronger than her mam, I reckon. She'll be all right. She'll be all right with me.'

Wordlessly, the doctor patted Luke's shoulder and went towards his car.

Rosa was called in for the operation only a week later. It was a tense and anxious time for the family and visiting Rosa in the city hospital proved difficult with the war restrictions. There was no telephone at Clayton's Farm so it was the doctor who once again brought the news.

The moment he stepped out of his car and went towards Luke, who was standing near the cowshed, the old man knew the news was bad.

Dr Phillips shook his head sadly. 'I'm so sorry, Luke. She came through the operation itself well, but back on the ward she suffered a massive heart attack. There was nothing anyone could do.'

Luke nodded wordlessly.

'If it's any comfort, old friend, the end was quick. If she'd survived and the cancer had returned, she would have had a lingering and very painful death.'

'Aye, well.' Luke sniffed hard, but was unable to control the break in his voice. 'Aye well, that's summat to be thankful for.'

The family was devastated. It was almost worse than the loss of Ken, for that had been a possibility from the moment he volunteered. But that Rosa – laughing, good-hearted Rosa – should die so quickly was hard to take.

'If only we'd had more time,' May wept. 'I can't believe it.'

Luke, though suffering his loss inside, seemed on the surface to accept the blow more easily than May. He had seen a lot more of life – and of death – than his daughter.

'You couldn't have asked for her to go on suffering. She were nowt but skin and bone by the end. You wouldn't let an animal suffer like that, lass. Now would you?'

May shook her head and murmured the very same words her daughter had used only months earlier. 'But it's so unfair, Dad. It's so unfair.'

Anna's grief was silent. She shed her tears in private, anxious not to add to her grandfather's grief or to upset her mother even more. May did her best to take over the running of the farmhouse, but Rosa, born to be a farmer's wife, was a hard act to follow.

May wept through the days. 'I can't get the Yorkshire puddings to rise like Mam did,' she moaned on the first Sunday after the funeral. 'I've burnt the meat and the gravy's lumpy.'

'Ne'er mind, love,' Luke said placidly. 'That range oven's always been a bit temperamental. Even your mam used to grumble about it. You'll soon get the hang of it, though.'

'But that's just it. I don't want to get the hang of it,' May wailed. 'I want to go back to Lincoln. I want to go home.'

Luke said nothing, but Anna had seen the deep hurt in his eyes. That his daughter should consider the little terraced house in a back street of the city to be home, instead of the farm where she had been born and brought up, cut the old man to the quick.

Anna's confidant was Jed, who came to see her the morning after the funeral. 'I'm real sorry about your gran, Anna. She was a lovely lady. Always so friendly. And cook – by heck, I've never tasted apple pasties like hers. Even me auntie Sue can't make 'em like Mrs Clayton could.' He tried to lighten the gravity of their conversation by adding, 'But don't you tell 'er I said so, else she'll chase me with me uncle's shotgun.'

Anna smiled thinly. Then Jed, trying to draw her out, said soberly, 'It must be very hard for you. First your dad and now your gran. Difficult for all your family. Look – ' he hesitated, his face reddening – 'if there's ever owt I can do to help you, you've only got to say. I aren't very good with words, but – but I'm a good listener. Sometimes – well – sometimes it helps just to be able to talk about it. And maybe you can't talk about it at home because – well – they're upset an' all. I don't mean I'm not,' he went on swiftly, lest she should misunderstand him. 'She'll be badly missed round here. Everybody liked her.'

The number of mourners at the funeral had told Anna that. The line following the coffin had stretched a hundred yards or more.

'But, well—' Jed was still stumbling on, trying in his youthful way to bring comfort to the young girl, 'I weren't family.'

Anna smiled at him through her tears. 'Thanks, Jed,' she said huskily. 'You're – very kind.'

Jed became her constant companion. Luke had taught her about sheep, but it was Jed she watched hedging and ditching, he who helped her with a broody hen and watched as the eggs cracked and little yellow chicks emerged. It was Jed who showed her how to milk the cows and helped her overcome her fear of their restless hooves.

'I won't ever like them as much as the sheep.' She laughed. 'But I'm not quite so scared of them now. Thanks to you.'

'You've got gentle fingers. You'd make a good milkmaid.'

Anna pulled a face. 'I'd rather be a shepherdess. That's what I really want to be.'

He took her fishing in the stretch of the River Brant that ran through both her grandfather's farm and his uncle's. And it was Jed who stood with his arm about her shoulders, comforting her whenever any of their animals were loaded into the back of the lorry to be driven to market.

'How's ya mam?' he asked gently one day.

Anna shrugged. 'She's running the house better now.'

She even managed to smile. 'Her cooking's improved, but she still cries a lot.' Anna's voice broke a little as she added, 'She – wants to go back to the city.'

Jed looked down at her, his blue eyes sober. 'What about you?' he asked softly. 'Do you want to go back?'

Vehemently, Anna shook her head. 'No. I never want to go back. I want to stay here for ever and ever.'

It was the dream of an eleven-year-old child, but silently Jed prayed that her wish would still be the same when Anna was grown. 'I hope you do,' he said softly.

Thirty-Four

Clayton's Farm, handed down through the generations from Luke's great-grandfather, was situated a few miles to the south of Lincoln. It had passed from son to son, but now there were only May and Anna to take it on should anything happen to Luke. The old man couldn't hide the fact that his dearest wish was to see them both living back at the farm for good.

'It's silly to keep paying rent on an empty house in the city,' Luke told May bluntly.

'But we'll be going back,' May argued, trying to hold out.

'Look, love,' Luke said, trying to be more gentle, 'even if you do go back to town one day – ' the words were said reluctantly, but he had to accept the fact that it was a strong possibility. If his daughter had her way, she'd be back to city life in a trice – 'surely you'd be better to have a fresh start in a different house? Do you really want to take that little lass' – Luke almost choked on the words – 'back to a house full of memories of her daddy? Do *you* want to go back there?'

May sighed. 'I don't know, Dad. Sometimes my memories of Ken are so vivid it's almost as if he's going to walk into the room at any minute. At others, it seems as if all those years were just a dream and never really happened.'

'Well, they did and you've a lovely daughter to prove

it. We've all got our memories – that's what keeps us going,' Luke said, thinking back down the years to all the happy times he'd spent with his beloved Rosa. 'Hold on to them, May, don't ever lose them. But it doesn't mean we have to stop living. You've still got a lot of your life left and Ken wouldn't have wanted you to mourn him for ever. And that little lass has got all of hers to come yet. Let her choose the path she wants to take, May.' He put his head on one side and regarded her solemnly. 'I didn't stand in the way of you marrying Ken Milton and letting him take you to live in the city, even though I wanted you to stay here.'

Easy tears filled May's eyes. 'You didn't like him, Dad, did you?'

Luke sighed. 'Not at first, no, but I think it was only because I knew he'd take you away from us. Later I came to see that he was a fine young man. A good husband and father.'

'Just because he volunteered for the war – like you did years ago?' There was a bitter edge to her tone now.

Luke sighed, but was honest enough to admit, 'Well, I saw then that he had the qualities I admire in a feller. It was a pity it took a war to show me that, but that was my pig-headedness. I'll own up to that.'

So, May relinquished the tenancy of the terraced house in Lincoln and moved their belongings and bits of furniture into the rambling farmhouse.

For most of the time the war seemed very far away, with only the drone of aircraft overhead to remind them. And, of course, the rationing, as May, who had now taken over the running of the household, was ever quick to tell them. But, living on a farm, they were luckier than most. By 1942 the last of Luke's young farmhands had joined the army, leaving only Luke and an old man who had worked on Clayton's Farm all his life. And even he was able to work less and less.

'Tis the arthritis in me old bones,' he complained. 'I'm not as young as I used to be.'

Despite her sympathy for the old farmhand, Anna always wanted to giggle when she heard him say that. Not about the arthritis, but about his age. Was anyone ever as young as they once were? she thought.

Jed helped whenever he could, but his uncle's farm was short-handed too.

'I don't know why they all want to go rushing off,' Luke grumbled. 'They're in a reserved occupation. Just wanting to play the hero.'

'Well, you did,' May retorted and added bitterly, 'and so did Ken.'

'Aye, you're right, lass.' The old man's eyes softened. 'I suppose I should understand better than anyone. Anyway,' he went on briskly, 'we're to have a couple of Land Army girls. Can you do with 'em in the house?'

May smiled and Luke realized how hard May was trying to be more like her mother. Rosa had wanted nothing more from life than to be a good farmer's wife. To their disappointment, Luke and Rosa had only been blessed with one child, though they would have loved more. After a difficult birth with May, Dr Phillips had warned Rosa not to have any more children. So Rosa contented herself with her husband, her daughter and the extended family of their farmworkers and all the extra help that came at haymaking, harvest and shearing. Rosa was at her happiest when she had an army to feed.

May hadn't quite got to that level yet, but she said

now, 'It'll be lovely to have some young folks about the place. Company for Anna too.' *And me as well*, she thought privately.

The sight of the two Land Army girls climbing out of the back of the lorry a few days later was a welcome one for Luke; May, too, smiled a greeting, but their reasons were very different. Luke was glad to see more help arriving, even if he expected it to take a few weeks for the two girls to settle in and learn the ropes. May was just glad to see two young women nearer her own age, who looked as if they might bring a little fun and laughter to the back of beyond, which was how she thought of Clayton's Farm.

May hurried out to greet them. The girls were dressed identically in the Women's Land Army 'uniform': open-necked shirts, green pullovers, brown corduroy knee breeches, long thick fawn socks and brown brogues.

'Hello. I'm May Milton. Come along in. You must be hungry. How far have you come?'

The two girls were bouncy, bubbly and quite pretty in a brash sort of way. The shorter of the two, who had blue eyes, shoulder-length blonde hair and a round, merry face, held out her hand. 'Hello, I'm Betty Purves.'

'Better known as Purvey the Curvy, because she curves in all the right places,' the other girl said. 'And I'm Rita Mackinder.' Rita was tall with short, curly dark brown hair and brown eyes. 'The skinny one.'

May shook hands with them. 'You're both very welcome. Come along in, do.'

The girls heaved their luggage from the back of the lorry and waved a cheery goodbye to the driver.

'Don't forget the dance next Saturday, Harry,' Betty called after him.

'It's a date, love.' He waved as he started the engine.

'Oh you!' Rita pretended indignation. 'How many fellers do you need? What about Douglas?'

Betty patted her long golden hair. 'Safety in numbers, pet. Come on, where's that tea the nice lady was offering? I'm parched.'

Later, when Anna and Luke walked into the house together, the kitchen was alive with noisy laughter. May, her eyes more alight than they had been for months, said, 'Oh, come and meet these two. They're a scream. They ought to be on the stage.'

When the introductions were done, Luke said, 'Well now, where are you two lasses from then?'

'Me? I'm from up north,' Betty said. 'Near Newcastle, but Rita here, she's from Sheffield. We've never been to Lincolnshire before. Neither of us.' She pulled a comical face. 'I thought it was supposed to be flat, but we tried walking up Steep Hill in Lincoln last week. I don't call that flat!'

Anna stared at the two girls, fascinated by the way they talked. She'd heard a Yorkshire voice before, but never a Geordie accent. The way Betty's lilting voice rose at the end of each sentence, almost as if she was asking a question, delighted the young girl.

Luke was chuckling. 'It's flat in the south of the county, in the fens and also along the east coast. But we've got the Wolds and the Lincoln Heights to give us a few hills.' He nodded at them both. 'Not like where you come from, I admit, but it suits us.'

Rita nudged Betty. 'It'll be safe for you.' They both laughed and Betty's face was tinged with pink.

'We were on a farm in Derbyshire until last month and she was driving a tractor on a steep slope. Going down hill, like this – ' Rita sloped her hand to demonstrate – 'and ended up in the river at the bottom. The farmer weren't right pleased.'

'Remind me not to let you loose in the field that borders the Brant then,' Luke said, but his eyes were twinkling.

'You can talk, Rita Mackinder. What about you and cows then?' Betty leant across the table towards Luke and now it was Rita's turn to look embarrassed. 'I hope you've got hundreds of cows, Mister. Our Rita loves 'em. Can't *wait* to get her hands on them.' Laughing, she pretended she was milking a cow.

'We've only got seventeen now, but most of them are good milkers.'

Betty hooted with laughter and dug her friend in the ribs. 'There you are, Reet. You'll be all right.'

Mystified, Luke, May and Anna stared at the two girls. Anna was the first to realize the joke. 'She's teasing you, isn't she? You don't really like them, do you?'

Rita pulled a wry face. 'Sorry, no. I don't. I got kicked badly at the farm in Derbyshire and I've been frightened of them ever since.'

'Never mind,' Anna said kindly. 'You can help with the sheep, can't she, Grandpa?'

'Course she can, love. We don't want anyone being hurt here.'

'You'll like sheep. They're lovely and gentle.'

'You're very kind,' Rita said, serious for a moment, 'but I wouldn't want it to look as if I'm trying to get out of doing summat I'm supposed to.'

Luke laughed. 'Don't worry, lass, we won't think that of you. Besides – ' his eyes twinkled – 'there's plenty else you can do.'

They joined in his laughter. It was the happiest sound the farmhouse kitchen had heard in months.

'We're going to a dance next Saturday in Lincoln,' Betty told May. 'My feller's picking us up. Why don't you come with us?'

The two girls had settled in remarkably quickly and now everyone felt they were part of the family.

'Oh, I don't know. It – it wouldn't seem right. I – I lost my husband at Dunkirk and then my mother died soon after . . .'

Looking unusually serious, Betty said gently, 'You can't live in the past, pet.'

'Well, no, but . . . It just seems a little too soon. That's all.'

'How about letting Anna come with us, then?'

Now May shook her head firmly. 'Oh no. She's far too young.'

'Is she?' Betty sounded surprised. 'How old is she?'

'Thirteen.'

'Thirteen! I thought she was at least fifteen. She looks it.'

'She's tall for her age. She's grown even in this last year. I expect it's living on the farm. She's filled out.'

Betty laughed as she ran her hands down her own body. 'And in all the right places. I'll have a rival for Miss Curvy, nineteen forty-two, if I don't watch it.' They laughed and then Betty added, 'But, yeah, you're right. She is a bit young to be going to dances, specially in the city. We get a lot of the RAF lads there.' Betty's eyes sparkled at the thought. 'Tell you what, though. We'll take her to the pictures sometime. My feller's got something to do with one of the cinemas there. He'll tell us when there's a nice film on we can take her to. You'd let her go there with us, wouldn't you?'

May nodded. 'That'd be very kind of you.'

'Oh, go on.' Betty flapped her hand at May. 'We love it here. You're very good to us and as for Pops . . .' It was the name that Betty had christened Luke. 'He's a real poppet.'

May laughed. She'd never heard her father referred to as 'a poppet' before, but the endearment suited him. Her face sobered as she said pensively, 'I wish you could have met my mother. You'd have loved her.'

Betty couldn't bear anyone to be maudlin for more than a couple of minutes, so she patted May's hand and said, 'I'm sure we would. I bet you take after her, don't you?'

May sighed. 'I really wish I did. But I – I don't think I'm quite as strong a character as she was.' She bit her lip, reluctant to confide even to the friendly Betty that she hated the life on the farm. She was only biding her time until the war was over and she could go back home.

'Must be off,' Betty said, not one for analysing life too closely. 'Mustn't keep the cows waiting. I still can't remember all their names. And as for the sheep . . . I never knew anyone to give names to their sheep before.'

May laughed now. 'We don't. Cows have always had names, but naming the sheep was Anna. She loves them.'

'And that dog, Buster. He never leaves her side, does he? He was missing the other afternoon and I asked Pops where he was. "Oh he'll be down at the school," he said, "waiting for Anna to come out." And sure enough, there he was, loping alongside of her when she rode into the yard on her bike.'

At that moment, Anna and Buster were out in the fields with Luke's flock of thirty ewes and their twenty-four lambs.

Anna stood with her hand on Buster's head. 'The lambs'll have to go in a month or two,' she told the dog sadly. 'Most of them. But I think Grandpa is going to keep three female lambs to build up his flock. That's nice, isn't it?'

Beside her the dog looked up at her adoringly, his long pink tongue lolling. He gave a little bark, as if he understood her every word. 'Come on, boy, we'd better go home. We've got those two little lambs to feed that lost their mother.'

Minutes later, Betty stood watching as Anna prepared a bottle to feed the lambs. 'You really love the silly creatures, don't you, pet?' she teased the young girl, shaking her head and pretending to be mystified. 'Can't understand why. They never do what you want 'em to do. If you want 'em to go to the right, they'll go left, sure as eggs.'

Anna only grinned as she held a motherless lamb firmly under her arm to feed it with a bottle.

'Take no notice of her,' she pretended to whisper to the lamb, but making sure that Betty heard. 'She dun't know what she's talking about.'

Betty laughed. 'You could be right there, pet. But give me a tractor to drive any day. Least I can steer it where I want it to go.'

Anna looked up and grinned saucily. ''Cept when you nearly drove it into the river last week. When you first came here, Rita said you'd done the same thing in Derbyshire.'

Betty pulled a face. 'Well, yeah, I did that time, but I didn't with your grandpa's tractor. I only got a bit too close. And don't you go telling Pops, else he'll not let me drive it again.'

Anna giggled. 'As long as you are nice to my sheep.'

Betty laughed. 'Little minx!' she said fondly and then winked. 'It's a deal.'

They heard the noise of Betty's feller's car even before it turned into the yard gate. The roar of an engine being driven at full speed coming closer and closer down the lane, the skid of tyres as it swung in through the gate and the squeal of brakes as it came to a stop. Luke came out of the barn and stood frowning at the sleek, open-topped sports car standing in the middle of his yard.

The driver hoisted himself up and agilely swung his legs over the low door without opening it. He came towards Luke, his hand outstretched. He was dressed in a checked suit and a trilby and sported a neat moustache.

'Douglas Whittaker, sir. How do?'

Luke took the proffered hand, but glanced down at the man's brown and white shoes. 'Not the place for those, young feller. You'll get 'em messed up.'

Douglas laughed. Although he was young compared with Luke, he was in his late thirties. He gave off the appearance of being a man of the world. Luke's knowing eyes narrowed as he took in Douglas Whittaker's appearance. So this was Betty's feller. He hoped it wasn't serious. Luke was becoming fond of the two Land Army girls and this wasn't the sort of man he would like to see courting anyone belonging to him. He gave a grunt. It was nowt to do with him, he told himself sharply. 'Come along in while you wait for the lasses. 'Spect they're still titivating.'

Douglas guffawed. 'Making themselves beautiful for me, eh? That's what I like to hear.' He pulled a gold cigarette case from his pocket, snapped it open and held it out towards Luke. 'Do you smoke, sir?'

Luke eyed the long, slim cigarettes. American, by the look of them. 'Only a pipe,' he murmured. And then, remembering his manners, added, 'Thanks all the same.'

'What brand of baccy do you smoke? I can get you some.' Douglas tapped the side of his nose and winked. 'Know what I mean?'

Oh yes, Luke knew what he meant. He was a black marketeer by the sound of it. Luke had heard about the goings on, but he'd never been approached directly before.

He turned his back on Douglas as he replied shortly, 'I don't smoke a lot. I've plenty for what I need.'

This time he added no word of thanks.

As he ushered the visitor into the farmhouse kitchen, May hurried forward, wiping her floury hands on her apron. 'You must be Betty's young man. Do come in. I don't think they'll be long.'

In the corner by the range, Anna was feeding a lamb with a bottle.

'Hello, young lady.' Douglas knelt beside her and touched the animal's fine, woolly coat. Buster, sitting close by on the hearth, gave a deep-throated growl. Hearing it, Luke almost laughed aloud. *You and me both, boy*, he thought, but he said nothing.

Anna, however, spoke sternly to the dog. 'Stop it, Buster. This is Betty's friend. Naughty dog.'

Buster lay down, his nose on his paws, but he continued to eye the stranger with suspicion.

There was the sound of clattering high heels on the

stairs and Betty and Rita, dressed in pretty cotton dresses, swept into the kitchen.

Douglas held his arms wide. 'Well, well. Now if that isn't worth waiting for.' His gaze swept them up and down and then his grin widened. 'But if I'm not much mistaken, you're not quite dressed yet, are you?'

Betty and Rita exchanged a glance. 'Cheek of the devil,' Betty said, fluffing her hair.

Douglas laughed, holding out his hands in supplication. 'No offence, ladies.' He fished in his pocket and pulled out two packages. 'I just thought perhaps you could make use of these.'

Tearing open their gifts, the girls exclaimed over the nylon stockings, whilst May watched enviously and glanced down at her own thick lisle ones. Betty threw her arms round Douglas. 'Oh, you darling. I might have known. There's nothing you can't get, if you've a mind, is there?' She drew back and glanced at Luke and then at May. She prodded Douglas in the chest. 'So if there's anything you want, he's your man.'

'If I'd known there was another lovely young lady, I'd have brought another pair.' Douglas gave a little bow towards May and murmured, 'Maybe next time, eh?'

May smiled uncertainly but Luke's only response was to turn on his heel and leave the house.

Thirty-Five

Douglas became a regular visitor to the farm, along with other 'followers' of the two girls. One was a very good-looking RAF pilot with wavy black hair.

'He looks like a film star,' Anna breathed, watching him with wide eyes.

'Aye aye,' Betty said, winking mischievously. 'Our Anna might only be thirteen but she knows a good-looking feller when she sees one. I'll have to keep me eye on you, pet, else you'll be stealing them from under my nose with those lovely eyes of yours.'

'Oh I reckon you're safe, our Betty,' Rita chirped up. 'Anna's got a boyfriend.'

Anna turned wide eyes on the grinning girl. 'What do you mean? I haven't got a boyfriend.'

'Haven't you? You could have fooled me. Well, I know a very nice young feller who'd like to fill the part.'

'Who?'

'Jed, of course.'

'*Jed?* But he works here. And he's heaps older than me.'

'Yeah, course he is. All of five years, but it doesn't stop him making sheep's eyes at you. Oops, sorry for the pun.'

'He doesn't,' Anna denied, but could not help blushing.

*

'You know Charlie, the pilot officer,' Betty said one evening, only a week later.

'That handsome one with black hair?' Anna asked as May looked up enquiringly.

Betty nodded, biting her lip. 'His plane never came back. Went down somewhere over the Channel, they say. The whole crew are missing.'

'That's terrible,' May said, her hand to her mouth to still its trembling. 'Oh the poor boy. He was only nineteen, wasn't he?'

Anna bent her head over the rug she was learning to make from scraps of material so that the others would not see the tears in her eyes. To think that that lovely-looking young man was now dead brought back vividly all the sadness about her own daddy.

Betty nodded. 'Yeah.' She sat for a moment as if lost in thought, then she stood up quickly, 'Still, life has to go on, pet, hasn't it? At least there's no chance of that happening to good old Douglas.'

In his chair in the corner, Luke shook his newspaper and sniffed.

'What was that, Pops?' Betty said.

'Nothing,' came the short reply. 'Nothing at all.'

'Are you serious about this Douglas?' Luke asked after supper the following evening.

'Me?' Betty laughed. 'I'm not serious about any feller, Pops.' She beamed at him. 'Only you, mebbe.'

They all laughed, but no one had missed the underlying message of Luke's question. Betty put her head on one side. 'You don't like him.' It was a statement rather than a question.

Luke shrugged but said nothing.

Betty laughed again. 'I'll take that as a "no" then, shall I?'

Now Luke muttered, 'Seems a bit of a flash type to me. What I'd call a spiv.'

'Dad!' May exclaimed, scandalized at her father's blunt remark, but Betty only grinned. 'You could say that, Pops, yes.' She winked at Luke, as if sharing a secret. 'But he's good for a pair of stockings now and again, chocolates and even a new dress when my clothing coupons run out, to say nothing of keeping me well supplied with knicker elastic.'

Luke grunted and bit hard on the end of his pipe. He tried to look disapproving, drawing his shaggy white eyebrows together, but even Anna could see that he was having difficulty hiding the amused twinkle in his eyes. He removed his pipe from his mouth and jabbed the end of it towards Betty. 'Just be careful, lass, that's all.'

'I will, Pops, don't you worry,' Betty said merrily in her lilting accent, yet there was an underlying seriousness to her tone. 'He'd have to get up early to get one over on us Geordie lasses.'

May pursed her lips and said primly, 'It sounds to me as if it's you that's taking advantage of Douglas's generosity.'

Betty's eyebrows rose and she glanced at Luke and then back to May. Betty opened her mouth to make some retort but evidently thought better of it and closed it again, but suddenly there was a pink tinge to her cheeks and her eyes sparkled with anger.

'How's he come to be in these parts?' Luke put in, trying to smooth over the awkwardness. 'He's a Londoner by the sound of him, ain't he?'

'Yes. He worked in the West End theatres, but when the war started the audience figures dropped off and then the government closed all the theatres throughout the country. Course they opened up again after a few months, but even then what with the evacuation of a lot of people, the blackout and a lot of restrictions the government imposed, Dougie said it was hardly worthwhile opening. Anyway,' she went on, 'he'd got this mate in the Midlands, so he came up this way and now he's got a cinema in Lincoln and reckons he's doing very nicely, thank you.'

'You mean he owns it?' Luke asked.

Betty stared at him and blinked. 'Well, I never really asked him outright. But – well – he acts as if he does.'

Luke only reply was a disbelieving grunt.

'I think he seems rather nice,' May ventured, though she cast a nervous glance at her father. 'He's taking us all to the pictures on Friday night. He's asked me to go too.' She glanced at Betty. 'I – I hope you don't mind.'

'Course I don't, pet,' Betty said, her good humour restored. 'The more the merrier.'

It was certainly a merry outing on the following Friday evening. Douglas arrived with his usual flurry.

'I'm so sorry I can't fit you all into my car,' Douglas said. 'Maybe Anna could squeeze in the back seat, but it won't take all three of you ladies.'

'That's all right,' May said. 'We'll take the bus into town and meet you and Betty somewhere.'

'Nonsense,' Douglas retorted. 'You're our guests. You and Anna must come with me.' He turned to Betty. 'Sweetheart, you and Rita won't mind catching the bus just this once, eh?'

Betty glared at him but then, seeing the disappointment on Anna's face as if she feared the whole outing was suddenly in jeopardy, she shrugged her plump shoulders and smiled. Wagging her finger playfully at him, she said, 'Just this once then, mind.'

Douglas was a charming and attentive host. He took them for tea in a small cafe before the film. As they left, he crooked both his arms and offered one to Betty and the other to May. Rita and Anna fell into step behind them and, laughing, they walked towards the cinema.

As they stepped into the foyer a youth of seventeen or so was waiting for them.

'Here he is,' Douglas boomed, obviously expecting the boy to be there. 'Ladies, may I introduce my son, Bruce. Bruce, this is Betty, Rita and May. And this . . .' he gestured with a flourish, 'is May's daughter, Anna. Now I'll get the tickets. Front row circle and you two young ones can sit together.'

Bruce was thin, gangly some might have said. He had dark brown eyes and carrot-coloured hair. As often happened with his colouring, his face was covered with freckles. He grinned a welcome and nodded. 'Hello.'

Betty pulled her hand from Douglas's arm. 'I didn't know you had a son,' she said tartly. 'Got a wife hidden away somewhere an' all?'

For a moment Douglas's mask of jollity slipped. His mouth tightened and his eyes were resentful. 'For your information,' he snapped, 'I'm a widower. My wife died giving birth to our son.'

Betty, red in the face, was immediately contrite. 'I'm sorry.' She turned to the boy too. 'Oh pet, I am sorry.'

Anna's glance had gone at once to the boy. He had an odd expression on his face. He was looking at his father, Anna thought, as if he were surprised at what

Douglas had said. *But surely*, she thought, *he must know how his mother died?* Feeling for him, she moved to his side and, trying to change the subject, whispered, 'It looks like you're lumbered with me. I – I hope you don't mind.'

The boy dragged his gaze away from his father, who had gone to the box office and was now leaning forward to talk to the girl behind the glass. Bruce looked at her for a moment and then grinned suddenly. 'Course not. Pretty girl like you.' He leant closer. 'You've got lovely eyes. Almost violet, aren't they? Anybody ever told you that?'

Anna blushed and glanced down. Unused to compliments from strangers, she did not know how to handle it. *He's like his dad*, she thought, envying the boy his confident manner. *He's very different to Jed.* Jed was kind and always ready to help her but he was quiet and shy. This youth was outgoing, ready to take the lead and anything but shy.

'Come on,' he was saying. 'Let's go and find the best seats.'

'But – but we haven't got our tickets yet.'

'Ne'er mind about that. Dad's fixing it.' He took her hand and began to pull her towards the stairs leading up to the circle. 'Come on.'

'But won't the girl inside want to see our tickets?' Anna remembered her father taking them to the pictures. The usherette had inspected their tickets and torn them in half before guiding them down the steps to their seats with the narrow beam of light from her torch. Tears threatened at the memory, but Bruce was saying, 'Nah. Me dad runs this place. The girls all know me. I'm always here.'

Her eyes wide, Anna asked, 'Does he own it?'

The boy glanced at her, seemed to ponder for a moment and then said, 'Not exactly.' He seemed to be choosing his words carefully. 'But, like I say, he runs it.'

'I see.' Anna wasn't sure she did. But she surmised that Douglas must work for the people who did own it, that he was some kind of manager.

By the time they had chosen their seats, the adults had caught up. Their faces illuminated by the light from the screen, they sat in a line in the front row of the circle, Douglas between Betty and May, then Rita, Anna and, finally, Bruce on the end of the row.

Anna leant forward and glanced along the row. Douglas was laughing again. He was leaning towards her mother, whispering to her. May was smiling and nodding. Anna leant further forward to see Betty on Douglas's other side. She was staring straight ahead at the screen with, for her, a morose expression on her face.

In the intermission between the feature film and the supporting picture, the Pathé News boomed out the latest about the war, how the RAF had begun a round-the-clock bombing campaign. Sitting two seats away, Anna heard her mother's gulp and glanced to her left to see that May's head was bowed and that she had covered her face with her hands.

'There, there, May. Don't cry,' she heard Douglas say as he proffered a white handkerchief. Then Anna saw him put his arms along the back of the seat and around May's shoulders. He now sat half twisted towards May, his back towards Betty.

Throughout the whole of the second film, Betty stared stonily at the screen, looking neither to right nor left and speaking to no one.

Thirty-Six

They left Bruce on the steps of the cinema. 'You go straight home, boy,' Douglas instructed. 'I have to take these lovely ladies home and I might be late.' Anna caught him winking at his son.

Douglas had borrowed a bigger car so that he could take them all home together. As he drove, he sang at the top of his voice, but the three women and Anna were silent. When they arrived at the farm, May, sensing the atmosphere, hustled Anna upstairs to bed, with a hurried, 'Thank you for a lovely evening.'

Rita too yawned and said, 'Well, I'm for bed too. Nighty-night.'

'Don't I even get a cup of cocoa?' Douglas asked, pretending peevishness as the door closed behind the others, leaving him alone with Betty.

Betty flung her handbag on the table, sat down in Luke's chair by the range, kicked off her shoes and began to massage her feet. She glanced up at Douglas. 'You'll get a thick ear, m'lad, unless I get an explanation. And it'd better be good.'

Feigning innocence, Douglas said, 'Now what have I done?' Before Betty could answer, he grinned and wagged his forefinger at her. 'Oho, I do believe the lady's jealous. Just because I was kind to little May.'

'Jealous? Me? Huh, don't flatter yourself. It's nothing to do with May. It's your son I want to know about. You never told me you was married.' She glared up at him. 'That you'd *been* married.' She corrected herself, but even so her look suggested that she doubted his story. She nodded at him. 'I saw how your son looked. Surprised, that's what. As if he'd never been told. Now, sorry, but I don't believe a lad of his age hadn't been told before now that his mother had died having him. And if he hadn't,' she went on pointedly, 'then it wasn't a very nice way to break the news to the lad, was it?'

Douglas sighed and sat down opposite her. Adopting a hangdog look, he said, 'Betty, you're a woman of the world.'

Betty grimaced comically. 'Aye, aye, there's something coming if the flattery starts.'

Douglas gave an exaggerated sigh. 'Like I say, you'd understand, but I wasn't sure that May and her family would.'

Betty raised an eyebrow. 'Oh aye. It matters what May thinks, does it?'

'Not just May. All of them. You're living here and I want to keep seeing you. I want to be able to come here. And I'm not sure the old man likes me much anyway.' He laughed. 'I didn't want anything else rocking the boat.'

'So?'

'Well, it's not something a chap likes to admit. Dents the old confidence a bit. My wife left me five years ago. Ran off with some wide boy . . .'

Betty laughed inwardly. She liked Douglas. He was all right for a laugh and a good touch for the odd pair of nylons and other scarcities that made a girl's life a little easier in wartime, but she had no illusions about him. A wide boy, indeed! Seemed the former Mrs

Whittaker went for the same type each time, then. For if ever there was a wide boy it was Douglas himself. Old Pops was no fool. Betty smiled inwardly. He'd sussed out Douglas Whittaker from the moment he'd clapped eyes on him.

She managed to keep her face straight but she couldn't keep the sarcasm from her tone. 'Oh, I'm sorry. Left her lad an' all, did she? Tut, tut. Some women. I don't know. Divorced, are you then?'

'Yes, yes, that's it. We're divorced.'

She eyed him shrewdly, wondering. Still, it didn't make any difference to her. She was only out for a bit of fun. She was never going to be serious about a man like Douglas Whittaker.

Now that handsome pilot officer, Charlie – the one whose plane had gone down – now she could have been serious about him, poor boy.

Betty banished the unhappy thought and smiled. 'Well, pet, I won't tell anyone. Your secret's safe with me.'

Douglas leant across the hearth and planted a kiss on her mouth. 'You're a smasher, Betty. Now, about that cocoa . . .'

On the following Sunday afternoon Douglas brought Bruce out to the farm. 'He's done nothing but talk about you since Friday,' Douglas whispered to Anna. 'Quite smitten, he is.'

Anna blushed. At school the girls teased each other about different boys and Anna had a crush on a boy who sat two desks in front of her. She would sit in class staring at the back of his head and daydreaming until she earned a sharp reprimand from the teacher. But now here was Bruce's father telling her that his son was 'smitten' with her.

'Don't you tell him I said so, though,' Douglas was saying. 'It'll embarrass him. You know what lads of his age are like.'

She didn't really. The older boys at school took no notice of the younger girls, though she had to admit one or two had winked at her as they passed her in the corridor. There was really only Jed and he didn't count.

'Take him and show him the animals. He'd like to have a look around,' Douglas urged. 'Now, where's Betty?'

'She and Rita have gone on a bike ride. She thought you weren't coming today.'

'Ah yes, that's right. I did say I might not be able to make it, but then I found I could.' His smile widened. 'Then I'll just go and talk to your pretty mother, shall I?'

Anna nodded as Douglas beckoned his son over. 'Now you two, off you go and enjoy yourselves. Don't do anything I wouldn't, eh?' He guffawed loudly.

He turned towards the back door of the farmhouse, where May had appeared in the doorway. Arms outstretched, he walked towards her. 'Ah, May, how lovely you look.'

Anna watched the tinge of pink in her mother's cheeks and heard her girlish, nervous laugh. 'Betty's not here . . .'

Douglas lowered his voice, but Anna's sharp ears still heard him say, 'I know. I was hoping she wouldn't be. It's you I came to see. And I had to bring the lad. I hope you don't mind . . .'

'Of course not. He's very welcome. You both are.'

Anna watched them disappear inside. Then she

turned to Bruce. 'What do you want to see? Cows? Pigs? The sheep?'

The boy shrugged and kicked a stone. 'Don't mind. Let's just go for a walk, eh?'

'Right. Well, we'll see the sheep as we go. We've some lovely lambs . . .' Her face sobered. 'But they've to go soon.'

'To the market, you mean?'

Anna took a deep breath as she nodded. 'For slaughter.'

Bruce laughed and drew his hand across his throat, making a gurgling sound. Anna smiled thinly, but deep down she didn't think it was funny at all.

As they walked through the pasture, she saw Bruce eyeing the lambs. 'You've got a lot. How much do you get for each one then?'

Anna stared at him. '*I* don't know. They're Grandpa's.'

'Yeah, but you live here, don't you? It'll all be yours one day, won't it, when the old man snuffs it?' He glanced at her. 'Or has he got other grandchildren?'

Anna shook her head. 'No – no. There's only me. They only had one daughter, me mam.'

'So the farm'll go to your mam and then to you, won't it?'

'I – suppose so.' Anna was hesitant. She didn't even like to think about Grandpa dying. She'd lost her father and then her grandmother so recently that the thought of another death terrified her.

Bruce interrupted her thoughts. 'You ought to be taking an interest in the place.'

'I do. I help out a lot when I'm not at school. You can watch us do the milking later, if you like.'

'Yeah, that'd be fun,' he said, but his tone sounded

insincere. Almost sarcastic. Then he brightened. 'Come on, you can show me all the fields your grandpa owns.'

'There's a lot,' Anna said. 'I don't think we've time to see them all.'

There was a glint in the boy's eye as he glanced about, surveying all the land around him. 'He owns all this?' He waved his hand.

'Yes. Right down to the river.'

'The river? Great! Can we go fishing?' Now he was really interested. 'I like fishing.'

'I – I don't know. I'd have to ask Grandpa.'

'I like seeing fish wriggle on the end of me line and then—' He brought his hand down in a chopping movement, demonstrating how he killed his catch.

As they walked on, he pushed his hands into his pockets and walked with a swagger. 'I'm going in the army as soon as I'm eighteen.'

'How old are you now?'

'I was seventeen last month. Roll on next year. I can't wait to get at 'em.'

Anna glanced at him. 'Who?'

'Jerry, of course.'

'Oh.'

They walked in silence until they came to the river bank and stood looking down at the flowing water.

'I bet there's plenty of fish in there,' he said.

Anna bit her lip. 'We'll have to be getting back. It'll be teatime soon and then there's the milking.'

Bruce turned towards her and put his hands on her shoulders. He looked down into her upturned face. Then without warning, he bent and pressed his mouth hard on hers. Shocked, Anna tried to pull away, but found that he was gripping her shoulders so firmly she could not move.

'There,' he said as he drew away. 'Bet that's the first time you've been kissed properly, ain't it?'

Her mind reeling, Anna could find no words. Bruce laughed softly and, still with his arm about her shoulders, began to lead her back towards the farm.

And that was how Luke saw them as they came into the yard.

Thirty-Seven

When Douglas and Bruce had departed in a cloud of fumes, the sound of the noisy sports car echoing long after they had roared up the lane, Luke said, 'She's too young to be having the likes of him putting his arm around her. Put a stop to it, May, or I will.'

'Oh, Dad, it's only a bit of harmless fun. He's the first boyfriend she's had.'

'Boyfriend?' Luke almost shouted. 'At thirteen? Have you taken leave of your senses, May?'

'She's just flattered by the attentions of a good-looking lad, that's all.'

Luke's shaggy eyebrows almost covered his eyes as he frowned. He bit down hard on his pipe. 'Not the only one, is she?' he muttered. Then he jabbed the end of his pipe towards his daughter. 'I mean it, May. I don't want her getting romantic notions at her age.'

May flushed and bit her thumbnail, but she argued with her father no further. Luke turned away, satisfied that he had made his point and that it would be obeyed. But if he could have read May's rebellious thoughts at that moment, he would not have been so content. As he walked away, May glared after him. *If you think I'm going to risk wrecking my chances of going back to live in the city by upsetting Douglas and his son, then you've got another think coming. I'm a grown woman and I'll bring my daughter up how* I *like, not how you say.*

Later, when Betty and Rita had returned and they were all seated round the supper table, Luke was still unable to get the two visitors out of his mind. 'I'd like to know where he gets his petrol from.'

Betty laughed. 'Oho, don't ask, Pops. Don't ask.' Then she winked. 'But if there's anything you want, you can be sure Douglas Whittaker will know where to get it. Only no questions asked, if you know what I mean.'

'Yes,' Luke said grimly, 'I think I do.' He glanced at May, who had lowered her head when the conversation had turned to Douglas. 'You're very quiet, lass.'

Her head shot up. 'Oh. I – er – no. I mean, I didn't mean to be.' She was flustered and red in the face.

'Know what I think,' Betty said, cradling her cup in her palms. 'I reckon Douglas is sweet on our May here.'

'Oh no,' May said quickly, but her blush deepened. 'He's your young man, Betty. I wouldn't want you to think . . .'

Betty flapped her hand. 'Don't worry about that, May. There's plenty more fish in the sea. And Douglas Whittaker's no great catch.' Then, realizing how that might sound, she added hastily, 'Not as far as I'm concerned anyway. I promise you, he's just a laugh. Besides, he's a bit old for me. No offence, love.'

'None taken,' May murmured. She was older than Betty by about ten years. She was much nearer Douglas's age than the young Land Army girl. Betty's eyes clouded as she added, 'I'm not getting serious about anyone. Not while this war's on.'

'Love 'em and leave 'em, that's Betty's motto,' Rita laughed.

Betty crashed her cup into its saucer and stood up suddenly. 'It's – it's them that leave us, isn't it?'

She turned and rushed from the room. They heard the back door bang. Rita looked after her thoughtfully. 'I think,' she said slowly, 'that despite what she says she was getting rather fond of Charlie.'

May gasped. 'The – the one who got shot down?'

Rita nodded.

'Oh,' May breathed. 'Poor Betty.'

'Aye,' Luke growled at his daughter. 'And it'll be poor you, if you take up with that – that spiv!'

May hung her head.

Despite Luke's warning, May couldn't help liking Douglas. She looked forward to his visits to the farm and she felt more comfortable now that she knew Betty did not regard him as her boyfriend. May liked the two girls who had come to live with them and help on the farm. She didn't want to offend either of them, especially the forthright Betty, whose tongue, Luke said, could mow a ten-acre field without a scythe.

Douglas began to take May out – just the two of them – roaring off up the lane in his car. He even took her away for a weekend, staying away Friday and Saturday nights, during which time Luke glowered morosely and then refused to speak to May for three days afterwards. Douglas tried his best to win the old man over, bringing him tobacco and even a can or two of precious petrol.

'No thanks,' Luke said tersely. 'I don't hold with black market stuff.'

Douglas laughed, but shrugged. 'Don't tell me you

don't get a bit of extra meat from under the counter now and again.'

'We have all we need. We live on a farm,' Luke reminded him.

'That's exactly it,' Douglas said and jabbed his finger towards Luke. For a brief moment, Douglas's grey eyes were as hard as flint. 'You're lucky, but some of us are really suffering because of the shortages. Can you blame us for wanting to make life a bit easier?'

Luke's glance travelled slowly up and down the smartly dressed man before him. He said nothing, just sniffed as if to say: *You look as if you're really suffering!* Then he shrugged. 'That's your business and no concern of mine. Just don't ask me to get involved, that's all. And don't' – now it was Luke who wagged his finger at Douglas – 'involve my daughter either.'

Douglas threw back his head and laughed loudly. 'She doesn't refuse the nylons and the chocolates I bring.'

Luke turned away frowning. He was pretty sure Douglas was into the black market. Oh, maybe not in a big way. But Luke felt sure that he was on the fringes of petty villainy. He didn't like May's involvement with him or the way her eyes sparkled when she heard that noisy contraption swing into the yard.

But there was not a lot Luke could do about it.

When Douglas visited the farm at the weekends, he usually brought Bruce with him.

'I've brought you some chocolates,' Bruce said.

'Oh, how lovely.' Anna smiled. 'How kind of you. It – it must have used up all your coupons.'

Bruce shrugged and grinned. 'You're worth it.'

Across the yard, Anna was aware of Jed glowering at them. Hastily she said, 'I'll just take these indoors and then we'll go for a walk.'

As they strolled together by the river, Bruce took hold of Anna's hand, whilst Buster ran ahead, exploring for rabbits. She felt her face glowing pink, but did not pull away. It was nice to have an older boyfriend; nice to be able to boast about him to her best friend, Jean. And walking hand in hand with him made her feel really grown up.

'Has he kissed you yet?' Jean asked eagerly every Monday morning when she knew Bruce had been to the farm.

'Oh yes,' Anna said airily, giving the impression that it happened all the time. 'And when we go for walks, we hold hands.'

Jean nudged her. 'Has he tried – well – you know?'

Anna put her nose in the air. 'Course not. He's not like that. He's nice.'

'Does he know you're only thirteen? 'Cos you look older. Mebbe he thinks you're as old as him.'

Anna shrugged. 'Dunno. But I'm not going to tell him.' They giggled together.

And now, here she was once more walking with him. Maybe there'd be even more to tell Jean on Monday morning . . .

'What have you been doing with yourself this week?' Bruce broke into her dreams.

'Oh, the usual. You know, school and helping Grandpa.'

'When are the lambs going then?' Bruce asked her as they walked through the meadow, watching the lambs playing.

'Next week,' Anna said dolefully. 'They're coming for them next Monday.'

'A week tomorrow, you mean?'

Anna nodded as she pulled her hand from his and crept towards one of the lambs suckling its mother. Neither the sheep nor the lamb moved, not even when Anna stroked the lamb. Buster trotted up and stood close by, watching. 'Come and feel their lovely coats,' Anna said to Bruce. 'Isn't it a shame they have to be – to be—?'

He moved carefully across the grass towards her, but when he was about three feet from her and the sheep, Anna heard Buster growl softly. She turned to look down at him. He was crouching, his eyes on Bruce, as if ready to spring.

'Don't be silly, Buster. It's only Bruce.'

Bruce gave a nervous laugh. 'I don't reckon that dog likes me.' He grinned. 'Reckon he's jealous.'

Anna's eyes widened as she looked at him, 'Jealous?' she began and then realized what he meant. She blushed. 'Don't be silly. You ought to make friends with him. You never pet him.'

Bruce laughed. 'I don't want me hand bitten off.'

'Take no notice of Buster. He won't hurt you. Not while I'm here anyway. But he's only doing his job.'

Bruce glanced at her. 'What do you mean?'

'It's his job to protect the sheep.'

Bruce eyed the dog thoughtfully.

'Come on,' Anna encouraged. 'Feel how soft their wool is.'

Bruce, keeping a wary eye on the dog, moved forward and bent to stroke the lamb. The lamb stopped suckling and allowed Bruce to pick it up. 'Cute little fellers, aren't they?'

Anna giggled. 'Yeah. Except that one's a girl.'

Suddenly, Buster growled again and began to bark. Frightened, the lamb bleated and struggled in Bruce's grasp. 'It's all right, boy,' he said to the dog. 'I'm not going to run off with it.' He laughed as he set the young animal down on its spindly legs. 'They're heavier than I thought they'd be,' he murmured as the lamb trotted away to join in a game with the others.

'They're like children, aren't they?' Anna smiled. 'Look at them, playing just like little children in a playground.'

'Yeah,' Bruce murmured, draping his arm across her shoulders. 'But they're worth a bit more than a load of screaming kids.'

Anna said nothing. She felt uncomfortable that Bruce kept referring to how much things were worth. The sheep, the crops they were growing – even the fish in the river. Everything seemed to have a price tag as far as Bruce was concerned.

'We ought to come fishing one day,' he'd remarked. 'Me dad could get a good price for fresh fish in the markets.'

Maybe it was because his father was a businessman, Anna told herself, finding excuses for him. It was just his way, that was all.

As they began to walk back towards the farmhouse, Bruce glanced back over his shoulder. 'Yeah, your old man's got a bob or two coming his way next week when he sends this little lot to market.'

Thirty-Eight

The following Sunday Bruce came again with his father.

'Come on,' he said, catching hold of Anna's hand. 'Me dad says I can take you for a drive in the car while he's talking to your mam.'

'Drive?' Anna gasped. 'Can you drive?'

'Course I can.' The youth swaggered. 'Come on. We'll have some fun. Get your mam to pack us a picnic hamper. We'll go off for the day.'

'I don't know,' Anna said doubtfully. 'I ought to stay and help Grandpa. The lambs are going tomorrow. I told you.'

Bruce blinked, as if he had forgotten. 'Oh. Oh yes, I remember. You said last week.' He frowned. 'Why do you have to help? What have you got to do?'

'Grandpa sometimes round them all up and brings them down to the barn. It saves time in the morning, if they're all together. Ready for when the lorries come.'

'Oh.'

'I'll ask him, though. He might not bother.'

'You're not going and that's final.'

'But Grandpa—'

'Don't argue, lass. I don't want you going in that car with him. He's not safe.'

'You can't say that. You don't know what sort of a driver he is.'

'I can make a pretty good guess. It's bad enough your mother going off in the thing wi' 'im.' He jerked his thumb towards the farmhouse. 'There's not a lot I can do about that—'

'Except not speak to her for days on end when she comes back,' Anna said rashly.

'Now, now, lass. That's not like you to be cheeky to me.'

Anna was ashamed. 'I'm sorry, Grandpa, but we only wanted to go for a picnic.'

'Well . . .' Luke was still reluctant. He didn't like Douglas or his son. But he could hardly stop the youngsters spending time together. Even though in his heart of hearts he would like to have done so. 'That's all right,' he said now. 'You can walk down to the river bank. There's some nice spots there for a picnic. Me and your grannie often used to take a picnic down there—'

He turned away abruptly and Anna gazed after him, sorry to have revived poignant memories. 'We won't be late, Grandpa. I'll be back in time to help with the milking.'

As he walked away, Luke raised his hand in acknowledgement but he did not look back.

It had been a lovely afternoon down by the river. They'd sat on a rug close together, their shoulders touching. It was peaceful and quiet.

'You wouldn't think there was a war on, would you?' Bruce said. Then he'd turned and kissed her, pressing her onto her back. 'You're lovely,' he'd murmured against her mouth. His hand caressed her waist and then moved up to her breast.

'Don't!' Anna said sharply and sat up.

For a moment, Bruce's face was like thunder and Anna felt a tiny shiver of fear. But then he was smiling. 'Sorry. I keep forgetting you're only thirteen. You look older.' He sat up too, resting his arms on his knees.

Anna was relieved, yet there was a little tinge of regret. After all, he was her boyfriend. At least, that was what she told Jean and the other girls at school. He lit a cigarette and sat smoking it.

'Can I – can I have a puff?'

He turned and looked at her. 'You're not old enough to smoke – ' he paused deliberately and then added – 'either.'

Anna felt the colour suffuse her face and she hung her head.

She heard him laugh softly. Then he was holding out the cigarette to her. 'Here, have a go.'

She took it and drew on it. The smoke stung the back of her throat and she began to cough, feeling as if she were choking. He slapped her hard on the back.

'Don't take it down the first time, you daft thing.'

She was purple in the face and it took some moments for her to recover enough to speak. 'What on earth pleasure is there in that?' she wheezed. 'It's horrible.'

Bruce was grinning at her. 'You'd probably get to like it.' He glanced at her out of the corner of his eye. 'Given time.'

Anna had the distinct feeling that he was not talking just about smoking.

*

That night Anna was restless and sleep was fitful. She tossed and turned, thinking over what had happened between her and Bruce. She felt as if she had behaved like a silly little schoolgirl. He'd only wanted a harmless cuddle, she told herself. He would never ask her to go too far, she was sure. And now she'd probably lost him. He'd find another, more mature girl who would let him love her.

She sat up in bed suddenly. Her bedroom window faced out over the yard and she could hear Buster barking. Maybe there was an intruder. There'd been a lot of thefts from nearby farms recently. Chickens, ducks and geese, even a piglet or two, anything that would sell on the black market to give hard pressed housewives a little extra meat for their families.

Anna was about to get out of bed to wake her grandfather, when she realized Buster had stopped. She listened for a few moments longer and then lay down. It couldn't have been anything serious or the dog would still be trying to raise the alarm. Her anxieties over Bruce diverted by the brief disturbance, within minutes Anna was asleep.

As she stepped into the kitchen the following morning, Luke and May turned to greet her.

'What is it?' she asked at once. She could see by the look on their faces that something was wrong.

'It's Buster,' Luke began, putting his hand on her shoulder.

'Buster? Why? What's happened?' She made as if to rush outside, but Luke's hand restrained her.

'There's summat the matter with him. I don't know

what. He was spark out when I went out first thing this morning, just lying in the yard near his kennel. But not inside it. Looks as if he's been out there all night.'

'He's not—. You don't mean he's—?' She couldn't bring herself to voice her worst fear.

'No, he's not dead. In fact, he's woken up, but he's staggering around. If he were a man, I'd say he was drunk.' Luke shook his head. 'But he's not right. I'll have to take him into the vet as soon as they've been for the lambs.'

'Can't we go now?' Anna was frantic.

Luke shook his head. 'No, we'll have to round up the lambs ourselves. Buster's going to be no use this morning. Ya mam's agreed that you'll have to stay off school today to help.'

'I wouldn't have gone anyway,' Anna said firmly. 'Not until I know what's the matter with Buster.'

'Get your breakfast and then go with your grandpa—' May began, but Anna was already hurrying from the house. 'I've got to see Buster.'

The dog was staggering about near his kennel looking very sorry for himself. She ran her hands over his coat and he made a half-hearted attempt to lick her.

'What is it, boy? What's the matter, eh? I wish you could tell us.'

Luke appeared and came to stand beside her, scratching his head in puzzlement. 'I can't mek it out, love. We'll have to get him to the vet. Only thing is – I haven't much petrol.'

'There's a can in the barn that Douglas left for you.'

Luke's mouth tightened. 'I'm not using that—'

Anna sprang up and caught hold of his arm. 'Oh please, Grandpa. Just this once. For Buster. Please.'

'All right.' Luke gave in, but added sternly, 'But

don't you go telling that feller or his son, else he'll think he's got the better of me.'

Anna hugged him. 'I won't, Grandpa. I won't.'

'Now, go and get some breakfast and then join me and the girls in the fields. I need all the help I can get this morning to round up those lambs.'

'There's three missing. I know there is.' Betty was adamant. 'We've got nineteen and there should be twenty-two.'

'Are you sure you haven't miscounted, lass?' Luke said. 'The little blighters keep moving about.'

Betty shook her head. 'No. Rita helped me and we counted 'em out of this pen and into that one.' The lambs that were being sent for slaughter were all in the barn now.

'What about the three I'm keeping to rear? The ones I marked with red paint.'

Betty and Rita glanced at each other. 'There's only two in the field with red paint on their backs,' Betty said. 'But we left another female lamb there. We knew you wanted to keep three back. We started with twenty-five, didn't we?'

Luke nodded.

'So,' she went on, 'take away the three that we've left in the field for rearing and we should have twenty-two and we haven't. We've only got nineteen.'

They all looked at the lambs milling about in the makeshift pen inside the barn. There was no lamb with a red paint mark on its back.

Luke scratched his head. 'Well, I dunno. We'd better go and have a look round the fields.' Then he muttered, 'Just when we could have done with Buster.' He looked round. 'I don't suppose he's recovered enough to help us, has he, Anna?'

Anna shook her head. She had gone straight to look at the dog on returning to the yard. 'He's in his kennel. Sleeping.'

Luke glanced at her, then turned on his heel and left the barn. Anna, Betty and Rita exchanged a worried look and then went to peer out of the door. They saw Luke bend down and reach into the kennel. Then he straightened up and came back towards them. He was smiling. 'He's sleeping right enough. I can't understand it. There doesn't seem much wrong with him.'

'But you're still going to take him to the vet, aren't you?'

'Well—' Luke hesitated.

'Oh please, Grandpa.'

'All right then. As soon as they've been for the lambs.'

'We'd better get back to the fields and see if we can find the other three,' Betty said and laughed. 'Now I know how Bo Peep felt.'

'They'll be down a dyke side somewhere, I expect,' Anna said confidently as she and the two girls set off, leaving Luke to wait in the yard for the lorry.

But Anna was wrong. They scoured the fields and the dykes but there was no sign of the three missing lambs. Tired and dispirited, they went back to the farmyard. The lorry had just arrived and the lambs were being shepherded into the back of the vehicle. As soon as they were loaded and the lorry had trundled its way down the narrow lane from the farm, Anna turned to Luke. '*Now* can we take Buster to the vet?'

*

'Well, I can't find anything physically wrong with him, Luke,' the vet, who was an old friend, said. He was a portly man in his early sixties who had been the local vet for 'more years than he cared to remember', as he always said. He smiled at Anna, who was standing close by, a worried expression on her face.

'I knew it was a waste of time and petrol bringing him,' Luke grumbled.

'Hold on a minute.' The vet looked at Luke over the top of his spectacles. 'I hadn't quite finished. As I said, there's nothing physically wrong with him and without taking blood samples to prove it, I can't be sure, but I'd take an educated guess that this dog's been drugged.'

'Drugged! Who on earth—?' Luke began and then, as realization began to dawn, his mouth tightened and his eyes sparked anger. 'That explains it, then.'

'Explains what?' the vet asked.

'I sent my lambs to slaughter this morning and three were missing. Someone must have come in the night and stolen them.'

'And drugged the dog to stop him barking, you mean.'

Luke nodded. Anna pulled at his sleeve. 'Grandpa, I remember now. I should have said before, but with everything happening I forgot.'

They both turned to look at her. 'What, lass?'

'Last night. Before I fell asleep, I heard Buster barking. I was just going to get out of bed and come and fetch you but – but he stopped. Oh Grandpa, if only I'd come and woken you, then – then—'

Luke put his arm around her. 'It's not your fault, lass. You weren't to know. Mind you, I would have gone and had a look. Buster's a good guard dog. He only barks for a reason.' He nodded again. 'That'd be it. They'd come and drug him first, stop him barking a warning when they went into the fields to pinch me sheep. We never tie him up, you see. If he'd heard a disturbance out in the fields, he'd have been off like a rocket.'

'Sounds to me as if it was someone who knew just what they were doing,' the vet said mildly.

'Yes,' Luke said grimly. 'It does, doesn't it?'

Thirty-Nine

'Dad, how can you possibly accuse Douglas of such a thing?' May was angry and tearful.

'I'm not.' The words were grudging.

'Yes, you are. You've never liked him. Just because he's smart and – and has a fancy car.'

'And dabbles in the black market,' Luke shot back. 'He admitted that himself.'

'Yes, and you weren't above using the petrol he brought you when you needed it.'

Luke said nothing but gave a low growl, sounding very like Buster when Douglas or Bruce were around. He glanced at Betty across the supper table. 'You're not saying much, lass. You know him better than any of us. What do you reckon? Am I being unfair?'

Betty regarded him with her clear, blue eyes. 'I honestly don't know. I know he wheels and deals, if you know what I mean. But I didn't think he'd stoop to theft. I know one thing, though.' She glanced across at May. 'I don't know if he's stolen your sheep, but I do know he's causing trouble between you and your family. And that alone makes me sorry I ever brought him here.'

'Well, I'm not,' May said boldly and glared at her father. 'And don't you go saying anything to him, Dad. You've no proof. I look forward to him coming. And his lad. We'd be buried alive out here, if it wasn't for them coming at a weekend. I never wanted to stay on the farm. Why do you think I married Ken and moved to the city? And now, because of this blasted war, I've had to come back.' Tears of anger and frustration poured down May's face as she rushed from the room and ran up the stairs.

For the quiet, usually docile May to react in such a way shocked them all.

'Oh dear,' Betty said. 'I think she's got it bad.'

'Oh dear indeed,' Luke muttered as he got up from the table.

Nothing was said about the lambs when Douglas and Bruce arrived as usual for Sunday dinner, after which Douglas took May for a drive in his car and Bruce and Anna walked to the river bank.

'What sort of a price did your grandpa get for his lambs then?' Bruce asked as soon as they were alone. They walked side by side, he with his hands in his pockets, Anna with her arm through his.

'*I* don't know,' Anna said.

Bruce grinned. 'I thought you might be in for a bit of extra pocket money if he was feeling generous.'

It was on the tip of her tongue to confide in him, to tell him that three lambs had been lost and that the vet suspected their dog had been drugged. But the knowledge that her grandfather would be angry kept her silent.

'Don't you go saying anything to either of them when they come,' Luke had demanded of them all. 'You hear me, May? And you too, Anna.'

He didn't even need to press the point home to the two Land Army girls. To May and Anna's dismay, it seemed as if he trusted the two girls more than his own flesh and blood.

Over the next few weeks nothing more was stolen from Clayton's Farm, but Luke heard that several of the farms nearby were missing chickens and geese on a regular basis.

'They don't take many at a time,' Jed told Luke, 'but me uncle's lost four hens now. He reckons that whoever's doing it thinks that out of fifty hens or so we won't notice a couple have gone. But it's getting regular and it always happens at a weekend.'

Luke eyed him shrewdly. 'Aye, it's when these townies come out to the countryside. You've seen the two that come to our place?'

Jed nodded, his mouth tightening at the thought of Bruce.

'I don't mind telling you, Jed lad, I'm not keen on them. Too flash for my liking, but the girls like the company.'

'I'd noticed,' Jed said dryly and Luke cast him a shrewd look.

'Ah,' he said slowly, knowingly. 'Like that, is it, lad?'

'Aye, Mr Clayton. As you say, it's like that.'

Jed turned away, but Luke watched him go and chewed thoughtfully on his pipe. Now there was a lad he'd be happy to let Anna go to the ends of the earth with. Because he knew she'd be safe with Jed and, what's more, Jed would always bring her back home.

'Not long now before I join the army,' Bruce told Anna towards the end of the year.

The war was now three years old and yet there was no talk of it ending soon. There had been the heartening news of Monty's triumph at El Alamein and, for once, the sound of church bells was heard in celebration. But still the fighting continued.

'I – I'll miss you,' Anna said.

'I'll be home on leave in me smart uniform. All the girls like a man in uniform.'

'I – like you anyway,' Anna said quietly and Bruce squeezed her arm. There was a pause and then she asked, 'Will you have to go abroad? To – to where the fighting is?'

''Spect so.'

'You will be careful, won't you?'

Bruce stopped and turned to face her. He put his hands on her shoulders and kissed her gently on the lips. 'Course I will, as long as I know you're my girl.' He raised his head and looked about him, his sweeping glance taking in all the land around them. All the land that belonged to her grandfather. Then he murmured, so low that Anna only just caught his words. 'And there's all this for me to come back to.'

The following spring Bruce went into the army. Anna missed him and counted the days to his next leave. When he came home he was full of tales of service life.

'The training's hard, but I love it.' He flexed his arms. 'You should see my muscles. And look – I brought this to show you.' From a sheath attached to his belt, he pulled out a long, cruel-looking weapon. 'This is a bayonet. You fix it to the end of your gun and have to run at sacks of straw and thrust it in.' He demonstrated with vicious delight. 'You have to imagine it's the enemy.'

Anna gasped, scandalized. 'They teach you to do that to someone? You could kill them.'

'That's the general idea.' Bruce eyed her scathingly. 'What do you think war is? A picnic? Living out here in the back of beyond, you're sheltered from what's really going on. Oh, you hear the planes and read the papers, but you don't know what it's really like.' His eyes were shining as he added, 'I can't wait to get out there. I just hope it's not all over by the time I get overseas. I want to get at 'em.'

Anna shuddered. He was right, she knew he was. It was people like him, with that kind of attitude, who could win the war. It needed fearless people like him, but this didn't stop her being appalled by the brutality of it. To her it seemed that Bruce was actually relishing the idea of killing.

'Of course I know what war is,' Anna was stung to retort. 'I should do. I lost my dad, didn't I? But I didn't realize you had to – had to—' She gulped back the tears as the sudden, horrifying picture of her lovely father being trained in hand-to-hand fighting came into her mind.

'It's either us or them,' Bruce was saying harshly. 'You've got to get them first before they get you.'

'Yes,' Anna murmured, unable to take her eyes off the bayonet. Had her father been killed in such a way, too gentle to be the first to strike?

'I've got me own knife an' all, but it's not standard issue, so I have to be careful the Sarge doesn't see it.'

Now he showed her a short, dagger-like knife. 'This is better up close.' He made an upward, stabbing movement. 'Straight through the heart.'

'I don't want to talk about it any more,' she said, turning away.

'Hey, I'm sorry,' Bruce said at once, putting his arm around her. 'I was forgetting about your dad. I'm sorry, Anna, honestly.' He adopted a hangdog expression, like a little boy caught scrumping apples. 'Forgiven?'

Anna smiled and nodded. 'Yeah, you're forgiven.'

Even though Bruce was away, Douglas still came every weekend, bringing nylons, chocolates and flowers for May and for Betty and Rita too. He still brought Luke's favourite brand of tobacco, but the old man refused to touch it.

It was lambing time again, and after school and at weekends Anna was out in the fields or in the barn with her grandfather and the two Land Army girls.

'Do you know,' Betty said with a comical expression, 'if anyone'd've told me before the war that I'd be sitting in a barn in the middle of the night, dressed in these awful clothes, helping bring lambs into the world, I'd've said they'd gone off their rocker.' Luke, Rita and Anna laughed, but Betty added seriously, 'But I'll tell you something, I wouldn't have missed this for the world.'

There was a cosy intimacy in the warm darkness of the barn. Strangely, the feeling was still there even when they were out in the bitter cold when sheep gave birth in the fields. The four of them were united in helping the ewes and preserving the young, fragile lives. Three lambs had to be suckled by hand and Anna had charge of these in the big farmhouse kitchen. Luke taught her how to feed the lambs with a bottle and keep them warm near the huge range. One ewe, the mother of twin lambs, had died and another had rejected her offspring.

'Isn't it sad,' Betty remarked, tears in her eyes as she stroked the soft wool of the little creature's coat, 'when a mother rejects her own?'

Anna held the lamb close and laid her cheek against its woolly warmth. 'I'll look after you,' she whispered. 'I'll look after you all.'

Forty

Life on Clayton's Farm went on much the same through the seasons; lambing, shearing, haymaking, harvest and then the autumn threshing, ploughing and seeding. And then the whole routine began again. By this time, it was obvious to them all that it was May that Douglas now came to see, not Betty. Luke tolerated his visits, always hoping that something would happen to put a stop to them. He hoped that petrol would get even scarcer, but the 'wide boy' never seemed to go short of anything.

The happy atmosphere of the farmhouse was irrevocably torn asunder the Sunday evening just after the New Year of 1944 when May arrived home after a weekend with Douglas in the city, her eyes sparkling like the huge diamond on her fourth finger.

Luke took one look at the ring, glared at Douglas and then stormed out of the house, slamming the back door with such force that the whole house seemed to rattle.

Douglas laughed. 'Oh dear, I don't think my future father-in-law likes me.'

May tucked her arm through his and gazed up adoringly at him. 'Don't worry, he'll come round. Anyway, we won't be living here, will we?'

Her eyes still shining, May turned to Anna. 'Darling, we'll be going home. When Douglas and I are married, we'll be going back to live in Lincoln.'

For a moment Anna felt sick. It wasn't that she didn't like Douglas, she did, but not enough for him to take her father's place.

'You mean – we're going back to – to the house we had in Lincoln?'

'No, no, of course not. I gave up the tenancy on that. No, we'll be going to live in Douglas's house.'

Douglas came towards Anna and put his arm about her shoulder, squeezing her to his side. 'We'll get a new house for the four of us. And you can help us choose it. Now, that'd be nice, wouldn't it?'

Anna's gaze was on her mother's face. 'But what about Grandpa? We can't leave him all alone here.'

'He's got Betty and Rita.'

'Yes, but when the war's over, they'll be going home. They won't want to stay here.'

For a moment, May's face clouded. 'Oh, I hadn't thought of that.' She glanced at Betty and Rita, who, up until this moment had remained silent. 'I thought you liked it here. I thought you'd be staying.'

The two Land Army girls glanced at each other and then shook their heads. 'We do like it,' Betty said, 'more than we thought we would, I have to admit that. But no, once this lot's over, we'll be going home. I – I miss my family.'

'Me too,' Rita said quietly.

'Oh.' May was crestfallen.

Douglas hugged her. 'Don't worry, darling. The old man will be all right. He'll get a housekeeper and there'll be plenty of men coming back from the war looking for work. He'll be fine.'

Anna bit her lip, torn between concern for her grandfather and the delicious thought of seeing Bruce every day. And yet the farm was where she belonged.

She took a deep breath and before she really knew what she was doing, she said, 'I'll stay with Grandpa.'

The look of relief on Douglas's face was obvious, but May was still worried. 'But you're only a child—'

'I'm not. I'll be fifteen in a few weeks. I think I can leave school at Easter. Old enough to get a job. Well, this will be my job. I'll work for Grandpa and look after him.'

May bit her lip and murmured, 'I'll talk to Dad. I really wanted to go back to the city but I suppose we *could* all live here—' Her voice trailed away in disappointment.

After Douglas had left, Betty said sharply, 'I wouldn't bank on it, if I were you. I don't think Pops will ever come round to liking Douglas.'

Helplessly, May spread her hands. 'I can't see *why*. Douglas has been nothing but generous.'

'That's maybe it,' Betty said. 'He flashes his money about and your dad doesn't like the fact that Doug is probably dealing just outside the law.'

'Is he?' May asked ingenuously. Betty shrugged her plump shoulders and said, 'I wouldn't like to ask. Dougie's got a bit of a temper on him if he's crossed.'

May's eyes widened. 'Has he? I've never seen it.'

'Well, you wouldn't, would you?' Then she added ominously, 'Not yet.' She shook her head. 'I'm sorry to say it, May, but you know me. I've got to say what I think and I think you're making a big mistake. Dougie's all right for a bit of fun, like I've always said, but that's all. Marrying him might be the worst thing you've ever done.'

May gave a nervous laugh. 'You're only jealous.'

'No, I'm not, May,' Betty said seriously. 'Not a bit. Look, me an' Reet care about this family. We're very fond of all of you and I just don't think he's right for you. That's all.'

May's lips were tight as she said, 'Well, let me be the best judge of that.'

Betty stood up and shrugged. 'Have it your way then, but don't say I didn't warn you. Come on, Reet, let's give Pops a hand.'

The two girls left the room and May and Anna were left staring silently at each other. May's wonderful news had not been met with the delight she had hoped for.

Two days later at breakfast, Luke made a startling announcement. 'If you marry that feller, May, I'm changing me will.'

Betty got up from the table. 'If you want to discuss private family business, me an' Reet—'

'Sit down,' Luke said sharply. 'You might as well hear it. If this war goes on much longer, it might even concern you, in a way. As I was saying, I'll change me will and leave it all to Anna. But' – he turned towards his granddaughter, his shaggy white eyebrows meeting in a frown – 'there's a condition. You will have no more to do with that son of his. That Bruce. I won't have' – Luke glanced around the table now, prodding his knife in the air – 'either of them getting their hands on my farm. You hear me?'

May was sitting with her mouth wide open, stunned by the depth of her father's dislike for her fiancé. Betty and Rita glanced uncomfortably at each other, but said nothing. Only Anna cried out, 'Oh, Grandpa, don't you like Bruce?'

'No, I don't like either of them. And that's the truth. So' – he rose and rested his hands on the table, leaning forward – 'it's up to you now. I've said me piece and I'll say no more. If you want to marry that – that wide boy, May, go ahead. But you won't get my blessing – or the farm. And you, Anna, there'll be a condition in my will that you only get it if you don't marry Bruce Whittaker.'

As the door closed behind Luke, May whispered, 'Can he do that? Can he put that sort of thing in a will? About Anna, I mean?'

Betty shrugged. 'I don't know, but he's going to try. That's obvious. Come on, Reet, we'd better get working.'

Once again, May and Anna were left staring helplessly at each other across the table.

The happy atmosphere at Clayton's Farm was gone. Luke only spoke to May when it was absolutely necessary, and then in clipped tones. On the surface he treated Anna no differently, yet the girl could feel the tension, knew that he was waiting for her to discuss the matter further with him; waiting for her to give him her promise.

Bruce was due home on leave for the weekend and this time Anna had no compunction in pouring out the whole story to him. She knew May would have told Douglas by now.

'That's blackmail,' Bruce said. 'I hope you're not going to take notice of the silly old fool.'

Despite her anguish over her grandfather's ultimatum, Anna felt a thrill run through her to think that Bruce thought so much about her that he didn't care whether she inherited the farm or not. His next words took away some of that thrill. 'You could always contest the will when the time came. You're his only relative, aren't you?'

Anna nodded.

'Well, then you could always say he was going senile when he made it. I think you'd have a pretty strong case.'

Anna gasped. 'I couldn't say something like that about Grandpa. Specially when it's not true.'

Bruce shrugged and said callously, 'He wouldn't know, would he? He'd be dead by then.'

As they returned to the farmyard hand in hand, Douglas roared in through the gate, bringing his car to a squealing halt. May, breathless and laughing, allowed him to help her from the car.

'Anna, come and help me get the tea ready.'

'We'll stay out here and have a smoke. I know the old man doesn't like cigarette smoke.' Douglas laughed. 'I don't want to upset him any more.' He held out his cigarette case to Bruce, who took one and lit it.

As Anna and her mother moved into the house, May glanced back. 'Isn't it nice to see father and son getting on so well?' she said wistfully and Anna knew she was thinking of the growing rift between herself and her own father.

'Don't worry, Mam. Maybe Grandpa will come round once he sees how happy you are with Douglas.'

May sighed. 'Perhaps you're right. He didn't like your daddy when I first met him, but he came round in the end. But – but this seems different. I've never seen your grandfather so – so determined. No, Anna, I don't think he will ever come to like Douglas. If I marry him and you continue to see Bruce, we'll lose the farm.

Somehow, my father will see to that.' Then her glance went to the window as she watched Douglas talking to his son. 'But Douglas has told me I'm not to worry about it. He's not bothered. He can provide for all of us, he says.' Her cheeks were pink with pleasure as she added shyly, 'It's me he wants, he says, not the farm.'

Anna, too, glanced out of the window, watching Douglas lean nonchalantly against his car whilst his son was talking earnestly to him, his head bent towards him.

'What do you think they're talking about?'

May smiled. 'I don't know, but it looks pretty serious. Maybe they're planning to buy that house in Lincoln Douglas has promised.'

'Mmm,' Anna said thoughtfully. 'Maybe.'

Douglas and Bruce left just after ten. 'I'll have to get the lad back home. He has to be up early in the morning to get back to camp.' He guffawed. 'Can't have him going AWOL.'

By half past ten everyone was in bed in the farmhouse; the only being left awake was Buster on guard outside in the yard.

Anna was drifting into sleep when the sound of barking startled her into full wakefulness. This time, she did not hesitate but sprang from the bed and, barefoot, rushed along the landing to knock on her grandfather's bedroom door.

'Grandpa, Grandpa – Buster's barking.'

'Right, lass,' her grandfather's voice sounded through the door. 'I'm on me way.'

Anna rushed back to her bedroom to pull on trousers and a warm jumper over her pyjamas. By the time she emerged again from her room, her grandfather was halfway down the stairs and Betty, Rita and May had appeared at their bedroom doors.

'What is it?'

'What's the matter?'

'It's Buster barking. Maybe it's those poachers again.'

'Right,' said Betty. 'Let's get 'em.'

Downstairs they found Luke opening the back door, his twelve-bore shotgun in his hand.

'Oh, Dad, do be careful,' May cried.

Luke turned briefly. 'You stay here. All of you.'

'I'm coming with you,' Betty said firmly and Rita and Anna said in unison, 'So am I.'

'All right. But keep well back. I don't want to shoot you by mistake. But I mean to get these beggars. Whoever they are,' he added grimly.

They stood together in the yard for a few moments, listening, until their eyes became accustomed to the dark. Buster had now ceased barking and came to stand beside his master. Briefly, Luke fondled the dog's head and murmured, 'Good boy. Good dog. Quiet now.'

Now they could hear the squawking from the henhouse.

'It could be a fox,' Rita whispered.

'Aye,' Luke said grimly, 'but Mr Fox is still a poacher.'

Luke moved forward, the others following, but keeping their distance as he had instructed. The noise of the terrified hens got louder as they neared the henhouse. Luke raised his gun and pointed it to the sky. Then he fired it, the report echoing through the night.

The girls, standing near the corner of the barn, saw two shadowy figures moving near the henhouse. One was running away, climbing over the fence and into the lane, but the other was crouching low and coming straight towards Luke.

'Stop or I'll shoot,' Luke said and lowered his gun.

The figure spoke, but the girls were too far away to hear what he said. They heard Luke say, 'You!' before the man reached him, knocked the gun aside and punched the old man viciously in the stomach. Luke groaned and slumped to the ground.

'Grandpa!' Anna cried and began to run forward, Betty and Rita close behind her.

The attacker stood over Luke for a second, his face masked by a balaclava. Then he turned and ran across the grass towards the fence, whilst Betty blundered after him, shouting obscenities.

'You bastard. Wait till I get me hands on you. Hit a poor old man, would you?'

But he was too fast for any of them. He vaulted the fence and when, panting, Betty reached it, she could only hear his feet pounding down the lane, receding into the distance. Moments later, she heard the sound of a vehicle's engine and knew that they had escaped.

Furious that she had not at least been able to catch up with one of them, Betty returned to where Anna and Rita were crouching beside Luke. Anna was crying, saying over and over, 'Grandpa. Oh, Grandpa.'

As Betty reached them, Rita stood up and began to run towards the barn. 'I'm going for the doctor, Bet. He's been stabbed. Get May—'

For a moment Betty could not move. She gazed down at the inert form. 'Stabbed?' she repeated stupidly. Anna's hands were moving over Luke's body. 'He's bleeding. There's blood everywhere. Oh, Betty, do something. Please, do something!'

Galvanized, Betty leapt forward and began to run towards the house. 'I'll get your mam and a torch. We need some light—'

May was waiting anxiously, hovering near the back door.

'Your dad's been hurt. Stabbed,' Betty said briefly. 'Bring a torch and a towel. I'll get some blankets off my bed—'

May, too, repeated incredulously, 'Stabbed?'

'Yes. Hurry. Reet's gone for the doc.'

Betty, with May hurrying after her, returned to Anna to find the girl still weeping over the still form of the old man.

'Now, now,' Betty said kindly. 'Crying won't help him. Come on, love, stop that noise.'

'Oh Betty, I – I think he's dead. I – I've tried to feel his pulse and – and I can't find one.'

'Course he isn't, love.' But when Betty shone the torch into Luke's face and saw his wide, staring eyes and his mouth gagging open she knew the girl was right. She went through the motions of feeling for a pulse, first in his wrist and then his neck. She even put her cheek to his chest, desperate to hear the merest flicker of a heartbeat. There was nothing.

Slowly Betty stood up and took hold of Anna's arm. 'Come on, love,' she said quietly. 'There's nothing more we can do.'

'What? What do you mean?' May's voice rose hysterically.

'I'm so sorry, May. He's dead.' Betty put her other arm around May and tried to lead them both away, but May fought her off and fell to her knees beside her father. She rocked backwards and forwards and then bent her head and kissed his cheek. Anna looked down once more and then buried her face against Betty's comforting shoulder.

At last May stood up. 'Can't we carry him into the house? We – we can't leave him here.'

'Better not move him, love,' Betty said. 'Not till the doctor and the police have seen him.'

'The police?'

'It's a police matter now, May. Your father's been murdered.'

May closed her eyes and groaned whilst Anna sobbed into Betty's shoulder.

There was no sleep to be had for anyone the rest of that night. May sat in the kitchen, dry-eyed now, a wooden figure at the table, her arms resting on its surface, just staring into the distance. Anna curled up in her grandfather's chair near the range, alternately crying and raging against whoever had done this dreadful thing.

'All for a few hens,' she kept saying angrily. 'His life for a few miserable hens.'

May said nothing, whilst Betty made endless cups of tea and Rita looked after the doctor and then the village bobby, who had come to the farm on his bicycle.

'Bad business, this,' he said, sitting at the table in front of May and opening his notebook. 'I'm sorry to put you through this, May, but I'll have to ask you some questions.' He glanced round the room, intimating that he would need to question them all.

'Can't it wait?' Betty asked tartly. 'You can see what a state they're both in.' Then she muttered, 'The state we're all in, if it comes to that. Me and Reet were very fond of old Pops.' Tears filled her eyes, but she dashed them away impatiently. It was no time for her to indulge in tears. She had to be strong for the others. Later, in the privacy of the room she shared with Rita, she would weep for the old man, but for now . . .

'I'm sorry, miss,' the policeman, Reg Hamlin, was saying, 'but statements are best taken as soon as possible after the event. I've had to send word to my superiors in Lincoln. It'll be out of my hands soon, but they'll expect me to have made a start. Besides' – he glanced sympathetically towards May and Anna – 'I'm a friend of the family, like, and I thought they'd rather talk to me than a stranger.'

'But they can't think properly.'

'Things can always be altered later, but it's best to make a start now,' Reg said with kindly firmness, 'while it's all still clear in their minds.'

One by one he listened to what they had to say, but the sum total of all their statements didn't amount to anything very helpful.

Reg left as a red dawn was breaking over the farmhouse.

Forty-One

Of course there had to be a post-mortem and an inquest, the outcome of which confirmed that Luke had been stabbed with a knife or similar weapon by 'a person or persons unknown'. Hearing it, Anna shuddered, remembering the bayonet that Bruce had shown her.

Douglas had arrived as usual the following Sunday and was appalled to hear the news. 'Darling May,' he said, taking her into his arms, 'you should have let me know. I would have come at once. You need a man at a time like this.'

May clung to him and Anna turned away, wishing that Bruce had come with his father. She could do with a strong shoulder to cry on too. But his brief leave was over and he had had to report back to camp.

Sensing her feelings, Betty hugged her. 'Chin up, love. Pops wouldn't have wanted you to grieve for too long. Once they've let us bury him—'

'Oh Betty, don't. I can't bear to think of him being put in the cold earth.'

'He'll be next to your gran though, won't he? He'll be with her now. And he'd want to know that you were carrying on the farm. For him. You will, won't you?'

'I – don't know what Mam wants to do. She's never liked the farm, so now . . .' Anna's voice trailed away sadly.

'You don't mean she'll sell it?' Betty was shocked.

Anna shook her head miserably. 'I don't know what she'll do.'

If, at that moment, they could have heard the conversation between May and Douglas, they would have been even more uneasy.

'Don't you worry about a thing, May. I'll see to everything. Just tell me what you want doing, darling, about the funeral, I mean, and I'll arrange it all.'

'Oh Douglas, you are good. I don't know what I'd do without you.'

'You won't have to do without me, May. I'll stay here with you, if you like.'

'Would you? But what about your work?'

'I'll have to go back into town tomorrow and sort out a few things, but if I can arrange it, I'll stay the rest of the week and help you. I – er – take it you'll have to see your father's solicitor?'

'I hadn't thought about that, but yes, I expect so—. Oh!'

'What? What is it?'

'I wonder if he changed his will like he threatened.'

Douglas forced a laugh. 'Surely not. I thought that was just an idle threat to make you throw me over.'

May shook her head and said soberly, 'My father never made idle threats.'

Douglas's face darkened and there was a glint of anger in his eyes. 'I didn't think he would move so fast—' Hastily, he altered his words, 'What I mean is, I didn't think he'd really carry out his threat. Not against his own daughter.' He thought for a moment and then said, 'But if he has, he'll have left it to Anna instead, won't he?'

'Maybe.' May was still doubtful.

Douglas's face cleared. 'There you are then. It's the same thing. She can't run it, though, can she? She's only fifteen. The best thing you could both do, May, is to sell the farm and come and live with me in Lincoln.'

'He – he might have put in some clause that it can't be sold. He threatened to leave it to Anna on the condition that she had no more to do with – with Bruce.'

Now Douglas could scarcely hide his anger. In a tight voice he said, 'Did he, indeed?' But he forced himself to smile and to say in a tender tone, 'Then the sooner you find out just how things stand the better. I'll take you into the city with me tomorrow and you can call and see the solicitor. How's that?'

'Oh, Douglas,' May breathed and said again, 'I don't know what I'd do without you.'

Bruce wangled compassionate leave to attend the funeral.

'I had to tell a little white lie to get here,' he told Anna. 'I said it was my stepmother's father.' He laughed. 'Mind you, by the look of them' – he nodded to where May was walking down the church path, clinging to Douglas's arm – 'it doesn't look as if it'll be long before she really is.'

Anna said nothing. The day, for her, was a tumult of emotions. She had lost her beloved grandfather and it seemed only yesterday that she had lost both her father and her grandmother. And whilst Anna could see that her mother needed Douglas's support, she was uncomfortable when she remembered that Luke had disliked the man so intensely that he had threatened to cut his own daughter out of his will.

Nor had he approved of the young man walking at her side, taking her cold hand in his and squeezing it sympathetically. Anna sighed as she and Bruce fell into step behind her mother and Douglas to follow the coffin into the church. After the funeral, she knew the solicitor would be coming to the farm to read the will in keeping with the old-fashioned custom. Maybe then they would learn just how deep Luke's resentment had gone.

Betty and Rita were walking behind her and Bruce, and behind them it seemed as if half the local population had come to Luke Clayton's funeral. Even Reg Hamlin, in plain clothes, was standing to one side watching all the mourners.

'I shall be there,' he had told May and Betty the day before when he had visited the farm, 'with my Inspector. I'd be attending old Luke's passing anyway, but I shall be in a semi-official capacity.'

'Why?' May had asked.

'It's just possible that the killers might be there.'

'Really?' Betty had put in. 'Then I'll keep me beady eye open an' all, pet.'

Several people returned to the farm for sandwiches and cups of tea, with something a little stronger for the men.

'You can't have a wake without a drop of the hard stuff,' Douglas had told May. 'Leave it to me.'

As the mourners began to drift away, Douglas said, 'Bruce and I should go too, May. That solicitor chappie looks to be getting a bit agitated. We'd better let him have his bit of the limelight.'

'Oh Douglas, don't go. You've every right to stay. You're – you're my fiancé.'

Douglas patted her hand. 'No, May. I don't want to

intrude. You can tell me later. I'll run Bruce to the station but I'll come back tonight. That's if you want me to?'

'Of course I do. And will you – will you stay?'

Douglas put his arms round her and held her close. 'Of course I will, darling.'

'And we'll make ourselves scarce, too,' Betty said. 'This is family business.'

The solicitor's clipped tones butted in. 'No, Miss Purves and Miss Mackinder too. I shall need you to be present.'

The two Land Army girls exchanged a puzzled glance, then shrugged and sat down at the table, where the solicitor, Mr Davey, had already seated himself at one end and was setting out his papers in front of him.

'We'll go, May,' Douglas whispered and kissed her cheek. 'Chin up, darling. It'll be all right. I know it will. 'Bye for now.'

As the solicitor's voice droned through all the legal jargon of the will, the nub of Luke's wishes became clear. Although no mention was made of either Douglas or Bruce Whittaker by name, Luke's suspicions had overshadowed his thinking and his decisions. The will had been made and signed only a month earlier.

The solicitor laid down the paper. 'To sum up briefly,' he said now in his own words, 'Mr Clayton has left two thousand pounds to his daughter, May Milton, together with bequests of two hundred pounds each to Miss Purves and Miss Mackinder. The remainder of his estate is to be held in trust for his granddaughter, Anna Milton, until she attains the age of twenty-five.'

'Twenty-five!' May cried, her voice high-pitched with indignation. 'Why twenty-five for Heaven's sake? Why not twenty-one?'

'Mr Clayton felt that twenty-five was a more mature age for such decisions.'

The three women and Anna glanced at one another. May turned towards Mr Davey. 'So what you mean is that he's turning me out and expecting Anna to live here on her own and run the farm until she's twenty-five?'

'No, no, my dear lady. The reason he has, er – ' the man cleared his throat in obvious embarrassment – 'bypassed you and left everything to his granddaughter is that he believed you intend to marry quite soon.'

'Ah, now we have the real reason.' May's eyes glittered with anger now.

'He also mentioned to me,' the man went on calmly, no doubt used to being in situations where the dear departed's will did not meet with unmitigated delight from the rest of the family, 'that you had never had much interest in the farm, but, he said, he believed that his granddaughter did.' He fixed May with a beady look. 'Is that so, Mrs Milton?'

May was flustered now. 'Well, yes, I suppose so. But I'm his daughter. I have a right—'

Mr Davey shook his head. 'I'm sorry, dear lady, but his wishes are crystal clear and the will is solid. I helped draft it myself.'

'And you mean we can't even sell the farm?'

Mr Davey shook his head. 'He appointed one of my partners and myself as his executors and trustees. When Miss Anna reaches twenty-five the farm will be hers to do what she likes with it. But until that time—' He spread his hands and his gesture said the rest.

There was nothing that could be done to challenge Luke's will.

Forty-Two

'A measly two thousand pounds!' Douglas almost shouted at May when she told him the news. 'But you're his daughter, for God's sake.' Then, realizing his error, he put his arms about her. 'I'm sorry. It's not my place to say a word. But I'm so angry on your behalf. I know how dreadfully hurt you must feel. And I feel so responsible too, darling. If it wasn't for me—'

May nestled against his chest. 'It doesn't matter. I'm not interested in the farm. He knew that.'

'But he's left it so that it can't be sold, hasn't he? Left it so – so tied up – ' Douglas's tone was bitter once more – 'that you can't do anything with it. Not a blasted thing.' He held her away from him and looked down into her upturned face. 'What exactly are you going to do?'

'Well, for the moment,' May began hesitantly, unsure how he would greet her plans, 'I thought we could live here at the farm.'

Douglas raised his eyebrows and said sarcastically, 'Oh – and will your daughter allow that?'

May stared at him, not knowing how to react. Then Douglas laughed loudly and drew her to him again. 'Darling, I'm only teasing. Of course, you must stay here, at least for the time being. But once the war is over, well, then we'll see.'

'Why? What do you mean?'

'You don't want to go on living here for ever, do you? I thought you wanted to get back to the city.'

'You know I do,' May said slowly, 'but I can hardly leave a fifteen-year-old girl living here on her own, now can I?'

'What you ought to do is to put a manager in here until such time as she can sell the blasted place.'

May gasped. 'Douglas!'

'Well, you said yourself that you don't want to stay here.'

'I know, but Anna does.'

'She's said so?'

'Yes.'

Douglas's mouth was suddenly a thin, hard line. 'Then your daughter will have to do as she's told. As you have said, darling, she's only fifteen and you, May, are her mother.'

'I'm not going back to the city. I love it here. It belongs to me. Grandfather wanted me to have the farm and I want to live here.'

'And you think you know all about farming do you? You think you'll be able to run this place single-handed?' Douglas sneered.

Anna faced him. 'No, of course I don't. But Betty and Rita are here for a while and—'

'A couple of Land Army girls?'

'And,' Anna continued, 'there's Mr Tomalin – Jed's uncle – at the next farm. He'll help me. He's said so. And, and—' she added in a low tone, 'there's Jed.' She wasn't so sure that she could rely on Jed's help any more. His attitude had been decidedly frosty towards her ever since Bruce and she had become close.

'But you're only fifteen, Anna,' May said. 'I can't go and live in Lincoln and leave you here.' She glanced helplessly towards Douglas. 'I can't.'

'What's wrong with you and Douglas living here?' Betty asked. 'Seems to me that's the simple answer.'

Douglas shot her a vitriolic glance. 'I'm a city dweller. My work's in the city. I couldn't drive back and forth every day. It's difficult enough getting hold of the petrol to get here at weekends as it is. Tell you what, though.' His face suddenly brightened. 'Why don't we buy a place in the city? It's quite a good time to be buying. There's your two thousand pounds, May.' He took her hand and kissed it, smiling into her face. 'We could get a very nice house in Lincoln for that.'

Before May could answer, Betty put in, 'And you'd be selling your place, too, would you?' Her stare was fixed on Douglas's face. He laughed with feigned embarrassment. 'I'm afraid I've nothing to sell. Bruce and I live in rented accommodation.' He pulled an apologetic expression.

May smiled and patted his hand. 'Don't worry. At least my father didn't leave me penniless. Or homeless. We've always a home here, haven't we?'

Above her head, Douglas looked up to meet Anna's troubled gaze. 'Of course we have.' He smiled.

But the smile did not reach his eyes.

Without her grandfather, the farm was not the same place to Anna. Even though the work continued as before with the guidance of Luke's friend and neighbour, Bill Tomalin, she missed the old man dreadfully. Her mother, too, was unhappy. Douglas's visits were fewer. Some weekends, as he was leaving, he would say, 'May, I'm sorry, darling, but I just can't get the petrol to come all the way out here next weekend.'

When he did not come, May moped and cast resentful eyes at Anna, as if it were all her fault.

Only Betty and Rita carried on much as before, though even they missed 'Pops'.

Anna left school and began to work full-time on the farm.

'Ya'll wear a path between your farm and mine, lass,' Bill Tomalin remarked.

Anna smiled. 'I'm sorry to keep bothering you—'

'No bother, lass. Luke'd be proud of the way you're handling things. A slip of a lass like you and you're more or less running that place, aren't ya?'

Though he didn't say so outright, Anna knew he was hinting that he understood May had no interest in the farm. It had been the talk of the district since Luke's death.

Loyally not mentioning her mother, Anna said, 'I couldn't do it without Betty and Rita.'

Bill eyed her soberly. 'Aye, but they'll soon be gone, lass, won't they, when the war's over. Still,' he brightened, 'When the fellers get demobbed, there'll be plenty looking for work.'

Anna nodded. 'But how much longer is the war going on?'

Bill sighed. 'I can't tell you that, lass. I only wish I could. But I'll let you have Jed whenever I can spare him.'

If he'll come, Anna thought, but she smiled and thanked him.

*

'I've got what they call embarkation leave. When I get back, I'll be going overseas.'

Bruce had arrived that Friday evening with his father. When he told her the news, Anna's eyes were wide with fear. 'Where are you going?'

Bruce shrugged. 'Dunno.' Then he grinned, 'And if I did, I couldn't tell you.'

'But I'll be able to write to you?'

'Yeah, course you will. I've got the address written on a bit of paper somewhere. You write to BFPO, I think it is.'

'Whatever's that?'

'British Forces Post Office. And then it gets sent to wherever we are.'

'Oh.' Anna was silent and then asked in a small, doubtful voice. 'Do you think you'll ever get it?'

'Course I will.' He put his arm around her shoulders. 'You write every week and I'll do the same. If I can, that is.' He grinned. 'But I'll be so busy sticking it to Jerry' – he made a stabbing movement as if thrusting his bayonet into the enemy – 'that I might not get much time. Anyway, let's not think about that. Let's go for a walk around *your* farm.'

He laughed and, for a brief moment, Anna felt a twinge of uneasiness at his attitude, but she brushed it aside when he added, 'Come on, let's make the most of my last day.'

Despite her inner sadness, Anna was to look back on that day as one of the happiest she had spent with Bruce. He was kind and attentive, kissing her gently and holding her hand. They talked and laughed and when she shed a few tears over her grandfather, he held her close, stroked her hair and murmured words of comfort.

When Douglas and his son left late on the Sunday night, Anna clung to Bruce. 'You will take care?'

He laughed. 'Don't worry about me. Them Jerries won't get me. It's them that'll have to watch out when I get over there.' He tapped her chin gently. 'Just you remember that you're my girl. I want to know that you're here waiting for me to come home to.'

'Of course I am,' she breathed, feeling a thrill of pleasure run through her.

Douglas revved the car engine and Bruce hopped into the passenger seat. The car roared out of the gate as May and Anna stood waving goodbye. They stood there in the empty yard, listening to the sound grow fainter and fainter.

May put her arm around Anna's shoulder and drew her back into the farmhouse. 'Anna,' she began, biting her lip, 'there's something I have to tell you. Douglas wants me to go back into town with him sometimes. Not every week,' she added hastily, 'but just now and again. You don't mind, do you? Betty and Rita will be here to look after you.'

'That's fine, Mam,' Anna said brightly. But she guessed that May's visits would get longer and longer until she was hardly at the farm at all.

Forty-Three

The tide of the war seemed to be turning in favour of the Allies. At the beginning of June they had entered Rome and only days later the newsreels of the D-Day landing had given everyone new hope. The pictures of the troops landing on the beaches were cheered loudly in every cinema. And as the soldiers pressed inland, Anna wondered if Bruce was there with them. Desperately she scanned the screen for a glimpse of him, but amongst the thousands of servicemen she could not really hope to see him.

But then Hitler launched a new and terrible weapon upon the south of England, the V-1 flying bomb, and a mass evacuation of children from the target area of the pilotless weapons began again.

'Will they get here, do you think?' Anna asked fearfully.

'Don't think so,' Betty said practically. 'They haven't got the range. It's just the south that'll get it. Them poor devils in London have had more than their fair share, I reckon. Fancy having to cope with doodlebugs after all they went through in the Blitz.' She cast a wry glance at Douglas. 'Bet you're glad you moved up here, aren't you?'

Douglas put his arm around May and smiled down at her. 'It was the best thing I've ever done in my life.'

Watching them together, Anna thought: *He really*

does love Mam, I'm sure he does. He's so generous. Maybe Grandpa was wrong about him after all. He never stops buying things for Mam and spoiling her.

May was always dressed in the latest fashion – thanks to Douglas. He bought material and employed a dressmaker to make dresses and costumes for her.

'My future wife's not going to be dressed in utility clothes. Mind you,' he added, winking saucily, 'I must say I like the idea of the shorter skirt to save on material.'

And he brought gifts to the farm too. The day he came with a box of oranges, the Land Army girls and Anna fell on them with squeals of glee. 'I'm not going to ask how you got 'em,' Betty declared, peeling one and biting into the segments. She closed her eyes in ecstasy. 'I'm just glad you did.'

In August Paris was liberated and everyone began to hope that soon the war would be over. Plans for a better Britain were already being talked about. New homes were to be built and a National Health Service that would bring equal health care for all was promised.

And soon, Anna prayed, Bruce would be home. She longed to see him again. She wrote to him every week, just as she had said she would. His letters were not so frequent, but she understood why and forgave him.

I reckon I'll sign on as a regular after the war, he wrote. *I love the army life.*

Anna wrote back to him in a panic. *But what about us?*

His reply was a long time coming and Anna was in a torment of uncertainty. He didn't love her any more. He'd found someone else. A sophisticated, chic French girl perhaps, like the pictures she'd seen in the magazines Betty and Rita brought home.

What do you mean 'What about us?' he wrote at last. *You're my girl, aren't you? We'll get married and you can come with me. It'd be a great life, travelling all over the world. You'd love it. You don't want to live on the farm for ever. And even if you did – which I hope you won't – you won't need me around. You'll always have the faithful Jed.*

Jed had been classed as being in a reserved occupation, much to Bruce's scathing disgust.

He's yeller, he had scoffed in a letter home to Anna. *He ought to be out here getting a taste of what being a real man is like.*

As Anna had expected, May spent more and more time in Lincoln with Douglas, but they still came at the weekend sometimes and then May would stay the rest of the week with Anna, whilst Douglas went back to the city alone.

'We'll have a lovely Christmas this year,' May promised. 'The war might be over by then and Bruce could be home. We'll make it really special.'

But the war was not over by Christmas, though towards the end of November Bruce did get leave and came home for a blissful weekend with Anna.

As they said their goodbyes on the Sunday evening, Anna clung to him. 'Do take care.'

'Course I will. It'll soon be over.'

'But – but you said you might stay in the army. Did you really mean it?'

Bruce shrugged. 'Dunno yet. I might. Look, sorry, I've got to go. Dad's waiting in the car.'

He kissed her hard on the mouth and then he was gone.

*

The following morning Betty came bursting into the kitchen.

'There's three hens gone missing. That beggar – whoever he is – must be back again,' Betty said angrily. 'I thought we'd got rid of him. Nothing much has happened lately.'

'How do you know? Have you counted them?' Rita asked.

'I have now,' Betty said. 'I got suspicious when I couldn't find Speckly.' Betty's favourite was a black and white speckled hen.

'They could have wandered off somewhere,' May suggested. 'Laying their eggs under a hedge, I shouldn't wonder.'

Betty pressed her lips together as she shook her head. 'No. Speckly comes to me to be fed every morning.' The girl was adamant. 'She's gone, I tell you.' And she glared belligerently at May as if it were her fault. 'She'll be plucked and roasted and lying on somebody's plate now.' She glowered as she muttered, 'Somewhere in the city, I shouldn't wonder.'

'What? What do you mean by that, Betty?' May asked sharply, but the girl turned away and left the house, slamming the back door behind her.

'What did she mean?' May asked, glancing between Rita and Anna.

Rita got up. 'I'd best get on.' As she too left the house, May stared after her.

'What did Betty mean? Do you know, Anna?'

Slowly Anna said, 'I think she's hinting that poor Speckly – and probably everything else that's gone missing over the months from the farms around here – has ended up on the black market in the city.'

'Well, yes, I expect it has. We all know that, but –

but she seemed to be hinting at something else. Something more—'

Mother and daughter stared at each other.

'Douglas! She thinks it's Douglas, doesn't she?' May's fingers fluttered to cover her mouth. 'Oh, how could she?' Then suddenly May's eyes sparkled with anger. 'It's more likely she's got some feller in tow who's wheeling and dealing and she's supplying him with our stock. Huh! The cheek. Accusing my Douglas. She's still jealous, that's what. Just because it's me he comes to see now and not her.'

Now it was Anna who did not know how to answer.

May refused to speak to either Betty or Rita for the rest of the week, and by the time Douglas arrived again on the Saturday afternoon she had packed her suitcase and was waiting for him, wearing her hat and coat in readiness.

'We're going straight back to town,' she informed him before he had scarcely got out of the car.

'Why? What's the matter? Trouble?'

'I'll tell you later. Come on, we're going.'

Anna had never seen her mother so forceful. May turned briefly towards her daughter. 'I don't know when I'll be back. You'll – you'll be all right?' There was a moment's brief hesitation in her resolve.

Anna nodded as Douglas lifted his shoulders and spread his arms in a helpless gesture. But he was laughing again as he climbed back into the car. 'Your wish is my command, ma'am.'

As they disappeared down the lane in a cloud of exhaust fumes, Betty came to stand beside Anna. Putting her arm around the young girl, she said, 'I'm sorry

I've upset your mam, but I'm not apologizing for suspecting him. Have you noticed that stuff seems to disappear only after a weekend and only when him and his lad have been?'

Anna gasped and turned to face Betty. 'You mean you think Bruce was involved too?'

Betty watched her with serious eyes. Then she nodded. 'I'm sorry, pet, but—'

Anna pulled away from Betty. 'How could you? Mam was right. It's not them. It's *you*, but you want everyone to *think* it's them.'

'Me?' Betty's face was red, not with guilt but with anger. 'How dare you think that of me? Why, if Pops was still here—'

Tears glistened in Anna's eyes. 'Don't you dare even mention his name.'

'What's going on?' Rita said, coming across the yard.

Betty swung round. 'This little madam is accusing me of stealing.'

Rita's mouth dropped open. Then she laughed. 'Don't be daft, Anna. Betty wouldn't take a ha'penny that didn't belong to her. You should know better than that.'

Now it was Anna's turn to flush with embarrassment. 'All right then, but she's no need to go accusing others.'

Puzzled, Rita glanced from Anna to Betty and back again. 'Others? What others?'

'Douglas and – and Bruce.'

'Ah, well now, there you have me because I'm afraid I have to agree with her.'

Now it was Anna's turn to glance from one to the other as she said falteringly, 'You – you do?'

Rita nodded. 'Sorry, love, but yes, I do.'

Betty was gentle now as she could see that Anna was genuinely distressed and confused. 'Actually, it's more Bruce than Douglas, but I reckon his dad was in on it and all. He was the only one with the transport. Think about it, pet. We had a spate of livestock going from all the farms around here, didn't we? And then, for a while, nothing. All the time Bruce was away doing his basic training. And then when he comes home on leave – three hens go missing.'

'Bill told me yesterday that he lost a piglet last weekend an' all. Same time as our hens went. The weekend Bruce was home on leave.'

Anna closed her eyes and groaned. 'It's not true. It's not. I won't believe it.'

'I'm sorry, love,' Betty said again, 'but I think it's more that you don't want to believe it. Don't you?'

Anna was quiet for the rest of the week. She didn't ignore Betty and Rita, who did their best to act normally, but she was unhappy. She liked Betty and Rita. Her grandpa had too – he'd thought the world of them and trusted them completely. But, she remembered uncomfortably, he had not liked Douglas or his son. Anna sighed. But she loved Bruce and wanted to believe in him. He had gone away again, back abroad, and she didn't want to write this sort of thing in a letter. If only he would come home on leave again, she could sort it all out with him and prove his innocence. And Douglas's too.

The week dragged by. She missed Bruce and now she missed her mother. But for the two Land Army girls' insinuations, it could have been a happy week. Betty and Rita were good workers and despite the atmosphere between them and Anna they still carried out the work as they always had done.

Privately, Betty said to Rita, 'For two pins I'd walk out, but I'm doing it for Pops.'

'Anna's all right. I know she likes Bruce, but I reckon she's wavering.'

Betty's tough line softened. 'Poor kid. She's only young. She doesn't know what to believe.' Her tone hardened again. 'But May's old enough to know better.'

Rita laughed. 'Come on, Bet. You fell for him once.'

Betty grinned. 'Nearly, I admit it. But,' she tapped the side of her nose knowingly, 'I never let myself get so carried away that I can't suss out what they're like. And I soon started to see that Mr Douglas Whittaker wasn't quite all he was cracked up to be.' She sighed and added, 'But May—' She needed to say no more. They both knew that May was so besotted with Douglas that she could see no wrong in him.

'We ought to work on Anna,' Rita said seriously.

Betty shrugged. 'I don't expect she'll believe us. When her own mother is so taken up with the father you can hardly expect her to turn against the son, can you?'

'It's worth a try, even if only for poor old Pops,' Rita said solemnly. 'It's what he would have wanted us to do.'

The girls' plans to get Anna to see what they believed was the truth were dashed when May returned home three weeks later, flashing a wedding ring.

'We were married by special licence, Anna,' May said, her face glowing with happiness. 'I'm sorry you couldn't be there, but Douglas says we'll make it up to you. You and Bruce, next time he's home.'

'Well, that's it, then,' Betty said, folding her arms with a gesture of finality. 'You'll not be wanting us around any longer.'

'As you wish, Betty,' May said stiffly.

'Oh now, come on, Betty.' Douglas put his arm around her shoulders. She stiffened beneath his touch. 'May's told me of your suspicions and yes, you're quite right to suspect me—'

'Douglas!' May's eyes were wide, but he was laughing.

'Oh, I'm not perfect, May darling, I'll be the first to admit it and yes, I do a bit of dealing on the black market, but I wouldn't stoop to stealing. Specially not from May. I'd be a fool wouldn't I?'

'What about that lad of yours then?' Betty persisted. 'Is he pure and lily white an' all?' she added sarcastically.

Douglas was still standing with his arm draped around her. His face was close to hers. As she looked up, she was sure she saw a fleeting malicious glint in his eyes, but it was gone in an instant and she wondered if she had imagined it.

Douglas forced himself to laugh again. 'No young feller of his age is pure and lily white, as you put it, but he's not a bad lad.'

Betty moved away from him as she glanced at May. 'I still think it would be better if we left. Now you've got a husband to help you with the farm work, you won't need us.' There was the merest hint of sarcasm in her tone and everyone noticed it. Only Douglas guffawed. 'Me? Milk cows and muck out the henhouse? I think not. Besides, May and I will be spending most of our time in Lincoln. Won't we, darling? We've got a nice house in view – a semi-detached in a nice part of the city.' He turned towards Anna, as if suddenly realizing he had not included her in their plans. 'You'll love it, Anna. And we'll have your room decorated just as you'd like it.'

Anna smiled weakly and murmured, 'That's very kind of you, but I must stay here.' She turned to Betty and Rita. 'Please don't leave me. I couldn't manage on my own.' But before either of them could answer, Douglas said, 'It'd be far better if you could sell the lot. This place is a millstone round your neck. A young girl like you should be out having fun, not slaving away out here in the back of beyond. If it hadn't been for that vindictive old man, you could be well off and having the time of your life.'

Anna gasped. 'I love the farm. I'll never sell it. Never.'

Now Douglas couldn't hide his anger. 'Well, you'll be on your own then because your mother and I have no intention of living here.'

May bit her lip and glanced anxiously between her new husband and her daughter. But she said nothing. She made no attempt to deny Douglas's words.

Anna's dark violet eyes filled with tears as she murmured again, 'Betty, please don't go.'

The two older girls glanced at each other and, as if reaching mutual agreement, Betty sighed and said, 'All right, pet. We'll stay a bit longer.'

As it turned out they only stayed a few more months, for in the following May the war ended and when demobilization began, as Betty had predicted, there were plenty of men looking for work.

Anna's heart sang. Bruce would be coming home and then everything would be all right.

Forty-Four

'I 'spect we'll be going home soon, then,' Betty said.

They had all been to the street party in the village to celebrate VE Day and had returned home to the farm tired, but elated that the war was finally over.

'I don't expect they'll let us go just yet. Not till demob starts and there's fellers back home to take our places,' Rita said.

Betty nodded. ''Spect you're right. They'll tell us when, I suppose.'

'You'll stay till after shearing, won't you? Even if we get new fellers, they won't be as good as you.'

'Could I have that in writing please, ma'am?' Betty quipped. 'I might need a good reference when I go back home and start looking for work.'

It was Jed who took charge at shearing time.

'He's a born natural with them shears,' his uncle said proudly. 'He's won prizes for it, y'know.'

Anna was fascinated to watch Jed at work. He was firm but gentle with the sheep. There was no panic or rough handling, but his strength kept them under control as he rolled them over and began to shear, the fleece falling off.

'Like a knife through butter,' Betty, standing beside Anna, murmured. 'He's good, isn't he?'

Anna nodded. For a brief moment there was a lump

in her throat. Things had not been the same between her and Jed over the last months and she missed his easy friendship.

'Yes, he is good,' she said and meant it about more than just sheep shearing. He had taught her so much, she realized. It had been Jed who had shown her how to fold the fleeces, Jed who had helped her at dipping time when she had not wanted to plunge the poor creatures right into the dip.

'You've got to do it, Anna, for their own sake,' he'd explained gently. 'You don't want to see 'em with ticks or lice or, worse still, sheep scab, do you?'

And despite the rift between them over Bruce, he was still here, still helping her, even though she had the uncomfortable feeling that he was now doing it more for her grandfather's memory than for her.

'I don't like leaving you, Anna,' Betty said worriedly when the day came in the autumn for both her and Rita to leave. Their former, easy relationship had never been fully restored since Betty's accusations, yet both Land Army girls were genuinely fond of Anna – and May, too, though they were exasperated by the older woman's blind worship of Douglas.

'Can't she see him for what he is? A wide boy. A spiv. If only she'd listened to Pops. He knew, bless him. Oh, how I wish I'd never brought Douglas Whittaker here. I could kick myself. If I'd thought for one minute—' Betty said more than once, but never now in front of Anna. 'And what'll happen when Bruce gets home I shudder to think.'

'It's not our worry,' Rita tried to tell her.

'No, I know. But when I think about Pops—' It was

all Betty needed to say for them to lapse into a sorrowful silence, until Rita said practically, 'There's nothing more we can do, Bet. Time to go home and pick up our own lives.'

And now the day had come. Their belongings were all packed and they were in the yard waiting for the lorry that was coming to pick them up. Anna hugged them both in turn, all discord forgotten. Tears were running down her face. 'I wish you weren't going. You've been wonderful.'

'I just hope these two new fellers you've got are going to be all right.'

Anna smiled through her tears. 'Well, it isn't as if I don't know them. Jed is still here – ' she pulled a face – 'well, now and again. And I went to school with Phil – one of the new hands – though he is a bit older than me. Grandpa knew his family, so I know he would have approved.'

There was an awkward silence as if all of them were thinking the same thing. Luke would not have approved of May's marriage or of the fact that Anna was longing for the day when Bruce returned.

Betty nodded, comforted by Anna's words. 'They do seem nice lads,' she said, 'and at least if you say Pops would have approved of *them*—' She didn't finish the sentence and what she didn't say seemed to hang in the air between them.

'Here's the lorry,' Rita said and there was a further flurry of hugs and goodbyes and promises to write. As the lorry drew out of the yard, Anna followed it into the lane and stood waving until it turned a corner and disappeared from her sight. Slowly she walked back into the silent farmhouse and wandered from room to room. She would be sleeping here alone now and, though the fact didn't frighten her, she knew she would be very lonely.

Oh, if only, she thought, *Bruce would come home.*

The months dragged on and another Christmas came and went. Whilst May and Douglas spent Christmas Day and Boxing Day with her, there was nothing festive about the atmosphere in the farmhouse.

Anna did her best, cooking a goose with all the other Christmas fare that rationing would allow, but Douglas seemed ill at ease and fidgeting to get back to town. And May too no longer belonged at Clayton's Farm – if she ever had, Anna thought wryly.

There was no word of Bruce being home on leave or even of a date for his demob.

'Do you think he's signed on? He said he was going to.'

Douglas frowned. 'He'd better not have done, else I'll have something to say about that.'

Near the time of May's birthday in May, she and Douglas arrived at the farmhouse unexpectedly one weekend.

'Come on,' Douglas said, 'pack your case. We're taking you back to town.'

'But, I can't leave—'

'Of course you can. Phil and Maurice will manage for a few days.' He smiled as he leant towards her. 'And we've got a surprise for you.'

'What?'

'Aha, you'll have to wait and see. Wouldn't be a surprise if we told you, would it?'

Anna was still doubtful, but when May said persuasively, 'Oh please come, Anna, you haven't seen our house yet,' she gave in.

'I can't stay long though. There's sheep dipping to do soon and I don't think the lads'll manage on their own.'

'We'll see, we'll see,' Douglas said and Anna saw him wink at May. As she packed an overnight bag, Anna began to feel excited. It would be nice to go to Lincoln, to go shopping. Perhaps they'd even go to Douglas's cinema together and see a film. She'd like that. Perhaps that was the surprise.

May showed her all over the semi-detached house she and Douglas had bought. Their new home was set on a road leading up the hill on the northern side of the city. Anna buried the thought that her mother's money had paid for it.

'They're lovely houses, aren't they?' May enthused, flinging open the door of one of the three bedrooms. 'And this is your room. We've had decorators in specially. Do you like it?' she asked eagerly.

Anna glanced around at the pink-flowered wallpaper, the pink bedspread and matching curtains fluttering at the window. 'It's – it's lovely, Mam, but—' She turned her gaze towards her mother. 'But I won't be living here. I'll have to stay at the farm.'

May flapped her hands. 'But that's only for a few years. Until you can sell it and come and live in the city with us. You might even be able to come before, if you put a manager in. Then you can get a nice job in an office and—'

Anna shook her head. 'Mam, I don't want to work in an office. I want to work on the farm. I love it there. Besides, I couldn't sell Grandpa's farm.'

'Oh, Anna, surely you're not serious? You can't really mean that you want to live out there? All on your own?'

'I won't be on my own.'

'You will be at night when the workers have gone home. And we can't keep driving out to the farm. Petrol's still in short supply, you know.'

'Bruce will be with me.'

May laughed. 'You can forget that, you silly goose. Bruce won't want to live in the back of beyond any more than his father does.' May shook her head and added bitterly, 'If that stupid old man hadn't tied everything up so tightly that we can't sell the place for years, we'd be living in clover now.'

Anna glanced around her. The words were out before she could stop them. 'You don't look to be doing so badly, Mam.'

'Anna!' May was appalled. 'How dare you speak to me like that?'

'You shouldn't speak about Grandpa like that.' Tears filled the girl's eyes. 'He loved us. Both of us.'

May sniffed. 'You, maybe, but I'm not so sure about me.'

Appalled, Anna stared at her. 'Of course he loved you, Mam. Look how they took us in at the start of the war and – and looked after us when Daddy—'

'I know, I know, but – ' May bit her lip – 'I always felt that was more your grannie's doing than *his*.'

Anna was adamant. She shook her head. 'No, no, you're wrong. I know you are. He wanted the best for you. I know he did. And as for him not liking Douglas, well, maybe then it was only because he was concerned about you getting involved with someone else so soon after Daddy—'

May said bitterly, 'Oh, you don't know the half of it, Anna. How could you? I've told you before that he didn't like your father when I first met him.'

'I know, but he came round, didn't he?'

'He was against me marrying him because Ken didn't want to live on the farm. It was always because of the farm.'

'But – but he was always nice to Daddy.'

May laughed wryly. 'Oh yes, after we had you. He came round very quickly when we gave him a grandchild. He even wanted me to christen you Anna Clayton Milton, but I drew the line at that. Such a mouthful. But he was quite happy then to think that there was someone else to pass his precious farm on to.' She paused and then added pointedly, 'He was right, wasn't he?'

Anna nodded slowly and said huskily, but with a firmness that her mother could not fail to notice, 'Yes, he was.' Then she added, 'I'm sorry, Mam, I didn't mean to cheek you.'

'I should think so too. Douglas was right. He said you had a stubborn streak in you. Well, my girl' – May put her hand on Anna's shoulder and propelled her from the room – 'there's someone downstairs waiting to see you who might change your mind for you.'

As they stepped into the sitting room Anna gasped aloud, for standing in front of the fireplace, resplendent in his army uniform, was Bruce.

Anna flew across the room, her arms outstretched. Bruce caught her and swung her round.

'How's my best girl?' he laughed and, though both

Douglas and May were watching, he kissed Anna firmly on the mouth, ignoring her blushing protest.

They had a wonderful weekend. Anna and May went round the city shops on the Saturday and in the evening they went to the cinema, Douglas having procured the best seats in the front of the circle.

On the Sunday May packed a picnic and they went to the Arboretum, sitting on the grass in the warm September sunshine.

'When do you have to go back?' Anna asked Bruce for the first time. Until this moment she hadn't wanted to broach the subject.

Bruce lay back and put his hands behind his head. 'Wednesday morning. Four whole days of leave.'

'You won't be going abroad again, will you?'

'Dunno,' Bruce said, squinting up at her. 'I told you, I thought I might sign on after the war. Well, I've made up my mind. I'm going to become a regular. I like the army life.'

'Oh, but what about—?' she began and then bit her lip.'

Bruce grinned. 'What about what?'

'Oh nothing.' She glanced away from him and pulled at the grass.

Bruce sat up. Softly, he said, 'You were going to say, "What about us?" weren't you?'

'Well,' she said hesitantly then added hastily, 'but maybe you don't want – I mean—'

'Of course I want. You're my girl, aren't you?'

Anna blushed and nodded.

'We can write to each other and when I come home on leave—'

'Never mind about that.' Douglas raised his voice and both Anna and Bruce realized that, though he had been lying back with his eyes closed, he had been listening to every word of their conversation. 'Never mind about that,' he said again, sitting up. 'What you want to do is to get married. The pair of you—'

Now May sat up. 'Oh no, Douglas. Anna's far too young. She's only seventeen. There's plenty of time—'

'No, there isn't,' Douglas almost snapped. 'This war should have shown you that, May. Youngsters have to grab their happiness. Just think about it. They haven't even got to save up for a home of their own.' He spread his hands. 'Anna's already got one. The farm. They can live on the farm. And you' – he jabbed his finger towards his son – 'can forget about signing on for years. What more could you want than a life in the country? You'll be set up for life, the pair of you.'

'But you said—' May began, but Anna saw Douglas glare at his wife. 'Never mind what I said. If it's what they both want, then why make them wait, eh?'

Still May hesitated as she looked across at Anna. 'Is it what you want, love?'

'Well—' she glanced at Bruce. He was staring at his father as if he thought Douglas had taken leave of his senses.

Ignoring him, Douglas boomed, 'Of course it is,' as if the matter had been decided. 'Come on,' he said, getting up. 'It's getting chilly. Let's go home. Bruce, you help me pack up the picnic things. You two go and sit in the car. We'll manage.'

As Anna and her mother walked down the slope to where the car was parked on the road, she glanced back. Douglas was wagging his finger in Bruce's face, whilst his son stared wordlessly at his father. It looked as if Douglas was telling his son exactly what he must do and that Bruce was not daring to argue.

Later, after their evening meal, Anna managed to whisper to Bruce. 'Will you take me back to the farm tomorrow morning? I have to get back and we need to talk.'

Bruce nodded.

Forty-Five

'You don't have to marry me, you know. Never mind what your dad says,' Anna said as they drove back to the farm.

'Who said I didn't want to marry you?'

'No one, but—'

'Well, then, what are you going on about?' Bruce snapped and Anna glanced at him and then fell silent.

They did not speak for the rest of the journey and when they drew to a stop in the yard, Bruce leapt out saying, 'I'll bring your things in. You'd better go and make sure those lads you left in charge haven't killed off half your stock.'

As Anna climbed out and began to walk towards the house, Bruce flung up the lid of the boot and reached inside. For no particular reason, she glanced into the boot as Bruce was lifting out her bag.

Beneath it, lying in the well of the boot, Anna was sure she saw two or three chicken feathers. Bruce slammed the lid. Anna stopped and stared at him.

'How've they got in there?'

'Eh? Come again?'

'Those feathers? In the boot? How've they got in there?'

For a moment, Bruce glared at her, 'I don't know what you're talking about.'

She pointed. 'In there. There's some chicken feathers.'

'Don't be daft. You're seeing things.'

'Open the boot then. See for yourself. There's definitely feathers in the boot.'

Frowning, Bruce opened the lid once more and glanced inside.

'There! Look!'

Bruce slammed the lid once more. 'So what? Them hen feathers get everywhere. So does their flipping muck. Last time I came here I got a right rollocking from my Sergeant when I got back to camp 'cos there was chicken muck on my boots.'

Somehow he had turned the accusation against her, but for the rest of the day Anna could not put the memory out of her mind. The thought that perhaps Betty had been right after all crept insidiously into her brain.

Bruce, however, seemed to have put the incident out of his mind. As dusk fell, he said, 'I'd better be getting back to town then.' He slipped his arm around her waist. 'Unless you want me to stay the night. It must get lonely for you—'

Anna shook her head. 'No, you'd better go. It wouldn't be right, you staying here. People would talk and I don't think Mam'd like it.'

'Dad'd talk her round. Oh, go on, Anna, let me stay.'

'Well, you could sleep in the spare room.'

'The spare room? I'm not sleeping in any spare room.'

Anna gasped as his meaning became clear. 'Oh no,' she said firmly now, 'in that case, you're not staying.'

Bruce let his arm fall away. 'Please yourself. There's plenty wouldn't turn down an offer like that.'

Anna gasped. 'What – what do you mean?'

Bruce grinned. 'What do you think I mean?'

'That you – you've been with other girls?'

Bruce opened his mouth to retort and then suddenly he closed it again, then frowned slightly, almost as if he realized just what he had been going to say and had caught himself just in time. 'I didn't say that, did I?'

'No, but—'

'Don't jump to conclusions. All I said was, there's plenty wouldn't turn down the offer. Right?'

'All right,' Anna said in a small voice. Once again he had gained the upper hand in an argument.

'So? Do I stay or do I go?'

This time he could not argue when Anna turned away from him. 'You'd better go.'

From the kitchen she heard the car roar off up the lane until she could hear its sound no more.

Suddenly, she felt incredibly lonely and regretted her prim refusal of Bruce's company.

The following morning, her eyes still heavy with sleep after a restless night, Anna went out into the yard. Clanging noises were coming from the cowshed. The morning milking was already under way.

She peeked round the door to see Jed sitting with his head pressed against a cow's side, the milk spurting into the bucket. He was whistling softly.

'Morning, Jed,' Anna said quietly, so as not to startle the cow.

Jed twisted his head sideways. 'Morning, Anna. Had a nice weekend?' The question was not quite the polite enquiry it might have been. There was a hint of sarcasm in his tone and no friendly smile to accompany it.

She gave a swift nod, but lowered her eyes. 'Everything been all right here?'

'Fine. Phil's away up the fields to check the sheep.' His reply was terse and to the point.

'I'll have breakfast ready for you all. How long will you be finishing milking?'

''Bout half an hour.'

She was sitting in the kitchen, cupping a mug of tea in her hands and watching Jed devour a plateful of bacon, eggs and fried bread, when Phil burst in through the back door.

'You know those lambs you kept back from going to market? To increase the stock?' he began at once. Anna turned to look up at him and Jed stopped eating, his fork suspended halfway between the plate and his mouth.

Anna rose slowly, guessing what he was going to say. 'Yes?'

'One's missing.'

Anna closed her eyes and groaned. 'Oh no!'

Jed's face was grim. Hurriedly he finished his meal and rose to his feet. 'We'd best have a good look round, but if we can't find it, I reckon you ought to report it to the police this time, Anna.'

Anna shuddered. He was right, of course, but the memory of the chicken feathers in the back of Douglas's car was all too vivid.

Forty-Six

Over the next few weeks no letters came from Bruce and Anna could not bring herself to write to him either. Perhaps their romance was over, she thought dully, almost before it had really begun.

Douglas and May came out to the farm most weekends and never left without trying to persuade her to move to the city to live with them.

'Why won't you agree to put a manager in here? That young fellow, Jed, he'd be ideal. I know he's only young but he's got his uncle close by,' Douglas said more than once, always angling his suggestions to appear as if he only had Anna's best interests at heart. 'It's no life for a young girl like you stuck out here. Living all alone. Your mother's worried sick about you. Think of your mother, Anna. You're being very selfish, you know.'

Anna said nothing but sighed inwardly. It was amazing, she thought, how both Douglas and Bruce seemed to turn everything around to being someone else's fault.

But Anna didn't want to go. Oh yes, some nights she felt very lonely, but usually she was so tired that she went to bed early and slept the sound sleep of someone who had worked hard all day in the open air. Winter had been the worst with the long dark nights, but always the memory of Luke made her determined to stay. Her grandfather had left Clayton's Farm to her.

He knew she loved it and he had trusted her to carry on the family tradition. And now it was summer again, a year on from the end of the war. Things were getting better and there was plenty of work to keep her busy.

'I'll not let you down, Grandpa,' she whispered into the darkness as she lay in bed. 'I'll never sell your farm. Never.'

'Bruce is coming home on leave next week,' Douglas told Anna toward the end of June. Has he told you?'

'No. He – he hasn't written lately.'

Douglas frowned. 'Not written? Well, I'll have something to say about that when I see him.' He patted Anna's shoulder. 'Don't worry, love. You know what young fellers are. I expect he's not much of a letter writer.' He gave a bellowing guffaw. 'Takes after his dad.'

Anna smiled weakly.

'Tell you what,' Douglas said, 'instead of you coming into town, we'll all come out here. Make a nice change, wouldn't it, May, to have a weekend in the country?'

'Whatever you say, dear.'

Anna glanced at her mother, but May avoided meeting her daughter's eyes. Anna made up her mind to try to speak to her mother alone. There was something different about May. She looked on edge, nervous and agitated, and every time Douglas spoke to her she seemed to jump. She was wearing more make-up than usual, Anna noticed, the powder plastered thickly onto her cheeks. May had always spurned artificial aids, Anna thought, remembering how proud her mother had been of her smooth, flawless skin. A good face cream and a touch of pale pink lipstick was all she'd ever needed had been her proud boast. But now the make-up was thick and poorly applied. And, Anna noticed, May's thumbnail was bitten down to the quick.

But during the day Douglas never left May's side and Anna had no chance to speak to her mother alone. As the car sped away that evening, Anna had the irrational feeling that Douglas had stayed close to May deliberately. He had been his usual charming and attentive self, but there was something more. Something that Anna could not quite put her finger on . . .

On the following Friday Anna threw open the windows in the room that had once been her grandparent's bedroom and also in the tiny spare room.

'He can sleep here,' she muttered. 'He's not getting into my bed, whatever he thinks.'

She put fresh linen on the beds and a posy of flowers in the main room to greet her mother.

'Is *he* coming?' Jed asked morosely as he ate his ploughman's lunch sitting at the scrubbed table in Anna's kitchen. His eyes followed her busy movements between table and range as she prepared a special evening meal.

'Who?' She looked up, startled.

'Him? Bruce whatever-his-name-is?'

Anna tried to hide her smile, but unsuccessfully. It sounded for all the world as if Jed was jealous. 'He's on leave, but they're all coming.' She giggled. 'My reputation will be quite safe.'

Jed glowered at her and bit deeply into his bread and cheese.

A few moments' uncomfortable silence went by before Jed blurted out, 'Are you serious about him?'

It was on the tip of her tongue to say, 'What's it to do with you?' but something in his tone stopped her. They'd been friends ever since the day her grandfather had introduced him to her when she had come to live on the farm with her mother at the beginning of the war. Lately their easy friendship had been strained, but now he sounded like the old Jed.

She sighed and sat down opposite him. 'To tell you the truth, Jed, I don't know. Not now. A while back, I would have said "yes" straight away, but now—'

Jed's tone became gentle as if he sensed her dilemma and really wanted to help. 'I'm always here if you want to talk about it.'

Anna felt a lump in her throat. 'Thanks,' she said huskily. There was silence between them once more, but now it was a companionable one. 'Have you got a girlfriend, Jed?'

'Oh, dozens of 'em,' he said airily. 'They're queuing up, y'know.'

Anna laughed. 'I can believe that.'

Jed's smile faded as he regarded her seriously. 'I was only joking. No, Anna, there's no one.' As she met his steady gaze across the table, Anna felt a shiver run through her. She was not so naive now that she didn't recognize the look in his dark eyes.

She had not been mistaken earlier. It had most definitely been jealousy in Jed's tone when he had spoken of Bruce.

'Here we are then,' Douglas boomed as he offered his hand to May to help her from the car. Anna hurried forward. She glanced briefly at Bruce as he sprang from the back seat, but it was to her mother she went with her arms outstretched. She kissed May's cheek and then stood back to look at her. May's smile was tremulous and there was a wary look in her eyes. She met Anna's gaze and glanced towards her husband, then swiftly back to Anna. The girl had the strangest feeling that her mother was trying to tell her something. Trying to warn her, almost.

Anna linked her arm through May's and drew her towards the house, promising herself that during this weekend she would definitely get her mother on her own and find out what was troubling her. Because she was sure now that something was bothering May.

'Hey, don't I even get a kiss after all this time?' Bruce spread his arms wide.

'Later,' she teased, forcing a gaiety that she wasn't feeling, 'when there's not so many people about.'

She was uncomfortably aware that not only were her mother and Douglas there to see, but that Jed was watching from the cowhouse door.

'I'll look forward to it.' Bruce pretended to leer.

'Come along in,' Anna chattered brightly, trying to hide her disquiet. 'I've cooked you a meal and we'll have it in the front room as a special treat. I've even lit a fire. It's still cold in the evenings, isn't it, even though it's June?'

The two men were not following them into the house but had remained standing by the car. Douglas was gesticulating and almost shaking his fist in Bruce's face. A few fractured words and partial sentences drifted across the yard to her, but made no sense.

'. . . all this . . . make her . . . just do it . . . think of . . . I'll take care . . . as I say . . .'

But Anna's mind was on her mother so she paid no

heed to whatever the argument was between father and son. As she drew her mother into the kitchen, she asked quickly, 'Are you all right, Mam? You don't look – well.'

May glanced nervously through the kitchen window, but already Douglas was moving towards the back door. 'I'll tell you sometime. Not now.' Suddenly she gripped Anna's hands and whispered urgently, 'Be careful, Anna, oh, do be careful . . .' May's voice faded away as Douglas came into the kitchen, rubbing his hands together and moving towards the table laden with roast leg of lamb, fresh mint sauce and steaming vegetables.

'Now, isn't that a welcome sight? Beats life in barracks any day, doesn't it, boy? The sooner you get yourself demobbed and back here the better.' He turned and winked at Anna. 'You've got everything very nice, love, and this dinner looks a treat.'

There was a tense atmosphere around the dining table with only Douglas keeping up a hearty attempt at conversation.

Bruce kept his head down, almost shovelling the food into his mouth.

'Where's your manners, boy?' Douglas berated him. 'You've not been brought up to eat like a pig. Is that what they teach you in the army?'

May picked at her main course and refused the pudding. As she rose at the end of the meal to help Anna clear away, Douglas's hand shot out. 'Let the youngsters do that. Let's you and me go for a little walk in the moonlight, eh?'

May bit her lip, glanced anxiously towards Anna, but said meekly, 'I'll get my coat.'

'And you, m'lad' – Douglas jabbed his finger towards

Bruce – 'can stay and help Anna with all this washing up.' Then he bent towards his son and mumbled something close to his ear that Anna couldn't catch.

As they worked together side by side in the scullery, Bruce said, 'I'm sorry I haven't written.' He sounded so genuinely contrite that Anna glanced over her shoulder as she stood at the sink, her hands deep in the washing-up water. He looked like a naughty little boy who had been caught scrumping apples. She smiled. 'Me too. I – I didn't know what to say after – last time.'

Bruce flung down the tea towel and, standing behind her, he put his arms about her and nuzzled her neck. 'I know. I'm sorry. Am I forgiven?'

She felt the familiar thrill of excitement surge through her as she turned and put her hands about his neck, oblivious to the fact that she was dripping soapsuds onto the back of his uniform.

'Of course,' she said huskily.

His mouth came down hard upon hers, so hard that it bruised her lips. 'I want you, Anna. Oh, how I want you.'

Forty-Seven

When her mother and Douglas returned from their walk, Anna and Bruce were sitting before the dying embers of the front-room fire, with Buster lying on the hearth rug between them. As May and Douglas came in, the dog raised his head and gave a low growl. Sitting beside him, Anna stroked his silky head soothingly and shushed him.

'Look at this pair of lovebirds,' Douglas laughed. 'Sitting here in the dark. They've been too busy to light the lamp.' He chuckled suggestively.

'I'll do it,' May said and reached up to lift down the lamp that hung from a hook in the ceiling.

'Leave it, love,' Douglas said, giving an exaggerated yawn. 'I don't know about you, but I'm for bed anyway. Must be the country air. Night, you two. Come along, May.' As if confident of her immediate obedience, he turned and left the room. May hesitated, glancing meaningfully at her daughter. Anna scrambled up from the hearthrug.

'Do you want some cocoa, Mam? I'll make some.'

'No—' May began and then changed her mind. 'Yes. That would be nice, dear. 'I'll – er – come and help you.'

As they passed through the narrow hallway towards the kitchen, they heard Douglas shouting from the top of the stairs. 'May? Are you coming, May?'

'We're just going to make some cocoa. I'll – I'll bring you some up.'

'Never mind about cocoa, May. Come on up to bed.' There was a slight pause. 'Now!'

Anna gasped and opened her mouth, but her mother put her fingers to her lips and whispered, 'Don't say anything, Anna. Please. I must go. We'll talk tomorrow.' Hurriedly, she kissed her daughter's cheek and turned towards the stairs, calling, 'Just coming, dear.'

Anna returned to the front room, concerned for her mother.

'I thought you'd gone to make cocoa,' Bruce said.

'What? Oh, sorry. Mam changed her mind. She's gone up. Do you want some?'

'No.' Bruce grinned and got up, moving towards a cupboard in the sideboard. 'I'd like something a bit stronger. Now – ' he was bending down opening the door of the sideboard – 'if I remember rightly, the old man kept a bottle of whisky somewhere in here. Ah yes.' He lifted out a bottle triumphantly. 'Here it is.' Then he reached for two of her grandmother's best cut-glass tumblers from the shelf above the sideboard. 'Want some?'

'No, thanks.' Anna gave a shudder. 'I don't like the stuff.'

'How do you know? I bet you've never tried it.'

'I have,' she said, with a wry smile. 'When I was quite little I drank some from that very cupboard and made myself terribly sick. I can't even bear the smell of it.'

Bruce laughed as he poured himself a generous measure. 'Come on, try a bit. You might like it now you're grown up.'

'No, thanks.'

She sat close to Bruce on the sofa, resting her head against his shoulder whilst he drank. 'Mind you, I'd have preferred a beer. Have you got any?'

'No. I never thought. Sorry.'

'Well, just mind you get some for next time I'm home on leave.' He tweaked her nose playfully and she laughed.

There was silence between them as Bruce seemed to concentrate more and more on drinking. He had refilled his glass three times when Anna said, 'I'm going to bed.'

Eyes half closed, Bruce took another swallow and nodded.

'Night, then,' she said. 'Come on, Buster. Let's put you out and lock up.'

The dog rose obediently, but followed her with his tail between his legs. At the back door, he refused to go outside. Anna laughed. 'I've spoiled you, haven't I? Letting you sleep on my bedroom floor when no one else is here.'

The dog gave a knowing bark, as if he knew exactly what she was saying and then, to prove it, he turned and scampered towards the stairs, bounding up them and into her bedroom. Anna gave in, hoping that her mother wouldn't find out. Besides, it would create far more commotion to try to drag the dog down the stairs again than to let him stay.

Anna was just drifting off to sleep when she heard Buster's low growl. She sat up in bed and heard the familiar squeak of the doorknob. The door opened slowly and Buster's growl grew louder. The door stopped moving, as if whoever it was coming in, had heard the dog and had hesitated.

Anna's heart was thumping. 'Who is it?'

She heard the door click shut and soft footsteps going

along the landing towards the tiny spare bedroom. She knew it had been Bruce coming to say goodnight.

She snuggled down, smiling to herself. Tomorrow night she would make sure that Buster slept in her room again.

'Good boy,' she whispered into the darkness and heard his soft, answering whine.

The morning milking had been done and the breakfast laid by the time that any of her bleary-eyed guests appeared.

'Oh, pour us a strong cuppa, Anna love,' Bruce said, sitting down at the kitchen table and dropping his aching head into his hands.

Jed, sitting on the opposite side of the table eating his breakfast, eyed him disgustedly.

'And you can take that look off your face, mate. Ain't you ever had a skinful?'

'Oh aye, more 'n once,' Jed said airily, 'but I can hold me liquor. Thought you army wallahs could an' all.'

'I could drink you under the table any day,' Bruce sneered.

'Betcha,' Jed muttered, through a mouthful of egg and bacon.

'Right, you're on. Tonight, down the pub.'

Jed's eyes sparkled as he nodded. 'Betcha ten bob I'm the one carrying you home.'

'You're on.'

Anna banged the cup and saucer down on the table in front of Bruce. 'Haven't you both got summat better to do with your money than drink yourself senseless and then lose ten bob into the bargain?'

Bruce grinned up at her. 'I shan't lose ten bob. I'll be winning it.'

'Huh!' Anna gave a snort, exasperated with them both. She turned on Jed. 'I'm surprised at you, Jed. And don't think you can be late for morning milking tomorrow.'

'I won't be.' He grinned at her and added saucily, 'Boss.'

'Oh, you!' Anna flounced out of the kitchen, leaving each young man to savour the thought of beating his rival.

Anna was busy all the morning and had no chance to speak to her mother alone. She paused only once when passing through the yard, amused to see that Bruce was trying to make friends with Buster.

'Here, boy. Here, look what I've got for you. A nice piece of meat.'

She chuckled softly to herself. *Bruce is trying to befriend my guard dog*, she thought, *in the hope that he'll let him into my room tonight.*

And in the afternoon, when Bruce said, 'Let's go for a walk,' she agreed readily. 'We'll take Buster. He could do with a long run.' She whistled, but there was no answering bark, no sound of paws scampering towards her.

'Where is he?' Anna murmured, glancing round the yard.

Bruce laughed. 'Looks like he's gone for his own long run. Come on. Let's not waste time looking for him. He'll be somewhere chasing rabbits.'

It was a beautiful, peaceful afternoon as they walked along, their arms around each other. Beneath the shade of two tall trees, they stopped and Bruce turned to take her into his arms.

'I reckon you're even prettier than I remembered,' he said and kissed the tip of her nose. 'I'm going to give that Jed a run for his money tonight. Let him know you're my girl. He can keep his eyes off you.'

Anna laughed aloud. 'What, Jed? Don't be daft.' But she couldn't help a faint tinge of pink coming into her cheeks.

'Well, just you remember if he starts anything, you're my girl. And you can tell him that. Mind you, I reckon he'll get the message tonight, after I've finished with him.'

She laughed again. 'You're as daft as each other. The pair of you. Besides, Buster will look after me. He's my guard dog.' It was an oblique reference to the previous night and for a moment Bruce drew back and looked straight into her eyes. 'Yes, he is, isn't he?'

'Where the devil is he? Where's Bruce?' Douglas ranted after tea.

'He's gone down to the pub,' Anna said.

'The pub? When he's got a lovely girl like you here sitting on her own.' Douglas's mouth was a grim line. 'I'll have a word or two to say to him when he gets back.' He frowned. 'That lad's getting out of hand since he's been in the army. Thinks he can disobey me.'

'Why?' Anna asked innocently. 'Did you ask him to stay in tonight?'

'What? Oh – er – no. Not exactly, but it would only have been polite when he's your guest and he has only one more day here.'

Anna shrugged. 'I don't mind.'

'Well, you should,' Douglas snapped. Then he forced a smile. 'What I mean, love, is don't you want to see as much of your young man as you can?'

'Of course I do, but I know how young men like their pint.' She forbore to tell Douglas about the wager between Bruce and Jed. It would only cause more trouble. 'I'm sure he won't be late,' she added, placatingly. *Now I'm doing it*, Anna thought. *I'm doing just what Mum does. Trying to keep the peace. Trying to keep Douglas happy.*

'He'd better not be,' she heard Douglas mutter beneath his breath. Then he seemed to recover his good humour as he said, 'How about a game of rummy? May, find the cards.'

'Yes, dear,' May said and got up obediently.

Forty-Eight

Anna awoke with a start to find a hand covering her mouth. She tried to call out, to scream, but the hand stifled any sound other than a noise in her throat. She flailed wildly, clutching at her assailant, trying to wrestle him off her.

'Shut up, you idiot. It's only me.' Bruce's voice came out of the blackness. 'If you don't make a noise I'll take my hand away.'

Alcohol fumes were wafting in her face, making her feel sick. She stopped struggling and lay quiescent. Slowly Bruce removed his hand and she breathed more easily. 'What do you think you're doing?' she hissed angrily, but kept her voice low. She had no more wish to wake her mother and Douglas than he had.

Bruce was pulling at the bedclothes, trying to climb in beside her. 'No!' she cried. 'Don't! Go away. Go back to your own bed – you're not getting in here.' Her voice rose in fear.

At once his hand was clamped back on her mouth. And then, suddenly, she felt something cold and sharp against her neck. 'Shut up,' he slurred. 'Just lie back and enjoy it. You know you want it.'

No, no, her mind screamed, but she was unable to utter more than a guttural noise.

'Lie still and stop struggling, or you'll get what that blasted dog of yours got.'

Now her eyes were becoming accustomed to the gloom. In the moonlight she could see his shape above her, but not his features. Buster? What had he done to Buster? She thrashed her head from side to side, tried to hit him, but now he was pinning her down, his whole body weight on top of her.

Anna tried to resist him, tried to throw him off, but he was too heavy, too strong. She couldn't breathe, couldn't summon up an ounce of strength now. Then she managed to get her left hand free and she tried to claw away his hand, but her fingers touched the cold thin thing that he was still holding against her neck. She winced as pain shot through two of her fingers. And then, in her mind's eye, she saw the bayonet he had shown her that day down by the river. Bruce was holding the long, sharp blade close to her throat and threatening to do to her what he had done to her dog. *Oh Buster, Buster! Where are you? What has he done to you?*

Bruce was flinging the bedclothes off her now and pulling up her nightgown. Then he was lying on top of her once more and she could feel his nakedness next to her trembling skin. Then, with his knees, he spread her legs wide and thrust himself into her. She felt a searing pain and tried to cry out. His fingers, still pressing on her mouth, slipped between her teeth and she bit down hard. He gave a yelp and reared up above her. He raised his hand and dealt her a blow across the side of her face that almost knocked her senseless.

But she was still aware of the pain in her groin that went on and on as he rutted like a ram at a ewe.

She must have blacked out completely for when she became aware of the pain once more he was gone. She was lying uncovered on her bed, shivering and weeping uncontrollably. Stiffly, feeling as if she had been battered, Anna crawled off the bed and lurched to the dressing table. With shaking fingers she managed to light a candle. She held it up and looked down at herself in horror. There was blood everywhere, on her nightie and on the bed. Most of it seemed to be coming from the deep cuts on her fingers. Sobbing, she pulled open a drawer and found a handkerchief to bind round her hand.

Aching in every part of her body and bent almost double, she shuffled to the door. She was about to open it and call for her mother when she realized that Bruce could be still out there – waiting for her. Instead, she dragged a chair across to the door and wedged it under the door handle. Then she staggered to the washstand and, setting the candle down, poured cold water into the bowl. She washed herself between her legs, trying to cleanse away the stickiness and the smell of him. She scrubbed herself until she was sore, but however hard she tried she could never wash away what Bruce had done to her.

Anna lay huddled in her bed for the rest of the night, alternately sobbing and falling into nightmarish sleep, only to wake with a start, imagining his weight on top of her and breaking into a cold sweat of fear and loathing. As dawn filtered into her room, she hauled herself off the bed and staggered towards the full-length mirror in the door of her wardrobe. A pathetic sight met her eyes. The left side of her face was swollen, her eye almost closed. Blood spattered her nightdress and drenched the handkerchief around her fingers. Bruises on her arms and legs pained her, but the worst pain was the dreadful soreness between her legs and in her groin.

Once more she tried to wash herself, whimpering like a whipped animal. It was time to get up, to start the day. She should be downstairs by now in the kitchen, stoking up the fire in the range, getting the breakfast . . . But Anna could not bring herself to leave her room. She lay on the bed again, her knees drawn up to her chin, arms wrapped around herself, shivering and cowering in fear as she heard footsteps hurrying along the landing and stopping outside her door . . .

When May opened the kitchen door, she looked round in surprise. No cheerful fire burned in the range's grate. There were no breakfast dishes on the table, no smell of frying bacon. The room was cold and empty. She crossed to the back door and opened it. She stood listening. From across the yard she could hear clattering in the cowhouse. Morning milking was under way. She turned back, pulled on a pair of wellingtons that stood in the scullery and crossed the yard.

Resting her arms on the lower half of the stable door, she called, 'Morning, Jed. Is Anna here?'

Jed glanced up from his place beside a cow. May was startled by the look on his face. The young man was unusually pale and there was distress in his eyes and a tightness round his usually laughing mouth. He rose, put the bucket of milk at a safe distance from the cow's restless feet and came towards her. As he came closer, she could see that his left eye was half-closed and an ugly bruise was swelling around it. His lower lip was cut.

'Whatever—?' she began but Jed interrupted, 'I haven't seen her, but I need to as soon as I can. I knocked on the back door earlier, but there didn't seem to be anyone about. I thought she – she'd maybe slept late.' His mouth seemed to tighten even more. 'I thought mebbe she – she's with him.'

He made no effort to hide the resentment in his tone.

May stared at him. Trembling, she asked, 'What – what do you mean, Jed? With him?'

He sighed and then said, 'We had a stupid bet on last night. Him and me – that we could drink each other under the table. Well, it got a bit nasty. He was saying things about Anna – things I didn't like and then we got into a fight.'

'Over Anna?'

Jed lowered his head and mumbled, 'Well, yes.'

'Is that why you wanted to see her?'

Jed shook his head, his eyes sad. 'It wasn't to do with that. I've found Buster.'

May smiled. 'Oh, she will be pleased. She was worried last night. He'd run off and . . .' Her voice faded as she realized that Jed's expression was grim. Her hand fluttered to her throat. 'What? What is it?'

'He's been killed. Someone's – knifed him.'

'Killed?' May's voice was a squeak.

Jed nodded. 'Yes. It looks like he's been stabbed,' he said slowly, his dark gaze fastened on May's face.

May gave a little cry of alarm. 'Oh no!' she breathed.

No words were needed. They were both remembering the result of the post-mortem on Luke Clayton.

Killed by person or persons unknown, stabbed with a knife or similar weapon.

'I must go and find her,' May whispered. She stumbled away, back across the yard and into the house.

Wrenching off her boots, she ran through the kitchen, up the stairs and along the landing. Outside Anna's room, she paused a moment to catch her breath, leaning against the door jamb. Then she tried the doorknob. It turned, but the door would not open.

'Anna,' she cried, hammering on the wood. 'Anna, open the door.'

Anna heard her name being called as if from a distance. Then she became aware of a banging on her bedroom door. For a moment she cowered lower beneath the bedcovers, but then, as the voice penetrated her distraught mind, she realized.

'Mam! Oh, Mam.' She struggled off the bed and stumbled across the room, pulling away the chair so that the door opened at once and May almost fell into the room.

'Anna, what—?' May began, but as she saw the state of her daughter, she staggered and would have fallen had not Anna reached out and caught hold of her. They clung together until May led her gently to the bed and made her sit down.

'The door,' Anna whispered hoarsely. 'Shut the door.'

May did so, once more inserting the chair under the knob as Anna had done. Only then did Anna breathe more easily. May came and sat beside her and enfolded her in her embrace, rocking her to and fro like a small child. 'Oh, my darling, what have I done? What *have* I done?'

Anna lifted her tear-streaked face to look into her mother's. 'It's not your fault.'

Tears were running down May's face too now. 'It is.

It is. If I had only listened to your grandfather. He knew, didn't he? He could see what they were like.'

'What – what do you mean?' Anna asked huskily. 'They?'

'Bruce did this to you, didn't he?'

Anna nodded.

'Did he – I mean—?'

Anna squeezed her eyes tightly shut, trying to blot out the nightmare. She nodded. 'He held a knife to my throat.' She held out her hand, still with its rough, blood-soaked wrapping. 'I – I tried to fight him off, but I cut my fingers on the – the blade.'

Her mother gave a deep-throated groan of despair. 'Oh, my darling, my baby.' They clung to each other, seeking solace, but there was none they could give each other.

Forty-Nine

'What did you mean when you said Grandpa knew what "they" were like?' A little later, when they had hugged each other and tried to reassure each other, Anna was calmer.

Silently, May drew back from her and pulled up the sleeves of her blouse. Anna gasped as she saw the bruises on her mother's forearms, one purple, a recent injury, and two now yellow and fading.

Anna gasped. 'He – he hits you? Douglas?'

May nodded. 'When something doesn't suit him.'

'I knew there was something wrong. I knew it. But I could never seem to get you alone to talk to you. He always seemed to be in the way.'

May nodded, tears in her eyes. 'I know. He made me promise not to tell you. Told me that it would be the worse for me – and for you – if I did. But I was going to tell you, if only we could have had a few moments alone.'

'How long has it been going on?'

'It started just after I'd bought the house. He was fine before we got married and afterwards, until – until . . . Oh, Anna, I gave him all of the two thousand pounds your grandfather left me. After that, once he'd got it all, he – he started being nasty. Oh, what a fool I've been.'

'What are we going to do?' Anna whispered.

May sighed, shrugged helplessly and said, 'I don't know.'

'Leave him. Come and live here with me. Oh Mam, come home.'

'He'd never let me alone, Anna. He swore he'd never let me go. I married him, didn't I?' she added bitterly.

They sat together until they heard footsteps pass by the bedroom door and go downstairs. They held their breath.

'That's Douglas going down for his breakfast,' May whispered. 'He'll get a shock, won't he? No fire, no dutiful wife waiting to serve him.'

'You'd better go down. I don't want him going for you again because – because of me.'

At that moment a bellow came from the bottom of the stairs. 'May? Where are you?'

May jumped at the sound, but did not get up at once. 'What are you going to do? Do you want me to stay here with you? I'll see if I can get them to go back to town without me.'

'I want to get in the bath, then I'll come down. Where's – where's Bruce?'

May shook her head. 'I don't know.' Now she did stand up and held out her hand. 'Come on, I'll help you into the bathroom and make sure you've locked the door before I go down.'

'Where on earth have you been, May? And where's my breakfast? Where's Anna?'

Her anger emboldened May to say, 'You might well ask where Anna is.'

Douglas frowned. 'What do you mean by that?'

'Your precious son forced himself on her last night.

He raped her, Douglas, there's no other way to put it. Your Bruce raped my little girl.'

Douglas stared at her for a moment and then threw back his head and laughed. 'That's my boy. I never thought he had it in him to go through with it. So that's why he went to the pub – to get a bit of Dutch courage.'

Now it was May's turn to stare at him, aghast. Her voice trembled as she said, 'What do you mean "go through with it"?' You can't mean – oh you can't – that he – that you *planned* it?'

'Well, not rape exactly, only that he should seduce her.'

'Why? In God's name – why? She liked him. She really liked him. But now—'

'Mmm.' Douglas's eyes were calculating. 'Yes, I see that. Maybe he's gone a bit too far.'

'A bit too far?' May's voice rose hysterically. 'Do you have any idea what it means for a woman to be violated like that? Especially a young girl. A *virgin*!'

'Oh, come now, May. Don't be so melodramatic. She's led him on. You can't deny that. And when a young feller's blood is up—'

'How dare you? How dare you suggest that it's Anna's fault?' she screamed.

Now Douglas's eyes were glittering. 'Oh, I dare because that is what happened.' He grabbed her by the shoulders, his strong grip bruising her. 'Do you hear me? *That is what happened*.'

May gasped and stared up at him with wide, frightened eyes.

'And now,' he said ominously, 'they'll have to get married, won't they?'

'Married?' May's voice was a squeak. 'Oh no. Not now. She'll not marry him now.'

'Oh, but she will, May,' Douglas said calmly. His quiet tone was far more menacing than if he had been shouting. 'Anna will marry Bruce and then, one day, this farm will be his.'

May felt as if the breath had been knocked from her body. 'No,' she managed to gasp at last. 'Never! Over my dead body.'

Douglas laughed, but without humour. 'And even that, my dear May, can be arranged.'

At once the vision of Buster's still form came into May's imagination and then a more horrifying picture pushed its way to the forefront of her mind.

The memory of her father, Luke, lying on the ground, stabbed and bleeding to death.

May closed her eyes and groaned. 'Oh no! No,' she moaned more to herself than to the man who still held her in his grasp. 'Don't let it be true. Not that. Oh please, not that.'

Douglas let go of her suddenly so that she staggered and almost fell. She put out her hand and steadied herself against the kitchen table.

'Now, how about getting me some breakfast and when Bruce and Anna show themselves, we'll begin to make arrangements. Maybe we can get a special licence. If not, then it will have to be the next time he comes home on leave.'

May moved woodenly towards the range and took up the frying pan, wishing she had the temerity to hit him over the head with it. But she didn't. She was weak. She despised herself now. It had been her weakness – her need to have a man to love and protect and care for her – that had led her beloved daughter and herself into this mess.

She cooked breakfast for Douglas, wishing she had

rat poison handy. Douglas sat at the table and opened his newspaper as if nothing untoward had happened.

'Thank you,' he said sarcastically, as she banged the plate of eggs, bacon and fried bread in front of him. He glanced round the table. 'Where's the tomato sauce?'

Obediently, May fetched it from the pantry. She poured a cup of tea for him and one for herself, but couldn't bring herself to eat anything. Revulsion against this man and his son choked her.

The kitchen door opened and a tousle-headed, yawning Bruce appeared. 'Morning,' he muttered and dropped into a chair at the table.

May stared at him in astonishment, then crashed her cup into the saucer. Bruce winced at the sudden noise and, frowning, glanced up.

'Do you have to make such a noise?' he grumbled. 'My head's fit to burst.'

May gaped at him. 'I don't believe this,' she murmured. Was she dreaming? Was this all some terrible nightmare that no one else but herself was experiencing? But no, it was true. At this moment Anna was in the bath trying to scrub away all traces of her attacker – the young man, who sat so calmly before her now, waiting for his breakfast . . .

May sprang to her feet. 'How can you sit there,' she shrieked, 'as if nothing's happened?' She shook her head in bewilderment as Bruce gaped up at her, uncomprehending. 'Don't tell me you can't remember? That you were so drunk—?'

'Can't remember what?' Bruce glanced at his father. 'Do you know what she's on about?'

'It seems,' Douglas drawled, 'that Anna is accusing you of raping her last night.'

Bruce stared at him. He opened his mouth to say

something, but at that moment the door opened and all eyes turned to see Anna standing there.

For a moment, they all seemed turned to stone. The bruise on the side of Anna's face was swollen and darkening and the two fingers on her left hand were wrapped in a clean white handkerchief.

May moved suddenly and rushed to put her arms around Anna and draw her into the room. 'Come and sit down, darling.'

Stiffly, her gaze fastened on Bruce's face, Anna moved across the room and stood on the hearth rug. Facing the two men defiantly, she said, 'Leave this house. Both of you. My mother's staying here with me and—'

As if catapulted, both men sprang up and faced them.

'Oh no, she's not,' Douglas said.

'Mam,' Anna said quietly, 'go and fetch Buster.'

'Oh darling,' May said tearfully, 'I can't. He – Jed found him. Someone killed Buster.'

Briefly, Anna's gaze swivelled to look at her mother. 'Killed him? How?'

'With – with a knife.'

Anna stared at her and then slowly her gaze came back to Bruce's face. 'You! You killed him. Didn't you? Didn't you?' Suddenly Anna launched herself at him, her arms flailing, but Bruce caught her easily and held her wrists. She kicked out at him, catching him on the shin, but he wound his leg around her and brought her down in a crude tackle. He pinioned her arms to the floor and straddled her body. 'Want some more of what you had last night, do you?'

'No, no,' May shouted, trying to pull him away from Anna, but now Douglas grasped May from behind, pinning her arms to her sides and holding her fast. Tears coursed down May's face. 'Anna, Anna—' she cried, watching with horrified eyes whilst her daughter struggled to throw Bruce off her, but he held her easily, laughing cruelly. 'Yeah, go on, struggle all you like. You won't get the better of me.' He glanced round to look triumphantly at May and his father. 'We've got you both just where we want you now, haven't we?'

Whether it was because Bruce relaxed his concentration for a brief moment or because Anna made one last superhuman effort, but somehow she freed her leg from beneath him, bent her knee and, pressing her foot and elbow against the floor managed to roll him over. Without waiting for him to recover from her surprise move, she brought her knee up viciously into his groin, so that Bruce gave a cry of pain and doubled over, writhing on the floor.

Anna scrambled to her feet and turned towards her mother.

'Leave me,' May gasped. 'Don't worry about me, darling. I mean it. Just go. Go on. Run, Anna. Get away from here. Run, Anna, just *run* . . .'

1963

Fifty

'Who on earth were those two lunatics? They knocked me off my bike,' Tony asked his mother indignantly.

Bertha smiled. 'Oh, we had a very nice chat.'

Tony looked at her in surprise. '*You* did? You've been chatting to complete strangers?'

Bertha nodded, looking very pleased with herself.

'Who were they?'

'A father and son called Whittaker.' Her smile widened maliciously. 'They came looking for someone. I'll give you three guesses who. Did you see the younger feller?'

'Not really. It was all too quick. I just saw two men in the car. I got their number plate, though. Reckon I'll have a word with PC Jenkins—'

'I wouldn't, because they might be doing us a big favour.'

Tony eyed her. It was a long time since he had seen his mother with a gleam in her eye. She was excited about something.

Tony frowned. 'What's going on, Mam? And what do you mean "they came looking for someone"?'

'Exactly what I say. The younger feller – well, the older one too mebbe, though his hair's grey now – but the younger feller had bright red hair. Copper coloured. *Just like the girl's.*'

Tony stared at her. 'You mean – Maisie?'

'Course I mean Maisie. What other little trollop around here has red hair?'

'They came looking for Maisie?'

'Well, I suppose it was more *her*, Anna. They didn't even know about Maisie. Didn't even know Anna had been pregnant. Thrilled, the young feller was, to think he was a dad. And the old one kept saying, "I've got a granddaughter. Just think, I'm a granddad." Of course, they wanted to see them straight away . . .'

'And you told them?' Now Tony was incredulous.

'Course I did . . .'

Tony's face was thunderous. 'Why, Mam? When you know that's who she must have run away from? That's who she must be so frightened of.'

Suddenly, Bertha's expression was ugly. 'Why should I care? Why should I protect her? Your dad's fancy piece . . .'

The truth was filtering through Tony's mind now. He pointed accusingly at his mother. 'You've lied to me. All these years you've tried to make me believe that – that Maisie was *his* child and my *half-sister*. But she wasn't, was she, Mam? 'Cos now you're saying that this red-haired feller that turned up today was her dad.' He paused a moment and then added again incredulously, 'Why, Mam? Why?'

Now Bertha was truculent, trying to justify herself. 'Well, I thought she was. Men are all the same. Why else would he have brought the little trollop home with him that night if he wasn't getting his oats there? Or at least hoping to. All right, mebbe Maisie isn't his, but I bet they've been at it all these years since.'

Tony's last glance at his mother, before he turned and left the house, was a mixture of contempt and pity.

As he began to walk up the track, he saw Maisie

running pell-mell towards him, her hair flying, her skirt above her knees.

'Tony, Tony, hurry—' Even before she reached him he could see that she was crying hysterically. He caught her and held her. 'What is it? Is it your mam? Did those two men frighten her?'

'No – yes – it's worse. Your dad. He – he tried to defend her and one of them had got a knife—' Maisie could say no more as sobs racked her.

'Oh my God,' Tony breathed. 'Is he hurt?'

Maisie could only nod. Releasing her, Tony began to run up the track, pausing only to say, 'Go to the house. Use the phone. Get help.'

Maisie rushed into the house, ignoring Bertha, and grabbed the phone.

''Ere, 'ere, what do you think you're doing, miss?' Bertha protested, but the girl, still crying, ignored her. With shaking fingers, she dialled Pat's number. The district nurse was the only person she could think of to ring. She was certainly the nearest. The ringing tone seemed to sound in her ears for ages, until Pat's breathless voice said, 'Hello. You just caught me. I was on my way out. Who is it?'

'It's Mr Eddie . . . I mean, this is Maisie. Mr Eddie's been hurt. Stabbed—' Dimly the girl heard the listening Bertha cry out.

'I'll come at once,' was all Pat said.

Maisie replaced the receiver in its cradle and turned to face Bertha who was staring disbelievingly at her.

'What do you mean stabbed?'

Now that Pat was on her way, Maisie was managing to control her hysteria. Pat would help Mr Eddie. She was a nurse. If anyone could save him, it would be Pat.

'Those two men. They grabbed me mam and me and

Mr Eddie tried to help us. The younger one had a knife. He went for Mr Eddie and – and stabbed him in the stomach.'

Bertha felt for the edge of the table and sat down heavily, staring unseeingly ahead. Maisie turned and left the house, running back up the hill.

Left alone, Bertha sat motionless. What had she done? she asked herself silently. She had sought to wreak revenge on Anna and her daughter. She had waited years for the right moment and when the two strangers had turned up on her doorstep, looking for Anna, Bertha had believed they had been heaven-sent. And now her husband was lying injured, possibly fatally.

Reluctantly, the bitter, twisted woman was forced to face the truth. All those years ago Anna had obviously had good reason to run away. Bertha could make a good guess at why. So, when he brought her home, Eddie hadn't known her. It was the truth he had told her. It was just him being kind. She thought back down all the years. He had always been kind. It was his nature. Look how he'd rushed to help all those folks at the time of the floods. He'd had no need. They were nothing to him. But that was Eddie.

He'd never said an unkind thing about her father, not even when Bert Tinker had been sent to prison. Throughout their marriage, he had never raised his hand to her, not once, yet she had given him cause. Oh yes, she had given him cause all right. He'd done his best to be a good husband, but she'd not let him. And now . . .

Bertha dragged herself up.

For the first time in many years she would have to climb the track and go over the hill.

*

Pat arrived, breathless and anxious in the yard. Flinging her bicycle against the wall, she dragged her medical bag from its strap on the back of the bicycle and ran up the hill.

Arriving at the top, she saw the sorry scene below her and, though her heart would not let her believe it, she knew already that Eddie was gone. She could see Anna cradling him in her arms, her head bent over him, whilst Tony, who was standing close by, held Maisie, trying to comfort her. A few steps away from the group stood the lonely figure of Bertha, isolated and cut off from the others.

Pat's fears were justified. When she knelt beside Eddie, she knew before she even touched him, that he was dead. Sadly, she looked up to meet Anna's tear-filled eyes and shook her head.

She was aware that Bertha turned and walked away.

They had to leave Eddie lying there until the police came and, even then, they were allowed no more to do with the body. It was too big an incident for the local bobby to handle. An Inspector came from Ludthorpe and, later, a Detective Chief Inspector from Lincoln. There seemed to be policemen everywhere, searching the ground minutely, taking statements from Anna, Maisie and Tony. And from Bertha.

Anna told them briefly all the events that had led to her flight from home. 'I was a coward,' she said flatly. 'She told me to go, to run – and I did, but I left my poor mother to take the brunt of their fury. God knows what happened to her. I expect they killed her too.'

The Sergeant taking her statement said, 'What do you mean, love, "killed her too"?'

'Someone killed my dog, Buster, that night. I suspect it was Bruce and – and then I realized that he – probably helped by his father – had been the poacher and that they – ' she swallowed painfully – 'had probably killed my grandfather.'

The officer's face was grim. 'Well, if it's any consolation – and I don't suppose it is – we'll get 'em. Oh, we'll get 'em, sure as eggs is eggs. And we'll investigate everything you've told us. Specially the bit about your granddad.'

Anna regarded him with such pleading in her dark, violet eyes that even the tough Sergeant was moved. 'Could you find out about my mother? Please?'

'I'll do what I can, love. Now, give me any addresses you know.'

'There's the farm.' She gave the address. 'And there was a house in Lincoln.' She paused frowning, but little by little she remembered the road and then the number.

'We'll check that too,' the Sergeant promised. He was about to put away his notebook when Anna added, 'And then there's the cinema, of course.'

Maisie, who was hovering nearby, and the Sergeant spoke at the same time. 'The cinema?'

Anna nodded. 'Yes, Douglas had something to do with running one of the cinemas in the city.' She wrinkled her forehead. 'I can't remember what they called it.'

Maisie gave a little cry and clapped her hand over her mouth, her eyes wide as she stared at her mother. 'It must be the man who saw us at the ABC cinema. That's where we went in Lincoln to see Billy Fury. Oh, Mam, it's all my fault.'

Fifty-One

Maisie was inconsolable at the thought that her disobedience had brought about such tragic consequences.

Anna tried to comfort her. 'It's not your fault, darling. I should have told you everything, then you would have understood. You're old enough now. I shouldn't have kept you locked away for years. Or myself, for that matter.' She sighed. 'I should have faced things a long time ago.'

Even Tony, who was distraught and grieving too, tried to reassure Maisie. 'I'm as much to blame. I knew your mam didn't want you going out, specially not to Lincoln, yet I took you there.' He paused and scratched his head in a gesture so like Eddie's that Anna felt a lump in her throat. 'But the only people who are really to blame,' Tony went on, his tone hardening, 'are Douglas Whittaker and his son.'

'My father.' Maisie wept. 'Fancy having *him* for a father.'

Tony tried to smile, though the sadness never left his eyes. 'That's not your fault either. And you've got Anna for your mother. You couldn't have a better mother than her. Now, come on.' He shook her gently by the shoulders. 'You've got to be strong. And the best thing you can do for your mam now is to help us find *her* mam.'

*

'They've caught them,' Tony told Anna and Maisie two weeks later, 'trying to leave the country.'

Anna nodded. It was a hollow victory; it couldn't bring Eddie back, or her grandfather, or compensate for the lost seventeen years of her life. 'I've been such a coward, hiding myself away all these years. Not even caring enough to find my own mother.'

'You were only seventeen or so when you came here, weren't you? You shouldn't blame yourself.'

She smiled tremulously at him. 'You're just like your father, Tony,' she told him huskily. 'So kind. You're still trying to comfort us even when you must be hurting so dreadfully.'

Tony's voice was unsteady. 'I'll take that as a compliment, shall I?'

Anna nodded. 'Oh yes. Most definitely. I – I've never met a nicer man than Eddie. Only my own father and grandfather came close.' There was a pause before Anna asked tentatively, afraid to hear the answer, 'Have the police said any more to you about my – my mother?'

Tony shook his head. 'They wouldn't tell me, would they? They'd come to you.'

Anna sighed deeply. 'I suppose so. I did so hope that . . .' Her voice trailed away. Then more firmly she asked, 'Would you do something for me?'

'Of course.'

'Would you ask PC Jenkins what's happening? Actually, he might tell you more readily than me. You're not so closely involved. He might just tell you something that he wouldn't want to tell me.'

Tony nodded. 'I'll try.' He was about to turn away when he paused and said quietly, 'Poor Pat's taken my dad's death badly, hasn't she?'

Anna nodded. 'I – I think she loved your father. I

think part of her always had done from the time they were young.'

Tony's mouth hardened as he said, 'I wish me mam was half as upset. I don't think she cared about him at all. Her only worry is whether she's been left the farm.'

Anna gasped, shocked that Bertha could be quite so heartless. Even after all she knew about her, she hadn't expected that. 'Has he left a will?'

Tony nodded. 'We've an appointment at the solicitors in Ludthorpe tomorrow. Wish me luck because if it's all in her name, I don't reckon I'll be staying.'

'Oh Tony, don't say that.'

'I mean it. For years, Anna, I've tried to understand her, to stand by her, even side with her against me dad sometimes, although I never liked doing that. But do you know, she's misled me all these years.' His gaze met Anna's steadily. He hesitated, wondering whether now was the time to speak out. Anna looked puzzled, so he took a deep breath and plunged on. 'She always said she believed that Maisie was my father's child and that Maisie was my half-sister. Anna – I hope you won't be angry – but my feelings for Maisie aren't a brother's. It made me feel – ' he paused again searching for the right word – 'dirty. Unnatural. Wicked.'

'Oh, Tony.' There was no anger in Anna's tone, only sadness. Now she understood his strange, erratic behaviour. He had been suffering a turmoil of emotions caused, so unnecessarily, by his mother's lies.

'I promise you,' she said softly, 'on Maisie's life that she is not your half-sister.'

He nodded. 'Oh, I know that now.' He smiled ruefully. 'And if I'd been sensible about it, I'd have asked you before. And believed you. But when your own mother drills it into you from the age of ten or so that you were – you were – that you and my father . . .' He faltered.

Anna smiled sadly. 'I know,' she said. 'I know.'

Tony pulled off the cap he was wearing, ran his fingers through his hair and then pulled the cap on again. 'Of course, I don't know how Maisie feels about me,' he said. 'It might all be hopeless anyway.'

'She's very fond of you.'

'I know, but I have to remember that she's not mixed with other fellers much. Only the lads at school.'

Anna grimaced. 'That's my fault.'

'Oh, I didn't mean—' he began, but she held up her hand. 'It's all right, Tony,' she said. 'It's the truth. And as for Maisie, just give her a little more time, eh?'

He smiled. 'I seem to have been waiting for ever for her to grow up.'

They smiled understandingly at each other.

'Well,' he said briskly. 'This won't get the work done. I'd better go.'

'Good luck for tomorrow,' she called as he turned away.

Over his shoulder he grinned. 'I might need it because I could be gone by tomorrow night.'

As he walked away, Anna murmured, 'Me too.'

Eddie's will contained a shock for Bertha, a pleasant surprise for Tony and a different kind of shock for Anna.

'He's left the farm to me,' Tony told her happily as he held out an envelope to her. 'And the solicitor's sent you a letter.'

Anna eyed the long legal envelope suspiciously. 'Me? Why me?'

'Go on, open it. You'll see.' The young man could hardly contain his excitement, his obvious pleasure.

Anna rubbed her palms down the sides of her skirt, feeling suddenly nervous. Yet, by the look on Tony's face, the letter didn't contain bad news. Surely Tony wouldn't be throwing them out of the cottage? Not after what he had said about his feelings for Maisie. And yet . . .

Tony could contain himself no longer, couldn't wait for her to open the letter and read the news for herself. 'He's left you this cottage and a bit of land round it.'

Anna stared at him. 'Me? Oh no, he can't do that.'

'Well, he has,' Tony was grinning from ear to ear. 'And it's all legal and there's not a thing anyone can do about it.'

'Do you mind?' she asked swiftly.

He laughed. 'Course not. I'm delighted. It means you'll stay here.' He paused, realizing that the capture of the two men Anna had feared for years meant that she was now free to go wherever she chose. She might want to leave. 'You will stay, won't you?'

Anna smiled and reached out to take the envelope. 'Of course, only—' She stopped, afraid that what she had to say would hurt him. 'I must let Maisie have more freedom. It's time she spread her wings. You do see that, don't you?'

A fleeting look of pain crossed his face, but he nodded. 'I've always thought,' he said carefully, 'that if you let birds fly free, they'll come home all the more readily. I think it applies to people too, don't you?'

How sensible Tony was, Anna thought. She nodded. 'We'll have to let her decide.'

'I know,' he whispered. 'I know.'

She touched his arm. 'It'll come right. I know it will.'

He smiled, but the doubt was still deep in his eyes.

Changing the subject Anna asked, 'What about your mother?'

Tony shrugged. 'She's hopping mad, of course, but I think deep down she half expected it. He's left her some money and I've to pay her a monthly allowance – which I would have done anyway,' he added hastily.

Anna nodded. 'So she's staying on the farm?'

Now Tony laughed. 'Oh no. She's packing her belongings this very minute. She can't wait to get away. She's moving into Ludthorpe. Going to live with her sister for a start.'

The smile began slowly on Anna's mouth, spreading until it lit up the whole of her face. Now she could open the envelope. Reading the words of Eddie's generous and, yes, loving gesture, Anna felt a happiness and contentment flooding through her that she had never expected to feel ever again. Although her feelings were tinged with sadness that her current fortune had come about because of Eddie's death, she knew he would want her to be happy. It was all Eddie Appleyard had ever wanted for her.

There was only one cloud in her otherwise clear blue sky.

What had become of her mother?

Fifty-Two

PC Jenkins wheeled his bicycle down the track towards the little cottage. He leant it against the wall and knocked on the door. While he waited for an answer, he looked about him. Sheep grazed on the slope of the field in the sunshine. It was an idyllic scene and he wished he had better news for the young woman who was now opening the door to him.

Anna smiled a welcome. 'Come in, Mr Jenkins. You must have known I've got the kettle on.'

The constable stepped into the kitchen, laid his helmet on the table and sat down whilst Anna mashed the tea and set out home-made biscuits on a plate.

'I'll come straight to the point, Anna. We've been making enquiries about your mam, but we can't – at the moment – trace her.'

Anna sighed and sat down. She busied herself pouring the tea, but could not hide her disappointment. 'Well, I'm sure you've done your best. I can't ask more than that.'

'Oh we're not giving up. Be assured of that. Besides, we're still building a case against the two we've got in custody.' His eyes narrowed. 'From the bit you were able to tell us, it seems there's a lot more wants looking into.' He nodded knowingly. 'A lot more.'

Anna looked him straight in the eyes. 'Tell me honestly – do you think she's dead?'

He sighed. 'I don't know, love, and that's the truth, but we want to find out anyway. If she's alive, she could help us with our enquiries.' He smiled at the use of the official-sounding term. Then his expression sobered. 'If she's not, then we shall be making enquiries into the nature of her death.'

Anna nodded, unable to speak for the lump in her throat. It was defeatist, she knew, but knowing the Whittakers as she did, she could hold out no hope that her mother was still alive.

'There's one thing we did find out that might interest you. That cinema you thought he owned or at least managed—'

Anna looked up. 'Yes?'

'Seems he had nowt to do with it at all. I've talked to the chap who runs it and he remembers him well. "Oh him," he said. "That fly-by-night! He's nothing to do with this place and never has been. He fancied himself as something of an entrepreneur or whatever they call it. Reckoned he knew all the stars and used to stand outside the front there when there was a big name appearing here, making out he knew them and that it was all down to him that they'd come here. And he used to chat up the girls in the box office to get the best seats in the house. Lots of folks thought he owned the place. Oh yes, I remember Douglas Whittaker all right," he said, "I'd like to get me hands on him myself." '

Anna tried to smile, but her thoughts were still on her mother.

PC Jenkins must have read her mind for he touched her hand and said softly, 'Don't give up hope yet, love. We'll keep searching, I promise you.'

*

Eddie's death had hit Pat Jessop hard. She had stood close to the graveside during his interment, weeping openly, not caring who saw her. Beside her stood a grim-faced Maisie.

Anna stood alone beneath the shadow of a tree some distance from the other mourners around the grave. She had slipped into the back of the church at the last moment, quietly and unobserved. But Maisie had had no such compunction. Boldly, she had marched into the church to sit beside Pat. She had walked out with Pat and followed the coffin to watch it being lowered into the earth. Her eyes were dry, but bright with anger, her mouth tight. Though her arm was linked through Pat's, it was Tony's face that Maisie's glance sought constantly.

Tony was standing, white-faced, beside his mother, his mouth set in a hard line. Only his brown eyes showed any sign of the tumult of emotion raging inside him. Deliberately he avoided meeting Maisie's eyes, even though he could feel her glance upon him.

His overriding emotion was anger. Anger that his father should have been killed. Why should a kind, considerate man like Eddie Appleyard have his life snatched away so violently by a vicious thug?

But there were so many other emotions struggling within him. He felt sorry for Maisie – her natural father had been the one to take the life of the man who had been more than a father to her. And for Anna now there was understanding. Her fear had been justified. Yet he couldn't help wishing that she had had the courage to confide in his father and him too. Perhaps if they had known all about it, they could have prevented the tragedy.

And his mother. Oh, what about his mother? His

loyalty and, yes, his love for his mother was being sorely tested now that he knew her part in the terrible events. Her vindictiveness towards Anna had led to his father's death.

And he felt guilt too. Guilt because, even in the midst of his grief, his heart was leaping with joy at the knowledge that Maisie was not his half-sister.

It had been difficult to assess Bertha's feelings that day. She had stood at the side of the grave, her face expressionless, and afterwards she had got into the funeral car with her sister, Lucy, and been driven back to Ludthorpe, offering no refreshment back at the farm. It had been left to Anna to invite Tony and Pat back to the little cottage, the cottage that was now rightfully hers.

Pat had sat outside the front door, an untouched cup of tea in her hands, just staring across the fields towards the sun as it began to sink in the sky.

Anna sat down beside her. 'He loved this view.'

'He loved a lot of things. He loved this farm, his land, his son and, once, I suppose – ', there was a strange reluctance in her tone as she went on – 'he must have loved Bertha.' She paused and then said quietly, 'And he loved you, Anna.' As Anna opened her mouth to protest, Pat hurried on, 'Oh, I don't mean in the way Bertha accused him of. No, as a dear friend, or even a daughter perhaps. The same way he loved Maisie. Do you know what I mean?'

Anna, tears choking her throat, nodded.

Then, quite simply and without any shame, Pat said, 'And I loved him and in *exactly* the way Bertha thought.' She sighed. 'Such a pity he never knew.'

Huskily, Anna said, 'I think he did, Pat. I'm sure he did.'

Pat smiled through her tears as she whispered, 'I hope so.'

Life settled into a new routine. Bertha was gone and Tony now lived alone in the farmhouse, though he seemed to spend far more time with Anna and Maisie in the little cottage than he did in his own home.

'We need more help on the farm and – ' he smiled ruefully – 'I need some sort of a housekeeper, or at least someone to come in to cook and clean for me. And to wash and iron my clothes. I'm beginning to smell.'

Maisie pretended to sniff the air. 'No worse than usual,' she quipped.

'Well, I could do that,' Anna said, but Tony shook his head. 'No, you've enough to do about the farm and when you get back here. Specially looking after madam here. That's a full-time job.'

'Ta very much,' Maisie tossed her curls and pretended indignation. 'You know what you need?'

'What's that?'

'A wife.'

'You could be right. You applying for the job then?'

The banter was spoken light-heartedly, yet Anna was aware of an undercurrent between them.

'Who me?' Maisie feigned astonishment, her eyes wide. 'What makes you think I want to bury myself here? My teachers say I've already got enough qualifications to get into teacher-training college.'

'Is that what you want to do?' Anna asked.

Questioned directly, Maisie faltered. 'I'm thinking about it? I want to get my A levels first, though.'

Anna glanced at Tony. His eyes were lowered and she could not read their expression, but by the slump in his shoulders she knew that Maisie's words had dashed his hopes even further. But, strangely, Maisie did not look exactly ecstatic about her own tentative plans either.

I wonder, Anna thought.

Anna was sitting outside the front door of her cottage, watching a glorious sunset. The sun slipped down slowly, streaking the sky with burnished gold. Maisie had taken her homework – reading two chapters of *Pride and Prejudice* – to sit beside the stream. Anna could just see her, on the bank, head bent, engrossed in her book.

Something, she wasn't sure what, perhaps a movement or a slight sound, made her look to her left, up the hill. Tony was walking towards her. He waved and she lifted her hand in response.

He reached her and sat beside her. For a few moments they watched the sunset together in silence. Then he said gently, 'Anna, there's someone to see you.'

She turned, a moment's fear leaping into her eyes before she remembered. There was no longer any need to be afraid. All the years of hiding were over.

'Who?'

Tony glanced up the track and Anna followed his line of vision. Coming down the hill was the slight figure of a woman. Anna's heart seemed to stop and then began to thud erratically. She rose slowly, her gaze still on the figure coming closer and closer.

Then she gave a cry, held out her arms and began to run up the hill.

'Mam! Oh, Mam!'

Fifty-Three

There was so much to say and yet, for the moment, they could say nothing.

'I'll go and tell Maisie,' Tony said tactfully. 'We'll give you a few moments.'

As he turned away, Anna cried, 'Oh, Mam, can you ever forgive me?'

'It's you who need to forgive me, Anna.' Easy tears welled in May's eyes and, in spite of her obvious joy at seeing her daughter again, she still seemed anxious and unsure.

'But I left you with – with them. I ran away,' Anna insisted.

'When I told you to run, I didn't mean you to go right away,' May said. 'Why didn't you go to Jed? He would have helped you. He was frantic when he found you had gone. And then, when we couldn't find you—'

Anna lifted her head slightly and whispered his name softly for the first time in years. 'Jed. Oh, Jed.' Her voice broke as she added, 'Mam – I couldn't. I was so – so ashamed.'

May's face was still haunted by the memories. 'If it was anyone's fault, it was mine. I should have known better. I should have listened to your grandfather. And to Betty and Rita.'

They sat down together outside the cottage, mother and daughter watching the golden sunset with their arms around one another, as if, never again, would they allow themselves to be parted.

'But you,' May went on, stroking Anna's hair tenderly, 'you were just an innocent young girl, full of romantic dreams that were smashed in a violent and terrible way. No wonder you wanted to run and hide from everything and – and everyone. Oh, Anna –' May's voice cracked – 'did you hate me? Did you blame me?'

'Blame you? Oh, Mam! Never. Not for one moment. But I thought you would be ashamed of me, that it had been somehow my fault.'

'No,' May whispered. 'Oh no, it wasn't you. It was them. Both of them.'

'I felt so guilty though, and so – so cowardly, running away like that. Just leaving you. What –' she stumbled again over his name – 'what did Jed do when he found out what had happened?'

May stared straight ahead, watching the glorious colours, the blue and gold and pink, realizing that over the years since Anna had gone, she had never even noticed a sunset. Her life had been dark and gloomy and so very sad. She gave a deep sigh and said, 'Jed didn't know. I – I couldn't tell him, Anna. If he'd known and he'd caught up with Bruce – or even Douglas for that matter – there would have been murder done and an innocent boy would have gone to the gallows, or at best served life imprisonment, just because he loved you. I couldn't risk Jed knowing. So – no one knew.'

For once, Anna thought, *her mother had shown surprising strength in her decision.*

'And he – he still doesn't know?'

May turned and looked deeply into the lovely eyes

of her daughter, eyes that were so like her own. 'Not all of it. Not – not why you ran away. You should tell him that yourself. But Jed knows I've found you, Anna, and he wants to see you.' She smiled. 'He would have come today if I'd let him.'

Anna closed her eyes. 'Soon,' she whispered, her heart lifting at the thought of seeing him again. 'I'll see him soon, I promise. But just now—' Her voice faded away.

'So, tell me – what happened to you, my darling? Where did you go?' May asked unsteadily. Her new-found happiness was hard to believe after all the years of anguish.

'Oh Mam.' Anna closed her eyes, trying to blot out the memories, yet they had to be relived. For her mother's sake. May had a right to know, so haltingly, she began to tell her sorry tale.

'I just ran – like you told me to. I thought about going to the city, but then, big though it is, I thought they might find me. Douglas had his cronies there and all I could think of was getting as far away as I could. So I struck across country, living rough, sleeping in barns, stealing food.' She smiled grimly. 'I had no identity card, no ration book. But I thought if I could get to the coast, maybe to Grimsby, I could stow away on a ship. It was a stupid idea, but I didn't care where I went or even what happened to me.' Anna paused, remembering vividly her feeling of hopelessness, not caring then if she lived or died. If it hadn't been for Eddie . . .

She took a deep breath and went on.

'I got as far as Horncastle and it was market day. I set about stealing some food. How I never got caught, I don't know, but I didn't. And then – then there was a young woman who left her handbag on the edge of one of the stalls whilst she moved away to look at something. Before I realized what I was doing, I'd snatched it up and walked away with it in the opposite direction. My heart was thudding. I expected any minute that someone would shout, would come running after me, but nothing happened. Perhaps part of me even wanted to get caught. I don't know. I walked and walked, never looking back, just taking the first road that took me out of the town. I didn't even know where I was heading.' Anna licked her lips and paused in telling what to her was another shameful episode in her story. 'I know it was wrong, Mam. I'm not a thief, yet after what had happened to me stealing seemed nothing.'

'No,' May said huskily, 'it wasn't wrong.' There was a pause and then May prompted. 'And what did you find in the handbag?'

Anna shook her head in wonderment. 'You'll not believe this, Mam. I could hardly believe my luck. I still felt so guilty and yet – yet it seemed – meant to happen.'

'What did? What do you mean?'

'The girl's identity card and her ration book were in the handbag. And do you know – ' even now after all the intervening years there was incredulity in Anna's voice – 'do you know, her name was Annabel Woods.'

May gasped. 'So – so you called yourself Anna Woods?'

Anna nodded. 'I just hope the real Annabel Woods didn't get into too much trouble. I hoped she'd be able to replace the lost items.'

Now there was a long silence between them until, haltingly now, Anna came to the part where she had been standing in Ludthorpe marketplace on a cold, wet evening just before Christmas . . .

When she had finished, Anna said, 'Now you must tell me what happened to you.'

May's voice was unsteady. 'I had to take the beatings for a while. I tried several times to get away, but he always found me and dragged me back, and then, suddenly, about two years after you'd gone, he stopped hitting me and became much nicer. Just like he had been in the early days.' She glanced at Anna as she added, bitterly, 'But there was a reason. He'd found out that if you were declared dead, then – then I was your next of kin and could inherit the farm. That's what they were after all the time. The farm. They'd planned it all.'

'So what happened?'

'At first, because we couldn't sell it, we put a manager in. The farm did well and earned quite a good living for us. But Douglas wanted the lump sum. He wanted to buy the cinema he was involved in.'

At this point, Anna interrupted her mother's tale to tell her what PC Jenkins had said.

'It doesn't surprise me.' May's mouth was grim. 'Believe me, Douglas Whittaker owned very little that had been legitimately bought, unless,' she added bitterly, 'it was something I'd paid for.'

Anna said nothing.

'When you'd been missing a few years he consulted a solicitor. But he must have been advised to wait a little longer. I think he was told that we ought to make more effort to find you first. So the farm had to stay in your name and we couldn't sell it, only continue to work it.' She sighed. 'Douglas was furious, so the beatings began again for a while. And then he stopped again, though the cruelty still continued, but it was only verbal now.'

'Only!' Anna cried.

'It – it wasn't so bad.' May tried to sound brave, but her mouth trembled. All she had ever wanted was to be taken care of, but instead she had lived with a brutal, greedy man.

'Poor Mam,' Anna murmured. Then, taking a deep breath, she asked, 'What about Bruce?'

'He stayed in the army and only came home on leave. And when he did, the conversation was always about finding you. Of course, part of me wanted you found – desperately – but on the other hand, I wanted you to stay hidden. I was so afraid that if they did find you—' She needed to say no more. Anna shuddered.

'Did Douglas go back to the solicitor again?'

'Yes, and the second time – oh, Anna – ' tears filled May's eyes – 'I didn't really understand it all. I still don't. Douglas handled everything, but I had to swear an oath in front of an independent solicitor that I believed you to be dead and that I was your next of kin. Eventually probate was granted and – and the farm came to me.' May covered her face with her hands and wept. 'Douglas made me sell it. I lost Clayton's Farm, Anna.' She shuddered. 'Your grandfather must be turning in his grave.'

'Oh, Mam, don't. Grandpa would have understood. He loved you. He wouldn't blame you.'

'But I blame myself,' May whispered hoarsely. 'And the worst of it is it needn't have happened. Douglas didn't have the power to make me do anything, if only I'd known it.'

'What do you mean?'

May was shamefaced. 'I was never properly married to him. It – it seems he never got a divorce from his first wife. Oh, Anna, how could I have been so stupid?'

Anna did not answer her directly but asked instead, 'Who – who has the farm now?'

Through her tears, May was able to smile. 'Jed.'

'Jed!' Anna was startled. But then, as the realization seeped in, she said again, but softly now, 'Jed.'

Again there was a long silence before May asked, 'How did Douglas and Bruce find you after all this time? No one has told me.'

Anna explained that her rebellious teenage daughter had persuaded Tony to take her to Lincoln to see one of her idols.

'It wasn't their fault. I'd kept her hidden away so long without any explanation. She was bound to break out sooner or later. I see that now. I'm not really sure what happened exactly. All Maisie knows is that they were outside the cinema and a photographer took pictures of the queue. Tony thinks perhaps the picture appeared in the *Echo* complete with Maisie's name and where she lived and they came looking.' Her voice hardened. 'Of course, when they got to the farm, Bertha couldn't wait to tell them where I was. I expect she saw for herself then, the likeness of Maisie to – to Bruce.'

'Is she like him?' May asked, sounding as if she hated the idea.

Anna smiled. 'She has his red hair and his brown eyes, but, thankfully, that's the only way she resembles him.' Anna squeezed her mother's hand. 'You'll love her, Mam. I know you will.'

They glanced across the grass to see Maisie and Tony walking towards them. Anna caught her breath. Tony's arm was around Maisie's shoulder and Maisie's was around his waist. As they drew closer, Anna felt tears fill her eyes, but now, after all these years, they were tears of joy.

Tony's face was shining with happiness and Maisie was blushing as she laughed up at him.

It's all right, she thought. *Everything's going to be all right*. As they drew near, Anna, with one arm still around her mother, held out her hand towards Maisie.

'Darling,' she said, 'come and meet your grandmother.'

Without Sin

For Robena and Fred Hill,

my sister and brother-in-law

Acknowledgements

The Workhouse at Southwell, Nottinghamshire, which has been magnificently restored by the National Trust, is the inspiration for the setting of this novel. However, the characters and story are entirely fictitious and have no relation whatsoever to any inmates or staff, past or present.

My love and thanks, as always, to my family and friends for their constant support, help and encouragement.

One

June 1910

'You're not going to leave us here? Not in this place?' Meg turned her wide green eyes accusingly on her father. 'You can't.'

Beyond the black wrought-iron gates, the three-storey, red-brick building surrounded by high walls was an ominous threat. Its regimented rows of windows were like watching eyes. The young girl, face like a thunderstorm, wild long red hair, glanced at her mother, willing her to say something. But Sarah's pale face was expressionless, her eyes dull with defeat. Her thin frame drooped with weariness, yet she held one arm protectively around the mound of her belly. Sarah's time was near and she was anxious to have a decent place for her confinement. Despite their dire circumstances, Sarah didn't want to lose this baby. She'd lost so many that even the humiliation of the workhouse was better than giving birth in a ditch. Beside her, five-year-old Bobbie sucked his thumb and said nothing. He gripped his mother's hand tightly, his huge brown eyes glancing nervously between his sister and father.

Reuben Kirkland passed his hand wearily across his brow. 'I've no choice, Meggie. I'm sorry, we've nowhere else to go and till I can find work again . . .' His voice trailed away and he avoided meeting his daughter's belligerent gaze.

Reuben's sudden dismissal from his work as a wagoner at Middleditch Farm had come as a shock to all the family, but Meg was the only one who had dared to voice her indignation. Sarah had said nothing.

'Why, Dad?' Meg had challenged him the previous evening when, still in their cosy tied cottage, Reuben had brought home the devastating news. 'What's happened? And what about me?' Meg worked for the farmer's wife in the dairy, but she helped with outdoor work too, at haymaking and harvest and at potato-picking time. 'Am I to go an' all?'

Wordlessly, Reuben had nodded.

Meg bit her lip, casting about in her mind. Was it her fault? Had she done something wrong, something so dreadful that her whole family were being put out of their home? Eyes downcast, Reuben had muttered bitterly, 'It's the missis. Got her knife into me, she has. The mester'd've been all right, but her with her tittle-tattling.' He had spat the last words out with unusual viciousness.

Fresh hope had surged in Meg as she cried out eagerly, 'But what about Miss Alice? She's my friend. Her dad'd listen to her. She'll not let him turn us out.'

Her father had refused to listen. He'd turned away towards the back door, wrenched it open and disappeared through it. Meg had stared after him. Then she'd felt her mother's light touch on her arm. 'Leave it, love,' Sarah had said softly, speaking for the first time.

Why? Why? *Why?* Meg had wanted to scream. But her mother's pinched face and tear-filled eyes had stilled her angry outburst. Instead, she'd been sorely tempted to run to the farmhouse, to bang on the door and demand to be told the reason for her father's dismissal.

And, more importantly, her own. She was sure there had been nothing wrong when she'd left the dairy earlier that evening. The mistress – Mrs Mabel Smallwood – was a hard employer. She was strict and humourless, but she'd never been cruel or unjust.

Meg couldn't understand the sudden, soul-destroying change in their fortunes. How had they come to this? A sorry little group in the pale light of early summer, standing outside imposing gates. The workhouse lay on the outskirts of the small town of South Monkford, the nearest place to Middleditch Farm and the home they had been obliged to leave. They'd left at dawn, tramping the five miles here. As they walked, the rising sun heralded a warm day. Pale pink wild roses dappled the hedgerows and elderflower bushes were laden with their heavy cream blossom. Birds flew overhead in frantic frenzy to feed their young. But Meg saw none of it.

'Why can't we look for work?' the girl persisted, in no mood to 'leave it' as her mother suggested. 'You and me, Dad? There must be something. It's shearing time. There must be plenty of work—'

'I'm a wagoner, Meg. 'Osses is all I know about. What would I know about sheep?'

'But—'

'We've been sacked without a reference. Both of us.'

Meg gasped. That was the worst thing that could possibly happen. New employers always, but always, demanded a reference from the previous master or mistress. Without it, finding work was almost impossible except for the most menial, disgusting of jobs.

Like in the workhouse.

Standing at the gate, which seemed to the young girl like the bars of a prison, Meg shuddered. 'Why, Dad?' she whispered, once more searching her mind for something – anything – she might have done wrong. 'What's happened? It's not because of me, is it?'

She knew she was often pert and saucy, but the mistress wouldn't dismiss the whole family just because the dairymaid was a bit cheeky sometimes, would she? More than likely, Mabel Smallwood would have let Meg feel the back of her hand.

Then a far more worrying thought came into the girl's mind.

'You're a bad influence on my lass,' Mrs Smallwood had said more than once. 'She should be making friends of her own age. Nice girls who aren't fluttering their eyelashes at the farm lads half the time.'

'Alice talks to the farmhands, missis,' Meg would begin defiantly. Wasn't it from Alice that Meg had learned to laugh and flirt with the boys? 'So why can't I?'

'I'll hear no more of that sort of talk from you, miss. My Alice is different. She knows how to behave, knows where to draw the line. I can trust my Alice.' Her tone implied that she did not trust Meg. 'But how can you know at your age? Fifteen, indeed! Playing with fire, my girl, that's what you are. You'll come to a bad end, if you don't watch out. You mark my words.'

Remembering all this, Meg, suddenly afraid, asked her father, 'Is it to do with Alice? Is it because I'm friends with Alice and the missis doesn't like it?'

Beside her, Sarah gave a little sob and covered her mouth with her fingers. Reuben glared at Meg for an instant and then his gaze fell away. He turned towards his wife. 'I'm sorry, Sarah. Truly. I – I will come back for you. But I must get right away from here so – so that I can find work. You do understand, don't you?'

White-faced, Sarah lifted her head slowly and stared back at him. She bit her lip so hard that she drew blood, but she made no gesture of understanding. Her eyes held only suffering and silent reproach.

Meg gasped. Her mother's look was directed, not at her as she had feared, but at Reuben. Sarah held her husband entirely responsible for their predicament. Meg pressed her lips together, making her firm jawline even more pronounced with new determination. 'Well, you needn't think we're going in there, Dad, cos we're not. I'm going back to the farm. I'm going to see Miss Alice. She'll speak up for us. I know she will.'

She started to turn away but her father's hand shot out and gripped her arm. 'You'll do no such thing, girl. You'll go in there with your mam and your brother and you'll look after them. You hear me?'

Meg gaped at him and twisted her arm free. 'You're hurting me.'

Reuben was at once contrite. 'I'm sorry, love—' He rubbed his forehead distractedly. 'I just don't know which way to turn. Now, be a good girl, Meggie, and take care of your mam and Bobbie. Will you do that for me, eh?' His brown eyes were pleading with her. He touched her face gently and Meg was lost.

'Oh, Dad!' She flung herself against him, hugging him. Muffled against him she said, 'You will come back for us, won't you? Promise?'

For a brief moment, Reuben held her close whilst Meg clung to him. She felt his chest heave beneath her cheek, heard the gulping sound in his throat, but then, without warning, he tore himself from her, turned and stumbled away.

'Dad,' Meg cried, 'Dad, don't go. Don't leave us . . .' But Reuben hurried on and though the forlorn little family stood staring after him, not once did he look back.

Two

The small, whitewashed cottage on Middleditch Farm, owned by George Smallwood, had been home to the Kirkland family for the past three years. Meg's childhood had been punctuated by moves almost every year as her father shifted from farm to farm. With a new home in a strange place, a different school where she was cast adrift in a playground full of strangers with scarcely a friendly face amongst them, Meg had learned early to rely on no one but herself. Often she had been the butt of bullies, the object of ridicule for her bright red hair and her second-hand clothes.

'Look at carrot tops,' some boy would tease, pulling her red curls. The name would be taken up by them all – even the girls.

'A' them clothes your mam's hand-me-downs?' A jeering ring would form around her in the playground and the laughter and the pointing would begin. 'Look at 'er shoes. Reckon they're 'er dad's.'

'I've seen better shoes on 'osses.'

That most of the other children were similarly dressed to Meg didn't seem to matter. She was the new girl, the object of derision, fair game for the bullies.

As a little girl Meg had worked hard to become one of them, to earn friends, but as she grew older she learned not to care. She would stick her nose in the air and make some scathing retort. She became handy with her fists and many a time a harassed teacher had to prevent the red-haired she cat from pulling the hair of her opponent out by its roots. But at the age of ten Meg learned another way to deal with the taunts and jibes. She joined in the teasing directed at herself. She was the first to say, 'This is me mam's old skirt –' then she would pull a wry face and add – 'and you should see the bloomers I have to wear.' Instead of using her fists, Meg used her lively wit. She would laugh the loudest at herself, but behind the laughter in her green eyes, there was a hint of steel. Meg was learning fast how to stand on her own two feet in an unkind world.

There was only one reason why Meg was still goaded into using her fists now and then – if anyone dared to tease little Bobbie. Then his assailant would end up with a bloody nose and running to his mother.

'She hit me. That big girl hit me.'

Meg would clench her fists, narrow her eyes and, gritting her teeth, turn to face the irate mother.

'You're old enough to know better than to hit a little chap half your size.'

'Then your little chap shouldn't hit my brother.'

'My Arthur wouldn't do a thing like that.'

'Then why has Bobbie got a black eye?'

''Spect you did it and you're trying to put the blame on someone else.'

Meg would take a step closer and the older woman would back away, intimidated by the young firebrand. 'I *never* hit my brother.'

'All right, all right, but you leave my Arthur alone.'

'I will.' Then Meg would add ominously, 'As long as he leaves our Bobbie alone, an' all.'

When Meg was twelve, Reuben found work as head wagoner to George Smallwood and brought his family to the cottage that came with the job. Reuben was good with horses, loved them and understood them. Meg loved them too, the way the huge shires shook their great heads, snorted and stamped their heavy hooves. She loved their power, their might.

'You'd make a good wagoner, Meggie,' her father told her proudly and then spoilt it by adding, 'if only you were a lad.'

Meg did not go back to school. She was old enough now to be employed on the same farm and soon she was under Mrs Mabel Smallwood's eagle eye in the dairy. But Meg had never known such happiness and contentment. She worked hard, though she rarely earned even the most grudging praise from the farmer's wife.

And at last she found a real friend in the Smallwoods' daughter.

Although Alice – buxom, fair-haired, blue-eyed and pink-cheeked – was five years older than Meg, she was kind to the young girl. There were no girls of a similar age to Alice on the neighbouring farms, so the two were thrown together even in their spare time. Though there was not much of that for either of them, Meg thought wryly. Alice took Meg to the big church in South Monkford every Sunday morning. They knelt together demurely during the service, but on the walk home Meg watched as Alice smiled coyly at the youths gathered near the church wall, laughing and talking whilst they watched the girls parading in their Sunday best.

'Come for a walk with us, Alice.' One spotty-faced youth was a particular admirer, but Alice only tossed her hair and stuck her nose in the air. 'What? With you, Harry Warner?'

The young man grinned. 'I was all right to walk out with last Sunday.'

Alice laughed her tinkling laugh and dimpled her cheeks. 'That was last week.'

'Oho, someone else, is there?' He pressed his hand to his chest. 'My heart is broken.'

'I'm sure Lizzie Lucas will help it mend.'

'Lizzie Lucas means nothing to me.'

'That's not what I've heard.' Tossing her hair, Alice linked her arm through Meg's and, with a cheery wave to all the watching youths, walked down the lane, swinging her hips. Meg, too, turned, grinned saucily at the lads and then tried to copy Alice's provocative walk.

Middleditch Farm lay in the rolling countryside of east Nottinghamshire. The nearest town was South Monkford, with narrow streets of shops and a market held on Wednesdays and Saturdays. On the outskirts was a racecourse that was becoming quite famous and it was George Smallwood's ambition to own a racehorse one day.

'You'll look after it for me, Kirkland,' the farmer would say, clapping Reuben on the back. 'We'll rear a winner, eh?'

And several times a year, when there was a big meeting on, George and his wagoner would disappear for a day at the races. On those days Meg would lie in her bed at night under the eaves and listen to her father stumbling about in the room below when he arrived home late and much the worse for drink. Her mother would be tight-lipped for days afterwards, but there was little Sarah could do about it when it was their employer who was the ringleader in such escapades.

The family's three years at Middleditch Farm had been the longest they had stayed anywhere that Meg could remember. And they had certainly been the happiest years for her. But suddenly, disastrously, that had all changed. And Meg was very much afraid that somehow it was all her fault.

Had Mabel Smallwood found out about last Sunday's picnic, when she and Alice had taken sandwiches, cakes and beer into the recreation ground beyond the church? They had sat on the grass in the sunshine, talking dreamily about the kind of man they'd like to marry, when they'd been startled by two youths from the town whom Alice knew vaguely.

'Well, well, well, if it isn't the lovely Alice Smallwood. And who's this?' The taller of the two young men had turned his attention to Meg, but it had been Alice who had invited the lads to join their picnic. The four youngsters had had a merry afternoon. There'd been a little flirting, a little horseplay and when they parted in the early evening, a chaste kiss. Though it had all been innocent enough, Mrs Smallwood wouldn't think so. And, Meg thought fearfully, she would not blame her own daughter. In her eyes, Alice could do no wrong. No, the mistress would lay any blame squarely on Meg's head. But without going back to Middleditch Farm, there was little Meg could do to find out if this was the reason for their sudden dismissal.

One day, the young girl vowed, *I will find out. And I'll tell Mrs Mabel Smallwood exactly what I think of her – and her precious daughter*. For what hurt Meg more than anything was the growing realization that, whatever had happened to cause this catastrophe, Alice – her dear friend and confidante – had not spoken up for her.

That hurt the young girl much more than the fact that she and her mother and brother had now to enter the much-feared workhouse.

Lifting her head with a show of defiance, Meg said,

'Come on, Mam – Bobbie. We'd best go and knock at the door.'

She pushed open the heavy gate and marched up a long, straight path leading through an orchard and neatly cultivated vegetable gardens. Sarah, with Bobbie holding her hand, trailed listlessly behind her. They passed between high walls surrounding yards on either side of the main entrance at the front of the building and then climbed wide, stone steps to the white pillared door. Meg rang the bell. Somewhere deep inside they heard a faint clanging. It seemed an age until the door was thrown open and the biggest man whom Meg had ever seen stood there looking down on them.

Isaac Pendleton, master of South Monkford workhouse, was six feet tall with a girth that seemed almost the same measurement. A large, bulbous nose dominated his florid face. His lips were fleshy and wet and heavy jowls bulged out over the starched white collar. His dark hair, greying at the temples, was thinning and smoothed over his crown in a vain attempt to cover advancing baldness. Yet his eyes seemed kindly.

'What's this? What's this? Ragamuffins knocking at my front door?' His voice was as large as his frame, deep and resonant. He was dressed in a dark, sober suit, but a multi-coloured waistcoat, stretched tightly over his ample chest, lightened his otherwise sombre appearance. Looped across it was a gold watch chain. It was as if his position demanded that he dress with sobriety and authority, yet his waistcoat revealed a more flamboyant side to his nature.

Sarah quailed and Bobbie shrank against his mother's skirts, but Meg stood her ground and gazed boldly up at him. She opened her mouth, but before she could speak the master boomed, 'Round the back with you.

You'll find someone there to direct you.' He seemed about to shut the door in their faces, but then he hesitated. His gaze roamed over Meg's face and hair.

'By,' he murmured, 'but you'll be a beauty one day an' no mistake.' Then his glance went beyond Meg to Sarah's face.

Though at present she was pale with distress and heavy with child, Isaac Pendleton, who prided himself on being a veritable connoisseur of women, could see beyond Sarah's temporary weariness. She was undoubtedly feeling humiliated too, he thought, at having to present herself at his door, but she was a pretty, gentle-looking creature with lovely eyes.

Isaac smiled. 'My dear lady, pray come in.' He bent closer, as if sharing a confidence. 'We'll break the rules for once, shall we? This is the main door to the guardians' meeting room and to my apartments. It's not normally used by the – er – inmates. But come in – come in.' He extended a long arm and ushered the reluctant little family inside.

Isaac Pendleton was not at all what Meg had expected the workhouse master to be like. From the imposing look of the building's walls and windows from the outside, she'd expected the man in charge to be as threatening, treating people down on their luck as idle, good-for-nothings. Yet this man was leading them down a room, past the long, polished table to a door at the far end on the left-hand side. Reaching it, he paused and turned. Putting his finger to his lips, he chuckled, 'Now, not a word to the others, mind, else they'll all expect to use the front door. Go through here and out of the door on the right into the yard and then to the buildings on the far side. That's the way you should have come in.' He beamed benevolently down at them. 'The porter's lodge is at the end near the entrance gate. See old Albert Conroy. He'll admit you and then arrange for someone to take you to the bath room and fit you out with uniforms.' He took Sarah's hand and raised it to his lips. 'Don't fret, my dear lady. You'll be well looked after here. You and your little ones.'

For the first time since Reuben had brought home the dreadful news, Sarah managed a weak smile. 'You're very kind,' she murmured and a faint tinge of pink touched her pale cheeks.

Three

They crossed the yard towards a door in the high wall – the door by which they should have entered the workhouse. Near it, at the end of a row of buildings, was the porter's lodge. As they approached, an old man appeared. He was scowling at them, his bushy white eyebrows drawn together. Several days' growth of grizzled beard gave him the look of an unkempt tramp. His clothes, crumpled and threadbare, hung loosely on him.

'And where might you three 'ave come from? I didn't see you come in.' His voice was gruff and accusing. He walked with a limp that gave him a curious rolling gait, like a sailor who has just stepped ashore after weeks at sea.

Bobbie cowered behind Sarah, burying his face against her skirt. 'Mam,' he wailed. 'Mammy!'

Surprised, the old man looked down him. 'No need for that, little feller. I ain't gonna hurt yer.' His voice, though still growly, was now kindly.

Meg stepped forward, protective of her little brother as ever, protective now of her mother too. 'We came to the wrong door,' Meg explained and treated him to her most winning smile, 'but we've been told to report to you. Are you Mr Conroy?'

The old man stared at her for a minute. White-haired, wizened and crippled with arthritis, Albert Conroy lived out his existence in the lodge near the workhouse's back gate, by which the inmates entered and left. Each night it was Albert who admitted the vagrants and directed them to the bath room. From there they went to the casual ward, where they were allowed a meal and to stay overnight in return for several hours' work the following day. And it was Albert who saw other folks enter the building, never to leave again until they were carried out in a plain, rough pauper's coffin.

Few stayed to talk to old Albert and even fewer gave him the courtesy of addressing him by name. And now here was this pretty little thing calling him 'Mr Conroy' just as if he were some toff in fancy clothes. He rubbed the back of his hand across his nose and mouth and sniffed. He tried a toothless smile, but found he had almost forgotten how to summon one up.

'Aye, I am.' His voice quavered. 'Long time since anyone called me "Mr Conroy".' He paused and then added wistfully, 'Time was when I was "Albert" to mi friends, but now it's just "Conroy" or just "eh-up, you".'

Meg put her head on one side. 'Wouldn't it sound cheeky of someone like me to call you by your Christian name?'

Albert's eyes watered. 'Nah. Not a bit. I'd – I'd like to be called Albert by a pretty young wench like you.'

Meg held out her hand. 'Albert it is, then. I'm Meg Kirkland and this is my mam and my little brother, Bobbie.'

The smile, long unused, quivered on his mouth and his voice was unsteady as he said, 'Pleased to meet yer, mi duck, though I'm sorry to see you in a place like this.'

'We won't be here long,' Meg said, forcing a cheerfulness she didn't feel for the sake of her mother and

Bobbie. 'But as you can see –' she gestured towards her mother's obvious condition – 'mi mam needs somewhere to stay.' Then she added quickly, 'Mi dad's gone to look for work and then he'll be coming back to fetch us.'

For a moment the old man looked doubtful, but then he said, 'Aye, course he will, mi duck, course he will.' More briskly, he added, 'Now, let's get down to business . . .'

They followed Albert into the porter's lodge, a grand-sounding name for what turned out to be one small, square room where the old man obviously lived.

'They let me sleep here and eat here,' he said with a note of pride, as if to live in this cold, sparsely furnished room was a privilege. Perhaps it was, Meg thought, for him, though she couldn't imagine a harsher fate than to end her days in such a way.

Just inside the door of his lodge was a table and open upon it was a ledger. A list of names was neatly written in copperplate script on each page. Albert picked up a pen and, poised to write, looked up at Meg. 'Now, tell me your full names, starting with yer mam.'

He wrote down the information with painfully slow deliberation, yet he was justifiably proud of the finished result. He asked a few more questions and then stood back, looking down with satisfaction at the neat rows of writing.

'It's beautiful handwriting,' Meg said.

'I allus did have a good hand,' Albert murmured. 'And I like to keep mi book nice. The guardians always ask to see it when they 'ave one of their meetings here. I teks it across to the committee room and the master shows them it.'

'I wish I could write like that,' Meg said.

'Oh, it's just practice, that's all,' the old man said

modestly, but Meg could tell he was gratified by her praise. 'Right, now I'd better get her ladyship to tek you to the bath room and so on.'

'Who's "her ladyship"?'

Albert guffawed wheezily. 'Waters.'

'Is she in charge?'

'She'd like to think she is. Nah. She's an inmate – just like me. Mind you, the silly woman 'ad the chance to leave years ago, but wouldn't.'

'Wouldn't leave?' Meg was incredulous. 'Why ever not?'

'Ah, well now, it was like this—' He seemed about to launch into a long story, but one glance at Sarah's face, white with fatigue, changed his mind. 'Mebbe I'll tell you all about it one day, but now I reckon you'd best get yer mam settled. She looks fair done in. Ah, here comes Waters. How that woman knows when there's new folks arrived beats me, but she always does. Nowt seems to get past her beady eyes.'

The woman coming across the yard towards them was more what Meg had imagined those in authority in the workhouse might be. Thin-faced with a beak-like nose and small, ferret eyes, she snapped, 'How did you get in? I saw you coming across the yard.'

'We came in the other way. Sorry,' Meg smiled winningly, trying not to let slip that they'd come in by the front door. 'We saw a gentleman who told us where to come.'

Waters looked puzzled and Meg hurried on, explaining. 'He was very tall and – and big, but he was ever so nice and—'

The woman's eyes widened. 'Mr Pendleton? You saw Mr Pendleton?'

'I don't know his name, but he was very kind.'

'It must have been Mr Pendleton.' Then Waters gave a start, her mind obviously working fast. 'You – you don't mean you went to the front door?' she asked, appalled by the newcomers' audacity.

'Er – well,' Meg stammered.

'What Miss Pendleton'll say, I don't know,' Waters muttered, sniffing her disapproval.

'The man – Mr Pendleton – didn't seem to mind,' Meg insisted. 'He was very nice about it. Who is he?'

The woman's tone was suddenly reverential. 'Mr Pendleton is the master of the workhouse. He's a wonderful man.' For a brief moment her eyes softened. 'A wonderful man.' But the look was gone in an instant and her eyes hardened again. 'And you'd do well to remember it, girl.'

Waters moved into Albert's lodge and ran her finger down the list of names in his ledger, noting the new arrivals.

'So –' her disapproving glance raked them up and down, taking in the faded work clothes, the shabby, dusty boots – 'homeless, are you?'

Meg and her mother exchanged a glance and the girl's mouth tightened as she was obliged to say bitterly, 'Yes.' Then in a rush she gabbled, 'But mi dad's gone looking for work. We won't be here long. He'll soon be back for us.'

'That's what they all say, but they're still here years later.'

'Well, *we* won't be.' Meg was belligerent. 'He'll come back.' She turned towards her mother. 'Won't he, Mam?'

But Sarah only hung her head whilst the other woman sniffed yet again. 'How old are you, girl?'

'Fifteen.'

The woman grunted, dissatisfied with her answer. 'You look older,' she said, eyeing Meg suspiciously. 'Sure you're not trying to make out you're younger than you really are just to get out of a bit of work?'

Meg tossed her head. 'I'm not frightened of work. I've worked on a farm for three years. I'm sixteen next month.'

The woman's lips stretched in what passed for a smile, though it did not reach her eyes. They were steel grey, cold and hard. 'My name is Ursula Waters, but we're all called by our surnames in here. That is –' she paused and hesitated fractionally, before adding – 'unless the master decides to call you by your Christian name.'

Pertly, Meg asked, 'And do we call him by his Christian name then?'

Ursula Waters gasped. 'The very idea! You've a mite too much to say for yourself, child.'

'I'm not a child,' Meg retorted hotly.

'You're a child in here if you're only fifteen. It's the rules.' Ursula leant closer. 'Are you sure you're not older?'

For the first time, Sarah spoke. Haltingly, her voice husky with shame and despair, she said, 'She is only fifteen, ma'am. I assure you.'

Meg turned and stared at her. Why was Sarah kow-towing to this harridan? It was obvious the woman was only an inmate too – though probably an inmate who held some sort of position. No doubt the woman enjoyed special privileges because of it. But Waters was no better than they were, Meg thought. She opened her mouth to retort, but caught her mother's warning glance and closed it again, pressing her lips together.

Bobbie, sucking his thumb, began to whimper and tug at Sarah's skirt.

'I'd better fetch Miss Pendleton. She's the matron and Mr Pendleton's sister.' Unbending enough to impart a little information in which she seemed to take great pride, Ursula Waters said, 'Poor Mr Pendleton lost his wife some years ago and his sister came to take her place as matron. Of course, it's quite unusual for that to happen. The master and the matron are usually man and wife, but the guardians' committee gave special consent. They didn't want to lose Mr Pendleton as master, you see.'

Meg nodded, pretending to understand.

'Wait here whilst I fetch matron.' Waters glanced down at Bobbie with distaste, sniffed once more and left the room.

'What a dragon!' Meg burst out, almost before the woman was out of earshot.

'Hush, Meg,' Sarah whispered. 'Don't make things worse than they already are, there's a dear.'

Meg looked at her mother. 'Mam, was it my fault . . .?' she began, but Sarah was bending over Bobbie, trying to quieten his crying, and at that moment Miss Pendleton bustled in, followed closely by Ursula Walters.

Letitia Pendleton was younger than her brother. Meg guessed she was about forty, but Isaac Pendleton had looked over fifty. The matron was small and round, and dressed in an ankle-length, dark blue dress with broad, starched white cuffs. A white bib apron covered the dress and she wore thick dark stockings and lace-up shoes with small heels. Her hair was completely covered with a starched white square of cloth, which fell in a triangular shape at the back of her head. Her face was plump, her cheeks round and rosy, but it was not the rosiness of good health, rather of too much indulgence, especially from a bottle. Young as she was, Meg recognized the signs. Farmer Smallwood had just such a look. Like her brother, Letitia Pendleton had hazel eyes that twinkled merrily. Once again, Meg was surprised. To her, Ursula Waters was the epitome of workhouse authority – the type everyone on the outside dreaded – not this buxom, smiling woman, who reminded the girl more of a fat and jolly farmer's wife. Not that Mrs Smallwood had been like that; she had been thin and wiry and shrewish. Meg pushed away the painful memories that threatened to overwhelm her.

'Now then, who have we here?' the matron greeted them.

Her glance lingered a moment on Sarah's swollen stomach. Then her gaze fell upon Bobbie, whose cheeks were now stained with tears. He was hiccuping miserably and sucking his thumb hard.

Letitia Pendleton's eyes softened. 'Poor little chap,' she said, taking his hand. 'I bet you're hungry, aren't you? You come along with me.'

'Oh, I don't think—' Sarah began.

'I'm sorry, my dear,' the matron said, but there was understanding in her tone. 'It's the rule in here. You all have to be segregated. Women, men – and the children.'

'You'll do as you're told,' Ursula put in sharply. 'It's the master's rules.'

'I tell you what,' Miss Pendleton said kindly. 'Maybe he can stay with you until the medical officer has seen you tomorrow morning, but then I'm afraid he will have to go with the other children.'

Meg noticed that Ursula's lips pursed even more tightly and her eyes flashed with anger. But she said nothing.

Sarah was close to tears, desperation on her face, but

Bobbie, with his small hand in the matron's plump grasp, had stopped crying. He was looking up at Miss Pendleton and she was smiling down at him with such compassion in her eyes, such fondness, that, to Meg's surprise, a tremulous smile hovered on the child's mouth.

'Do you look after the little ones, Matron?' she asked.

Letitia looked up, reluctantly dragging her gaze away from the little boy, but before she could answer, Ursula snapped, 'Mind your tongue, girl. Just remember who you're talking to. It's not your place to be asking questions. Not in here.'

'It's all right, Waters. The girl is concerned for her brother. That's only natural and very commendable too.'

Again Ursula sniffed her disapproval but said no more. Letitia turned back to Meg. 'The schoolmistress and I have care of the children between us. She teaches the younger ones during the day, whilst the older ones go to the local school. Outside school hours we share the supervision of all the children.'

'The schoolmistress?' Meg asked. 'Is she –' she glanced meaningfully at Ursula – 'nice?'

Meg saw that the matron pursed her mouth to prevent a smile. 'Louisa Daley? Oh yes, she's nice. Only young and the little ones love her.' Letitia glanced at Ursula. There was something pointed in the look that Meg couldn't understand as the matron added, 'We *all* do.' And she noticed that an angry flush crept up Ursula's scrawny neck and into her face.

Meg felt herself relax. She turned and touched her mother's arm. 'That's all right then, isn't it, Mam? Bobbie will be all right.'

Sarah's eyes lingered on her small son. She touched

his hair and then, not trusting herself to speak, she nodded.

'Now,' the matron said briskly, 'Let's get you admitted to the receiving ward. Waters, have you got all their details from Conroy?'

'Of course I have.'

Meg was surprised at the insolence in Ursula's tone. It was almost as if she was in charge – not the matron – and yet Meg knew that this could not be the case.

'They were all born within the county.' She sniffed – a sound that Meg was already coming to know very well when the woman was expressing her disgust. 'Though they've moved about a lot. Like gypsies.' On Ursula's lips the word implied disgrace.

'Mi dad's a farm worker. A wagoner,' Meg retorted defiantly, lifting her chin higher. For a brief moment there was a note of pride in her tone as she spoke of her father, remembering the position he had held, the respect his skill with horses had commanded. But then the pride faded from her tone when she relived the moment he'd told them that he'd been dismissed. 'We – we moved about a bit with his job, but we've been at – at the last place –' she couldn't bring herself to say the name of Middleditch Farm – 'for the last three years.'

'Well,' Letitia said, 'that'll make it easier for the guardians to decide. In the meantime, we'll get you settled in. Come along.'

'Goodbye, Albert,' Meg said to the old man, who had remained silent ever since Ursula Waters had stepped into his room.

''Bye, mi duck. For now.'

They followed the matron and Ursula across the yard, which was enclosed on all sides either by the buildings or walls and solid gates.

Meg shivered as she looked about her and once again the feeling of guilt swept through her. Was it her impertinent tongue that had landed them here? Or had it been because of her friendship with Alice? The thought of the girl she had liked so much was like a knife in her heart. Alice had betrayed her. She had done nothing to help Meg and her family. Surely, Alice could have done something.

Oh, Dad, Meg begged silently, *come back for us. Don't leave us in this place. Please come back, Dad. Please.*

Four

'Take your clothes off.'

Appalled, Meg stared at Ursula. 'All of them?'

'Yes. You wear the workhouse uniform whilst you're in here.'

'But – but what happens to our own clothes?'

'We have them cleaned.' Ursula eyed the newcomers up and down, assessing them. 'Fumigated in some cases. Just in case you're riddled with lice and—'

'We most certainly are not,' Meg said, deeply insulted. She turned to her mother. 'Tell her, Mam.'

But Sarah only murmured, 'Do as Miss Waters tells you, love. Don't make a fuss.'

'I'm not making a fuss, I just want to know what happens to our clothes. Miss Alice gave me this dress and . . .'

At once her mother's face was bleak and Meg was sorry she'd brought back memories of the comfortable, happy life that had been so suddenly and brutally torn away from them. She bit her lip. She still couldn't believe that Miss Alice had been party to their dismissal.

'We label all your clothes,' Letitia said and Meg felt the matron was trying to lessen Ursula's harshness. 'You'll get them back when you leave.'

Meg heard Ursula mutter darkly, 'If you leave.'

'That's all right, then,' Meg said, addressing her remark to the matron and ignoring Ursula. 'We won't be without them very long. We'll soon be out of here.' She felt embarrassed as Ursula stood watching them undress, gaping at Sarah's swollen belly.

'When are you due, Kirkland?' Ursula asked, once more taking the lead. To Meg's surprise, it was the matron who was helping Bobbie out of his clothes, smiling down at him and talking to him in gentle, reassuring tones, whilst Ursula stood to one side as if to have to touch the newcomers offended her.

Quietly, Sarah said, 'Sometime this month, I think.'

'The medical officer will inspect you tomorrow morning and classify you.' Then Meg saw Ursula lean towards the matron. 'If you ask me that girl ought to be classed as an able-bodied woman. She's no child.'

Meg felt them gazing at her young breasts, slim waist and firm, rounded buttocks. She faced them boldly, but it was hard to do so. Being naked took away her last vestige of dignity, leaving her humiliated and vulnerable. 'I've told you, I am fifteen – nearly sixteen – and I'm not afraid of work. I don't want to be with the children.'

'We'll see what the medical officer thinks,' was all the matron would say. 'Now, let's get you bathed and don't forget to wash your hair.' She bundled up their clothes and the few possessions they had brought with them. 'Here you are, Waters. See these are washed and properly labelled.'

The look of distaste on Ursula's face as she was forced to take their clothing made Meg want to laugh out loud for the first time.

'Bet that's the last we see of them,' she muttered, though not loud enough for the matron to hear as Ursula disappeared through the door.

The matron was bending towards Bobbie. 'Come on, little man, you come with me.'

'I'll wash Bobbie,' Meg began, but Miss Pendleton said firmly, 'You help your mother and see to yourself. He'll be fine with me.'

She led Bobbie away. Sarah and Meg looked helplessly at each other as they listened for his protesting wails. But Bobbie made no sound and trotted off, his hand happily in the matron's plump grasp.

Sarah closed her eyes and swayed. She might have fallen if Meg hadn't been quick to steady her. 'Let's get ourselves bathed quick, Mam, and then perhaps we can go and find him.'

Sarah nodded weakly and allowed Meg to help her.

It was the first time that Meg had seen her mother's body. Standing naked in the lukewarm water, she tried to avert her gaze, tried to leave her mother some shred of dignity.

But what self-respect was there left for either of them in this place?

When they were bathed and their hair washed, but still wet and clinging, Ursula returned. She handed them coarse scratchy underwear and the grey dress and white apron that were the uniform of the workhouse, saying, 'You can keep your own boots.'

'Where's Bobbie? Where's she taken him?' Meg demanded when they were fully clothed once more.

'If by "she" you mean matron, then she'll have taken him to the children's dormitory, I expect.'

Meg glanced at her mother, willing her to stand up to these people, but Sarah seemed to have lost her spirit completely. Meg could hardly believe the change in her. Sarah had always been quiet, but content with her lot and happy with her husband and young family, despite the sadness of losing three babies. She'd always had a gentle smile on her face and, even when Meg had been her naughtiest, Sarah had never raised her voice. Her chastisement had been a disappointed admonishment that had always left Meg feeling guilty at having hurt her mother by her wilfulness. But now Sarah was defeated by the shame of entering a place which she'd been taught since childhood was the ultimate in degradation.

So it was the young girl who turned back to face Ursula. *She's like a jailer*, Meg thought. 'Matron said he could stay with us. At least until tomorrow.'

'It's the rules,' Ursula snapped. 'Everyone's classified and segregated in here. Until the medical officer's seen you, you'll be in the receiving ward.' She pointed upwards, indicating the room on the next floor up, directly above their heads. 'He classifies you and then you go into the dormitories in the main building.' With a sideways flick of her head, she gestured towards the long, three-storey building across the yard. She ticked off the categories of inmates on her fingers. 'At the far end there's the able-bodied men's day room on the ground floor with their dormitories above on the first and second floors. Next to that are the old and infirm men. Then on the ground floor there's the clerk's office and the master's room. Right in the centre of the building is the guardians' committee room with the school room behind it and above them are the master's bedroom and the children's dormitory. Still on the ground floor is the kitchen, then the old women and then right at this end there's the able-bodied women.'

'Where are the children? Where will Bobbie be?' Meg demanded.

'He'll spend most of the time in the school room or the dormitory, but they're allowed into the women's exercise yards.'

'Are those at the front of the building, behind those walls?'

'Yes. That's where the privies are too. And there's a privy in this back courtyard too. Here, next to the bath room.'

For the first time Sarah spoke. 'Will I be allowed to put Bobbie to bed?'

Ursula shook her head and Sarah's shoulders drooped even more.

'I'll show you upstairs. You're going to be a bit crowded in the receiving ward. It's the casual ward where the vagrants stay overnight, as well as people like you waiting to be admitted. Come along.'

The small dormitory was jammed with beds – if they could be called beds, for they were nothing more than rough hessian bags filled with straw, grubby grey blankets and a lumpy pillow on the floor. Meg and her mother were obliged to share, and later on, through that first night they huddled together, hardly sleeping in their anxiety over Bobbie.

'He'll be all right, Mam. Miss Pendleton was kind to him. Much nicer than the dragon.'

In the darkness, Sarah buried her head against Meg's shoulder and wept. With her arms about her mother, Meg lay staring into the darkness, listening to the snuffling and snoring of the other women. Real sleep was impossible and she dozed fitfully, waking in the early light of the following morning still unable to accept what had happened to her family in the short space of the last thirty-six hours.

Was it really only the night before last that her father

had come home with the news that they had to leave their home?

I wish I could have seen Miss Alice. Perhaps her mam or her dad stopped her seeing me. I can't believe she wouldn't have tried to help us, Meg thought, trying to find excuses for the older girl. She still did not want to believe that Alice, her bright, vivacious friend, had really deserted her so cruelly. Perhaps it hadn't been Alice's fault. Perhaps . . .

Somewhere a loud bell was being rung, disturbing her thoughts. The other women in the room were stirring.

'Come on, Mam,' Meg said, gently shaking her mother awake. 'We have to get up.'

Meg and Sarah stood side by side, submitting to the medical officer's thorough examination. Once more they were obliged to be almost naked before a stranger, with Miss Pendleton standing in the background. And Ursula was there again, by the door, her beady eyes missing nothing.

'Now, Mrs Kirkland,' the doctor said, 'I think your baby will come very soon, so only light duties for you. But I shall put you with the able-bodied women. Matron –' he half turned towards the woman standing behind him – 'you'll see to it?'

'Of course, Doctor. She can help in the kitchen, preparing vegetables and such.'

'Excellent, excellent. She can be allowed to sit down to do that.' It was an order rather than a suggestion.

'Whatever you say, Doctor.'

'She could pick oakum,' Ursula put in, a malicious smile on her face. 'She can sit down to do that.'

The doctor frowned at Ursula. He could not interfere directly with the internal running of the workhouse, even if he wanted to. But unpicking lengths of old, tarred rope, though a sedentary occupation, was painful work resulting in raw and bleeding fingers.

He sighed as he beckoned Meg forward. 'Now then, young lady, let's have a look at you.'

Dr Collins was young, only in his early thirties, Meg guessed. He was very good-looking and, as he examined even her most secret places, Meg grew hotter and hotter with embarrassment. He was tall with fair curly hair and the brightest blue eyes that Meg had ever seen in a man.

Moments later he pronounced her, 'Fit as a flea and strong as an ox. Now –' he glanced down at his papers before adding – 'Meg, you're fifteen, but sixteen next month.'

'Yes, sir, and I don't want to be with the children. I can work. I—'

'Hold your tongue, girl,' Ursula snapped from her place by the door, but the doctor held up his hand, smiling at the girl standing before him.

'What I was going to suggest is that you should be with the children for the first month—'

'Oh, we won't be here as long as that. Mi dad will be back for us. I know he will.'

'I'm sure he will, but just in case he – er – encounters a few difficulties, we'll plan for a little longer, shall we?'

Meg stared into the man's blue eyes and saw sympathy there. A lump came into her throat and she nodded. 'All right,' she agreed huskily.

'What I suggest is that you should help the schoolmistress with the little ones. She is responsible not only for the teaching, but for the general care of the children too. I'm sure Miss Daley would be glad of some help and –' he leant towards Meg and lowered his voice – 'you'll be near your little brother for a while. Help him settle in. The little chap looked none too happy when I saw him earlier.'

Meg realized suddenly that the doctor was trying to do her a favour. She beamed at him, her whole demeanour changing in an instant. Her eyes shone and her cheeks dimpled prettily. It was like the sun appearing after a rain shower. 'Thank you, sir. Oh, thank you,' she breathed.

The doctor stared at her for a moment, then blinked, glanced down and shuffled his papers. Clearing his throat, he said, 'Don't mention it. I can see that you are a nice family, who've hit a bad patch in your lives.' He looked up again and smiled, once more in control of himself. 'I hope you're right and that your father returns for you very soon.' He glanced towards Sarah. 'Perhaps by then he'll have become a father again. In the meantime, we'll take good care of you all.'

Outside the infirmary, where they had been summoned for the medical officer's examination, Meg helped her mother down the stone steps.

'I don't believe this place, Mam.'

Sarah drew in a deep breath. 'Why? What do you mean?'

'Most of them are so nice, Mr Pendleton, the doctor, even Miss Pendleton isn't a bad old stick. But that Waters is a dragon. I thought they'd all be like that. I mean, everyone's always so frightened of the workhouse. It's like a terrible shadow hanging over anyone who can't work or falls sick.'

'It's the shame, Meg. That's the worst thing. And you're right. A lot of places are dreadful, with awful people running them. When I was a girl, we heard terrible stories about this place. It was our worst nightmare that we'd end up in here. And now –' tears threatened – 'here I am.'

Meg put her arm around her mother and hugged her close. 'Don't worry, Mam. Dad'll soon be back. He'll find work and come back for us.'

Sarah's only answer was a sob and a slight shake of her head.

Reaching the foot of the stairs, they stepped out into the men's backyard and Meg glanced about her. There was a pump in the centre of the wide open space and three or four men were queuing at it, bending their heads down and opening their mouths to drink. Others strolled around the yard in twos and threes, hands in their pockets and chatting together, but their shoulders were hunched, their heads bent forward. One or two walked alone, a defeated look on their faces. To one side older men, bent and crippled with age, shuffled along. But in the middle of the yard, youths, who must have been sixteen or more to be classed along with the men, played a rowdy game of football with a stone.

Meg looked about her, half-hoping to see someone she knew, but at the same time hoping no one would recognize her. One of the young lads glanced across at her and, giving the stone a last kick, left the game and swaggered towards her, grinning cheekily. 'By heck, it's nice to see a pretty girl in here. Where've you come from?'

Meg put her nose in the air and said loftily, 'What's that to do with you?'

The lad laughed, showing surprisingly even white teeth. His face creased and his brown eyes twinkled. He was thin, but wiry and energetic with thick brown curly hair cut short. He shrugged his shoulders. 'Nowt, just interested that's all. No offence meant.'

Meg capitulated and grinned back at him. 'None taken. Just that we've done nothing but answer questions since we got here.'

The youth nodded. 'I guess it's like that, but I wouldn't know.'

Now Meg was intrigued. 'Why? Didn't you have to answer a lot of questions when you came in?'

He laughed again. 'Nope. I was born in here. Me mam died having me, so they tell me. I've been here all me life.'

'Oh, how terrible!' The words escaped from Meg's mouth before she could stop them.

'Is it?' he asked solemnly, the laughter dying on his face. 'I've never known owt else.'

'No,' Meg said slowly, beginning to understand. 'I see that now.'

'Meg,' Sarah began, 'we ought to go. I – I need to sit down.'

At once Meg was contrite. 'I'm sorry, Mam.' With Sarah leaning heavily against her, they began to move back towards the gate in the wall, which led from the men's courtyard into the women's.

Meg glanced back over her shoulder towards the youth. 'What's your name?'

'Jake. What's yours?'

'Meg. I'll see you again.'

He pulled a face and lifted his shoulders. 'Not much chance. *They'll* see to that. But I'll watch out for you.' He winked at her. 'There are ways – if you know 'em.'

Meg nodded, wondering who 'they' were, but she could stay no longer. Sarah was looking pale and had deep purple shadows beneath her eyes. 'Come on, Mam. We'll find the dormitory and you can lie down.'

'But she needs to rest. Look at her.' Meg flung out her arm towards her mother as she stood facing Ursula Waters. 'She's done in.'

'She can't lie down in the dormitory during the daytime. If she's ill, she should report to the infirmary. And she's not, else the doctor would have said.'

'She's not ill, just exhausted.'

The woman pursed her thin mouth. 'I'm sorry. There's nothing I can do about it.'

'You don't want to, you mean,' Meg muttered.

'What did you say?' Ursula snapped.

'Nothing,' Meg answered morosely. How she would like to give this woman a mouthful, but she realized her runaway tongue would only make matters worse, especially for her poor mother.

Ursula sniffed. 'She's supposed to start work in the kitchens.' She glanced at Sarah, who was sitting on the chair and looking as if she was about to fall off it at any moment. Sarah's pallor must have touched even Ursula's hard heart, for she relented enough to say, 'I'll see what matron says.'

'Thank you,' Meg said, with more than a hint of sarcasm.

Ursula glared at her for a moment, before turning and leaving the room.

'Never mind what that dragon says, Mam. Come and lie down. Here, these are our beds next to each other.'

In the able women's dormitory the beds were still straw palliasses with rough grey blankets and one pillow, but the mattresses were now sitting on a four-legged wooden frame.

Sarah allowed Meg to help her to one, where she lay back and gave a weary sigh.

Meg sat beside her holding her hand, concerned by its feeling of limp clamminess. Letitia appeared beside them and stood for a moment, looking down at Sarah. Then she gave a brief nod.

'We'll let her rest today, but tomorrow she must try to do a little work. And the following day you'll have to be interviewed by the board of guardians. That's when their next meeting is.'

Sarah lay quite still, her eyes closed, and made no sign that she had even heard the matron. Letitia Pendleton glanced at Meg. 'But you go with Waters, Kirkland. She'll introduce you to Miss Daley, the schoolmistress. I'm sure she'll be glad of your help. She's run ragged by the little tykes.' But the matron spoke the last few words with a fond smile.

Meg rose, bent and kissed her mother's damp forehead and followed Ursula out of the room. 'Where's Bobbie? Is he all right?' she asked.

'Of course he's all right,' Ursula snapped. 'Why shouldn't he be?'

'No reason,' Meg said swiftly. 'I just thought – I just thought he might be missing Mam.'

'Well, he isn't. He stayed with matron last night. She keeps a truckle bed in her room in case any of the little ones are fretful the first night in a strange place.' She sniffed. 'Though goodness knows why. It's spoiling the little brats, to my mind.'

Meg bit her lip. She wasn't sure of the matron's motives. It sounded, on the surface, as if the woman was kindness itself, but surely, she thought, if Miss

Pendleton had really had Bobbie's best interests at heart, she would have let him stay with his mother and sister.

Keeping her tone polite and deferential, Meg asked, 'Couldn't he have stayed with us? Like she promised?'

'It was better to make the break straight away. We must stick to the rules. The master's rules.' Ursula's words were a pious chant. 'The place would soon be in an uproar if we didn't.

Meg said nothing, but she wondered if it had been the matron or Ursula Waters who had enforced a rule that was harsh enough to keep a lost, lonely, little five-year-old boy from his mother.

Ursula led the way along passages and through doors until they came to a large room which Meg recognized. This was the guardians' meeting room – the room through which they had passed when they had arrived. There was a large door at the end, opposite the entrance door through which Meg and her family had first come in. Behind it, Meg could already hear the noise of children.

Ursula opened the door and stepped inside. Meg was close on her heels, anxious to see Bobbie.

'Quiet!' Ursula bellowed, making Meg and everyone in the room jump. Twenty pairs of eyes turned to look at her, including those of the harassed young schoolmistress.

Suddenly there was the scrape of a stool being pushed back and a little figure hurtled towards them, flinging himself against Meg.

'Bobbie, oh, Bobbie,' she cried, hugging him.

'Stop that this instant.' Ursula grabbed the child's arm and pulled him away. 'If you're to help Miss Daley, Kirkland, you must treat your brother just like all the other children. Do you understand?'

Giving Bobbie a quick smile, Meg said, 'Go back to your place.' She bent close and whispered in his ear. 'I'm to help the teacher, so I'll be with you every day. But we'll have to behave.'

Understanding quickly, the little boy nodded solemnly. He turned, glanced up at Ursula and mumbled, 'Sorry, miss.' Then he trotted back meekly to his seat next to a boy with a shaven head and scabs on his face.

To see her mischievous, sunny-natured little brother so docile and in such a place as this broke Meg's heart.

Five

Miss Daley didn't look much older than she was, Meg thought, though surely the schoolmistress must be in her mid-twenties at least. She was small and slim with gentle eyes. Her black hair was fastened up into a bun on the back of her head, though curly tendrils escaped onto her forehead. She wore a navy blue costume with a fitted jacket and beneath it a blue and white striped blouse. Her pretty face with a small nose and perfectly shaped mouth was marred by a perpetual worried frown that creased her forehead.

As soon as Ursula had left the room, closing the door behind her, Louisa reached out to Meg.

'I'm so pleased to see you. I've been asking for some help for ages, but the guardians won't approve the employment of another teacher. And they keep telling me there's no one suitable amongst the women here, which,' she added wryly, 'I don't believe. But, there you are.' Louisa smiled and the anxiety left her face for a brief moment.

Meg warmed to her at once. 'What am I to call you?'

'Miss Daley or just miss in front of the children.' Louisa leant closer and lowered her voice, 'But in private please call me Louisa. And you're Meg, aren't you?'

Meg nodded. 'Yes, but I thought we had to be called by our surnames?'

'Ah – well – yes. And in front of the class I'm afraid

that is the name I'll have to use. Kirkland, isn't it? You're Bobbie's sister?'

Meg nodded.

'Good, good. Now for today if you would just help in general, but this evening, when the children are in bed, I should like to give you a few tests and then I can assess what you will be able to do in the way of teaching.'

'Teaching? You're going to let me help with the teaching?' Meg's eyes were shining.

'It depends,' was all Louisa would say. 'I can't promise until I see what you can do.'

For the first time in her young life, Meg wished that she had not been so eager to leave school and start working. Perhaps she too could have had a career like this smart young woman.

In the middle of the morning the door to the school room was flung open and the huge figure of the master filled the doorway. With one accord the children scrambled to their feet and stood in silence, their heads bowed. One or two of the little ones trembled.

'Miss Daley,' Isaac's deep voice boomed. 'I see you have a new helper. What a pretty picture you both make.' He moved forward into the room towards them, totally ignoring the children. For him they did not exist.

He stood close to Miss Daley and took her hand. The young woman blushed and looked as if she would like to pull away, but did not dare.

'Bring your little friend to see me whilst the children take their exercise after lunch, my dear.'

He raised her hand to his lips and then, without waiting for any kind of reply so sure was he of her obedience, the master turned and walked back down the room. As the door closed behind him, Louisa closed her eyes and shivered. 'One of these days,' she murmured. 'One of these days.'

'What?' Meg said before she thought to stop herself. 'What do you mean?'

Startled, as if she had forgotten Meg's presence, Louisa's eyes flew open. 'What? Oh – oh, nothing.' She took a deep breath before she said briskly, 'Now, please see that each child has a slate and I'll write on the board what I want them to copy.'

The morning passed quickly and soon the children were being given their lunch and sent out into the women's back courtyard.

'Poor little mites,' Louisa murmured as she and Meg ushered them through the door and watched one or two rushing towards the women there. 'It's the only time they get to see their mothers.'

To Meg's surprise, most of the children stayed together and began to play a game. 'What about those? Don't they want to find their mams?'

Louisa glanced at her and then looked back at the group of children. The girls had found a long piece of old rope. Two of the girls, one at either end, turned the rope and the others queued up to take turns at skipping in and out. All of them took up the chant, 'One, two, buckle my shoe; three, four, knock at the door . . .'

At her side, Louisa said quietly, 'They're the ones who haven't got any mothers. They're the orphans.'

Horrified, Meg stared at her. 'You mean – you mean they've got no one? No father either?'

Louisa, her gaze still on the skipping children, shook her head. Then with a sigh she said, 'Come on. We'd better go and see Mr Pendleton.'

From the yard they went in through the back entrance, turned left along the passage past the kitchen and went into the committee room. Instead of turning left again back into the school room, Louisa led the way across the room to a door on the opposite side, along a short passageway and turned to the right. There were two doors close together, one to the left and one directly in front of them. Louisa gestured towards the one on the left. 'That one's the clerk's office. You won't see much of him. He comes in each weekday, but he – he doesn't live in.' There was a note of envy in the young woman's voice. Louisa raised her hand to knock on the door facing them. 'This one's the master's room.'

At the sound of Isaac's booming voice, the two young women glanced at each other and, taking a deep breath, Louisa opened the door.

'Ah, my dear, come in, come in,' the master welcomed as they sidled into the room. 'Come and sit down. You, too, my dear,' he held out his arm invitingly to Meg.

The room seemed to be used mainly as an office. A large leather-topped desk occupied the centre of the room and behind it was a swivel chair that looked battered and well worn. Meg smothered an impudent laugh as she imagined the poor chair suffering Mr Pendleton's bulk. No wonder it looked in such a sorry state.

The surface of the desk was littered with untidy heaps of papers, a silver inkstand, a glass tray for pens and a long, thin cane like the one the headmaster at Meg's last school had always kept near at hand.

At the far end of the room a fire burned in the grate and above it an ornate mantelpiece held ornaments and framed photographs of stiff-backed figures, self-conscious as they faced the camera. In front of the fireplace was a lumpy yet comfortable-looking sofa with battered easy chairs on either side. As Meg moved closer, she saw that one of the photographs was of the master. His round face was solemn as befitted the serious business of sitting for a photographer – yet it was unmistakably a much younger, fitter-looking Isaac Pendleton. There were two other photographs. One was of a thin-faced, shy-looking young woman with fluffy fair hair. But it was the other that caught and held Meg's attention. The girl in the picture was very pretty with a sweet face and beautiful dark hair cascading in curls and waves down to her waist. Meg stared in astonishment. The photograph, she was sure, was of Letitia Pendleton.

The master waved Louisa and Meg to the sofa, where they sat side by side as if seeking reassurance from each other. The big man took one of the easy chairs. He beamed at them. 'Well now, this is nice. Shall I ring for some tea?'

Louisa shook her head. 'That's very kind of you, sir, but we really only have a few minutes. The children—'

'Ah yes. Of course, the children,' he murmured. 'We mustn't forget the children, must we?' Then his smile widened as he glanced at Meg. 'But now that you have a helper, my dear, perhaps you will have a little more free time, eh?'

Without warning, he leant across and squeezed Louisa's knee. Meg almost gasped aloud as she saw Louisa flush. To Meg's amazement, the young woman made no attempt to move the master's hand.

I'd have slapped him, Meg thought disgustedly. *The dirty old man.*

'It – it's very kind of you to permit Kirkland to help in the classroom,' was all Louisa said.

'I've been thinking about it for a while, but we had to wait until someone suitable arrived, didn't we?' Now he looked directly at Meg. 'And how is your dear mother, my child?'

Meg ran her tongue nervously around her lips, forcing herself to be respectful. 'Matron has allowed her to rest today, sir.'

'Good, good. I'll try to visit her myself later.'

'I'm sorry, but we must go,' Louisa said, standing up. The master's hand was dislodged from her knee and he too rose.

'You must let me know how your little helper shapes up.'

Louisa inclined her head obediently and began to move towards the door. Meg sprang to her feet and followed close behind, anxious not to be left alone with Isaac Pendleton. The big man lumbered forward, opening the door for them with a great flourish. 'I'll see you again, my dears, very soon.'

As the door closed behind them and they hurried back along the passageway, through the committee room towards the school room, Louisa murmured, 'I'm sorry you had to see that, Meg. It – it's not what you think. At least – not on my part.'

'Then why don't you say something – tell him – slap his hand away? I would,' Meg declared.

Louisa gasped and stopped in her tracks. Shocked, she turned to stare at Meg. 'You don't know what you're saying.' She shook her head. 'What d'you think would happen if I did that? I'd be dismissed at once. And without a reference.'

Meg stared as the young schoolmistress went on, 'We all have to do just as we're told in here. The inmates, the staff, everyone.'

'Why?'

'Why do you think? We'll be turned out into the street if we don't.'

'Haven't you any family to go to?'

Louisa's face was downcast. 'I – I've a widowed mother,' she muttered, but the confidence was shared reluctantly. 'She's not well and can't work. It's only because I've got this job that she can stay in her own home. Otherwise . . .'

She said no more, but Meg understood the implication. Otherwise, Louisa's mother would be forced to end her days as an inmate of the infirm women's dormitory.

The children clattered back into the classroom and Bobbie ran straight to Meg to be picked up and hugged. Though Louisa glanced at them, she said nothing.

Meg soon realized that Louisa's time was totally taken up with caring for and teaching the children. The children's dormitory was on the first floor, just across the landing from the master's bedroom, and the young schoolmistress slept in a tiny room at the far end of the dormitory.

'Don't you get any time off?' Meg asked, finding that she too was expected to be with the children all day long.

'One day a month when I go to see my mother.'

'Does she live nearby?'

'Yes. In the town.'

'Don't you get any time to yourself in the evenings when they're in bed?'

'I . . .' Louisa began and then bit her lip. 'I – have to be with them. They're still my responsibility.' She bowed her head, avoiding Meg's questioning gaze.

'Well, it seems unfair to me. I'd've thought you could have had a bit of time off in the evenings.' Meg was beginning to see how easy her life on the farm had been in comparison with this young woman's existence. An existence that was perhaps now going to be hers too, she thought with dread.

Six

Sarah, Meg and Bobbie stood before the guardians' committee. A row of bewhiskered, rotund gentlemen sat on the other side of the long table. The only faces they knew were those of the master and the medical officer. Dr Collins was not officially a member of the board, but he was frequently asked to sit in on their meetings to give his opinion and the findings of his examinations of those applying for admission.

A portly, red-faced man with bushy grey sideburns, sitting in the centre of the row, took charge of the meeting. He tapped on the table to bring the guardians to order. Then, in a gravelly voice, he asked Sarah for their names and demanded that she explain how they had come to present themselves at the workhouse door.

Sarah's face was deathly white, her eyes huge pools of suffering and shame. Her head sank lower and she spoke in a whisper.

'Speak up, woman. I can scarcely hear you.'

Meg put her arm about her mother's shoulders and faced the row of disapproving faces. 'My father's employers turned us out of our home. They dismissed him and me too. But don't ask me why because no one will tell me.'

'Who were your employers, girl?'

'Mr and Mrs Smallwood at Middleditch Farm.'

'Smallwood? I know him,' the chairman said. 'Meet

him at the races now and then. He's a decent enough chap.' He turned towards his colleagues on the board, first one way and then the other. 'A good man. Yes, yes, a good man.' Frowning, he turned back to Meg. 'Your father – or you – must have seriously displeased him in some way for a man like Smallwood to dismiss you. Without a reference, I take it.'

Meg was forced to nod.

'Humph,' the man grunted. 'That says it all, in my opinion.'

Suddenly, Sarah gave a little cry and leant heavily against Meg. She clutched at her stomach and bent forward.

'Mam, what is it . . . ?' Meg began, but her mother's weight was too much for the girl to hold and Sarah slipped to the floor in a faint.

At once, Dr Collins rose and came round the end of the table. Isaac Pendleton, too, was instantly on his feet. He pointed at Bobbie. 'You, little boy. Run and find the matron.'

But Bobbie stood transfixed. He took no notice of the master and began to whimper, squatting down beside his mother and shaking her. 'Mam, Mam . . .'

'I'll go,' Meg muttered now that the doctor was bending down beside Sarah. Without waiting for permission, she whirled around and ran towards the door.

Dr Collins took Sarah's limp wrist in one hand and placed the palm of his other over the mound of her stomach. Several of the guardians shuffled their papers and looked away in embarrassment. They murmured amongst themselves and then the chairman said, 'Well, that seems to settle it. You'd better admit the family, Master. We'll review their situation once this woman has been delivered of her child.' He cleared his throat and stroked his right sideburn. 'Another mouth for the parish to feed, I'll be bound.' He went on muttering and grumbling under his breath. 'Something should be done about these people who have no more sense than to go on breeding even when they cannot support themselves.'

Isaac Pendleton cleared his throat. 'Mr Finch – I have checked our books and there is no record of this family having been in the workhouse in the last few years. Some misfortune has befallen them. I'm sure it's only temporary and—'

'That's as maybe,' Mr Finch interrupted gruffly, 'but they should make provision for misfortune.'

Isaac frowned, but bit back his words. Theobald Finch lived in the Hall, the largest house in South Monkford. He owned almost half the commercial properties along the High Street as well as cottages and houses in other parts of the town. He had considerable influence in the community, yet there was no love lost between the chairman of the board of guardians and the master of the workhouse. They had clashed on all sorts of matters on numerous occasions. Indeed, Isaac knew that Theobald Finch would have him removed from his post if he could, but there were reasons why Theobald would make no move against him. Isaac allowed himself a satisfied smirk. His position was safe. He knew that and – better still – he was aware that Theobald Finch knew it too. Besides, the rest of the board members liked Isaac Pendleton. The workhouse had never been run as efficiently or economically as it was under his authority. They would never agree to his dismissal without reason. Just because the two men disliked each other was not a good enough motive in their opinion. In fact, it amused the other members of the board to watch the two men needling each other whenever they got the chance. Theobald was glaring at Isaac now. He nodded towards the prone form on the floor. 'One of your lady friends, is she, Pendleton? I wouldn't put it past you . . .'

But at that moment Meg rushed back into the room, followed by Miss Pendleton and Waters, and in the general hubbub that followed whatever Theobald had been about to say was lost.

The matron bent down over Sarah and held a small bottle beneath her nose. In a moment Sarah began to splutter and revive. After a few minutes Meg and Waters were able to help her up.

'Take her to the infirmary, if you please, Matron,' Dr Collins said. 'She's going into labour. I'll come along in a few minutes when you've got her into bed.'

Although Miss Pendleton laughed and tapped the doctor playfully on his arm, there was an undercurrent of huffiness as she said, 'There's no need for that, Doctor. I'm sure me and Waters know what we're doing. We've delivered more babies into the world than you've got patients.'

'I'm sure you have, Miss Pendleton.' The young doctor smiled placatingly. 'I'm sure you have, but—'

'We'll send for you if we need you, Doctor,' the matron said and though she was still smiling there was a firmness to her tone that forbade him to overstep his authority. Within these walls her brother and she were in supreme charge.

'Quite so, Matron,' Mr Finch, who had been listening to the exchange, put in. 'We don't want the bill for your services here getting any longer than it has to be, Doctor.'

'I wouldn't dream of charging anything in this case,' Dr Collins said mildly. 'But as you wish, Matron, as you wish.' So saying, he walked back to his seat behind the table.

As the matron and Waters helped Sarah towards the door, Meg and Bobbie, holding hands, fell into step behind them.

'You, girl. Kirkland –' Meg turned to see the master pointing at her – 'take your brother and go back to the classroom.'

'Oh, but I want to go with Mam—' Meg began.

Dr Collins sprang to his feet again and beamed at Meg. 'Now, Meg, your mother is in good hands, so how about I come with you and say hello to all the children, eh?' He turned and smiled charmingly at the chairman. 'And no, Mr Finch, there will be no charge.'

He moved towards Meg and Bobbie and, stepping between them, put an arm around each of their shoulders. As he ushered them towards the double doors at the end of the room leading into the school room, he whispered in Meg's ear, 'Don't worry, my dear, I'll hang around here for a while and make sure your mother's all right before I leave. Now, here we are, I'm sure the lovely Miss Daley will be delighted to see you back.'

He removed his arms from around them and threw open the doors with a flourish. There was a scraping of stools as all the children stood up. Meg saw Louisa look up, dread on her face, but when the young schoolmistress saw who was standing there, a pretty, pink blush tinged her cheeks.

The doctor moved between the rows of desks, not even glancing down at the children as he passed between their ranks. His gaze was all for Louisa Daley.

*

Meg's mind was hardly on her job during the rest of the morning. She longed for lunchtime so that she could run across to the infirmary and see how her mother was. Dr Collins, after a long, whispered conversation with Louisa, still did not leave the classroom. He pretended to be interested in the children's work, but his glance strayed every few seconds back to the schoolmistress. The blush on Louisa's face deepened.

A few minutes before twelve, the door flew open and a flustered Waters, cap awry and hair falling from its prim bun, appeared.

'Doctor – thank goodness I've found you. Please come at once. The baby – it's not breathing. Matron's tried everything, but—'

He stayed to hear no more but was through the door and gone before anyone else could move. Meg dropped the slate she had been holding and, picking up her skirts, fled after him, almost knocking Waters over in her haste.

'Meg! Kirkland!' Louisa began, but the girl had no intention of heeding her. 'What is it?' Louisa asked Ursula. 'What's happening?'

'Kirkland's mother's had her baby.'

'And?'

Waters glanced round the room at the twenty pairs of staring eyes. Her gaze came back to meet Louisa's. She said no more but lifted her shoulders in a helpless shrug.

Louisa closed her eyes and gave a groan. She opened them to find Bobbie tugging at her skirt. 'Mammy? I want my mammy. Where's Meg gone?'

Louisa knelt on the rough wooden floor and drew the little boy into her arms.

*

Meg heard her mother's wailing as she raced up the stairs to the infirmary which was situated across the men's backyard and above the bake house.

How many times before had she heard that sobbing? Three, was it, or four? The young girl couldn't be sure. There had been a couple of times when she had been very little and had not understood what had happened. Then, when Bobbie had been three and she thirteen, Meg had understood only too well. Her mother's pregnancy had ended in a stillbirth and Sarah's raging tears.

And now, in this awful place, it had happened again.

Later, Meg was allowed to sit beside her mother's bed and hold her hand.

'Just a few moments,' Matron said gently. 'Then you must leave her to rest. She's had a bad time, poor thing.'

'Can Bobbie come and see her?'

'Best not. But don't you worry about him. I'll look after Bobbie. He can have his tea with me in my room.'

Meg smiled wanly, surprised at Miss Pendleton's kindness.

'I'll go and find him now and tell him what's happened. He's too young to understand. Good thing, really.'

Meg nodded, a huge lump in her throat and her eyes full of tears. As Miss Pendleton left the room, Meg leant towards her mother. 'Mam,' she whispered softly, 'Mam – how are you feeling?'

Sarah, her face flushed from the effort of giving birth and from her weeping when all her efforts had come to naught, lay still, her eyes closed.

'Do you – do you want me to go and find Dad?' Meg suggested. 'I could—'

Now Sarah roused herself. 'No!' Her voice was surprisingly strong. 'No,' she said again as she sank back. 'You look after Bobbie. There's a good girl. Ne'er mind about your dad.'

'But – but he'll want to know.'

Sarah was silent now, her eyes closed.

'He ought to know,' Meg insisted and when her mother did not answer, she pressed again, 'Mam?'

'Leave it, Meg. There's a good girl. Just leave it, will you?'

Meg sat beside her for a few moments more, chewing her little finger agitatedly. Her dad ought to be told. Whatever had happened, he would want to know. Perhaps he had already found work and, as soon as her mother was well, they could all leave here and be together again.

When she could see that Sarah was sleeping, Meg crept away. As she stepped out of the doorway at the bottom of the stairs and into the yard, a figure emerged out of the shadows.

'Hello, again. I thought it was you I saw running across the yard earlier.'

It was the boy who had spoken to her on the day they had arrived. Now, what was his name? Frowning, Meg tried to remember.

'It's Jake,' he said helpfully, grinning at her through the gloom. 'Don't tell me you've forgotten already.'

'Sorry,' Meg smiled faintly. 'I'm not thinking straight. It's me mam.'

At once the boy's face sobered. 'Is she poorly?'

'Well, sort of. She – she's just had a baby, only . . .' She bit her lip to stop it quivering, but failed. Tears spilled over and ran down her cheeks.

'Aw, don't cry. A babby's nice, even in here.' Awkward with embarrassment, the boy put his arm about her and she rested her face against his shoulder.

'I know, but – but it was born dead.'

Jake could think of nothing to say to comfort her, but his arm tightened about her.

They stood together in the empty yard in the growing dusk. Then suddenly, the silence was shattered as a window on the first floor was thrown up and the master leant out.

'Hey, you there. What do you think you're doing?'

Startled, the two youngsters looked up.

'Oh heck,' Jake said, his arm falling away from around Meg. 'Now we're in for it.'

Isaac's deep voice echoed across the yard. 'My office now. The pair of you.'

Then the window was slammed down with such a force that the small glass panes rattled.

Seven

They stood together outside the door of the master's office. Jake was trembling.

'What are you so frightened of?' Meg asked. 'What can he do to us?'

Jake glanced at her, then looked down at the floor. 'It'll be a beating for me. Or – or the punishment cell. He can't wait to send me there. Mind you – he should get the guardians' agreement before he does that.' Then he muttered beneath his breath, 'But usually he doesn't bother.'

'What – what'll he do to me?'

Again Jake glanced swiftly and then looked away again. Then he shrugged. 'Nothing, probably. If – if you're nice to him.'

'Nice to him? What do you mean?'

'I dunno really. I just know that he's not so strict on the girls. And you're new here, so if you smile prettily at him and say you're sorry, mebbe you'll get away with it.'

The door flew open and Isaac stood there. He looked nothing like the kindly, avuncular figure he had seemed before. Now he resembled a raging bull.

'You, boy, in here.'

As Jake stepped forward, Meg did so too, but the master said sharply, 'No, you stay there, girl. I'll see you in a moment.'

The second that Jake stepped into the room the door was slammed behind him, but because the master was shouting Meg could hear every word.

'How many beatings do I have to give you, boy, before you learn the rules? Eh? Eh? Answer me that. It's not as if you've any excuse. You've been here all your life. You were born here, yet you still flout the rules at every end and turn. And don't expect Miss Pendleton to come running to your aid. Not this time when I tell her what you've done. Such disgusting behaviour with a young and innocent wench. In broad daylight and in the middle of the yard too. Have you no shame, boy?'

Meg heard Jake's muttered response, but she could not make out the words. His voice was too low.

'Upset, you say? Of course the lass was upset. Her mother has just lost her baby. But that's no excuse for what you were trying to do.'

Again, a low reply from Jake.

'Comfort?' Isaac laughed cruelly. 'I know the kind of "comfort" you had in mind, you dirty little tyke. Taking advantage of the poor lass when she was upset. That's what you were doing.'

Another murmur from Jake and then the sound of a slap. 'Don't answer me back, boy. And like I say, it'll be no good running to matron. Not this time. You may have been her blue-eyed boy up to now, but when she hears you've been after a young girl, then she'll have no more sympathy for you. You mark my words. You'll have blotted your copybook with her good an' proper.'

Meg blinked. The master sounded gleeful, as if he had been waiting for just such an occasion.

'It's the cell for you, boy, for a couple of days and nothing to eat but bread and water. Let's see if that'll curb your beastly desires.'

This time, Meg heard Jake argue. 'You can't do that. Not without the guardians' say-so.'

Isaac's answering bellow seemed to shake the door. 'How dare you argue with me?'

Heavy footsteps moved across the room, then came the sound of something swishing through the air. Meg shuddered, knowing that the master had picked up the cane from his desk. 'Bend over, boy. We'll see what a good thrashing can do for you. I don't need to ask the guardians' permission for that!'

Meg was forced to stand listening to every swipe of the cane. They seemed to go on and on, yet Jake made no sound. Not a cry, not even a whimper.

When she could bear it no longer, she turned and ran out into the men's backyard, looking wildly to right and left. But the dusk had deepened. It was almost dark now and the yard was deserted. Then she heard a noise behind her in the building and turned to see a strange man just inside the entrance locking the door to the left of the master's room. He turned and came towards her, stepping out into the evening air. A tall, thin man dressed in a dark suit with a starched white collar. His face was pale and gaunt and he stooped slightly, as if he spent too much time indoors bending over his books and ledgers. He paused for a moment and straightened up, taking in a deep breath as if it were the first time he had breathed fresh air that day.

'Sir – oh, sir,' she cried. The man jumped and blinked. He took a step back, startled by the girl rushing towards him. 'Please help us. The master. He's thrashing a boy. Jake. Oh, please stop him. Please do something.'

The man's lips curled. 'Jake Bosley?'

'I – I don't know his second name. Only that he's called Jake.'

The man nodded and said curtly, 'That'll be him, all right. Trouble, he is, with a capital T. You'd do best to keep your distance from him.' He bent closer, squinting at her through the darkness. 'I haven't seen you before. Just come in, have you?'

Meg nodded. 'Three days ago.'

'So how do you know Jake?'

'I don't. At least, I mean, I met him in here. In the yard.'

'What's he done?' Again the man's lips were tight with anticipated disapproval.

'He was trying to comfort me. My mother's just – just lost her baby and I was upset. He only put his arm around me.'

'Put – his – arm – round – you!' The man was scandalized.

'Well, yes. I was crying and—'

'He's not even supposed to talk to you, let alone have physical contact. Where do you think it would lead if we allowed that sort of thing to go on? Why do you think we separate the men from the women? Oh no, I'm sorry, girl, but there's nothing I can do. And let me tell you, even if I could I wouldn't. Bosley deserves every bit of punishment he gets. And if you've any sense, you'll get back to the women's quarters pretty sharpish and stay there.'

Meg stared at him in disbelief for a moment, then her shoulders dropped with defeat. 'I – I can't. I was told to wait outside the master's room.'

'Then I suggest you get back there at once.'

Without another word the man stepped aside, walked

around her and crossed the yard into the darkness. With the sound of finality, the entrance door banged behind him as he left. Dragging her feet, Meg went back into the building to wait outside the master's room.

The sound of the beating had stopped, but Isaac was still shouting. 'Get yourself to the cell.'

The door opened and Meg, her eyes widening, gasped in horror. Jake emerged slowly, hardly able to walk. Tears streamed down his face, but still he made no sound.

Instinctively, Meg reached out to him. 'Oh, Jake, I'm so sorry . . .'

The boy shrank from her, avoiding her touch. He turned his head away and moved towards the door. She watched him go, sick at heart to think that he hated her now. But at the doorway, hidden from Isaac Pendleton's view, he turned and smiled. Though his mouth still trembled he winked at her. He glanced back at the door to the master's room and, as Isaac appeared, he turned away abruptly.

'Come in, Kirkland,' the master said. His voice was still stern, but he was no longer shouting.

Trembling and biting her lip, Meg moved forward and entered the room. Isaac closed the door firmly behind her.

'Now, my dear—' Suddenly, his tone was very different. He smiled down at her and put his hand on her shoulder. 'Come along and sit by the fire and we'll have a little chat, shall we?' He guided her towards the sofa and pressed her to sit down. Then he sat down close by, leaning towards her. Putting his fat hand on her knee, he said, 'You've not been here long, so I'm not going to punish you. Not this time, but you must understand and obey the rules we have here.'

Meg stared at him, meeting his gaze fearlessly. She steeled herself not to shrink away from him, though his touch seemed to burn through her skirt. She wanted to push his hand away, to stand up and scream at him to leave her alone. Instead she narrowed her eyes and gritted her teeth.

'You must know by now that men and women are separated. Oh, I know it seems hard, especially if there are husbands and wives in here, but there are good reasons. You see, my dear girl, boys and men of all ages for that matter, especially the sort that we have in here, cannot resist their animal urges. A boy like Jake has to be taught a lesson. One day he'll thank me. Oh yes, he will.' He nodded agreement with himself, a satisfied smile stretching his thick lips. 'Jake Bosley will leave here one day a fine upstanding young man and it will all be thanks to me.'

Meg could bear his touch no longer. She stood up suddenly and his hand fell from her knee. There was a fleeting look of anger on his face, but Meg said swiftly, 'Master, I'm so sorry I broke the rules and I promise you it will never happen again. But you must believe me – we were doing nothing wrong. I swear it. I was very upset and he – Jake – was being very kind to me.'

Isaac smiled sadly. 'Oh, my dear child, how young and innocent you are. But there, there.' He took hold of her hand and patted it. Meg wanted to snatch her hand away; his touch made her flesh crawl. 'I'm here to protect you. Now, you run along and have your supper with the children.' He leant towards her as if sharing a confidence. 'When they're all in bed, I'd like you to do something for me. Just to show me how really sorry you are.' His tone was silky. Meg was silent, holding her breath, afraid of what he was going to say. 'I'd like you to stay up in the dormitory with the children so that Miss Daley is free. And you'll tell her that I'd like to see her, won't you?'

'Oh, but Miss Daley's going to give me some tests tonight. To – to see if I can help teach.'

For a fleeting moment, Isaac's face was like thunder, then he forced a laugh and said, 'Well, well, how very conscientious of our little schoolmarm. But you tell her from me that she can do that another time. Now –' suddenly he pulled her close to him, so that she felt his stale breath on her face – 'you'll do that for me, little Meg, won't you? And we'll say no more about what happened in the yard, eh?'

It was a threat, yet for once there was nothing she could do but nod her head in agreement, even though she hated herself for giving in.

Eight

When Meg burst into the children's dormitory, Louisa Daley put a finger to her lips. Most of the children were already asleep and the others were drowsy, just on the point of falling into a kinder world than they knew in their waking hours.

'I've had to put little Betsy Arnold into my room. She's got the most awful cough. Matron has given me some medicine for her, but it doesn't seem to be doing much good.'

'Miss Daley, Louisa—' Meg began urgently.

'Yes, yes, I know what you're going to say, but I haven't forgotten. We can sit quietly in my room. We'll be on hand for Betsy then. I'll test you on arithmetic tonight. Your written English is very good—'

'No, no, you don't understand—'

'Oh, my dear.' Louisa took Meg's trembling hands in hers. 'Here I am prattling on about schoolwork and I haven't asked how your mother is.'

'She's poorly, but I think she'll be all right. But she – she lost the baby.' For a moment Meg's thoughts were diverted from the message she carried. 'It was a boy too. I think Dad would have like another boy. He was that thrilled when Bobbie was born.'

'Oh, Meg, I'm so sorry. No wonder you don't want to work. I do understand that you really wouldn't be able to concentrate—'

'It's not that. Oh, Louisa, it's the master.'

Louisa paled. 'What – what about the master?'

The words came tumbling out. 'I'm so sorry, Louisa, if it's my fault. You see, I was coming down from the infirmary after seeing Mam and Jake Bosley was in the yard. He – he saw me crying and tried to comfort me and the master saw us.'

Louisa shuddered. 'That man sees everything,' she murmured bitterly. 'From his bedroom and the landing on this floor he can see all the yards. Oh, I can tell you, Isaac Pendleton misses nothing. I only wish I'd thought to warn you, my dear. I suppose he's punishing you both in some way, is he?'

'He – he thrashed Jake.'

Louisa closed her eyes for a moment and sighed. 'Poor Jake, but it's not the first time and I don't expect it will be the last. However many beatings he has, it doesn't seem to dampen his spirit for long.' She paused and then looked into Meg's green gaze. 'What about you? What is your punishment?'

'He – he asked me to look after the children tonight while you – while you—' Meg bit her lip.

Flatly, Louisa finished the sentence for her. 'While I take some time off.'

Wordlessly, Meg nodded.

'It's not your fault, Meg. He's been hounding me for weeks. Ever since I came here, in fact.' Louisa grimaced wryly. 'I think he's got me in mind for the position of Mrs Pendleton number two.'

Meg stared at her in disbelief. 'You wouldn't,' she breathed. 'Oh, you wouldn't marry *him*!'

Louisa laughed and for a brief moment the ridiculous thought drove away Meg's sadness and she began to laugh too. They leant against each other, overcome by a fit of girlish giggles. Drying her eyes at last, Louisa said, 'Well, I'd better go. I daren't refuse. Let's just hope I can keep him at arms' length. Where is he? In his office?' She shuddered and inclined her head in the direction of the master's bedroom across the landing. 'I certainly don't fancy going to his room across there. Now,' she went on more briskly, 'you will look after poor little Betsy, won't you?' Suddenly, there was a spark of mischief in her brown eyes. 'Of course,' she said slowly and deliberately, 'if you're *really* worried about her, you'll have to come and fetch me. Won't you, Meg?' she added pointedly.

Meg giggled again, the conspiracy between them chasing away some of her sadness about her mother and her anxiety over Jake. She didn't like being the cause of the boy's punishment. Especially when he had tried to be so kind to her.

'When shall I come down for you then?'

'Oh, in about an hour.'

'But there isn't a clock. How shall I know the time?'

'I'll leave you my watch,' the young schoolmistress said, unfastening the fob watch she always wore pinned just above her left breast and pressing it into Meg's hand. 'Don't lose it,' she said. 'My father gave it to me. It's all I have to remember him by.'

Louisa hurried away, dreading her mission, yet anxious not to frustrate the master any further.

Meg placed Louisa's watch on the battered chest of drawers and sat down beside the small bed where Betsy lay. The child was restless, her breathing rasping and laboured. Meg poured a little water from the china ewer into the bowl and dipped a flannel into it. Wringing most of the water from it, she dabbed at the child's hot face.

She remembered her mother doing this for Bobbie when he'd had a fever. Betsy opened her eyes and stared up fearfully.

'It's all right,' Meg soothed. 'Miss Daley's had to go down to the master's office. I'm here to look after you.'

The fear faded from Betsy's blue eyes as Meg smoothed the damp tendrils of fair hair back from the young girl's forehead. 'Try to sleep,' she whispered.

'I want my mammy,' Betsy said, her mouth quivering. The girl looked about ten years old. She was very thin and, at this moment, very poorly.

'Where is she? In the women's section?'

Betsy shook her head and bit her lip. 'No, she died.'

'Oh, I'm sorry,' was all Meg could say. After a pause she asked, 'What about your dad? Where's he?'

'He's gone away.'

Meg nodded. 'Yes, so's mine. He's gone to look for work and then he'll come back for us.'

'That's what my dad said.' Betsy's voice trembled. 'But he's been gone two years.'

Meg bit her lip. She didn't know what to say to comfort the child, so she just sat beside her and held her hand. Betsy slept fitfully, dozing for a few moments then tossing and turning with fever and whimpering pitifully. The minutes crawled by. Meg kept looking at Louisa's watch hardly able to believe that the time was going so slowly. Once she held it to her ear to see if it was still going. Reassured by the low tick-tick-tick, she was about to replace it on the top of the cabinet, when Betsy reached out her hand.

'Let me hear it,' she said.

Meg held the watch close to the little girl's ear. Betsy's tiny mouth trembled and tears welled in her eyes.

'My daddy had a watch like that. He – he used to let me listen to it.'

Meg held it there for a few moments until Betsy was asleep once more. She seemed calmer now and her face was not so flushed. Carefully, Meg placed the watch back on top of the chest, noting the time as she did so. Another five minutes, she decided, and then, if Betsy was still asleep, she would creep away and go down to the master's office. Now even the seconds dragged and Meg fidgeted, agitatedly biting the nail of her little finger. When only three minutes had passed, she jumped up, unable to wait a second longer. With one last glance at Betsy, she crept towards the door. Its creaking echoed in the silence and Meg held her breath, sure that it would wake not only the sick little girl, but half the dormitory too. As quietly as she could, she pulled the door to and tiptoed down the centre of the long room. On either side, the children slept on straw mattresses in wooden beds pushed close together. Curled beneath rough blankets, some slept silently, while others snuffled and muttered in their sleep. Bobbie, Meg noticed thankfully, was one of those sleeping peacefully, but in the end bed nearest the door to the landing, she could hear muffled sobs. Meg paused, wanting to comfort the child, yet not liking to linger. She was nervous enough about lying to the master, even if it was to save Louisa from his clutches. What if he insisted on coming up to the dormitory to see Betsy for himself and found her asleep and looking, if anything, better not worse?

Meg moved on, out onto the landing and down the stairs. At the bottom she stood outside the master's office door. She paused a moment, listening for the sound of voices from beyond the door.

She could hear nothing.

Her heart pounding, Meg took a deep breath and rapped urgently on the door. Isaac Pendleton's exasperated voice called, 'Come in.'

Meg rushed into the room. 'Oh, Miss Daley, do come. It's Betsy. I'm sure she's worse. I didn't know what to do.'

Louisa was sitting on the sofa with the master close beside her, his arm around her shoulders. She stood up at once and placed the cup and saucer she was holding on the low table. Then she turned to face Meg. 'I'll come at once.' She glanced down at Isaac. 'I'm so sorry, but I must go. The child is very sick. I really shouldn't have left her . . .'

Isaac struggled to his feet. He put his arm around her again and hugged her to him. 'Your concern does you credit, my dear.' Then he turned frosty eyes upon Meg. 'But you should have fetched the matron, girl. Miss Daley deserves a night off now and again. She works far too hard as it is.' His eyes narrowed and Meg read the threat in them. Suddenly, he was once again the bull-necked, angry tyrant wielding power over all the people in his charge – staff and inmates alike. 'If I'm to allow you to continue as Miss Daley's assistant, you'll have to cope better than this.'

Meg dropped her gaze. 'I'm sorry, sir,' she said meekly for the second time that day. 'I – I was just so frightened. Betsy's breathing. It sounds awful . . .'

Louisa eased herself away from Isaac. 'I'd better go. Perhaps, if she settles again, I can come back.'

'Please do, my dear.' Isaac's voice was husky, but with one last squeeze he released her.

Louisa hurried across the room towards Meg, who dared not meet her gaze, so terrified was she that she would break into nervous laughter. 'Come, Kirkland,' Louisa said sharply, keeping up the pretence of being annoyed at the girl's interruption.

Only when the door had closed behind them and they were hurrying up the stairs, their hands pressed to their mouths to stop their laughter, did Louisa touch Meg's arm and whisper, 'Thank you. Oh, thank you, Meg.'

'I was terrified he'd come with us because she's asleep.'

'Oh, you needn't worry about the master coming to see the children,' Louisa whispered. 'He rarely concerns himself with them, except,' she added wryly, 'to administer punishments.'

'But he came to the school room.' Before Louisa could reply, Meg answered her own question. 'Oh, I see. He came to see *you* – not the children.'

'Exactly,' Louisa said dryly.

They crept down the dormitory and into Louisa's room. The candle was guttering, sizzling and casting eerie, dancing shadows around the room, but Betsy was still asleep.

Louisa lit another candle and then gently felt the child's brow. 'I don't think she's quite so hot.'

'I bathed her face,' Meg whispered and Louisa nodded approval. She straightened up and stood looking down at the child for a moment before saying, 'I think we can leave her to sleep now.' She glanced round the tiny room as she added, 'But I'm afraid we're going to have to leave testing your arithmetic for tonight. We shall disturb her if we stay here and I really daren't go back down to the school room. It's too near his office . . .' Louisa's voice trailed away, but Meg understood. 'Maybe tomorrow.'

'It's all right,' Meg smiled. 'I want to try to see me mam again before I go to bed.'

'Off you go then, dear,' Louisa waved her towards the door, then paused and said, 'Oh, just before you go, where is my watch?'

Meg pointed towards the chest. 'It's on the top there—' she began and then her mouth fell open in horror.

The watch was not there.

Nine

'Where is it? Where's my watch? What have you done with it?' Louisa's voice rose hysterically, no thought now for the sick Betsy or even the sleeping children in the dormitory. 'Have you stolen it?'

Thunderstruck and hurt beyond words that anyone could think such a thing of her, Meg gasped. She felt her face turning fiery red and knew that Louisa would see it as guilt.

'No,' she cried as, in the bed behind them, Betsy stirred and whimpered. But Meg was beyond caring too. 'How dare you accuse me of such a thing? I'd never take a penny that didn't belong to me. I'd starve first.' Dramatically, she held out her arms wide. 'You can search me. Go on, search me.'

'You'd hardly have it on you, would you?' Louisa muttered. 'You must have hidden it somewhere.'

In a moment the blossoming friendship between Meg and the young schoolmistress was torn asunder. Meg shook her head in fear and disbelief. What was happening to her? From living in a cosy cottage with her mother, father and brother she had been brought to this – a pauper cast into the workhouse by her own father, stripped of her clothes and possessions, separated from her family. And now, worse even than all that, she was being branded a thief.

She thrust her face towards Louisa. 'Well, I haven't.'

But Louisa stood her ground. 'Then where is it? You'd better find it and be quick about it.' The schoolmistress's pretty face was suddenly pale with anger, her eyes no longer soft and kindly, but dark with suspicion.

Wildly, Meg looked about her. What could have happened to the watch? Had someone crept into the room whilst she had been downstairs fetching Louisa? Had one of the children—?

Betsy stirred and murmured. 'Daddy – I want my daddy.'

Meg elbowed Louisa aside and wrenched back the covers. There, clutched in Betsy's small hands and held lovingly close to her heaving chest, lay Louisa's watch.

'So that's where you hid it.'

'I did not *hide* it,' Meg almost spat out the words. 'I told you – I left it on the top of the chest when I came to find you. Betsy must have reached for it.'

'Don't try to put the blame on this poor child. She's too ill to have got out of the bed.'

'Well, she can't have been. I did show it to her – I admit that – I held it to her ear and she listened to its ticking. She said it reminded her of her daddy because he had one like it. It seemed to comfort her because she fell asleep then.'

For a moment, Louisa stared at Meg then looked down at the watch and then back to Meg's face. She was struggling with her thoughts. Now that it had been found, she realized she had been far too hasty in her judgement.

'Oh, Meg, I'm sorry. I shouldn't have accused you. Please forgive me. I—'

Meg held up her hand, palms outwards. 'Oh no, don't start that. You called me a thief and I'll never forgive you. And don't expect me to help you any more.

Not—' she added slowly and deliberately, 'with *anything*.' She jerked her head towards the door and her meaning and gesture were clear. *Don't*, she was implying, *expect me to help you with the master*.

'Oh, Meg, please—'

'Don't "Oh, Meg" me!'

'But what about the school? What about you?'

'I wouldn't work for you if they *paid* me,' the girl said vehemently. With that, she moved towards the door.

'Meg, please don't go like this. Let's talk about it.'

'There's nothing to say. Too much has been said already.' With a worldly wisdom beyond her tender years, Meg said, 'You can't unsay what you said, Miss Daley.' She glanced back briefly. 'And don't you be taking it out on our Bobbie, 'cos if you do –' her eyes narrowed – 'you'll regret it.'

'You're hardly in a position to threaten me, Meg.'

'Oh, I'm not threatening you, miss. I'm *promising* you.'

Meg marched through the dormitory and out of the door at the far end, then ran lightly down the stairs. She paused for a moment outside the master's office, wondering if she dared to let him know that the child was not as bad as she had made out and that Louisa Daley was free.

But then she rejected the idea. It would only mean that she had to remain with the children and she didn't want to do that. She wanted to avoid having to see Louisa Daley any more than she was forced.

'Oh, Dad,' she murmured aloud, 'please come back for us soon and take us away from this place.'

*

Sarah's recovery was slow and made more so by the fact that she was sunk in misery and despair. Each day for the following week, flouting the rules, Meg visited her mother in the infirmary.

'I so wanted this baby,' Sarah whispered to Meg. 'I know it's an awful place for a child to be born, but – but I wanted something to remember your daddy by.'

Meg leant closer. 'What do you mean, Mam? You make it sound as if Dad isn't coming back.'

Sarah plucked nervously at the rough blanket covering her, her eyes downcast.

'Mam?' Meg prompted, but still her mother did not answer. She closed her eyes and lay back against the hard, lumpy pillow and sighed.

Meg went on. 'I'm sorry, Mam, but I'll have to go. I'm working in the gardens today.' True to her word, she had refused to enter the school room again. The morning after her quarrel with Louisa, she had marched boldly to the master's office and rapped sharply on the door.

'Come in, come in,' his voice had boomed and Meg opened the door and stepped up to his desk. Standing before him, she felt no fear; she was still smarting with anger from Louisa's unfair accusation.

'I'm sorry, sir,' she began with her most winning smile. She crossed her fingers behind her back at the lie she was about to tell, 'but I don't think I'm suited to teaching. I haven't got Miss Daley's patience.' That part, at least, was true. 'I think I'm better suited to working in the kitchens or even outside, sir. It's what I'm used to.'

Isaac frowned. 'Oh? And what makes you think you can pick and choose what job you do here? If I say you'll help in the school room, then help in the school room you will.'

Meg lowered her head so that he would not see the flash of anger in her green eyes. 'Yes, sir,' she said meekly. She waited, holding her breath. She risked glancing at him through her long eyelashes. He was regarding her thoughtfully. His chair creaked as he leant back in it and laced his fingers across his paunch.

His tone was deceptively mild as he asked, 'Have you displeased Miss Daley? The truth now, girl, because I can ask her, you know. And she –' he paused as if savouring the thought of the schoolmistress – 'will tell me.'

Quickly, as if the very idea appalled her, Meg said, 'Oh, I do hope not, sir. She's a lovely lady and I wouldn't want to upset her.' Meg was shocked by how easily the lies slipped from her lips. She had always prided herself on being truthful and honest, but if she were to be branded as no better than a thief and a liar just because her family had hit hard times, then . . .

Isaac smiled. 'I'm glad you think so, my dear. She is indeed a wonderful, wonderful young woman.' He ran his tongue around his lips. 'Then what is it?'

'It was last night, sir. When she – when you and she – when I was left alone with the children, specially with little Betsy, who was so sick. I – I was frightened of doing something wrong. Of – of displeasing you.'

'But help wasn't far away.' A hint of sarcasm entered his tone. 'As you so ably proved.'

'I know and I'm very sorry for spoiling your evening, sir. I should've fetched the matron, but being new here I didn't know what was the right thing to do and – and Miss Daley'd said that she was responsible for the children.' Meg babbled on, her fingers still tightly crossed, praying that the master would not question Louisa Daley about what had happened and why the new girl now didn't want the best job in the place but would rather scrub floors on her knees or work outside in all weathers. 'And besides,' Meg ended, 'I really don't think I'm clever enough.'

'Oh well.' Isaac shrugged his huge shoulders. 'In that case the guardians would have been unlikely to give their consent to the arrangement. So, we'd better find you something else to do, hadn't we?'

Now Meg explained to her mother. 'There's three of us girls they've let go into the gardens to do the weeding. I've been doing nothing but scrub floors and stone steps all week and it's been so good to be outdoors again today. The men and the boys do the heavy digging and the planting. Mind you, I could do the digging if they'd let me. Do you remember, Mam, how me and Miss Alice used to look after their vegetable patch?' The words were out before she had stopped to think.

Sarah gave a sob and turned her face away, burying it in the pillow.

'Mam – Mam – I'm sorry. I shouldn't have mentioned it.' Meg's voice faltered. 'I shouldn't have reminded you of the times when we were happy.' She touched her mother's shaking shoulder, castigating herself for her thoughtlessness. 'But we'll be happy again, Mam. I know we will. When Dad comes back . . .'

Her mother's sobs grew louder. The door opened and Miss Pendleton bustled in. 'Now, now, we can't have this. Have you been upsetting your mam, Kirkland? What have you been saying to her?'

Meg's expression was all innocence. 'I was just telling her I was working in the garden.'

'Ah yes.' Miss Pendleton pursed her lips. 'I don't approve of my brother making you young girls work out of doors. There's plenty of indoor work for you women.' She sniffed. 'But of course *I* have no say in the matter. But just you mind you keep your distance from the men because Isaac watches from the windows of his room.' She wagged her finger at Meg. 'He'll know if you get up to any shenanigans.' There was suddenly a strange, bitter note in her voice. 'Oh yes, he'll know, all right.'

Meg stood up and eased her aching back. The patch of earth near her feet was clear, though the other two girls were still squatting down, tearing weeds from the ground.

'That's my bit done ready for the men. I'll tell 'em, shall I?' Meg tossed her head towards where a man and a youth were pointing some of the brickwork in the wall. The youth was Jake.

Mary, one of the other girls, stood up. 'You'll get into trouble,' she warned as she glanced nervously towards the windows. 'He'll be watching.'

'Not if he's in his office on the ground floor. He can't see us from there,' Meg said reasonably.

Mary was still nervous. 'Yeah, but you don't know he's in his office, do you? He could be in his bedroom. He can see *everything* from up there.'

Meg gazed up at the first-floor windows in the centre of the building, where she knew the master's bedroom to be. 'Can't see him.'

'Huh,' Mary said scathingly as she picked up her bucket of weeds. 'He'll not let you see him, you daft 'aporth. He'll stand well back, but he'll be up there.

You mark my words. Come on, Kitty, 'ave yer finished? If madam here's going to get 'erself into trouble, I'm off. I don't want to be part of it.'

As the two girls walked away, Meg hid behind the trunk of a tree and beneath its branches. She peered up at the building. *If I can't see him*, she thought with a grin, *then he can't see me*.

'Jake,' she called softly. 'Jake!'

He looked round from where he was kneeling down, smoothing cement into cracks in the wall. She watched him searching for the owner of the voice, but he could not see her behind the tree trunk. Keeping a careful watch on the windows, Meg took a step from her hiding place. 'Jake,' she called again. 'Over here.'

Beneath the wall he, too, was hidden, but if he once stepped away from its shelter he could easily be seen from the second floor of the building.

She saw his quick grin as he got to his feet and moved to the end of the wall. Then he ran swiftly to the first tree and, like her, hid behind its trunk. Then he dodged from tree to tree until he was standing a few feet away from her. They each remained hidden behind a trunk, but they could talk.

'Jake, I'm so sorry about what happened before.'

He shrugged and grinned at her. 'Don't matter. I've 'ad plenty of beatings off of him in mi time. One more meks no difference.'

'Mebbe so,' she countered. 'But I don't like being the cause of you getting another.'

'Forget it. I have.' Then he smiled ruefully, ''Cept I've still got the stripes across mi backside.'

She grimaced in sympathy, then added, 'I just wanted to tell you that I'm getting out of here as soon as I can. I'm going to look for my dad.'

'You'll have to ask permission from the master,' Jake said. 'Do you think he'll let you go?'

Meg's face was grimly determined. 'He'd better 'cos I'm going whether he likes it or not!'

The boy looked envious for a moment. 'Wish I could get out of here an' all.'

'Well, why don't you? Why don't you come with me?'

He stared at her for a moment before a huge grin spread across his thin face. 'D'you know, I reckon I just might at that.'

Ten

'You go and ask him first,' Jake said.

'Getting cold feet?' Meg teased. It had taken them both a few days to pluck up courage to face the master.

'No.' His answer was swift. Too swift, for he avoided meeting her gaze. Meg realized it was a big step for the boy, who had never been beyond the workhouse walls.

'Look,' Meg said, serious now. 'I won't think any the worse of you if you do change your mind—'

'No,' he said firmly. 'I'm coming with you. It's time I got out of here. Don't know why I haven't done it before.'

Meg grinned. ''Cos you needed someone like me to give you a push, that's why.'

Soberly, Jake nodded. 'You could be right, at that.'

'I'm surprised they haven't *sent* you out before now. How old are you?'

'Sixteen.'

'Then why haven't they found work for you in the town?'

Jake shrugged then joked, ''Spect the matron wouldn't let them send her precious boy away.'

Meg laughed. 'Is that what she calls you? Her precious boy?'

'Yeah.' He looked embarrassed for a moment and then added, 'But she makes a fuss of all the little boys – not just me.'

'Perhaps you're special to her, though, if you've been here all your life.'

'Suppose so.' There was a pause before he added, 'Well? Are you going to ask him or what?'

'Please,' Meg began as she stood before Isaac Pendleton's desk, adopting what she hoped was her most winning smile, 'may I have your permission to leave the workhouse on Saturday?'

'Why?' Isaac's tone was not encouraging.

'I want to find my dad and tell him about Mam. I want to see if he's found work yet and I want him to come and see her. He can come to see her, can't he?'

Isaac leant his elbows on the desk and steepled his fingers together. 'We allow visits on Sunday afternoons, but under supervision in the committee room and only for one hour.'

Meg's instinct was to protest, but she nodded sensibly. 'I understand.'

Isaac appeared to be thinking. 'As long as you're not thinking of trying to remove your mother. She's still rather poorly and needs to rest.'

Meg shook her head. 'Oh no. Matron and the doctor are being very kind to her. It's just – just that I think my dad ought to know and – and about the baby.'

Isaac cleared his throat. 'Well – er – yes. Very well then, but you must be back here by six o'clock. Is that understood?'

'Oh yes, sir. Thank you, sir.'

Jake was not so fortunate in his request. 'Oh no, boy,' the master said at once. 'You're not going anywhere. At least, not –' he frowned as he added – 'on the same day as young Meg Kirkland.' He gave a hearty laugh, but somehow there was no humour in the sound. 'Think I don't know what the two of you are up to?'

Jake tried to adopt an innocent expression, but realizing he was failing he decided to be truthful. 'Yes, sir, I admit I did want to go the same day as M—'. He corrected himself quickly. 'Kirkland – because I thought she'd be able to help me. I've never been outside, sir, and – well – I wouldn't know how to go on.'

The big man moved towards Jake, who held his breath, half-expecting a clout around the ears. But Isaac put his hand on the boy's shoulder. 'We haven't always seen eye to eye, Bosley, but it might surprise you to know that actually I admire your spirit. I've felt it my duty to see that you were brought up properly. I've tried to be – well – a father figure for you.' He paused, as if expecting Jake to assure him that he had indeed been like a father and that he, Jake, would be eternally grateful. But no such words of appreciation were forthcoming from the boy. Jake could not imagine that a real father – however strict and stern – would have given him the beatings and sent him to the punishment cell with the same frequency that Isaac Pendleton had done.

'We would miss you if you left, especially,' Isaac added with emphasis, 'the matron. She has always – er – been good to you, hasn't she?' Now Jake was able to say with sincerity, 'Oh yes, sir, yes, she has,' for Letitia had been just what he imagined a mother would be. But Jake's heart sank. Was he expected to stay here the whole of his life?

Isaac cleared his throat. 'Of course the day will come when you must go out into the world and earn your own living. That day is not far away. Indeed, the guardians were only recently discussing the cases of several boys and girls of your age who really should no longer be a burden on the parish. You are fit and healthy and able to do a man's work now. Our only problem is – finding suitable employment for you.' He tapped the side of his nose. 'But never fear, Bosley, that is in hand at this very moment.'

'Yes, sir,' Jake's voice was hoarse. He didn't know whether to laugh or cry. He wanted to leave, oh, how he wanted to leave the workhouse and yet he didn't know what sort of a life awaited him beyond its walls.

Tentatively, he tried again. 'But don't you think, sir, that you could see your way clear to let me go out with Kirkland? Just for a day. Just to get the feel of – of what it's like out there.'

Isaac frowned. 'It wouldn't be right to let you go with a girl, Bosley. And especially, not with her. Not after what I witnessed the other day. Oh no. I couldn't trust you. Either of you. No, I'm sorry. The answer is "no".'

Later Jake told Meg. Her response shocked him. 'Then why don't you just come with me? Run away?'

'Where would we go?'

Meg thought a minute. 'We could go back to the farm where we used to live. Miss Alice would help me.' She bit her lip, unsure for a moment. Part of her did not want to think badly of her former friend. 'I still don't think she had anything to do with us being thrown out. I reckon it was her mam – or her dad. Not Alice.'

'Well, there's one way for you to find out,' Jake said.

Meg nodded solemnly. 'I intend to.'

'So, when are we going then?'

Meg's eyes shone. 'You'll do it? You'll come.'

Jake nodded. 'Even if we have to come back at night, I reckon it'll be worth a beating.'

'Saturday,' Meg said firmly. 'There's a race meeting

this Saturday and I'll bet anything that's where my dad will be.'

'Why?'

Patiently, Meg explained. 'Mi dad worked with horses – farm horses, of course – but Mr Smallwood often used to take mi dad with him to the races. The mester was a great one for the races. Dad used to say that Mr Smallwood wanted to buy a racehorse, but that the missis wouldn't let him. Anyway, Dad got to know a lot of the farmers who liked going to the meetings. He knew one or two of the racehorse owners, an' all. I reckon that's where he'll be trying to find work.'

Jake's eyes shone. 'I wouldn't mind working with 'osses.'

'There you are then,' Meg said triumphantly. 'We'll go to the races on Saturday.'

Jake grinned. 'I say, don't it sound grand?'

Meg thought it best not to tell either her mother or Bobbie what she intended to do. Bobbie might cry and make a fuss and beg to be taken too and Sarah would more than likely forbid her to go.

Very early on the Saturday morning, before it was even light and before anyone else was about, Meg crept out of the women's dormitory. Carrying her clothes, she slipped like a wraith down the stone stairs in her bare feet and into the tiny room where the washing benches were. Shivering, she splashed her face and hands with cold water and dressed quickly. Then she ran silently across the exercise yard at the front of the building to the privies at the far corner. When she had finished she crept along the wall to the door leading out into the gardens and the orchard. She held her breath a moment, fearing that it might be locked against her, but it opened with a creak. Meg glanced back at the windows of the building. No face – that she could see in this light – appeared and no light glowed. The inmates, the staff, and even the master were all still in their beds.

Carefully, she pulled the door shut behind her and narrowed her eyes, squinting through the poor light to see if Jake had yet appeared from the men's yard. The door from which Meg had emerged was at the end of the wall nearest to the path running down at the side of the orchard and leading out onto the main road into the town. Jake would come out of one of the doors furthest away from the path. She was about to move stealthily along the wall when a sound behind her made her jump.

'Psst. I'm here.' Jake hissed and Meg turned to see him peeping round the corner of the wall.

She went to him. 'You ready?'

'Ready as I'll ever be, but I reckon I'll be in trouble tonight. I'll've missed roll-call. I've got one of the lads to answer for me, but if he's spotted, he'll get a thrashing an' all.'

Meg laughed softly. 'Mebbe you won't be coming back tonight. Mebbe you won't ever be coming back again. Come on, let's not stand here chatting. Time we was on our way before anyone else gets up.'

She grabbed his hand and they ran down the path and onto the road. Not until they had turned the corner and were out of sight of the workhouse, did they both breathe more easily.

They turned to each other and laughed aloud.

'We did it. We really did it!' Jake shouted joyously and began to caper along the grass verge at the side of the road. 'I'm free. I'm free. Look at me, I'm free.'

Meg laughed and skipped along beside him. The night

her father had told them that the whole family had to leave their home Meg's life had changed dramatically. But now, as the sun rose behind them, streaking the eastern sky with apricot light, Meg dared to feel happy again.

After Jake's euphoria at being out of the workhouse had settled down, he asked, 'Where are we going first then?'

'The farm,' Meg replied determinedly.

As they walked the five miles to Middleditch Farm, the sun came up.

'Going to be a nice day,' Meg remarked, but all she got out of Jake was a grunt. He was saying little, too preoccupied with looking about him, drinking in the sights and sounds and even the smells of the countryside. A farmer's horse and cart passed them and Jake stood back on the grass verge, as close to the hedge as he could get, eyeing the big shire with trepidation.

'I thought you said you liked horses,' Meg teased.

'Not a big bugger like that!' Jake burst out.

'Language,' Meg admonished playfully. 'What would Miss Pendleton say if she heard you?'

Jade grinned and stepped back into the road as the horse clip-clopped away. 'She'd pat my head and tell me not to be a naughty boy.'

'Wouldn't she report you to her brother?'

Jake guffawed. 'What? The matron? Report me? Or any of the boys? Never.'

'Why not?'

Jake glanced at her. 'You ain't been here long enough to understand the set-up, have you?'

'What do you mean? The set-up?'

'The master likes the ladies – and the girls. All of 'em. He's kind and generous to them, but us fellers, well, he'd take his cane to any one of us or send us to the punishment room soon as look at us. But Miss Pendleton – well – she likes the little boys. Oh, she's no time for the men. Wouldn't give them the time of day, but she loves the lads. Mek a good pair, don't they, the Pendletons?'

The memory of the matron taking Bobbie away, separating the little boy from his family, was vivid in Meg's mind. She stopped suddenly and stared at Jake. She wasn't quite sure why and couldn't have put it into words, but all at once she felt very uncomfortable about the matron's actions. 'What – what do you mean, she *likes* the little boys?'

'Eh?' Jake stopped too and turned to face her. Puzzled, he stared at her for a moment. Then his expression cleared and he laughed. 'Oh, she doesn't do owt funny with them, if that's what you're thinking.'

'I – I don't quite know what I am thinking. It – it just sounded a bit odd. You know.'

Jake nodded. He possessed a depth of understanding that was surprising not only for his age, but also considering the fact that he had spent his entire life within the confines of the workhouse. But, Meg supposed, being in the company of older men he must have heard and learnt a lot. As if answering her unspoken question, he said, 'Funny sort of life, I suppose, being an orphan and brought up in that place, but you meet all sorts. The inmates are mostly nice to us kids and – well—' He looked down and scuffed the toe of his boot on the road in embarrassment. 'I suppose the matron is the nearest us kids've got to a mam.'

Meg was thoughtful for a moment before she said

slowly, 'I suppose so and, if I think about it, that's what mams do.'

'What?'

Meg grinned. 'Protect their kids from the father if he's the strict sort.'

Jake's mouth dropped open. 'Well, I wouldn't like Mester Pendleton as my dad.' He recalled his recent conversation with the master. 'Mebbe that's how he likes to think of himself, but he's not *my* idea of a dad.'

'No.' Meg's agreement was heartfelt. 'Nor mine.' She had mixed feelings about her father at the moment. She still felt very bitter about the way he had deserted his family, but, trying to give him the benefit of the doubt, she thought that perhaps it wasn't his fault. *Maybe*, she thought with dread, *it was mine and I might be about to find out*. As they rounded a bend, Meg said, 'This is it. This is where we used to live. Middleditch Farm.'

Eleven

'What are you going to do?' Jake asked, his eyes wide as he stared around the farmyard.

Hens scratched for food, pigs grunted and squealed in a nearby sty and from the cowhouse came the clanking of buckets, the sounds of morning milking.

'See the missis first.' Meg squinted at the sun to gauge the time. 'She'll be in the dairy by now.' She turned to Jake. 'Come as far as the door with me, but don't step inside. She's a tartar for things being kept clean is the missis.'

Obediently, Jake followed Meg as she marched towards the door of a building attached to the farmhouse.

'Wait here,' she told him as she cleaned her boots on a metal scraper. Then she pushed open the door and peered inside. Mrs Smallwood was already busy with the first batch of warm milk and didn't hear the door open and close. Meg walked towards her.

'Missis—' Meg began. The woman jumped and the heavy container of milk began to slip from her grasp. Meg leapt forward and steadied it, saving it from being dropped and all the precious milk being lost. But she was unprepared for the vitriolic look in the woman's eyes as Mrs Smallwood recovered her senses and realized who had startled her.

'You!' she gasped and snatched the container out of

Meg's grasp, slopping milk onto the floor. 'Get out of my sight. You're not wanted here. You or your blasted family.'

Now Meg gasped with shock. 'What did I do wrong? Please – tell me. What was it I did that was so terrible you threw us all out?'

The woman avoided Meg's direct gaze, but the pleading tone and the genuine bewilderment in the girl's voice must have touched even Mabel Smallwood's hardened heart.

She banged the metal milk churn to the floor. 'I – I didn't like your friendship with our – our Alice.'

It was an excuse, Meg could tell. It was not the truth – at least, not the whole truth – but the young girl could hardly challenge the lie. All she could say was, 'But if only you'd told me, missis, serious like, I mean. I'd – I'd have stopped it.'

Now Mabel met her gaze. 'I doubt it.'

'Then – then why didn't you just sack me? Why did it have to be my dad as well? Did you really have to turn our whole family out of our home just because I was too friendly with your daughter?'

The woman's patience snapped and now she shouted out the truth. 'It wasn't you. It wasn't you at all. It was your father – God rot him!'

'My – my dad? What – what did he do?'

Mabel glared at her, resentment in her eyes, her mouth tight with bitterness. 'You'll find out. Oh, you'll find out soon enough.' She turned her back on Meg in final dismissal.

'But—'

'Clear off.' Mabel waved her hand driving the girl away. 'Just leave. I don't want to talk about it any more.'

Daringly, Meg stood her ground. 'I want to see Alice. I want—'

Mabel whirled round on her, waving her arms above her head and yelling. 'Get out of here, I say. Get out.'

Meg went. Outside the dairy, she stood, white-faced and shaking.

'Whatever was all that about?' Jake asked. 'I could hear 'er shrieking from here.'

Meg bit her lip and glanced back at the closed door. 'I'm not sure. But at least I've found out one thing.'

'What's that?'

'It wasn't me that caused all the trouble. It was mi dad.' She shook her head slowly, as if she couldn't really take it in. 'Goodness knows what he could have done that was so bad. The missis has always had a sharp tongue, but now . . .' Meg's voice faded away.

As they moved away across the yard towards the gate back onto the road, Jake felt a horrible sense of foreboding, as if no good would come of this visit. He was suddenly afraid for Meg and what she might find out.

'So, what do we do now?'

Meg frowned and glanced about her. 'If the mester's about—'

'Oho, you're asking fer trouble now. If the missis is like that, what's he going to be like?'

'He's not as bad as her.' Her face cleared. 'He'll be in the cowhouse, milking. Come on.'

This time, they both stepped into the building. For a moment Meg paused, breathing in the familiar smells. With all that had happened, she hadn't realized just how much she'd missed the farm.

Glancing a little fearfully at the restless cows in the stalls, Jake, close behind her, whispered, 'Is that him?'

Halfway down the row, they could just see the back of a man sitting on a stool, his head resting against the cow's belly, his hands moving rhythmically as he drew the milk.

Meg shook her head. 'No, that's not him.'

The sound of her voice must have reached the man, for he stood up and turned towards them.

'Hey,' Jake said loudly. 'It's Ron from the workhouse. Hello, Ron. So this is where you've been disappearing to every day.'

The man, tall, thin and slightly stooping, grinned and began to move towards them.'

'Best move yer bucket, mister, else she'll have it over, will Buttercup,' Meg advised.

'Oh aye, right you are.' He bent and picked up the bucket from beneath the cow and moved it to safety.

'What you doing 'ere, young Jake? Come fer a job, 'ave yer?'

Jake grinned. 'Wish I had, Ron. No, I've – I've come out without permission. You won't tell, will yer?'

'Course I won't.' He glanced from one to the other. 'But what *are* you doing here?' His face clouded. 'You ain't come looking fer me. There's nowt wrong wi' mi missis back at the house, is there?'

Jake shook his head. 'I've come with Meg. She used to work here. Used to live here till these folks turned her whole family out. She's come to try to find out where 'er dad is.'

The man scratched his head. 'Well, there's no one else here 'cept me an' the mester and the missis, of course. He took me on a couple of days ago and I'm right grateful. He ses if I prove miself, he'll let us have a cottage he's got vacant. Eh, but it'll be grand to fetch me missis and the bairns out o' that place.'

Meg's eyes filled with tears and there was a sudden lump in her throat. 'That'd be our cottage.'

Ron looked awkward and shuffled his feet.

'It's all right,' Meg said swiftly. 'You tek it, if you get the chance. They're hardly likely to let us back. Anyway,' she went on, trying to sound bright and hopeful even though she felt anything but, 'where's Mr Smallwood? I'll talk to him. Or Miss Alice. Is she about?'

'The mester's gone to the races. Went early, he did.' Now a mystified expression crossed Ron's face. 'And Miss – who did you say?'

'Miss Alice. Their daughter.'

Ron shook his head. 'There's nobody else here. Only Mr and Mrs Smallwood. There's no daughter living here. Not that I've seen.'

'Maybe you just haven't seen her if you've only been here a couple of days,' Jake put in.

But it was Meg who shook her head now. 'Oh no, if she was here, you'd have seen her all right.'

Now Meg was more mystified than ever.

Although the racing wasn't due to start until the early afternoon, the ground was already humming with activity.

'I just can't understand what can have happened to Miss Alice,' Meg murmured, still puzzled.

'Maybe she's just gone on holiday,' Jake suggested, trying to be helpful. Not that he had any personal experience of holidays, but he had heard them talked about. Miss Pendleton sometimes went on holiday to visit her sister, who lived in London. At such times Jake had tried to keep out of the master's way as much as possible when his champion was not there.

'The Smallwoods don't have holidays. They hardly ever leave the farm and then only for a day. I've never known any one of them go away for longer than that.'

Jake had run out of suggestions, so they walked on towards the stables in silence.

Horses were arriving early to give their stable lads time to settle them into the surroundings. The trainers would arrive a little later in time to walk the course so they could advise their jockeys on how to run the race.

'Why's this Mr Smallwood come so early if it don't start till this afternoon?' Jake asked.

'He likes to mingle with the trainers and talk to the owners. I told you, he fancies being an owner one day.' Meg bit her lip. 'He always promised mi dad that he'd put him in charge of his racehorse – if he ever got one.'

Wide-eyed with wonder, Jake was staring about him. 'I wonder if there's any jobs as stable lads going?'

Meg laughed. 'You're frightened of horses. What good would you be?'

Jake grinned. 'I could learn. It's only 'cos I've never had the chance to be around them.' He narrowed his eyes and watched a young lad leading a sleek chestnut past. 'Beautiful animals, aren't they?'

'Yeah,' Meg agreed. Her eyes were misty as her gaze followed the magnificent creature. 'Dad once said that if I'd been a boy he'd've tried to get me a job as a stable lad.'

'Would you have liked that?'

Meg nodded and her voice was husky as she answered, 'Yeah. Yeah, I would.'

They wandered around the ground unchallenged. Meg had got them in through a break in the fence she knew about. 'I used to beg mi dad to take me with them when they came to the races, but he never would. Said the master and the missis wouldn't approve. But I used to skive off school and come anyway. It was more difficult when I was working at the farm. There was more work for me when the master and Dad were away for the whole day.' She grinned widely. 'But I managed it a few times.'

'Did they ever catch you?' Jake's life was ruled by the fear of getting caught doing something wrong. The threat of Isaac Pendleton was never far away. Even though he was at this moment enjoying himself as never before in his young life, the day was marred by the thought of the punishment he would get if he was found out. And he was sure that he would be.

Suddenly, Meg clutched Jake's arm. 'Quick, turn round and keep walking.'

'Why? What's—' Jake began but found himself being dragged round and propelled in the opposite direction.

'It's the mester.'

Jake turned pale. 'Not – not Mr Pendleton?'

'No. Mr Smallwood.'

Jake glanced over his shoulder towards the burly figure of the farmer, standing close to the rails. He was talking to two other men and they were laughing heartily.

'But I thought you *wanted* to speak to him? You were looking for him at the farm.'

'Well, yes. And maybe I will. Later. But if I speak to him now he'll likely get us sent out of here. And I want to stay a bit longer.' She thought quickly. 'Look, if anybody ses anything to us – asks us what we're doing here, just tell 'em – just tell 'em that – that you're stable lad for Mr Smith.'

'Who's Mr Smith when he's at home?'

'He's one of the biggest owners and he employs a lot

of stable lads. No one'll know whether you're really one of his or not.'

'Wish I was,' Jake muttered. 'But what about you?'

'Say I'm your sister and you've brought me along for the day.' She grinned. 'With Mr Smith's permission, of course.'

Jake still looked doubtful, but he nodded.

Meg glanced briefly over her shoulder. 'We're out of his sight now, I reckon, and . . .'

She stopped suddenly and clutched Jake's arm again.

'I wish you'd stop doing that, Meg. You ain't 'alf got a grip on you, for a girl. It hurts. Gerroff.'

Meg's gaze was fixed on a figure walking towards them.

'There, look,' she cried excitedly and pointed with a trembling finger. 'That's mi dad.'

She plunged forward, dragging Jake with her. 'Dad, Dad—' she began.

Then suddenly she stopped. She felt as if someone had thumped her hard just below her ribs and knocked all the breath from her body. Her eyes widened in shock and she gasped. The colour drained from her face and her grip on Jake's arm slackened.

Jake pulled free and rubbed his arm where her strong fingers had dug deep. 'Where? Which one is he?' He followed the line of her startled gaze and saw a tall, thin man walking towards them. He was dressed in what was obviously his Sunday best suit and he carried his cap in his hand. His light brown hair was ruffled by the breeze, but he was unaware for he had eyes for nothing and no one except the person walking beside him. He had his arm around the shoulders of a fair-haired young woman and they were looking into each other's eyes as they walked and laughing together. The sound of the girl's tinkling, flirtatious laugh reached Meg and Jake. The man bent towards the woman and touched her forehead with his lips.

Beside him, Jake heard Meg's strangled whisper. 'Miss Alice. It's mi dad and Miss Alice.'

Twelve

As if drawn by Meg's intense gaze, Reuben Kirkland's eyes met hers. He stopped and, puzzled, for she had not yet noticed Meg, Alice looked up at him. Then she too saw what had caught and held his attention. For a moment, all four of them stared at one another and then Meg leapt forward, covering the distance between them in an instant.

She launched herself at her father and pummelled his chest, crying and shrieking. 'How could you? How could you do this? And with her? Of all people, with *her*!'

Reuben caught hold of her flailing fists and tried to hold her, but her rage lent her strength and now Meg turned upon Alice. She grabbed the girl's hair and yanked it from its pins as if she would wrench it from her head.

'You slut! You trollop, you – you—' The vulgar names tumbled from her mouth until there was a small crowd gathering around them. Alice retaliated with a few punches of her own, one catching Meg on the mouth and drawing blood from her lip. At last Reuben pulled his daughter away from Alice, who was now crying and trembling.

Jake did nothing. He certainly wasn't going to help the man. If he'd done anything, he would have waded in beside Meg, but she seemed to be doing very nicely, thank you, on her own. If the scene had not been so obviously traumatic for Meg, it was comical. In fact, several uninvolved onlookers were laughing.

'Better than a peep show, this is,' Jake heard one remark.

'Aye, I like to see two women having a scrap,' another agreed. 'Much more fun than fellers.'

Holding the panting women apart, Reuben glanced about him. 'Show's over, folks,' he said grimly. 'Come on, let's go somewhere quieter where we can talk.'

'Talk?' Meg screamed. 'Talk? What is there to talk about? I see it all now. No wonder me poor mam seemed so – so defeated. All her spirit gone. She must have known and I thought it was just 'cos she was expecting an' . . .' A bitter smile came to Meg's mouth as she added sarcastically, 'Oh, and by the way she had the bairn. But you'll be pleased to know it was born dead.'

Reuben had the grace to wince. 'I never wished that on her, Meggie.'

'Don't call me that,' Meg spat at him. Angry tears filled her eyes and there was a catch in her voice as she added, 'Don't ever call me that again.'

Reuben's eyes were anguished. 'Meg, please try to understand. Alice and I fell in love. We – we have to be together.'

'That's why you got the sack, isn't it? Because of her?'

Seeing she was a little calmer now, Reuben relaxed his hold on his daughter and put his arms around Alice. Seeing his action, Meg felt sick. Alice clung to him, her blue eyes full of tears and her hair wild and fluffy about her face.

'They found out, Alice's mam and dad,' Reuben said.

'And so they threw us all out,' Meg added bitterly.

'And me.' Alice spoke up for the first time. 'They threw me out an' all.'

'My heart bleeds for you,' Meg fired back. For a moment she closed her eyes and shook her head, still hardly able to grasp the truth. 'I thought you were my friend, Alice. How could you do this to me? To all my family? To my mam and to little Bobbie? How could you stand by and see us put in the workhouse? You were my one hope. It was really you I came looking for today. I thought if there was anyone who would try to help us, it'd be you.'

'Like your dad says, we fell in love. I love your dad and he loves me and we want to be together, no matter what.'

Slowly Meg nodded. 'No matter who gets hurt, eh? You don't care about anybody but yourselves, do you? Well, I hope you rot in hell, the pair of you.'

Rage carried her through, held her up whilst she turned her back on them and marched away. With one last glance at them, Jake turned and followed Meg.

It wasn't until they had reached and crawled through the hole in the fence that Meg sat on the ground. She drew her knees up, wrapped her arms around them and dropped her head, hiding her face against her skirt. Her shoulders heaved with racking sobs.

Jake could think of nothing to say so he sat beside her and put his arms about her. They stayed like that until Meg's weeping subsided. At last she raised her face, ravaged by tears, and whispered, 'I'll never trust anyone ever again.'

*

A little later, Meg, calmer now, said, 'We might as well go back. There's nothing else to stay out here for.'

'Suppose not,' Jake agreed reluctantly. 'But I was enjoying miself. At least,' he added swiftly, 'I was until that happened.'

Meg tried to smile, but it was a feeble effort. At this moment she felt as if she would never smile properly again.

'Come on then,' Jake said, scrambling up. 'If we can sneak back in before dinner time, we just might get away with it.'

'I needn't sneak in. I had permission,' she reminded him.

Jake wrinkled his brow thoughtfully. 'Tell you what, I'll go in through the hole in the hedge into the orchard and start working there.' He grinned swiftly at her. 'You're not the only one who knows about holes in things to get in and out.'

There was no answering smile from Meg, but she did ask, 'I thought you said you'd never been out before?'

'*I* haven't, but I know a few who have.' He paused and then asked, 'Do – do you think you could leave it a bit before you come back in? Just – just so it doesn't look as if we've been out together. If I have been missed, then—'

'Course I will. I don't want you to get another thrashing. I feel bad enough about the one you did get.'

'Don't.' Jake grinned and squeezed her arm. 'You've got more than enough to worry about without thinking about me.' He bit his lip and looked at her uncertainly, then away.

'What?' she asked, realizing that there was still something on his mind.

'Look, Meg, would you mind . . . ? I mean, while we've been sitting here, I've been thinking—'

'While I've been making a complete fool of miself,' she said bitterly.

'No.' Jake's tone was gentle. 'You haven't made a fool of yourself. You could never do that. Not to me.' He pulled her close and for a moment she rested her head against his shoulder.

'Good job old Pendleton can't see us now,' Jake murmured as he bent his head. With the awkwardness of youth and the clumsiness of the first time, he kissed her. Startled, Meg drew back and stared at him.

'Sorry,' Jake mumbled, his face fiery red.

'No.' Meg took his hand. 'Don't say that,' she whispered. There was an awkward pause between them before Meg prompted, 'What was it you wanted to ask me?'

On safer ground, Jake's embarrassment subsided. 'I just wondered if you'd mind if I had a talk to Ron when he comes home tonight. See if there's any jobs going at that farm.'

'Why should I mind?'

'It just seemed – well – a bit unkind to be trying to get a job there when the only reason there might be one going is because you got the sack.'

Meg's mouth was tight as she said, 'Don't you worry about that, Jake. You go ahead. Don't bother about me or anybody else. You look out for yourself.' Her tone was icy as she added, 'It's what I'm going to do from now on. Me, miself and I – that's who I'm going to look after,' she declared and, as a hasty afterthought, she added, 'And mi Mam and Bobbie, of course.'

*

On her return to the workhouse, Meg worked with a fury. She scrubbed the stone steps of the staircases and the flags of the passageways until her knees were sore and her hands bleeding. Her tears were gone. She refused to cry over her father ever again, but there was a heavy feeling in her chest as if a huge lump was stuck there.

When she walked into the women's day room for her supper, she was surprised yet gladdened to see her mother sitting beside the fire. Miss Pendleton was bustling around Sarah, tucking a rug around her knees and handing her some socks.

'We have to do all the mending for the men. Not much use at that sort of thing – men. You're not fit to do heavy work yet, but you can darn these.' At that moment, Miss Pendleton caught sight of Meg. 'And look who's here. Your girl's back.' She raised her voice. 'Had a nice time out, Kirkland? Did you find yourself a job?'

Meg bit her lip and shook her head.

'Ah well, not to worry. Tell you what,' the woman added as a thought came into her mind, 'next time you get permission to go out, go into the town to the tailor's shop. It's owned by a Mr Rodwell. He's walking out with a friend of mine – Miss Finch.' The woman paused and laughed loudly. 'Mind you, they've been engaged for five or six years and there's still no sign of wedding bells. Anyway, I hear he's looking for a young woman to work in his shop. He's started to stock ladies' underwear and finds a lot of his customers are too embarrassed to be served by a man. Tell him I sent you, Kirkland.'

Meg tried to smile as she thanked the matron politely.

Letitia Pendleton nodded. 'You can sit and talk to

your mam for a bit, but,' she added, handing Meg a pile of socks too, 'you can make yourself useful while you're doing it. And now I must see to my little boys.'

As she began to move away, Sarah looked up with pleading eyes. 'Matron, how is Bobbie? Please – can I see him?'

'Not today, Kirkland. You'll see him tomorrow when the chaplain comes to hold the Sunday service in the committee room – your little lad can spend the rest of the afternoon with you.' Letitia's eyes softened. 'He's a grand little chap. I've quite taken to him. Don't you worry. I'll look after him.'

As soon as the woman had left the room, Sarah whispered, 'Meg, have you seen Bobbie? Is he all right?'

Meg shook her head. 'No, Mam, not today. I – I've been out.'

Sarah nodded, 'Yes, I heard the matron say so. You've been looking for work?'

'Well,' Meg said slowly, 'not exactly. I – I went looking for Dad.'

Sarah seemed to slump in her chair and some of the socks slid from her lap. She closed her eyes and gave a low moan. 'Oh, Meggie, I wish you hadn't done that.'

There was silence and Meg bit her lip as she watched the anguish on her mother's face. Sarah was silent, asking no questions. If she had been in her mother's place, the questions would have been tumbling out of her mouth. *Did you see him? Has he found work? When is he coming back for us? And when – oh, when – can we get out of this place?*

But Sarah asked nothing and sat with her head in her hands. Now Meg was sure. 'Mam? You knew, didn't you? You knew about – about *her*?' Meg couldn't even

bring herself to speak her former friend's name, so great was the hurt of Alice's betrayal.

Sarah sighed heavily and admitted, 'Yes, yes, I knew.'

'How long has it been going on?'

'I don't know. I've known for about a month, but it must have been going on a lot longer than that.' She paused and then whispered, 'Oh, Meggie, I wish you hadn't found out. Don't hate him—'

'Don't hate him?' Meg's voice rose and some of the other women looked up, but the girl was oblivious to their curious glances. 'Oh, I hate him all right. And her. I hate them both. But don't you worry, Mam. I'll get a job and I'll get us out of here. You, me and Bobbie.'

She jumped up and piled the socks she had been given to darn onto her mother's lap. 'I'll go right now and see the master.'

'Oh, Meg—' Sarah began, but her daughter was paying no heed.

She planted a kiss on her mother's forehead and patted her hand. 'Don't worry, Mam. I'll take care of everything.'

She turned away and was about to hurry across the room when the door was flung open and the man she sought stood there, filling the frame.

'Good evening, ladies, good evening. And how are we all on this fine night?'

Feet shuffled and chairs scraped as all the women stood up and chorused, 'Good evening, Master.' Even Sarah struggled to her feet, the socks spilling from her knee.

'Sit down, sit down, ladies, do,' Isaac boomed and glanced around the room. His gaze came to rest on Sarah as she sank back into her chair. Meg bent and retrieved the socks from the floor.

Isaac pulled up a chair and sat down beside Sarah.

'Sir,' Meg began, 'I was just coming to see you. Please – may I have your permission to go out again on Monday?'

'Ah, well now, I don't know about that. We can't have you going out too often, Kirkland. Your poor mother needs you here.' He took hold of Sarah's hand and held it.

Meg was sure she heard stifled laughter from the women behind her, but the girl was too intent on her goal to worry about it at the moment. 'Matron has given me the name of someone who might give me a job.'

Isaac turned his watery blue eyes on Sarah. 'What do you say, my dear?' he asked smoothly, still holding her hand. 'Shall we let her go, eh?'

'If you please, sir,' Sarah said softly, 'I'd be very grateful. Meg is a good girl and is only trying to look after us.'

Isaac started back, pretending shock. 'Oh, my dear lady, you wound me deeply. Don't you think that is what we're trying to do here? To look after you?'

Sarah lowered her head and said huskily, 'Yes, yes, of course, I didn't mean . . .'

Isaac patted her hand and laughed. 'No, no, of course, you didn't. I was only teasing. Of course, she can go.'

Despite the turmoil of the day, Meg rewarded the master with her widest smile, which lit up her green eyes and dimpled her cheeks. 'Thank you, Master.'

The master gazed at her and, as she dipped a curtsy and moved towards the door, Isaac murmured, 'By, but she'll be a beauty one day and no mistake.'

Hearing him, the girl's mother shuddered.

Thirteen

After supper most of the women, weary from their day's work, began to drift up to the dormitory.

'I'll just get some more coal in, Mam,' Meg said. 'You go on up. I shan't be long.'

Carrying the coal bucket, Meg slipped down the stairs and across the yard towards the coal store. It was the one building in the row that stood between the men's and women's yards and was accessible from both. She and Jake had arranged to meet there under cover of darkness.

'There you are.' His voice came out of the blackness. 'I thought you weren't coming.'

'The master came to the day room and then there was supper. I couldn't get away.'

'Like I told you. He likes the women.'

'He seems to have taken a fancy to me mam. He was sitting beside her, holding her hand.'

'You want to watch him.'

'But I thought he was after Miss Daley.'

Jake laughed softly. 'He's after owt in skirts. But I don't reckon he'll get far with the schoolmarm. She's sweet on the doctor.'

Meg was thoughtful. 'Mm. I noticed that.'

Side by side they shovelled coal.

'Look, we still might get caught meeting here,' Jake whispered. 'Next time, let's meet in the dead room.'

Meg was startled. 'The what?'

'It's a room right at the end of this row of buildings in the men's yard, where they put the dead 'uns.' She saw his white, even teeth shining through the gloom as he grinned. 'There's only empty coffins in there.'

Meg shuddered. 'You sure?'

'Well, not *all* the time. If someone dies—'

'Ugh!'

'But it's safe. No one'll go in there.'

'Don't blame 'em,' she muttered, with feeling. She paused and then added, 'All right then. Anything to save you another thrashing. Did you get into trouble today?'

'No, I was lucky. I slipped into the orchard and started working and nobody seemed to have missed me.'

'Not even Miss Pendleton?' Meg asked saucily.

She heard his low chuckle. 'No, though she did say, "I haven't seen you all day," at suppertime. Gave me a right scare. I thought she was going to ask where I'd been. And I can't lie – specially not to her.' He leant closer. 'They reckon the reason she makes such a fuss of the lads is 'cos years ago, when she was a young girl, she had a baby boy.'

Meg gasped. 'What? You mean – you mean she wasn't married?'

'Yeah.'

'What happened to it?'

'Don't know. Mebbe it died or was taken away from her. You know, adopted.'

'Or maybe,' Meg said thoughtfully, 'it was sent to the workhouse.'

Jake stared at her through the darkness. 'I'd never thought of that.'

'So that's why she loves all the little boys who come in here.' Meg felt a sudden surge of sympathy for the woman. 'Poor old Letitia.'

Jake chuckled softly. 'Daft name, isn't it? What parents in their right mind would call their daughter "Letitia"?'

Meg was defensive. 'I think it's quite a pretty name. Besides, Isaac's not much better.'

'Yeah, but his name does suit him. Look, I'll have to be off. Don't want to get caught now, seeing as I got away with mi little expedition into the big wide world.'

'Did you enjoy it?'

He was solemn now. 'I would have if it hadn't been for meeting your dad and you being so upset.'

'Seems mi mam has known about his carryings on for a month or more,' Meg said bitterly and added incredulously, 'And she doesn't seem to blame him.'

'What? Do you mean she doesn't *mind*?'

'Oh, she minds all right, but she said to me, "Don't blame him, Meg." I can't understand her. I really can't. If I was her, I'd want to kill 'em both.' Beneath her breath she muttered, 'I felt like it anyway.'

There was silence between them for a while, the only sounds the scraping of the metal shovels on the stone floor and the tumbling of pieces of coal into the buckets.

'Anyway, I'm going out again on Monday. Miss Pendleton's given me the name of someone who might give me a job.'

'Well, good luck. Wish I could find one.'

'Have you spoken to Ron yet?'

'No.'

'Why not?'

'I – I dunno, really.'

'Jake,' Meg said firmly, 'just do it.'

'Matron –' Meg stood before Letitia Pendleton on the Monday morning and adopted her most docile and pleading expression – 'do you think I could be allowed to wear my own clothes? Just today. The master has given me permission to go and see Mr Rodwell and – and seeing as he's a friend of yours, or rather a friend of your friend – I do want to be a credit to you.'

Letitia laughed and her chins wobbled. 'I see. Workhouse uniform not good enough for you, eh?'

Meg caught the twinkle in the older woman's eyes and said coyly, 'But I scrub floors in these clothes, Matron.'

'No disgrace in honest hard work.' Letitia pondered for a moment and then said, 'Very well, then. See Waters and tell her you have my permission.'

'Oh, I don't know about that. It's most unusual.' Ursula pursed her thin lips with disapproval.

'But matron said I could.'

'Strikes me you're trying to hide the fact that you come from the workhouse. Trying to fool a would-be employer into thinking you're better than you are.'

'Of course I'm not,' Meg replied heatedly. 'Miss Pendleton's recommended me to go and see this Mr Rodwell. That's hardly hiding the fact that I'm here, is it? Ask her, ask the matron if you don't believe me.'

Ursula sniffed. 'She's not here to ask. She's gone out for the day.' She made no move to find Meg's belongings.

'Well, who would you believe? Mr Pendleton?' Meg persisted.

'We mustn't worry the master about such a matter.'

'Yes, we must, if you're not going to let me have them.' Meg reached out and grabbed hold of Ursula's thin arm. 'Come on. We'll go and see him this very minute.'

To the older woman's consternation, she found herself being dragged out of the storeroom, across the men's yard and into the door leading directly to the master's office. 'Kirkland, I don't think we should—'

'You should have thought about that before you refused to obey the matron's orders.' Meg paused briefly and stuck her face close to Ursula's. 'And they *were* her orders.'

'Oh well, in that case—'

'No, no. Too late now. We'll ask the master and we'll do what he says. Whatever it is.' Meg had already raised her hand to knock on the door, but now Ursula reached up and grasped hold of it.

'No – please – don't. I don't want to cause trouble.'

'You don't want to cause trouble for yourself, you mean. You couldn't care less about me. But I bet you've suddenly realized that the master – new though I am here – will take my side.'

Suddenly, Ursula's face twisted into ugliness. 'Of course he will. He can't resist a pretty face. Well, let me tell you something. When I first came here, I was young and pretty too. Oh yes, you can hardly believe it, can you? Well, it's true. And he couldn't resist *me*. But now I'm older, he's cast me aside and he's after the younger ones.' Now it was Ursula who hissed in Meg's face. 'You want to watch out for yourself else you'll end up like me. But why should I care? I'll get you your clothes and much good may they do you.'

She twisted her arm out of Meg's grasp and went back the way they had come, with Meg following her more slowly.

It felt wonderful to Meg to be dressed in her own clothes – again; to feel soft underwear against her skin instead of the rough, scratchy garments the workhouse provided. She'd lost weight since coming here and her dress hung loosely on her, but beneath her shawl it didn't show too badly. The clothes had been crumpled when Ursula handed them to her, but the use of a hot iron in the wash house had made them look much better.

Meg paused at the porter's lodge. 'Albert, I have permission to go out. I'm going after a job.'

The old man hauled himself out of his chair and limped to open the gate for her. He remembered the lass coming in with her mam and her little brother. The poor woman had been heavy with child and now, by all accounts, she'd lost the bairn.

'You look as pretty as a picture, mi duck,' he told Meg, knowing she would not sneer at him daring to compliment her. Not like some of the women in here who laughed in his face if he even spoke to them. Trollops, the lot of 'em, to his mind, but not this lass and her mam. They were a nice family. 'Mind you're back by six o'clock, won't yer? Shouldn't like to see you in trouble.'

Meg smiled at him, dimpling prettily. 'I will, Albert.'

As he closed the gate behind her, she turned and waved and he called, 'Good luck wi' yer job.'

There was a spring in Meg's step as she walked down

the long cinder path to the road. She breathed in deeply, savouring the fresh morning air. Oh, what it was to be free, out in the open. She hadn't realized just how much the workhouse confined her. How damp and cold and oppressive it was to be inside those thick walls and behind the iron bars of the huge gates. She felt like a caged bird within its confines, but out here she could fly free.

Meg found herself sending up an ardent prayer. *Please let me get this job! Please let me get it and then I can get Mam and Bobbie out of that place.*

Fourteen

Meg walked down the High Street in the centre of the town. Already the street was busy: ladies in long skirts and white blouses were moving from shop to shop with baskets on their arms. Two young girls, carrying school books, stood chatting in the middle of the road, whilst a youth with a bicycle stood leaning on it, trying to catch the eye of one of the girls. He raised his cap to Meg, but she put her nose in the air in haughty rejection, tossing back her long red hair beneath the beribboned straw boater.

Outside the General Stores stood the proprietor, in a white jacket and a long white apron that reached down to his ankles.

'Good morning, good morning . . .' Meg heard him greeting the folk passing his shop.

She walked on, past the newsagent's with a rack of the day's papers hanging to one side of the door, past the ironmonger's with pots and pans, buckets and mops in the window, to the shop next door, where the sign read 'T. RODWELL & SON, Tailor and Outfitter'. It was a double-fronted shop, with the door in the centre between two windows.

Meg paused and peered in. Her heart was beating fast and her hands felt clammy. Inside she could see a man standing behind the counter. He was thin with receding dark hair and dressed in a sober suit with a waistcoat, a stiff-collared white shirt and a plain tie. He was serving a customer and as Meg glanced at the man in front of the counter, she gasped. It was Theobald Finch, the chairman of the board of guardians at the workhouse. Meg bit her lip, uncertain what she should do. Should she wait out here until Mr Finch had left or should she go inside and stand quietly at the rear of the shop until Mr Rodwell was free?

Deciding that the latter course of action was perhaps the safest – she didn't want to be accused of hanging about in the street in a suspicious manner – Meg opened the shop door. The bell clanged loudly and both men turned to look at her. Meg closed the door carefully, though the bell clanged again. She turned to face them.

'Good morning.' She smiled. 'I've come to see Mr Rodwell. Would you like me to wait outside?'

Closer now, she could see that the tailor was younger than she had expected him to be. She had imagined an elderly man, but Mr Rodwell looked to be in his early forties. He had a sallow complexion and his pale hazel eyes were large behind thick spectacles.

He blinked several times, but did not smile. 'No, no,' he said in a soft voice. 'That won't be necessary. Just wait over there, if you please, and I'll be with you shortly.'

'Thank you, sir.'

She moved to the far end of the long shop, aware that Mr Finch was still watching her. 'I know you, don't I? I've seen you before somewhere.'

Meg thought it politic to drop a small curtsy. 'You interviewed me and my family, sir, a week or two back. We – I'm from the workhouse.'

'Ah, yes. I remember you now. Your mother fainted, did she not?'

'Yes, sir.'

'And is she recovered now?'

'She is getting better, thank you, sir. But she – she lost the baby.'

'Ah.' The large man said again, but without a word of sympathy. He lost interest in her and turned back to choosing the material for his new suit. Meg waited, trying to curb her natural impatience. She watched how Mr Rodwell flicked through a swatch of fabric, giving his customer details of the make-up of each piece. 'Now this one is a fine worsted. And this one a coarser weave but very hard-wearing and this one . . .' And so on until Meg's head spun. There'd be a lot to learn, she thought, and wondered if she wouldn't be better to seek employment on another farm. At least she understood that work and there might be a cottage for her family . . .

At last Mr Finch made up his mind. 'That one, Percy. That's the one.'

'A wise choice, if I may say so.' The tailor inclined his head. It was almost a bow – but not quite. 'I'll order the cloth. Now, would you like me to take your measurements?'

'Not today, Percy. I'm in a hurry.'

Who'd have thought it, Meg thought, amused, *considering the time he's taken to choose? I must have been standing here for ten minutes or more.*

'I'd like to see the material again,' Theobald said. 'You know, in a full piece, just to make sure I like it. You can take my measurements then. Good day to you, Percy.'

'Good day, Theobald.'

Theobald opened the shop door with a flourish and then turned back. 'I'll see you later. I believe you're dining with us tonight.'

'That is so.'

Theobald's smile broadened. 'Clara is looking forward to it.'

Percy Rodwell gave a thin smile and dipped his head once more.

When the door had closed behind his customer, the tailor turned towards Meg. For a few moments he scrutinized her, taking in her appearance from head to toe. When his gaze finally met her green eyes, he seemed a little startled and blinked rapidly.

'You – you wanted to see me?'

Meg moved forward. 'Yes, sir. Miss Pendleton sent me. She said she's a friend of yours. Or rather,' she added hastily, 'a friend of Miss Finch's.'

'I hadn't realized they were friendly. I rather thought—' He paused and then asked, 'Why did Miss Pendleton send you to see me?'

'She thought you might have a job for me.'

Percy frowned. 'A job? For you?'

'She thought you were going to start stocking ladies' – er – garments and that perhaps your customers might prefer to be served by a woman.'

Percy allowed himself a small amused smile. Meg had the feeling it was because she had referred to herself as a 'woman'.

'That is correct,' he said in his soft voice. He cleared his throat and now he avoided her direct gaze. 'But I had it in mind to employ someone a little more – er – mature than yourself.'

Meg made sure that disappointment showed keenly on her face. 'I see,' she whispered and hung her head. Then she gave a huge sigh and glanced around the shop. 'What a shame! I'd've loved to work here. To have learnt all about fabrics and such. It must be so interesting.' She turned her brilliant eyes upon him and sighed again. 'But, of course, if I don't suit—'

'Well, now –' Percy was flustered – 'I didn't say that exactly.' He cleared his throat nervously. 'We – er – could discuss it. Yes, yes, we can discuss it.'

For the next half an hour, Percy Rodwell questioned Meg closely about herself, her family and her background. When he heard that her only experience of work had been as a dairymaid, doubt crossed his face once more.

Meg leapt in quickly. 'I realize you might prefer someone with experience in this kind of work, but I am honest and reliable and quick to learn and –' she ran her tongue around her lips and suggested craftily – 'and you could train me in *your* ways, couldn't you?'

He glanced at her. 'Well, there is that, I suppose.' He pondered for what seemed to the anxious girl an interminable time. At last he said, 'Very well, then. I'll speak to Miss Pendleton about you and if her comments are satisfactory, I'll take you. But it will be for a trial period, mind.'

Meg's eyes shone. 'I understand. And thank you, sir. I won't let you down, I promise.'

'We shall see, we shall see,' Percy said. 'Present yourself here at eight thirty sharp next Monday morning – one week from today – and we shall see.'

As she left the shop, Meg glanced back at the building. Two dummies, fully clothed in men's suits, stood in one of the windows. The other window displayed shirts, ties and socks. She glanced upwards and saw that the smaller windows on the first floor were very dirty. It was obvious that the upper floor was used only as a storeroom or perhaps a workroom. She wondered if there were enough rooms to make some into living quarters.

Meg skipped all the way back to the workhouse. She couldn't wait to tell her mam and Bobbie. The only thing worrying her was whether Miss Pendleton would speak well of her. But she had not upset the matron. Waters would have been a different matter and maybe even Mr Pendleton would not give her a glowing reference exactly, but she was sure that Miss Pendleton would speak well of her.

Albert was waiting for her when she rang the bell at the back gate to the workhouse. 'How did yer get on then?'

'Mr Rodwell's going to give me a trial. I'm to start next Monday.'

'He's a decent sort.'

'Mr Rodwell? Do you know him, Albert?'

The old man sniffed. 'I know most folks round here. Used to be an oddjob man in these parts, till I couldn't work any more.'

'And you . . . you . . .' Meg hesitated. She couldn't imagine that Albert had ever bought a suit at the tailor's. Albert finished her sentence for her. 'I worked for him now and again. Not in the shop, o' course. At his house.'

Meg kept her face the picture of innocence. 'Oh, so he doesn't live above the shop, then?'

'Used to do. Years ago.' This was the most talkative that Albert Conroy had been in years. But this pretty young girl had shown him such respect, kindness even. 'When his dad had the shop before 'im the whole family lived upstairs. But Percy moved into a little cottage near the church a few years back.' He sniffed. 'When he got hisself engaged to Miss Clara Finch.'

Meg smiled back at him and leant closer to share a secret. 'Mr Finch was in the shop when I got there. I had to wait for him to leave and as he went he said –' she mimicked Mr Finch's cultured tones – '"I believe you're dining with us tonight," and when Mr Rodwell nodded, Mr Finch said, "Clara is looking forward to it." '

Albert's smile widened, stretching his face more than it been for years. 'Been hengaged for six years or so, they have.'

'Six years!'

Albert chuckled, a wheezing sound. 'Aye. Not one to rush into anything, isn't Percy Rodwell.'

'But six years! I wouldn't wait six years,' Meg declared. 'Not for any man.'

Albert eyed her. 'Shouldn't think you'd 'ave to, mi duck. Have you seen Miss Finch?'

Meg shook her head and Albert chuckled again. 'Well, wait till you do and then you'll see why Percy's in no hurry to tie the knot.'

Laughing, Meg skipped on her way feeling more light-hearted than she had done since the day they had entered the workhouse. She went into the wash house and took off her own clothes. As she dressed once more in the workhouse uniform, she smiled to herself. She wouldn't have to dress in these awful garments for much longer. Soon she would be handling the fine fabrics in Mr Rodwell's shop.

She focused her thoughts on the future and refused to think about her father and Alice. Now she had new hope. Her mother was getting better. Sarah would be sad for a little while about the loss of her baby but soon . . .

Waters was standing in the doorway of the bath

room. 'You'd better come, Meg. Miss Daley is asking to see you.'

'Well, I don't want to see her,' Meg said abruptly.

'I think you should, Meg.'

The girl looked at her in surprise. Waters's tone was kindlier and she had called her Meg. Her attitude was so out of character that Meg was alarmed.

'What is it? What's wrong?' But the woman had turned away and all she said was, 'Miss Daley's in the children's dormitory. You'd better hurry.'

Cold fear clutched at Meg's heart.

Fifteen

Meg ran up the stairs and burst into the dormitory. The children were getting ready for bed, the bigger ones helping the little ones. Meg glanced around wildly, but she could not see her brother.

'Where's Bobbie? And where's Miss Daley?'

She knew some of the children by name now from her brief time spent in the school room. One of the older girls came towards her. 'Miss Daley's in her room.' She pointed to the far end of the dormitory to the room where Meg had looked after the sick child.

'Is she with Betsy?' Meg asked.

The girl shook her head. 'No. Betsy's better. Look, she's in her bed over there.'

Now Meg could see the thin, pale little girl sitting up in bed. Betsy held out her arms towards Meg and tears welled in her eyes. 'Meg,' she called, her voice trembling.

Sighing inwardly, Meg crossed the room to stand by her bed.

'I'm so sorry I caused trouble. I didn't mean to steal the watch. I – I just wanted to hear its tick. It – it reminded me of me dad.'

'It doesn't matter,' Meg said. She had neither the time nor the patience to listen to Betsy. There was only one thing on her mind. 'Do you know where Bobbie is?'

'In there. Miss Daley's looking after him. He's poorly.'

Meg's heart pounded anxiously. She had been right to be fearful. She ran down the long room to the closed door, ignoring Betsy's pleading, 'Meg, say you forgive me . . .'

Meg didn't even knock, but rushed straight into the schoolmistress's bedroom. The room was stifling and Meg's gaze went at once to the bed where Bobbie lay. His face was flushed and though his eyes were closed he was writhing and moaning. His nose was very sore and looked as if it had been bleeding. Miss Daley was bending over him, sponging his face. She glanced round at Meg but all she said when she saw who it was, 'You shouldn't be here. It might be infectious. He's quite sick.'

'What is it? What's the matter?'

'I don't know.'

'Has matron seen him? Have you called the doctor?'

'Meg,' Louisa said gently, 'they don't call the doctor for every minor childish ailment.'

'That's not a minor illness,' Meg said heatedly. 'Just look at him!'

'Well, yes. His pulse is weak, I have to admit, but then children can be terribly sick one minute and fine the next.'

Meg's mouth was a grim line as she whispered, 'If anything happens to our Bobbie, I'll know who to blame, won't I?'

'Meg—' Louisa began, but the girl whirled around and was gone from the room. She had to find her mother.

As she neared the women's day room, Meg could hear her mother's hysterical crying. When she rushed into the room, she saw Sarah in the middle of the room wringing her hands and wailing. The other women were clustered around her, but standing beside her was Isaac Pendleton. He was holding her hand and patting it.

'Now, now, my dear. Don't fret. Matron will take care of little Bobbie. He'll be good hands.'

Catching sight of her daughter, Sarah wailed afresh. 'Meg, oh, Meg. What are we to do? Bobbie's ill.'

'I know. I've seen him.'

Isaac Pendleton looked round, a flash of annoyance in his eyes. 'You had no right to go anywhere near the child. If it's something infectious, we could have an epidemic on our hands.'

'Then why isn't he in the infirmary with the matron?' Meg flashed back.

Surprise flickered briefly across Isaac's face. Before he could open his mouth to refute Meg's statement, she said, 'He's in Miss Daley's room at the end of the dormitory and I don't think the matron has even seen him yet.'

'But I thought—' Isaac began. He looked back at Sarah. 'I thought it was matron who told you.'

Sarah shook her head. 'No, no, it was Waters.'

'Waters! She had no right . . .' He broke off, gave Sarah's hand a final pat and added, 'Leave this to me.' He took hold of Meg's arm roughly and propelled her across the room. 'And you, young lady, had better come with me.'

'Why won't they let me see him?' Sarah wailed. 'I'm his mother.'

Meg glanced back over her shoulder to see that some of the other women in the day room were clustering round her mother and one was putting her arms about

Sarah's shoulders. At least, she thought, her mother was being comforted.

'Where – where are you taking me?' Meg was a little afraid to be alone with the master. He was a strange mixture. One moment he was charming and benevolent, the next a frightening, vengeful figure.

'To see if what you say is true. I've been hearing about you, miss. How you throw folks' kindness in their faces.'

Meg gasped. 'Me? I'd never do that.'

He stopped suddenly and pulled her round to face him. 'Then what's this I hear about you refusing to do the nice little job I found you in the school room? Where's your gratitude for that, eh? I had thought it was that Miss Daley found you unsuitable, but she tells me that it is you who have the gall to refuse to work with her.'

'I—'

'Don't bother trying to drum up some fancy tale.'

'But you don't understand—'

'I understand only too well, my girl. Ungrateful little chit that you are.'

'No, I'm not,' Meg was stung to retort boldly. 'I'm not ungrateful.'

Suddenly his attitude changed and he stood gazing down at her. 'By heck,' he murmured, 'but you're a bonny wench and a fiery one. I'd like to have the taming of you. If only you were older I'd let you show me just how grateful you can be—' He frowned and seemed to shake himself. 'Come along,' he said more briskly, but now the anger had gone from his voice. 'Let's find out what's to do with the little chap and see if we can put your poor mam's mind at rest. She's a bonny little woman, your mam.'

Isaac strode through the children's dormitory and opened the door into Miss Daley's room. Meg peered beneath his arm, her glance going at once towards the bed. But she could not see Bobbie, for now Miss Pendleton was there and bending over him.

'What's to do, then, Letitia?' Isaac boomed. His sister turned an anxious face towards him and Meg caught her breath. There were tears in the matron's eyes.

'I think it could be diphtheria, Isaac. He's very poorly, the poor little mite.'

'Then we must have him moved at once to the infirmary and you must isolate him and yourself, Letitia. There's no other course of action. We don't want an outbreak. The guardians would be most displeased . . .'

The hours dragged by. Darkness fell and supper passed, though Sarah and Meg could eat nothing. The other women were silent, leaving them alone with their worries.

'If only they'd let us see him,' Sarah moaned constantly and Meg bit her lip. Several times, Meg went outside and through the gate into the men's yard to stand in front of the long row of buildings across the yard from the main workhouse. She stared up at the dimly lit windows of the infirmary on the first floor above the bake house. She knew that was where they had taken Bobbie.

On her fifth visit outside, when she had been standing in the darkness for some time, a soft voice spoke behind her in the shadows. 'Meg? Meg, is that you?'

It was Jake. He had slipped out of the men's quarters and along the side of the wall. He was standing near the door into the room at the end of the row. 'Come on. Quick.'

With one last glance up at the windows, Meg ran lightly towards him.

'In here.' Jake took her hand and pulled her into the small room and closed the door. As her eyes became accustomed to the dark, Meg could just make out the shape of three coffins lying across trestles. 'Is there – is there anyone in them?'

'Nah. No one's died lately.'

Meg breathed more easily.

'Now, tell me – what's going on?' Jake whispered.

'It's Bobbie. He's sick and – and they won't let us see him.'

'That's usual, Meg. They won't let any of the mams see their kids, even if they're ill.'

'But if only they'd let Mam go to him. She could nurse him. She needn't mix with the other women until – until he's better again.'

'But that'd mean she didn't work, wouldn't it?'

'She's not working anyway. Not really. She's not well enough yet.'

'There you are then.' He tried to comfort her with common sense. 'They don't want her catching summat, do they?'

'But no one can look after him better than his own mam,' Meg cried passionately.

There was a long silence until Jake mumbled, 'I wouldn't know about that.'

Her mind on Bobbie, Meg didn't notice the sadness in his tone. Instead she said, 'I mean, you'd think they'd be glad of the help. You'd think they'd prefer the mother to look after him instead of the matron having to devote all her time to one child.'

'But it's what Miss Pendleton always does.' Jake paused significantly before adding, 'Specially if it's a little boy.'

'They've not even let us know if the doctor's been,' Meg ranted. Suddenly she made up her mind. 'I can't stand this. I'm going to see the master.'

'Meg . . .' Jake called after her, but she had wrenched open the door and was running across the men's yard. Moments later she was knocking urgently on the master's office. There was no reply, so she rapped again. Nothing.

She hesitated only a moment before running up the stairs to the master's bedroom. Before she could lose her nerve, she knocked on that door and Isaac's voice boomed, 'Come in.'

Meg opened the door and stepped into the room. Immediately, she understood the reason for Isaac's impatience. He was sitting on the sofa before a blazing log fire with his arm along the back of the sofa around a woman, whose head rested on his shoulder. The sound of weeping reached Meg and, as she recognized the woman's dark brown hair, she gasped aloud. 'Mam – what are you doing here?'

Gently, Isaac disentangled himself and stood up. Though irritation still showed in his eyes, he managed to say smoothly, 'Come in, my dear. Come and sit down. We didn't know where to find you.'

'I – I've been in the yard. I was trying to – I wanted to feel as close as I could to Bobbie.'

She moved forwards stiffly and sat down, her gaze going to her mother. But Sarah was sitting hunched up on the sofa, her hands covering her face.

'Mam – what are you doing here?' The sight of her mother with the master's arm around her had disturbed

Meg. But at Isaac's next words any qualms she had about her mother were driven from the girl's mind.

'My dear,' he said in a solemn tone, 'we have bad news, I'm afraid. Little Bobbie died an hour ago.'

Meg felt as if her heart had stopped beating. She began to shiver uncontrollably. 'Oh no, no. Not that. Not Bobbie too.'

Sixteen

They were used to death in the workhouse. It happened to the young as well as in the dormitories for the old and infirm, where death was to be expected. Indeed, many elderly folk, too infirm to work, knew that they were entering the workhouse to die.

And, amongst the young, many were undernourished and weak when they arrived. In such conditions, infectious diseases spread rapidly and there was little care available beyond a perfunctory visit from the doctor and the ministrations of the matron. One whole section of the local cemetery, where paupers were buried, gave testament to this fact. A flat area, broken only by gentle mounds with no marked graves, no headstones erected by loving relatives, spoke of the desperate circumstances of the departed. No one mourned them, no one had cared enough about them in life to give them shelter and now no one cared about them in death.

But Meg cared. She was incensed that her little brother should have been allowed to die. For the first time since the misunderstanding over the watch, Meg sought out Louisa Daley. She found her alone in the classroom before the start of morning lessons.

'You killed him,' she cried passionately. Fists clenched, she stormed towards the young schoolmistress. 'You *let* him die.'

Louisa blanched. She stepped back behind the desk,

trying to put a barrier between herself and the distraught girl. 'Meg, there was nothing that could have been done. It – it was diphtheria. Philip – Dr Collins – said so.'

'Ah yes! Dr Collins!' Meg's eyes blazed. 'Too busy paying court to you to attend to his patients.'

Louisa gasped. 'That's not fair.'

'Not fair? Not *fair*? Is it fair that my poor mam has lost four babies and now her little boy? And I've lost my Bobbie.' Tears threatened to choke her, but anger carried her on. She shook her fist in Louisa's face. 'First, you call me a thief and then you let my brother die. I won't forget this. I swear – one day – I'll make you pay.'

She turned away but then swung back to deliver one last salvo. 'And don't you dare to think of coming to his funeral.'

It was the custom for the matron and the schoolmistress to attend the funeral of any child who had been in their care. But this time Meg made sure that Louisa Daley knew she was not wanted.

Sarah and Meg stood beside each other after the brief and soulless committal of the pathetically small rough wooden coffin into the cold earth. Only one other person attended the brief service held at the graveside: the matron. She stood on the opposite side of the deep hole, holding a handkerchief to her face.

'Another of my little boys gone,' she wept.

Meg wanted to shout: *He wasn't yours. He was ours. Mam's and mine*. But she said nothing. The woman's sorrow was genuine and, strangely, the fact that someone else was grieving for little Bobbie seemed to comfort Sarah. It was she who stepped around the grave and took Letitia's arm to lead her gently away. Poor Sarah had become so used to heartache in her life that she expected it now.

With one last glance down into the grave, Meg whispered, 'Goodnight, my darling little brother. Sleep tight.' It was what she'd always said to him when she'd tucked him in bed at night. She was heartsore that even that small, loving action had been denied to her, and to Sarah too, during the past few weeks. Only the matron – or Louisa Daley – had had that privilege. Meg turned away, tears blurring her vision, and stumbled after the two women.

It was only then that she remembered. Today was her sixteenth birthday.

On their return to the workhouse, Jake was hovering near the gate leading from the men's yard into the women's.

Letitia put her arm around him and hugged him to her, even though he was as tall as she was now. Her little Jake. She'd cared for him since the day he was born. She wouldn't lose him. Jake would always be with her. 'What are you doing here, Jake? If the master sees you—'

'Sorry, Matron, but – but—' He nodded towards Meg and her mother, now crossing the yard towards the back door into the women's quarters. 'I wanted to see how Meg and her mam were.'

Letitia shook her head. 'Ah, poor souls.' She glanced across the yard and then up to the windows of her brother's rooms. Then she smiled at the anxious boy in front of her. 'You're a good boy, Jake.' She patted his cheek and seemed to come to a swift decision. 'I know. Walk across the yard with me. You can have a few minutes with the lass just inside the back door. If he sees you with me, he'll not say anything.'

Jake grinned at her. 'You're a diamond, Matron.'

The woman's round cheeks flushed and for a moment tears sparkled in her eyes. Then she smiled fondly. 'And you're a rogue, Jake Bosley. You know how to twist me round your little finger, don't you? Always have done.' But she turned and walked across the yard, Jake falling into step beside her. 'Now, don't let me down,' she murmured as they walked. 'Only a few minutes, mind.'

The two young people were left alone just inside the back entrance.

'You all right?' Jake asked softly. Meg nodded, unable to speak for a moment.

'And – and your mam?'

Meg sighed. 'Sad. We both are. But—'

'What?' Jake pressed gently.

'It was funny, really. Miss Pendleton seemed even more upset than us.'

Jake shrugged. 'She always is when one of the little ones dies.'

There was silence between them until Jake asked hesitantly, 'Shall you – shall you try to find yer dad again? To tell him about Bobbie, I mean?'

Meg gave an explosive snort. 'No, I shan't. He doesn't care about us. Any of us. Made that plain, hasn't he? I don't care if I never set eyes on him again.'

'I just thought – well – he is Bobbie's dad and I thought he ought to know.'

Meg thrust her face close to Jake's. 'He doesn't deserve to know anything,' she hissed. 'And if you want me an' you to go on being friends, then shut up about him. As far as I'm concerned, I haven't got a dad. Not any more.'

Jake blinked at her vitriolic words. Then, despite himself, he grinned. 'By, no wonder you're a redhead. Fiery, aren't yer?'

But Meg could not share his attempt at fun. She glowered at him. 'Yeah, I'm fiery. Looks like I'm going to have to be to get anywhere in this world. I'm on me own now, aren't I?'

'You've still got yer mam.' The wistfulness in his tone was lost on Meg, who was too wrapped up in her own tragedies. She pulled a face. 'By the look of things, it's going to be me looking after her, not the other way about.'

Jake gave a weak smile and shuffled his feet in embarrassment. 'You – you can count on me, Meg. I'll always be there for you.'

Meg stared at him for a moment and then softened enough to touch his arm and say huskily, 'Thanks, Jake, but let's face it, you don't know much about the world outside these walls, do yer? And I'm damned if I'm staying in the workhouse the rest of me life.'

Jake squared his shoulders and puffed out his thin chest as far as he could. 'Neither am I,' he declared boldly. 'I've talked to Ron and I'm off to see the mester at the farm come Monday. And if he teks me on, Ron says I can move in with him and his family in the little cottage—' He stopped suddenly, appalled to realize that he was talking about Meg's former home. 'Oh, I'm sorry.'

'Don't be,' she said harshly. 'Look after yourself, Jake.' She smiled wistfully as she added, 'Try and get the little room above the kitchen. It was mine and it was always warm from the chimney above the range. And – and think of me.' She turned away to run up the stairs, her hobnailed boots clattering on the stone steps.

Jake gazed after her. 'Oh, I will, Meg,' he whispered, even though she could not hear him. 'I'll think of you all the time.'

Meg was waiting outside Mr Rodwell's tailor's shop well before opening time the following Monday. It was a wet morning and cool for July. The wind whistled round the corner, making her shiver. She hopped from one foot to the other, trying to keep warm, and was thankful when at last she saw a figure hurrying up the street, his umbrella held low in front of him against the driving rain. He didn't see her until he was almost at the door and lifted his umbrella, searching in his pocket for the keys to his shop.

'Ah, there you are,' Percy said.

'Yes, sir. Here I am.'

'Dear me, you must be soaked. Come in quickly . . .' He fumbled with the keys, dropping them to the ground in his haste. Meg bent and picked them up, handing them to him with a smile. She was about to say: *Don't worry about me, Mr Rodwell. I'm used to working out in all weathers. A bit of rain doesn't bother me.* But then she thought better of it. Instead, she smiled shyly. 'It's very kind of you to be so concerned, Mr Rodwell.'

At last he got the door open and held it for her to step inside ahead of him. 'Have you been waiting long?'

'A bit,' she said, as if reluctant to admit it. 'I didn't want to be late.'

'Very commendable, my dear,' Percy said, a smile creasing his thin face. 'But I don't like to think of you standing in the cold waiting for me.'

He moved about the shop opening the window blinds and letting in what early-morning light there was on this dull day. Then he beckoned her to the back of the shop and ushered her through a door and into his workroom. Meg glanced about her.

The place was very untidy. Bits of fabric were scattered all over the floor. A length of cloth, marked with chalk lines, lay on the long table with a huge pair of scissors waiting to be used. A yardstick and measuring tapes were thrown down haphazardly and cottons and threads were heaped on a shelf nearby. A tailor's dummy stood in one corner, draped with a half-finished jacket, and at one end of the table was a Singer sewing machine, the gold lettering gleaming against the black of the machine.

Before she stopped to think, Meg cried out, 'Oh, you've got a sewing machine!'

'Er – well – yes,' Percy murmured. 'The tools of my trade, you know.' He cleared his throat. 'Now, first of all, I must light the stove. I like it lit most days – even in summer. This is a cold building and I like my customers to have a feeling of warmth when they step into the shop.'

Meg had noticed the stove in the back corner of the shop as she had walked through. It was similar to the one at the workhouse, which she had learnt how to light and keep stoked.

'I'll do that for you, Mr Rodwell,' she offered, taking off her outdoor coat.

He glanced doubtfully at the white cotton blouse she was wearing. She had ironed it so carefully the previous evening. 'It's a very dirty job,' he warned.

Meg smiled sweetly at him and was gratified when Percy blinked rapidly. 'I brought my apron just in case,' she told him. 'And I'll be sure to roll my sleeves up.'

'Well, if you're sure, it would be a help. I have to

admit,' he confided, 'it's a job I hate doing. My hands get so rough and then – when I have to work . . .' He gestured towards the table and the tailor's dummy.

Meg nodded. 'I understand. You must keep your hands nice.' She glanced around. 'Just tell me where I can find paper, kindling and coal.'

Percy gestured towards a door at the far end of the workshop. 'That leads into a backyard, Miss – er – Kirkland. The coal store is out there and you'll find all you need.' He seemed about to say more, but then glanced away from her. 'Please – er – have a look around while you're out there. So – so that you know where everything is.'

Meg opened the back door and stepped outside. On either side high walls separated the tailor's backyard from the next-door premises. To the left would be the ironmonger's, Meg realized, and on the right – by the appetizing smell that was already wafting over the wall – there must be a bakery. Immediately to her left in the yard was a wooden lean-to used as a scullery. As Meg pushed open the door, it scraped on the dusty floor. *The whole place wants a good scrub*, she said to herself and couldn't prevent a wry smile as she thought of Mrs Smallwood's face if she were to see this place. Meg's smile faded. She didn't want to be reminded of the past – not any of it.

At the end of the yard were two doors into brick-built outbuildings and a gate in the wall, which led into the alley running between the backyards of this street and the next. One door was the coal store. The other, Meg found, was the privy. Now she understood Mr Rodwell's suggestion that she should familiarize herself with the premises. He had been too shy to tell her directly where the privy was, but knew she would find it for herself. She smiled as she picked up newspaper, kindling and a bucket of coal and returned to the shop.

'Find everything?' Percy enquired, hovering near the stove.

'Yes thank you, sir,' she said, demurely dropping her eyes and making no reference to the delicate matter of the whereabouts of the privy.

'Good, good,' Percy said, rubbing his long-fingered hands together. 'I'll – erm—' He paused, not quite knowing what to do with himself now that Meg had taken over his usual first task of the morning. 'I'll sort out the money for the drawer.'

Very soon Meg had a good fire going in the stove and the shop began to feel warmer. She washed her hands in the tiny scullery and hung up her apron on a hook behind the door, pulled down her sleeves, smoothed her hair in the cracked mirror on the wall and went back inside.

The first customer of the day had entered the shop and was standing in front of the counter talking to Mr Rodwell. Meg went to stand behind the counter, keeping a discreet distance from both Mr Rodwell and his male customer. But she was close enough to do his bidding should he need her. She waited patiently until the satisfied customer left the shop, a parcel under his arm.

Mr Rodwell turned and smiled at her over his steel-rimmed spectacles. 'Well done, Miss Kirkland.'

Meg glanced back at the fire. 'It's quite an easy stove to light,' she said. 'Not so temperamental as the one at the—'

'Now, now, there's no need for us to mention – ahem – where you are obliged to reside at this moment in time. No need at all.'

'You're very kind, Mr Rodwell.'

There was a pause before Percy added, 'Actually, I wasn't referring to the fire at all. No, I meant you were right to wait quietly whilst I served my customer. It was well done, my dear. Very well done indeed.'

Now Meg lifted her face and gave Mr Rodwell the full benefit of her most dazzling smile.

Seventeen

Later in the morning, when the shop was empty, Percy cleared his throat and said tentatively, 'I – erm – heard about your loss. Your little brother. Miss Pendleton called in on Saturday and she told me. I was very sorry to hear it.' He glanced at her, his pale eyes sympathetic behind his spectacles.

Meg wanted to ask what the matron had said about her. Had she given her a good reference? But at the mention of her brother, tears filled her eyes. She only had to think of little Bobbie and the tears came all too readily. There was no need for pretence now – her grief was all too genuine. 'Thank you,' she said huskily.

'I – erm – would have quite understood if you'd needed a few more days before starting your employment with me.'

Meg shook her head firmly. 'No – thank you – it's very thoughtful of you, but it's best to keep busy.'

'I just thought that perhaps your mother might need you . . .' Percy's voice trailed away.

'There are plenty of people at the – plenty of people *there* to comfort her.' For some reason that Meg could not quite understand, the vision of Isaac Pendleton with his arm around her mother's shoulders flashed into her mind. The picture made her feel uncomfortable.

Percy was nodding. 'Quite so,' he murmured. 'But

it's not quite like having a member of your own family close by, is it?'

Carefully, Meg rolled fabric back onto a bolt of cloth that Percy had had on the counter to show to a customer. Meg took a deep breath. In control of her emotions once more and now pretending innocence, she asked, 'Have you any family, Mr Rodwell?'

'What?' He was startled as if he was unused to having anyone ask personal questions. 'Who? Me? Oh well, no, not really. I – erm – did have once. Of course I did. But I was an only child and since my parents died there has been no one.'

Now Meg feigned surprise, even though she knew the answer well enough. 'You mean – you're not married?'

Percy blinked rapidly, took off his spectacles, polished them vigorously with a tiny cloth he carried in his waistcoat pocket and then perched them back on his nose. 'Oh, dear me, no. Certainly not. Well, that is to say, I – erm – may one day decide to – erm – embark upon the sea of matrimony.' He shook his head. 'But it's a big step. A very big step.'

Meg smiled coyly. 'Well, she'd be a very lucky lady to have you as a husband, Mr Rodwell.'

Percy blinked again.

During the hour the shop was closed for lunch, Percy explained his reasons for wanting to employ a female assistant. 'I've found it increasingly difficult to do my work in the back room and look after the shop too. Interruptions, you know. If I have to stop the machine in the middle of a long seam, it can spoil it completely.'

Meg smiled and nodded. Percy Rodwell was obviously

a perfectionist in his work if not in the cleanliness and tidiness of his premises. But if he let her stay . . .

He was speaking again. 'And I want to expand – well – alter things round a bit. It was Miss Finch's idea that I should stock women's apparel. She suggested that I should make the right-hand side of the shop into the ladies' section, whilst this side –' he waved his arms about, demonstrating – 'should stay as the men's.'

Meg glanced around her. 'Are you going to put a counter this side too? For me . . .' She hesitated then, with a coy tilt to her head, went on, 'I mean – for your assistant to serve at?'

'Yes, yes, that's a very good idea.' He was all enthusiasm. 'Miss Pinkerton . . .' He broke off to ask, 'Do you know Miss Pinkerton?'

Meg shook her head.

'She's a dressmaker and milliner. She lives in a little cottage just by the church, near where I live, actually. Well, she has always made garments for Clara – Miss Finch – and my fiancée has persuaded her to make dresses and costumes – even coats – to order for me.'

'And hats?'

'Oh yes, eventually, hats too, I'm sure.'

'Ladies like nice hats,' Meg volunteered and again Percy's pale eyes rested thoughtfully upon her.

About mid-afternoon, a woman entered the shop. Meg looked up and smiled, ready to offer her services and eager to show Mr Rodwell what she could do. But Percy hurried forward at once, his hands outstretched towards the woman. 'My dear, I'm so glad you've called. There's someone I'd like you to meet.' He put his arm around the woman without actually touching her, but shepherding her towards the counter, where Meg was standing. 'My dear, this is Miss Kirkland. She's – erm – on trial for a month and I am proposing to train her to serve the – erm – ladies' items I am planning to stock.' Now he smiled at Meg. 'Miss Kirkland, this is Miss Finch.'

Meg smiled and bobbed a respectful curtsy. In a quiet, demure voice, she said, 'I'm honoured to make your acquaintance, Miss Finch.' *So this*, Meg was thinking, *is Miss Clara Finch, Mr Rodwell's fiancée and Miss Pendleton's friend.* Meg had expected Mr Rodwell's fiancée to be a pretty young woman, slim and dressed in fashionable clothes with a sweet smile and adoring eyes when she looked up at her intended. But the woman before her was nothing like Meg's romantic imaginings. Clara Finch was thin and angular with cold grey eyes, a beak-like nose and a small, pursed mouth. She was dressed in a dark purple costume that admittedly was well made and expensive, but it was drab and unbecoming. The woman – *she must be forty if she's a day*, Meg thought – carried her hands folded neatly in front of her at waist height. Meg felt Clara's hard gaze appraising her. When she spoke, Clara's tone was shrill and sharp, her words clipped. 'I don't know why you wanted a woman working here at all, Percy. Haven't I promised to help you out now and then if you need it? And you most certainly don't want –' she nodded at Meg with a swift pecking movement of her head – 'a young girl and one from *that place*.' The last two words were spoken scathingly.

Meg felt the colour rising into her face, but defiantly she lifted her chin. Though her green eyes sparked with anger she kept her tone submissive and courteous. 'My family have fallen on hard times, ma'am, through no fault of their own.'

Mentally, she crossed her fingers, praying that Miss Finch did not know the truth about their misfortune. But Mr Finch was a crony of Mr Smallwood's. They went to the race meeting together . . .

Meg's heart fell as she saw the gleam of malice in Miss Finch's eyes. 'Indeed?' Clara said, her tone laced with sarcasm. 'That's not what I heard.'

Beside her, Percy began to fidget. 'Oh, now come, my dear, all that is merely idle gossip and speculation.'

Clara whipped round to face him, making Percy blink rapidly. 'Percy, I have never indulged in idle gossip. You should know me better than that.'

'Of course, my dear. I'm sorry, I did not mean to imply—'

A little mollified, she nodded. 'Very well.' Then she turned her attention back to Meg. 'Your father, girl, brought shame to a decent, well-brought up young woman, Alice Smallwood, besides causing his family to become an expense on the parish.' She leant across the counter, closer to Meg. 'Your father, girl, should be horsewhipped.'

Meg stood her ground and returned the woman's gaze steadily. 'I entirely agree with you, ma'am. And I'd cheer on any person who cared to do it.'

Now it was Miss Finch who looked startled and, for a brief moment, nonplussed. But she recovered herself quickly and took refuge in finding fault. 'You are too bold, miss. You have too much to say for yourself.' She turned to her fiancé. 'If you want my opinion, Percy, you'd do better to look elsewhere for your counter assistant. Someone more mature would be far more suitable.'

'Oh, but Clara – my dear – Miss Pendleton herself

recommended the girl. I thought – she being your friend – that you would approve.'

Clara sniffed dismissively. 'Letitia Pendleton would like to class herself as my friend, but I have no wish to be associated with such a person. She has tried before to ally herself to my family. But it won't work. Oh, dear me, no. No, Percy, be guided by me. The ladies you hope to attract to your establishment would much prefer an older person to serve them and someone more refined. This girl was nothing but a milkmaid. What can she hope to know about fine fabrics and the kind of garments that *ladies* wear?'

Percy blinked. He glanced in embarrassment towards Meg and then took hold of Clara's arm and drew her away from the counter. He leant closer to her to whisper, but Meg's sharp ears still caught his words. 'But my dear, the child has suffered most grievously. The family was turned out of their home. Oh, I know, I know, he – the father – no doubt deserved it, but it is hardly his poor wife's fault, is it? And certainly this girl is not to blame. You've heard for yourself how bitter she is. And worse than that, the mother lost the child she was expecting and only this week the little boy died in the – in the – in *that place*.'

Clara's eyes shifted towards Meg and then widened. 'What of?'

'What?' Percy was mystified.

'What of? What did the boy die of?'

Percy shrugged. 'I don't know . . .' Now they both gazed at Meg.

Meg bit her lip. She knew only too well that her brother had died of diphtheria, but would Miss Pendleton and her brother want the fact known? An epidemic in the workhouse was something to be feared. Already there were two more suspected cases amongst the children, but the matron had isolated them at once and Dr Collins visited daily. But Meg didn't want Mr Rodwell or Miss Finch to hear about it any more than Isaac wanted it known beyond the workhouse walls. She faced them squarely. 'I don't know. You'd have to ask the doctor – or the matron.'

'Well, I hope it was nothing infectious, girl,' Clara said and took a step backwards. 'I think I'll be going, Percy. I'll see you tonight.'

'Thank you, my dear. I shall look forward to it.'

'Don't be late. Theobald hates unpunctuality.'

As the shop bell tinkled at her departure, Meg busied herself with tidying the shelves. She could not trust herself to meet Percy's eyes. She knew her runaway tongue was in danger of saying far more than it ought to.

The work was not as physically hard as farm work and yet, for some reason, Meg found it very tiring. Maybe it was having to be quiet and polite all day long, with a smile permanently plastered on her face. She was constantly alert, trying to anticipate Mr Rodwell's every need. There was so much to learn, much more than she had ever dreamed. All the different garments, the different sizes, different fabrics and qualities. And when the new stock began to arrive – stock that was new even to Percy and something of a mystery to him – Meg was busier than ever. He was already looking to her to take charge of it. To price it and put it away. Even to display it, although he was still embarrassed to have ladies' undergarments on show. A new counter had been installed on the right-hand side of the shop and all the drawers and shelves behind were given over to women's wear. Meg lost count of the number of times she climbed the stairs to the cluttered rooms above the shop to dump piles of men's vests, long johns, socks and shirts to make room for the ladies' garments. But at least now she could see the rooms on the first floor for herself. She had been right; they were only used as storerooms and untidy, higgledy-piggledy storerooms at that! They weren't even proper stockrooms, Meg realized. Oh, she'd taken plenty of old stock up, but she had never once seen Percy bring anything down into the shop. The rooms were just a dumping ground for rubbish, she was sure.

She would ask him, Meg determined, if she could tidy the rooms out, give them a good clean and sort out all the stock. If she worked hard and pleased him, he would take her on permanently as his assistant and then she could ask him if she and her mother might live above the shop. She would tell him how much better it would be to have someone living on the premises. She could light the stove before he even arrived. She could sweep and dust and clean the shop after it closed. He wouldn't have to stay late at night to do these tasks, as she knew he often did.

Percy was speaking to her, dragging her back from her plans. 'When you serve the customers, Miss Kirkland, you must let them know – delicately, of course – that we now stock such – erm – items.' He waved his hand towards the drawers containing ladies' underwear.

Meg smiled to herself and was crafty enough not to explain every little detail about the new stock to her employer. The less he knew about ladies' apparel the more he would need to rely upon her.

She was enjoying the work, but every night her head whirled until it ached with all the information she had tried to absorb. And there were still chores in the workhouse awaiting her at night.

On the Saturday evening at the end of her third week working in the tailor's shop, Meg trudged wearily home. *Home!* she thought in disgust as the huge building loomed out of the dusk. *Fancy having to call the workhouse 'home'*. They had been in the workhouse now for almost seven weeks and Meg was even more desperate to leave it than she had been when they had first been admitted. Then she had truly believed that they would only be there for a few days at the most.

'If I ever meet up with him again,' she vowed, thinking of her father, who had caused all this, 'I'll kill him. And *her*.'

She still wasn't sure which betrayal hurt her the most: her father's or her friend's.

But tonight, as she opened the gate into the yard, her steps quickened. Something was banishing her tiredness and unhappy thoughts. She couldn't wait to tell her mother. She had left the shop that evening, calling, 'Goodnight,' to Mr Rodwell and leaving him to close up. In the street she had paused for a moment to glance up at the windows above the shop. If they were all cleared out, as she planned, there was plenty of room for her and her mother to live up there. She hugged the idea to herself, feeling more positive and hopeful than she had for weeks. As she hurried through the workhouse gate and across the yard, she was vaguely aware of someone calling her name. But, intent on sharing her wonderful idea with her mother, she paid no heed and ran inside and up the steps into the women's day room.

'Mam,' she cried, flinging open the door. 'Mam,

where are you? I've had the most marvellous idea. If only . . .'

She stopped, hesitating in the doorway as her gaze swept around the room. Several faces turned towards her, others did not look up, and Meg had the strange feeling that it was deliberate. No one spoke.

'Where is she? Where's my mam?' she asked of no one in particular. Now everyone lowered their gaze and turned away. Only one woman stood up and stumbled across the room towards her.

Ursula Waters stood before her. Her thin, bony hands clasped Meg's shoulders, her fingers digging painfully into the girl's flesh. Young and strong, Meg quickly shook her off.

'You ask where she is?' Ursula shrieked, her eyes wild, spittle showering Meg's face. 'As if you didn't know. You've planned it, I bet. You're a scheming little hussy and she's no better than she should be.'

'Waters, I don't know what you're on about.'

But Ursula continued to scream at her, tears now coursing down her thin, lined cheeks. 'Fancy, a mother who's just lost her child, two, if you count the miscarriage. And look at her now. Carrying on like a common trollop off the streets. I felt sorry for her. I did. I did. But not any more. Oh, not any more.'

Now it was Meg who gripped the woman's shoulders firmly. 'Waters, I don't know what you're talking about. Just tell me – where is my mam?'

Waters's face contorted into an ugly grimace. 'With *him*,' she spat. 'With the master.'

Meg blinked, still unable to understand why Ursula was so upset. 'She's gone to see him, you mean? What about? Is something wrong?'

'Oho, there's something wrong all right, but not the

way you mean,' Ursula said bitterly. 'Oh no, everything's all right for her. Very "all right" now.'

'I don't understand.'

'She's gone to him.'

'Yes, you said that, but—'

'Moved in with him. Moved her belongings into his room. She's – she's *with* him. Your mother is Mr Pendleton's new – new *fancy woman.*'

Eighteen

Meg's mouth dropped open and she stared at the woman in front of her in horror. 'Wha– what do you mean?'

Ursula's lip curled. 'You know exactly what I mean! A girl of your age and brought up on a farm too. Oh, don't play the innocent with me.'

Vaguely, Meg heard a movement behind her. Someone else had come into the room, but she hardly noticed. She was so caught up by the terrible things this vindictive woman was saying about her mother. 'But – but my mam would never – she wouldn't . . .' Meg was incensed. Her green eyes blazed and she raised her hand as if to strike Ursula. But before the blow could land, someone standing behind her caught hold of her wrist and held it fast.

'Don't, Meg.' Jake's voice was soft in her ear. 'It'll cause you more trouble. Come away. Leave her.'

Meg struggled against his grasp, but Jake held on grimly. He put his arm about her waist and dragged her bodily from the room, whilst Meg still shouted and cursed at Ursula. She shook her fist. 'You wicked, evil woman to say such things. I'll – I'll . . .' But she could think of nothing bad enough to threaten.

'Come away, Meg,' Jake urged, all the while pulling her out of the room. Once in the passageway, he pulled the door shut and leant against it, barring her way back inside. 'Just calm down, will yer?' He spoke firmly now. 'And I'll explain it all.'

'What is there to explain? She's got it wrong. My mam wouldn't . . .' She fell silent, her mouth open. She squinted in the half-light of the passageway to see Jake's face more clearly. His expression was sober, pitying almost. 'She wouldn't . . .' she protested again, but now her voice was feeble and cold uncertainty was stealing over her. She shivered and Jake drew her close. Her head resting on his shoulder, neither of them caring for once who saw them, Jake whispered, 'What she says is true.' As he said the words Meg stiffened and would have pushed away from him, but he held her firmly. 'Not – not perhaps like she's making it sound. That dried-up old prune is jealous. That's what's the matter with her. Just 'cos your mam is young and pretty and old Isaac is taken with her. Who can blame him, eh?'

Now Meg sobbed against his neck and clung to him. 'Oh, Jake, it's not true, is it? She wouldn't – couldn't – take up with a man like Mr Pendleton.' She paused and then added in a pitiful tone that tore at the boy's heart, 'Could she?'

Jake stroked her hair tenderly. 'Isaac likes the ladies. Always has. But he's kind to 'em. Even when he – well – when he moves on to the next, he sees that they're well cared for. He finds them a job in the town or even a job here.'

Slowly Meg raised her head and looked at him. Her mind was working again. 'You mean – that Waters was once – you know?' It was what the woman herself had implied, but Meg hadn't believed it possible.

Jake nodded. 'It was before I can remember, but that's what they say. After, he tried to set her up with a nice little job in the town. Working in a little shop, they said. Ever such a nice, genteel sort of job, but she wouldn't go. She wanted to stay here in the workhouse. Can you believe it?'

Meg swallowed and said huskily, 'Yes, yes, I can. I see it all now. I see why she's – she's so bitter. She still loves him and it must hurt her to see him take up with younger women.' She felt a fleeting pity for the lonely spinster. Then another thought struck her. 'But I thought Mr Pendleton had his eye on *her* . . .' She couldn't bring herself to say Louisa Daley's name but there was no need, for Jake laughed softly. 'The school-marm, you mean?'

Meg nodded.

'Oh aye, well he had. But the young doctor's got in there first and I 'spect old Isaac doesn't want to upset him. Dr Collins does the workhouse quite a few favours. He attends folk here without sending in a bill a lot of the time, but I reckon it's because he can see Miss Daley when he visits.'

Meg sighed and shook her head. 'It's all too much for me. I can't take it in. Me mam. How could she? How *could* she?' She shuddered at the thought of her mother lying beside Isaac Pendleton in his bed. 'It's disgusting. *She's* disgusting.'

'Aw, don't be like that, Meg. Your mam must be feeling so bad, what with losing her baby, then her little lad . . .' Jake bit his lip, not wanting to refer directly to her father's desertion, yet the thought was in both their minds. 'And Isaac will be kind to her. He's a good man, really.'

'How can you say that after the way he beat you? That was cruel.'

Jake shrugged. He had known no other life than within the walls of the workhouse. He had no means of comparison. 'I've sometimes thought he's a bit harder on me than the other lads, but then –' he grinned – 'I'm more trouble to him than they are. And I've always got the matron on my side.'

'She likes you,' Meg murmured absentmindedly, her mind still in a tumult of emotions concerning her own problems. 'She's not what I imagined the matron in the workhouse would be. I thought she'd be horrible. More like Waters.'

'Aw, come on, Meg. Poor old Waters is an unhappy woman.'

Meg stared at him. 'How is it,' she asked slowly, 'that you seem so – so sensible and – and knowing, when you've never hardly been outside the workhouse?'

Jake tweaked her nose playfully. 'I've always kept mi eyes and mi ears open. I've met lots of fellers in here and they all had a story to tell and they've liked talking to me. About their lives, their families and how they'd come to be in here. Well, I listened, Meg, and I learned. I learned a bit of readin' and writin' in the school room but I learned a lot more about life by listening to them fellers.' Now his ready smile widened. 'And now I'm not going to be here for much longer. That's why I came looking for you, to tell you.'

Meg suddenly realized that Jake should have been nowhere near the women's quarters. His news must be important for him to take such a risk.

'I've got that job on Smallwood's farm. I start on Monday.' His eyes were shining. 'Only one more day, Meg, and I'm out of here. And it's all thanks to you. If you hadn't taken me out wi' you that day, I might have been stuck in here for the rest of mi life. But now I'm getting out and I ain't coming back. Not ever.'

Meg felt a lump in her throat that had nothing to do

with the news about her mother. She touched his shoulder. 'I'm glad, Jake. Real glad for you. But I'll miss you.'

He laughed aloud. 'Oh, you'll still be seeing me. I'll be down to that there shop you're working in to get the mester there to mek me mi first proper suit. You see if I don't.'

Meg couldn't bring herself to seek out her mother. She didn't want to speak to her or even see her. And she certainly didn't want to encounter Isaac Pendleton. That night she lay in the narrow bed in the women's dormitory. The empty bed beside her, where her mother had slept, taunted her. Meg stared into the darkness, listening to the breathing, snores, even murmurings of the other women in the room. Sometime during the early hours of the morning she must have dozed fitfully, but when it was time to get up she awoke with a blinding headache. She was sorry it was Sunday. She wanted nothing more than to escape to the sanctuary of the tailor's shop. But she had to endure the glances and the whisperings of the other women, the long walk into the town to morning service and another long, restless night.

Unable to face breakfast on the Monday morning, she was about to slip out of the gate when she heard Albert's voice.

''Morning, lass. Now, you weren't going off wi'out saying ta-ta to me, were you?'

Meg sighed inwardly and turned to face the old man limping towards her. She tried to smile, opened her mouth to speak, but before she could utter a word, he said, 'Aw, lass, what's wrong? You ill?'

Meg bit her lip and shook her head. 'No,' she said huskily. 'I didn't sleep too well.'

'Ah!' was all the old man said, but somehow he managed to put such a depth of understanding into that one sound that Meg's eyes filled with tears. Impatiently, she dashed them away with the back of her hand, determined not to let anyone see her cry. At least, anyone other than Jake.

She glanced at Albert and saw the sympathy in the old man's rheumy eyes. 'You – you know, don't you?'

Albert nodded.

Bitterly, Meg said, 'I suppose everyone knows.'

'Aye well, you can't keep secrets, lass, in a place like this. But look at it this way, yer mam'll be well looked after. I'll say that for 'im, if he teks to a young woman, he treats 'em well, treats 'em fair. And I'll tell you summat else an' all, he doesn't cast 'em aside when he's done wi' 'em either. He sets 'em up in some nice little job that should see them all right for the rest of their days, so to speak.'

'That's what Jake said,' Meg murmured.

'Well, 'e's right.'

Meg bit her lip, but the words would not be held in. 'But it's the shame, Albert. How could she? My *mother*? That's not how she's always brought us—' She pulled in a shuddering breath when the appalling truth hit her. She was now the only child left. 'It's not how she's always brought *me* up to behave.'

'No, lass, I don't expect she did. But life has dealt her a lot of bitter blows lately, hasn't it? She's down there –' he pointed towards the ground – 'in the depths of despair and old Pendleton can be very kind when he wants to be.'

Meg turned away. They all seemed to be on Isaac

Pendleton's side. No one seemed to understand how she felt. But she answered Albert politely. 'Thank you for talking to me, Albert.'

'Tha's all right, lass. Any time.'

As she walked away from the shadow of the workhouse towards the town, the young girl's mind was in a turmoil. She could scarcely take in all that had happened. And she still couldn't believe what they were saying about her mother.

Her little family had been hard-working, honest, trustworthy and loving towards one another. And now, in the space of only a few weeks, her father had deserted them for a pretty face and a flighty nature. Because of his betrayal, not only of his family, but of his employers too, they had lost their home and their livelihood and faced the shame of the workhouse. Another baby had been lost and then poor little Bobbie had died. Yet Meg knew she could have faced all that if only she still had her mother. But what Sarah had done was beyond forgiveness. Meg had felt bitter and unforgiving towards her father, but it was nothing compared to how she now felt about her mother.

As she neared the shop and saw Mr Rodwell opening up the door, Meg made herself a promise. *I'll see mi mam tonight and, if it's true what they're saying, then that's it. I don't want anything to do with her ever again.*

And I'll tell her so.

Nineteen

Meg worked hard that day, throwing herself into each task with a kind of desperation. She was aware of Percy's anxious glances and knew he could sense that something was not quite right. But he said nothing; perhaps he thought the cause was 'women's troubles', a subject far too delicate for any man, especially a bachelor, to approach.

Meg worked on, never pausing to give herself time to think, to dwell on the hardships and disappointments life was throwing at her. The only person she spared a brief thought for was Jake, but even thinking of him starting his new job at the farm revived her own bitter memories. She unpacked all the new stock as it arrived and arranged it. She dressed the right-hand window, which Percy had now given over to ladies' wear. She stayed on long after the shop had closed to sweep and tidy up and she even made a start on the storerooms above, in the hope that she could persuade Percy to let the rooms to her. If only she had a proper home for her mam to come to, she was sure that she could persuade Sarah to leave Isaac Pendleton. Meg still hadn't given up hope entirely.

'There's a lot of stuff up there, Mr Rodwell. Is it to be thrown out?'

'Oh, dear me, no. I couldn't throw any of it away. I mean, someone might ask for something one day . . .'

Despite her inner unhappiness, Meg found herself smiling. When pigs might fly, she thought, but said demurely, 'How about offering some of the things for sale at less money? I mean, you could even put some in the window showing the marked-down price. You know how the farmers who come into the town on market day love a bargain. And they're not the sort to want fancy clothes.' She giggled mischievously and her green eyes twinkled at him. 'Some of those long johns I've carted upstairs to the storerooms are just what the old farmers still wear. I used to see Mr Smallwood's hanging on the line on wash day.'

Percy stared at her. 'Do you know, Miss Kirkland, I think you could be right. How clever of you to think of it. We'll do it. Yes – yes – we'll do it.'

Late in the afternoon the shop bell clanged and Meg looked up, hoping that it was a female customer for her to serve. In spite of her own worries, she really enjoyed serving in the shop, guiding the customers towards their purchases, giving an honest appraisal, handing out compliments when something was just right, a tactful, 'Perhaps you might like to try this instead . . .' when something really didn't suit.

'Always try to be honest with your customers, but do it in such a way that they hardly notice that you're really saying, "That looks absolutely dreadful and I wouldn't let you walk out of my shop wearing it in a hundred years,"' Percy had taught her. It had made her laugh when he had said it. Today she didn't feel like laughing, but she plastered a welcoming smile on to her face as she glanced up to see who had entered the shop.

Her smile faded when she saw Clara Finch advancing towards the counter, her hands folded neatly in front of her, her lips pursed to nothingness.

'My dear,' Percy greeted her, hurrying out from behind his counter. 'What a nice surprise.'

'I don't think it will be, Percy, when I've said my piece.'

Percy gave a nervous laugh. 'Oh dear, that sounds ominous. What have I done now?' His tone was jovial and yet Meg had the feeling that there was a hint of truth in his statement, as if he often did things that displeased his fiancée.

'It's not so much what *you've* done, Percy, but you are perhaps guilty of a lapse in common sense.'

He looked perplexed. Miss Finch's gaze was fixed on Meg's face and slowly Percy followed suit. Under their scrutiny, Meg could not prevent the colour rising into her face, but she lifted her chin defiantly and stared back at the woman.

'Look at her, Percy. Just look at that bold, brazen look. My goodness, girl, you've a lot to learn. But, if I have any say in the matter, you won't be learning it in this establishment. Oh, dear me, no.'

'Clara, my dear, whatever's the matter? And what has it to do with Miss Kirkland?'

'I've just had a visit from Miss Pendleton.' The lips pursed even tighter. 'The wretched woman seems to think that she has some right to be called a friend of the family, when really –' she broke off and muttered – 'but that's another matter.' She cleared her throat and said loudly, 'My brother has some standing in the community and I pride myself too that I am a respectable, God-fearing woman—'

'My dear, of course you are. Who could doubt that fact?' Percy murmured. He had now looked away from Meg and was anxiously scanning the face of his intended.

Clara turned her eyes accusingly upon Percy for a moment, and under their steely gaze he blinked rapidly. 'You seem to have forgotten that fact when you brought this – this hussy to work in your establishment. It reflects on me as your future wife whom you employ, you know.'

Percy gasped. 'Oh, now come, my dear. Miss Kirkland is doing very nicely. The customers – the lady customers, that is – seem most pleased with how she—'

'Do they indeed? You surprise me, Percy. But then, perhaps I ought not to be surprised. Perhaps they do not know what *I* know.'

'What – what you know, Clara?' Percy stuttered, any composure he'd tried to cling to now draining away.

'Yes, Percy. What I know. I don't suppose she has told you herself, has she?'

Percy glanced briefly at Meg and quailed afresh. The girl's face was fiery with embarrassment, but there was now a spark of defiant anger in those fine green eyes. He felt trapped between the two of them and feared an unseemly scene. Respectable though his fiancée claimed to be, he'd once witnessed her screaming like a fishwife when one of her housemaids had committed some offence. The experience had unnerved him and made him unwilling to set a firm date for their wedding.

'No,' Clara continued, 'I see that she has not.'

'Erm,' Percy began, glancing worriedly from one to the other, his greatest fear that a customer would enter the shop. 'Perhaps you would like to go into the workroom to talk together. It would be better—'

'What I have to say can be said here, Percy. I don't mind who hears me.'

'That's what I was afraid of,' Percy muttered.

'What did you say?' Clara flashed at him.

'Nothing, my dear,' Percy said mildly, but the worried frown did not leave his forehead.

'Well, then.' Clara turned her attention back to Meg. 'What have you to say for yourself, miss?'

Meg took a deep breath and willed herself to speak calmly and respectfully. This was her employer's fiancée. Percy would side with Clara. It was natural. So, she, Meg, would have to be very careful what she said and how she said it. 'Miss Finch, I can hardly bring myself to speak of it, it pains me so much. To think that my own mother would act in such a way.' Meg hung her head as if she bore the full burden of guilt. 'How am I ever to hold my head up again in respectable society?' she whispered, trying desperately to give the impression that she was throwing herself upon the other woman's mercy. For a moment it seemed as if she might have succeeded, for Miss Finch appeared nonplussed by the girl's dignified answer. But Clara was not yet finished. Her mouth twisted into a sneer. 'And then, of course, there was your father running off with a girl half his age.'

Meg kept her eyes downcast and her chin trembled. She nodded and allowed tears to splash onto her hands, which she gripped tightly in front of her. Her voice husky, she said, 'I know. Oh, Miss Finch, I hardly know how to bear it all. If it hadn't been for the kindness of Mr Rodwell putting his trust in me, then – then I truly believe I would not have wanted to live any longer . . .' She raised her eyes, brimming with tears. 'But surely a Christian woman like yourself can see that none of it is my fault. What can I do? What *can* I do?'

'There, there, my dear girl,' Percy interposed. 'We'll say no more about it. Erm – whatever it is.' Percy was still partially in the dark. He had no idea what the two women were talking about. He could only murmur, 'Please, don't distress yourself.'

Clara whirled around to face him. 'Her mother has become Isaac Pendleton's latest – latest *paramour*.'

Percy blinked and stared down at her for a moment. Then he glanced at Meg and back again to Clara.

'Well?' Clara demanded. 'What have you to say about *that*?'

Percy frowned and shifted his weight from one foot to the other. 'Erm, well. I don't really think it is any of our business, my dear. Not really.'

'Not – our – business?' Clara's voice was rising shrilly and Percy put out his hands, palms outwards, trying to placate her.

'What I mean is – as Miss Kirkland says – it is not her fault—'

'One is judged by the company one keeps,' Clara said piously. 'People will talk, Percy. Believe you me, people will talk and your customers, at least all the *lady* customers you are hoping to attract, will go elsewhere.'

For a moment Percy looked helpless and then, gripping the tape measure that always dangled around his neck during working hours, he straightened up and declared, 'Well, I'll just have to take that risk, won't I, my dear? I am not prepared to punish this poor girl for something that she hasn't done. She is to be pitied, not blamed.'

Now it was Clara's face that coloured, so vividly her complexion was almost purple. 'Well, really!' was all she could utter for a few moments. Then the tirade began. 'You disappoint me, Percy. I would have hoped for better things from you, really I would—' The shop doorbell clanged and a woman entered the shop, but Clara, in full flow now, did not notice. 'How can you even consider employing a girl with such connections? Bad blood will out, Percy. Mark my words, it's in the breed.' On and on she ranted until even the woman who had entered the shop began to look embarrassed and seemed about to leave.

Meg moved around the counter, eased her way past Clara and stepped towards the newcomer. 'May I help you, madam?' she asked politely as if nothing untoward was going on behind her.

The woman glanced towards Clara. 'I – er—' she began hesitantly. 'I was looking for a new hat. I understand that Mr Rodwell is beginning to stock ladies' fashions and I wondered . . .'

Meg shook her head apologetically. 'I'm sorry, madam. At the moment we don't stock hats although we may do so in the future.' Meg spoke carefully, smoothing out the local dialect from her speech. 'But we do have a wonderful selection of undergarments, if you would care to take a look,' she added hopefully.

But the customer shook her head, stepped backwards and fumbled for the door handle. Casting one last look towards Clara, she murmured, 'Perhaps another time . . .' turned and hurried out.

'There, you see?' Clara said at once, gesturing towards the shop door through which the potential customer had just disappeared. 'That woman didn't want to be served by a chit of a girl. Really, Percy, can't you see further than the end of your nose? Ladies want to be served by an older woman. Someone who is discreet and *respectable*. The kind of woman you need to employ is a genteel kind of woman who has become impoverished through no fault of her own.'

'Surely Miss Kirkland fits that description?'

'I said, "impoverished", Percy. Not a pauper from

the workhouse!' She glared at him, but when he made no reply, she gave an exasperated 'Huh!' and turned towards the door. She pulled it open and looked back to launch one last parting shot. 'You haven't heard the last of this, Percy Rodwell. If you won't listen to me, then perhaps you'll listen to my brother.' Her face twisted into a sneer as she added, 'After all, he does own these premises.'

With that, she swept out, slamming the door so hard behind her that the bell shuddered on its spring for several moments.

Meg was appalled at what she had heard. In her view the woman was hysterical – mad. Even if she disapproved passionately of her fiancé's employment of Meg, she herself had shown a surprising lack of decorum. But Meg knew she must be careful what she said to Percy. Clara was still his fiancée. She must not forget that.

Now that the shop was empty, she turned tearful eyes towards him. 'Oh, Mr Rodwell, I hadn't realized how my family's troubles might reflect upon you.' She pulled in a deep breath and took a risk. 'I should leave at once. I'd hate to lose you custom because of – because of—' Now she allowed the tears to flow freely down her face. She pulled out her handkerchief and covered her face, sobbing uncontrollably into it.

She felt Percy move to her side and his tentative touch on her shoulder. 'There, there, my dear. Please don't cry. I wouldn't dream of you leaving. You're doing very nicely here. Very nicely. Don't worry any more about – about Miss Finch. I will talk to her. Yes – yes, I will talk to her again. She has my best interests at heart. I know that, but – well – perhaps . . .' His voice trailed away but then he added more firmly, 'But there must be no more talk of you leaving.'

'Oh, thank you, Mr Rodwell. You are good. Thank you.'

He patted her shoulder again and murmured, 'There, there.'

Behind her handkerchief, Meg smiled.

Twenty

Her heart in her mouth, Meg knocked on the door of Isaac Pendleton's office. Trying to keep her anger, disgust even, in check, she adopted a docile image. When his voice boomed out telling her to enter, she opened the door and smiled as she stepped into the room.

'Ah, Meg, my dear girl.' Isaac rose from behind his desk and came towards her, his arms outstretched.

Meg shuddered but managed to hide her revulsion. 'I wondered, sir,' she began meekly, 'if I might see my mother, if you please?'

'Of *course* you can, my dear. You don't need to ask. My door is always open to you.' He put his arm around her shoulder and pulled her against the bulge of his stomach. 'After all, we are almost family now, aren't we? I expect you've heard that your mother has made me the happiest of men by agreeing to become my – er – um – *friend*?'

Meg had to clamp her mouth tightly shut to prevent the vitriolic words that were tumbling around in her mind from spilling out. 'Where – is she?' she managed to stammer.

'In my room upstairs. Run along and see her, my dear. I'll be along shortly.'

Meg managed a weak smile as she pulled herself away from him and left the room.

The stairs leading to the first floor were just outside

the master's room. As Meg put her foot on the first step, she heard a movement above her and glanced up to see Louisa Daley coming down towards her. Meg stood aside and waited until the schoolmistress passed by. At the foot of the stairs, Louisa paused. She smiled uncertainly. 'Meg,' she began hesitantly. There was a pleading tone in her voice but Meg only glared back at her, her expression frosty and unforgiving. 'Meg, please – can't we be friends again? I am so sorry. What more can I say?'

'There's nothing you can say that can undo what happened.'

'But I've apologized about the watch. And as for Bobbie – well – Philip – Dr Collins said there was nothing he could've done even if he'd been called in earlier.'

'There might have been,' Meg insisted. 'You shouldn't have tried to look after him yourself. You should've told matron sooner. At least she really cares about the children.'

'How can you say that? *I* care, Meg. Really I do.'

The girl was stony-faced and unforgiving.

'Won't you believe me, Meg? I truly am so sorry. I know you don't want to come back to the school room – that you've found a nice post in the town. Do you like it? Are they kind to you?'

'What do you care if they're kind to me or not? We're just paupers to you. Not even worth your precious doctor's attention. And I'm just a common thief, aren't I?'

'Oh, Meg, please—'

'Let me pass.'

Louisa remained where she was, blocking Meg's path to the stairs. 'You're going to see your mother?'

'That's none of your business.'

Louisa touched Meg's arm, still trying to make amends. 'Things will be better for her now. For you both, now that you're under Mr Pendleton's protection. You needn't think of yourselves as being in the workhouse any more.'

Meg's face contorted. 'You don't think I condone what she's doing, do you?'

'But you'll be set for life now. Isaac – Mr Pendleton – looks after his – his ladies. He—'

Meg thrust her face close to Louisa's. 'Then why didn't you climb into his bed?'

Louisa gasped and drew back. Meg pushed her aside. 'I've nothing more to say to you.' Without looking back she lifted her skirts and ran up the stairs.

'How could you, Mam? How could you do it? After all you've taught me.'

'Oh, Meggie, please don't judge me.' Sarah came towards her daughter, beseeching her for understanding. But Meg refused to reach out to her mother. She couldn't bear to touch her. Even when Sarah put her arms about her and laid her face against Meg's shoulder, she did not move, but held herself rigid, refusing to return her mother's embrace.

'I feel so alone,' Sarah whispered. 'I need someone to take care of me. Of us.'

'You've got me. I'll take care of you. I've got a good job in town—' Mentally, Meg crossed her fingers, hoping that this was still the truth now Miss Finch had made clear her disapproval. Maybe, with the hold her family had over her fiancé, in more ways than one, Clara might yet persuade Percy to dismiss Meg. The accusation was out of her mouth before she could stop herself. 'But I might not have now because of what you've done.'

Astonished, Sarah pulled back and stared at Meg. 'What – whatever do you mean?'

Unable to hold back her frustration, Meg blurted out, 'Mr Rodwell's fiancée is Miss Finch and she's friendly with Miss Pendleton and she knows that you – that you've become what she calls Mr Pendleton's latest "paramour". And all them down there—' Momentarily, in her anger, her care for her grammar deserted her as she flung out her hand in the vague direction of where the women's day room was on the floor below. 'They all know. You should've seen them last night when I came home. And as for Waters, she nearly attacked me.' She forbore to tell her mother that if it hadn't been for Jake, it would have been she who attacked Waters, not the other way about. 'One way or another the whole town will know soon,' she went on, sparing her mother nothing. 'And if what Miss Finch says is true, then the ladies will stop frequenting Mr Rodwell's shop.' She paused and then drove the knife home. 'And then they might persuade their menfolk to stop too and then where will he be? Not needing an assistant, that's where.'

'But Isaac's kind and generous and he says he'll look after you too. He'll look after us both. He wants you to go back into the school room with Miss Daley.' Sarah gripped Meg's arm, pleading desperately. 'Oh, Meg, please, do what he asks. He'll set us up for life. He's got contacts. He can arrange for you to become a teacher. Just think about that, Meg.'

The door opened quietly behind them, but they were

both so caught up in their conversation that neither of them noticed who was standing there.

'No, I won't think about it. I don't need to. I'm not letting that man rule our lives. Oh, Mam—' Now it was Meg who took hold of her mother's shoulders and gave her a gentle shake as if trying to instil some sense into the distraught woman, who, in her view, was making a tragic mistake. 'I do understand how you must feel, truly. After everything that's happened, but please don't do this. Don't become Isaac Pendleton's mistress. He'll cast you off eventually, just like he did Waters. Then where will you be?'

Sarah shook her head. 'He's not like that. He – he looks after – even if . . .' Her voiced trailed away.

'Look, I was going to tell you last night. There's some rooms above Mr Rodwell's shop that I'm sure aren't used. I'll ask him if we can live there. Just you and me. I'm sure he'll say "yes".'

Slowly, Sarah shook her head and whispered, 'Meg, I'm sorry, but I need—'

Meg pulled away from her mother. Her green eyes filled with disgust. 'Then you're no better than a – than a *whore*. If you stay here with him, I want nothing more to do with you. Do you hear me?' Though her voice broke on the final words, she cried, 'If you stay here, I don't want to see you ever again.'

The figure in the doorway moved into the room. This time it was not Meg's ally, Jake, but Isaac Pendleton, who had heard every word of Meg's final outburst. 'I think, young lady, you've said quite enough.'

Sarah gasped in horror, realizing what he must have overheard, but Isaac moved forward to stand beside her and put his arm around her. 'Your mother's quite right.

I intended to look after you both. But not now. Oh, I'll take care of your mother, but not you. From this moment on, my girl, you're on your own.'

Sarah clutched at the front of Isaac's coat. 'Oh, please, Isaac, don't cast her out into the streets.'

For a moment, he said nothing and Meg could see his internal struggle on his face. 'Very well, since it is you who ask, my dear, she can stay in the workhouse for the time being.' He turned back to Meg, his face purple with rage, his eyes bulging. 'But you will have none of the special privileges you *might* have enjoyed.'

'I don't want them,' Meg spat back. With one last glance at her mother, she whirled around and ran from the room. As she did so, all she heard was her mother's pleading, 'Oh, Meggie, please don't go. Not like this . . .'

Twenty-One

'Oh, Mr Rodwell, what am I to do? I'm so ashamed of my mother.'

Meg had told Percy everything that had happened the previous evening. Now she covered her face with her hands, but she peeped through her fingers to watch his reaction. Percy was agitated. He removed his spectacles, polished them and replaced them. He cleared his throat. 'Well, my dear. I can see how you're placed. It is unfortunate. Most unfortunate.'

Meg sobbed.

'Now, now, don't take on so. I didn't mean to imply that it was your fault. But, of course, whilst you are still at the – still *there* . . .'

Now was the moment. It had come sooner than she'd dared to hope. Meg took a deep breath. 'Sir, I know it's a dreadful imposition and if you say no then I will quite understand. As you say, whilst I am still living at the workhouse . . .' She gulped back a sob, her mouth trembling. 'And now I've stood up to the master, he's – he's going to make life so difficult for me – I wondered . . .' She allowed the words to come tumbling out, erratic and desperate. 'I just wondered – the rooms above the shop. Could I perhaps live in one of them? I'd only need one. And I could keep an eye on the shop all the time, have the stove lit every morning for you and do the cleaning at night after we've closed.

Oh, Mr Rodwell, sir, please – please would you consider it?'

Percy stared at her as if she had taken leave of her senses. 'But – but they're not suitable. I mean, they're in a dreadful state. They're not habitable.'

Meg hung her head and was at once full of pretended contrition. 'I shouldn't have asked. You haven't even said you're keeping me on. I haven't completed my trial period. I was taking too much for granted. I'm sorry.'

Percy was still staring at her as if he was suddenly seeing something that he hadn't noticed before. Nervously, he cleared his throat. 'No – no, it's not that. Miss Kirkland – Meg – I am quite satisfied with your work. Very satisfied, in fact.' He gripped the tape measure hanging around his neck. 'It's just . . .' He stopped and stared at her again.

In a small, pathetic voice, Meg said, 'It's just that Miss Finch wouldn't agree.'

Percy shook his head emphatically. 'No, it's not that either. Miss Finch has nothing to do with the running of my business.' He paused and then added, almost grimly, 'Not yet, anyway.'

'But it would make it very awkward for you, I see that. I'm really sorry, I shouldn't have asked you. I wouldn't have done if I hadn't been so desperate.' Tears filled her eyes again. She made a great play of dabbing her face, squaring her shoulders and smiling bravely through her tears. 'I'll think of something. Now, shall I make us a cup of tea and tidy the workroom? You must have worked very late last night, Mr Rodwell. I see the suit for Mr Pickering is almost finished.'

Percy nodded absently. 'He wants a final fitting today,' he murmured, 'And the suit finished as soon as possible. I think he plans to wear it for the next race meeting.'

'Oh yes,' Meg murmured. Unbidden, the memory of her last visit to the racecourse and the picture of Alice clinging to her father's arm pushed its way into her mind. Banishing it swiftly, she widened her smile and was gratified to see Percy blinking in its radiance. 'Then you'll be needing that cup of tea and, if you want to carry on working on it, I can hold the fort in the shop.' Seeing his mouth open to protest, she added at once, 'I can always fetch you if a gentleman requires you particularly.'

The morning passed with Meg's mind in a turmoil. Every time Percy emerged from the workroom, she looked up eagerly to see if he was going to say anything. But he avoided meeting her gaze and only spoke to her when he required her to do something. By the middle of the afternoon Meg was losing heart and by the time for her to leave came he had still not said any more about her idea.

Dispirited, she trudged towards the workhouse. Albert met her at the gateway. 'I'm sorry, lass, but mester's given orders you've to be sent straight to the punishment room.'

Meg gasped. 'Why?'

The old man shrugged his shoulders. 'Search me, lass. I'd go there miself instead of you, if I could, but—'

'Oh, Albert.' Now genuine tears filled her eyes. She was touched by the old man's thoughtfulness.

He patted her shoulder with rough kindness. 'There, there, lass. You've done summat to upset him and you'll have to pay. Thing is, old Isaac's fine and dandy, generous to a fault, when we'm all doing his bidding.

But cross him –' the old man shook his head – 'and there's hell to pay.'

Meg's eyes widened. 'He's not going to keep me locked up so that I can't go to work, is he?'

Albert looked at her sorrowfully. 'Three days, he said. On bread and water.'

Meg stared at him, her mind working quickly. She glanced round the deserted yard and then up at the windows of the master's rooms, which overlooked the back of the main building. There was no shadowy figure standing there. *Too busy with me mam*, Meg thought bitterly. She stepped closer to Albert. 'Go back into your lodge. You haven't seen me, right?'

'Aw, lass, what're you up to now? It won't do no good, yer know. Yer'll only get yersel' into more trouble.'

'Don't worry about me, but I don't want him taking it out on you. Just do one thing for me.'

'What's that, lass?'

'Tell Jake I've gone.'

'He's not here no more, mi duck. He's living in at the farm now.'

'Well – when you do see him, then.'

Albert sighed. 'All right. But what are you going to do?'

'Best you don't know.'

'I wouldn't tell—' he began indignantly.

'I know you wouldn't,' Meg said swiftly. 'It's not that it's just – well – I don't want him even *thinking* you know.'

The old man sighed. 'All right – but you will take care of yoursel', won't you?'

Meg grinned at him through the dusk. 'Oh, I'll do that

all right, Albert. And – and thanks for – for everything.' Briefly, she gripped his hands in hers.

'I ain't done nowt,' the old man sniffed, sounding suspiciously tearful.

'You've done more than you know.' Impulsively, she leant forward and kissed his cheek. Then she was gone, running across the yard and up the stairs to the women's dormitory. She held her breath as she opened the door. She was lucky – the room was empty. The women would all be at supper. That was where she should be. If anyone missed her . . . Then she remembered. She would not be missed, for they would probably all know by now that she'd been banished to the punishment room. If no one but Albert had seen her come back from work, then there was still time for her to escape.

Hurriedly, she gathered together her belongings. It didn't take more than a minute or two – there was precious little to gather – and then she was creeping back down the stairs and scurrying across the yard, afraid that at any moment the master's voice would boom out. Thank goodness she'd been allowed to wear her own clothes to go to work in. At least she had those. She reached the gate out of the yard again. Albert had gone back into his lodge and closed the door. She looked briefly through the window and saw him sitting at the table, a plate of food in front of him, but he wasn't eating. He was just sitting, his arms resting on the table and staring into space. He didn't even glance towards the window.

Meg crept out of the yard and into the lane. She slipped like a silent wraith along the side wall and then began to run as fast as she could away from the workhouse.

She ran and ran until her lungs were bursting and she could run no more. When she reached the shop, the premises were in darkness. Percy Rodwell had gone home. Meg crept down the passageway at the side of the shop and let herself into the yard at the back. She tried the door into the workshop, but, as she'd expected, it was locked and bolted. But she found that the door to the lean-to scullery was unlocked. There was little in there worth stealing and Percy didn't bother to secure it. Meg shivered as she felt her way around in the darkness. Even though the August night was balmy and warm, it would get colder in the early morning, but she had her thick shawl and all the clothes she possessed, though they were pathetically few. She did not want to lie on the brick floor, so she spread a layer of clothing on the top of the table and curled up on it with her shawl covering her. She wished now that she'd been brave enough to steal a blanket from the dormitory, but she had not dared. Isaac would have her sent to prison for theft. He'd do anything, she thought, to get back at her for the things she'd said.

Meg slept fitfully, waking every so often, cold and shivering. She was pleased to see the pale light of dawn creeping in through the grimy windows. She sat up and climbed stiffly down from the table. Her feet were like blocks of ice and had no feeling. She stamped them and threw her arms about herself, trying to get warm.

She opened the door and listened. Already she could hear movement from the other yards in the row of houses and shops, so she went out to the pump in the middle of Percy's yard. The handle squeaked and icy, fresh water streamed from the spout. She splashed her face, shivering anew as she did, and then took a long drink. Next she visited the privy and then returned to the scullery to try to make herself look presentable. It was fortunate, she thought, that she had taken to coming round to the back entrance each morning. Percy would see nothing unusual when he opened the back door to find her standing there.

Meg had no idea what the day would bring. How long could she stay in the scullery without Percy finding out? And what would he do when he did?

One thing Meg did know: no matter what happened, she would never, ever go back to the workhouse. She would sooner die of starvation and cold.

Twenty-Two

Meg spent four more nights in the scullery before she managed to take the spare door-key from the hook behind the back door on the Saturday evening. Each night she left as usual by the front door, calling out a cheery 'Goodnight' to Percy and set off in the direction of the workhouse. But she only went as far as the end of the street, where she waited until Percy left the shop, carefully locking the door behind him. Then, in the darkness, she crept back into the yard and let herself into the workroom by the back door. Not daring to light a lamp or even a candle in case someone should see the light, Meg felt her way through to the shop and huddled down by the stove. Though the floor was uncomfortable, at least she was warm throughout the night now.

She was awake early each morning. She'd washed and tidied herself and was standing outside the back door when Percy arrived for the day's work.

'Good morning, Meg – Miss Kirkland.' As he held open the door for her and she passed close to him to step inside, he touched her shoulder. 'You look tired, my dear. Are – are things still the same?'

Meg nodded. 'I haven't seen my mother since – since that night.' It was the truth, if not the whole truth. She did not tell him that she hadn't been back to the workhouse since then, for he would surely ask questions. As it was, she lived in dread that Miss Pendleton would have told Miss Finch that Meg Kirkland had left the institution.

'Dear, dear,' the kindly man murmured. 'What a state of affairs, to be sure.' He went through to the front of the shop, shaking his head sadly and leaving Meg to start the day's work.

The stove was soon revived each morning for now Meg was able to keep it going through the night. She just hoped Percy wouldn't notice that the shop was warmer than usual when he arrived. Later that day she was able to sneak upstairs to fetch a man's woollen vest and a pair of long johns from the old stock. These would keep her warm during the nights. It could still be surprisingly cold at two o'clock in the morning. She'd look a strange sight, but she didn't care. There was no one to see her. She also found two moth-eaten blankets and stowed these and the garments near the top of the stairs, where she could easily find them in the dark when she returned each night.

Meg had no means of washing and drying her clothes and by the end of two weeks her dress was decidedly grubby. Percy must have noticed. Late one afternoon he handed her a parcel and, avoiding her eyes, murmured, 'I thought it would be nice for you to wear some kind of uniform. I . . . er . . . hope these . . . um . . . garments will fit.'

'Oh, *thank* you, Mr Rodwell,' Meg said as she unwrapped a long black skirt and a white cotton blouse. Her gratitude was heartfelt, but even Percy could not guess just how much the gift of the clothing meant to her.

Meg managed to remain undiscovered for almost four weeks. Sundays were the worst. Then she wandered the streets, her stomach rolling with hunger, for she had no money to buy anything. The small wage that Percy paid her was soon gone. She was relying now only on the bread rolls that Percy bought from the bakery for their midday meal.

'It's too far for you to go home in the middle of the day,' he'd said when she had first begun working for him. 'But you'll get a good meal at night, won't you?' Meg had smiled, wondering what he would think to the workhouse supper of bread and porridge. The best meal of the day there was the one at midday which she was now missing: boiled meat, peas and potatoes.

After four weeks the strain of living in such harsh conditions was taking its toll. One morning, exhausted by a fitful night's sleep, she awoke with a start to find Percy bending over her as she lay on the floor near the stove.

'Meg?' His tone was more concerned than angry. 'Whatever are you doing here? And – and how did you get in?' Then he straightened up and, staring down at her strange garb and the makeshift bed of old blankets on the floor by the stove, realization spread across his face. 'Oh, my dear girl, you've been sleeping here, haven't you?'

Meg scrambled to her feet with difficulty. Her limbs were stiff and cold. 'Oh, please, Mr Rodwell. Please forgive me. I've done no harm, honestly. Please don't be cross—'

'I'm not, my dear. I'm just so sorry you didn't trust me enough to tell me. If I'd known then . . .' He took off his spectacles, polished them and replaced them on the bridge of his nose.

'I had to leave the workhouse, Mr Rodwell. Mr Pendleton was going to shut me in the punishment room on bread and water for three days. He wasn't even going to let me come to work.' Meg said, standing now and trying to smooth her hair. She knew what a ridiculous sight she must look, with an old man's woollen vest pulled over her own clothes and a pair of long johns peeping out from beneath her skirt. Percy looked her up and down and the corners of his mouth twitched. He tried to control himself, but he smiled and then he chuckled and finally he was laughing out loud. Meg joined in and they were both shaking with laughter until tears ran down their faces.

'Oh, Meg, what a sight you look!'

'I know,' she spluttered. 'But they are warm. I found them upstairs. It's not your best stock. I wouldn't have used that.'

'Oh, my dear girl,' Percy said, wiping his eyes, 'I wouldn't have minded if you had. It'd've been worth it. I don't know when I last laughed so much.' And they dissolved into laughter afresh.

'Now,' Percy said at last, 'go and make yourself presentable through the back and then you must go next door to the bakery and buy whatever you would like to eat. I don't suppose you've had any breakfast, have you?' He looked down at her with mock severity, but there was still a twinkle in his eyes. Then the twinkle faded as he added, 'In fact, if I'm not much mistaken, you haven't been eating properly for some time, have you?'

Meg shook head.

'Right, you go and get whatever you want. Tell Mr Wilkins to put it on my account. And then we'll talk.'

'Yes, Mr Rodwell,' Meg said meekly, hanging her head.

*

Later in the morning, when there was a lull in the number of customers coming into the shop, Percy once more went through his spectacle-polishing routine. Meg had noticed by now that this was a nervous habit of his when he was anxious. He seemed to do it a lot, she thought, when Miss Finch came into the shop.

'Now, we must decide what we are going to do.'

Meg waited, chewing her little finger, her heart thumping painfully. Was he going to dismiss her and send her back to the workhouse? The punishment room awaiting her was, to her mind, far worse than the discomfort she'd suffered recently sleeping on the floor of his shop.

'Don't send me back there, Mr Rodwell, please . . .'

He looked at her and blinked rapidly. 'My dear girl, nothing was further from my mind. I wouldn't dream of sending you back – there.'

'You're – you're not going to dismiss me then?'

Percy shook his head. 'Certainly not. You're doing very nicely here and the ladies seem to like you.' He paused, then glanced away as he murmured, 'Well, most of them anyway.' And Meg knew that he was thinking about Miss Finch. 'No, no, I was just wondering where we could find lodgings for you in the town. I mean, I'd take you home with me, but – well – it wouldn't be right. You do understand, don't you?'

Meg nodded. She bit her lip and then plunged in, repeating her previous request. 'Mr Rodwell – please – would you let me use the rooms above the shop? I'd clean them out and make them habitable and – and I'd be on hand to look after the shop. I could keep the stove going all night in the winter—'

'Ah, so that's why the shop has been so warm every morning,' Percy said thoughtfully. 'I see now.'

'And it would be good to have someone living on the premises, wouldn't it?' Meg rushed on, but her heart sank when Percy shook his head. 'It wouldn't be right, a young girl like you living on her own here.'

'I'd be all right. Really I would. Oh, please, Mr Rodwell, won't you think about it?'

'Well . . .' he seemed to be wavering and Meg pressed home her point. 'I could clean the shop after hours and sort out all the stock. I'd enjoy that, really I would. Oh, please, do say yes.'

He stared at her for a several moments before slowly he nodded. 'Very well, then, but –' he wagged his forefinger at her – 'there's just one thing.' Meg held her breath as he continued, 'You're not staying here any longer. Until we've got those two rooms upstairs habitable, you are coming home with me.' He smiled archly at her. 'I'll risk my reputation, if you'll risk yours.'

Meg laughed and thanked him prettily, but she did not voice what she was thinking.

Whatever was Miss Finch going to say about that when she heard? As hear she surely would.

Twenty-Three

Clara Finch had plenty to say. From the workroom, where she was carefully sewing buttons onto the jacket of a suit, Meg heard it all.

'Percy Rodwell, have you taken leave of your senses entirely?' the woman almost screamed at him. 'You mean to tell me that you're going to let that slut of a girl live over the shop? You're trusting her to be alone here? Well, I declare I've heard everything now.'

Percy's tone was calm. 'The girl is no slut. She and her family have hit hard times.'

'No slut, you say. Like mother, like daughter, I say.'

In the workroom, Meg winced and her resolve against her mother hardened.

'I really couldn't pass comment on her mother, Clara,' Percy was saying, his voice low. 'I've never met the poor woman, but just remember she's lost her husband and two of her children. Can't you find it in your heart to be a little more sympathetic?'

Clara snorted in a most unladylike manner. 'You make it sound as if her husband died. Well, I don't know what that chit of a girl has told you, but he didn't.' By now Meg had crept closer to the door leading from the workroom into the shop. It was ajar and she peeped through the open slit to see Clara prod Percy in the chest with a sharp, bony fingertip. 'He ran off with another woman. Morals no better than a tomcat's, if you ask me. And now the mother has taken up with Isaac Pendleton.'

'Clara,' Percy cut in, 'nobody is asking you.'

There was a moment's stunned silence and then her voice shrilled. 'Percy Rodwell, how dare you speak to me like that?'

'My dear—' Percy began.

'Don't you "my dear" me,' Clara shot back. 'The scheming little hussy is taking you for a fool, Percy. But if you're too blind to see it, then so be it. But don't come running to me for sympathy when she runs off with all the takings.'

'She won't do that,' he said confidently and the listening girl felt a warm glow of gratitude flood through her.

'Don't my opinions count for anything with you, Percy?'

There was the slightest of pauses before Percy answered. It sounded to Meg as if he was having to force the words out. 'Of course, my dear,' he said mildly, 'but I think I am a better judge of character than you give me credit for.'

Clara's laugh was hard and brittle. 'You're a fool, Percy. A fool over a pretty face. Just like a lot of men. Though I'd've thought better of you. But . . .' She paused deliberately, then added, 'If you won't listen to me, your fiancée, then perhaps you'll listen to my brother.' Percy did not respond this time and Clara added pointedly, 'Don't forget, *my dear* –' the endearment was heavy with sarcasm – 'that he owns these premises. I think he has a right to say who occupies them, don't you?'

Meg heard the swish of the woman's skirts as she moved and then the sound of the shop doorbell. Now, through the crack, she could see Clara standing near the door, her hand on the doorknob, about to leave. Then she saw the woman turn back to deliver one last parting shot. 'Don't force my brother to do something we might all regret, Percy.'

She left the shop, slamming the door behind her so that the bell bounced crossly.

Meg pulled open the door and stepped into the shop. 'Oh, Mr Rodwell, I couldn't help overhearing. I'm so sorry. I should leave at once.' She moved closer to him and looked appealingly up into his face. Huskily, she said, 'I can't bear to be the cause of trouble between you and your fiancée.'

Percy was still staring at the closed door through which Clara had departed. 'Don't concern yourself, my dear,' Percy murmured.

Behind the round, steel-rimmed spectacles, Percy's hazel eyes had a thoughtful, far-away look.

For the rest of the day there was a tense atmosphere in the shop. Customers came and went and were served with the usual polite efficiency, yet between Percy and Meg there was constraint. They were both waiting for the arrival of Theobald Finch. Meg didn't know what to expect and Percy did not share his thoughts with her. Yet they were both jumpy, and each time the shop doorbell clanged they turned towards it, holding their breath until they recognized the newcomer.

Mid-afternoon, Meg was alone in the shop whilst Percy worked in the back room. The bell clanged and Meg looked up to see Jake standing in the open doorway, grinning widely. There was no one in the shop to see, apart from Percy, so she hurried towards him, her hands outstretched.

'Jake – how are you? How are you getting on at the farm? Have you settled in with Ron and his family? Oh, do tell me everything.'

'It's great,' he began, closing the door and coming further into the shop. 'They're really nice people, the Smallwoods.' He sounded surprised after what Meg had told him.

Meg sighed. 'I suppose they are. It was my dad and Alice caused the trouble, if I'm honest.' She changed the subject, away from painful memories. 'Tell me what you're doing.'

'All sorts. I like the milking the best. Never thought I'd tek to cows, but they're nice creatures when you get used to 'em.'

'Do – do you help in the dairy?'

'A bit, if the missis is short-handed. She's got a girl working there, but Mrs Smallwood ses she's useless. I reckon she's going to get rid of her before long.' There was a pause before he said, 'I was thinking I might tell her about Betsy.'

'Betsy! But she's not old enough.'

'She's twelve – nearly thirteen.'

'Is she? I thought she was only about ten.'

'She's very small for her age. But she's wiry and stronger than she looks.'

'She'll need to be to work in Mrs Smallwood's dairy,' Meg said tartly. Her feelings towards the young girl were mixed. She knew she shouldn't blame Betsy for the mix-up over Louisa Daley's watch – the girl had been very ill and had hardly realized what she was doing. But if it hadn't been for Betsy, Meg might now have been training to be a proper teacher with Louisa as her friend. But then, of course, there had been Bobbie . . .

Jake broke into her thoughts. 'I've moved in with Ron and his family and I've got the little bedroom you told me about.' He touched her arm. 'I think about you when I'm lying in bed at night. Was it your bed? Is – is that where you slept.'

Meg nodded, a lump in her throat. 'I 'spect so. I shouldn't think the Smallwoods have refurnished the place.'

Jake laughed. 'No, they haven't.' Then his voice softened as he said, 'But I'm glad they haven't if I'm sleeping in your bed. It – it makes me feel closer to you.' Colour crept into his face as he added. 'I – I miss you, Meggie.'

It was the endearing pet name her father had called her. When her family life had fallen apart, she had vowed never to let anyone else call her that. Yet for some reason she didn't mind Jake using it.

'And I miss you, but I'm glad you like it there,' she said brightly. Then she added wryly, 'Mind you don't do anything to upset the missis and get yourself thrown out, that's all.'

Jake's face was sober now, the wide grin gone. 'I've been up to the workhouse.'

Meg dropped her gaze and began to turn away, but Jake caught hold of her arm and held on to her, forcing her to remain where she was. 'Meg, I've seen your mam. She's desperate to see you – to know if you're all right.'

Meg glared at him. 'She should have thought of that before she got into Isaac Pendleton's bed.'

'Oh, Meggie, don't be so hard on her. What else has she got left?'

'She's got me,' Meg said passionately and struck

herself in the chest with her clenched fist. 'I'd never've let her down. Not like she's let me down.' Meg was leaning towards him now, shouting in his face. 'She brought me up to believe that I shouldn't let a man – any man – touch me before I'd got a wedding band on me finger. And then just look what she does.'

'Well–' Jake shifted uncomfortably from one foot to the other – 'that's different.'

'Why is it?' she shot back.

'Because – because it just is. I mean – when you're a young girl and it's your first time an' that.'

'When you're a virgin, you mean?'

Jake's face flamed as he nodded.

Meg's face twisted. 'It's no different. She's – she's a whore.'

Softly Jake said, 'She's still yer mam and she loves you.'

Now Meg pulled herself away from him. 'Well, I don't love her any more. I hate her and I never want to see her again. And you can tell her that.'

Jake shook his head. 'I'll do no such thing.' He sighed and said gently, 'Look, I can understand why you're feeling hurt, but in time you'll feel different.'

'No, I won't. I never forgive and I never forget.'

She turned away and went to stand behind the counter, but there was more between them now than just the physical barrier. Jake stood awkwardly, still near the door, whilst Meg stood behind the counter glowering, and that was how Percy saw them as he came in. He glanced from one to the other.

'Jake's just leaving, Mr Rodwell. Goodbye, Jake,' she added pointedly and picked up a bolt of cloth, turning her back on him as she replaced it on a shelf behind the counter.

Jake nodded to Percy, pulled on his cap, and opened the door just as someone else was about to enter. He stood aside and allowed Theobald Finch to step inside, then left without another word.

'Now, Percy, what's all this about? You've quite upset the old girl, don'tcha know.' Theobald said the last three words as if they were one. His glance alighted on Meg. 'And – er – is this the young lady in question?' He frowned as he added, 'I know you, don't I? Weren't you the lass at the workhouse whose mam fainted?' This was the second time that Theobald Finch had recognized her by remembering that incident. Meg bit her lip.

Percy leapt to her aid. 'That's beside the point, Theo. Meg has come to work for me here in the shop. As you know, I am expanding my business into ladies' – erm – apparel and I need a female assistant.'

'But surely, Percy, old man, someone a little older would be more suitable.' They were talking about her now as if she wasn't there, but Meg stood her ground, wanting – needing – to know just what was being said.

'Meg is quick and willing to learn. I can teach her my ways. The way I want things doing.'

'Well, yes, I can see that might have its advantages,' Theo conceded.

Percy removed his spectacles, polished them and replaced them. 'I really can't see what Clara is so upset about.'

Theobald cleared his throat, glanced briefly at Meg and then dropped his gaze. 'Give us a moment, girl—'

'Her name is Miss Kirkland,' Percy almost snapped.

Theobald Finch stared at her. 'Ah,' he said, 'now I do recall. Your family used to work for Smallwood. Is that right?'

Reluctantly, Meg nodded.

'And your father seduced their young daughter?'

Rashly, and not knowing really why she did when her own feelings for him were so bitter, Meg leapt to her father's defence. 'Alice Smallwood was a flirt. It wasn't all his doing. She – she led him on and – and he fell for a pretty face.'

Theo eyed her and nodded slowly. 'And that's not all, is it? Your mother's taken up with Isaac Pendleton, I hear. And what about you? Are you setting your cap at Percy here? Think he's a good catch, do you?'

'Now, look here—' Percy began, but Theobald held up his hand.

'Percy, old chap, I think perhaps – in all the circumstances – it might be best if you dispensed with this girl's services.'

Percy was quite calm and all hesitation gone as he said, 'No, Theo. I'm sorry, but I will not. Meg is to remain here and she is to live in the rooms upstairs and if that doesn't suit you then . . .' He left the sentence hanging in the air between them, an unresolved contention.

'Well now, let's not be too hasty. Think the matter over, Percy, there's a good fellow.' Theo patted his future brother-in-law on the shoulder and, completely ignoring Meg, turned and strode towards the door, pausing only to say, 'Think it over, I'm sure you'll come round to our way of thinking, Percy, if you know what's good for you.' Then he pulled open the door and was gone.

Before the sound of the shop bell had died away, Meg said, 'There's nothing else for it.' She looked up at Percy with soulful eyes. 'I'll just have to go back to the workhouse.'

'I won't hear of it. I'm not going to be bullied into doing something I don't want to do.'

'Oh, Mr Rodwell,' Meg breathed, a catch in her voice, 'you don't know how much that means to me.' She turned her bright gaze on him and Percy blinked.

Then she dropped her gaze and gave an exaggerated sigh. 'But Miss Finch is your fiancée. I don't want to cause trouble between you.'

She felt him touch her shoulder lightly and when she looked up at him again, she saw that he was smiling. Softly, he said, 'I think the trouble was already there long before you arrived, my dear. You've just made me see things so much more clearly. Oh yes – so *much* more clearly.'

Twenty-Four

Late that evening they left the shop together, Meg walking beside Percy along the street, clutching her belongings. They were pathetically few and Meg felt ashamed.

'Here we are,' Percy said, opening the gate into the tiny front garden of a cottage in a row of similar houses. He opened the front door and stood aside for her to enter. 'Please,' he said, smiling down at her, 'come in.'

Meg stepped into a small, dark hallway and waited whilst Percy closed and bolted the door. 'Wait here,' he said, 'whilst I light a lamp and then I'll show you round.'

The cottage was small, but clean and neat and tidy. It could have been cosy, but to Meg's eye it lacked a woman's touch. There were no pretty cushions on the sofa, few ornaments, and what pictures there were on the plain, whitewashed walls were dark and dreary. Meg itched to place fresh flowers on the sideboard and to light a cheery fire in the grate in the small front parlour. The room looked as if it was never used, merely dusted once a week, the square of carpet in the centre brushed and the hearthrug shaken. But as she followed Percy through the hallway again and into the long, narrow kitchen at the back of the house, she realized that the front room was the only sitting room. *He must use it*, she thought, yet *it looks so forlorn, so unloved.*

The kitchen, too, was sparse, adequate only for a

single man's needs. The feeling of loneliness made Meg shudder. Used to family life and even to the workhouse, where it was impossible to be alone for more than five minutes in the day, Meg couldn't imagine coming home to an empty house and a cheerless grate. It must be awful, she thought, to have no one to talk to, no one with whom to share the day's news.

A tiny twisting staircase led up out of the kitchen to two bedrooms.

'The first one's mine, but this is a spare room. There are sheets in the cupboard. I hope they'll not be damp,' Percy added worriedly. 'No one's been in here for a long time.'

Meg smiled and glanced around her. It was the largest bedroom she had ever slept in. 'It'll be fine, Mr Rodwell. I'm very grateful.'

'Please –' he gestured towards the small fireplace – 'light a fire. I had both chimneys swept only last month, so you shouldn't have any trouble getting it going.'

'It doesn't seem right to be lighting a fire in a bedroom in summer,' Meg murmured.

'Well, we're into September now.' Percy smiled. 'And nights start to turn a little autumnal. Besides, it feels cold and musty in here. Not being used, I expect. No, no, Meg. Light a fire, do – it'll help air the room. There are sticks and coal in the backyard. You do that and make up the bed while I find us something to eat.'

Half an hour later, Meg sat on the bed watching the shadows cast by the flames dancing on the ceiling. She felt herself growing drowsy. The bed felt so comfortable and she was warm . . . She shook herself awake, yawning and rubbing her eyes, then went down the stairs, opening the door at the bottom and stepping straight into the kitchen.

Meg gasped in surprise. The table to one side of the narrow kitchen was laid and Percy was placing steaming dishes of meat and vegetables on top.

'Come and sit down, Meg.'

'Oh, Mr Rodwell. I never thought – I mean – of course, living on your own . . .' Her voice trailed away, not quite sure if she was saying the right thing.

'Needs must, my dear. Of course, it would be nice to be married. To have a wife to come home to . . .' Now it was Percy's voice that faded away and he bowed his head and clasped his hands together to say grace.

He began to serve the food, but Meg jumped up. 'Please – let me.'

When she had finished serving them both, she sat down again opposite him and they smiled at each other. They ate in silence, yet it was a companionable silence. At the end of the meal, Meg stood up. 'Now, I'll do the washing up. You go and sit in the front room and read your paper. That's what—' She stopped suddenly. She had been about to say, 'That's what my father liked to do,' but she bit back the words that reminded her so cruelly of happier times.

'That's very thoughtful of you, Meg,' Percy said, 'but it's chilly in there and it's hardly worth lighting a fire at this time of night just for one. I usually sit in here until bedtime.' Meg glanced around, but there were only the two wooden chairs that they had sat on at the table. There was no easy armchair for the man of the house. 'I always light one on a Sunday, but we can light one tonight if you like, now that you're here too,' he added. There was suddenly an eager note to his voice and he even half rose out of his chair, as if to go this very minute to fetch paper, sticks and coal.

'No, no, please, don't trouble on my account. If you don't mind, when I've washed the pots, I'll go to bed. I – I am rather tired.'

'Of course,' Percy said, understanding. 'You can't have been sleeping very well for the past few nights.' He put his head on one side. 'Just how long have you been sleeping at the shop?'

Meg bit her lip. 'Nearly four weeks. For the first two nights I slept in the scullery.'

'You must have been frozen out there.' Percy was appalled. 'Even summer nights can be very cold. Why ever didn't you tell me?'

'I wish now I had, but – but—'

Gently he said, 'You thought I would send you back to the workhouse.'

Meg nodded and Percy sighed. 'Well,' he said slowly, 'if I'm honest with you, that's very well what I might have done. At least, I would have encouraged you to go back there until we could have sorted out somewhere for you to live.'

'I was – I was going to ask you if we could *both* live above the shop. My mother and me. But when I got back to the workhouse, on the very night I was going to tell her of my idea, well, she'd – she'd—'

Percy patted her hand. 'There, there, don't distress yourself. Now, you get to bed. I'll see to the pots—'

'No, no, please let me do them.'

'Very well. But then you must get some rest.'

The following morning Meg awoke with a sore throat and a throbbing head. Her nose itched until she sneezed again and again and her eyes watered.

She dressed and went downstairs.

'My dear girl,' Percy said at once when he saw her. 'You look dreadful.' Then swiftly he rephrased his tactless remark. 'Oh, I'm sorry, but you do look ill.'

'I think I have a cold cubbing,' she said thickly and sneezed again.

Percy stepped back quickly. 'Oh dear, I do hope the sheets weren't damp. Look, you must stay at home today.'

'No, I'll be all right,' Meg said, wiping her eyes and sniffing loudly.

'No, no, I insist. Besides,' he added swiftly as he saw she was about to argue once more, 'it doesn't do to be in the shop with a heavy cold. I know because I've had to be there on a couple of occasions when I really should have stayed away. The customers don't like it.' Then hastily, lest she should think that all he cared about was his customers, he added, 'And you'll get better much quicker if you rest. Have a day in bed, Meg.'

'A day in bed!' Meg squeaked. Usually a healthy child, she could not remember ever having stayed in bed during the daytime.

Percy smiled and nodded. 'Yes, go on. Spoil yourself. Tell you what, before I go to the shop I'll fetch you some fresh lemons. Put the juice in some hot water and drink it as hot as you can. And I think –' he went towards a kitchen cupboard and pulled open the door – 'ah yes, I thought so.' He picked up a jar and held it out to her. 'There's some honey here. Hot lemon and honey. That'll help.'

Meg wiped her eyes. Whether her tears were a result of her cold or sprang from his thoughtfulness, even she could not tell.

*

Meg slept most of the day away, but towards late afternoon she had two visitors. The first was Clara Finch, who banged on the door until, woken from a deep sleep, Meg staggered downstairs to open the front door. Bleary-eyed, her hair hanging unkempt about her face and dressed only in her nightgown, Meg opened the door, to be pushed roughly aside as the other woman barged her way in.

Slamming the door behind her, Clara leant against it and surveyed the barefoot girl before her.

'This is a fine how-de-do.' Her mouth tight, her cold eyes raked Meg from head to toe. 'No wonder Percy was reluctant to tell me where you were. Well, you might fool him, miss, but you don't fool me. You can get your things together and get out of this house this minute.'

Meg sneezed, loudly and juicily. Clara pressed herself back against the door, but there was nowhere to go. 'Really, girl,' she admonished, 'haven't you a handkerchief?' Meg sniffed and Clara answered her own question with an exasperated sigh. 'No, I don't suppose you have. Here, take mine.'

Meg took the clean delicate lace handkerchief that Clara held out to her. She blew her nose, saturating the tiny square of linen in seconds.

'Thank you,' she said politely. All her 'ems' sounded like 'bees' as she added, 'But I'b not going anywhere. Mr Rodwell gave be perbission to stay in bed today. I'b sure I'll be a lot better toborrow. I'b only staying here till the roobs above the shop are ready.'

Clara's mouth turned down at the corners. 'If you think I'm going to stand by and let you move in over the shop, you'd better think again.' She took a step towards Meg and then, remembering the girl's cold, pulled back. 'The workhouse is where you belong, girl. You and your kind. And I'll see you back there, no matter how long it takes me. I know what you're up to. You think you can wheedle your way into Percy's affections. Getting him to feel sorry for you and bringing you home with him. What will people say? Have you stopped to think what harm it might do to his reputation? To his business, even? When folks get to know you're here – alone in this house with him – his business will suffer. Specially, this new venture of his with ladies' apparel. What self-respecting lady is going to frequent his establishment with a little slut like you behind the counter to serve them?' Her beady eyes narrowed. 'I can see your game. You think he's a good catch, don't you? A bachelor with a nice little business. You're no better than your mother.'

'I'b not like by bother,' Meg cried thickly. She sneezed and, to her frustration, tears ran down her face. She didn't want Clara Finch to think she was crying, but this heavy cold was making her feel wretched.

'No?' Clara raised her eyebrows. 'So you intend to try to get a ring on your finger, do you?' She held out her bony fingers, on one of which was a solid gold band inlaid with the blue enamel initials CF and PR. Between the two sets of letters were two tiny stones, a ruby and an emerald. 'Well, this is his ring and that's where it's staying. On *my* finger.'

Before she could stop herself, Meg said, 'He doesn't seeb in buch of a hurry to get the wedding ring to go with it onto your finger, though, does he?'

Shocked, Clara gasped. 'How dare you? Just wait till I tell Percy how rude you've been to me. You might as well pack your bags this very minute. You'll be out on the street by nightfall.' She smiled maliciously. 'Back in the workhouse even quicker than I could have hoped.' With that, she pulled open the door and left, slamming it behind her.

Meg sneezed and groaned aloud. How could she have let her foolish tongue run away with her? She went into the kitchen and cut one of the two lemons which Percy had left on the table. Then she squeezed the juice into a mug and added a teaspoonful of honey and poured hot water into it from the kettle that was kept permanently on the hob. Carefully, she carried the mug back up the stairs and snuggled back beneath the bedclothes. Sipping the liquid, she found that the tang of the lemon cleared her blocked nose and the honey eased her sore throat. The fire, built up that morning by Percy before he left for work and added to by Meg with the coal he had left, was still casting a warm glow about the room. It crackled comfortingly and shadows danced on the ceiling and walls as the daylight faded.

Meg leant back against the pillows and sighed. Warm and drowsy, she was about to drift into sleep when another knocking at the front door roused her.

'If it's that old biddy back again, I'm just not answering it,' she muttered, frowning, and pushed herself further beneath the bedclothes. But the knocking persisted and then she heard a voice calling – a young voice, a voice she recognized. 'Meg? Meg, where are you?'

'Jake!' She sat up, flung back the covers and swung her feet to the floor. 'I'm coming,' she called. 'I'm coming.'

'What are you doing here? Shouldn't you be at work?' she asked as she opened the front door. 'Come in, quick, before all the gossiping old biddies down the street see you.'

Jake stepped inside and pulled off his cap. He glanced

around the small hallway and peered through the half-open doorway into the front room. 'Nice little place, Meg. Getting your feet under the table, are you?'

Did she imagine it, or was there a trace of sarcasm to his tone?

'Don't you start,' she pouted. 'I've just had that dragon of a fiancée of his round here telling me to pack mi bags.'

'Can't blame her. News travels fast – half the town's talking about the pretty young lass old Mester Rodwell has taken on in his shop and moved into his house an' all.'

'He's not that old,' Meg retorted.

Jake stared at her, his face sober now. 'I was only joking. Oh, Meg, you're not really setting your cap at him, are you?'

Meg stared back. The thought hadn't entered her head. Oh yes, she'd made up to him, but only to get a job, to get the rooms over the shop to live in. She'd never thought about anything further than that.

But now she did. First Miss Finch and now Jake was suggesting so much more. Meg's eyes narrowed thoughtfully and a slow smile began to spread across her face.

'And what if I am?' she said softly.

Disgust flitted across his face. 'You're not serious?'

Her only answer was to shrug.

'How can you even think of doing such a thing? Specially after the way you've treated your own mam. You've called her all sorts and yet now you're thinking of climbing into an old man's bed. Ugh!'

'I wouldn't do what mi mam's doing,' she cried hotly. 'Oh no! If I get into Percy Rodwell's bed – or any other man's – there'll be a wedding ring on mi finger first. You can take bets on that, Jake Bosley!'

Twenty-Five

'You have today off as well,' Percy insisted the following morning.

'But I feel much better.'

'And you look much better, but I'd be happier if you had at least another day's rest. We don't want it turning into a nasty cough.'

Meg giggled. 'Well, you could always rub my chest for me.'

Percy blinked and stared at her for a moment.

'I'm sorry – I shouldn't have said that. It – it was a family joke if anyone got a bad cough. Mam used to rub goose grease on to our chests and – and—' She let tears fill her eyes and she turned away, saying in a husky, trembling voice, 'I forgot where I was for the moment. I'm so sorry.'

Yet again, he patted her shoulder awkwardly. 'There, there, don't let it upset you.'

Meg was not upset. She was angry – with herself. She had been too forward, too bold. Percy wasn't the sort of man she could joke with like that. Not like Isaac Pendleton, she thought wryly. He'd've been only too ready to take her up on the offer! The thought made her shudder. She still could not believe that her pretty young mother could become the mistress of such a man.

'You stay here – just for today, at any rate, and we'll see how you are in the morning.'

'All right,' she agreed meekly, but her mind was busy. She'd had a restless night that was not altogether caused by her cold. Nothing had been said about Miss Finch's visit either to the shop or to the house. Percy had not remarked on it and Meg had no intention of telling him about either of her visitors. But their remarks, their insinuations, had given her ideas. Ideas she meant to put into practice that very day.

Percy Rodwell opened the door to his home in the evening and thought he had stepped into the wrong house. An appetizing smell of cooking drifted into the hallway from the kitchen and through the open door into the front room he could see a fire blazing in the grate. On the small table in the window stood a vase of flowers. Percy blinked and reeled, momentarily unsteady on his feet. It felt as if he had stepped back into his childhood and he half expected, when he stepped into the kitchen, to see his mother bending down to take a crusty brown loaf out of the range oven. But, as he pushed open the door, it was Meg who straightened up, her face flushed – not with fever now but from the heat of the oven. In her hands she held a tin of sizzling roast potatoes. A stew bubbled in a pan on the hob.

'Oh,' she said, catching sight of him. 'I'd hoped to have it all on the table by the time you came in. But it's all nearly ready. Sit down.'

'Meg – what . . .?'

'I wanted to thank you for all you've done for me. All I could find was a bit of stewing beef and a few vegetables. But there was flour and fat in the pantry and some fallen apples. Did someone give you those?'

Mesmerized, Percy nodded absently, but he did as she bade him and sat down at the table.

'I've made some pastry so there's apple pie for afters.'

In a dream, Percy picked up his knife and fork and began to eat. Then, blinking as if to bring himself back to reality, he said, 'I'm sorry, I haven't asked how you're feeling.'

'Much better,' she said, sitting down opposite him. 'How was your day? Have you been busy in the shop?'

'Mm,' he nodded, his mouth full. 'Two or three ladies came in and asked specifically for you.'

Meg looked up at him, her eyes wide. 'Did they really?'

'Mm,' he said once more and did not speak again until his plate was clear. 'My, that was good. I never seem to get my stews to taste like that. Whatever do you put in it to give it that . . . that . . . ? Oh, I don't know. It's just got a special taste.'

'Ah,' said Meg, gathering the dirty plates together and bending down to bring the apple pie out of the oven to the table. 'Now that would be telling. We women have to have our little secrets,' she said coyly. 'Or you'd be able to do very nicely without us, wouldn't you?'

Percy smiled. 'I don't think so, Meg,' he murmured appreciatively as the smell of hot apple pie assailed his nostrils. To his surprise he heard himself saying rashly, 'I don't think I'd even want to try to manage without you now.'

Meg hid her triumphant smile. 'I feel so much better, I'll come back to work tomorrow. I can't have my lady customers kept waiting.'

'There's no hurry. I told them you might not be back until the beginning of next week. They all said they'd call again then.'

Carefully, Meg said, 'So – er – who were these ladies?'

Percy wrinkled his forehead as he recalled their names. 'Miss Robinson – you know, the fussy little spinster?' Meg nodded. 'She didn't want me to serve her. She was blushing as she came into the shop, and when she saw there was only me behind the counter she got very flustered.'

Meg laughed. 'Oh, poor thing. Who else?'

'Let me see – Mrs Newton and – oh yes – there was that young woman who's the schoolmistress at the – erm – at the workhouse.'

Meg's head shot up. 'Louisa? Miss Daley? She came into the shop?'

'Yes. She asked for you, but she didn't say why she wanted you. I supposed it was to buy something.'

'Maybe,' Meg said thoughtfully.

'Unless, of course, it was a message from your mother.'

Meg's mouth hardened. 'Whatever it was, I don't want to know. I don't want messages from my mother and I certainly don't want to see Louisa Daley.'

'Why? I thought she seemed quite a nice girl. The sort that might be a nice friend for you.'

'I thought she was my friend – once upon a time. But she betrayed me.'

'Betrayed you?'

Meg bit her lip, wondering whether she dared to confide in Percy. Was she taking too much of a risk? Would he believe her or begin to think that perhaps his fiancée was right after all?

She took a deep breath and the words came spilling out. She told him how she had been left in charge of Betsy and all that had happened.

'She accused me – me! – of taking her father's watch,' Meg finished indignantly and her eyes blazed. 'And no one – *no one* – accuses me of theft.'

In the face of her vehemence, Percy blinked.

The following morning, Percy said, 'Why don't you have another day off?' He smiled sheepishly. 'It – it was rather nice to come home to a warm house and a meal ready and waiting.'

Meg laughed. 'I'll do the same for you tonight. It'll be a pleasure, but—' She bit her lip.

'But what?' Percy asked anxiously.

'There's not much food left and – I'm sorry – but I haven't any money—'

'Oh, good heavens. What am I thinking of? Wait a moment . . .'

He went back up the stairs and Meg heard him opening a drawer in the chest in his bedroom. Moments later he returned and pressed several coins into her hand. 'Buy whatever you need.' He put his hand up. 'Don't tell me. It'll be a nice surprise.'

'Is there anything you don't like?'

Percy wrinkled his brow. 'I can't think of anything. I'm not a fussy eater.'

They smiled at each other.

Percy opened the door of his house eagerly that night. For the first time in years – not since before his mother had died – it felt like a home. He sniffed the air appreciatively. Something smelt good, but he couldn't decide just what it was . . .

'Roast pork, sage and onion stuffing and apple

sauce,' Meg told him moments later as he stood in the kitchen watching her. 'I used the rest of those fallen apples.' Her cheeks were rosy, her eyes bright. And, he realized with a jolt, she looked completely at home in his tiny kitchen.

'Sit down. I won't be a minute . . .'

'Not before I've put this outside the back door to chill.' Percy smiled as he produced a bottle of white wine from the bag he was carrying.

Meg's eyes widened. 'Oh! How very grand we'll be tonight. I know the posh folks drink wine, but I never have. Oh, Mr Rodwell, what a treat.'

'Please,' he said hesitantly, 'won't you call me Percy?' Then he added hastily, 'Not in the shop, of course, but when we're here. On our own.'

Meg's green eyes sparkled and Percy Rodwell was lost.

Twenty-Six

'Hello, lad, what yer doing here?' Albert Conroy greeted Jake on Sunday afternoon as he opened the gate for him. 'Can't keep away from us, eh?' He laughed wheezily.

Jake grinned. Like Meg, he had always had time for the old man whom many ignored. 'Something like that, Albert. You all right?'

'Oh ar, same as ever,' Albert said, resigned to his lot. He would never leave the workhouse, but there was no use in railing against what he couldn't change. He closed the gate and limped painfully back to the door of his lodge. 'Like a cuppa, would yer? Kettle's on the boil.'

Jake laughed. 'I don't remember a time when your kettle wasn't on the boil. Go on then.' Still chuckling, Jake followed the old man into the tiny room that was old Albert's home. Carefully, Jake laid a package on the table. 'I've brought you some eggs. Don't worry, I ain't pinched 'em. The missis said I could.'

Tears filled Albert's eyes. 'Aw, lad, that's kind of yer. A' yer sure? Don't you want to give 'em to – well – to someone else?' It was a long time since anyone had thought enough about him to bring him a gift.

Jake wrinkled his brow, pretending to think. 'No, can't say as I do. Go on, you daft old devil. I brought 'em for *you*.'

Albert sniffed and touched the package with trembling fingers. 'Thanks, lad.'

Moments later they sat together, Albert in the dilapidated armchair, Jake perched on a stool with a loose leg. Jake stirred the tea in the cracked mug, looking down into the swirling, dark brown liquid.

'Penny for 'em, lad.'

There was a silence before Jake said dolefully, 'I don't reckon they're worth a penny, Albert.'

'Wha's up? Don't tell me you're missing this place.'

Jake smiled, but it wasn't his usual wide grin. 'No. I miss some of the people, but no, not the place, even though it's the only home I've ever had.'

'Are they good to you, these folks you're working for?'

Jake nodded. 'Aye, the mester's all right. She's a bit of a tartar, but Meg warned me about her . . .' His voice trailed away and Albert watched his face.

'Ah,' the old man breathed. 'It's that lass, is it?'

Jake's head shot up. 'What?' He met Albert's steady, knowing gaze and realized denial was futile. He glanced away and sighed as he nodded. 'I don't know what to do. She won't listen to me.'

'How d'yer mean?'

Jake sighed. 'She's run away from here—'

'I know that. I saw her the night she came back when he –' Albert jerked his thumb towards the master's room – 'was going to lock her in the punishment room. She took off then and I ain't seen or heard from her since.'

There was a long silence between them until Jake blurted out, 'It's because of her mother. Meg doesn't . . . approve of her mother being with old man Pendleton.'

Albert shrugged philosophically. 'Can't blame the poor woman for seeking a bit of comfort. Had enough sorrow in her life just lately to turn her mind, if you ask me.' He sniffed. 'I like that little lass, but I reckon she ought to be grateful that someone's being kind to 'er mam and looking after her. And he does look after his lady friends, yer know. I'll say that for 'im.' Albert sniffed. 'Though I ain't got much else to say in his favour.' There was a pause before the older man pressed Jake to say more. 'Why's she so upset about it?'

'She – she says it's not how her mother brought her up. Meg feels betrayed, I suppose.'

'Aye, aye,' the old man murmured. 'And so soon after her dad ran off. Must have hit the lass hard. They've both brought her up to believe one thing, then she sees 'em doing the opposite. Both of 'em. It's a lot for a young lass to come to terms with. And, aye, mebbe to forgive an' all. You'll have to understand that, Jake.'

'I do, but – but she's doing the same thing herself now.' His mouth tightened. 'Talk about pot calling kettle black!' When Albert looked puzzled, Jake went on. 'She's gone to work for Mr Rodwell, the tailor and – and she's moved into his house.' Jake's face was tortured as he added, 'She's living with him, Albert. She's *living* with him.'

The old man could find nothing to say except, 'Aw, lad. Aw, lad.'

'How is she? Have you seen her? Where is she living?' The anxious questions tumbled out of Sarah's mouth.

Jake perched nervously on the edge of the sofa in Isaac Pendleton's office. The only occasions he had ever visited this room were when he had been in trouble. Usually such visits had ended with a thrashing or being sent to the punishment room across the yard, 'for his own good' as Isaac always put it.

'It hurts me far more than it hurts you, boy.' Isaac had always made a great play of being in loco parentis. 'You have no father to guide you and so it falls to me to fill that role. It pains me, really it does, boy, but if you're to make something of yourself in this world then one day you will thank me.'

At the time Jake couldn't imagine that he would ever have reason to thank the big man who seemed to wield the cane with such relish.

'It's what your father – whoever he was – would have wanted me to do. He'd have wanted me to make a man of you.' And the cane would swish through the air, landing on the thin trousers that offered no protection. The only solace Jake had ever had was that after Isaac's 'ministrations', Miss Pendleton would seek him out and clasp him tightly to her ample bosom, promising that she would have words with her brother. 'He's too harsh on you,' she would sob, stroking Jake's hair. 'You must try to be a good boy and not make him angry. He thinks it's his job to mould you into a fine young man. And you will be a fine young man, Jake. Oh, you will be.' And she would hug him all the tighter.

It was not lost on Jake that neither Letitia nor Isaac ever made reference to his mother. Perhaps, he thought sorrowfully, a young, unmarried girl giving birth in the workhouse and then dying and leaving her child to their tender mercies was not even worth a second thought.

'Is she all right?' Sarah prompted again.

Jake sighed. He hated having to be the one to tell the poor woman what her daughter was doing and, even worse, that Meg didn't want to see her own mother. He tried to soften the blow, but without deliberately lying. 'She's been ill. Had a heavy cold and – and Mr Rodwell's let her stay at his house.'

Sarah stared at him. 'But – but – he lives alone, doesn't he? I mean – he's engaged to Miss Finch, isn't he? *She* doesn't live there, does she?'

Jake was obliged to shake his head.

Sarah was silent for a moment as the implications unravelled themselves in her mind. Then she covered her mouth with trembling fingers. 'Oh no!' she breathed. 'You mean – you mean that Meg is living there alone with Mr Rodwell.'

Again Jake just nodded.

'But what will people say? I mean, they're saying enough about me. I don't matter, but Meg—' She paused again and her eyes widened. 'This is all my fault, isn't it? She's doing this to pay me back.' Sarah closed her eyes and rocked backwards and forwards. 'She was disgusted at me and yet now she's harming herself. No one will believe that nothing's going on between them.' Her eyes flew open again as she asked breathlessly, 'Does Miss Finch know?'

''Fraid so.'

Sarah groaned, then she brightened visibly. 'But maybe that's just as well. She'll either put a stop to it or – or give her approval and if his fiancée approves then people can't think . . .'

Her voice trailed away as she saw Jake's solemn expression. 'Nothing will stop the talk, missis. It's already started.'

'Now, Percy, I've come to get this matter sorted out once and for all.' Clara appeared at the shop the following morning and faced Percy across the counter. 'About this girl—'

At that moment Meg appeared from the workroom. Hearing the woman's shrill voice, she came through at once. 'You mean "this girl", Miss Finch?'

'I'm talking to my fiancé. This has nothing to do with you.'

'I think it has everything to do with me, Miss Finch. Mr Rodwell was kind enough to give me a bed in his spare room for a couple of nights whilst I get the rooms above the shop cleaned out. Then I'll be moving in here.'

'Over my dead body,' Clara spat. 'You should be back in the workhouse, where you belong.' Her lip curled. 'I'm sure you could usurp your mother's place if you smile nicely at the master. He likes young flesh. Only trouble is, he can't often get it.'

'Clara! Really, that's quite enough.'

She rounded on Percy. 'There's no one here. None of your precious customers, who, let me tell you, will soon stop coming in here when they hear about your carryings on.'

'And what carryings on would those be, Clara? And from whom are they going to hear it?' Percy's tone was deceptively mild, for there was a warning glint in his eyes. But if she saw it, Clara took no notice.

'Percy, I'm warning you. Get rid of this girl. If you don't – then – then—'

'Then what, Clara?'

'Our engagement is at an end.'

Meg stood still, hardly daring to breathe. She had not expected matters to come to a head so quickly. It was what she wanted, but not like this. Miss Finch – and her brother – could do untold harm to Percy and his business. And that was not what Meg wanted at all.

She moved forward to stand beside Percy. It gave the impression that the two of them were ranged on one side, facing Clara together.

'Oh, please, Miss Finch. If you really don't want me to live here, then . . . then . . .' She forced the tears to fill her fine eyes and spill down her cheeks. 'Then – I'll go back to the workhouse. But, please, don't ask Mr Rodwell to dismiss me. I'm trying so very hard and I do want to better myself.'

Now Clara turned her vitriol against Meg. 'Oho, I've no doubt you want to better yourself, girl. But don't think I can't see through your schemes, even if Percy here is too blind. I know what you're up to.'

As if mystified, Meg shook her head and widened her eyes innocently. 'I don't know what you mean, Miss Finch. All I know is that my father has betrayed his wife and family and now my mother . . .' She gulped and pressed her fingers to her mouth, as if the shame was too much to be spoken of aloud.

'Exactly. Your mother is no better than she should be. And you, I've no doubt, are going down the same path to ruination. Well, you're not dragging my Percy with you. Not whilst there's breath in my body, you're not.'

Percy's voice was calm, yet there was an unusual firmness in his tone as he said, 'No one is dragging me anywhere. I can make up my own mind, especially about my business. Meg—'

He got no further for Clara interrupted him with a wild screech. 'Oh, "Meg", is it now? So I was right all along.'

Percy continued as if she had not spoken. 'Meg will remain in my employment and she will continue to live in my house. In my opinion,' he went on, his steady gaze meeting Clara's hostile glare, 'the rooms above here are quite unsuitable for anyone to inhabit.'

Clara gave a gasp and tottered backwards. She seemed about to fall, but she recovered herself. Pressing the palm of her hand to her chest as if she had a terrible pain there, she rasped, 'I do declare, Percy, you've quite taken leave of your senses.'

When he made no move to go around the counter to her or even to say anything further, her eyes narrowed and she nodded. 'Very well then. You leave me no alternative. I will not be a party to this – this disgrace. As I said, Percy, you may consider our engagement to be at an end.'

They stared at one another for a few moments before he nodded slowly and said quietly, 'As you wish, Clara.'

With one last surge of energy, Clara Finch shook her fist at him. 'You've not heard the last of this, Percy Rodwell. Wait till my brother hears. Then we'll see if you will still have a business.'

As the sound of the shop bell died away after Clara's indignant departure, Meg said, 'Oh, Percy, I didn't want that to happen. Go after her. Make it up with her. Please. I couldn't bear to be the cause of you being unhappy.'

Slowly, Percy turned to look down at her and there was a note of surprise in his tone as he said, 'Don't worry yourself about that, my dear. In fact, all I am feeling at this precise moment is an overwhelming sense of relief.'

Twenty-Seven

Percy closed the shop and they set off along the street.

'I'll just call in at the General Stores,' he said. 'Get a bottle of wine. This calls for a celebration.'

Meg looked up at him. 'A celebration?' Even she was surprised. 'You mean – I mean – I thought you'd be devastated.'

'Do I look devastated?'

'No,' Meg agreed, trying to keep her face straight. Percy was smiling, but then that was his right. She must not let her own feelings show, the flutterings of excitement in the pit of her stomach as her plan began to form and take shape and, yes, began to happen.

'When we get home . . .' He savoured the words. 'When we get home, if you make the meal, I'll light the fire in the front room and we – we'll have a nice, cosy evening together.' Suddenly, he was unsure. 'Is – is that all right?'

She smiled radiantly. 'Of course it is. Just what we both need.' *Thank goodness*, Meg was thinking, *that I had already planned a special meal tonight*.

Percy stopped outside the grocer's. 'What wine should I get? White or red?'

'But we've some left from last night—'

He waved aside her protest. 'I want to celebrate,' he said firmly.

'Well, it's roast chicken.'

His eyes sparkled. 'My favourite,' he murmured. 'White, then.'

Left alone outside the shop for a few moments, Meg began to feel less confident. What if Miss Finch made real trouble for Percy? What if her brother was so incensed that he threw Percy out of his shop? What then?

'Here we are.' He was back beside her and her doubts faded. In the short time that she had known him, she had never seen him look so happy or relaxed.

Some time later as they sat opposite each other across the narrow kitchen table, Percy confirmed her thoughts. He raised his glass to her in a toast. 'That was a lovely meal and I'll tell you something, Meg, I don't know when I last felt as happy as this. I feel as if I've been let out of prison.'

Huskily she said, 'I know just how you feel. That's how I felt the day I left the workhouse. And I owe all that to you. I'm only sorry that it's caused trouble between you and your fiancée. You – you will make it up with her, won't you? I mean her brother owns your shop premises. What if – what if he turns you out?' At last, she was voicing her greatest fear.

'I don't think he'll do that. He knows it would be difficult to find another tenant. The building needs a lot spending on it and Theobald Finch doesn't like spending money.'

'Haven't you ever tried to – to buy it from him?'

'My father – he started the business – tried to years ago, and I tried too, but the only way I was ever going to get it was to . . .' His voice faded away.

'What?' Meg prompted. 'Go on.'

Reluctantly, Percy admitted, 'Theo promised to give me the title deeds to the shop on my marriage to Clara. It – it was to be our wedding present.'

Meg gasped. 'And now you've lost that all because of me.'

'No, no,' Percy assured her. 'You mustn't think that. You've done me a favour. I think I always knew marriage between Clara Finch and me wasn't right, else why would I have kept putting off the wedding date every time she tried to suggest one? She would have had us married four years ago but I –' he smiled sheepishly at Meg – 'but I kept finding excuses.'

'Did you?' Meg said and smiled at him, her wonderful, breathtaking smile. It took poor Percy Rodwell's breath away and left his senses reeling. 'No,' he said, shaking his head slowly. There was a new-found certainty in his tone. 'No, I won't be trying to make it up with Miss Finch.' He raised his glass. 'I'm glad it's happened. Truly I am. So, I want to make a toast, Meg. To my new assistant, to the new ladies' wear and – and to freedom. Our freedom.'

Smiling, Meg touched his glass with her own. 'Here's to us, Percy,' she said softly.

'He's broken off his engagement to Miss Finch. The missus heard it in town.'

On the following Sunday afternoon, Jake brought the news to the workhouse, to Meg's mother. Sarah gasped. 'Why? Is it anything to do with Meg?'

Jake's face clouded as he shrugged. 'Who knows?'

'What have you heard?'

'Just that Miss Finch was so angry about Mr Rodwell employing Meg and then taking her to live with him that she threatened him. If he didn't get rid of Meg, their engagement was off.'

'And?'

'He insisted he wasn't going to sack Meg and that she was going to continue living at his house. Meg'd asked him if she could live in the rooms above the shop, but Miss Finch wouldn't hear of that either.' Jake glanced at Sarah and debated whether to tell her the whole story.

'You know the last time she came here?' he began tentatively. Sarah nodded, tears filling her eyes. 'The night after she found out about me and – and Isaac?' she whispered. 'That's the last time I saw her.'

'Yes. Well, she was coming to tell you that she'd had the idea of asking Mr Rodwell if you could both live above the shop. You and her. She said she wanted to look after you.' As Sarah covered her face with her hands, Jake said swiftly, 'I'm sorry, I shouldn't have told you that.'

'Yes, yes, you should. Oh, poor Meg. No wonder she's angry with me. Do – do you think she will ever forgive me?'

'Of course she will. Give her time. You're her mam.' He tried to make his voice sound hopeful and positive, but in his heart he wasn't sure. Although he thought Meg was wrong, a tiny part of him could understand how she must feel.

'I don't think so,' Sarah murmured sadly. 'First her dad and then me. We've both let her down. I don't think she will ever forgive either of us.'

Jake said nothing.

'Now, Percy, this is a fine how-de-do. Let's see if we can sort it out, man to man, eh?' Theobald Finch stood in the centre of the shop first thing on the Monday morning a week after his sister had arrived home to tell him that Percy had broken off their engagement. Hating confrontation, Theobald had deliberately left the matter for a few days, hoping that Percy would see sense and beg Clara's forgiveness. But a week had passed and there had been no sign of Percy coming, cap in hand, to the Hall.

Meg, serving a lady at her own small counter, had glanced up when he entered. It was the moment she had been dreading. There was only one other person she feared seeing more than Theobald Finch – Jake. But he hadn't been near the shop, even though by this time she believed he must have heard the gossip. Ron's wife came regularly to the bakery next door. There was no doubt she would have carried home the news with great glee. And Meg could imagine Mrs Smallwood's reaction. 'Aye well, I allus said she'd come to a bad end, that one. Blood will out.'

Oh yes, Jake would know by now, and if he knew, then everyone at the workhouse would soon hear of it too.

'Would you care to step into the workroom, Theo. We shall be more private there.'

Theobald gave a loud guffaw. 'I don't reckon there's anything I have to say that half the town don't know already, Percy.' He glanced towards Meg and her customer. 'Morning, Mrs Cartwright. Fine morning for a juicy bit of gossip.'

The woman glared at him, two pink spots appearing suddenly in her cheeks. 'Well, really!' She gathered her belongings and stormed from the shop, leaving Meg calling after her. 'But, madam . . .'

Mrs Cartwright paused at the door to turn and say, 'I have never been treated so abominably in my life. I shall never set foot inside this shop again.'

The shop bell clanged huffily as she slammed the door behind her.

'Oh, dear me,' Theobald remarked, his tone heavy with sarcasm, 'the lady seems somewhat offended. You'll have to be more careful, Percy, else you'll soon have no customers left, my dear fellow.'

Percy sighed. 'Please, Theo, come through—'

'I'm quite comfortable here, thank you. Now, about this other little matter. Look here, Percy, I don't want there to be trouble between us. Make it up with Clara, there's a good fellow. Now, what do you say?'

There was a long silence whilst the two men stared at each other. Meg held her breath. Quite calmly, but very firmly, Percy said, 'No, Theo. I'm sorry, but I no longer think marriage between Clara and me would work.'

'You mean – you're jilting her? My sister is being jilted by a penny-pinching upstart like you?'

Percy did not answer, but continued to meet Theobald's hostile eyes with a steady gaze. At last he spoke. 'So,' he asked slowly, 'are you going to give me notice?'

'I've a good mind to . . .' Theobald began but then, glancing about him, he seemed to think better of it. 'But this is business. I'm not a man to let private matters interfere with business. You've always been a good tenant, Percy. No, no, we'll keep business entirely separate.' Slowly Meg let out the breath she seemed to have been holding for ages. 'But,' Theobald warned, 'you've not heard the last of this. Oh, dear me, no.'

When he had gone, Meg said, 'I thought he was going to turn you out.'

Percy, his gaze following the portly man down the street, said slowly, 'No, he's more got more business acumen than that.'

'Does – does he own a lot of the shops?'

'The four shops in this row – the bakery, this one, the ironmonger's and the greengrocer's beyond that.

And then he owns several other properties about the town. Houses and cottages mainly. A whole row of them in Mint Street and one or two near the church, including . . .' He had been about to say more but at that moment the shop bell clanged and one of Percy's best customers entered. Percy hurried forward.

'Good morning, sir, good morning. Your suit's ready for you. If you'd care to step this way into the workroom . . .'

'Why don't you go down to the shop and see Meg yourself?' Jake suggested to Sarah.

'Oh no, I couldn't. If she doesn't want to see me, then . . .' She closed her eyes and sighed heavily. 'Besides, I don't want to embarrass her. If she's well settled in a good job, it's – it's better that I keep out of the way.' Sarah's voice was forlorn as she murmured, 'I'd only shame her.'

Jake took Sarah's thin hand as he declared stoutly, 'You couldn't shame anyone. She's being very silly and unkind and I'm going to tell her so.'

'Oh no, Jake, you mustn't. You're a good, thoughtful boy, but you really mustn't.'

'I shall. She should be grateful to have a mother like you. I – I would be.'

Sarah smiled sadly and stroked his hair. 'No wonder everyone here likes you so much. We all miss you.'

'Even old man Pendleton? I bet he misses the exercise with his cane.'

Sarah laughed for the first time in months. 'Oh, Jake, you bad boy. But it's Miss Pendleton I feel sorry for. She really misses you and weeps when you don't visit.'

'She's the same with all the boys.'

Sarah shook her head. 'No, I don't think so. You're special to her.'

'Well, I was here the longest.' He grinned, delighting in his own newly found freedom. There was only one thing marring his complete happiness. Meg.

'Is it true what they say?' he went on, trying not to think of her.

'What about?'

'That the matron had a little boy of her own once.' His voice dropped to a whisper. 'Even though she was never married.'

'Oh, I don't know about that, Jake. And I wouldn't dare to ask. Mr Pendleton is very kind to me, but I wouldn't like to pry into his private life.' She leant closer to Jake and whispered. 'I asked about his wife once and he snapped my head off and told me never to mention her name again.'

'Perhaps it's too painful for him to talk about her.'

'What happened to her? Did she die?'

Jake wrinkled his brow. 'That's what they say, but it happened about the time I was born. They say that's why Miss Pendleton came here to take her place as the matron. It's not usual, you know. A brother and sister being master and matron. It's usually man and wife, but after his missis died the guardians let Miss Pendleton come.' He stood up. 'And talking of her, I'd better go and see her.' He grinned. 'Don't want her in tears 'cos I didn't see her while I was here.'

Jake was as good as his word. The following day he asked George Smallwood for a little time off during the afternoon to go into the town.

'Aye, lad. Tek the pony and trap. He could do with

an outing and that way –' the big man laughed – 'you'll be back quicker.'

When Jake entered the tailor's shop, there were three customers and he was obliged to wait to speak to Meg. She was serving two customers at once, running along the counter from one to the other, whilst on the other side of the shop Percy was unrolling a piece of suiting to show a gentleman.

By the time the place was empty, Jake had been kicking his heels for ten minutes and his irritation with Meg had grown.

'Hello, young man,' Percy, the first to be free, greeted him jovially. 'Come to be measured for a new suit have you?'

'I've come to see Meg,' Jake replied curtly.

Percy glanced across at the one woman customer left in the shop and saw Meg carefully writing in the customers' ledger. Most of the townsfolk had accounts at the shop and paid at the end of each month. 'I don't think she'll be much longer.'

As the woman left, Percy said, 'Take Jake into the back. You can make us all a nice cup of tea, Meg. I'm parched after all that talking. We've been quite busy this afternoon, haven't we?'

As soon as the door closed between them and Percy, Jake could contain his anger no longer. 'Oh, "Meg" now, is it? When's the wedding set for then?'

Meg glared at him. 'Don't be stupid, Jake.'

'If anyone's being stupid, it's you, Meg Kirkland. Why haven't you been to see your mam? You're making her so unhappy.'

'*I'm* making *her* unhappy? What about what she's done to me? You only seem to think about her. What about me?'

'You seem to be doing very nicely for yourself. I don't think you need my help or my sympathy. But she does.'

'Then you can be her son. Hers and her fancy man's.' She thrust her face close to his. 'Because I'm no longer her daughter.'

Twenty-Eight

'Meg, are you happy here?' Percy interrupted her thoughts as they sat together in the cosy front room after a superb Christmas dinner, which Meg had cooked: goose and all the trimmings followed by plum pudding and mince pies. It had been a quiet day with just the two of them, but a welcome one, for the days and weeks leading up to Christmas had been busy at the shop. But now, in the quietness of the little house, her work done, Meg couldn't stop the memories intruding: pictures of the Christmases they'd spent at Middleditch Farm when Mrs Smallwood had invited the Kirkland family to the farmhouse. Her table had always been laden with all manner of food and, for once, she'd not minded Meg's friendship with Alice. The girls had helped her in the kitchen in the morning and then, later in the afternoon, the two families would join in the games that Meg and Alice devised. There had been warmth and laughter, but, Meg wondered now, had that been when her father had first cast his eye at Alice? And Jake – she hardly dared to think of him. It would be the first Christmas he'd ever known outside the workhouse. He'd be at the farm with the Smallwoods and Ron's family.

For a moment an acute longing to be with Jake threatened to overwhelm her. Then she heard Percy's tentative voice asking her, 'Are you happy here?'

Meg plastered a bright smile on her face. 'Of course I am. Who wouldn't be? Living in a nice little house like this and I love working in the shop. Handling all those lovely clothes—'

'You can have anything you want, you know. From the shop. If there's anything – anything at all—'

'Oh, I didn't mean it to sound as if I was asking for anything,' Meg said hurriedly. 'Please don't think I was dropping hints. You've given me such a beautiful shawl as a Christmas gift. It's far too good for me.'

Percy smiled and shook his head. 'Nothing's too good for you, Meg.' His gaze never left her face. 'And I would never think – for one moment – that you were dropping hints. You're not that sort of girl.'

Meg dropped her gaze and for a moment shame swept through her. How guileless he was. Could he really not see through her schemes?

There was a long pause before he said, 'Meg—' and then stopped again.

'Yes, Percy?'

'I . . . erm . . . just asked because . . . I . . . erm . . . wondered if our . . . well . . . our arrangement is causing you any embarrassment. I mean, we know that people are talking. I'm just concerned for your reputation, that's all.'

Meg put her head on one side and said coyly, 'And what about your reputation?'

Now Percy laughed. 'I don't think mine will suffer too badly, do you? I expect half the men in the town wish they were in my shoes.'

Meg lowered her head to hide her smile, but to Percy the action appeared to be one of modesty. 'You're a lovely young woman, Meg, and I wouldn't want to be the cause of making matters worse for you. You've suffered enough this past year. All I want to do is to take care of you.'

She looked up. 'You are doing, Percy. You've been wonderful, but I'm only sorry that me coming here seems to have caused trouble for you.'

'Don't ever think that. I'm – I'm pleased it happened. Pleased you came and – yes – I'm pleased my engagement to Miss Finch is at an end. I saw her in her true light in her treatment of you.'

Suddenly, he launched himself out of his armchair and fell on his knees in front of her. 'Oh, Meg, Meg,' he cried passionately, 'you must know how I feel about you. How I care for you. How I – love you!'

'Oh – oh! I had no idea,' Meg squeaked and widened her green eyes. She hoped she sounded suitably surprised and with just the right amount of pleasure. But in truth it was neither sudden nor a surprise. It was what she had planned to happen. 'Oh, Percy.' She leant forward and took hold of his hands. 'Do you – do you really care for me?'

'I've never felt this way about anyone before in my whole life,' he said ardently.

Meg couldn't resist saying saucily, 'Not even Miss Finch?'

'Especially not Miss Finch. I know I'm a lot older than you, but – but I just want to look after you. Would you . . . oh, Meg, will you marry me?'

'Don't you know I care for you too?' She was careful not to use the word 'love'. 'You've been so kind to me, so generous. I'd be honoured to be your wife.'

Behind the thick spectacles Percy blinked his surprise. 'You would? Are you sure? Really sure? I mean – I thought – perhaps that young man who comes to the shop. Jake—'

'Him!' Her tone was scathing, trying to blot out the sudden image of Jake beneath the mistletoe at Middleditch Farm. Oh, how she wished—. No, no, she didn't. She mustn't even think of Jake. She was on the verge of getting exactly what she had planned for these last few months. She must not think of Jake – not now. 'He disapproves of me. He's taken my mother's side. He doesn't realize how much she's hurt me.'

Percy, his eyes wet with happiness behind the thick spectacles, patted her hand. 'You don't know how happy you've made me, my dear. I want everyone in the world to be as happy as I am at this moment. When we're married, Meg, your mother can come here. She won't have to stay with Isaac Pendleton. She can live with us. Would that make you happy?'

Now Meg's tears of gratitude were genuine and she felt a surge of guilt, suddenly ashamed of her scheming. 'Oh, Percy, thank you. Thank you.' She flung her arms about his neck and kissed his cheek. In that moment she silently vowed that she would be a good wife to this kind and generous man. She could trust Percy Rodwell not to hurt her. He would take care of her. It was all she wanted, she told herself as she closed her eyes and buried deep inside her any feelings she had ever had for Jake Bosley.

Jake burst into the master's room without even knocking. He stood in the doorway, panting. It was New Year's Day and he had run all the way from the farm, rage and frustration spurring him on.

From her place on the sofa in front of the fire, Sarah looked up, and Isaac rose from behind his desk.

'What's this? What's this? Bursting in here without a by your leave? Is the place on fire, boy?'

Gasping, Jake's glance went beyond the master and found Sarah's startled gaze. 'She's only going to marry him, that's what!' he blurted out.

Sarah's mouth dropped open and she fell back against the cushions, her hand to her chest as if, suddenly, she found it difficult to breathe.

'Who? What?' Mesmerized, Isaac glanced round at Sarah and then back to Jake. 'Who are you talking about, boy?'

'Meg! She's going to marry Percy Rodwell.'

'Meg is? But – but he's engaged to Miss Finch.'

'He broke it off. Weeks – months – ago. And now . . .' His voice broke and he was unable to carry on.

Isaac leant on the desk towards Jake, resting on his knuckles. 'You mean to tell me,' he said slowly, frowning heavily, 'that Percy Rodwell broke off his engagement to Miss Finch in order to marry Meg?'

Jake nodded, his own expression as grim as the older man's.

Isaac sank down into his chair again and leant back, his hands clasped in front of his ample stomach. 'Well, well,' he said as he recovered from the surprise. 'All I can say is that he'll rue the day he married that little slut instead of Miss Finch, who is a fine woman of some standing in this town. And let me tell you, boy –' Now he wagged his forefinger at Jake as if he were somehow responsible – 'her brother, Mr Theobald Finch, will not stand by and see his sister slighted in such a way. Oh, dear me, no. Mr Percy Rodwell had better watch out, that's all I can say.'

Behind him, Sarah wept silently into her handkerchief.

The banns were read in the local church on the first three Sundays in May. Because Meg was under the age of consent, the vicar had sought Sarah's permission. She was reluctant to give it, but believing it was what her daughter wanted, she signed the form. Percy and Meg were to be married early in the morning on the last Friday of the month. The wedding was only three days away when Meg put on her best hat and coat and walked up the road towards the workhouse.

She couldn't help remembering the first time she had approached it. Though it was barely a year ago so much had happened since. She was almost seventeen now, yet she felt so much older and painfully wiser. With that knowledge had come bitterness and resentment. But today, at Percy's insistence, she was going to see her mother. Where Jake had failed, Percy – and all that he had to offer – had persuaded her to heal the breach.

'Hello, lass. Come to see yer mam, 'ave yer?' Albert greeted her at the gate. 'And what's this I hear about you getting wed? I thought you was waiting for me.'

Meg laughed. 'Oh, Albert, I'm far too old for you.' The old man laughed wheezily, but then his face sobered. 'I 'spect you'd like a word with yer mam without *him* earwigging, wouldn't yer?'

Meg nodded.

'Right. You wait in my little room here and I'll go and find one of the young 'uns to tek a message to yer mam.'

The old man limped away and Meg sat down in his lodge to wait. Peering out through the open door a few moments later, she saw a little girl skip across the yard towards the main building and old Albert returning.

'There, that's done. You can have this place to yerselves for a nice little chat. I'll make mysel' scarce.'

He brewed tea, hot and strong, and then said, 'She'll be along in a minute so I'll go and have a chinwag with one or two of the fellers in the orchard. Little walk'll do me good and I can still keep me eye out for folk coming up the path.'

After Albert had gone, Meg waited, her nervous fingers twisting her gloves. She rehearsed the words she intended to say to her mother. *If you come with me now, we'll say no more about you and* him. *Folks'll forget in time and living with Percy and me . . .*

A shadow appeared in the doorway and Meg looked up. It was not her mother who stood there, but Ursula Waters.

'So,' she said, stepping into the tiny room, 'you want to see your mother, do you? Well, I'm very sorry, but your mother does not want to see you.'

Meg rose slowly to face her. She tried to tell herself that no one in the workhouse had any power over her now, but still she found she was trembling. Then anger strengthened her resolve and swept away her fear. 'I've come to take her away from here. She's coming to live with me.'

'To live with you and your new husband, you mean. Oh, I think not. The master . . . wants her. He won't let her go.'

Meg raised her eyebrows. 'I'd've thought you'd have been only too pleased to be rid of her.' She paused and then added, with deliberate cruelty, 'There might be room in his bed again for you, then.'

Ursula's face worked as she struggled to control her emotions. She clenched and unclenched her hands. 'I want . . .' she gasped, 'him to be happy. That's all I want out of life now. Him to be happy. And if she – if she makes him happy – then—'

'And what happens when he tires of her? When a younger, prettier woman comes into the workhouse and he casts her aside? Just like he did to you?'

Even as the words left her lips, Meg knew she had said too much. The woman flew at her with flailing fists, catching her a glancing blow on the side of the head. But the young girl was much stronger and fitter. She caught and held the hysterical woman's wrists and, though Ursula writhed and twisted in Meg's grasp, she could not break free.

'Now, listen to me. You just go and tell my mother I want to see her.'

'No,' Ursula screamed at her. 'He won't want her to see you. *She* doesn't want to see you. She told me.'

For the first time, Meg was unsure. 'Is – is that true?'

'Of course it's true.' Ursula was calming down a little now, though Meg still kept tight hold of her.

'Is he going to marry her?'

'Marry her?' Ursula sneered. 'He'll not marry her – or anyone. Besides, she's not free. She's still married to your father, isn't she?'

'But if she wasn't, would he marry her then?'

Slowly, Ursula shook her head. 'He can't.'

'Can't? Why can't he?'

'Because . . . because,' the woman blurted out, 'he's still married.'

'Still married? But – but I thought his wife died.'

'No. She ran off. Couldn't stand it in the workhouse. She was the matron before – before Miss Pendleton came – but she hated it. She ran off with one of the fellers that was in here. That was when . . . that was when the master turned to me. I looked after him. I cared for him. I would never have left him.'

Meg stared at her. 'Do you know, Waters,' she said slowly, as she released her grasp, 'I feel sorry for you, I—'

Ursula's face was ugly again. 'Don't you feel sorry for me,' she spat. 'I could have left this place years ago – if I'd wanted. He'd have set me up in the town, but I couldn't bear to leave him. Just to be near him. That's all I ask and to see that no one – *no one* – ever hurts him again.' She thrust her face close to Meg's. 'I won't let them. Do you hear?'

'Yes,' Meg answered quietly, 'I hear.'

'Save your pity for yourself. You're going to need it if you marry Percy Rodwell. You're stealing another woman's man, with your green eyes and flaming hair. Seducing him with the promise of your young body.' Ursula glanced Meg up and down and her mouth twisted with jealousy. 'You mark my words.' She stood back, a smug expression on her face. 'You'll live to regret the day you marry Percy Rodwell.'

Twenty-Nine

Jake hovered at the door into the dairy, waiting for Mabel Smallwood to glance up and see him. He'd finished helping Ron with the evening milking and should, at this moment, have been making his way back to the little cottage for his evening meal with Ron's family. But there was something more important on his mind than eating. In fact, his thoughts were tearing him apart and robbing him of his appetite.

Meg was getting married tomorrow and he had to try and prevent it. She wouldn't listen to him, but she might listen to her mother. If only he could persuade Sarah to make the first move, to go and see her daughter in the shop, then maybe . . .

'Hello, lad, what're you after?'

'Sorry to bother you, missis, but I need to go into town. Urgent, like. And the mester's not about to ask.'

Mabel sniffed. 'Ain't that just like him. Never about when you want him. What's so urgent then?'

'I – er – have to see someone.'

Mabel glanced at him sharply. 'You seem to be needing to "see someone" a lot just lately. Got a girl, have yer?'

Jake shook his head, but he felt the colour creeping up his face. 'I want to see someone at the workhouse.'

Mabel sniffed her disapproval once more. 'Should've thought you'd've been pleased to shake the dust of that place off yer feet. Can't understand why you still want to keep going back.'

'I don't really, missis. It's just . . .' He sighed. 'Well, there's just something I have to do and if I don't do it today, it'll be too late . . .' His voice trailed away as if already he was anticipating failure.

Again, Mabel's glance seemed to bore into his soul and read his mind. 'Ah, I know. It's that wretched girl, isn't it? You're seeing that Meg creature.'

'She's not a creature,' he flashed back, unable to stop himself.

'Oho, so that's it, is it? You've got yer eye on her yourself, 'ave yer?' Suddenly her face softened. 'Look, Jake, you're a good lad. Me and the mester have taken to you, but don't get yourself mixed up with that family, if you'll take my advice. They're trouble. The lot of 'em. There's bad blood there. It's in the breed.' She paused, glanced away and then, coming closer, said in a low voice, 'You'll get hurt by them, lad. Same as me and the mester have been hurt. I don't often talk about it and I'll skelp the lugs off yer if I hear you've breathed a word about it to anyone, but it near broke our hearts when that bugger seduced our daughter. Oh, she could be a bit flighty, our Alice, I know that, but she wasn't a bad girl. But 'im.' She cupped her hands, thumbs touching as if encircling someone's neck. 'If I ever see him again, I'll swing for him.' She took a deep breath, calming herself. Then she turned away, shrugging her shoulders. 'But, it's up to you, lad. I'll not stop you going. Do what you have to do, but I'm warning you, it'll bring you heartache being involved with that family.'

'Thanks, missis. I'll be as quick as I can . . .'

Before she could say any more, he turned and ran

across the yard and into the road towards the town and the workhouse. He ran most of the way, stopping only to catch his breath when he could run no more. At last he was hurrying through the gate, pausing only to greet Albert briefly, then across the yard and in through the back entrance. He halted near the clerk's office door, cocking his head on one side, listening intently. He didn't want to run into the master: he wanted to catch Sarah alone. There was no sound coming from inside the clerk's office, no murmur of voices. No doubt the clerk was in there busily writing in all the numerous ledgers, keeping all the official records of the workhouse up to date. The door of the master's office was directly in front of Jake as he stood hesitating, whilst to his right the stairs led to the first floor. He put his foot on the bottom step, debating where the most likely place to find Sarah was. He bit his lip. During the daytime, she would probably be downstairs in the office, but there was also more likelihood of Isaac being there too. He took a step up the stairs and as he did so something – a movement perhaps – made him glance up.

Ursula was standing at the top of the stairs. 'What do you want here? You've no business here now.'

She descended the stairs until she was standing three steps above Jake, effectively barring his way. 'I expect it's matron you've come to see, is it? Can't keep away, can you?'

'None of your business,' he retorted boldly. As an inmate, he would not have dared to speak to Waters in such a way. She still had influence over the master and she was a tittle-tattle, if ever there was one. 'I've come to see Mrs Kirkland.'

There was a sudden malicious gleam in the woman's eyes. 'About that trollop of a daughter of hers, is it?

Well, I can save you the trouble. Mrs Kirkland wants no more to do with her daughter. And the master agrees with her. The wretched girl has made her bed. She can lie in it.'

The picture Ursula drew was in Jake's mind too – Meg in Percy Rodwell's bed, lying beside him, him turning to her . . . Jake shuddered.

Ursula's keen eyes were boring into his thoughts. 'No,' she whispered. 'Not a pretty thought, is it? Specially not for you. Sweet on her, aren't you? I saw you together when you were here. Sneaking around at night, meeting in the dead room—'

'Please, just let me see Mrs Kirkland. We might still be able to stop her—'

Ursula took two more steps down and grasped Jake's coat. 'Be off with you, else I'll call the master. She doesn't want to see her daughter – or you.'

'I don't believe you—'

Jake never finished his plea for, with a violent push that caught him off balance, Ursula sent him flying off the step to land sprawling on the floor. 'Be off with you and don't come back here again, or you'll find yourself in the punishment room . . .'

At that instant, a figure appeared in the entrance door: a figure who gave a cry of alarm and bent over Jake at once.

'Waters! What are you doing?' Letitia cradled Jake in her fat arms. 'There, there. Are you hurt, my precious boy?'

'He's trying to make trouble. I was telling him to let well alone, but he slipped and fell off the step. He'd do best to stay away from here, wouldn't he, Matron, or he might hear things he didn't ought to.'

'Hold your tongue, woman.' For once Letitia was in command. 'Or it'll be me telling the master.'

Ursula sniffed and pushed her way past the pair of them. 'Suit yourself, but just remember – I've been here a long time. A very long time . . .'

As the woman walked away, the matron muttered beneath her breath, 'Too long,' but then her attention came back to Jake. 'Are you sure you're not hurt?' Letitia's face crumpled, tears filled her eyes and ran down her plump cheeks and she held on to Jake even more tightly as if she would never let him go . . .

A little later Jake walked away from the workhouse, his thoughts in tumult. He had failed in his attempt to see Meg's mother, yet he could not believe that it was Sarah who'd said she did not want to see her daughter. On the occasions he had spoken to her, she had been desperate for news of Meg and longing for the rift between them to be healed. Jake sighed heavily as he trudged along. There was one last thing he could do, though he didn't hold out much hope of success.

He would go and see Meg one more time and plead with her not to marry Percy.

Jake held his breath as he knocked on the door of Percy's cottage. Meg might be at home now preparing their evening meal whilst Percy was still at the shop. Suddenly the door opened and she was standing before him.

'Jake!'

He couldn't tell from her expression if she was pleased to see him.

'Meg – I must talk to you.'

She frowned. 'If you've come to try to persuade me to change my mind, you're wasting your time.'

'Look, let me come in. We can't talk here on the doorstep.'

Meg glanced up and down the street. 'No, I don't want the nosy beggars round here gossiping about me.'

'Huh,' Jake muttered wryly. 'I should think there's plenty of that going on already. A bit more won't make a ha'porth of difference.'

'Oh well, if you're going to be like that.' Meg glared at him and Jake sighed. 'I'm not. Oh, Meggie, please – please let me in. There's something I must say to you.'

'If it's about Percy—'

'Just let me in, will you?'

'All right,' she said grudgingly and held the door a little wider for him to step inside.

'Meg, please don't do it,' he began at once. 'Work for him, live with him if you must.' His agony at the very thought was plain on his face, yet he pressed on. 'But please – don't marry him.'

'Give me one good reason why I shouldn't.' Facing him in the tiny hallway, Meg ticked off her own reasons on her fingers. 'He loves me, he's kind to me, he's got a nice little home and a good business. What more could I –' her face twisted with bitterness – 'a girl from the workhouse, hope for?'

Jake's face was white. 'But you don't love him, do you?'

'Love?' She was scathing. 'What do you know about love?'

'I know I love you,' he said simply and she gaped at

him. He caught hold of her hands and held them fast. 'Don't do it, Meg. Don't marry him. Marry me.'

'You?'

'Yes, me. Is that such an awful thought?'

'No,' she whispered. 'It's not an awful thought at all. It's just that I – I hadn't realized.' Her eyes filled with tears and she squeezed his hands in return. 'Oh, Jake, I can't.'

'You mean you don't love me,' Jake said harshly.

'I – I – oh, Jake, you shouldn't ask me that. You really shouldn't – not now.'

'Come away with me. Come now. Ron and his missis'll take you in . . .'

Meg was shaking her head and laughing, a little hysterically, through her tears. 'If they did, they'd soon find themselves homeless when the missis found out. We'd all end up back in the workhouse, Jake. She'd see to that.'

'So – it's no, is it? You're really going to marry him.'

Meg bit her lower lip so hard that she drew blood, but she nodded, tears splashing down her cheeks as she did so.

'Then it's goodbye, Meg, 'cos I shan't see you again if you marry him.'

'Oh, Jake,' she cried, 'don't say that. Please – I thought you were my friend.'

'I am your friend. More than you will ever know.'

'Then don't desert me. Please, Jake.'

Slowly, he shook his head. 'I can't stand to see you marry him,' he said huskily. 'And I don't like the way you're treating your mother.'

'But I went to see her. I did. Honestly. I waited for her in Albert's lodge. But Waters came and told me that

Mam didn't want to see me. That she never wanted to see me again.'

Jake's face softened a little. 'You went to see her? You really went?'

'Percy said I should.'

Jake's expression hardened again. He snatched his hands away. 'Oh, so it wasn't because of what I said, because *I* asked you to go and see her? Only because *Percy* –' he spat out the name – 'asked you.'

'Oh, Jake, don't – please don't be like this. I can't bear it.'

He pushed past her and opened the door, almost falling out into the dusk of evening in his haste to get away.

'Jake, Jake, please don't go. Not like this.'

But he did not answer her, did not even look back as he stumbled away, tears blinding him.

He had never been so hurt. Nothing in his life in the workhouse, not even the master's beatings, had hurt this much. Meg's arrival had brought him such hope, made him see that he could escape from the shame of his birth. It had been she who'd encouraged him to seek a life outside the workhouse. But for her, he would still be locked away behind the high walls with no kind of future. Her will, her determination, had given him courage, had given him hope and, yes, had given him someone to love, someone with whom he had dreamed of sharing the rest of his life.

And now, by some reasoning of her own that he would never understand, Meg was tying herself to a man old enough to be her father. Jake's mouth twisted. He was sure that the only reason she was marrying Percy Rodwell was for security. A security that he, Jake

Bosley, a lowly paid farm labourer, born and raised in the workhouse, could never give her.

No one came to their wedding early the following morning. There was no best man, no bridesmaid, and the verger and a churchwarden were obliged to act as witnesses. As Percy and Meg made their vows, their voices echoed eerily in the cavernous surroundings of the vast church. But Percy smiled down happily at his young bride, oblivious to the absence of relatives or friends. Only, as they walked down the pathway after the ceremony, did Meg fancy she saw the figure of a woman hovering beneath the shadow of some trees and wondered – for a fleeting moment – if it was her mother.

'Percy . . .' she began, turning to him to catch his attention, but when she looked back the figure – if it had ever been there – had disappeared.

There was to be no honeymoon – Percy decreed that the shop could not be closed – so they returned home, ate a hasty breakfast and went together to the shop.

About mid-afternoon, a stranger dressed in a black morning suit with a top hat and ebony cane entered the shop.

'Mr Percy Rodwell?' he enquired in a superior voice.

'Yes, sir. What can I do for you?' Percy hurried forward, almost rubbing his hands at the thought of the custom such a gentleman might bring to his shop.

The man produced a long, brown envelope, which he held out towards Percy with an exaggerated flourish.

'I am from the firm of Baggerley, Snape & Proust, solicitors, and I am requested by one of the partners, namely Mr Snape, to hand you this letter personally.'

Percy blinked, glanced at the envelope and then at the man and then back to the envelope before stretching out trembling fingers to take it.

'Good day to you, Mr Rodwell.' Having accomplished his task, the man raised his hat and left the shop, leaving Percy holding the envelope as if it might burn him.

'What is it?' Meg asked, moving forward.

'I – er – don't know.'

'Then hadn't you better open it?' she said practically. She slid her arm through his. 'Perhaps some rich old aunt has died and left you a fortune. Have you got any rich old aunts?'

Percy shook his head. 'I – er – don't think so.' He was still staring at the envelope.

'Go on, Percy. Open it. Do.'

He pulled open the flap and took out a single sheet of headed paper. As he read the letter, the colour drained from his face. When he looked up, his eyes were shocked. 'It's Clara, Miss Finch. She . . . she's suing me. For breach of promise.'

Thirty

'How can she?' Meg demanded when the initial shock had worn off a little, though Percy was still trembling. 'It was her who broke it off. I heard her myself threaten that, if you didn't sack me, the engagement was at an end. You didn't break it off, Percy. She did.'

'Well, yes, I suppose so, but . . .' His diffidence had returned. It seemed as if the very mention of Clara's name robbed him of every scrap of self-confidence.

'But what?'

He shrugged and said flatly, 'I don't know.'

'What're you going to do?'

'See my solicitor, I suppose.'

'It's not one of them, is it? Snape and what's 'is name?'

Percy shook his head. 'No, no. I go to a Mr Henderson the other side of the town. It's the firm my father always used. I was going to see him anyway soon about changing my will, so I suppose—'

'Go now, Percy. This minute. I can mind the shop.'

'Oh, I don't know about that, Meg.'

'It's almost dinner time and we don't get many customers between one and two. Go on, Percy.'

'But he – Mr Henderson – might be at lunch too.'

'Well, at least go to his office. If he's not there, make an appointment for when he is.'

'Yes, yes, you're right, my dear. Of course you are. It was just – just—'

'Just what?'

He took her hand. 'This is our wedding day and I planned to close the shop early so that we could go home. Have a nice long evening together . . .'

He said no more, but she understood his meaning. Involuntarily, she shuddered and was mortified that Percy noticed.

He touched her cheek. 'Oh, my dear, there's nothing to be afraid of. I wouldn't hurt you for the world.'

'I know that,' she told him. It was the part of getting married to him that she'd tried to blot out of her mind. She would do her duty to her husband, she would submit to him, but not for her the joy of giving herself to the man she loved . . .

Her mind shied away from what she knew she must endure later. Now she said, 'Do go, Percy. The sooner you go, the sooner Mr Henderson will be able to put your mind at rest.'

Mr Henderson was unable to put Percy's mind at ease.

'He thinks she has a case,' Percy told Meg worriedly when he arrived back at the shop later in the afternoon. He'd waited through the firm's lunch hour for an appointment at two o'clock. By the time he'd talked to the solicitor and trudged back across the town, it was already four thirty.

'Oh no,' Meg breathed, her eyes wide and anxious.

'We'll close now and go home. I'll tell you all about it there. But –' Percy shook his head sadly – 'it's not going to be the kind of evening I'd planned.'

Indeed, it spoilt their day. Neither of them could eat the special meal that Meg prepared and later, in their bed, Percy's lovemaking was fumbling and over so quickly that he wept against her neck.

Sleepless, Meg stared into the blackness and knew she had made the most terrible mistake of her life.

'Oh, Jake,' she whispered into the silence of the night, 'what have I done?'

The case was the scandal of the district. Several months had passed since their wedding and now the case was due to be heard in the imposing courthouse in the town during the first days of November.

Meg felt sick every time she thought about it.

At the workhouse Sarah was kept in ignorance of the events in her daughter's life. Isaac threatened everyone who came into contact with Sarah that, should they breathe a word about it to her, he would make their life utter misery. Since life in the workhouse was not easy by any standards, their tongues were stilled. So Sarah lived in blissful ignorance of Meg's troubles, believing her daughter happily married and well cared for. There was no doubting that the last of Sarah's hopes was true: Percy cared for Meg deeply and refused her nothing. And Meg was careful to play her part. She was a good and dutiful wife. She cooked, washed, ironed and cleaned his house and helped him in the shop. To their delight, the number of customers entering the shop had increased rather than decreased as they had both feared might happen.

Despite the worry of the impending court case, Percy was amused. 'Nothing like a bit of scandal to get the ladies of the town through our door.'

'As long as they keep coming once all this is over,' Meg said wryly.

'Oh, they will. We sell good-quality merchandise. They'll keep coming back for more.'

Meg glanced at him but said nothing. She believed it was curiosity that, for the moment, brought the good ladies of South Monkford into Percy's shop.

It seemed that Meg was right, if the number of women who crowded into the public gallery on the first morning of the case was anything to go by. By half-past nine the gallery was crowded and several people were already having to stand to watch the proceedings when Judge Henry Ashton, an elderly, severe-looking gentleman, took his place.

Meg sat in the front of the public gallery. Percy had not wanted her to attend and they'd almost had their first argument over the matter.

'I need you to stay at the shop,' he had said.

'Believe me, Percy, there'll be no customers that day. They'll all be at court and so,' she had added firmly, 'shall I.'

Although he said no more, Meg had the feeling that the real reason behind Percy's request that she stay away arose from the embarrassment he might feel at her hearing all that would be said in court.

She'd put her hand on his arm and said gently, 'Percy, whatever happens in that court, I know the truth. I could see for myself that a union between you and Miss Finch would have brought you nothing but unhappiness. Even if I hadn't come along, I believe you should not have married her, though I can see that you would probably have done so eventually.'

Percy gripped her hand. 'All I want you to know, my

dear, is how very much I love you. You will remember that, won't you?'

'Of course I will, Percy.'

If Meg had been in love with Percy herself then Mr Snape's opening speech on behalf of the plaintiff might have caused her considerable heartache. He spoke with theatrical eloquence of the romance between his client and the defendant.

'Here, your honour, we have something of a novel situation. This is the first time that such an action has been brought in the County Court in South Monkford. But, just in case any of you are in any doubt, I can assure you that these proceedings are right and proper under section 64 of the County Courts Act of 1898, giving County Courts jurisdiction in such a case with the consent of both parties.' Mr Snape puffed out his chest, grasped the lapels of his gown and continued.

'Your honour, I represent the plaintiff. Miss Clara Finch is a lady of genteel birth living under the protection of her brother, Mr Theobald Finch, a much-respected pillar of the society of this town. He and his family have lived at the Hall in South Monkford for four generations. During that time the family has served this community in a variety of ways. I will not take up your valuable time with all the positions of trust and authority which Miss Finch's family has held over the years. Suffice it to say that Mr Theobald Finch is a town councillor and has served as mayor on one occasion, with his sister, Miss Finch, acting as his lady mayoress. He is the chairman of the board of guardians of South Monkford workhouse and he is a churchwarden at St Michael's as well as a member of the board of governors for our local school. So, gentlemen, you see the kind of family of which Miss Finch is a much loved and respected member. She has involved herself in good works in the town, supporting her brother in all that he does and being a devoted member of the church.

'Now, as for – er – Mr – er—' Here, Mr Snape paused and shuffled his papers as if the name of the defendant was not even worth remembering. 'Ah yes – Mr Percy Rodwell . . .' He grimaced and spoke the name as if it pained him to do so. 'His family has lived in the town for a much shorter period of time. His parents moved to the town, I understand, in the year of 1868, shortly before Mr Rodwell's birth. He was born, I understand, in the rooms above the tailor's shop which his father rented, mark you, from the Finch family. Eventually, Mr Rodwell followed his father into the tailoring business and became the sole proprietor on his father's death in 1898. His mother, with whom the defendant continued to live, died in 1903, and since that time he has lived alone in a small house on Church Street. Mark you well, then, gentlemen –' Mr Snape made another extravagant gesture around the courtroom towards Percy and his eyes came to rest with a benign smile upon his client, Miss Clara Finch – 'the difference between the backgrounds of these two people. The one, my client, coming as she does from a genteel, upper-class home, being a property owner and landowner in her own right with a comfortable income as well as the sole beneficiary of her brother's will. The defendant –' again the man's tone changed rapidly from deference to derision – 'is a man of – trade.' The last word was spoken as if its utterance left a nasty taste in his mouth and there was a ripple of laughter around the courtroom. The judge looked crossly over the top of his spectacles at the sound and the noise subsided.

'About eight years ago –' Mr Snape gripped the lapels of his gown again – 'Mr Rodwell, who of course was known to the family through his tenancy of Mr Finch's properties, began to pay court to Miss Finch.' There was the sound of laughter, quickly stifled.

'At this stage, it has to be said—' Mr Snape's tone made it sound as if he were reluctant to say this – 'it has to be said that the defendant conducted the courtship with decorum. He approached Mr Finch for his permission and, this being given, he began to call at the Hall on a Sunday afternoon and sometimes on a Saturday evening after the close of – er – his business to dine with the family. During the first two years he observed the proprieties, the niceties, of such a courtship, their meetings always being in the presence of a third party.'

Again, from the public gallery came the sound of muffled laughter.

'Six years ago the couple, with Mr Finch's approval, became officially engaged. An announcement was made in the newspaper informing the whole world of the impending nuptials.' Mr Snape waved a newspaper in the air. 'And a small dinner party was held at the Hall to celebrate the event. If necessary, I can call several witnesses who were present on this happy occasion.'

He paused, cleared his throat and continued. 'The defendant purchased a ring. Not a ring of any great value, I hasten to add, though Miss Finch—' he inclined his head towards his client with an ingratiating smile – 'declared herself happy with the token of their betrothal.' He cast a baleful glance at Percy, who was sitting with his head bowed and hands clasped before him. 'Of course, my client would not say so for herself, but she is a modest soul, not of a grasping or a self-seeking nature. Miss Finch,' he declared resonantly, 'was most certainly not attaching herself to the defendant for his money.'

Now for the first time Mr Snape turned slowly and deliberately raised his eyes to seek out Meg, sitting in the front row of the gallery and it seemed to her that every eye in the vast room turned to look at her.

Thirty-One

Mr Snape's opening speech continued until the judge adjourned for lunch.

By the time Meg had struggled through the throng, ignoring the nudges and whispers around her, and fought her way to Percy and Mr Henderson, she was seething. 'It's not what he's saying,' she ranted, pacing up and down the small room, 'it's the way he's saying it. He's so scathing, so . . . so . . .' She couldn't think of the words to describe the way in which Mr Snape was besmirching poor Percy's character. 'So . . . awful,' she finished.

She sat down beside Percy and took his hand in hers. 'Oh, Percy, this is all because of me. I'm so sorry.' Whilst she knew, deep in her heart, that she was not in love with Percy Rodwell and never would be, she was very fond of the man who had been so kind to her. Watching her, Mr Henderson recognized her concern as being genuine. About Percy's regard for his young wife he had never been in doubt, but until this moment he had been unsure of the young woman's. Now Mr Henderson smiled, knowing that later on that day – if Mr Snape ever finished his opening speech – he would be able to stand up and speak just as eloquently as his adversary, safe in the knowledge that there was real affection between the couple.

After lunch the courtroom filled up again, buzzing

with excited chatter. Many there had never been inside a court before and none had ever seen a breach of promise case.

'She's a hard-faced shrew, that Clara Finch,' the few men there muttered to one another, their sympathies all with the defendant when they compared his former fiancée with his pretty young bride. 'Only thing is, I can't see what that young lass sees in him.'

'Money, that's what. He may not be in Theobald Finch's league, but he's a good catch as far as that young 'un's concerned. She's from the workhouse, they say.'

'Wasn't it her father who ran off with farmer Smallwood's daughter . . . ?'

And so the gossiping and the tittle-tattling went on, the men siding with Percy, whilst the women, for the most part, found themselves siding with the jilted woman.

As the judge entered the room, all present rose as the whispering subsided and every eye turned eagerly towards Mr Snape. What juicy morsels would he reveal this afternoon?

Mr Snape resumed his demolition of Percy's character subtly but effectively. He went into lengthy detail about the courtship's progress. According to his client, every attempt on her part to set a date for the marriage had been met by prevarication from the defendant. 'His excuses ranged –' here Mr Snape waved his hands expressively – 'from being too occupied with building up his business – a business in which, I might add, your honour, my client made it only too obvious that she would be willing, nay happy, to help. The defendant –' not once, Meg noticed, did Mr Snape refer to Percy by his name now – 'also gave the excuse that his home was not suitable for a lady of Miss Finch's standing in the community.' Here Mr Snape paused and smirked. 'For once, your honour, I find myself in agreement with the defendant.'

Though the judge did not even smile, this time he made no move to quell the ripple of laughter that ran around the court.

'So we come to the events leading up to this unhappy breach of promise action. The defendant, in his wisdom,' Mr Snape added sarcastically, 'decided to employ a young girl from the workhouse. Perhaps –' he spread his hands again – 'he wished to act charitably, to give a pauper the chance of a lifetime. Perhaps we should not condemn him for that action.' It was the closest the man had come to praising Percy, yet Meg could still detect the sarcasm in his tone. At his next words, she realized his intention. 'And oh, your honour, what a chance of a lifetime that turned out to be.'

'This young . . .' he paused, searching for the right word to describe Meg. 'This scheming hussy –' a startled gasp echoed through the courtroom – 'played upon the defendant's sympathies. She seduced him, your honour. There is no other way to describe—'

'That's not true!' Meg was on her feet, shouting at the prosecuting solicitor. 'Don't listen to him, your honour. It's not true what he's saying about me or about Percy – Mr Rodwell.'

An excited buzz ran through the public gallery and the judge banged on his bench with his gavel.

'Young woman, sit down or else I shall have you put out of court.'

'But, sir—'

Another angry bang. 'It'll be a charge for contempt of court if you utter another word. Sit down and be quiet.'

Meg glanced towards where Percy was sitting with his head in his hands. Mr Henderson was looking at her and frowning. He gave a little shake of his head and patted his hand in the air, indicating that she should sit down. Then he put his fingers to his lips. Meg subsided back into her seat, her face red. Now everyone was looking at her. She could feel their stares on the back of her neck and hear the whispers. The judge banged again and there was silence.

'Pray continue, Mr Snape.'

Mr Snape gave a little bow towards the bench. 'Thank you, your honour.' He glanced towards his opponent and Percy and then briefly up to the front row of the gallery towards where Meg was sitting. Smirking, he said, 'May I crave your indulgence, your honour. The girl is, of course, so *very* young!' It was neatly done, turning Meg's impetuous outburst against her.

The judge, whose white bushy eyebrows were almost meeting above the bridge of his nose in a frown, merely grunted and nodded to the plaintiff's lawyer to proceed.

Mr Snape droned on for another hour, extolling the virtues of his client as a woman of independent means, of a certain standing in the community who would bring nothing but respectability and stability to her future husband in both his personal and business life. In comparison, he painted a lurid picture of Meg as a woman who would bring disgrace and eventual ruin to the defendant.

At last he sat down and the court buzzed again, until Mr Henderson rose slowly to commence his opening speech.

'Much has been made of the plaintiff's standing in the community, but let us, for a moment, consider the position of my client. Mr Rodwell' – Mr Henderson stressed the use of Percy's name – 'was born here, in this town, in the rooms above the premises where he now conducts his business. He now lives in a small town house on Church Street. A modest dwelling by some standards –' he glanced towards the prosecution – 'that is true. Mr Rodwell is not a wealthy man. He makes no claims to be. He is, indeed, a modest man in all ways. Modest in wealth, modest in character. And, following in his family's footsteps, he runs a modest enterprise in, as we have heard, rented property. Rented, as we have also heard, your honour, from the plaintiff's brother. I'm sure there is no one in this courtroom' – Mr Henderson's glance swept the public gallery and around the court – 'who would deny that my client runs a respectable, though modest, tailoring business' – his voice became a little louder and his tone firmer, 'in a fair and honest manner. But consider for a moment, if you will, the position my client must have found himself in some eight years ago. We are led to believe that it was my client, Mr Rodwell, who began to court the plaintiff. In fact, your honour, it was the plaintiff who made the first – er – shall we say – approach to my client. Of course, there is no shame in this. Was it not our late and much lamented Queen Victoria – correct me if I am wrong – who was obliged to make the proposal of marriage to her beloved Albert because of her superior position?'

Now there was a gale of laughter around the courtroom and the judge banged his gavel irritably.

'As we have heard, the plaintiff is a genteel and respectable lady. But when she invited Mr Rodwell to dine at the Hall with herself and her brother, was that not placing my client in something of a dilemma? Apart from not wishing – quite understandably – to upset this genteel and respectable lady, he is also her brother's tenant and would feel, no doubt, under some kind of obligation to accept their kind invitation.' He paused to allow these thoughts to filter into the minds of all those listening. Meg glanced at Clara and saw her whispering urgently in her solicitor's ear, but Mr Snape was shaking his head and patting her arm as if to quieten her. Meg smiled wryly. Miss Finch wanted to argue with the opposition's statements just as she herself had done so rashly.

'Events moved on,' Mr Henderson continued, 'and the invitations to dine, to parties, to Sunday afternoon outings became more frequent, so frequent, in fact, with refusal unthinkable, that in the eyes of the community there must be some kind of – er – *understanding* between the plaintiff and my client. This modest and unassuming man found himself drawn into a relationship with the plaintiff that had really not been of his making. But let us be fair – we must not forget that the plaintiff is a genteel lady. I have no doubt that her motives were *most* respectable.'

Again a ripple of laughter ran through the courtroom, quickly silenced by the judge's frown.

'Perhaps at this time the plaintiff's brother – my client's landlord – took a hand in moving matters forward by pointing out to my client that his frequent visits to the home of the lady in question were putting her reputation at risk. Now, imagine my modest and unassuming client's feelings at this point. He has no wish to offend his landlord. The lady in question is . . .'

Here Mr Henderson paused and turned to look at

Clara. He regarded her for some moments, his silence drawing the attention of everyone present to her: to her gaunt face, to her hooked nose, to her hard, beady eyes, to her thin and shapeless figure. He cleared his throat and continued, '. . . as we have been repeatedly told, is a genteel and respectable lady. And Mr Rodwell had, at that time, no other – er – prospect.'

There was a titter from the gallery.

'He lived alone and ran his business alone. His only social life was comprised of invitations from the plaintiff. And so he becomes betrothed to this lady of means, of standing in the community, and the event is duly celebrated and becomes common knowledge. But this engagement, your honour, lasts six years. It would appear to an outsider, would it not, that there was nothing to stand in the way of the nuptials between these two – er – young lovers?'

More laughter from those present and even the judge allowed his lips to twitch.

'But if the prosecution is to be believed it was my client who prevaricated, with the weak excuse that he had nothing to offer his lady love. And indeed –' Mr Henderson puffed out his chest and gestured towards Clara – 'in comparison with this lady of independent means, of superior standing in the community, what has a modest tailor in rented business premises and living in a tiny cottage got to offer her?

'But in all this, your honour, we have not heard one word of the emotions between the plaintiff and my client. Oh, much has been made of the plaintiff's suitability. Who could argue that she is an undoubted catch?'

Now there was loud, insulting laughter from the gallery. The judge bowed his head as if to hide his face.

Then he banged his gavel, but there was still stifled sniggering from the gallery.

'We have heard no mention of love between them, of unbridled passion that could not wait for blissful union—'

'Mr Henderson,' the judge warned, and Percy's solicitor bowed, acknowledging that his turn of phrase might be becoming indelicate.

'Your honour,' he murmured. 'But then,' he continued, 'into my client's life comes this young woman – an impoverished young woman, your honour, with not a penny to her name, with nothing to offer a prospective husband. She has no standing in the community, she comes from the workhouse.' He paused to allow this information to sink in. 'But one day, in an effort to pull herself out of the mire, she dresses herself in the only clothes she has and walks all the way into town to Mr Rodwell's shop. She has been told, by a friend of the plaintiff's I might add, Miss Pendleton, the matron at the workhouse' – Clara whispered urgently into Mr Snape's ear, but Mr Henderson continued – 'that Mr Rodwell might be looking for a female assistant to serve his lady customers with . . .' Mr Henderson coughed delicately, 'underwear. And so, with a hopeful heart, this young girl sets out to better her circumstances with no further thought in her pretty head than that of securing a respectable, though lowly, position and being able to support herself and her poor mother.

'My client, altruistic and kindly, takes her on trial. On trial, mark you. But the young woman rapidly proves her worth. She is lively, warm-hearted, has a natural empathy with the customers and she is willing to do anything that is asked of her.'

There was a loud guffaw from a man standing at the

back of the public gallery. 'I bet she is!' He was quickly shushed by those around him. Ignoring the interruption with a look of contempt, Mr Henderson continued, 'But this young woman's strong instinct to be independent, not to be a burden on the parish any longer than she must, leads her to seek shelter at night in the shop.' Cleverly, the solicitor glossed over Meg's reason for leaving the workhouse. 'When he finds out, her kindly employer, far from dismissing her as his fiancée demanded he should, takes this girl to his home and gives her shelter. In return for his kindness, his trust in her, the young woman brings comfort and affection into his life. His world is suddenly a sunnier place and he falls hopelessly in love with her. But his love is not hopeless for, to his great surprise and delight, the young woman returns his affection.'

Mr Henderson stood for a moment shaking his head sadly. 'But now, of course, we come to the crux of the matter and why we find ourselves here in this courtroom today. The engagement that we are led to believe existed between the plaintiff and my client.'

At this there was an explosive snort of rage from Clara and nervous laughter from the public gallery. Again Meg noticed Mr Snape patting Clara's hand to quieten her.

'The truth of the matter is, your honour' – Mr Henderson rested on his knuckles on the table in front of him, leaning towards the judge and looking directly at him as his sonorous voice echoed round the room – 'that it was, in fact, the plaintiff who broke off the so-called engagement when my client refused to accede to her wishes. Wishes, your honour, which included the dismissal of the young woman from both his home and from his place of business. The plaintiff' – he now waved his hand dramatically in the direction of Clara Finch – 'cared nothing for the welfare of this young woman. Where she could have helped and supported her betrothed in giving the poor girl a chance in life, the plaintiff was vindictive and jealous. She resorted to emotional blackmail. Her very words, your honour, were—' Here he paused dramatically and held up a piece of paper from which he read, " 'If you do not dismiss the girl, Percy, then our engagement is at an end." '

He threw the paper down on the table in disgust. 'Your honour, I appreciate the difficulty facing you—'

'Thank you for your concern, Mr Henderson,' the judge remarked dryly. 'I am sure I shall rise to the occasion.' He allowed himself a small smile and glanced over the top of his spectacles towards the gallery. He was rewarded by laughter and someone even dared to clap.

'Quite so, your honour, but if I may be permitted to stress the point, it was the *plaintiff* and not the defendant who terminated their betrothal because he would not obey her. Now' – he straightened up and smiled benignly – 'if I am not mistaken, the vows contained in the marriage service do contain the word "obey". But am I not right in thinking that this particular vow is made, not by the man, but by the woman, who promises to "love, honour and obey"?' Mr Henderson paused again as if waiting for someone, anyone, to contradict him. When no one did, he added in silky tones, 'Not a very auspicious start to married life between the plaintiff and the defendant, eh?

'And one last point, your honour—'

The judge glanced at the huge clock on the back wall of the public gallery. 'Do you anticipate this taking very long, Mr Henderson?'

'No, your honour, just a few moments more.'

'Very well,' the judge said resignedly and settled back in his chair, his fingers linked in front of him.

'And my last point is this. My client is an honourable man – the sort of man who would have sacrificed his own happiness for the sake of keeping his word and his promises. But would it not have been the act of a *dishonourable* man to have continued in this relationship, to have gone through with marriage to a woman he no longer loved, purely for the sake of keeping his word? *When all the time he would have been in love with another*. Some might say he's a fool. A fool to throw away all that marriage to the plaintiff might have brought him.' Mr Henderson ticked the items off on his fingers. 'A fine house to live in, ownership of his business premises, which, we have heard, was to form part of the marriage settlement. And, last but not least, no doubt he could look forward to a step up the ladder in the social life of this community. He gave up all that, your honour' – his tone was husky with emotion as he gestured towards Clara and then let his arm continue in a sweep until it came to rest pointing in Meg's direction – 'to follow his heart.'

Thirty-Two

That evening Jake read the newspaper avidly, where the case was being reported in detail.

'Look,' he burst out. 'Just look what they're saying about her. It's not true! Someone ought to tell them—'

'Oh aye, and what would you tell 'em, eh?' Mabel Smallwood said grimly. 'That she's whiter than white, 'cos let me tell you if she's anything like her father – and her mother by all accounts – then she isn't.'

Jake stared at her. Then his manner softened a little. Craftily, he said, 'What was she like before her father – went off?'

Mrs Smallwood sniffed and admitted grudgingly, 'All right, I suppose, though she was always a bit of a flirt. Eyeing all the lads and chatting to them.'

'But was there any real harm in her?'

'She was only a lass when she was here. She's grown up a bit since then.'

'She had to, didn't she?' Jake was being greatly daring, defying his mistress in such a way.

Mrs Smallwood glared at him and then dropped her gaze. 'Aye well, you could be right. But we couldn't keep the family on here. Not after . . .' She fell silent.

'I know,' Jake said, gently now. 'I do understand.'

She looked at him and said slowly, 'For a young 'un, you're a very understanding sort of lad.' Then, unusually, she smiled at him. 'But just you be careful with that little madam. She's a heartbreaker, that one.'

Jake turned away. He didn't answer her, but what he could have said was: *Thanks for the warning, missis, but it's too late. Meg's already broken mi heart.*

'I suppose you'll be wanting time off to go to the court tomorrow to hear the verdict?' When he made no response, she answered herself, flapping her hands at him. 'Oh, go on with you, then. Though what the mester'll say, I daren't think.'

Mr Smallwood said nothing. Like his wife, he had taken to the young lad. They both liked Ron and his family, but they were a family unit, complete in themselves. Jake was alone in the world and the couple – though they would never have admitted it, not even to each other – were missing their daughter. The following morning, George Smallwood appeared in the yard dressed in his going-to-town suit. Without preamble he said bluntly, 'The missis reckons you want to go into the courthouse today. That right?'

'I . . .' Jake began hesitantly and then decided to be bold. 'Yes, I do, sir. But only if I can get mi work done first. I wouldn't go otherwise.'

'You'll not get it all done afore you go, else you'll miss all the excitement.' The tall, rotund figure beamed down at him. 'I've a mind to go myself. Bonfire night last night and the verdict today. Reckon there could be a few fireworks in that courtroom if the verdict goes the wrong way. I've known Percy Rodwell all his life and his father before him. A quieter, more docile fellow you couldn't wish to meet. I just can't believe he's in the middle of such scandalous goings on.' He stroked his chin. 'And as for that lass . . .'

Jake waited, holding his breath, willing the man not

to say anything unkind about Meg because, if he did, then Jake might just forget himself and likely lose his job.

'As for that lass, she was a pert little thing when she worked for us, but I don't believe all the things they're saying about her in the papers.'

'No,' Jake told him solemnly. 'Neither do I.'

'Right then, run along home and put your better clothes on.'

'I – er – haven't got any other clothes than these.'

'What?' The farmer looked scandalized. 'Is that so?' When Jake nodded, George murmured, 'Oh aye, I was forgetting where you'd come from, lad. That old skinflint Pendleton wouldn't give you a decent suit to your back, I'll be bound.' He put his hand on Jake's shoulder. 'Tell you what, m'lad. When Percy Rodwell's back in his shop we'll have you kitted out with a new suit, eh? How about that then?'

Jake managed to summon a smile and thank him politely. He didn't want to tell his employer that he had vowed never to set foot in the shop again. Not while Meg was still there.

Unaware of the young man's dilemma, George boomed, 'Let's be off then. Get the pony and trap harnessed, Jake lad, and we'll be off. Don't want to miss the fun, eh?'

The fun, as George called it, had already started by the time they reached the courthouse. All the seats were taken in the public gallery and George and Jake were obliged to stand just inside the door, squeezed in at the back.

'Not a minute too soon,' George muttered. 'They've stopped anyone else coming in now.' Jake heard him with half an ear. He was craning his neck to catch sight of Meg. And then he saw her, sitting in the middle of the front row of the public gallery. But he could not see her face.

They had scarcely got settled before the judge came in and the proceedings began. It seemed that only the prosecution wished to call any witnesses and there was only one: Mr Theobald Finch.

'Why won't you let me speak up for you, Percy?' Meg had begged him. 'I heard her say it. I was there. She threatened to break off the engagement if you didn't sack me.'

'I don't want you involved, Meg dear.' Percy was firm. 'And besides, I'm not sure whether a wife is allowed to testify on her husband's behalf.' He patted her hand. 'You just sit in the gallery – quietly, mind. Mr Henderson says you could jeopardize whatever chance I have got if you anger the judge.'

Meg was contrite. 'Yes, I know. I'm sorry for my outburst yesterday. If I could apologize to the judge, I would. I was just so angry at all the lies that horrible Mr Snape was telling about you.'

'Well, that's what the prosecution and defence is all about. Though how the judge is going to make up his mind through it all, I don't know. Mr Henderson isn't exactly telling the plain, unvarnished truth either, now is he? He's angling things the way he wants them to look.'

Despite the seriousness of their situation, Meg giggled. 'No, he's very clever, isn't he? But surely the judge can see by just looking at Miss Finch that she's a dried-up old spinster, who's just out for revenge?'

And now, in the courtroom once more, Meg, completely unaware of Jake's presence a few paces behind her, was crossing her fingers and hoping that Mr Henderson's cleverness would win the day for Percy.

Theobald Finch gave his testimony precisely, clearly and, strangely, quite impartially. When responding to questions it was obvious that he was trying to be entirely truthful and would not allow himself either to be led by Mr Snape or trapped by Mr Henderson.

'My family has always found the Rodwells to be excellent tenants. I have nothing against the defendant in a business sense.'

Mr Snape was quick to leap in. 'But you have in a personal sense, haven't you, Mr Finch?'

Theobald cleared his throat and glanced briefly at the judge. 'All I can say is that the engagement between Rodwell and my sister was a definite fact. Rodwell came and asked for my permission and we held a party.'

When it came to Mr Henderson's turn to cross-examine Theobald, he asked, 'Why do you think it was that there was such a long delay between the couple becoming engaged and setting a date for the wedding?'

Theobald shrugged. 'I expect Rodwell felt unable to provide for my sister in the manner to which she had always been accustomed, as they say. I expect he was trying to get a bit more capital together. Buy a better house, perhaps. I don't really know. It was never discussed with me.'

'Do you mean to tell us, Mr Finch . . .' Mr Henderson glanced around the courtroom, surprise on his face. 'Do you really mean to tell us that your sister never discussed these matters with you?'

'Ar-humph,' Theobald shifted uncomfortably and ran his forefinger around his collar as if it was too tight. He was growing redder in the face with every minute. 'Well, she might have said something of the sort. That – that she didn't like his poky little house.'

Laughter rippled around the court and, hearing it for the first time, Jake was startled.

'Ah,' said Mr Henderson, satisfied. 'His poky little house, eh?'

'But we offered for him to live with us – at the Hall – after their marriage.'

'At the Hall? Really? And you also offered to give Mr Rodwell the deeds to the property where he conducts his tailoring business? Is that not so?'

'It is so,' Theobald replied.

'Then why do you suppose – with all this on offer to him – that a date was never set?'

'You tell me,' Theobald shot back. 'I don't understand it myself.'

Mr Henderson leant forward on his knuckles as he said slowly and deliberately, his gaze boring into Theobald's eyes, 'Do you suppose it could possibly be because – even before this young girl appeared on the scene – Mr Rodwell was unsure of his true feelings for the plaintiff? He was having doubts about committing himself to her – *for life*?'

'Yes – no – I mean – I – er – um – suppose it's – it's possible.' Poor Theobald was obliged to admit the fact and for a brief moment, Meg felt quite sorry for him. 'But then,' he volunteered, regaining his composure, 'he shouldn't have got engaged to her, should he?'

'No.' Mr Henderson nodded solemnly. 'I am obliged to agree with you there.' He paused and Meg held her breath. Was Mr Henderson giving up? Whatever was he thinking of, agreeing with Mr Finch?

But then Mr Henderson's smile was deceptively

benign. 'But is it not possible, Mr Finch,' he went on smoothly, 'that in the early days of their – er – romance, my client did have a genuine fondness for the plaintiff? Perhaps, it was only when she found that his poky little house – the place that had been Mr Rodwell's home for the greater part of his life – wasn't good enough for her to live in, when she began to make demands about whom he should or should not employ in his business, when she began to threaten . . .' He paused and then said quietly, 'Need I say more?'

Theobald Finch did not answer.

When all the speeches had been made, the witness heard and the plaintiff and the defendant had each appeared in the witness box to be examined and cross-examined, the judge adjourned the case over the weekend whilst he made his decision. As Meg stood to leave, she glanced up and her gaze met Jake's. She climbed the steps towards him, pushing through the chattering crowd who were filing out.

Her immediate reaction at the sight of him was to smile, but that faded when she saw his solemn face, the censure in his eyes. By the time she reached him, her mood was belligerent. There were enough people blaming her – she could tell by all the whispering and nudging – without Jake joining their number.

'What are you doing here? Come to gloat, have you?'

Jake opened his mouth to make some biting retort, but then he closed it again. He was shocked by the look on her face. She seemed genuinely distressed as she pushed her way past him, down the stairs, through the entrance hall and out onto the wide steps at the front of the building. She stood there, pulling in great gulps of fresh air as if she had not been able to breathe in the confines of the courtroom.

'He doesn't deserve all this,' she said as Jake came to stand beside her. 'He's a good man – a kind man – and that – that bitch is dragging his name through the mud.'

'And yours,' he murmured.

She gave a wry laugh. 'Mine? Oh, what does my name matter? My name's in the mire already. But his? Like I say, he doesn't deserve it.'

She turned and hurried away from him but not before Jake had seen the tears in her eyes. Perplexed, he stared after her and one of old Albert Conroy's sayings crept into his mind. 'Funny creatures, women. They take some understanding, lad.'

Well, Jake thought, his Meg did. He still thought of her as 'his' and probably always would. But had he misjudged her? Had he really got it all so very wrong?

Thirty-Three

On the day that the judge was to sum up the case and give his verdict, the public gallery was crowded again. Jake and George Smallwood were once more squeezed in at the very back. The hubbub in the courtroom ceased abruptly as the door below opened and the judge entered to take his place. He shuffled his papers and cleared his throat.

'This has been a difficult case,' he said at last. 'By the evidence presented, I am convinced that an engagement did exist between the parties and that that engagement was subsequently broken. But who broke it off? That is the question.' He cleared his throat and glanced around as if enjoying the suspense he was creating. *Get on with it*, Meg wanted to shout, but she kept her lips pressed together.

'We are told that the plaintiff threatened to end the engagement if her fiancé did not comply with her wishes in the matter of the employment of the young woman. One could' – he spread his hands expressively – 'deduce from this that, because her fiancé did not comply, then it was she who broke off the betrothal. The defendant took her at her word, so to speak. Now, mindful of the vagaries of a woman's mind . . .' At this there was heartfelt laughter from the men in the gallery and the judge allowed himself a small smile, 'we could assume that the lady did not mean what she said. That she was, indeed, only using it as a threat to get her own way.' He paused and seemed lost in his own thoughts for a moment. 'But the defendant *did* take her at her word. Called her bluff, as you might say. But what follows makes us think that even if we believe the so-called threat, then the defendant used this threat to break the engagement for his own ends. He had taken up with the girl and wanted to marry her and here, presented to him on a plate, was his excuse. He could, he thought, release himself from the now unwanted entanglement of his engagement in order to marry the girl.'

The courtroom was silent now, hanging on the judge's every word. He recapped at some length what had already been ably said by the two solicitors. One moment he seemed to be in favour of Clara, the next on Percy's side.

'After much deliberation,' he said at last, when the folk in the gallery were beginning to get restive, 'I feel bound to accept the plaintiff's story.' He paused to wait whilst the excited whispering from the women onlookers in the gallery subsided. Clara Finch's face was a picture. Eyes narrowed, she smirked with satisfaction, and glanced across towards where Percy was sitting with his head in his hands. Vindicated, she was almost preening.

'And . . .' The judge looked slowly round the whole courtroom before he said in ringing tones, 'I award her the sum of – one farthing.' He banged his gavel and stood up to leave.

There was a stunned silence and then a loud guffaw of laughter from all the men present whilst the ladies twittered with indignation.

'What does it mean?' Jake asked George Smallwood. 'I don't understand.'

'It means, lad, that the judge felt compelled to find in her favour, as they say.' When he saw that Jake was still frowning, he explained in simpler terms. 'That he believes Miss Finch's story. That Percy Rodwell did break their engagement to marry Meg. But in awarding her only one farthing in damages he's indicating that he doesn't really blame Percy one bit.' George laughed loudly. 'And I bet there's not a man here who wouldn't agree with him. Why, you've only got to look at that skinny spinster with her vicious tongue and your Meg to side with Percy. He's a lucky feller. That's what we're all thinking. Lucky to have escaped that biddy's clutches and lucky to be married to that young lass.'

Aye, my Meg, Jake was thinking bitterly. *But she's not 'my Meg' any longer. She's Percy Rodwell's*. And yes, Percy was a lucky fellow.

The unusual court case, the way it had been conducted and its surprising outcome were the gossip of the town for several days. Gradually, however, folk settled back into their normal routine and other matters took their attention. But for some life had changed dramatically. Clara Finch rarely ventured out of the Hall. She had been humiliated in front of the whole community and she felt she could never hold her head up again.

'I told you not to be so daft, bringing an action against him,' was her brother's comment. 'What can you expect when it's men making the judgement?'

'I expected justice,' Clara replied through clenched teeth. 'And I expected a little more support from you – my own brother. It was you who lost the case for me. Standing up there and sounding as if you sympathized with – with – *him*. I'll never forgive you for that, Theo. Never!'

'Well, it wasn't my idea to bring the case.' Theobald paused and eyed her speculatively. 'Where did you get the idea from anyway?'

'Why do you assume I got the idea from someone else?' she snapped back. 'Don't you think I've got a mind of my own? Don't you think I'm capable of thinking for myself?'

Theobald's answer was a disbelieving grunt. 'Well, *did* you think of it for yourself?'

'Not – exactly.'

'So?'

'Oh, if you must know I was taking tea in a cafe in the town with Letitia and—'

'Letitia?' Theobald was startled. 'Letitia Pendleton?'

'Of course Letitia Pendleton. How many other Letitias do we know?'

'Well! You do surprise me.' He cast her a keen look. 'I thought,' he said, and there was a pointed edge to his tone, 'that she wasn't good enough to be in your company.'

'No more she is,' Clara snapped, 'but if the wretched woman has the effrontery to join me at the table – without being asked, I might add – I can hardly make a scene in a public place.'

'Mm, well, you made quite a scene in a public court, didn't you, my dear?' If he hadn't been her brother, Clara would have thought he was revelling in her humiliation. 'But she's not the vindictive sort,' he murmured mildly. 'Not Letitia. Now, if you'd said it had been Isaac's idea—'

'Oh, and you'd know that, wouldn't you, Theo. If anyone'd know that, you would.'

Brother and sister glared at each other and, though not another word was spoken, ghosts from the past lay between them.

At last, Clara sighed. 'It wasn't Letitia.'

'Ha!' Theobald let out a sound of great satisfaction. 'I thought not. Then who was it? Was it Isaac?'

'No. She'd brought some woman with her from the workhouse. She works for Letitia – has quite a good position there, so I believe.' Clara was at pains not to let her brother think that she had been taking tea with a workhouse pauper. 'It was this woman's birthday. I forget her name. Walters or Waters or something like that. Letitia had brought her into town as a treat. Well, it was her suggestion. "If it was me," she said, "I'd sue him." And I'll tell you something, Theo. I'm not sorry. No, I'm not. In spite of that horrible judge, I'm glad I let the women of this town know just what men are capable of. They'll be on my side, I can assure you. And when I've finished with Percy Rodwell and his fancy piece, he'll wish he'd never been born!'

Percy and Meg settled into a contented routine. Each day they worked together in the shop until mid-afternoon, when Meg went home to the little cottage to prepare an evening meal and to do her housework. On Monday evenings she washed. On Tuesdays she ironed. On Wednesdays she cleaned the bedrooms and on Thursdays she cleaned the downstairs rooms. On Saturday evenings she lit a fire in the front room and they sat together companionably, Percy with his newspaper and Meg with her sewing and mending. On Sundays, when the shop was closed, they attended morning service at church and then after lunch they went for a walk, if the weather was good, or again sat together in the front room. And at night in the privacy of their bedroom, Meg would open her arms to Percy and submit herself to his trembling lovemaking.

It was a quiet, well-ordered life and Meg told herself it was what she wanted. She closed her mind to her former life. She determined never to think of her father or of her lost little brother. And she hardened her heart towards her mother.

If she doesn't want to see me, she told herself, *then I don't want to see her. I'll never think of her again. I won't even think about that place and the people she's chosen to live with. I shall wipe them from my mind.* The master, the matron, Louisa Daley, Waters – all of them. Even poor old Albert had to be banished from her thoughts, for if she were to allow herself to think about him, then unbidden memories of the others at the workhouse would creep into her mind.

But there was one whom, try as she might, she could not banish from her mind or her heart. Jake Bosley refused to be forgotten.

Though she was unaware of it, Jake was finding it just as hard to put Meg out of his thoughts. He buried himself in his work at the farm, labouring from dawn to dusk and falling into his narrow bed in the little room in Ron's cottage. But even there he could not forget her. Where he slept had been her room, her bed, even. Her head had rested on the very same pillow he now used. Her young, lithe body had made the hollows in the mattress where he now lay. Her hand had touched the doorknob. She had washed in the bowl and ewer on the washstand, and she had brushed her hair, staring at herself in the cracked mirror. And his pledge to keep away from her, to let her get on with the life she had chosen, was thwarted by the kindness of his employer. Mr Smallwood had not forgotten their conversation about Jake's clothing – or rather the lack of it.

Just before Christmas, he said, 'Now, lad, I promised you a Sunday best suit and the missis has agreed. We hadn't realized that you'd only got the clothes you stood up in.' He made a sound of disapproval. 'What that place is coming to, I don't know.' He nodded his head in the vague direction of where the workhouse stood across country from his farm. 'You'd think the parish could run to equipping a young lad out when he ventured into the world. Anyway, ne'er mind about that. We don't mind forking out for a new suit for you.' He smiled and nodded. 'You're a good lad and we're pleased with the way you're shaping up, so we hope you'll stay with us.'

Jake, feeling suddenly happier than he had done for months – ever since Meg had married Percy Rodwell in fact – beamed. 'Oh, I will, sir. You and the missis have been very good to me.'

'There's just one other thing. I know you like living with Ron – and they like having you – but he tells me his missis is expecting another bairn.' For a brief moment there was an expression of envious longing in the older man's face, but it cleared quickly as he went on. 'And they're going to be a bit short of room. We wondered if you'd consider moving into the farmhouse with me and the missis. There's . . . there's . . .' again a fleeting glimpse of deep pain, 'only the two of us now.'

Jake hesitated, torn between wanting to stay with Ron and his family in the house where Meg had once lived and yet at the same time longing to be freed from her ghostly presence in his room in the long night hours.

He smiled up at his employer. 'I'd be glad to, sir. I'll try not to be a trouble to you and your wife.'

'Oh, you won't be, lad, no more than . . .' George cleared his throat and swiftly changed the subject. 'Just one other thing. The missis will expect you to go to church with us every Sunday. You'd do that for her, lad, would you?'

Jake grinned. 'Of course, sir. I'll be able to show off me new suit.' As they walked across the yard together towards the house to tell Mabel Smallwood what had been arranged between them, George put his arm across the young man's shoulders and they laughed together.

Watching them from the window, Mabel, for all her hard exterior, felt a lump in her throat. 'Aye,' she murmured. 'He's the son you've never had, George. Let's hope he's a mite more biddable than that good-for-nothing daughter of ours.'

So, two days later, Jake stepped into Percy's shop to be measured for a new suit. It seemed as if his path and Meg's were destined to cross. It would not be possible for him never to see her, for he knew she attended church on Sundays and now he was expected to do the same.

Forget it, Jake told himself. *It's in the past. She's married and nothing can change that. She's lost to you and you'd better get on with your own life*. So Jake buried his feelings deep inside himself and when he walked into the shop, it was with a bright smile plastered on to his face and a cheery word on his lips, as if all that had gone before was forgotten – and forgiven.

Thirty-Four

'Do you know of anyone who'd come as a dairymaid?' Mabel asked Jake. He had been working at Middleditch Farm for almost two years and during that time he had longed to ask the missis if Betsy could come and work at the farm, but he had never quite been able to pluck up the courage. 'Ron's eldest lass might be all right in a year or two's time,' she was saying, 'but she's a mite young at the moment.' Mabel sighed. 'And I really need someone now.'

Jake grinned at her. For all the sharpness of her tongue, he had become very fond of the missis and the mester too. He was as happy as he could be living with them. It was the closest he would ever come, he thought, to having a real family. He felt – though he could never really know – that they treated him as they might have done their own son, and had treated their daughter, he supposed. Though how, Jake asked himself, Alice Smallwood could have run away from such a kind and loving home, was beyond him.

'I just might,' he answered Mabel now as his grin widened. 'That's if you don't mind having another workhouse brat under your roof.'

Mabel stared at him for a moment and then laughed aloud. 'Well now, I'll have to think on that 'cos I don't know if I could put up with another young 'un like you.' As their shared laughter faded, she said more seriously, 'What's she like, this lass you've got in mind? 'Cos I can see you've got someone. How old is she?'

'Nearly fourteen.'

She looked at him for a while with her head on one side and her tone sharpened. 'Got yer eye on her, have you? 'Cos I won't have any hanky-panky under my roof.'

'I don't think of little Betsy like that.' He wrinkled his forehead. ''Spect she's more like a sister to me than anything.'

'Mm.' Mabel sounded none too sure. Little Betsy would grow into a young woman and then what? Still, she could keep a sharp eye on them both. A much keener one, Mabel reminded herself bitterly, than she had on her own daughter.

'Tell her to come and see me then.'

'Aw, thanks, missis.'

He turned away as if to go to the workhouse that very minute, but Mabel asked, 'Who was your mam, then?'

'Dunno, really.' He shrugged. 'Some poor lass who got herself into trouble and I 'spect her family didn't want to know. That's if she had any.'

'What happened to her?'

'Eh?' He stared at her, mystified by her question.

'Well, I mean, did she die? Or – or did she – just leave you there?'

'Is that – is that what they do? Just – just leave their bairns there? As if they've never existed?' Despite his years in the workhouse, that thought had never entered his mind.

Mabel did not answer him but asked another question. 'Do you know her name?'

Slowly, Jake shook his head, his eyes still fixed on

her face. 'Never thought to ask. I – I just took it that she'd died having me – or soon after. And I supposed her name was Bosley.'

'And your father?'

'Huh! Some bastard who didn't want to know when he'd had his way. Sorry, missis, but you know what I mean.'

Mabel hid her smile. 'You're probably right. And maybe you're right not to want to find out. But if you ever did, there'd be your birth certificate. I expect the master has it at the workhouse.'

'Birth certificate?' Jake looked puzzled for a moment. 'I've heard the other chaps in the workhouse talk about them, but I didn't know I'd got one.'

'It's the law. Every birth, death or marriage has to be registered legally and a certificate issued.' She glanced at him. 'If you wanted me to, I could ask Mr Pendleton for it. I'd have a right to see it as your employer. But only if you wanted me to, Jake.'

'Oh, well. I dunno. I've never really thought about it.'

'Well, if you ever decide you'd like to find out a bit more, let me know. All right?'

'Mm. Yes, well, thanks, missis.'

'And in the meantime, go and tell Betsy to come and see me tomorrow afternoon.'

Now Jake was smiling once more.

'Hello, Dr Collins. What are you doing here? Somebody ill? I hope it's not Betsy, 'cos I might have found a job for her.'

As Jake opened the gate into the workhouse yard, he came face to face with the young doctor on his way out.

Philip Collins smiled and stood aside. 'My word, Jake, farming life certainly suits you. You've filled out in all the right places. I do believe you've grown taller too.'

Jake laughed. 'Fresh air and all that good food the missis piles on my plate.' He rubbed his stomach and licked his lips. 'By heck, but she's a fine cook.'

Philip laughed. 'I can see that. It's not a place I have to call very often. They're too healthy by half.'

'So who's ill here then?'

'Thankfully, at the moment, no one. Oh, the usual sniffles, but nothing serious. No, I – er – came to see my fiancée. She's only got another month to work here. Miss Daley and I are getting married in six weeks' time, at the end of August.'

'Congratulations.' Jake grinned. 'I had me eye on her miself. If I'd've been a bit older, you wouldn't have got a look in.'

Philip smiled, knowing that the young man was only teasing. Jake had not an ounce of conceit about him and wouldn't realize just what a good-looking fellow he had become. His dark brown eyes were the same as ever, mischievous and yet with a depth of compassion for others that had perhaps come about because of his own unfortunate start in life. Jake's face was still thin, but now weather-beaten to a healthy tan and his brown hair was streaked by the sun.

'I can believe that,' the doctor murmured, smiling too, but there was a hint of seriousness in his tone.

They side-stepped each other and were about to say goodbye, when they both turned back and began to speak at the same moment.

'There's something you could—'

'How's Meg's mother?

They both stopped and Philip gestured that Jake should say his piece first.

'I just wondered how Meg's mother – Mrs Kirkland – is. Is she – is she still with *him*?'

Philip allowed himself a wry smile. 'She is.' He seemed about to say more, but decided against it. Jake nodded briefly. He understood the young doctor's unspoken words. If the master was taken up with Sarah, he was less likely to be bothering Louisa Daley. And that suited Dr Collins. Now, answering Jake's first question, Philip said, 'She's not too good, really. But I think her problem . . .' he hesitated, not sure if he should be divulging this to a third person, 'is more emotional than physical. Oh, she's not robust at the best of times, but I think she misses Meg terribly. She's so hurt by Meg's rejection.'

Jake stared. 'But – but Meg came to see her, the day before she married Percy Rodwell. She was told that her mother didn't want to see her. Meg did try. And I tried to see her – Mrs Kirkland, I mean – too. But I got the same answer.'

Philip stared at him for a moment and then let out a long 'Ahhh'. He was thoughtful for a moment before saying slowly, 'Next time I see Sarah alone, I'll tell her that. In the meantime, could you do something for me?'

'Anything, doctor.'

'Louisa is also very distressed by her estrangement from Meg. She became very fond of the girl, even though they worked together for such a short time. Louisa has no close relatives now. Her mother died two months ago. She would dearly love Meg to be her matron of honour at our wedding. Would you ask Meg to let bygones be bygones, Jake? It would mean so much to Louisa.'

Jake pulled a face. 'I'll try.' But his tone lacked hope.

Philip nodded. 'You can only do your best. Good day, Jake. And I hope all goes well for Betsy. She's a sweet child.'

The doctor turned away and as Jake began to cross the yard Betsy herself came skipping towards him, a happy smile on her face. 'I saw you from the dormitory window. I was making the beds. I don't go to school any more now, you know. And guess what?' She jumped up and down excitedly in front of him, clapping her hands. 'Miss Daley's asked me to be her bridesmaid.'

Jake smiled at the little girl's joy. To him, he thought, Betsy would always be a little girl.

'That's wonderful.'

'She's having such a pretty dress made for me. And afterwards' – Betsy's eyes shone – 'she says I can keep it.'

Jake held out his arms to her and Betsy skipped into them to be enveloped in a bear hug.

'Now, I've got some even better news for you.'

Betsy giggled and looked up at him. 'Whatever could be better than being bridesmaid and wearing a pretty new dress?'

Jake looked down into her upturned face, into her dancing blue eyes. For the first time he saw how pretty she was, with small, delicate features, perfectly shaped. Her face was too thin and her skin too pale, but fresh air and Mrs Smallwood's cooking would soon alter that.

'How would you like to work as a dairymaid?'

Betsy's eyes widened and her mouth dropped open. Against him, Jake felt her heart thud. Her voice was an ecstatic squeak. 'With you? At your farm?'

Jake chuckled. 'It's not my farm, though I wish it was. No, the missis is looking for a young dairymaid and she asked me if I knew anyone. And I thought of you.'

'Oh, Jake, thank you, thank you, thank you.' She hugged him tightly.

'Hey, don't thank me yet. You'd only be on trial to start with. And she's quite a tartar when she wants to be, the missis. Mind you.' His grin widened. 'I get on with her all right.'

'You get on with everyone, Jake. Everyone likes you.'

Except the one person I want to like me, Jake was thinking, but he kept this to himself.

'You should hear matron going on about you and how she misses you.' Betsy leant closer and lowered her voice, even though there was no one else in the yard to overhear. 'You should see her while you're here.'

'Of course I will. Come on, we'll go together and tell her the good news.' He took hold of her hand, not caring now if the master was watching. At last he was out of Isaac Pendleton's clutches for ever. But out of habit he glanced up towards the upper-floor windows.

'You're quite safe,' Betsy said, her eyes sparkling with mischief. 'He's not here today.'

The smile spread across Jake's face. 'Right,' he said. 'I'll see matron and then I'll see Meg's mam. See how she is and then I can tell Meg. I've to see her later anyway.'

At the mention of Meg's name, Betsy let her hand fall away from Jake's. She stepped back and the sparkle was gone from her eyes.

Thirty-Five

Meg stared incredulously at Jake. 'She must be joking! Me be her matron of honour? And with that – that child – of all people – as her bridesmaid? Oh no. Never. Never in a million years.'

They were standing in the workroom at the back of the shop, talking in heated whispers for Percy had an important customer in the shop choosing some of the best fabric he stocked to be made into a suit. Ironically, it was for a gentleman who was to be one of the doctor's guests at the wedding.

'I don't understand you, Meg, honestly I don't. You're the most unforgiving person I've ever met. And whilst we're on the subject, your mam is making herself ill with worry about you and not seeing you.'

'I went,' Meg hissed back, justifying herself angrily, 'but *she* didn't want to see *me*.'

'I don't think that was true. I reckon it was the master who didn't want you seeing her.'

'Why?'

Jake shrugged. 'How should I know?'

There was a pause whilst they glared at each other.

'So,' Jake prompted at last, 'what are you going to do?'

'Do? What about?'

'About either of them? Both of them?'

'Nothing.'

'So, you're going to refuse to be Miss Daley's matron of honour and you won't go and see your mother?'

Meg stretched her mouth into a sarcastic smile. 'Correct. Now, if you'll excuse me, I think my husband' – her accent on the word was unmistakable – 'requires my help in the shop.'

Jake flinched and stared at her. Where was the lovely girl he had met when she had first come to the workhouse? Where had she gone?

He turned away, sick at heart. Without another word he marched through the shop and out of the front door, slamming it behind him with such force that the bell bounced and the glass rattled.

In the back room, Meg stood chewing her fingernail and fighting back the tears.

Meg did not tell Percy that Miss Daley wanted her to be her matron of honour, but when the card arrived inviting them both to the wedding, Percy was adamant that they should attend.

'Of course, I don't know Miss Daley all that well, but the doctor has been very good to me. He was very kind one winter when I was ill. We should go to his wedding when we've been invited.'

'But it's on a Saturday. We'd have to close the shop if we both went. Why don't you go, Percy, and I'll mind the shop?'

Percy pursed his lips. 'Oh no, my dear, that would never do. It would be most unseemly.'

Meg looked at him, her mind working quickly. 'But surely you don't want to go.' She paused significantly and then added slyly, 'Won't Miss Finch be there? And her brother? Surely you don't want to run into them?'

Percy blinked. 'Oh, I hadn't thought of that.'

Meg lifted her shoulders. 'I'd've thought it stood to reason that the doctor would invite them. They're such prominent figures in the town. Or so we were led to believe, weren't we?'

Percy looked worried. 'Well, yes. I suppose you're right. Perhaps it would be rather awkward if they were there too.'

'Of course it would. And we wouldn't want anything to spoil the doctor's wedding day, would we?'

'No, no, of course not.'

'Then I think it better if we politely decline owing to business commitments. They know that the shop is always open on a Saturday.'

'I suppose so.' But Percy was still frowning anxiously.

Meg patted his arm. 'Don't let it worry you. You can explain to the doctor when you see him. He'll understand.'

She turned away, a satisfied smile on her lips, knowing that once more she had got her own way.

On the day of the wedding not one customer entered the shop and Percy fretted. 'We could have gone. We should have gone.'

'It's too late now,' Meg said briskly, carefully folding a pair of ladies' bloomers. She was amused to see Percy averting his gaze. 'I expect there are a lot of our customers at the wedding if the number of hats I've been asked for this last two weeks is anything to go by. Really, Percy, we should begin to stock hats, you know. We'd do a brisk trade, I'm sure.'

'Mm.' Percy's mind was elsewhere.

'And it's so hot today. We never get many customers

when it's such good weather. They stay indoors out of the heat.'

Percy glanced out the window at the bright, sunlit street. 'At least she's got a nice day for her wedding,' he murmured. 'She's lucky after all the rain we've had recently.'

'Yes,' Meg said flatly. Deep in her heart, she was envious of Louisa. The doctor was a good catch and young and handsome too. And he was kind. It would be very easy to fall in love with Dr Philip Collins. Meg's eyes had a faraway look.

If she hadn't met him in the workhouse, if she hadn't been wearing that awful, degrading uniform, then perhaps . . .

'Do you want to go home, my dear? I can manage here.'

'Yes, I will.' Meg dragged herself back from her daydreaming and flashed him a brilliant smile, the smile that had bowled him over and still did. 'I've some shopping I'd like to do and then I'll go home and cook your favourite meal.'

She knew that the day would end with Percy's awkward lovemaking. But she could always pretend . . .

Back from his honeymoon and looking fit and not so tired as he normally did, Dr Collins called into the shop. Meg hurried towards him and held out her hands. She smiled and kissed him swiftly on both cheeks. Philip seemed a little startled and the colour crept into his face.

'We were so sorry not to be able to attend your wedding. You do understand, don't you? It would have meant closing the shop. I tried to persuade Percy to come alone, but he wouldn't hear of it.'

'Of course not,' Philip murmured, his gaze still upon her face, her hands still in his.

She leant closer, sharing a confidence. 'And it might have been very embarrassing if Miss Finch had been there. We didn't want anything to spoil your lovely day.'

Before Philip could answer, Percy came through from the back room, a tape measure dangling round his neck, pins sticking out from his lapel. 'Doctor – Philip – how are you? Did you enjoy your – er – honeymoon?'

Meg pulled her hands away.

'Yes, thank you. We went to the Lake District. The weather was perfect. It didn't rain once.'

Percy gave a small, embarrassed laugh. 'That's unusual for there, so they tell me. I mean, I've never been.'

'You should go, Percy. Take Meg. It would do you both good.'

Percy shook his head, glancing away. 'Oh, I – we – couldn't leave the shop.'

'I've explained to Philip,' Meg said, forcing gaiety into her tone as, boldly, she used the doctor's Christian name for the first time – Percy did, she told herself, so why shouldn't she, as his wife? – 'why we could not attend the wedding.'

'Yes, yes, we were very sorry.'

'We were too.' The doctor's glance rested on Meg again. 'Especially Louisa. She particularly wanted you there, Meg, even if you didn't feel able to be her matron of honour.'

'What?' Mystified, Percy glanced from one to the other.

'Louisa asked Meg to be her matron of honour.'

'Oh, Meg,' Percy was reproachful. 'Why ever did you

refuse? That was a great favour Miss Daley was bestowing upon you.'

Meg thought quickly and then she put her hands to her face, her eyes wide with surprise above them. 'Oh no, I'm so sorry. I didn't believe him.' She turned from one to the other. 'I thought Jake was teasing. You know what a tease he can be. Well, perhaps you don't. But – but Miss Daley – Louisa – didn't come herself. Nor even you, Philip, and I never thought for a moment it was true. Oh, how dreadful! What must she think of me?'

Tears filled her eyes and she covered the whole of her face with her hands, peeping between her fingers to gauge their reaction.

Philip put his arm about her awkwardly and she pretended to sob against his shoulder. 'Please, don't distress yourself. There's obviously been a misunderstanding. I see it now. We should have come ourselves. Not sent messages. Don't think about it any more. Tell you what,' he said, brightly, 'you must both come and have dinner with us one evening. After the shop has closed. There, what do you say?'

Meg pulled back a little and smiled tremulously, looking up into his face. 'You're so kind to me. I don't deserve it.'

His gaze was on her face. Seeing the tears shimmering in her eyes, her soft mouth trembling, the just-married young doctor was appalled to find that at that moment he wanted nothing more than to kiss that mouth. To gather this young girl into his arms and hold her close.

With a leap backwards, he snatched his arm away, as if the touch of her ignited something in him that made him tremble with fear and longing. 'That's fine, then. I'll – I'll speak to Louisa about it. And – and we'll arrange something.'

But the invitation to dine with the doctor and his bride never arrived. Percy was disappointed and, though he never voiced it, Meg felt he blamed her. More than once she caught him looking at her, reproach in his eyes.

Thirty-Six

'So, what do you think, missis? Will she do?'

Betsy had been at Middleditch Farm for over a month now and Jake was eager to know if the mistress planned to keep her. Already the thin, wan child was blossoming into a healthy young girl, with a bloom on her smooth cheeks and new roundness to her body. And all day long Betsy had a sparkle in her eyes, the sparkle of real happiness. Jake couldn't know – wasn't conceited enough for the thought ever to cross his mind – that Betsy's happiness had as much to do with his nearness as with her new life.

Mrs Smallwood, her back to him as she kneaded bread dough on the kitchen table, took a moment to answer, whilst Jake's heart began to drop. 'Aye,' she said at last. 'She'll do.'

'Aw, missis, thanks.' Jake put his arms around the woman's waist and rested his head against her back. 'You don't know what it'll mean to Betsy.'

'Oh, go on with you, you daft ha'porth.' She waved him away, wafting flour into the air. 'I just hope I'm not bringing trouble on myself having you two under the same roof.' Her voice dropped as she muttered, 'As if I haven't had enough in my time already.'

Jake stepped back, hurt by her insinuation. He moved round the table to face Mabel. 'I'd never do anything to hurt Betsy. She's like a little sister to me. Always has been.'

Mabel eyed him wryly. 'Really. Well, I don't think that's how she sees you. As a brother, I mean.'

Jake blinked. 'Eh?'

With fond impatience, Mabel said, 'She's besotted with you, lad. She idolizes you.' Pointedly, she added, 'And I wouldn't want to see you taking advantage of the lass.'

Gaping at her, still unable to believe what he was hearing, Jake shook his head. Hoarsely, he said, 'I wouldn't, missis. I promise you I wouldn't.'

'Mm,' Mabel's tone still held doubt. 'Mm, well, let's hope so.'

Recovering a little, Jake asked, 'So you're going to keep her on?'

Mabel nodded. 'If she carries on as she is now and – she behaves herself – then yes, I'm keeping her on.'

'Can I – can I tell her?'

Now Mabel smiled one of her rare smiles. 'Aye, all right then.'

'Just one thing—'

'What is it now? More favours?'

Jake grinned. 'I suppose so, yes. It's Betsy's birthday next week – on the fifteenth of September. She's fourteen. Would you make her a cake? I don't reckon she's ever had a birthday cake in her life.' He didn't add that he hadn't either. 'They didn't do that sort of thing in the workhouse.'

Mabel stared at him. Into her mind flashed the pictures of her own daughter. Alice at five, six, seven and then – jumping the years – at fourteen, blowing out the candles on her cake, surrounded by her friends. First little girls from school and then bigger, older girls as they all grew up together, filling the farmhouse with their chatter and laughter.

'Aye.' Mabel's voice was husky. 'I'll make her a cake. It's on a Sunday, so we'll have a surprise party for her. Don't you go telling her, though.'

His eyes shining, Jake shook his head at the wonder of it all. Just how had workhouse brats like him and Betsy fallen on their feet like they had? 'You're a good 'un, missis.'

'So get your thinking cap on and decide who you're going to invite. Kids from the workhouse, I suppose.'

Jake wrinkled his forehead. 'Maybe one or two, but I reckon she'd like Miss Daley, I mean Mrs Collins, to come. And the matron. Miss Pendleton was always kind to her.'

'Aye well, invite who you like lad.' She looked up sharply. 'As long as it's not *her*. I won't have that girl in my house.'

Jake's heart was heavy. Without her name being mentioned, he knew she was referring to Meg. 'No,' he said sadly. 'She wouldn't come anyway.'

'Good job an' all,' Mabel muttered, as she pounded the dough almost as if she wished it was Meg's head beneath her strong hands.

Jake didn't hurry out of the kitchen in search of Betsy. He walked slowly, deep in thought. Was it really true what the missis had said? Did little Betsy really like him? A smile began at the corners of his mouth and spread slowly into a broad grin. He squared his shoulders and felt as if he had grown an inch as he went in search of her.

*

'Now, you've got to blow out all the candles at once and make a wish. That's what my mam used to tell me to do when I was a little girl.'

Letitia was enjoying herself. Her round face was red from the heat in the farmhouse kitchen and with pleasure in the day. She was sitting between Jake and little Betsy – her two favourite children from the workhouse. Though Betsy wasn't so little any more. She'd filled out and looked so happy and contented that it brought tears to the matron's eyes. And as for her beloved Jake – it was taking her all her time not to keep putting an arm around him and hugging him to her – he was growing into such a handsome young man. A son that any mother would be proud of.

I haven't done such a bad job with these two, she thought. Though a workhouse was not the ideal place for children to grow up in, she'd always done her best for all the little ones. Tried to be the mother to them that they'd lost. Tried to take their mother's place. Especially with Jake . . . And now look at their happy, healthy, smiling faces. The sight brought a lump to her throat and tears to her eyes, but she dashed them away impatiently and said again, 'Come on, Betsy, all at one blow.'

Pink with excitement and happiness, Betsy took a deep breath and blew and everyone around the table clapped: Philip and Louisa Collins, two younger girls from the workhouse, the matron, Ron with his wife and their children, Mr and Mrs Smallwood and, most important of all to Betsy, Jake. They had each given her a little gift: a hair ribbon, a lace handkerchief, and a brush-and-comb set. The two younger girls had picked bunches of wild flowers on their way to the farm. Jake had given her a prayer book to carry on Sunday mornings now that they were both expected to attend church with the Smallwoods. She would treasure that most of all because it came from him. But the best gift of all was this party.

'Put your bridesmaid's dress on for your tea,' Jake had urged her earlier in the day.

'Oh, I couldn't. It's far too grand. I'd get it messed up helping the missis get the tea ready.'

'I'll help her today. It's your birthday. You can just sit and look pretty in your posh dress and watch.'

'But what will the missis think? What will she say?'

'Oh, I'll make it right with her,' Jake said vaguely, knowing already that it was fine with Mrs Smallwood. They had planned it together.

'How are we going to get her to dress up in her finery?' Mabel had asked and it had been Jake's idea that he should make out he would help with the tea whilst Betsy had a little time off on her special day.

Now, as she cut the cake with Mabel's help, Betsy was thinking: *I'll never have another party better than this. Not as long as I live, I won't.* She glanced up and caught Jake watching her. The fact that he was there, that they were living and working together, made her life perfect.

Modest, unassuming little Betsy dared not hope for any greater happiness.

After tea they played party games in the parlour. Blindfolding Betsy, Jake spun her round and she moved carefully around the room, arms outstretched, trying to find Jake and have an excuse to put her arms around him.

They almost didn't hear the knock at the back door for their noisy laughter.

'I'll go,' Mr Smallwood said, heaving his bulky frame out of the easy chair.

Philip grimaced. 'It'll be for me, I expect.' So it was no surprise that George's glance went directly to the doctor when he came back into the room.

'It's old Albert from the workhouse.' He glanced at his wife before saying. 'He ses Sarah Kirkland's very ill.'

'Did you know about this?' Philip asked the matron at once.

Letitia shook her head. 'No. I had no idea. Isaac's never said . . .' She glanced around, her eyes fearful that they were somehow blaming her for Sarah's illness. Then she added more briskly, 'I'll come with you, Doctor, if I may.'

'Of course. Come along, my pony and trap are in the yard.' He glanced at the others, all turned to stone by the news. 'Does anyone else want a ride back to the workhouse? You'll have to be quick.'

The two young girls scurried to get their shawls and Letitia bustled after them to find her own as Philip turned to his wife. 'My dear—' he began but Louisa interrupted, laying her hand on his arm. 'I can see myself home. You must go at once with Albert.'

Jake moved stiffly as if coming back to life after the shock. 'I'll – I'll see Miss – Mrs Collins home, Doctor.'

'No, really—' Louisa began, but Jake interrupted. 'It's all right. I'll have to go into the town anyway. I'll have to tell Meg.'

No one spoke and the happiness fell away from Betsy's face.

Thirty-Seven

'I don't believe you. It's all a tale to get me to come and see her.'

Jake eyed Meg with disgust. 'Do you really think I'd joke – play a game – with your mother's life? She's ill, I tell you. Old Albert came to the farm to fetch the doctor.'

'What was the doctor doing there?'

Jake sighed. 'If you must know, we were all there. At a party. Betsy's fourteen today.'

'Oh, very nice,' Meg said sarcastically, her eyes flashing. 'Very cosy.'

Jake's mouth hardened but he couldn't hide the hurt in his dark brown eyes. 'Well,' he said sharply. 'Are you coming?'

'I can't. Percy's going to Nottingham tomorrow to order stock. I've things to do.'

'I'll wait for you.'

'No need. I'm quite capable of walking up to the workhouse by myself.'

'But I want to make sure you go.' Jake was belligerent.

'Don't you trust me?' Her tone was skittish, but Jake's was blunt. 'No, I don't.'

Her face darkened. 'Well, you're right. I'm not going. I've Percy's meal to prepare and his suitcase to pack. He's staying overnight.'

Jake stepped forward and gripped her arm roughly. 'You're just making excuses. Percy Rodwell's not the sort of man to make a fuss when he knows your mam's ill. You can't fool me, Meg. You don't want to go. That's the truth of it, isn't it?'

She thrust her face close to his, spitting the words out. 'Yes, yes, yes. That's the truth. I don't want to go. I don't *want* to see her and I'm not *going* to see her.'

'And what,' he asked her quietly, 'happens if she dies? How will you feel then?'

There was silence between them as, close together, they glared into each other's eyes. Then she shook off his grip and turned away. 'Then I'll have to deal with it, won't I?'

There was nothing more he could do, nothing more he could say to persuade her. Jake turned away from her, sick at heart. He did not go home to the farm but trudged towards the looming shape of the workhouse, the place he had once called 'home'. He marvelled at how different his life was now and wondered how he had stuck it in that place for so long. But then, he reminded himself, he had known no different. He still might not have done, if it hadn't been for Meg.

He groaned and tried to close his mind to her. He didn't want to think of Meg now.

Albert was back in his lodge and he opened the gate to Jake. 'I've come to see how Mrs Kirkland is.'

The old man shook his head. 'She's badly. They've moved her across to the infirmary. Matron's with her, but they reckon—' He wiped his mouth with the back of his hand, glanced at Jake and then looked down at the ground. 'See, lad, I didn't like to say back there – at the farm – but it seems she tried to take her own life.

Slashed her wrists, they say. There's blood everywhere – up in his room.'

'Oh no,' Jake breathed and stood just inside the gate, uncertain what to do next. He glanced up at the windows of the master's rooms. 'Is *he* here?'

'Nah. Been away all day.' He gestured with his head. 'She knew when to pick her time to do it. Thought with him out all day and the matron off to the party, then she wouldn't be disturbed. It's lucky one of the women took her up a cup of tea and found her.'

'Is she – is she going to be all right?'

Old Albert shook his head sadly. 'It's touch and go, I reckon.'

Jake glanced beyond the old man, across the yard towards the door leading to the stairs up to the infirmary. As if reading his mind, Albert said, 'I wouldn't go up there, lad. The doc's still with her and the matron. Leave 'em to it, lad. Leave 'em to it. They'll do their best . . .'

It seemed that the combined efforts of the doctor and the matron were still not enough. Before Isaac had returned, red-faced from merrymaking and looking forward to a night of passion with his woman, Sarah had slipped away, sinking into a peaceful oblivion, released at last from all the heartache and sorrow her short life had brought her. Jake, sitting with Albert, heard the news from Ursula Waters.

She stood in the doorway. 'Well, he's got rid of his latest paramour, then.' Her tone was almost gleeful. Jake felt sickened. 'She thought he was going to cast her off. That's why she did it. There's a younger woman just come in here. He's been eyeing her up. I can tell.

Kirkland must have thought she was going to be cast aside, so she saved him the trouble. She couldn't bear it. Sooner slash her wrists than live without him.' She nodded knowingly, her eyes bright, a satisfied smile on her thin lips. 'That's how it would be. Oh, I know that's how it would be.'

Jake stared at her. 'Do you mean – she's gone? She – she's died?'

Ursula nodded.

Behind him, Albert sighed deeply and murmured, 'What a waste! A nice little woman. What a shame!'

Suddenly Jake launched himself at Ursula, knocking her backwards against the wall. 'You bitch. You're glad, aren't you? Glad she's out the way. You reckon you've still got a chance with him. You dried-up old hag! As if—'

With surprising strength, Albert grasped Jake around the waist and pulled him away. Ursula was gasping in fear, her eyes wide and frightened.

'Nay, lad, that's not the way,' Albert said, holding him firmly. 'It won't bring her back, more's the pity. And you –' His eyes were hard as he glared at the woman holding her hand to her flat chest – 'you can get out of my lodge.'

'You . . . you . . .' she gasped, 'have no right to speak to me like that. You're only the porter.'

'Oh, aye? And what great authority have you in the place, eh? Oh, get out, woman, else I might be tempted to let this lad have a go at yer.'

Ursula scuttled out, but before he relaxed his hold Albert asked softly, 'All right now, lad?'

Jake gave a muffled sob and nodded. With his arm still about him, Albert gently guided Jake to a chair and pushed him into it. 'Now then, what we need is a strong cup of tea with a drop of summat in it.' He tapped the side of his nose. 'But don't you go letting on to *him* that I've got a bottle of the hard stuff here, will yer. Else I'll end up in the punishment room.'

Jake said nothing, but dropped his head into his hands and groaned. 'Fancy her doing that. Poor, poor woman. She must have been heartbroken. Just wait till I see Meg. Wait till I get me hands on Meg.'

Jake's loud banging on the door of Percy Rodwell's cottage was enough to waken the street.

'Your mother's dead.' When Meg opened the door, the words came out far more bluntly than he had intended. 'She took her own life.'

Meg gasped and stared at him, the colour draining from her face. She stood rigidly as if turned to stone. She held her breath, waiting for the news to hit her. And then it came. Realization flooded through her like a tidal wave. 'Oh – oh – oh!' she gasped like a person drowning. She wrapped her arms around herself, bending over, doubled up as if in terrible pain.

Jake watched, his heart hardened against her. He could not bring himself to go to her and put his arms around her, could not comfort her, could not even touch her. At her next words, his disgust deepened.

'How could she? Oh, how could she do that?' Meg gasped. 'The shame!'

It was, of course, a criminal act to commit suicide and even though the criminal was beyond reach, society still exacted a cruel penalty. Sarah would be buried in unconsecrated ground with no stone to mark her grave.

'The shame is that her own daughter judged her and found her guilty and then deserted her. Even now you're not thinking of her, of how she must have felt, are you, Meg? Just yourself. It's always *you*, isn't it?'

Slowly, like an old woman, she pulled herself up to face him. 'Why? Why did she do it?'

He lifted his shoulders, a jerky, angry movement. 'Waters reckoned the master had his eye on a younger piece. If I'd thought for one moment that it wasn't the sort of thing yer mam'd do, then I might even think—'

'But she wouldn't do that. My mam wouldn't kill herself,' Meg blurted out.

Jake stared at her. 'Are you sure? I mean, she must have been so unhappy.'

'Was she? The last time I saw her – with *him* –' still, Meg was bitter – 'she looked much better. The only thing that was upsetting her was . . . was . . .' She dropped her gaze.

'Yes, go on, say it. Face it, Meg. The only thing upsetting her was – you!'

They glared at each other, breathing heavily, their eyes hostile.

'To think I once thought I loved you,' Jake whispered. 'And now you sicken me. You really do. And this caps it all. Even now you haven't got a kind word to say for her. Your own mother.'

'What about me? Did she think about me when she took up with him? She was just the latest in a long line of his – his – *whores*. You want to think yourself lucky, Jake Bosley. You want to be thankful you haven't got a mother to do that to you.'

It was the cruellest thing she could have said to him and it broke his heart. The instant the words were out of her mouth, Meg regretted them. But it was too late.

Thirty-Eight

'Dr Collins – can you spare me a moment?'

Seated in his pony and trap, Philip looked around to see who had called his name. 'Jake! How are you?' he said, stepping down and holding out his hand towards the young man hurrying towards him.

As they shook hands, Jake said, 'I'm fine.' His look belied his words, for there was a worried frown creasing his face and his eyes were dark with anxiety. 'But I need to talk to you. When could you spare me a few moments?'

Philip took the watch out of his waistcoat pocket and glanced at it. 'Not now, I'm afraid. I'm due up at the workhouse for a medical inspection.'

Jake's lips pressed together grimly. The mention of the workhouse only increased his worries. 'Later on today, then,' he persisted. 'I can meet you anywhere you say. Only not there. Not at the workhouse.'

Philip smiled, thinking that the young man's reluctance stemmed from his years within its walls. He wouldn't blame Jake for a moment if he never wanted to set foot in the place again. 'Is it a medical matter? Can you come to the surgery?'

'No, it's not. Not really.'

'Then come to the house after evening surgery. Say, eight o'clock. All right?'

'Fine. We'll have finished the evening milking by then, an' all. Thanks, Doctor.'

Louisa opened the door to Jake's knock.

'How nice to see you, Jake. Are you well? Are you happy at the farm? And how's little Betsy doing? Oh, dear me, what a lot of questions I'm throwing at you before you've hardly got through the door!' She laughed. 'Come in. I'm just about to serve coffee in the drawing room. Go on through. Philip's in there and I'll join you in a minute.'

The doctor and his wife now lived in a double-fronted detached house in an elegant area of South Monkford. Philip had one of the bay-windowed front rooms as his surgery, with the room behind it as his dispensary. Patients waited in the vast hall for their turn to see him. On the opposite side of the house was the Collinses' private sitting room and behind that the dining room, with a kitchen to the rear of the house.

Louisa now opened the door on the right-hand side of the hallway and ushered Jake into the sitting room. From a deep chair beside the fire, Philip rose and gestured towards a sofa. 'Come in, Jake, come in. Sit down, do. It's good to see you – and looking so well. The outdoor life certainly agrees with you.'

Jake smiled. For a moment some of the worry lining his face was chased away. He'd always liked the doctor and Louisa, too, and had it not been for the sombre reason for his visit, he would have been delighted to spend an evening in their company. But Jake was hardly aware of his surroundings: the oil paintings on the wall, the cabinet with its delicate china, the bulky sideboard, the heavy ruby velvet curtains . . . He was too anxious about the reason for his visit to notice any of it.

They had only just exchanged polite pleasantries by the time Louisa came back into the room, bearing a tray with coffee and a selection of fancy cakes and biscuits. Setting it down on a low table in front of the crackling log fire, she asked, 'How do you like your coffee, Jake?'

His rueful smile flickered briefly. 'I've never had any, Miss – Mrs Collins. They're tea drinkers at the farm and before . . .' He needed to say no more. Coffee was never served in the workhouse, at least not to the inmates.

'I'm sorry,' Louisa said at once. 'I didn't think. I'll put milk in for you, but try it without sugar first. I can always put some in if you find it bitter.'

When they were all settled, Philip leant back in his chair and said, 'Now, what is it you wanted to see me about?'

Jake glanced briefly at Louisa and then looked away again. Quick to understand, Louisa said, 'If you want to talk to Philip privately, then I'll go.'

'As long as it's not a medical matter, Jake, I have no secrets from my wife,' Philip said, glancing fondly across the hearth at her. 'You can speak freely.'

'It's – it's about Mrs Kirkland. Meg's mother.'

Again the doctor and his wife exchanged a glance – a concerned look now – before Philip prompted gently, 'Yes? What's troubling you? If it's about where she has to be buried, then I'm afraid there's nothing anyone can do. As a suicide, she had to be—'

'That's just it,' Jake burst out, relieved at last to be able to share his darkest fears. 'That's it exactly. *I don't think she committed suicide.*'

Philip sat up straight in his chair so suddenly that his

coffee slopped into the saucer. 'What? What did you say?'

Louisa gave a startled gasp and her eyes widened. She said nothing, but her horrified glance went from one to the other.

'I just don't think she's the type to have committed suicide. That's all.'

'Why not? What makes you think that?'

Jake took a deep breath. He was gratified that the doctor was taking him seriously and not dismissing his thoughts out of hand as wild imaginings. 'She wasn't the sort. Oh, I know she'd had an awful lot of tragedy in her life. Enough to make anyone give up hope, but – but – look, maybe I'm being stupid. Will you just tell me, where was she found? *How* was she found?'

Philip relaxed back into his chair. With a deep sigh, almost as if he shared some of the responsibility himself, he said, 'She was in bed. In the master's room, of course. He was late coming back home. She'd cut her wrists.' His eyes were dark with the memory of it. 'They called me, but there was nothing I could do. There was blood everywhere. I called the police. I had to, Jake. I couldn't cover up something like that even if I'd wanted to. It'd've jeopardized my career.' He paused and then muttered. 'But I did want to, if truth be known. Poor woman.'

Jake licked his lips. He didn't want his next words to sound as if he was accusing the doctor of not doing his job properly. 'And were you quite, quite sure that she had – had done it herself?'

Philip stared at him. 'Well . . .' he began and then stopped. He was staring at Jake and yet he was not seeing the young man in front of him. He was visualizing again the distressing scene in the bedroom as he'd found her. 'She'd cut her wrists.'

'But could someone else have done it? Done it to her?'

'Not without her fighting them off. And there was no indication of a struggle.'

'Could someone have done it to her while she was asleep?'

'No, no, she'd have woken up.' Philip shook his head and then, suddenly, he was very still as he added slowly, 'Unless she'd taken a sleeping draught.'

Jake leant forward now. 'Did she take sleeping draughts? Did you prescribe them for her?'

'Not since she lost the baby. No – no, I tell a lie. The last time I gave her some was when her son died. Little Bobbie.'

'Might she have had some left?'

'I don't think so. Matron has charge of all the drugs on the premises. She keeps them locked in a cupboard in the infirmary. She is very strict about that.'

'Who had keys to that cupboard?'

'The matron, the master, of course, and myself. As far as I know, no one else.' He looked keenly at Jake. 'Surely you're not suggesting one of them did it, are you?'

Jake stared at the doctor, but did not reply.

'My God!' Philip was shocked. 'You are!' He paused briefly and then asked bluntly. 'Who?'

'The master.'

'The master?' Philip and Louisa both spoke at once, then the doctor shook his head firmly, 'Oh no, Jake. I think you're wrong.'

'I just can't think Mrs Kirkland would do it,' Jake went on. 'Even Meg . . .' He faltered over her name and then his tone hardened as he added, 'Even Meg, who hasn't a good word to say for her poor mother, doesn't think so. Waters said Mrs Kirkland had done it because she was afraid the master was going to cast her aside. Like he did all his women eventually,' Jake went on bitterly. 'But I just can't believe it. Not Mrs Kirkland.'

The doctor sat forward in his chair and placed his cup on the table. Resting his elbows on his knees, he linked his fingers together and leant towards Jake. 'Let's just suppose for a moment that you're right. That there was foul play involving – as they say – a person or persons unknown. How do you think it could have been done?'

'I've been going over it in my mind and apart from believing that she wouldn't kill herself, I just thought it was an odd place for her to do it. I mean, if I wanted to kill myself by cutting my wrists, I'd've done it in the bath. I'd have gone to the bath room and done it there.'

'But you'd have risked being found.' Philip was playing devil's advocate.

'She risked being found in the master's bedroom. She didn't know what time he'd be coming home.'

'Maybe she did it hoping he'd find her in time,' Philip suggested. 'Maybe it was a cry for help.' He paused, and guilt swept through him that he had not noticed whether the poor woman was so depressed that she had been driven to suicide. 'Perhaps he was later than she thought in getting home and he was *too* late.'

They were bandying ideas between them, testing out Jake's terrible theory. Philip looked across at Louisa. 'Come on, love, help us out here. What would you – God forbid that you ever should – have done? *How* would you have done it?'

Louisa thought for a moment. 'Of course, you can't

tell how terrible she must have been feeling,' she said slowly, still not quite able to discount it as a suicide and unwittingly adding to her husband's sense of guilt. 'She'd lost her husband, her baby, Bobbie.' As she remembered the little boy, Louisa's eyes filled with tears. 'And then, when she opted to take what security she could as – as the master's –' she ran her tongue around her lips – 'the master's friend, her own daughter condemns her and deserts her.'

Philip sighed. 'Yes, when you put it like that, the poor soul had reason enough, didn't she?'

'And yet,' Louisa went on slowly, 'I have to agree that over the last weeks I was working there, she did seem happier. Oh, there was a sadness deep in her eyes, a sadness, I suspect, that would never have gone, but she looked better – she'd put on a little weight.' She glanced at Jake and explained, 'She'd gone so terribly thin after little Bobbie died, I feared for her then. But after the master took her in, well, she seemed better. If only Meg . . .' She stopped and glanced up at the two men. 'I'm sorry – I shouldn't be blaming poor Meg. She must be feeling dreadful.'

'Huh! Only for herself. She says her mother has humiliated and shamed her. Again!'

'That's just bravado. She's covering up her true feelings, I'm sure,' Louisa said gently. 'She must be feeling torn apart.'

Jake cast a disbelieving look at her. 'You're being too kind. Maybe you don't know Meg now like I do. She's changed. Become ruthless. She's just out for herself. Out for what she can get. Look how she duped poor old Percy Rodwell into marrying her.'

'Oh now, Jake, I think you are being unfair,' the

doctor put in. 'Percy is devoted to her. You only have to see him with her to know that.'

'I don't deny that, but is *she* as devoted to *him*?'

Philip stared at him.

Jake nodded and smiled grimly. 'No, you can't say she is, can you?'

Now there was silence between the three of them until Philip said slowly, 'So you really think there might be cause to doubt the apparent suicide?'

'Well, it's been bothering me. I just needed someone to talk it over with and I thought you'd be the best person. You'd seen her and you'd know if something hadn't seemed quite right.'

Philip frowned. 'It's strange you should say that because there was something at the very back of my mind niggling me and yet I couldn't quite put my finger on it. Look, do something for me, will you, both of you?'

Jake and Louisa looked at him, eager to help in any way they could. Philip grimaced. 'It's a bit of a gruesome thing to ask you, but can you make the action of cutting your wrists? I want to see how you would do it.'

They stared at him, then at each other and shrugged. But they each picked up one of the small cake knives, which Louisa had brought in on the tray.

'You first,' Jake nodded towards Louisa.

She held her hands in front of her, the knife in her right hand. Then she pretended to cut into her left wrist with a downward stroke so that, in reality, a cut would have appeared diagonally from the base of her thumb to just below her wrist bone. She switched the knife to her left hand and repeated the stroke, against with a diagonal, downwards gash.

'Mm, good,' Philip nodded. 'Now you, Jake. You're left-handed so it will be interesting to see if there's any difference.'

There wasn't. Jake made the stroke in the same direction and in the same place on each wrist as Louisa had done. When he had done, he looked up expectantly. Again, Philip nodded and picked up a knife himself. The result was still the same; a diagonal, downward stroke on the inside of his wrists. Jake and Louisa were watching him. Carefully, he laid the knife back on the table and linked his fingers once more before looking up at them to say quietly, 'That's what was niggling at me. The cuts on her wrists didn't seem right. They were diagonal, all right, but the other way. And the natural way to do it is the way we've demonstrated.'

'So – so you think someone else could have done it?' Jake said. 'If she'd taken a sleeping draught—'

'Or worse still, if she'd been *given* a sleeping draught.'

Louisa covered her mouth with trembling fingers. 'Oh, Philip, how dreadful. You really think someone might have killed her?'

Solemnly, Philip said, 'I don't like even to think it, but Jake has raised doubts in my mind too now and I'll have to take it further. I shall have to share my suspicions with the police. Now, Jake, I shall need your help. You, more than anyone, know the internal workings of that place. Who does what and who has access to different places? For instance, could anyone else at all have got hold of a sleeping draught from the infirmary?'

'I suppose anyone could if they'd had the chance to get hold of a set of keys. They could have got into the cupboard when matron wasn't looking, though Miss Pendleton,' he added swiftly, anxious that the woman who had always been so kind to him should not be blamed in any way, 'was always very particular about it being kept locked. And she always kept the keys with her. Had 'em on a chain around her waist.' Despite the seriousness of their conversation, Jake smiled. 'We always used to reckon she slept with it still on her.'

'What about the master? Was he so particular – so careful?'

Everything led back to Isaac Pendleton.

Jake shook his head. 'I – I don't know.' He was trying desperately to be impartial, to put aside the memory of the beatings he had suffered at the hands of the master.

Thirty-Nine

It was Percy who persuaded Meg that she should at least attend her mother's funeral.

'So you'd have me humiliated all over again, would you? You're as bad as Jake.' She pouted truculently.

He sighed. 'You won't be humiliated. It's not your fault she – she did what she did.'

'She committed suicide. Why don't you say it outright?'

Percy winced. 'Like I say, it's not your fault.'

'Jake thinks it is. He's blaming me because I didn't go to see her.'

Percy stared at her. 'But you did go. I persuaded you to go. You did go, Meg, didn't you?'

'Yes, yes,' she waved him aside impatiently. 'Of course I went, but Waters came and told me that my mother didn't want to see me.'

Percy blinked. 'Oh.' He was puzzled. He had never met Sarah, but he couldn't imagine any mother not wanting to see her own child.

But Meg's mind was no longer on her mother. She was filled with indignation against Jake. 'I don't know what he's trying to do to me. Stirring up trouble. Having the police come here to question me and then having to stand up in court and answer that man's questions. What do they think I've done? Murdered her?'

Ironically, it had been Mr Snape who had posed the questions to the witnesses.

'There had to be an inquest after a suicide,' Percy commented reasonably. 'And if Dr Collins wasn't happy, then the police had to look into it, didn't they?'

'But it was Jake who stirred it all up.'

'Well, they haven't found anything, have they? Nothing that proves any different. The police couldn't come up with any evidence of foul play. Nor could the doctor.'

'Of course they haven't. All that stuff about the cuts being the wrong way.' She made an angry gesture as if slashing her own wrists, first one way and then the other. 'As if that proves anything. You can do it either way.'

'I hope you'll never think of doing such a thing.' He was worried now. If the tendency was in Meg's blood . . .

'I wouldn't dream of shaming my family like that. Oh no, nothing will ever get me so down that I do away with myself.'

On the morning of the funeral Percy saw to it that Meg was dressed in black from head to toe. He himself wore a black suit and tie and insisted that the shop be closed all day as a mark of respect.

'She doesn't deserve any respect,' Meg glowered.

'Oh, Meg, show a little compassion for your poor mother.'

'And besides,' she went on as if he hadn't spoken, 'I thought folk round here didn't like women attending funerals.'

'I don't hold with that. I never have. We're going together.'

So Meg found herself obliged to go, but she was the only woman standing alongside Percy on the cold, windswept patch of ground just outside the churchyard boundary. The vicar intoned the words monotonously, his voice clearly indicating his own disapproval. He had no words of forgiveness or understanding for the dead woman or of comfort for her daughter. On the opposite side of the grave stood the only other three people to attend: Isaac Pendleton, Jake Bosley and Dr Collins.

Isaac's face was stony. He had taken it as a personal insult that Sarah had so hated her life with him that she preferred death. He glared accusingly across the grave at Meg, seeming to blame her as the plain wooden coffin – a pauper's – was lowered into the ground.

As the few mourners moved away, Isaac caught hold of Meg's arm and roughly swung her round to face him. 'Had you anything to do with this? Was it your meddling that caused it?'

Meg glared back at him. 'I could ask you the same question. What did you do to her to make her life so unbearable that she didn't want to live it any longer? She didn't show any sign of doing anything like that before. No, not even when my father went off and she lost the baby.' Meg was aware that both the doctor and Jake were near enough to overhear the conversation, as well as Percy, who was standing protectively by her side.

'She was depressed because the only member of her family left to her – you,' Isaac went on, 'refused to come and see her.'

'I came,' Meg was almost shouting now. 'I came to see her, but Waters told me that she didn't want to see me and that you didn't want me to visit her either. Not ever. Waters was adamant.' Unbidden, tears sprang to her eyes and though she tried to dash them away, Jake had seen them. His heart twisted. Had he been misjudging his beloved Meg all along? Did she – under all that bravado – really care?

'I'd never have said such a thing,' Isaac answered indignantly. 'In fact, I sent Waters down into the town – to the shop – to ask you to come and visit your mother.'

Meg stared at him. 'You did? Well, she never came.'

The doctor and Jake glanced at each other and stepped away from the others a little.

'He's lying,' Jake muttered. 'I bet he never did any such thing. Waters idolizes him. She'd do anything he asked – whatever it was. I bet he never asked her.'

'I think,' Philip murmured, 'that the master has some questions to answer. Have the police seen him? D'you know?'

Jake shrugged. 'I've no idea.'

'Then I'll have another word with Sergeant Donaldson.'

It all came to nothing.

Several weeks later Sergeant Donaldson told Philip, 'We can't find firm evidence that anyone other than the deceased had anything to do with her death. Oh yes, I grant you there's room for suspicion, but what we need is proof.'

'And we can't give you that?'

The sergeant shook his head. 'Sadly, no. I don't like to think of that poor woman being accused of suicide if it wasn't and, even worse, I don't like to think of a murderer still being at large. But . . .' He spread his large hands helplessly.

'I understand,' Philip said heavily. 'Thank you for trying, at least.'

'Aye well, Doctor, keep me posted. If you see any funny business going on at that place, you let me know, and we'll take another look.'

'Tell me, was the master interviewed?'

The sergeant nodded. 'The only thing he said of interest was that Mrs Kirkland had seemed listless and depressed when he left that morning. He tried to cheer her up, he said, promising to bring her a present back from the city. He was in Nottingham that day on business, it seems.'

'What about some of the others at the workhouse? Did you speak to them?'

'Oh yes. The matron, of course, and a woman called – now what was her name – Waters. Yes, that was it. Even old Albert. We asked him if anything unusual had happened. You know, had there been any visitors – that sort of thing.' The sergeant cleared his throat. 'We couldn't disregard anyone. Not even her daughter, seeing as there was some sort of estrangement between them.'

'What did Albert say? Had he seen anything out of the ordinary?'

The sergeant shook his head.

'And Waters – what about her?'

'She said she'd taken up a cup of hot milk at about eight o'clock and that Mrs Kirkland had said she was going to take one of the sleeping draughts you'd left her.' He leant forward and lowered his voice. 'But do you know what that woman, Waters, said then?'

Philip shook his head. The sergeant straightened up and sniffed disapprovingly. 'Well, I never thought to hear such things from a woman's mouth. I mean, it's not the sort of thing a lady would mention.'

'But you were conducting an enquiry,' Philip reminded him mildly. 'Maybe she thought she had to tell you everything.'

'Oh aye, I don't deny that. But it's what she said she'd said to Kirkland that – well, speaking frankly, Doctor – disgusted even a tough old nut like me. I thought I'd heard it all, seen it all.' He shook his head wonderingly.

'What was it she said?' Philip prompted.

'She told me that she'd said to Kirkland – that's what she called her – "Kirkland". Not *Mrs* Kirkland or even Sarah.'

Philip nodded. 'They call everyone by their surname in there.'

'Humph!' Sergeant Donaldson grunted disapprovingly. 'Take away every last shred of dignity, do they?'

' 'Fraid so.'

'Anyway, she'd said to the poor woman, "You'll not get any sleep when he gets home. He'll be wanting your services." Have you ever heard the like, Doctor? Spoke to her as if she was a common woman of the streets, and bold as brass she was an' all when she was telling me. Now, I know Mrs Kirkland was living with the master and that's nowt to do with me, but if there's summat going on up there that I ought to know about—'

'I'm sure there isn't, Sergeant. Mr Pendleton isn't keeping an immoral house, if that's what you're implying.'

'Well, it makes you think, doesn't it, when someone makes a remark like that. And she seems such a prim and proper woman, that Miss Waters, an' all.'

Philip smiled. 'Well, once upon a time she was Mr Pendleton's – er – lady friend, if you get my meaning.'

The sergeant nodded, understanding at once. He'd been a policeman a long time. Nothing surprised him and it took a great deal to shock him. 'A case of the green-eyed monster, is it?' For a moment there was silence between them before the sergeant sighed and said sadly, 'But I don't know what else we can do.'

Heavily, Philip agreed, 'No, I don't think there is anything.'

In the early evening of the same day, Philip made a house call next door but one to the Rodwells' home. It was his last call and though he knew Louisa would be waiting dinner for him, he felt obliged to call to see Meg. She opened the door and when she saw who was standing there, she smiled her wonderful smile, which made even the happily married doctor's heart miss a beat.

She drew him inside.

'I just called to break the news to you . . .' he began, but she was pulling him into the front room, where a welcoming fire burned, and pushing him gently onto the sofa.

'Let me get you a drink. You must be so tired after a long day. What would you like? Beer? Whisky?'

Philip held up his hands in protest. 'Oh no, no, I shouldn't.'

'But haven't you finished for the day? You don't hold an evening surgery on a Thursday, now do you?'

'Well, no, but I still shouldn't. If I get a call out—'

She laughed gaily. 'I'm not suggesting that you get

rolling drunk. Only a little nip to keep out the cold on the way home.'

'I really shouldn't. Louisa will be waiting dinner for me.'

'Half an hour won't hurt. Come on, take your coat off, else you won't feel the benefit when you go out.'

Suddenly feeling weary after a long day, Philip gave in and allowed her to take his coat and fetch him a tot of whisky. She sat down opposite him.

He leant back, relaxing into the comfortable chair, the weariness of the day washing over him in waves.

'I only came to tell you that the police are taking the matter of your mother's death no further. I am sorry.'

Meg shrugged. 'I didn't really expect they would. It was only Jake trying to salvage her reputation.' She still wasn't sure whether she was touched by Jake's concern or irritated by it.

There was a long silence before Philip murmured, 'I shouldn't keep you. You must be preparing dinner for Percy coming home.'

'Percy won't be coming home tonight. He's gone to London on business. We're going to begin stocking hats and he's gone to one of the well-known fashion houses. Of course, Miss Pinkerton is going to make them for us. She's such a clever little woman – even if she is a bit of a fussy old spinster.'

Meg was chattering as if she hadn't seen anyone to talk to for weeks and Philip suddenly realized how lonely she must be for company nearer her own age. If only, he thought, she would make it up with Louisa. He knew his wife would dearly love to be Meg's friend again.

He felt exhausted and was struggling to keep his eyes

open in front of the warm fire. The tot of whisky she had pressed upon him was already beginning to take effect. 'Shouldn't you have gone to London if it was to see ladies' hats?' he asked drowsily.

'Oh no,' Meg said softly, as she watched the doctor's eyes close completely and his head droop. 'Percy is much better at choosing ladies' apparel than ever I would be. He has such an eye for quality.'

She rescued the glass before it slipped out of his hand to the floor and then, smiling down at him, she rose quietly and fetched a blanket from her own bed to cover him.

She closed the door behind her gently, leaving him to sleep. As she went back to the kitchen, Meg was smiling to herself.

Now let's see how you like it, Louisa Collins, when your precious husband gets accused of something he didn't do.

Forty

When Philip woke, it took him a few moments to remember where he was. The fire in the grate had burned away and the room was cold. He glanced at the window and saw that it was dark outside. He pushed off the blanket and struggled to his feet, still half asleep. Then he pulled the watch from his pocket and blinked at it in the soft light from the gas lamp which Meg had left burning.

It was five minutes past midnight.

'Oh my goodness,' he said aloud. 'Louisa will be worried sick.' He stumbled towards the door and was about to pull it open and shout Meg's name, when he realized she would probably have gone to bed and be asleep by now. He went back and turned out the light and then tiptoed across the room, opening the door as quietly as he could. In the hall, everything was in darkness. He bit his lip, trying to remember where the coatstand was. He didn't want to blunder about in the darkness, knocking into things. His eyes slowly became accustomed to the gloom and in the light from the street lamp shining through the coloured leaded window he began to discern shapes. He reached out and felt for his coat on the pegs opposite and then found his hat on a shelf. He struggled into his coat and rammed his hat onto his head. Then he felt about for his doctor's bag. He had brought it into the house with him. He never left it unattended in the trap. His fingers closed around its handle and he picked it up.

Then another dilemma faced him. The front door was locked and bolted. If he were to go out that way, he would be leaving the sleeping girl upstairs with an unlocked front door. He felt near the doorknob and found the heavy key in the lock. Then he made sure that there was a letterbox cut into the door. Finding it, he breathed a sigh of relief, unlocked and unbolted the door and let himself out. He relocked the door and posted the key back through the letterbox. It dropped with a clatter onto the tiled floor.

Upstairs, Meg lay awake smiling into the darkness and listening to the sound of the pony's hooves ringing through the still night air as Dr Collins drove his trap away from her house.

Louisa was still up, dozing in the armchair by the fire's dying embers.

'Oh, poor you,' she murmured soothingly as she hurried into the hallway to help her husband out of his coat. 'I'll get you some hot milk with a little something in it. It'll help you sleep.'

Philip shuddered. How ironic her words were. If only she knew . . . And then he shivered again, praying that she would never know.

Seeing him shaking, Louisa asked, 'Are you cold, my dear? I can light the fire in the bedroom.' She did not ask what had kept him out so late, but took it for granted that he had been with a very sick patient or attending a difficult birth. Her implicit trust made Philip feel even more guilty.

'No, no.' He reached for her hand and held it to his cheek. 'We'll go straight up.'

She patted his hand. 'You get into bed and I'll bring your hot milk up. Do you want anything to eat?'

Philip shook his head and stumbled tiredly towards the stairs. He should tell her the truth, tell her exactly what happened. There was nothing to be ashamed of, nothing had happened between him and Meg.

Then why, he castigated himself, could he not bring himself to tell his wife about it?

The following morning, as soon as he had finished his surgery, Philip went out on his rounds. His first call was to the tailor's shop. As he entered the shop and closed the door behind him, he was startled when Percy appeared from the back room, the ever-present tape measure around his neck, his steel-rimmed spectacles perched on the end of his nose.

The tailor smiled in welcome and immediately Philip felt even more guilty than before. 'Dr Collins – how nice to see you in pleasanter circumstances.' The last time the two men had met had been at Sarah's burial.

'Yes, yes,' Philip said swiftly. 'I – er – need some new gloves. Very cold driving the trap, you know.' The truth was that he hadn't been able to find them that morning and feared he had left them at Meg's house.

'Of course,' Percy was saying. 'And you have to be out in all weathers, even at night.'

Philip jumped. Did he know? Had Meg told him? Had Percy found his gloves in his house? But the tailor's next remark was innocent enough. 'Meg will be sorry to have missed you. She's taken the morning off, now I'm back. She had to hold the fort alone yesterday and first thing this morning, but I caught an early train home and arrived about an hour ago.'

'You must be tired.'

'No, no. The hotel I stayed at last night was very comfortable. I slept surprisingly well.'

So did I, thought Philip ruefully. *Too well and in the wrong place.*

The gloves, which he didn't really need, purchased, Philip made his escape. Not knowing whether he was being extremely foolish or not, he went straight to see Meg at her home.

She opened the door wide, silently inviting him to step inside.

'No, no, I mustn't come in,' Philip began, but Meg smiled at him archly.

'Don't you trust me, Doctor?'

He did not reply, but inside his own mind he was saying: *It's myself I don't trust.* Instead he smiled thinly and asked, 'Did I leave my gloves here?'

'Yes.' She pulled the door wider. 'Come in while I fetch them.' She leant forward, glanced up and down the street and then whispered, 'I hid them, just in case Percy saw them and asked awkward questions.'

As he stepped into the hall – he could do no other if he wanted to retrieve his gloves – he said, 'You – you didn't tell Percy, then?'

Meg closed the door and leant against it, watching him. She widened her eyes. 'Of course not. Now,' she said briskly, 'have you time for a drink?'

'Oh no! No more of your drinks, Meg.' He held out his hand as if to ward her off. 'Besides, I must be on my way. I've patients to see.'

She moved closer to him and, though she wore no perfume, the smell of her enticed him. It was a natural, womanly smell. Earthy and inviting. She put her hands, palms flat, against his chest. 'What is more natural than that you should feel able to rest at a friend's house when you were so desperately tired? You told Louisa where you were, of course?'

'Well – no – I – er – no, I didn't.'

'Then it will be our little secret.' She made it sound as if there was much more to hide than what had actually happened. 'We must think of Louisa and Percy.'

Without another word being spoken, she fetched his gloves and handed them to him. He left the house, but as she closed the door after him, Meg was still smiling.

I'll get my revenge on you yet, Louisa Collins.

Another Christmas came and went and life in South Monkford settled into a routine. Percy and Meg worked side by side in their shop. To the surprise of them both – though neither of them ever voiced their private thoughts to the other – the number of their customers grew steadily as they increased the range of their stock. Meg had secretly worried that the scandal of the breach-of-promise court case would seriously affect their business. And, though he said nothing to her, Percy had been concerned too. But their fears had been unfounded. Even Theobald Finch continued to frequent the shop, though they never saw Clara. In fact, very few people of the town ever saw Miss Finch. She ventured out rarely and when she did she travelled to Nottingham, where, incognito, she could shop away from the nudges and whispers. That the townsfolk of South Monkford had better things to think of now never occurred to the embittered woman.

Meg threw herself into work at the shop and at

home. She learnt as much as she could about the business and persuaded Percy to teach her tailoring. At first he was reluctant. 'Oh no, it's no job for a woman. How would you do the measuring? No gentleman would like that.' But Meg was insistent and at last he allowed her to learn how to use the sewing machine. She filled her days deliberately. That way she had little time to think. She refused to dwell on the past, nor would she plan the future. She just lived from day to day, being a good wife to Percy and helping him to build the business.

That way, little time was left for her to think of Jake.

At the farm Jake couldn't believe his luck. Every morning he woke to marvel at his good fortune. He was well fed and doing a job he loved. And best of all, little Betsy – who had always been one of his favourites at the workhouse – blossomed before his eyes. And if his nights were disturbed by haunting dreams of a fiery red-haired girl with a wonderful smile, no one would have guessed it from the wide grin that was permanently on his face. Only if they had thought to look a little closer would they have seen the sadness deep in his brown eyes that would never quite go away.

At the workhouse, for the first time in many years, Isaac slept alone in the vast double bed. Much to Ursula's glee, no one replaced Sarah Kirkland in the master's affections and the lonely, obsessed spinster began to cherish hopes once more.

I knew he always loved me best, she told herself. *He needs me. I was right to stay here – to devote my life to caring for him. He'll turn to me again. I know he will. I just have to be patient and wait . . .*

So it was Ursula who took the master his meals, who ran errands for him, who whispered tales about the inmates into his ear. Things, she said, that he ought to know, had a right to know. Yet to her chagrin he hardly seemed aware of her existence. And certainly he never invited her into his bed again.

'I know what you're up to.' The matron was not so blind as her brother.

'Up to?' Ursula assumed an innocent expression. 'Whatever do you mean?'

'Pandering to him. Running after him. Well, it won't work. He was fond of Kirkland. Really fond. And he's missing her.'

'He'll forget her.' Ursula smirked. 'And when he does, I'll be there.'

Letitia cast her a disbelieving glance, but said no more. She was not a cruel woman though at that moment she was tempted to say: *He'll never take up with you again in a month of Sundays*. But Letitia held her tongue. If anything, she felt sorry for Waters. The woman had wasted her life, choosing to stay in the workhouse instead of making a life for herself outside its walls as Isaac would have helped her to do. But no, she'd rejected his offer, preferring to stay near him, forever hoping that one day he would . . .

Well, he wouldn't, Letitia knew, but she would say nothing against her brother. They were bound together by shared secrets from the past. And there were things, too, that Ursula Waters knew, so it would not do to cross her. Letitia was obliged to be content with her lot – she had made her bed and she had to lie in it. Isaac had been good to her and she was grateful to him. She was lucky – she knew she was. And she had her little boys to love and cherish.

There was only one thing that saddened her these

days. She didn't see Jake as often as she would have liked and even less since Sarah's death. He hadn't been to the workhouse since then and she missed him. Oh, how the matron missed seeing her special boy.

Forty-One

When Britain declared war on Germany in August 1914 the news came as a shock to the people of South Monkford. Events outside the town rarely troubled the serenity of their lives, but now events in a far-off country, which should have had nothing to do with them, had turned their cosy world upside-down. In a fever of patriotism young men, and even not-so-young men, rushed to volunteer. Sons, husbands and fathers – all were swept up in the fervour to enlist.

At Middleditch Farm Betsy and Mrs Smallwood were in a permanent state of anxiety lest Jake should be caught up in the excitement.

'He won't go, will he?' Betsy said a dozen times a day.

'I hope not.' Mrs Smallwood was unusually patient with the young girl's fears and constant questions. Betsy was only voicing Mabel's worries.

At last it was George Smallwood who dared to speak out. 'You'll not do anything daft, lad, will yer? Like joining up?'

Jake's face was sober. 'I've decided . . .' he paused and George, Mabel and Betsy stared at him, 'not to volunteer, but of course if they bring in – what do they call it?' He looked at George, who said, 'Conscription.'

'Yes, that's it. If they bring in conscription, then of course I'll have to go.'

'Mebbe you'll not have to, lad,' George said. 'They'll need workers to stay on the land. There'll likely be food shortages if it goes on for very long.'

'But they say it won't,' Mabel put in. 'They say it'll be all over by Christmas.'

'Aye well, I wouldn't hold mi breath, love, if I was you,' was George's only reply.

Jake said no more, but silently made up his own mind. If conscription did come in, he would go then – even before they sent for him. He would answer his country's call.

'We'll never cope with all these orders for suits, to say nothing of the underwear they're buying,' Percy said worriedly. Nothing was too good for their menfolk when they went to war, and wives and mothers flooded into the tailor's shop demanding the very best for their loved ones. 'What on earth they want new suits for to go into the army, I don't know. Mind you, folks are very particular round here, but they'll not be given a chance to wear them. Once they're given their uniform, that'll be it. They'll not see their own clothes again until . . .' His voice faded away. Already news of the carnage at the Front had reached the town.

'Just be thankful they do, Percy,' Meg said. 'And we've nearly sold out of ladies' hats. Poor Miss Pinkerton is working through the night sometimes just to keep up with the demands.'

Percy sighed. 'I expect the ladies want to look their best when they wave their menfolk off. To give them a pretty memory to carry with them.'

'Is there any chance we could get a contract for making uniforms?' Meg was thinking of their own business, thriving in spite of – or rather because of – the war. 'I could help you.'

'Oh no.' Percy shook his head. 'That's very specialized and besides –' he shuddered, the thought abhorrent to him – 'I wouldn't want to.'

'Wouldn't want to?' Meg repeated, surprised. 'But there must be a lot of money to be made.'

'I wouldn't want to make money out of such a tragedy as this war is going to be,' Percy said righteously.

Then you're a fool, Meg wanted to say, but for once she held her tongue. She was revelling in the turn of events. Her recent life had been just a dull routine of housework and working in the shop. Even learning tailoring skills had palled. But now there was some real excitement. 'We'll have to take on more staff. Can't you advertise for a tailor? It's you who needs the help making the garments. I can cope with serving the customers. But you've been working every night for weeks.' She stepped closer to him and smoothed back a lock of his hair – hair that was thinning prematurely, she noticed.

Percy looked askance at her. 'Take on someone else? Oh no, I couldn't do that. Besides, this rush is only temporary.'

But the demand for new suits, new clothes of all description was a surprisingly long time in diminishing. After weeks of working late into the night every night, by November Percy was looking tired and even thinner.

'I'm calling the doctor,' Meg declared and refused to listen to Percy's weak protests. 'You must stay in bed all day tomorrow and I'll get Ph— Dr Collins to call to see you.'

It had been almost two years since the night he had

fallen asleep in her home. She had seen Philip rarely since, and then only in public, when she would smile at him coyly and be gratified by the look of embarrassed confusion that coloured his face. He was a nice man, she told herself, and she shouldn't make sport of him. Yet, it was so tempting. Her life was so dull and what harm could a little flirtation with Louisa's husband do? It would just serve her right, Meg thought, still unable to forgive.

And now, with Percy's exhaustion, there was an excuse – a genuine reason – to send for him, but she had to make sure he would come. She wrote a polite note and sent it by an errand boy to Philip's surgery asking him to visit. *I will not be at home*, she wrote, *as I must keep the shop open. The front door will be unlocked.*

Meg smiled to herself as she folded the note and handed it to the grubby urchin to deliver for her.

The following morning Percy insisted, 'You must go to the shop. You must be there to explain to Mrs Heane why her son's suit isn't ready. The poor woman was in tears when she ordered it. "It might be that last suit I ever buy for him," she said.' Percy sighed heavily. 'I suppose I can see now why they're wanting the best for their boys. It might be the last chance they get. Tell her I'll have it done tomorrow without fail.'

'I'll do no such thing,' Meg countered. 'I'm waiting here until the doctor comes and as for you working today or tomorrow, well, we'll see what he says.'

Meg was gratified by the startled look on Philip's face when she opened the door.

'I thought—' he began.

'I know,' she said quickly. 'I didn't mean to be here, but I didn't like to leave him. Once my back is turned, he'll be out of that bed and struggling to the shop. And he really isn't well. He's been working so hard.' Her tone softened as she noticed the dark circles beneath Philip's eyes. 'As you have too, I can see.'

He stepped into the house with a sigh. 'There's a lot of illness about,' he murmured, as he pressed himself back against the wall of the narrow hallway to allow her to lead the way up the stairs. He was overwhelmed by the surge of emotion that coursed through him at her nearness. And worse, as she lifted her skirts to climb the stairs in front of him, he caught a glimpse of her neat ankle and the curve of her calf. He closed his eyes and paused for a moment, catching hold of the banister rail to steady himself. Then he took a deep breath and followed her, keeping his gaze firmly on each tread of the staircase.

At first, Percy refused to obey the doctor's advice. 'I can't stay in bed. I have work to do. Meg can't cope alone in the shop and there are suits to finish and . . .' He groaned, closed his eyes and lay back against the pillows.

'Two days in bed, that's all I'm asking,' Philip said. 'If you feel better, then you can get up, but I would still advise you to stay at home for at least another two days after that.'

'It's impossible,' Percy moaned.

'If you work yourself into an early grave, the suits won't get made, will they?' Philip said bluntly. 'And you're not being fair to Meg,' he added, though he kept his gaze firmly on his patient, not daring to meet her eyes. 'She can no doubt manage the shop alone for a day or two, but if you get really ill, how would she cope then? Have you thought of that?'

Percy sighed. 'I hadn't looked at it like that.'

'Then I think you should.'

'All right.' Percy capitulated with a weary smile. 'I'll do as you say, Doctor.'

'Good. And I'll make you up a tonic.' Now he was obliged to glance at Meg. 'Perhaps you could collect it from the surgery later. I'd offer to drop it in, but I'm so very busy.'

'Of course,' Meg said evenly.

It was almost dark by the time Meg left the shop and made her way towards the doctor's house. She raised the heavy brass knocker and let it fall with a loud thud that echoed through the house. She waited several moments before she heard light footsteps beyond the door. When it opened, she saw Louisa holding out both her hands in welcome.

'Oh, Meg, I'm so glad to see you. Come in.'

'I've only called to pick up some medicine for Percy,' Meg said stiffly as she stepped into the hallway.

Louisa closed the door and stood facing her. 'Meg,' she began tentatively, 'can't we let bygones be bygones? Can't we be friends again? I am more sorry than I can ever put into words about what happened between us.'

Meg's mind was working rapidly, calculating. Suddenly, she smiled her brilliant smile and even Louisa gasped at the swift transformation from sulky pout to friendly warmth. She had forgotten just how beautiful the young girl was.

Meg took her hands and squeezed them. 'Nothing would give me greater pleasure. And I – I'm sorry now that I wasn't at your wedding. When Jake told me you wanted me to be your matron of honour, I thought it was him trying to bring us together again. I'm sorry I didn't believe him.'

'I was hurt at the time, but let's put it all behind us. Just one thing: Jake Bosley is the most honest boy I know. You can trust him with your life.'

Meg's mouth hardened and Louisa suddenly feared that she had just lost the tentative beginning they had made. Then Meg shrugged her shoulders and it was as if she was shrugging Jake off too. 'I never see him now.'

'Don't you?' Louisa was surprised. 'Then you won't know.'

Meg's eyes were sharp with an interest she could not hide. 'Know what?'

'About him and Betsy?'

Unable to speak, as a sudden inexplicable fear tightened her throat, Meg shook her head, her wide eyes fixed on Louisa's face.

'They've got engaged.'

After a moment, Meg found her voice, but it was a high-pitched squeak. 'Engaged? But – but Betsy's only a child.'

Louisa was smiling. Betsy had been one of her favourites at the workhouse and was a regular visitor to Louisa's home now. She shook her head. 'Not any more, she isn't. She was always small for her age and looked a lot younger than she really was. She's sixteen now.'

Meg's mind was in a whirl. Jake – her Jake, for he *was* her Jake – was going to marry Betsy. The depth of the emotion that swept through her startled her. She didn't care about him any more, she told herself repeatedly, but now she knew that was all a lie. Foolishly, she had imagined that, even though she had married Percy to gain security, somehow Jake would always be there for her. He would always be her friend. *That he would always love her and her alone.*

'But he – he doesn't love her.'

'Of course he loves her,' Louisa said and Meg was appalled to realize she had spoken her thoughts aloud. She put her hand to her forehead and swayed.

'Come and sit down.' Louisa's arm was about her, leading her into their private sitting room. 'There,' she said, when Meg fell onto the sofa, 'I'll get some tea. I'm sorry, Meg.' She stood looking down at the girl with a mixture of pity and concern. She hadn't realized how deep Meg's bitterness was. 'I didn't think it would be such a shock for you, that it would affect you so much. You're happy for them, aren't you?'

Meg could not bring herself to reply.

The day after Percy returned to work, Clara Finch entered the shop. Percy gaped at her for a few seconds before recovering his composure enough to say, 'Good morning, Clara.'

Her thin lips tightened. 'Good morning – Mr Rodwell,' she said stiffly. Meg watched in amazement as, her hands folded in front of her at waist level, Clara advanced towards the counter.

'I'm setting up a ladies' circle to knit balaclavas, scarves and gloves for the troops. We will be meeting each week at the Hall and I shall require a regular supply of appropriate wool.' She sniffed. 'Of course, I would normally have taken my custom elsewhere, but in these dreadful times one has to forget one's own petty grievances and think of the greater good.'

'Quite so – Miss Finch,' Percy murmured. 'I shall be

happy to be of service. I will also undertake to supply the wool at cost price. Call it my contribution to your worthy endeavours.'

Clara inclined her head. 'Most generous. I will make sure my ladies know of your kind offer.'

Meg wanted to laugh at the stilted exchange of conversation between the two people who had once been betrothed to each other. But instead she carried a selection of different coloured wools to Percy, gave a polite nod towards Clara and returned to her place at the other side of the shop. She watched as Clara picked out the colour of wool she wanted and Percy noted it, promising to keep a good supply in stock at all times.

As Clara was about to leave, Percy bade her 'Good day,' and added pleasantly, 'give my kind regards to your brother.'

Clara, on her way towards the door, turned back. Her mouth pursed and her eyes hard she said, 'Neither of us require your "kind regards", Mr Rodwell.'

'I'm sorry. Mr Finch was perfectly pleasant the last time I saw him. I thought—'

'When did you see him? You had no occasion to see him. He patronizes a tailor in Nottingham now.'

Percy blinked, realizing too late that Clara had no idea that her brother still came into his shop.

'I – er – encountered him.'

'Where?'

'I – er—' Percy was floundering and Clara was swift to guess the truth.

'He's been in here, hasn't he?' She paused and when Percy did not answer immediately, she shrilled, 'Hasn't he?'

'Well, just once or twice.'

Clara's eyes narrowed. 'Well, he will not be coming into this shop again, you can count on that.'

With that parting shot, she stormed towards the door and out of the shop. The bell clanged weakly.

Forty-Two

What happened between Clara and her brother, neither Meg nor Percy ever knew, but Theobald Finch did not come into the shop again. The first Christmas of the war passed with no sign of the hostilities coming to an end as people had hoped. Over the months that followed the number of customers coming into the tailor's shop seemed to dwindle.

Where he'd once worried about not being able to cope with the pressure of work, Percy now fretted about the lack of orders. 'We're losing business. I haven't made a suit in weeks.'

'Business isn't so good at this time of the year just after Christmas. You've said so yourself. It'll perk up in the spring. And besides, a lot of the men have gone to war,' Meg pointed out. 'We were lucky to get all those orders for suits when we did.'

Percy's glance was reproachful. He still felt guilty about all the trade that this terrible war had brought him.

As the second Christmas of the war approached, the whole town seemed sunk in depression. In January 1916 a fierce debate took place in the House of Commons over conscription, single men to be recruited first. At Middleditch Farm Jake dropped his bombshell over supper one evening. 'I'm going to enlist and I want Betsy and me to get married before I go. That way, if owt happens, she'll get my pension . . .'

Betsy began to cry and George and Mabel stared at the young man.

'Well, Jake Bosley, that's a fine way to propose to a girl, I must say. There, there, lass –' Mabel reached across and patted Betsy's arm – 'don't take on so.'

'There's no need for you to go, lad,' George said. 'At least not yet. They're not calling up married men. If you and Betsy get married quick—'

Jake was shaking his head. 'That'd be cowardice and I've no wish to be given a white feather.' He tried to make a joke, 'Even if there are plenty blowing about the yard.'

But no one was laughing.

George sighed. 'Aye well, I can't say I blame you, lad. If I was forty years younger, then—'

'George!' Mabel was askance. 'I hope you'd do no such thing. You should be telling Jake to forget such nonsense, not encouraging him.' She turned to Jake and her expression softened. 'Jake, you're like a son to us.' For a moment her expression was pained. 'Our daughter is lost to us – as good as – and you, well, you and young Betsy have filled the void in our lives.'

Though a strict taskmaster, Mabel Smallwood could, on occasions, be as soft as the butter she churned in the dairy. She grasped Jake's hand and then Betsy's, as if by her actions she would bind them together. Her voice was husky as she said, 'There's nowt we'd like better, George and me, than to see you two settle down together. We've even talked about how to get you a little place of your own.' She glanced at George, who added, 'Aye, we reckon if we did a bit of alteration to the side of the house. Built on a hallway and another staircase and knocked a few holes in the walls, you could have the front room and the bedroom above it and be all self-contained. We'd add on a bit of a kitchen at the back, an' all. What do you say, now?'

Jake and Betsy, whose tears had miraculously dried, stared at each other.

'It's – very generous of you,' Jake faltered. 'We – we never expected anything like that.'

'No,' Mabel said tartly, becoming her usual self once more. 'And if we'd thought for an instant that you did expect it, well, you wouldn't be getting it.' She paused and then her smile took away some of the sharpness. 'If you see what I mean.'

Jake's expression, however, was still sober. 'Is this – I mean – does this offer still stand if I enlist?'

Mabel opened her mouth, but George cast her a warning glance and answered for them both. 'We're not the sort of folks to make conditions. Besides, you must do what your conscience tells you. I've never been one to come between a man and his conscience.'

Mabel shut her mouth and lowered her gaze. Jake had the feeling that she did not wholly agree with her husband. 'So,' George went on, 'even if you decide to go, we'll look after young Betsy here whilst you're gone and – God willing – when you come back, we'll build a home for you both.'

'I won't have her at my wedding. I won't, I won't.'

Jake had never seen the quiet, docile Betsy in such a temper. Trying to placate her, he said mildly, 'I don't suppose she'd come anyway. She wouldn't come to Dr and Mrs Collins's wedding, so I don't suppose she'd come to ours.'

Betsy was still tearful and truculent, which was unlike her. 'But you still want her to come. You still want her to be invited. And the missis doesn't want her here any more than I do. And they're paying for our wedding . . .'

Jake sighed. 'I know, I know. But the missis is a bit unfair blaming Meg for what her father did. And you – I can't understand why you don't want to ask her. I thought you and she were friends.'

'I'd rather Dr and Mrs Collins came to our wedding,' Betsy said stubbornly, skirting round the real reason why she didn't want Meg Rodwell spoiling her special day. 'And – and Meg doesn't speak to Mrs Collins, so it – it could make it awkward.' Betsy was jealous of Meg and always would be. She had witnessed how Jake looked at Meg and how, when her name was mentioned, his face altered.

'But they do now,' Jake insisted. 'Mrs Collins told me herself. Meg went to the surgery to pick up some medicine for Mr Rodwell and Mrs Collins saw her and they've made it up.'

'Oh.' Betsy looked crestfallen.

Jake eyed her closely. 'You don't look pleased.'

Betsy was silent. Jake put his arms around her and pulled her to him. 'Come on, my little love, out with it. What's really upsetting you?'

She clung to him, burying her face against his chest so that he had difficulty in deciphering her muffled words. 'You – you – like her, don't you?'

'We're friends.' Above her head, he grimaced. 'Well, we were. I'm not so sure now.'

'No – no, I mean, you really like her.' There followed two words that he could not hear, so he pulled back and cupped her tear-streaked face between his hands.

'Look at me, love,' he said gently. 'Come on, tell me what's troubling you. We mustn't have secrets.'

Tears welled in the young girl's eyes and trickled down her face. Tenderly, Jake wiped them away with his finger.

'You – you love her, don't you?'

Jake stared at her, battling with an inner turmoil that he hoped Betsy would never know of. He sighed and, telling her the truth but not quite the whole truth, he said, 'When I first met her, yes, I did like her. I liked her very much. If it hadn't been for her, I might still be shut up in that place. She gave me the courage to get out and make a life for miself outside the workhouse. But then –' he paused for a moment, inwardly mourning the loss of the spirited, fiery girl he had first met – 'she changed. I suppose – if I'm fair – it was because of all the things that happened to her, but even so there's no excuse for some of the things she's done.' His voice dropped to a whisper. 'Some things I can't forgive her for.'

In a small voice, Betsy said, 'So – so you – you're not in love with her?'

Neatly he avoided giving a direct answer, but nevertheless he was utterly sincere. 'I love *you*, Betsy. It's you I want to marry.'

Deep inside him he buried all thoughts of Meg forever. And even Betsy had the sense not to voice her deepest anxiety. She didn't ask aloud: *But if Meg weren't married to Percy Rodwell, what then?* Instead she wound her arms about Jake's neck and whispered. 'I love you so much, Jake.'

He kissed her and hugged her and did his best to drive away all thoughts of the beautiful girl with the red hair and the heart-stopping smile.

*

On a Saturday morning in March, Meg stood near the front of the shop, gazing unseeingly out of the window into the street.

Jake was getting married today. To Betsy, of all people. And they were going to live at the farm, treated like the Smallwoods' own family. They'd all be there, she thought. Philip and Louisa, Letitia Pendleton. Maybe even Isaac Pendleton and Theobald Finch, George Smallwood's racing cronies, would have been invited.

They'd all be there. All – but her.

The wedding was over and after the briefest of honeymoons Jake left to join the army.

George, shaking the young man's hand vigorously, could not speak for the huge fear constricting his throat.

Betsy and Mabel wept openly. 'Do take care,' they kept repeating, as if convincing themselves that if he kept a sharp eye open he could easily dodge the bullets.

Jake hugged them all in turn, keeping his last tender kiss for his young bride. 'I'm no great letter writer, Betsy, but I'll do mi best. Will you do something for me?'

Mute with misery, she nodded.

'Go and see Miss Pendleton now and again. Let her know how I'm faring.'

'Miss Pendleton? Matron?' Betsy was startled.

'Yes. She's always been good to me. She was the nearest I had to a mam before I came to live here at the farm.'

'But, but they used to beat you—'

Firmly, Jake shook his head. 'She didn't. He did, but

not her. Never her. If truth be known, she saved me from him several times.'

'Did she?'

Jake nodded. 'But then, she liked the little boys, didn't she?'

'Mm,' Betsy said slowly, remembering how it had been. 'But she always seemed to like you best.'

'Don't come to see me off. I want to think of you all here.' And so the Smallwoods and Betsy went on with their daily routine about the farm, trying not to think about Jake joining the line of marching men on their way to the station.

The streets of South Monkford were lined with cheering, flag-waving folk. As they passed, Jake glanced towards the tailor's shop and fancied he saw a glimpse of Meg beyond the shadowy window. But she did not come to the doorway to wave him goodbye.

Her smile would live only in his memory.

Inside the shop, standing in the shadows, Meg bit her fingernail down to the quick. He was going. Jake was going to the war. Meg had never felt so terrified in her life. If he was killed and she never had a chance to tell him . . .

Letitia Pendleton was waiting near the station. She pushed her way through the throng and grabbed Jake's arm, trying to pull him away from the lines of marching men.

'Don't go, Jake. You don't have to. Don't go.'

Gently, he tried to prise her clinging hands away, but she held on tightly.

'I have to, Miss Pendleton. I've enlisted. I'd be put in prison if I don't go now. Besides, I want to. It's my duty and I'll be called up soon enough anyway.'

Letitia sobbed. 'But – I – I might never see you again. And I've never told you . . .'

They'd reached the entrance to the station and the formal lines of marching men had broken up.

Jake stopped and turned to face her, smiling down at her. 'I know I've always been one of your favourites.'

Letitia was sobbing uncontrollably, her arms trying to enfold him. 'It's more than that. Jake, there's something you should know. Something I *want* you to know.'

'I have to go, Miss Pendleton. They're all getting on the train now.'

He planted a kiss on her round cheek, wet with tears. 'When I come back,' he promised, 'I'll come and see you.'

He pulled away from her and marched purposefully towards the station entrance and in through the archway.

'Jake . . . Jake . . .' Her cry followed him, echoing eerily. 'Don't go. I have to tell you . . .'

He marched on and, if she said more, Jake did not hear it.

Forty-Three

The war dragged on through 1916. The people of South Monkford scoured the casualty lists in the local paper and those with menfolk at the Front waited fearfully for the dreaded telegram.

Philip Collins enlisted, and whilst he tried to reassure his wife that in his work as a medical officer he would be comparatively safe, Louisa was not convinced.

'I know you. You'll be right there near the Front. In a field hospital.'

He could not deny the probability. Louisa clung to him and whispered against his neck, 'And I don't even have a child to remember you by.'

It was a great source of sadness to them both that they had not been blessed, as yet, with children.

'When I come back, it'll be different. I promise you.' But Louisa would not be comforted.

Philip battled in the days before his departure against saying goodbye to Meg. He couldn't get her out of his mind and the thought that he might never see her again drove him finally, against his better judgement, to visit her.

He decided to call at the shop so Percy would be there too. That way he would not be alone with her. But when he opened the door and stepped inside, the shop was empty. Percy must be here alone, Philip thought, moving towards the back room. But as he stepped inside it was Meg who raised her eyes from sewing buttons on an almost completed jacket.

'Philip!' she cried and jumped up at once. Scarcely realizing what he was doing, Philip held out his arms and she ran into them. He held her close, his face against her hair, breathing in the scent of her.

'Oh, Philip, you're going too, aren't you? Jake's gone and now you.' She was weeping against him and then he was kissing her; her forehead, her eyes and lastly, her mouth. She returned his kiss, clinging to him, pressing herself against him.

'Oh, Meg, Meg,' he was saying over and over. His kisses, passionate and yet poignant, awakened something in her that Meg had not known existed. This was real desire, this was passion. What she was suddenly feeling was totally different to her affection for Percy. And oh, how different it would be to be made love to by this handsome man with his broad shoulders and lithe body.

'Philip,' she gasped and drew him into the room.

What might have happened then had the shop doorbell not clanged warningly, Philip dared not think. Only later was he grateful that at that moment Percy had returned to the shop. Philip and Meg sprang apart, gazing breathlessly at each other until Meg smoothed her hair and opened the door.

'Percy,' she said with amazing calm, 'I'm so glad you're back. Dr Collins has called to say goodbye.'

If the doctor appeared dazed and slightly incoherent, Percy put it down to the young man's trepidation at what awaited him.

'Good luck, Doctor.' Percy shook Philip's hand, noticing its clammy feel. 'Come back to us safe and sound, won't you?'

Philip gulped and backed out of the shop. 'Yes, yes, thank you. Er – thank you, goodbye.'

'Oh dear,' Percy remarked, shaking his head sadly. 'He's terribly afraid of what might happen, isn't he?'

'Mm,' Meg agreed absently. She was not thinking of what might happen to Philip at the Front, but of what might happen when he came home again.

Jake had served almost a year in France when he received a wound that brought him back home. His knee was badly smashed and, whilst he would recover, he would forever walk with a stiff leg.

Whilst she hated the fact that Jake had been wounded, Betsy was ecstatic that, for him, the war was over.

'Did you see Dr Collins? Did he look after you in the hospital?'

Jake smiled indulgently at Betsy's naivety. 'No, love, I didn't see him. I 'spect he was in a different place to me.'

'Oh.' She was disappointed and then a worried frown creased her forehead. Now that her Jake was home, she could spare a thought for the safety of others. 'I hope he's all right.'

Meg too was thankful to hear that Jake had survived. She longed to see him, but the past kept them apart. Instead, she thought dreamily of the time that Philip would come home. And then, suddenly, miraculously, on the same day that the United States entered the war, Philip too was invalided out of the army. He had been caught in a gas attack and was considered no longer fit enough to undertake the onerous duties of a field hospital doctor.

'It's not as bad as they're making out,' he told Louisa. 'It's just affected my lungs, but I hope they'll improve – given time.' He tried to smile.

'Oh, Philip, you're not going back, are you? You've done your bit. More than your bit.'

He raised her hand to his lips. 'No, my dear. I'm back home now, but I'll soon be well enough to care for all my old patients here.'

And whilst he would never be quite as fit as he had been before the war, Dr Collins was soon riding round the town again in his pony and trap and calling on all his old friends.

But there was one place he did not dare to call. Though he thought of her often – every day – he did not call to see Meg.

By October 1918 the worldwide influenza epidemic had reached Britain and South Monkford. Dr Collins, still not completely fit himself, worked day and night to care for his patients. And just when the worst appeared to be over in the town Percy Rodwell succumbed.

'Get to bed at once,' Meg told him. 'And I'll fetch the doctor.'

'Don't worry the poor man,' Percy murmured, holding onto the counter to keep himself upright.

Meg held a cool hand to his forehead. 'You're burning up, Percy. Go straight home and get into bed. I'll close the shop early and go to the surgery. Maybe there's something he can prescribe.'

The front hall at the doctor's home, which served as a waiting room, was crowded. Louisa drew Meg through into their private quarters at the rear of the house. 'If you don't mind coming into the kitchen,' she whispered as she led the way, 'I'll make us a cup of tea, though I'll have to keep answering the front door.'

'Of course,' Meg said. 'But you mustn't bother about me, Louisa. You've enough to do.'

Louisa smiled. 'If I can't make a cup of tea for a friend, then it's a pity. Besides, I'm ready for one. I've been on my feet for two hours answering that door and placating frustrated patients.'

'I really can't stay long, though,' Meg said, peeling off her gloves and sitting down at the table whilst Louisa bustled about the kitchen, though still alert for the sound of the front-door bell. 'I've sent Percy home to bed. He's got this dreadful influenza. He looks terrible.'

'Oh dear.' Louisa turned sympathetic eyes on her friend. 'I'm sorry to hear that, but I'm sure Philip will visit him. It might be quite late, though.'

Meg shook her head. 'Percy doesn't want to trouble him. I've just come to see if Philip can give me something for him. That's all.'

'Here's your tea. I'll just slip in to see him between patients and ask, shall I? It'll save you waiting if you want to get back to Percy. Excuse me a moment.'

When Louisa had left the room, Meg looked about her. The kitchen was large, yet still cosy. Louisa was obviously the perfect housewife. The smell of freshly baked bread lingered in the air and judging by the remnants of their evening meal, taken before Philip started evening surgery, she was also an excellent cook. The house was vast, and though Meg had only seen Philip's surgery, their private sitting room and the kitchen, she imagined that all the other rooms were just as spacious and well furnished.

A sudden wave of envy swept through her. Why should Louisa have all this whilst she, Meg, lived in a poky little house with an old man as her husband? Once Percy had seemed a 'good catch' – a well-respected businessman in the town with his own shop and house. But then she had found that he didn't own the shop and that, whilst the townsfolk patronized it, he was nevertheless something of a figure of fun. Meg sighed. Now why couldn't she have captured someone like Philip? He was handsome as well as clever and he was revered in the community, whereas she feared that since the court case folk were secretly sniggering about Percy and his child bride. Why, why, why . . .

Louisa came hurrying back into the room. 'Philip says you're not to wait. Go home and he'll come and visit after surgery.'

Meg pushed away her envious thoughts and tried to smile, though it did not reach her eyes. Louisa, however, misinterpreted the shadow in her eyes as concern about Percy. She touched Meg's arm. 'Philip will come as soon as he can, my dear.'

When Meg arrived home, Percy had got into bed, but he was shivering uncontrollably. She stood by the bed looking down at him dispassionately. Lying there, his eyes closed, Percy looked gaunt and sickly. The ruthless thought crept its way unbidden into her mind. *If he dies, I'll be left this house and the business . . .*

'Water,' he whispered through cracked lips. 'Please . . .' Ill though he was, Percy Rodwell was the epitome of politeness.

Meg smiled and laid her cool hand on his forehead. 'Philip's on his way to see you. He'll tell me what I should do. But first I'll light the bedroom fire. It's so cold in here. That can't be good for you. And I'll heat a brick . . .'

When she had been ill as a child, Meg remembered

her mother heating a brick in the oven, wrapping it in a piece of cloth and placing it in the bed at her feet. She remembered feeling cosseted and loved by that one simple action.

By the time Philip, heavy eyed and grey with weariness, arrived, a cheerful fire was burning in the bedroom grate.

'He asked for water,' Meg said as she led the way upstairs, lifting her skirts daintily, 'but I wasn't sure if it was the right thing to do.'

'Yes, plenty of fluids. He must drink plenty, but hot drinks would be even better.'

She opened the bedroom door and ushered the doctor inside. As he stepped past her into the room, his arm brushed her breast. He paused a moment and looked down at her. Their eyes met and locked in an intense gaze. She heard him sigh as he dragged himself away and into the room.

'I – I'll get that drink for him now,' she murmured. 'And I'll make you something.'

Without waiting for him to argue, she closed the bedroom door and went down the narrow stairs. She heated milk and poured it out into two cups. Then in each one she put brown sugar and whisky. She carried one through to the front sitting room and placed it on a small table by the sofa. Then she poked the fire, making the flames dance and spark. She turned the gaslights down low so that the room was lit by the glow from the fire. Then she returned to the kitchen and carried the other cup of milk up to the bedroom.

'I've put a drop of whisky in it. Is that all right?'

'For the moment, but once he starts taking this medicine I'm leaving for him, don't give him any alcohol, will you?'

'Whatever you say,' Meg said meekly.

'Give him his first dose before he settles down for the night and then four times a day after meals. That's if he manages to eat anything, which I doubt very much. And I doubt either of you will get much sleep tonight. He'll be very restless until this fever breaks.'

Meg nodded. 'I'd already thought I might sleep in the other room. I'll probably disturb him all the more if I sleep in here.'

Philip glanced at her. She saw the struggle of emotion in his eyes. Hoarsely he said, 'But – but – you mustn't be too far away from him. You must keep a watch on him.'

'Of course I will.' Meg was indignant. 'I will look after him, Philip. Really, I will.'

A wicked little voice deep inside her whispered: *Are you trying to convince Philip – or yourself?*

'I know you will,' Philip murmured. He glanced back at his patient. 'Send me word if you need me again.'

'Thank you. And now,' she added briskly, 'you must come downstairs. I have a hot drink ready for you. It's in the front room. You go and get it before it's cold and I'll be down in a moment when I've helped Percy with his.'

She went to the far side of the bed and helped Percy to sit up against the pillows. She picked up the cup. Philip watched as she bent over her husband and held the cup to his lips. Percy sipped. Philip stood a moment watching the young woman's tender ministrations. Then he turned and left the bedroom without another word.

A few moments later Meg joined him in the small front parlour. Philip had finished his drink and was sitting staring into the fire. She sat beside him on the sofa.

'What did you put in that milk?' The small amount of alcohol coupled with his tiredness had already affected him.

Meg chuckled. 'Whisky. Like I put in Percy's.'

Philip rubbed his hand across his eyes. 'You'll have me drunk. That wouldn't look good to my patients.'

They stared at each other, both remembering what had happened the last time she had given him whisky to drink.

'I thought you'd probably finished for the night.' She curled up her feet beneath her and half turned towards him, putting her arm along the back of the sofa behind his head – not quite touching him, but very close.

He sighed. 'As far as I know at this moment, I have. But if I get called out in the night . . .'

'You're working far too hard.'

She leant forward and smoothed back a lock of his fair, curly hair that had fallen on to his forehead. Slowly, he turned to look at her. 'Oh, Meg,' he whispered.

Her mouth was only inches from his, her fingers still resting on his hair. She bent her head and kissed him, oh so gently, on the lips. A tender, featherlight kiss. She heard him moan and murmur yet again, 'Oh, Meg, Meg.'

He was kissing her ardently now, pressing her back against the cushions, lying on top of her . . .

Afterwards, he was ashamed and contrite. 'I'm so sorry, Meg. I – we – shouldn't have done that.'

Meg, her eyes shining, whispered, 'But it was wonderful. I've never known it like that. Not with Percy . . .'

'Don't.' Philip dropped his head into his hands and

groaned. 'Please – don't. I feel bad enough already. I'm so sorry, Meg. It will never happen again, I swear.'

'Why? I won't tell a soul. No one need know.'

Philip's ardent lovemaking had awakened a passion in her that she had never known before. She had forgotten everything in the searing ecstasy of the moment. She couldn't bear to think that this might be the one and only time she would know such a glorious feeling. 'Please, Philip. I love you, I adore you . . .' she pleaded.

He lifted his head and gazed at her and she saw that his face was wet with tears. 'Oh, Meg. We can't. We mustn't. Don't you see? We'd hurt too many people. I'd lose my career.'

'I'd never do anything to hurt you, Philip. Never. No one would ever know. Not from me.'

'But people have ways of finding out, especially in a small town like this. And besides – more important than all that – we're . . . we're being unfair to Percy and to Louisa.' As he spoke his wife's name, he dropped his head into his hands once more, whilst, unseen by him, Meg smiled.

Forty-Four

Despite his good intentions, Philip couldn't stay away from Meg. She was like one of his drugs, just as powerful and much, much more dangerous. Throughout Percy's illness he continued to visit, knowing that for the moment at least the neighbours would not question why his pony and trap were parked outside for an hour at a time.

Meg was in heaven. When he was not there, her body yearned for him with a physical ache. Thoughts of him filled her waking hours and her dreams at night. And in the brief, ecstatic moments they were together, all thoughts of Percy – even of Jake – and certainly of Louisa were driven from her mind. They couldn't help themselves, neither of them. But whilst Meg had no conscience, Philip was being torn apart by their deceit and infidelity.

'It has to stop, Meg,' he said a hundred times, but day after day, drawn by his fascination with her, he called again.

But on the tenth day, Meg opened the door with a worried frown on her face. 'He's worse.'

The doctor hurried up the stairs and into the main bedroom. He found his patient sinking into unconsciousness.

'Oh no!' Philip felt guilt overwhelm him, whilst behind him, Meg stood uncertainly in the doorway.

*

No one blamed the doctor for the deaths from influenza. The epidemic was worldwide. There had been several deaths already in South Monkford and now there was one more – Percy Rodwell.

Five days after Percy's death the armistice was signed, and whilst the whole country celebrated the end of the war Meg buried her husband.

After the funeral, Meg returned to the darkened house and sat in the front room alone, waiting for Philip. The curtains had been drawn all day, as was the custom in the neighbourhood when there had been a death in the house. Even the neighbours had drawn their curtains as a mark of respect when the horse-drawn hearse left Percy's cottage.

She knew he would come. She was sure he would come, but when she heard the pony and trap pull up outside the door and she peeped through a crack in the curtains, she was disappointed to see Louisa sitting beside him in the trap. Meg watched as Philip jumped down and then assisted his wife to alight. Together they came towards the front door as Meg opened it to greet them.

'My dear,' Louisa said, holding out her arms. 'We can't tell you how sorry we both are.'

Meg held herself stiffly in Louisa's embrace. Over the other woman's shoulder she met Philip's gaze briefly, but he lowered his head and refused to meet her eyes.

'Come in,' Meg said in a flat tone. 'I'll – I'll make some tea.'

'Let me,' Louisa offered. 'You go into the front room with Philip. I'm sure there are things you need to discuss – to ask him. We both want to help, Meg, in any way we can. You have only to ask.'

For a brief instant hysteria welled up inside Meg. She

wanted to laugh and cry aloud: *All I want is your husband. It's me he loves now – not you.* But she remained silent, gave a weak smile and opened the door into the front room.

'Thank you, Louisa,' she murmured. 'There – there are one or two – business matters that I'm sure Philip could give me some guidance on.'

Philip glanced uneasily from one to the other, but when his wife touched his arm and bade him follow Meg, he had no choice.

Inside the front room with the door closed, he stood stiffly behind the sofa, at once putting a barrier between them. Meg smiled and held out her hands to him. 'Why so distant? Come here.'

'Meg.' He frowned, shifting uncomfortably from one foot to the other. 'Don't. Please, don't. Not today of all days.'

'I'm sorry.' Meg was at once contrite. 'You're right, of course. We must let a decent interval elapse before—'

'Before nothing, Meg.' His voice was still a whisper, but there was no doubting the vehemence in his tone. 'It's got to stop. We can't go on. I can't go on deceiving Louisa and – and there's my career . . .'

Meg watched him. His face was tortured. He was suffering agonies. He wanted her still, yet his conscience was crucifying him. She went to him and took his hands in hers. They were cold and trembling.

'It's all right,' she whispered. 'Truly it is. I won't ask anything more from you. It is at an end if – if that is what you really want.' She was so sure that he would not take her seriously, so sure that he would not be able to resist her.

'It – it is.' The words came haltingly, as if he was

forcing them out, and she could see by the look in his eyes that it wasn't what he really wanted to say.

They heard Louisa's footsteps in the hallway and Meg released his hands and stepped away. 'It'll be our secret. I promise,' was her final whisper as she went towards the door to open it for Louisa to carry in the tea tray.

Placing it on a low table, Louisa poured the tea and handed round the cups. She kept up a flow of conversation, but Philip and Meg said little.

'We must be going,' Louisa said at last. She stood up and bent to pick up the tray, but Meg said at once, 'Leave that. I've nothing else to do today. I shan't reopen the shop until Monday.'

'Very well, my dear,' Louisa said, leaning forward and kissing Meg on the cheek. 'You know where we are should you need anything.'

Meg nodded, but as Philip gave her a chaste peck on the cheek, tears filled her eyes. She stood at the door as they climbed into the trap and moved away, then she closed the door and leant against it and allowed the tears to fall freely.

When Meg visited Percy's solicitors on the day after the funeral, as requested by Mr Henderson in a letter of condolence, a shock awaited her.

As expected, Percy had left all his worldly possessions to her, but the shock was that his possessions didn't amount to as much as she'd believed. It came as a thunderbolt to learn that Percy didn't own the terraced house, but that he rented it from none other than Theobald Finch.

Meg stared at the solicitor in horror. She licked her

dry lips and when she spoke her voice came out in a croak. 'I – I had wondered what might happen about the shop, but – but I hadn't realized that he – he didn't own his home. Oh, Mr Henderson, whatever am I to do? The Finches will throw me out, won't they?'

Mr Henderson shuffled his papers and cleared his throat. 'Well, well, I really couldn't say. All you can do, my dear lady, is to continue running your late husband's business . . .' He paused and then asked, 'You intend to do that, don't you?'

Meg nodded.

'And we'll just have to wait and see,' Mr Henderson went on, 'what happens when the lease comes up for renewal. I don't think your landlord can do anything at all until then.'

'And when is that, Mr Henderson?'

The solicitor consulted his papers once more. 'Ah yes, here we are. Your husband signed a new ten-year lease seven years ago, Mrs Rodwell, so there are still three years to run on both premises. The house and the shop.'

'So,' Meg said slowly, 'I have three years before I shall be homeless.'

'Oh, I wouldn't put it quite like that, my dear lady. Perhaps Mr Finch will agree to renew the lease in your name.'

Meg stood up. She pursed her mouth grimly. 'And pigs might fly, Mr Henderson,' she said bitterly.

Meg reopened the shop on the Monday after Percy's funeral. Her first customer was Jake. He came to stand in front of her, the counter between them.

'So, what will you do now?' he asked at last, offering

her no polite condolences. His face was tight, his eyes accusing. 'Now that you're a woman of means?'

'Huh!' Meg's expression was bitter.

'What? Not the wealthy woman you thought you were going to be?'

Meg glared at him. 'Go away, Jake, if that's all you've come for.'

She banged a box onto the counter and began to unpack a quantity of men's vests.

There was an awkward silence. Meg tried to carry on with her work as if he wasn't standing on the other side of the counter, but it was impossible. The tension between them grew until she burst out, 'Oh, very well then, if you must know. The shop and the house weren't his. He rented them *both* from Theobald Finch. So –' she nodded as she watched the change on Jake's face – 'as soon as the leases run out in three years' time, I shall be out on my ear. That please you, does it?'

'No, Meg, it doesn't. But a lot of folks round here'll say you've got your just deserts.'

'And you're one of them?' she flashed back.

Jake sighed heavily. 'Meg, you know how I once felt about you, but you changed so. Where was the lovely girl I met when you first came to the workhouse?' His tone was pensive as he added in a whisper, 'Where did she go, Meggie?'

The unexpected use of her pet name – the name she had been called as a little girl by her family – brought sudden tears to Meg's eyes. Impatiently, she brushed them away as she answered tartly, 'She grew up, Jake. She just grew up.'

Jake's gaze held hers as he shook his head slowly. 'But she changed, Meg. It was more than just growing up. She changed.'

'Well, you can talk. You've got your feet well and truly under the table at Middleditch Farm, haven't you?' She leant forward. 'Don't you realize, Jake, that you're every bit as bad as me? You're trapped for life there now, whether you want to be or not. You're just a replacement, Jake, you and Betsy, for the daughter they lost.' She moved round the counter and stood close to him, smiling coquettishly. She traced her forefinger down the side of his face. 'Don't tell me,' she asked huskily, 'that you really wanted to marry Betsy. You did it to please them, didn't you?'

Jake stepped back from her as if she'd slapped him. His face twisted with disgust and anger, yet, despite it all, her nearness disturbed him. The feelings he'd once had for Meg, though he thought them buried deep, were still there. No matter what she did or what she said, as long as he lived he would never be able to kill his love for her completely. And he hated her for it. Loved and hated her at the same time.

'Don't judge everyone by your own standards,' he spat at her, ''cos you haven't got any.' He thrust his face close to hers. 'You might be able to seduce a feller like Percy Rodwell, but you don't fool me.' He paused and then added with deliberate emphasis, 'And I'd've thought the doctor would have had more sense, an' all.'

Now Meg was genuinely shocked. 'What – what d'you mean?'

'Just because we live a bit out of town doesn't mean we don't hear all the gossip.' He nodded. 'Market day's a good place to hear all that's going on and then there's the race meetings when they're on . . .'

'And what've you heard?' Meg asked between gritted teeth.

'Oh –' Jake tried to make his tone nonchalant – 'just

that when Percy was ill, the doctor visited him more often than he visited any other patient. He attended his funeral and came here afterwards to visit you.'

'Yes, he did,' she snapped back. 'And he brought his *wife* with him.'

He shrugged. 'Mebbe she'd heard the rumours, an' all.'

'There was nothing to hear,' Meg countered, but an ugly flush crept up her neck and into her face. Seeing it, Jake knew the truth.

He turned and left the shop, wishing he'd never come near her. He vowed that he never would again.

She could rot in hell for all he cared.

Forty-Five

At the end of Meg's first week running the shop alone, her fears were realized when Theobald Finch called in just as she was about to close for the evening.

He raised his hat to her. 'Mrs Rodwell.'

Meg managed to summon up her most brilliant smile, yet her heart was thumping. She guessed what he was going to say even before he opened his mouth. Theobald cleared his throat. 'I find myself in something of an embarrassing situation. My sister is insisting I give you notice at once. Both here and at the house you occupy. The tenancy agreements, as you no doubt now know, are still in the name of Mr Rodwell's father with a note of transfer to his son, Percy, some seven years ago.'

Meg said nothing. Her hands were clammy and her knees were trembling. She felt sick.

'The lease expires,' Theobald went on, 'in three years' time.'

There was a long, ominous pause before Theobald added, 'I shall be unable to renew the lease in your name at that time.'

Meg found she had been holding her breath and now she released it. 'So,' she said heavily, 'you're giving me three years?'

He nodded. 'Yes. Unless, of course, you wish to leave before then. There is a clause in the lease which allows you to give me three months' notice.' His tone was hopeful. If she were to do that, his life at home with his sister would be much easier.

'I see.' Meg raised her head defiantly and, with what she hoped was the right degree of businesslike attitude, she said, 'I will give the matter serious thought, Mr Finch, and instruct my solicitor accordingly.'

As Theobald raised his hat and bade her 'Good day,' Meg could have sworn that a smile twitched at the corner of his mouth. He was so sure of himself, she thought. So sure that she was beaten.

Meg felt sick. Every morning when she got up she had to rush to the bowl on the washstand to retch into it. It left her feeling pale and shaky. *It's the worry of the business*, she told herself. Since Percy's death the number of customers was diminishing noticeably with each day that passed. Meg hadn't had a woman customer for over a fortnight and even the number of men coming into the shop was less and less. Even regular customers whom she had heard declare to Percy that they would never dream of going anywhere else for their new suits now never entered the shop.

Of course, Meg was no longer able to offer a made-to-measure service and perhaps that had affected the sales more than she'd thought possible. She'd advertised in the local paper for an experienced tailor but there'd been no replies. Not one.

Worse than anything, Meg had no one with whom to talk over her troubles. Jake was lost to her and she wouldn't dream of going anywhere near Louisa, even though she longed to see Philip.

Was it because of him that the townsfolk were keeping away from the shop that was now hers – at least for the next three years? Philip was well liked and respected in the town. Perhaps, even if they hadn't believed the gossip, they were cold-shouldering Meg because of it. Just in case the rumours had some truth . . . Oh, they were true, all right, Meg thought bitterly, but he wasn't man enough to leave his wife and set up home with her. His career, his standing in the community, were too precious to him. He wouldn't give up everything for love. She despised him for it and yet she still ached for his touch, the feel of his strong, firm body next to hers . . . Meg lifted her head defiantly. *I don't need him*, she told herself. *And I certainly don't need Jake. I'll make such a success of this business that in three years' time Theobald Finch would be a fool to turn me out – whatever his sister says.*

Meg held a sale of all the menswear in stock. She plastered sale tickets in the windows, but still her only customers were strangers from out of town, who came into South Monkford on market day. They knew nothing of the scandal surrounding the pretty young woman behind the counter in the tailor's shop. Gradually she reduced the stock and was able to order more women's clothes. Then she advertised in the local paper once more, informing all her customers that there'd be a grand reopening with discounts on all sales on the first day.

She worked hard, rearranging the interior of the shop and transforming the workroom into a fitting room for ladies to try on dresses, coats and hats. She re-dressed the window and, from one of her suppliers, bought a mannequin to grace the display.

On the day of the sale Meg awoke early and rushed once more to the bowl. *It's just anxiety*, she told herself. *There's nothing wrong with me that a good few customers coming through my door today won't put right.*

Unable to face breakfast – even nibbling a dry piece of toast made her feel queasy again – Meg left home early. Excitement churned in the pit of her stomach. Today would be the turning point in her life. She was sure of it. She had some lovely new stock. Fine silk underwear for the ladies of the town and now, too, she had the more serviceable type of garments worn by farmers' wives.

As nine o'clock came, Meg opened the shop door and looked out onto the pavement, fully expecting to see a few women queuing there to be first to acquire the generous bargains.

There was no one in the street and by ten thirty, she was losing heart. No one had come into her shop even though it was market day and the centre of the town was buzzing. At twelve o'clock she tried to eat the sandwiches she had brought with her, but her stomach heaved at each bite. She gave up and contented herself with a cup of tea whilst standing mournfully near the window to watch the people hurrying past.

She was in the lean-to scullery outside the back door when she heard the bell clang and eagerly she hurried back into the shop.

Betsy was standing uncertainly just inside the door. Meg's welcoming smile died on her lips. 'Oh. It's you,' she said unnecessarily. Betsy's face turned pink, but she moved towards the counter. 'I wondered if you stocked –' the girl lifted her head with a show of bravado and stared straight into Meg's eyes as she added proudly – 'special dresses?' She demonstrated, holding her hands out in front of her. 'With plenty of room in them?'

Meg gaped at her. 'You? You're expecting?'

Her eyes shining, Betsy nodded. 'I'm three months gone and Dr Collins says the sickness should stop soon.'

'Sickness? What sickness?'

Betsy smiled knowledgeably. 'You get a bit of sickness when you're expecting. Usually, just first thing in a morning.'

'Sickness?' Meg repeated stupidly. 'First – first thing in the morning?'

'Yes. But sometimes you can get it any time of the day. For a week or two I had it in the evening as well, but Dr Collins says it should all go after the first three months. Mind you, sometimes it lasts the whole nine months.' Betsy pulled a face. 'That's what Mrs Smallwood ses.'

There was a moment's silence before Meg managed to say weakly, 'Congratulations.'

'Thanks,' Betsy said, then asked again, 'Well, have you got anything I could wear?'

'Yes, one or two bits. They're expensive though. It's usually the toffs who buy special clothes . . .' She left the sentence hanging, but the unspoken words said: *Your sort usually make do and mend.*

But Betsy only smiled and her blush deepened. 'Jake wants me to have the best and Mrs Smallwood said she'd treat me to a proper frock.'

'Very generous, I'm sure.' Meg was consumed with jealousy. Not only was Betsy married to Jake, but she had the Smallwoods treating her like their own daughter, whilst she, Meg, was struggling to run a dying business and facing eviction in three years' time. She was hardly aware of what she was doing as she showed the garments to Betsy. When the girl finally left the shop, the niggling worry burst into her mind.

Sickness? First thing in the morning? Oh no. No. No!

*

Louisa opened the door at Meg's ring. She took Meg's cold hands into hers. 'My dear. How are you? You're looking very pale.'

'I – I've come to see Philip. Professionally.'

'You've timed it perfectly. The last patient is in with him now. Sit down, dear. I'm sure he won't be long.'

To Meg's dismay, Louisa sat beside her in the hallway and kept up an incessant chatter. Inside her head, Meg screamed: *Go away. Leave me alone*. But instead she sat silently, nodding every now and again, though her mind scarcely took in what Louisa was saying.

The consulting-room door opened and a man came out, nodded towards Louisa and left by the front door. Louisa got up and opened the door again.

'Meg's here, Philip. She needs to see you.' Smiling, she held the door open. 'Come in, Meg. I'll leave you to his tender mercies. Come and have a cup of tea with us when you've finished here.'

Mutely, Meg nodded, though she had no intention of staying in this house any longer than she had to.

When the door closed behind his wife, Philip and Meg stared at each other. For a moment there was silence between them until Meg blurted out in a hoarse whisper, 'I think I'm pregnant.'

Moments later, when Philip had confirmed her worst fears, she sat down opposite him again. Now Philip's face was as white as hers.

'Well,' Meg demanded, some of her spirit returning, 'what are you going to do about it?'

'Me?'

'Well, it's your child. You didn't think it could be Percy's, did you?'

Philip gasped. 'You – you don't know that.'

Meg smiled bitterly. 'Oh, I do. Believe me, I do know.'

If it was possible, he blanched even more. He swallowed painfully and now it was he who whispered, 'What are you going to do?'

'Well, I'm not going to some back-street butcher to get rid of it, if that's what you're asking. And you a doctor!'

'Of course I didn't mean that,' he said at once. 'That thought never entered my head.'

'Really!' Meg's tone was scathing. 'Well, it had mine.' She leant towards him. 'D'you mean to tell me you've never been asked to do it?'

He stared at her for a moment. 'Oh, I've been asked, but I have never agreed. Whatever the circumstances – you've got a new life growing, Meg, and it's precious. It has a right to live. Besides, it's not the sort of thing . . .' He said no more, but Meg knew. His precious career, she thought.

'So, what's its *father* going to do? Acknowledge it? Tell the world he's had an affair with one of his patients? Leave his wife to marry the mother of his child?' There was a brief pause whilst Philip stared at her, horror-struck.

'No,' Meg said quietly. 'I thought not.' She came to a swift decision. She was taking a risk, but it was a calculated risk. She must play her hand carefully. Oh, so carefully. She sighed heavily as she stood up to leave, as if she were obliged to shoulder the whole burden alone. 'Well, you're a lucky man, Dr Collins, because the world will think it's Percy's. *I* know it's not and *you* know it's not, but no one else need know.'

Philip too stood up. 'You – you'd do that? For me?'

She stepped close to him and looked up into his face. For a brief instant, in spite of himself, she saw the longing spark in his eyes. She was right. Even now, he still wanted her.

'I'm not all bad, Philip,' she whispered huskily. 'Whatever people might think.' She put her hands, palms flat, on the lapels of his jacket. 'There are people in this world that, if I had the power, I would wreak revenge upon. I admit that. But you're not one of them. Your secret is safe, Philip. I promise you that.'

If anything, she thought, *will win him back, this will. He'll soon be calling on me again in the little house in Church Street*. Now that she was to bear his child, when his own wife seemed unable to do so, she was so sure Philip would come back to her. But for now she must play the part.

She kissed him lightly on the lips, turned and went towards the door.

'Tell your wife I'm sorry I couldn't stay.' She paused, her hand on the doorknob. 'Goodnight – Dr Collins.'

Today had been a turning point in her life all right, Meg thought bitterly as she walked home through the dusk, but not in the way she had expected.

Forty-Six

When Meg could no longer hide her condition, the news spread through the town's grapevine with amazing speed. More customers – mostly women – came into the shop but they bought very little and Meg knew it was only an excuse to gape at her and to gossip about her later with their friends.

The sickness had abated, but now her waistline began to bulge noticeably. Her ankles swelled with standing behind the counter most of the day. But, worst of all, Philip had not been near her. Not once had he called at the shop or at the house. It seemed that he had taken her at her word and her scheme had misfired. Meg felt very alone and lonely with no one to care for and no one to care for her. *If only*, she thought, *I still had Jake*.

She was worried as to how she would cope when her time came, to say nothing of caring for the child afterwards. What would happen to the shop? *If there's a shop left by then*, she reminded herself bitterly. The bills were mounting. Her suppliers were pressing for payment and the quarterly rent was overdue. Any day she expected a visit from Mr Finch or his solicitor.

It was neither of them who came into the shop one morning, however. Clara Finch stood in front of Meg and stared at her, her gaze running slowly up and down Meg's bulging body.

'So he left you pregnant, did he?'

'Yes,' Meg answered, aware that the 'he' Clara was referring to was a totally different 'he' from the one in Meg's mind.

'When is it due?'

Meg licked her lips calculating swiftly. The whole town knew when Percy had fallen ill and then died. 'About – about the end of May, I think.'

'What are you going to do?'

Meg frowned. 'Do?'

'Yes, do? You are hardly in a position to bring up his child, are you? Are you going to have it adopted?'

Meg gasped. That thought had never entered her head. It was her child, her responsibility and after the initial shock, she had accepted the fact. 'No. Of course I'm not.'

Clara leant towards her and there was menace in her face and in her action. 'That child should have been mine. I should be carrying Percy's child – not you. You never loved him, you scheming hussy. You robbed me of my husband. And you robbed me of the chance to have his child.'

There were tears in Clara's eyes, tears of anger, tears of frustration and longing. She had never felt such loathing towards any human being as she did at this moment. The pain of Percy's rejection of her had been nothing compared with the hatred she now felt for Meg.

Slowly and deliberately she said, 'I want that child. I want *his* child. I loved him and I'll love his child. I can give it everything you can't.'

Meg gasped. She felt the urge to laugh outright. If only Clara knew the irony of the situation. Here she was, demanding that Meg hand over the baby to her because she thought it was Percy's. What would she do if Meg were to tell her that it wasn't? But all Meg said was, 'You must be mad. Give my baby to you? Never while there's breath in my body.'

Clara leant even closer. 'You will. One day, you will. I mean to have Percy's child and I will.'

'Your – your brother wouldn't let you.'

'Huh!' Clara stepped back now and her tone was scathing. 'Him! He'll not stop me. He'll do anything I say. There are things I could tell you – tell the world – about my dear brother. And one day I just might. But for now he'll do anything I say. And the first thing he'll do is give you notice. You haven't paid your rent for this quarter yet, have you? Well, if you read your lease – Percy's lease – you'll find that if you default on your rent, you'll be evicted. We've only to send in the bailiffs and you'll be declared a bankrupt.' She smiled triumphantly. 'And I dare say we're not the only people you owe money to.' When Meg did not answer, Clara nodded. 'I thought as much.'

She turned towards the door. 'You'll be hearing from Mr Snape very soon. But think about my offer, won't you? If you agree to my proposition, I'll see that you keep the shop and your home. And I'd see that you got all your customers back. That's something we could think about, isn't it? You see, I can be very generous when I want my own way. Very generous.'

As the shop door closed behind her, Meg was left staring after her. *Sell my baby? She wants me to sell my baby to her because she thinks it's Percy's.*

Meg closed the shop early that day. She walked home in a trance to sit before the fire in the front room, the outrageous proposal whirling around in her head. It was a monstrous idea and yet it was a way out for her. The solution to all her problems. If she gave her child to

Clara Finch, she would be free. She could leave here. She could go anywhere and start her life over again. She had no ties here now, none at all. Jake was lost to her and the bitter truth was that Philip would never leave his wife and jeopardize his career. There was nothing left for her in South Monkford.

And yet . . . And yet . . .

For days Meg pondered Clara's offer. Days in which the number of customers dwindled yet further until she saw no more than three during the whole of one week. And then they only bought small items of underwear. Meg was at her wits' end and she spent the whole of Sunday pacing up and down her front room.

If I don't get any customers this week, she decided in the early hours of Monday morning when she'd tossed and turned, sleepless through the night, *I'll do it. She can have it. What do I want with a baby anyway?*

She was tired and listless when she opened up the shop. To her surprise, at five past nine the shop doorbell clanged, as if awoken from a deep slumber. Meg looked up and smiled. The woman approaching the counter had never before entered the shop, but Meg recognized her. Mrs Davenport's husband was the current mayor of South Monkford and his lady mayoress needed numerous outfits and hats to attend functions throughout the year.

'I'm looking for an evening dress. I don't suppose you have anything, but I thought I'd ask before I went into Newark or Nottingham.'

Meg beamed. One of the last deliveries from her main supplier had contained three dresses suitable for evening wear and Meg was sure that at least one of them was the woman's size. 'I'll show you what I have, Mrs Davenport. Please, would you care to come into the fitting room and I'll bring them through to you.'

The next hour was happily spent whilst Mrs Davenport tried on all three dresses, but the effort was worthwhile for she left the shop having purchased two.

'I needed something rather urgently. We have a grand dinner to attend at the weekend and another early next week in Newark and my dressmaker wouldn't have the time to make two complete outfits. However, she will have time to make the alterations. Could you have both dresses delivered to Miss Pinkerton?'

'Yes, madam. I'll see she has them by tonight,' Meg promised. Since Percy's death she had made even more use of the fussy little spinster who was so clever with her needle and thread. She had even tried to persuade her to tackle making men's suits, but Miss Pinkerton had been thrown into a tizzy at the very idea. 'Oh, I couldn't. I couldn't possibly fit gentlemen.' The little woman had blushed at the mere thought.

Ten minutes after Mrs Davenport had departed the bell clanged again and another customer entered the shop. She made several purchases of underwear. After her came yet another and the steady stream of women customers went on throughout the day. By five o'clock Meg was tired but elated. If things went on like this . . .

The bell sounded again and she looked up to meet Clara's eyes. The woman stood before the counter, hands folded in front of her waist, her mouth pursed and her eyes hard. But today there was a glitter of excitement in them.

'So? Have you had a good day?'

Meg gaped at her as realization began to dawn, slowly at first and then in a rush. Seeing the understanding on

Meg's face, Clara smiled and nodded. 'It could be like that every day if you'd be sensible and give me what I want. You hand over your baby to me – boy or girl, I don't mind what it is – and I'll get Theobald to renew the lease on both your home and this shop in your name. And I guarantee that you'll have plenty of customers. *Just like you've had today.*' She leant towards Meg as if sharing a confidence, yet the action was more threatening than confiding. 'You see, I made a lot of new friends through my war work and they're more than willing to listen to my recommendations.' She paused and added with deliberate emphasis, 'What*ever* those recommendations might be.'

Meg understood now how, little by little, her number of customers had dwindled and then, miraculously, had suddenly been restored.

'So,' Clara asked, 'what about it?'

'Is it – would it be – legal?' was Meg's only question.

Clara waved her hand airily. 'Oh, we'll let Mr Snape sort all that out. He's always very helpful to our family.' For a moment her face darkened. 'He's only ever let us down once.' And Meg knew she was referring to the court case which, whilst technically Clara had won, had not been the resounding success she'd sought. 'Besides,' Clara added, almost as an afterthought, 'my brother and I own his office premises.'

Meg almost gasped aloud. Was there no end to the power the Finch family wielded in this town?

'Well?' Clara was pressing for her answer.

Unable to say aloud what she knew in her heart was a terrible, unforgivable thing, Meg merely nodded. Clara smiled triumphantly. 'You're very wise. You've made the right decision.'

As Clara left the shop, all Meg could think was: *Whatever will Jake say when he finds out?*

Meg was never far from Jake's thoughts. Try as he might, he could not cut her out of his memory, or even out of his life. He hadn't seen her for weeks, months now, yet he knew that she was expecting a child, knew too that she was facing difficulties in her business. Part of him longed to help her, to give her whatever support he could. Longed, once more, to be her friend. But another part – the harsher side of him – told him: *She's made her bed, let her lie in it.*

And now, on the same day that Meg gave her answer to Clara, Jake was about to become a father.

As they were getting into bed that night in their newly built part of the farmhouse, Betsy suddenly clutched at her stomach, bent over double and cried out.

'What is it? What's the matter?' Jake, who was already in bed, sat up.

'I think it's the baby.'

Jake flung back the covers, wrenched off his nightshirt and began to dress. 'Get into bed, love. I'll get the missis.'

Minutes later Mabel Smallwood walked calmly into the bedroom, Jake hovering anxiously behind her. 'Now, lad, this is no place for you. This is women's work. Off you go downstairs,' she said firmly, 'and leave this to us.'

'But shouldn't I go for the doctor? Or the midwife?'

'Not unless we need them. No need for unnecessary doctor's bills if we can manage perfectly well without them.'

Jake backed out of the room reluctantly. He raised his hand in a wave to Betsy, but she was already too busy coping with another contraction.

For Jake the waiting, in the room below, was agony. He paced the floor, straining to catch any sound from upstairs. He tried desperately to keep his mind on his wife, on Betsy, yet try as he might he could not help thinking about Meg too. When he'd heard the news of her pregnancy his first unbidden thought had been that he wished the child was his instead of Percy Rodwell's. He remembered that thought with shame. Yet still – even after all that had happened – he worried about Meg. She lived alone. What would happen when she went into labour? Would there be anyone there to take care of her?

He paced the floor harder, feeling guilty at even thinking of Meg at such a time. Betsy – he must think only of Betsy.

Forget Meg, he kept telling himself. *She's not worth the ground your Betsy walks on.* He loved Betsy, really he did. He wanted to protect her and make her happy, yet it was always Meg's face that haunted his dreams, Meg who was never far from his thoughts. Even when his wife was giving birth to their beautiful daughter, it was still Meg whom he could not forget.

Forty-Seven

During the third week of June Meg's son was born in the bedroom she'd shared with Percy. It was a difficult birth and the midwife insisted that she needed a doctor's help.

'I'm sending for Dr Collins,' she said firmly after Meg had laboured in vain for nine hours.

'No,' Meg had tried to protest, but exhausted by her efforts she was too weak to argue any more.

An hour or so later Philip entered the bedroom reluctantly, though he had no choice but to attend. There would have been raised eyebrows and questions asked if he had refused. And to send for another doctor would have taken too long and possibly endangered the lives of mother and baby.

Meg was in too much pain to care who was there. It was not until afterwards that she realized the irony. Philip had helped to bring his own son into the world.

Clara Finch was her one and only visitor. She came the day after the birth and stood by the side of Meg's bed.

'You shouldn't be feeding him yourself,' she said. Her face showed her distaste as she watched the tiny child suckling greedily at Meg's breast. Meg realized that the woman was afraid she would change her mind. Once her baby was born, in her arms and suckling at her breast, Meg's maternal instincts might be so powerful that . . .

She looked up at Clara. She stared at the thin, bitter face of the woman standing over her and wondered how she'd ever thought she could give her child up to her.

'I'm sorry,' she said quietly, but there was a new note of determination in her tone. 'I'm sorry, Miss Finch, but I can't let you have him. He's my baby and, whatever you do to me, I'll never let him go.'

Clara's face contorted with rage. If it hadn't been for the baby in her arms – the child she thought was Percy's – Meg believed the woman would have attacked her. Weak after the birth, Meg knew she would have had no defence. As it was, Clara – for she would not harm the child – had to content herself with an angry tirade and dire threats.

'I'll ruin you. You'll be homeless. Yes, yes, that's it. You'll be back in the workhouse where you belong. And this time there'll be no foolish Percy Rodwell to fall for your charms. Oh yes, and then we'll see, because you'll have no say in what happens to your child. Remember, your life in there is ruled by the master and—' she paused as she delivered her final, triumphant blow – 'by the board of guardians.'

Meg gasped. The woman was mad, quite mad. Did Clara really think that if she had Meg put back into the workhouse, she could then just take her child? Meg blanched. Remembering now just how it had been, she realized that with the co-operation of everyone concerned it was entirely possible. Illegal, probably, but Clara would not let that worry her. She had Mr Snape to worry for her about that.

As she left the bedroom, Clara shook her fist at Meg. 'You'll live to regret this. I'll have that child. One day – mark my words – I'll have that child.'

As she heard the woman go down the stairs and bang

the front door behind her, Meg laid her lips against the baby's head. 'I'm so sorry,' she whispered hoarsely. 'So sorry that I ever thought of giving you away. Forgive me.'

The baby slept in her arms, calmly unaware of the drama his arrival into the world had caused.

When she felt well enough, Meg walked to the surgery to see the doctor. There was nothing unusual about a young mother visiting her doctor and Louisa welcomed her with open arms.

'Let me hold him. Oh . . .' As she took the baby boy into her arms, Louisa's eyes shone and her face took on a soft glow. 'Oh, Meg, he's lovely – beautiful. How lucky you are.' For a moment her face clouded. Longing showed clearly in her face.

'What're you going to call him?'

'I – haven't decided on a name yet.'

'You're not calling him after his father, then?'

Meg gave a start and then realized that Louisa meant the name 'Percy'. She shook her head. 'No.'

Shyly, Louisa said, 'Well, some mothers call their baby boys after the doctor who attended them. I mean, you did have a bad time and Philip . . .' Her voice trailed away.

Meg almost laughed aloud. *If only you knew*, she thought. Instead she said brightly, 'I'll ask Philip what he thinks.'

'Do.' Louisa smiled. 'And I'll put the kettle on. Come and have tea with me afterwards.'

When it was her turn to go into the consulting room, Meg stood for a moment inside the door until Philip looked up and saw her there with his son in her arms.

She saw him start, the colour flood into his face and his anxious glance towards the door.

'It's all right. I'm the last patient. Louisa has gone back into the kitchen.'

But he was still agitated. 'Why have you come? Is something wrong?'

'No, but I wanted to ask you what you'd like me to call him.'

'Call him?' Philip said, a little stupidly.

'Well, yes, I thought you ought to approve. After all, he is—'

'Yes, yes,' Philip held up his hand, palm outwards, as if to fend her off.

Meg smiled mischievously, enjoying Philip's discomfiture. 'Louisa suggested I should call him after my doctor. How do you feel about that?'

Philip's look of absolute horror made her smile, but he misinterpreted her amusement, believing that was what she intended. He clasped his hands together. 'Oh, please, Meg. Don't do that. I beg you. There's – there's been gossip already and if – if you were to name him after me, then – then Louisa might begin to suspect.'

Meg put her head on one side, enjoying his discomfort. 'But it was she who suggested it.'

Beads of sweat shone on Philip's forehead. He caught hold of her hand. Tears in his eyes, he pleaded, 'Meg, please. Promise me you won't call him after me. It'd start the tongues wagging all over again. It could ruin my career. Look . . .' He stepped closer. 'I'll give you some money. I'll pay you a monthly allowance, if you like. Help you get away from here – anything . . .'

She stared at him, seeing him suddenly for what he was. A man who had given into his craving for her who yet was not man enough to stand by her now. He was selfish and self-centred. He'd been unfaithful to his wife, yet now all he really cared about was his precious career. He didn't want anything to do with his son. He had not even looked at the baby once since Meg had entered the room.

He wanted nothing to do with the child – or her. He wanted them both out of his life.

He hadn't loved her, Meg realized. He'd lusted after her. In a searing moment of truth, Meg saw herself too for what she had become. She did not like the picture. In the beginning she'd deliberately led Philip on, finding sweet revenge in seducing Louisa's husband. She'd betrayed her kind and devoted husband when Percy had needed her most. She looked down at the sweet, innocent infant in her arms, the child she had been tempted to give away. What sort of mother was she? What sort of woman was she? Shame swept through her.

By offering her money, Philip made her feel like a common woman of the streets, but she was worse than any of them. At least they did what they did with an open kind of honesty. She had been devious, manipulative, cruel to her poor mam . . . The list was endless. No wonder Jake – who'd once loved her – hated her. But no one hated her more at this moment than Meg herself.

She pulled herself free of Philip's pleading hands and took a step back. But the distance between them was so much greater now than that one step. Meg lifted her chin and her green eyes sparked with resolution.

'I don't want your money, Philip. Or you. I'll take care of *my* child.' Her lip curled with contempt. 'And don't worry yourself. Your dirty little secret's safe. I'd rather people think he's Percy's son than have you as his father.'

She turned and walked across the room towards the

door, pausing only to say, 'Oh – please give my apologies to your dear wife. I am unable to accept her invitation to take tea with her.'

When Meg felt well enough to reopen the shop, taking the child with her, customers were once more in short supply, no doubt under Clara's instruction. At the end of the week a letter came from Mr Snape to say that her landlord required her to vacate both the shop and her home unless she could pay the two months' rent she already owed and another month in advance. By the same post two letters came from suppliers threatening her with court action if their accounts weren't paid within fourteen days.

Late that evening, carrying the baby in her arms, Meg walked to the little cottage where the dressmaker, Miss Pinkerton, lived, along the road from her own home. It was almost dusk when she arrived and the nervous spinster peered out of her front-room curtains before she opened the door to her.

'Why, Mrs Rodwell, you're out late – and with the baby too. Come in, come in. Let me make you some tea.'

Miss Pinkerton bustled about her tiny kitchen and when they were sitting on either side of the fireplace in her front room, Meg said, 'Miss Pinkerton, I'll come straight to the point. I'm being evicted by the Finches.'

'Oh, my dear, I'm so sorry, but I have to say I'm not surprised. Clara Finch is a vindictive woman.' It was the second time that word had been used about Clara, Meg thought, but she said nothing about the latest reason for Clara's wrath. Miss Pinkerton believed that Miss Finch was still seeking revenge for what she considered a miscarriage of justice. 'So where will you go? What will you do?'

'I wondered if you would be interested in taking over the shop.'

'Oh!' The little woman nearly dropped her teacup in her surprise and blinked rapidly behind the thick lenses of her spectacles. Her reaction reminded Meg suddenly of Percy and she realized just how much she was missing her kindly protector. When she'd recovered a little, Miss Pinkerton shook her head. 'Oh, dear me, no. I'm too old to take on something like that. And besides,' she bit her lip. 'I may have to give up dressmaking altogether sooner than I had anticipated.' She touched the rim of her spectacles. 'My eyesight, you know. The fine stitching is getting too much for me.' She looked down at her hands holding the cup in her lap. 'I, too, am beginning to lose business.'

Meg's mind was working quickly. She leant forward. 'So why don't we join forces?'

Miss Pinkerton raised her head. 'I – don't understand.'

'You could still serve in a shop, couldn't you, whilst I took on all the sewing? Percy taught me a lot. I used to do quite a bit for him.'

'Dressmaking isn't the same as tailoring.'

'But I can sew well. And I still have Percy's sewing machine. He taught me how to use it. Don't you see? You could soon teach me dressmaking.'

'But Miss Finch? If she knew, wouldn't she . . .?' Miss Pinkerton's voice trailed away.

'She needn't know. I wouldn't be in the shop but in the back, or when I find another place to rent I could work at home, just like you always have.'

'But I'm too old—'

'How old are you?' Meg asked candidly.

'Fifty-five.'

'And what are you going to do for the rest of your life? How are you going to earn a living?'

'I – don't know. That's what's been worrying me. I own this house. My aunt left it to me, but once that's gone—'

'It'll be the workhouse,' Meg said bluntly. She saw the little woman shudder and pressed home her point. 'But it needn't be like that. I can give you advice about the shop. It's only failing because Miss Finch has set all her friends against me.'

'I know,' Miss Pinkerton said. 'She's tried to stop me doing any alteration work for you.'

Meg's face was grim. 'So you know I'm telling you the truth. I haven't failed in the business. I've been hounded out of it. The only problem I've got is finding somewhere else to live. They're turning me out of my home as well.'

'Well, you could come here,' Miss Pinkerton ventured tentatively, but Meg shook her head. 'No. It's very kind of you, but if we're to do this together and try to keep it from Miss Finch I could hardly live here, could I? She'd never let you take on the shop if she thought you were having anything to do with me.'

Miss Pinkerton's face brightened. 'I have a cousin lives in the street – Laurel Street – behind your shop. In fact' – she was getting quite excited now. Two spots of colour burned in her cheeks – 'I think if you go out of Florrie's yard and walk a little way along the passage-way that runs between the backyards, you can get into Mr Rodwell's – oh, I'm sorry, I still think of it as his.' The little woman noticed Meg's puzzlement. 'I'm sorry, I'm not explaining myself very well. My cousin lives alone since she lost her husband and she lets out two rooms, more for the company than anything else.' She leant forward as she added, 'And her last lodger has just left. She's looking for someone else.'

'But would she mind having a baby in the house?'

'Mind? She'd be thrilled, but you'd have to be prepared for the possibility that you might lose him.'

Meg's eyes widened and her heart thumped. Surely Miss Finch hadn't . . . ? But behind her spectacles, Miss Pinkerton's eyes were twinkling. 'My cousin, Florrie, will likely take complete charge of him.'

Meg smiled as she relaxed and murmured, 'I shall be very glad of her help.'

Forty-Eight

Events moved much faster than even Meg had dared to hope. Eliza Pinkerton took only two days to accept Meg's suggestion that she should take over the shop. The little spinster suddenly seemed revitalized, finding a new purpose in her drab, monotonous life.

'I have a little money put by,' she said. 'I'm sure I can pay off all your suppliers, although I won't be paying Theobald Finch your back rent.'

'I think he'll be only too pleased to relet the shop so quickly – and to be rid of me.' Meg told Eliza the current rent and advised, 'Don't let him put it up much more than that.'

'I won't. And now I'll take you to meet my cousin.'

Meg was apprehensive. What if Miss Pinkerton's cousin did not want such a scandalous woman beneath her roof? She need not have worried. Florrie Benedict was round and jolly – a big woman with an even bigger heart. She was energetic and forthright to the point of bluntness, but that frankness was tempered with a ready laugh.

'Oh, so you're the scarlet woman I've heard so much about. Bowling poor Percy Rodwell off his feet and pinching him from under Clara Finch's nose.' She laughed heartily, a deep belly laugh. 'Couldn't have happened to a nicer person.' She pulled a comical face. 'I've no time for the woman, never have had. And the power she and her brother wield in this town – well – there ought to be a law against it. My late husband worked for the council for a while and what Theobald Finch used to push through in the council meetings was nobody's business. Ought to have been investigated, if you ask me.' She laughed again. 'Still, nobody ever did. Now, let's have a look at this little babby of yours. See if we can tek to each other . . .'

Florrie took the child into her arms, nestling him against her ample bosom. She walked up and down the room with him, crooning softly. 'We'll get along just fine, won't we, my little man?' Looking up, she demanded, 'What's his name?'

'Robert Jake.'

Florrie's smile broadened. 'Now fancy that. My little grandson's called Robert. Isn't that strange? But my daughter lives down south and I don't see them very often.' She looked down again at the baby lying placidly in her arms. 'You'll be my little Robbie here, won't you?' As if answering her, the baby gurgled and waved his arms about and Florrie laughed loudly.

Meg moved her few belongings from Percy's house to Florrie's. The two rooms she'd been given upstairs were well furnished, so there was little in the way of furniture she needed to keep. It had belonged to Percy's parents, so was old and worn, and she sent most of it to the local saleroom, where it raised her a few precious shillings. For the first time since Percy had died Meg felt safe. She wanted to live quietly, away from prying eyes and vicious tongues. The fewer people who knew where she was the better. Eliza and Florrie revelled in the intrigue. Eliza didn't want the Finches to know Meg's whereabouts any more than Meg did. For the first time in her life Eliza Pinkerton was someone. She was the proprietor of a genteel shop and – with Clara Finch's innocent backing – her business flourished.

'I'm pleased to see you here, Miss Pinkerton. You deserve to do well. I'd just like to know where that little hussy has disappeared to. She still has something I want. Something I want very badly. If you hear word of her, you will let me know, won't you?'

Clara fixed the little woman with her steely stare, but Eliza blinked behind her thick glasses and smiled back innocently. 'Of course, Miss Finch. Now, may I show you my new line of gloves . . .'

Florrie, too, revelled in the deception. It was she who took Robert out in an old perambulator and all she said if anyone enquired about the baby was, 'Oh, this is little Robbie.' *It's not my fault*, she told herself, *if they think it's my grandson come to stay with me for a while, now is it?*

During the following months, Meg was perhaps the happiest she had been since that dreadful night her father had come home with the news that they must leave their home. Eliza gave her plenty of work and with practice, and under the dressmaker's patient guidance, Meg became skilled with her needle and with Percy's sewing machine. She rarely left the house during the daytime, but took exercise as dusk fell.

So life continued in the little terraced house, and if Meg was not exactly happy, then at least she was content.

There was only one person she really missed seeing – Jake. It hurt her to think that he would not even know where she was and, worse still, that he wouldn't even care.

*

Betsy considered herself the happiest woman alive. She had a husband whom she adored, she had the Smallwoods, who treated her like a daughter, and she had a beautiful baby girl of her own. If she still harboured doubts about Jake's love for her, she kept them buried deep. They never spoke of Meg, yet sometimes she caught Jake with a faraway look in his eyes and wondered if he was thinking about the vivacious girl he had loved. Did he love her still? Betsy tried not to think about it. At such times she would draw his attention to the baby. His eyes would soften and he would take the child into his arms and gaze at her as if he too couldn't quite believe his luck. There was certainly no doubting Jake Bosley's love for his daughter.

Letitia still came to the farm with the excuse of seeing the baby, yet Betsy knew it was still Jake that the matron came to see. Her gaze followed him everywhere and deep in her eyes there was sadness and a look of longing. Betsy, fulfilled and ecstatic in her role as a mother, felt sympathy for the unmarried, middle-aged woman, who would never know motherhood. Happily, secure and content now, Betsy did not begrudge Letitia her visits to the farm and her time spent with her precious boy and his new daughter.

It was as if Letitia had adopted the child as her granddaughter and when Jake and Betsy asked her, along with Mabel and George Smallwood, to stand as godparents for baby Fleur, the matron wept with joy.

They chose Fleur's christening day with care. 'We'll have it on the Sunday nearest to the first anniversary of armistice day,' Jake decided as he cradled his daughter. 'We're the lucky ones. Me and the doctor. We came back, but there's many a family with no cause for celebration. So many bairns,' he murmured, looking down in wonder at the child in his arms, 'who'll never see their fathers again.'

Betsy rested her head against his shoulder and wrapped her arms around Jake and the baby. 'I know, but you're here and you mustn't feel guilty because you survived. You owe it to all those men who died to make a good life – with us.' Betsy was determined to drive any thoughts of Meg out of his mind. She was very afraid that he still thought of the strong, wilful, passionate girl and she was right.

Even on the day of the christening, Meg was there, a shadow at the feast, though Jake prayed that no one else would guess. He had no idea where she was now and believed that perhaps she'd left the district. It hurt him to think that feelings were so bad between them that she had not even said goodbye. He'd have liked one last chance to make things right. On this happy day, it saddened him to think they had parted in such bitterness.

God bless you, Meggie, he prayed silently, *wherever you are.*

Things might have continued happily if Clara Finch had not been so determined to get her own way. After several months she was still no nearer finding out what had happened to the child she believed was rightly hers. In her twisted mind, she almost came to believe that he was hers, that she had actually given birth to Percy's child and that wicked girl had snatched him away from her.

At night she paced the floor of her bedroom, growing more and more agitated and creating her own fantasy world. 'He's mine, he's mine.' The words became like a mantra which she chanted in her mind.

The boy – wherever he was – was growing without the love of his rightful mother. Christmas and New Year had come and gone. Time was passing and he'd be almost nine months old already.

Theobald didn't realize the depth of his sister's inner turmoil. If he had, perhaps he'd have done something about it. But Theobald Finch was happy to turn a blind eye to Clara's ravings. He was content to rule the roost as the chairman of the board of guardians at the workhouse, to get his own way in the town council chamber, to drink with his friends, to go to race meetings and to collect the rents from all the properties he owned in the town. The only excitement he craved, apart from seeing the horse he'd backed romp home in first place, was the acquisition of more property.

'There's a row of houses in Laurel Street coming up for auction. Chap who owned them has died and the family want the money to divide between them,' he told his sister one evening over dinner, as they sat at either end of the long dining table. 'Should we bid for them? What do you think?'

Clara rose from the table, leaving her pudding untouched. She was especially agitated tonight. 'Oh, I can't enter into that now. I've far too much on my mind. You do what you think best, Theo. I really don't mind.'

Frowning slightly, Theobald watched her leave the room, but as the butler refilled his wine glass, he forgot all about his sister and her strange behaviour. 'Women!' was all he muttered.

Forty-Nine

The news of her landlord's death had thrown Florrie into a turmoil. 'His family are putting the whole row of houses up for auction.'

'You mean we're going to be evicted?' Meg's face paled.

Florrie scanned the letter she had received from Mr Snape, who was her landlord's solicitor. 'No – no, it says we'll be treated as "sitting tenants", whatever that means.'

Meg felt the fear subside. 'I think it means the ownership of the properties will change, but they'll take you on as their tenant. I heard Percy mention something about it once. I shouldn't worry—' she began, but then stopped.

Florrie was looking up from the letter with troubled eyes.

'What? What is it?' Meg asked.

'They – they want details of all the occupants of the house.'

The two women stared at each other and Meg felt her security slipping away. 'What are we going to do?' she whispered, her eyes wide.

Florrie bit her lip. 'I don't know. We must talk to Eliza.'

But Miss Pinkerton had no ready solution either.

'You see,' Florrie explained, 'folks round here must

be wondering whether little Robbie is really my grandson, since he's here all the time. No one's asked any awkward questions yet, but . . .' She left the unspoken words hanging in the air.

Meg finished the sentence for her. 'But they might if you've got to put down in writing who's living with you.'

Florrie nodded. 'I'm a straightforward sort of person, Meg. Never been frightened to say what I think, but I've never liked telling deliberate lies. Oh yes, I've been happy to go along with our little deception because it's what others have chosen to think. I've never *had* to lie about you being here. So it's never bothered me. But now . . .' Again she did not finish her sentence.

'Well, I wouldn't ask you to lie for me,' Meg said in a small voice, hoping in vain that Florrie would offer to do just that. When the offer was not forthcoming, Meg sighed and murmured, 'Perhaps I should think about moving away from here.'

'What do you mean, you can't find them?'

The hapless private detective whom Clara had hired stood in the middle of her drawing room, twirling his trilby between nervous fingers. 'I've made every endeavour, Miss Finch.'

Clara clicked her tongue against her teeth in exasperation. 'I doubt that, Mr Gregory, I really doubt that.'

'I don't think they can still be in this area, ma'am.'

'You don't think. You don't *think*! Mr Gregory, I'm paying you to be certain. And then I'm paying you to find out where exactly they are.' She paused and her eyes narrowed. 'Have you, for instance, asked Dr Collins if they're still on his list of patients?'

'Er – well – yes, ma'am, but doctors won't divulge any information about their patients.'

'But you did ask him?'

The man nodded. Clara's eyes gleamed. 'Then, to me, that means they're still here somewhere. If they weren't, he'd have said so. That wouldn't be divulging confidential information, surely.'

'I don't know . . .'

'Well, I do. They're still here. Somewhere – they're still here, I'm sure of it.' She was talking more to herself now than to the man. Suddenly she remembered that he was still standing there, awaiting her instructions. She pursed her mouth and said sarcastically, 'But it seems you aren't going to find them if you have, as you say, made every endeavour. So.' She rose and went to a small bureau from which she extracted some money. 'Here's your final payment. I no longer require your services.'

'Oh, but–'

'No buts, Mr Gregory. If you haven't found them after three months, then I don't think you're going to. I've paid you a lot of money and got nowhere and wasted a lot of time in the process. Good day to you.'

Mr Gregory knew himself dismissed.

After he'd gone, Clara paced the floor. Where now? Who could she turn to for help? Not her brother. She hadn't told him of her plans to take Meg's child and bring him up as her own. Theobald would be horrified, but he wouldn't – couldn't – stand in her way. Clara smiled grimly to herself. There were plenty of secrets from Theobald's past that she knew he would not want revealing. No, her brother wouldn't have a say in the matter.

'Mr Snape,' she said aloud to the empty room. 'He owes me a favour. I'll go and see Mr Snape.'

'Do sit down, my dear lady.'

Mr Snape ushered Clara into his office with the sycophantic attention he gave to all his female clients. He kept his personal feelings well hidden behind his professional mask. He disliked Clara Finch intensely. At the time of her case against Percy Rodwell, he had advised her not to proceed with the prosecution, but she had been adamant. They had all been left looking very silly and Mr Snape was not a man who liked to be made to look foolish.

Nevertheless, he sat behind his desk and asked, 'And how may I help you, Miss Finch?'

'I want to find that young woman who married Percy Rodwell.' She bit back any further explanation, but Mr Snape was not so easily deceived.

'Why should you wish to find her?' Mr Snape feared further trouble.

'That's my business,' Clara snapped. 'I just want you to tell me the best way to go about it.' Her eyes narrowed. 'She has something that rightly belongs to me.'

Mr Snape frowned. 'And what might that be?'

Clara opened her mouth. She was on the point of confiding in him and then thought better of it. All she said was, 'That does not concern you. At least,' she added, tempering her tone for she realized she might very well need this man's help over her plans to adopt the child – it wouldn't do to antagonize him, 'not for the moment.'

'The usual way to find a missing person is to hire a private detective—'

'I've done that. He was useless.'

Mr Snape sat staring at the woman in front of him, debating with himself whether he should tell her the information that had, by chance, that very morning come into his hands. He was dubious about her intentions. Clara Finch was a nasty piece of work. Her brother was a shrewd businessman, but a decent enough chap in general, but she – well – she was a vixen. What could she want with the widowed Mrs Rodwell? What did she mean when she said the young woman had something that rightly belonged to her? No doubt it was only some trinket or keepsake from the Rodwell house. Surely it could do no harm to tell her the whereabouts of Meg Rodwell and her son.

'As it happens,' he said, leaning back in his chair and linking his fingers in front of him, 'I think I can help you. I happen to know exactly where Mrs Rodwell is living.'

Clara almost jumped to her feet. 'You do?' Her eyes gleamed with excitement and triumph.

'Do you remember Mr Boyd? Your brother would know him. He owned quite a lot of property in the town and he was on the board of guardians.'

'Yes, yes, I know of him.' Clara was impatient to hear what she had waited months to learn, had paid good money to find out.

But Mr Snape was not to be hurried. 'As you know, he died recently and his family wish to sell some of his properties, in particular, a row of terraced houses on Laurel Street. Your brother is intending to buy them and asked me to make some enquiries about the occupants and so on.' He waved his hand and paused, still debating whether he really should divulge the information.

'Go on,' Clara insisted and Mr Snape sighed. The Finches were his wealthiest clients and the owners of his office.

'One of the tenants there – a Mrs Florence Benedict – has a lodger—'

Mr Snape got no further for now Clara did jump to her feet. 'It's them. I knew it! I knew they were still here somewhere, though how I've never seen or heard of them I don't know.' She held out her hand. 'Thank you, Mr Snape. Good day to you.'

Before Mr Snape could rise out of his chair to usher her out, she was gone, through the door and out into the street.

As she walked home, Clara felt like running and jumping for joy.

'I've got you, Meg Kirkland,' she muttered gleefully, refusing as ever to give the girl the name of "Rodwell". 'I've got you at last,' she wanted to shout aloud.

Fifty

For two days Clara pondered how she could entrap Meg. Now that she knew where Meg and the baby were, she was in no hurry. She didn't want to rush into doing something that would not work so she had to be sure that every move she made was the right one. The only thing that concerned her was that, if she moved too quickly, Meg might leave the district, taking her child with her.

'I must think this out carefully,' Clara muttered as she paced the drawing room alone. 'And Theobald must know nothing of what I'm about until it's done.' Her eyes narrowed as her thoughts moved from her brother to the workhouse. 'That's where she ought to be. Back in the workhouse, where she belongs. I'll go and see Isaac.' She smiled grimly. 'He'll help me. If he wants to keep his job, he'll find he has to help me.'

That afternoon she walked through the town to the workhouse. She paused a moment outside the austere building. She shuddered. She counted her blessings that she'd been born into the world she had been and would never know life as a workhouse inmate. Yet, so obsessed was she by the child that she had no compunction in seeing Meg back inside its walls.

Clara would stop at nothing to get her own way.

She opened the gate and was about to cross the courtyard when Albert Conroy stepped out of his lodge.

His bushy white eyebrows almost met in a frown when he recognized her.

'What d'you want? Come slumming, 'ave yer?'

The old man had no time for any of the Finch family. Years before he'd worked for a time for old man Finch, as he called Clara's father. He'd not been well treated and he thought this woman took after her father. Theobald wasn't so bad, he supposed. He was a bit of a bumbling old fool, really, except when it came to matters of business and then he was as sharp as a packet of needles.

Clara pursed her lips. 'I'd watch your tongue, if I were you. You enjoy something of a position with your own quarters here in the lodge.' She nodded towards the small room near the gate that was Albert's only home. 'That could all change, you know.'

Albert stared back at her insolently. He wasn't going to kowtow to the likes of Clara Finch. Own quarters, indeed! A poky little room with a tiny fireplace, for which he was allowed a meagre ration of coal. In return for which he was never off duty. He even had to get up in the middle of the night if the homeless came knocking at the workhouse door.

Albert sniffed, wiped his mouth with the back of his hand and said again, 'I work for the master, not you. I asked you what you wanted here.'

'I've come to see Mr Pendleton.'

'He's not here.'

'Miss Pendleton, then. She'll do.' Clara smiled maliciously. Letitia would be even more pliable than Isaac.

'She's not here either.'

Clara frowned. 'Are you being deliberately obstreperous?'

He grinned at her, showing blackened, worn-down teeth. 'I might be – if I knew what it meant.'

'Oh, get out of my way. I'll find them myself.'

Albert watched her go, laughing to himself. He'd got under her skin and that had been worth getting up for that morning.

Clara marched purposefully across the yard, but she wasn't really sure where to start looking for the matron. As she thrust open the door leading up the stairs to the infirmary and the matron's room, she almost knocked Ursula Waters flying.

'Oh, I'm sorry. Are you all right?'

Waters, holding her palm to her flat chest, nodded. Catching her breath, she said, 'Yes, thank you, ma'am. You startled me, that's all.'

Clara stood aside for the woman to pass her, but Ursula hesitated, asking, 'Can I help you, Miss Finch?'

'I doubt it. I came to see the master or the matron, but I've been told neither of them are here.' Her tone implied that she didn't believe it.

But Ursula shook her head, confirming Albert's words. 'No. I'm sorry, they're not.'

Clara sniffed. 'I was not aware that they were allowed to both leave their posts at once.'

'They've gone to a family funeral.' Ursula paused and then asked tentatively, 'Is there anything I can do to help?'

'I shouldn't think so, for a minute,' Clara said dismissively and turned to leave. 'Not unless you can make an admission for me.'

'Yes, I can do that, Miss Finch. When the matron isn't here, I'm in charge of anyone coming into the workhouse. Matron or the master sees them as soon as they get back, of course,' Ursula added quickly, remembering that Miss Finch was the chairman's sister. 'But in the meantime . . .'

Clara eyed her shrewdly. 'Are you trustworthy – er – Waters?'

Ursula preened. 'Mr Pendleton and the matron trust me implicitly. They couldn't do without me, they say. Ever since that woman –' Ursula's tone was scathing – 'that last paramour of his, died, he's depended on me. He's realized who really cares for him. She was just after what she could get out of him – they all were – whereas I—'

'What woman?' Clara interrupted sharply.

'That Kirkland woman. Sarah Kirkland – the mother of that – that girl.' Ursula nodded, a pecking movement. '*You* know who I mean, don't you?'

Clara eyed Ursula shrewdly. It might be even easier to make use of this woman, who was so anxious to please, than to try to persuade Isaac or his sister to help her.

'Er – when are the Pendletons due back?' she asked, with deceptive mildness.

'Not until the day after tomorrow. They've had to go to a family funeral somewhere. Halifax, I think they said.'

Clara's smile widened. *Time enough*, she was thinking excitedly. *Time enough. And when they come back and it's all accomplished, there won't be anything they can do about it.*

'I think there might very well be something you could do to help me. Is there somewhere you and I could talk privately, Waters?'

'We could use the committee room.'

They entered the huge room and moved down to the far end of the long table, where they sat together across one corner.

'Would you like some tea, Miss Finch?'

Clara was anxious to get on, but she wanted to humour the woman. She needed Waters to think herself an equal, at least for the moment.

'That would be nice,' Clara said, drawing off her gloves. 'Thank you.'

Whilst Ursula hurried to have tea brought in for herself and her important guest, Clara pondered how best to approach what she had in mind.

They chatted about inconsequential matters until the tea arrived. Stirring hers thoughtfully, Clara began, 'You mentioned Meg Kirkland . . .' For a moment, Ursula looked startled, surprised that Clara – of all people – should want to talk about the girl. 'How does Mr Pendleton feel about her now?'

'About Meg?' Ursula's voice was a high-pitched squeak.

Clara nodded.

'He – he never mentions her.'

'Do you suppose he's – er – fond of her.'

Immediately, there was a wild look in Ursula's eyes. '*Fond* of her? Fond of *her*?'

Clara nodded, watching the other woman's reactions closely. 'For the sake of her mother, I mean. He was fond of Sarah, I presume?'

Ursula wriggled her shoulders and Clara saw the jealousy flare in her eyes. 'I suppose so,' Ursula was forced to admit grudgingly. 'But she was no good for him. All she ever did was cry over her children. "All my dead babies," she'd say. "And now I've lost my lovely Meg too." '

'Didn't Meg come to see her mother?'

Waters's look was suddenly sly. 'No, never.' Now she avoided meeting Clara's direct gaze. 'And afterwards I think the master blamed her for – for that woman's suicide.'

It seemed, Clara thought shrewdly, as if Waters couldn't even bring herself to speak Sarah's name. She referred to her only as 'that woman'. Her hatred went deep, it seemed, as deep as did Clara's for the daughter.

'I think, Miss Waters –' the sudden deliberate use of the courtesy title did not go unnoticed by Ursula – 'that perhaps you could help me. But I need to know that I can trust you. Trust you implicitly.'

Ursula's eyes shone and she nodded enthusiastically. 'Anything I can do to help you, Miss Finch. Anything at all. And I know Mr Pendleton would approve. He thinks very highly of you. Of both you and your brother.'

Oh, indeed he does, Clara thought cynically to herself, *if he values his position here*. But she voiced nothing of her thoughts to Ursula.

'It seems that Meg is about to find herself homeless. Her and her child.' She bit back a tirade and managed to keep her voice calm. 'I am sure that the master would think you had done the girl a service by admitting her and the child to the workhouse.'

Ursula stared at her. 'She's still here? In South Monkford?'

Clara nodded. 'Has been all the time, apparently. Lodging in a house in Laurel Street. But the – er – house where she is living has recently changed hands.' There was no need for Waters to know that the contracts had not yet been signed and that, legally, the properties were not yet in Theobald Finch's possession. 'And the – er – new landlord,' Clara went on, 'doesn't allow his tenants to take in lodgers. Overcrowding and such. You understand?'

Ursula didn't, but she nodded, thinking it was expected of her.

'Now –' Clara leant forward – 'she'll be arriving here probably tomorrow. I want you to admit her and her child, but once they are segregated . . .' Clara ran her tongue nervously round her lips. She was suddenly unnerved by the look of astonishment on Waters's face, but she had gone too far to turn back now. 'I will take the child to live with me. The workhouse is no place for my Percy's son.'

For a long moment Ursula stared at Clara and slowly, very slowly, realization came to her. Despite all that had happened, Miss Finch still loved Percy Rodwell. Her love for him was as great as Ursula's own for Isaac Pendleton. No matter how much they were hurt, these two women were united in their undying devotion to their men.

'You – you want to – to take Mr Rodwell's son and – and bring him up as – as your own?'

Clara took a deep breath and prayed hard. 'Yes.'

Again, Waters just stared at her, trying to imagine how she would feel if Sarah had borne Isaac a child. Would she feel so charitable? Was her love great enough to take that child in and bring it up as her own? She couldn't answer her own questions at this moment, but later, in her lonely spinster's bed, she would think them through.

'My, my,' she murmured, her gaze still on Clara's face. 'You must have loved Mr Rodwell very much.'

'I did. He was my life. That – that girl's child is the child I should have had. He belongs to me.'

In her own obsession for Isaac, Ursula began to understand Clara's twisted reasoning. She nodded eagerly. 'What do you want me to do?'

'Just admit them and leave the rest to me.'

'They'll be here tomorrow, you say?'

'Yes. Well before the master and the matron return . . .'

Understanding at once, Ursula's eyes gleamed.

It happened with such speed that Meg thought she was in some terrible nightmare. Any moment she would wake up sweating and find herself safely in her bed at Mrs Benedict's, with Robbie sleeping soundly in his little cot beside her.

But this was no dream. This nightmare was only too real.

At the end of a long day, and with Robbie in bed, Florrie and Meg were sitting quietly by the fireside drinking cocoa when a loud knock came at the door.

'Now who can that be at this time of night?' Florrie said, setting down her cup and hurrying to the door. 'Sounds as if some poor soul is in trouble.'

Before she'd even reached the door, three men wearing balaclavas and carrying sticks rushed into the house. Doors were never locked in Laurel Street during the daytime and Florrie's habit was to lock up just before she went upstairs to bed.

'Here, what d'you think—'

Florrie's indignant question was never finished for one of the men pushed her in the chest as they rushed past her. She fell heavily to the floor, banging her head, and was knocked unconscious. Meg had hardly time to rise to her feet before two of the men grabbed her, held her fast and thrust a gag into her mouth.

'Get the kid,' were the only words spoken in a gruff voice.

Minutes later she was being bundled into the back of a cart as her squealing son was thrust into her arms.

'Shut him up,' ordered the gruff voice, 'else I will.'

A quieter voice spoke up. 'Don't hurt the kid. Remember?'

'Want the whole street coming out their doors, do yer?'

'No, but—'

'Gerrin and let's be off.'

The cart jolted away, whilst in the back a terrified Meg held her child close to her and tried to remove the gag from around her mouth.

'Leave that alone, else it'll be the worse for you,' came the voice again.

The men were anxious and agitated. One drove the cart whilst the others ran alongside it, their sticks at the ready.

But no one stopped them. No one ventured out of their houses. If anyone saw, they stayed within the safety of their homes. No one came to Meg's aid as the cart trundled up the street towards the outskirts of the town – and the workhouse.

Fifty-One

Just inside the gate the men paused.

'What about him?' One jerked his head towards the porter's lodge.

'I'll see to that old fool.' In the darkness Meg saw him brandish his stick. 'This'll keep him quiet.'

Suddenly Meg managed to free the gag from her mouth. 'Albert!' she yelled at the top of her voice. 'Albert—'

A rough hand fastened painfully over her mouth. 'Keep it shut if yer know what's good for you.'

As they were dragging her across the yard to the wash house, the door of the lodge opened and Albert peered out. 'What's going on . . . ? Ah!'

Meg heard the sound of a stick cracking against the old man's head and saw him crumple to the ground. She was sobbing now and trying to wriggle free, but the man held her fast. Robbie had been taken from her as they had pulled her roughly from the cart, but she could still hear his cries.

Someone opened the door into the wash house, where a light burned inside.

'Take her to the punishment room, but leave the child here with me.'

Meg recognized the woman's voice. Waters! But there was nothing she could say or do as she was pushed into the stark cell. She fell to the hard floor, where she lay panting and sobbing. The door slammed shut and she was alone in the cold and the dark.

Albert awoke to find himself back in his narrow bed. His head was throbbing and when he put up his hand he felt a lump on his forehead the size of an egg. Gingerly he sat up, then pulled himself to his feet. Other than the bump on his head, he seemed to be all right.

He blinked a few times in the pale morning light. Yes, he could see all right. He frowned, trying to remember. What had happened? Had he fallen out of bed and banged his head? Strange. How had he got back into his bed?

Then, slowly, he began to remember. He'd heard a noise outside in the yard – had heard the gate opening and had gone out to greet the new arrivals. The homeless could arrive at any time of the day or night, so it was nothing unusual for Albert to be wakened. But there was a struggle going on and he was sure someone – a woman – shouted his name.

Then he remembered no more.

Albert dressed slowly and made himself a cup of tea. One of the young lasses would bring him a bowl of porridge later. He opened the door and peered out into the yard, but all was quiet. At least, so he thought at first, but then he heard the faint sound of banging and shouting. He walked along the line of buildings, past the bath room, the coal store and the privies, even beyond the dead room and through the gate at the far end. The noise was growing louder. Someone was locked in the punishment cell.

'Help! Somebody help me. Please.'

Albert was outside the door now, but here he paused and bit his lip. If the master had put someone in there, he couldn't let them out.

But then he remembered: the master wasn't here. Nor matron. Then who . . . ?

Albert pressed his ear close to the door.

'Who is it? Who's in there?' he called softly.

'Albert? Oh, Albert, is that you? It's Meg.'

'Meg! Aw, lass, what on earth are you doin' in there?'

'I don't know. Three men came in the night and brought me here. Oh, Albert, they've taken my little boy . . .' She dissolved into heartbroken tears.

'I can't let you out, love. I daresn't.' He thought quickly. 'But I'll fetch help. I know someone who'll help us.'

'Albert – Albert . . .'

But now Meg's cries were in vain for Albert was hurrying back to his lodge. He knew just the person he must fetch.

'Jake! Jake! Wake up. There's someone knocking at our door.'

Jake felt Betsy shaking him.

'Wha . . .?' Bleary eyed, he pulled himself up and out of the bed. He stumbled across the room and down the narrow staircase. 'All right, all right. I'm coming. Where's the fire?'

His bare feet sticking out from beneath his nightshirt, his hair rumpled, and blinking in the early morning light, Jake was a comical sight as he opened the door. But Albert didn't laugh, didn't even notice.

'Jake, lad, thank God you're here. You must come at once. There's summat up at the workhouse. Summat not right. It's Meg . . .'

'Meg!'

Betsy, coming down the stairs behind Jake, heard the name and her heart sank. She craned her neck to see beyond Jake's shoulder, expecting to see the young woman standing there. But there was only Albert Conroy.

'Don't let him stand there on the doorstep,' she said at once, more fully awake than Jake. 'Bring him in. I'll make us all some breakfast. Come in, Mr Conroy, come in.'

'Ah, yes, sorry, Albert,' Jake mumbled opening the door wider. He rubbed his eyes, trying to wake himself up. 'Go into the kitchen. I'll just get dressed, then I'll be with you.'

Betsy, with a shawl over her nightgown, bustled into the kitchen. From upstairs came the first sounds of their little girl, Fleur, waking. Hearing her, old Albert frowned. A child. Yes, that was what had been bothering him. Meg had a child – a boy, he thought – yet he'd heard no sound of it. Where was the little chap? What had happened? He frowned, trying to remember. She'd said something about . . .

'That's a nasty bump you've got on your forehead, Mr Conroy. Let me put something on it for you.'

'Nay, lass. I'm fine.' He touched it gingerly. 'Had worse than that in mi time.' He glanced worriedly at the door leading to the staircase, willing Jake to hurry back.

It was only a few minutes before Jake reappeared, fully dressed, yet it seemed an age to the anxious old man.

'Now, what's up, Albert?' Jake asked.

'It's Meg.' He noticed the swift look between husband and wife and then they both turned their gaze on him. 'She's suddenly appeared back in the workhouse and she's locked in the punishment room.'

'Meg?' Jake repeated stupidly. 'But I thought she'd left the town. Gone away altogether.' Again he and Betsy exchanged a glance.

Albert shrugged. 'Well, I don't know about that. All I know is that she's locked in the punishment room and crying for help. She – she said something else.' He frowned, trying to remember. 'I know,' he said suddenly. 'She said, "Albert, they've taken my little boy." That's it! That's what she said.'

'Who'd taken him?'

Albert shook his head. 'I dunno, but she was in a right state, Jake. You've got to come and sort it out.'

'I don't think there's much I can do. If the master's put her there . . .'

'But he's not there. Matron neither. They're both away. At a family funeral or summat. Waters is in charge. Or at least she thinks she is.'

'Waters!' Jake pondered a moment. 'Waters,' he said again slowly as if jumbled thoughts were just beginning to straighten themselves out and make some kind of awful, terrifying sense. 'Come on, Albert,' he said grimly. 'We'd best get back there and be quick about it. If—'

'But – but what about your breakfast?' Betsy began.

'No time.' For a moment, Jake gripped her shoulders and looked into her eyes. 'Don't worry, love. I have to go. You do understand, don't you?'

Oh yes, she understood all right. Miserably, Betsy watched him go, walking alongside Albert, matching his steps to the old man's, even though she could see that he wanted to run ahead, to get there as quickly as he could. To get to Meg.

Betsy gave a sob and pressed her hand to her mouth, the tears blurring her eyes so that she could no longer see him.

When they entered the workhouse yard there was pandemonium. The tall figure of Isaac Pendleton was standing in the middle of the women's exercise yard with Letitia beside him, both still dressed in travelling clothes. Surrounding them were several women and a few men, all talking at once. Jake's heart sank. He'd have a hard time getting Meg out now, if the master was back in charge.

He put his hand on Albert's shoulder. 'You go back into your lodge,' he began, but the old man shook his head. 'No, I'm coming with you, lad. We've got to get this sorted out.'

With Albert close on his heels, Jake pushed his way through the throng towards Isaac, who was trying to placate the women and get them to speak one at a time.

'Quiet, quiet!' He bellowed and at last the tumult subsided.

At that moment, Jake reached his side. 'Where is she?'

The master looked down at him – he was still a good foot taller than the stockier built Jake.

'Where's who?'

'Meg. Meg Kirkland – sorry – Rodwell. Is she still here?'

Isaac shook his head. 'I wasn't aware that she was.'

Again, the women all began to talk at once. Isaac

spread his hands in a calming motion. 'Just explain, quietly, what has happened.'

'She's in the punishment cell, crying to be let out. She says they've taken her child.'

'Meg? Here?' Isaac was as surprised as anyone and Jake could see at once that it was genuine. Whatever had happened, the master had had nothing to do with it. Neither, by the surprised look on her face, had the matron.

'In the punishment room?' It was Letitia who spoke up now. 'But I don't understand. What is she doing here? And who put her in there?'

'Waters,' came the immediate reply of several voices.

'Waters!' Isaac and Letitia spoke together and then the matron added anxiously, 'She's got a little boy now, hasn't she? Where's he?'

The women glanced at each other worriedly. 'We don't know.'

Within minutes Meg had been released from the tiny room to fall, weeping hysterically, into Jake's arms.

'I'm taking her home,' he said in a tone that brooked no argument, not even from the master – the man who had ruled the whole of Jake's young life.

Isaac nodded bleakly. 'Take my pony and trap. It's still outside the front entrance.'

'Thank you, Master.' Old habits died hard and Jake still called the man by the name he always had.

'My baby! My Robbie! Where is he?' Meg cried as Jake led her away.

'We'll find him. I'll take you home. Betsy'll look after you and I'll come back here.'

She clutched at him. 'What about poor Mrs Benedict?

Those men. They pushed her over. She was on the floor. What's happened to her?'

'Mrs Benedict? Who's Mrs Benedict?'

'The woman I've been lodging with. Her house is in Laurel Street. Number fifteen. Maybe Robbie is back there with her.'

He helped her into the pony and trap and as he picked up the reins and turned the pony towards the road, he said, 'Now, tell me what happened.'

Swiftly, Meg explained but Jake was still mystified. 'Whoever would want to harm you in such a way?'

'Oh, I've plenty of enemies,' Meg said bitterly. 'I wouldn't be surprised if the master isn't behind it all.'

Jake shook his head. 'No,' he said slowly. 'I don't think he knows anything about it. I was watching him when the women were telling him about you. He was really surprised.'

'The matron, then. Maybe she wants to kidnap my little boy. You know how she loves little boys.'

'No, it's not her. I'd bet my life it's not her. ' He was silent for a moment. Slowly, he said, 'I think it's Waters. I should have seen it before. Why, *why* didn't I think of her?'

'Waters?'

Jake nodded but for the moment he said no more. He didn't want to tell her at this moment of the suspicions he'd always harboured about the death of Meg's mother. Only he had been suspecting the wrong person. It hadn't been the master at all. It had been Waters, jealous, embittered, twisted Waters. He could see it all now. It had been Waters who'd told Meg – and him – that her mother didn't want to see her any more. When all the time poor Sarah had been desperate to be reunited with her daughter. He should have realized – should have known that wasn't true. Then he'd suspected the master, but now he could see that he had known nothing of Waters's deception. Jake blamed himself for not realizing the truth before. And now he was sure too that it had been Waters who'd had something to do with Sarah's death. But he'd no proof – not yet – and to say any more now would only throw Meg into an even greater panic over her son.

They arrived at the farm. Jake drew the pony and trap to the door leading into his part of the house. He climbed down and held out his hand to Meg. For a moment, she did not move.

'Betsy won't want me here. She hates me and so does Mrs Smallwood.'

'They'll do what I ask them. Come on,' he said firmly.

As they moved towards the house, Betsy opened the door. When she saw Jake with his arm around Meg, her face paled, but he glanced up and smiled at her.

'Betsy, love. Look after Meg for a while, will you? Her little boy's missing. I have to go and look for him. I'll see the mester before I leave and there's something I want Ron to do for me. You'll be all right,' he added, though whether he was reassuring Meg or his wife, even he could not have said. 'Everything'll be all right. I promise.'

Fifty-Two

The child had not been found though the inmates – male and female – had searched everywhere they could think of. Waters had been found in the mangle room above the wash house, calmly sorting out the washing into piles for the women to iron during the day.

'Where is he?' Letitia demanded, puffing after her climb up the stone steps. 'Where's Meg's little boy?'

'Where he belongs.'

Letitia bit her lip. She wanted to take hold of the thin woman and shake her like a rat, but she kept calm. 'And where's that, Ursula?'

'He's quite safe. Waiting for his mother to come for him.'

'But – but she was here. Meg was here. He's not with her.'

Ursula's lip curled. 'She's not his mother. She's not fit to be anyone's mother.'

'Then who – ?'

Waters smirked. 'Miss Finch. She's his rightful mother. The child should have been hers. Hers and Percy Rodwell's.'

Letitia gasped and stared, wide-eyed, at the woman calmly folding clothes. 'Miss Finch? Clara? She – she's behind all this?'

Ursula nodded. 'I knew you and the master would agree. I mean, her brother's the chairman of the board of guardians, isn't he? I knew it must be all right to do whatever Miss Finch wanted.'

'Oh, Waters,' Letitia moaned. 'What have you done?'

'I've reunited a little boy with his rightful mother.'

'You mean, she has him? She has Meg's boy?'

'He's not Meg's boy. He belongs to Miss Finch.' Ursula's eyes were wild.

'Yes, yes.' Letitia placated her. 'Whatever you say. Then – then the child is with Miss Finch?'

'Not yet, but he will be. She'll be here for him today.' Suddenly Ursula seemed to realize that the matron should not be here. 'What're you doing back here? You're not supposed to be home until tomorrow.'

'We came back early.' Beneath her breath, Letitia muttered, 'And it's a good job we did.' Louder, she said, 'So where is he now?'

Ursula's look was sly. 'Where no one'll find him. Not until she comes for him.'

Letitia forced a smile. 'Well, that's all right then. You carry on here . . .' She turned and left the room, closing the door behind her. She glanced down and was thankful to see the key was in the lock. Quietly she turned it and then hurried down the stairs.

Out in the yard little groups of men and women were still standing about, talking anxiously.

'Where's the master?' Letitia called.

One woman detached herself from a group and came towards her. 'He's gone to the clerk's office. I think he's going to send for the police.'

'Yes, yes, but the little boy's still here – somewhere. Waters is locked in the mangle room.' Letitia pointed at one of the women. 'Go and stand outside the door and don't allow anyone to let her out. Not till I say so.'

'Right, Matron.' The woman hurried away as Letitia

raised her voice to the others. 'The child's still here somewhere. Get everyone looking.'

'But we've looked everywhere . . .'

'Well, look again. Keep looking. He's here, I tell you.' Then she added, 'Where's Jake? Has he come back?'

'He's with the master.'

Letitia found them both in the clerk's office, arguing with Mr Pearce. 'The boy is still here,' she interrupted.

The three men turned to look at her, but it was Jake who asked, 'Where?'

Letitia shook her head. 'She won't tell me.'

'Waters? You found her?'

Letitia nodded. 'I've locked her in the mangle room.' She glanced at Isaac. 'I don't understand it all, but it's to do with Miss Finch wanting Meg's boy.' Swiftly she repeated all that Ursula had said, ending, 'She thought she'd be pleasing you, Isaac.'

Jake waited to hear no more. He was out of the room and into the yard, marshalling a proper search party. Two hours later they had still not found the child.

'Master, could you persuade Waters to tell you where she's put him?'

'I'll try . . .' But even Isaac wasn't hopeful. Waters had, by now, discovered she'd been locked in and was making such a din that she could be heard down in the yard. She was shouting and screaming incoherently. 'I don't think I'll get much sense out of her.'

'There must be somewhere we've missed.' Jake turned to the searchers, who were standing about not knowing what to do next.

'You'd think we'd hear him crying, wouldn't you?' one woman said. 'Poor little mite.' Several women had tears in their eyes.

Albert came limping across the yard. 'Jake – I've just

thought. I bet no one's thought to look in the dead room.'

All eyes turned towards him as Jake said grimly, 'No, they haven't.' Before anyone else could say a word, he was running across the yard, through into the men's and towards the end of the line of buildings. He flung open the door and at once heard the sound of muffled sobbing coming from one of the coffins. He flung back the lid to see the little boy lying there. He picked him up and held him close, oblivious to the fact that the baby was soaking and smelt terrible.

'There, there, little man. You're safe now. We'll soon have you home with your mammy.'

He stepped out into the yard and everyone surged forward, but it was Letitia who, despite her size, reached Jake first, holding out her arms. 'Let me have him.' And as she took him into her arms, Jake heard her say, 'Oh, you poor little thing. My precious little boy.'

Tears stung Jake's eyes. It was what she'd always called him – all his life.

Letitia looked up. 'Go and tell Meg that he's safe, but leave him with me. Come back for him in a little while, Jake. He'll be safe with me, I promise.'

Jake nodded, a lump in his throat. 'I know that, Matron. Oh, I know that.'

He returned later to find Letitia in her room, cuddling the little boy. A tender smile on his face, Jake watched her bouncing the child on her knee.

'You used to do that to me,' he said softly.

Letitia looked up at him, her eyes misty. 'Fancy you remembering that. You can't have been very old.'

'There's a lot I remember, Matron. All the beatings

you saved me from, even though mebbe I deserved them.'

'Isaac was too hard on you. Harder on you than on anyone else, but maybe that was because . . .' She avoided meeting his gaze now.

'Because?' he prompted, but she pressed her lips together and shook her head. 'Oh, nothing,' was all she would say.

Jake sat down opposite and leant forward, smiling at the little boy. 'He's a grand little feller, isn't he?' The child turned and beamed at Jake. He seemed to have recovered remarkably quickly from his ordeal and was now gurgling happily. Jake caught his breath. For a fleeting moment, he thought he saw a strange likeness in the child. A likeness to someone he knew.

'What's the master going to do about Waters and this Miss Finch business?'

Letitia looked up at him, seeming suddenly nervous.

'He ought to report it all to the police,' Jake went on. 'What they tried to do must be against the law, mustn't it?'

'He will. He's going to.' Then suddenly she burst into sobs.

'What is it? What's the matter?'

'Can I trust you, Jake? I mean – really trust you?' Her eyes were imploring him. Something was causing her great distress.

'Of course you can,' he reassured her.

'You – you won't make trouble?'

'Well, it rather depends on what it is. If you're planning to say nothing about what's been going on here, then I'm not sure I can give you that promise.' He put his head on one side and regarded her thoughtfully. 'I suppose it has something to do with the Finches, has it? The fact that he's the chairman of the guardians? You and the master might lose your jobs if you report his sister?'

She sighed heavily and stroked the little boy's hair gently. The child leant his head against her bosom and began to suck his thumb. His eyes closed and he slept. His action was so trusting, so loving almost, that above his head tears now ran down Letitia's cheeks.

'Yes, that comes into it, but it's only part of it. I'll have to tell you, Jake, even – even if it means I'll – I'll be in trouble with Isaac. You see, my brother's had a hold over me all these years because – because of something in my past.' She still held the child close to her, rocking him gently, but her whole attention was now on the young man sitting in front of her. 'Oh, Jake, my precious boy, you won't hate me, will you?'

'Hate you?' Jake was puzzled. 'Why on earth should I do that? I've a lot to thank you for.'

Letitia was shaking her head. 'You mightn't think so when I've finished telling you.' She paused, as if summoning up the courage, the strength to speak of things she'd kept hidden for years. 'A long time ago,' she began haltingly, 'I had a baby boy.'

'Yes,' Jake said.

She looked up at him, startled. 'You – you knew?'

'It was said around the place that that was why you loved all the little boys because you'd had one and lost him.'

She stared at him and then slowly shook her head. 'Oh, I didn't lose him, Jake. But, you see, I wasn't married and my family –' her tone was suddenly bitter – 'my loving family wanted me to go away to have the baby and then give it up for adoption. But I wouldn't. I loved the baby's father desperately, but – but he came from a good family and – and he – well – he didn't want to know.'

It was a familiar, age-old story. Jake touched her arm. 'Go on.'

She took another deep breath. 'It happened about the time that Isaac's wife – left. He said that if I came here and took her place – as matron – so that he could keep his job, he'd let me have the baby here as long as I never let it be known that the child was mine. So – I went away, had the baby and came back here. Isaac took the child in as an orphan . . .' Her voice trailed away and she gazed into Jake's eyes.

'And what happened to your boy . . .?' Jake began and then realization began to seep into his mind. Pictures from the past came flitting into his mind and, suddenly, he knew. 'It's me, isn't it? I'm – I'm your – your son.'

Letitia nodded and whispered. 'Don't hate me, Jake. Please don't hate me.'

He stared at her for a moment. The revelation was overwhelming and yet he felt no bitterness towards her, certainly not hatred. She'd been given no choice. Like many girls before her and since, she had got into trouble and had been forced into what she had done.

'No,' he said hoarsely and touched her arm. 'No, I understand. I understand it all. Perhaps – the only thing I could have wished is that you'd told me before now. Years ago. I'd've loved to have known you were my mam.'

Fresh tears flooded down her face. 'I'm sorry, Jake. Oh, I'm so sorry, but Isaac forbade it and I was so afraid that if I told you he'd have me sent away from here and I'd never see you again.'

'I know, I know.' He put his arm around her shaking shoulders. 'And don't worry, he needn't know you've told me now. We'll keep it our little secret, eh? Nobody else need know, though I would like to tell Betsy. We – we don't keep secrets from each other. But she'll not say a word. I promise you.'

Letitia nodded.

'Well, well, this is a day for surprises and no mistake,' he joked, recovering himself a little, though he knew it would take him some time to realize that all these years he had had a mother and maybe a father too.

He hesitated a moment, but then he had to ask. 'Don't tell me if you really don't want to, but – but who was my father?'

'I – well – that's the trouble, you see. I mean, the trouble we've got now. What I'm leading up to tell you.'

'You mean there's more?' he teased and clapped his hand to his forehead. 'I don't know whether I can take much more in one day.'

But poor Letitia wasn't smiling. She was looking even more afraid. 'Your father was – is – Theobald Finch.'

'Theobald Finch!' Now Jake was astounded, rendered speechless. Letitia – his mother, as he must now think of her – nodded.

'Theobald Finch,' Jake repeated, wonderment in his tone. And then his voice hardened. 'And he deserted you. Wanted nothing to do with you – or me.' It was a statement of fact, not a question, but nevertheless, Letitia whispered, 'Yes.'

'But – but why? He had no ties. He wasn't married . . .' He paused briefly and then asked, 'Was he?'

'It – it was his parents – his father mainly – they were still alive then – and he said it was shaming the family name. He – his father, I mean – even said how did Theobald know the child was really his.' Here Letitia hung her head, reliving the shame she had felt then. 'I was so naive, Jake. So trusting. I loved him so much and – and I believed he loved me . . .' Her voice trailed away sadly as she relived her broken dreams.

Jake squeezed her shoulders. 'I don't blame you, not for a minute. But couldn't your family . . . Mr Pendleton . . .' Not yet could Jake think of the master as his uncle Isaac. 'Couldn't they have done something?'

Letitia shook her head miserably. 'Mr Finch, Theobald's father, was the chairman of the guardians in those days and Isaac feared for his job.'

'I see,' Jake said grimly. And he did. He understood it all. How a young girl had been seduced and abandoned just because the father of her lover held a position of power in the town. The same position that Theobald now held and, as Letitia began to speak again, Jake realized with horror that Theobald was now wielding that same power over other people's lives.

'I don't know what to do, Jake,' she began. 'Waters told me that Clara Finch wants to adopt Meg's boy. Has done ever since he was a baby. When he was born, she promised Meg everything – money, a house, even the shop – but Meg wouldn't give up her child.'

Jake stared at her. 'What on earth does Miss Finch want with the child?'

'She wants to bring him up as her own. She wants to bring up Percy's son. In some twisted way she thinks of him as the son she might have had with Percy. She wants him, Jake, and she'll stop at nothing to get him.'

'And Meg? You say she won't let her have him, even though – even though –' Jake was unwilling to voice the doubts in his mind, yet Letitia was being honest with him, he couldn't be any less so with her – 'Miss Finch used all sorts of . . . of . . .'

He hunted for the word and Letitia supplied it. 'Inducements?'

He nodded and then murmured, 'Well, well, wonders will never cease.'

'What?'

'Oh, nothing. I was just wondering why,' his tone hardened as he added, 'Meg didn't accept such a tempting offer.'

Letitia stared at him. To her, the reason was simple enough. 'She loves her little boy, that's why not.'

The child, still sleeping against her bosom, stirred and opened his eyes. At once, he beamed up at Jake.

'Besides,' Letitia said softly. 'Just look at him, Jake. He's no more Percy Rodwell's child than you are. I'm guessing, of course, but who does he remind you of?'

Jake stared at the boy, who reached out with chubby arms to be lifted onto Jake's knee, where he sat smiling up at him. Jake's gaze roamed over the boy's face. The fair curling hair, the bright blue eyes, the wide smile. Even in one so young, it was a reassuring kind of smile – a smile you could trust.

'My God,' Jake breathed. 'He's the spitting image of him, isn't he? I knew he reminded me of someone, but I couldn't think who it was.'

'It looks as if the rumours were true after all, Jake,' Letitia murmured.

He looked up and met her gaze. Solemnly he said, 'He's Dr Collins's son, isn't he?'

Fifty-Three

Meg reached out and took the boy from Jake and into her arms. She held him close and murmured endearments.

'Ron says Mrs Benedict's fine,' Jake reassured her. 'A few bruises, but angry more than hurt. She'll not let the matter rest, though, I can tell you, whatever the Pendletons do or don't do.'

Meg sighed with relief. 'I'm glad. She's been very good to me, but I don't suppose she wants me back. I was going to have to leave anyway soon. We had a letter from the new owner's solicitor. She's not going to be allowed to have lodgers.'

Jake was grinning. 'Well, I think you needn't worry about that any more. The new owner is Theobald Finch, and after what his sister's been up to I don't think he'll make any more trouble. In fact –' Jake wrinkled his forehead and added shrewdly – 'maybe he knew nothing about it. It might've been just Clara up to her tricks.'

'So – you mean, I can go back to Mrs Benedict's.'

Jake nodded. 'Whenever you're ready. I'll take you back in the cart.'

But Meg was shaking her head. 'No, no. I'll walk. I could do with some fresh air after that awful cell. And as for Robbie –' She stroked his hair and her eyes softened – 'well, to think of him being shut in that – that box.' She couldn't bring herself to call it a coffin.

'He'll soon forget about it,' Jake said gently. 'It'll soon seem like a bad dream for the little chap. That's all.'

'I hope so,' Meg said fervently. 'Oh, Jake, I don't know how to thank you.' She touched his arm.

Watching them together, Betsy's heart turned cold. There was a fire in Jake's eyes when he looked at Meg that Betsy had never seen before. It was never there when he looked at her. And she could see it too in Meg's eyes. It was as if they belonged together, as if only a cruel Fate kept them apart. Fate – and her, Betsy thought. If he wasn't married to her, then . . .

She turned away. She didn't want to see any more, didn't want to see the love in Jake's eyes when he looked at Meg. But he called to her, held out his arm. 'Come, Betsy, let's go with Meg to the gate. And bring Fleur to say "hello" to young Robbie here.'

Stony-faced, Betsy carried her daughter and watched as the two babies reached out their chubby arms to each other, gurgling and crowing. Jake and Meg looked on fondly, but it took Betsy all her resolve not to snatch her daughter away.

They walked to the end of the yard and stood awkwardly at the gate. Meg turned to Jake. There were tears in her eyes. 'I'm so sorry, Jake,' she said simply. 'For – for everything.'

Jake put his arms around her and held her and the little boy in her arms close to him. There was no need for words. His forgiveness was complete and Meg knew it. As Jake stepped back and looked down into Meg's upturned face, Betsy felt as if her heart would break. It was torture for her to watch Jake gently wipe away the tears on Meg's face. She almost turned and ran, yet something held her there.

'Be happy, Meggie,' Jake murmured.

She nodded and whispered hoarsely, 'You too, Jake. You too.' For a brief moment her eyes met Betsy's. 'Look after him,' she whispered.

She's giving him back to me, Betsy thought in surprise. *She knows she only has to say the word and he'll go with her, but she's not going to do that. She's not going to take him from me.* Unable to speak, Betsy nodded and moved closer to Jake. She put her arm around his waist, laying claim to him.

Meg nodded, gave one last tremulous smile to Jake and then turned away. She hitched up her little boy to sit on her hip and walked away from them down the lane without looking back.

Jake took Fleur into his arms. She was whimpering and holding out her arms towards the little boy, who was being carried away from her.

'There, there,' Jake said absently, his gaze still on Meg as she walked further and further away.

They watched until she turned the bend in the lane and was lost to their sight. Jake let out a deep sigh, as if, finally, he was letting Meg go. 'She'll be all right,' he murmured softly. 'She's a fighter, is Meg. She'll be –' his gaze still lingered on the spot in the lane where she had disappeared – 'fine.'

Then, seeming to shake himself, he pulled Betsy closer and kissed her forehead. Smiling down at her, he asked, 'Now then, wife, what's for mi tea?'